AUTHOR'S NOTE

The ABCs of What I Can Be includes existing careers, some of which can be found in The United States Department of Labor Occupational Outlook Handbook (https://www.bls.gov/ooh/a-z-index.htm), as well as hobbies and fanciful occupations. I hope to encourage children to try new things and ask themselves "What can I be?"

Caitlin McDonagh

An artist, a dentist, an EMT,
a Zumba instructor—it's fun to be me!

Zipper Maker

Z

Zumba Instructor

Zen Gardener

Xerophytic Gardener

Xylophone Player

X

X-ray Technician

Exobiologist

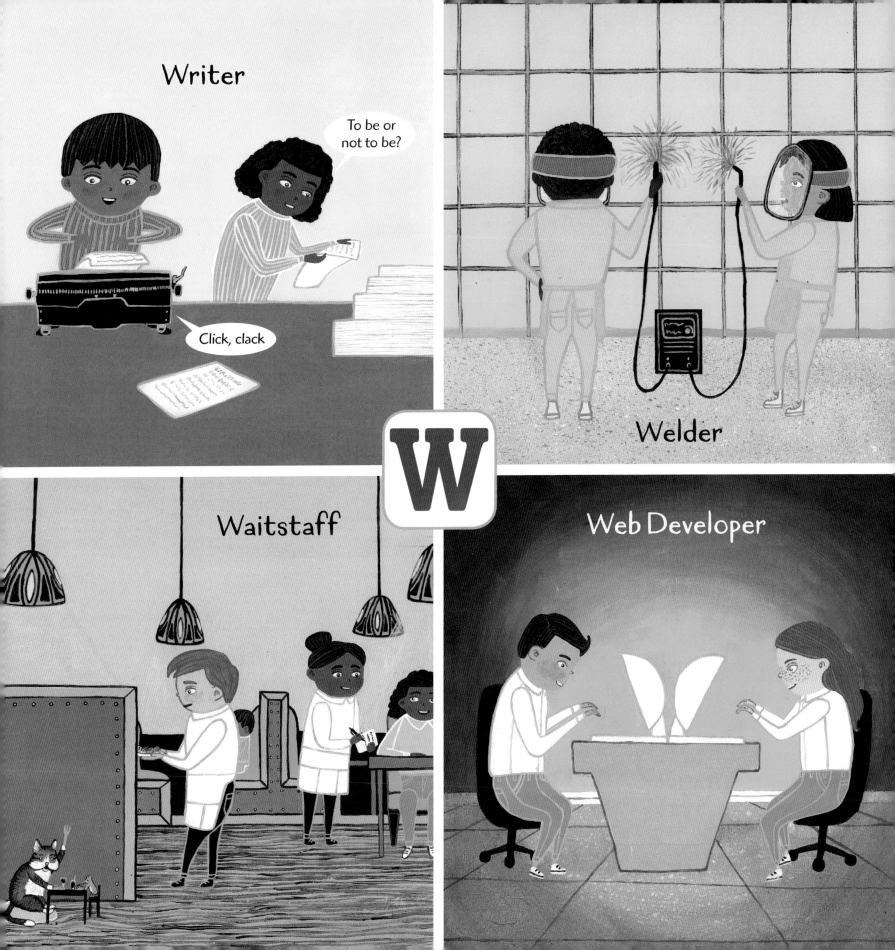

Upholsterer

Underground Miner

U

Underwater Researcher

Ukulele Player

Therapist

Toy Maker

T

Teacher

Tour Guide

Quiz Writer

Question #1

Question #2

Quarry Worker

Q

Quilter

Plumber

Police Officer

P

Politician

Photographer

Olympic Athlete

Office Worker

O

Oil Rigger

Ophthalmologist

Nail Technician

Nurse

N

Nanny

Nutritionist

FOOD ADVICE
#1. Eat your VEGGIE

Magician

Mathematician

Mechanic

Musician

Landscaper

Lawyer

Librarian

Lifeguard

Kiln Worker

Key Maker

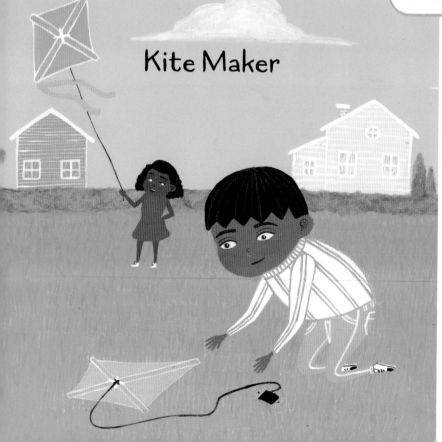

Kite Maker

Kennel Aide

Woof!

K

Hairdresser

H

Housekeeper

Hot-Air Balloon Pilot

Farmer

Fashion Designer

F

Firefighter

Florist

Engineer

Environmentalist

Electrician

Emergency Medical Technician (EMT)

E

Detective

Doctor

D

Dentist

Director

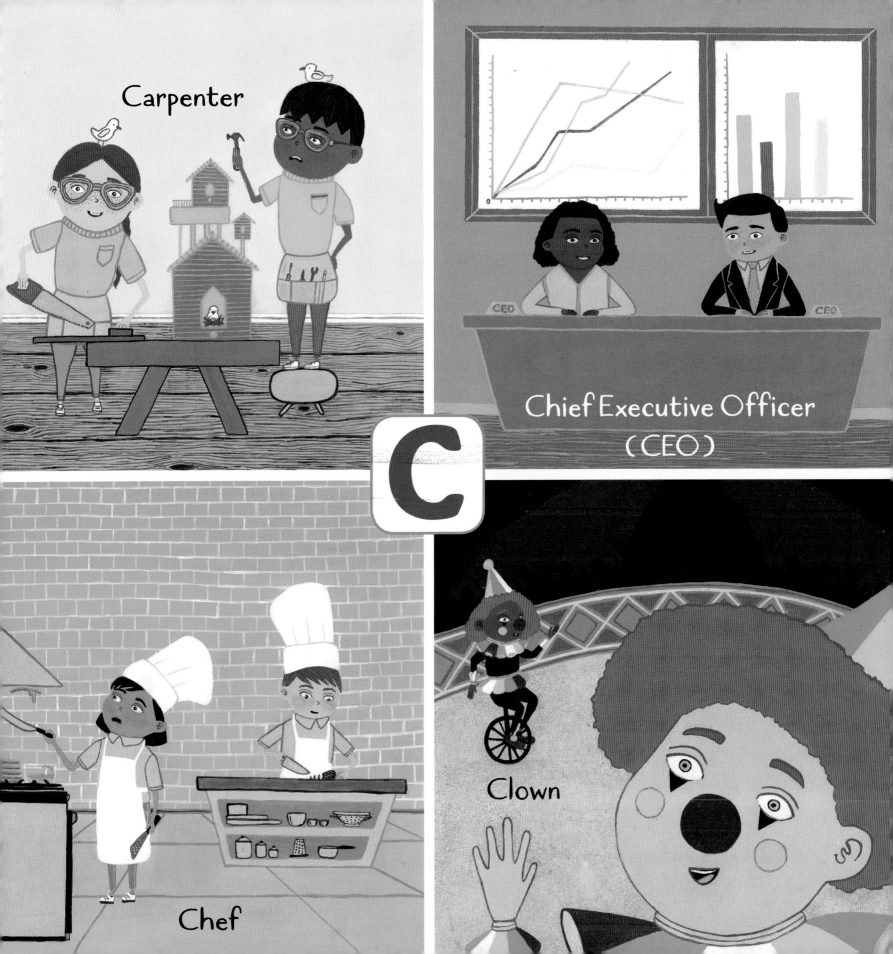

Carpenter

Chief Executive Officer
(CEO)

C

Chef

Clown

Ballet Dancer

Beekeeper

Biochemist

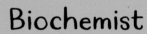

Bus Driver

B

Astronaut

Artist

Archaeologist

Athlete

Come along and you will see!

ABC, what can I be?

To my parents, John and Annette McDonagh

HOLIDAY HOUSE is registered in the U.S. Patent and Trademark Office.

Printed and Bound in August 2018 at Toppan LeeFung, DongGuan City, China.

The artwork was created with acrylic paint on gessoed illustration board.

www.holidayhouse.com

First Edition

1 3 5 7 9 10 8 6 4 2

Library of Congress Cataloging-in-Publication Data

Names: McDonagh, Caitlin, author, illustrator.
Title: The ABCs of what I can be / Caitlin McDonagh.
Description: First edition. | New York : Holiday House, [2018] | Summary:
Children dress up and imagine what they could be when they grow up—from
astronaut to dentist to mathematician to Zumba instructor.
Identifiers: LCCN 2017045485 | ISBN 9780823437825 (hardcover : alk. paper)
Subjects: | CYAC: Occupations—Fiction. | Alphabet.
Classification: LCC PZ7.1.M43434 Ab 2018 | DDC [E]—dc23 LC record available at https://lccn.loc.
gov/2017045485

HA
HA
HA

The ABCs
of What I Can Be

Caitlin McDonagh

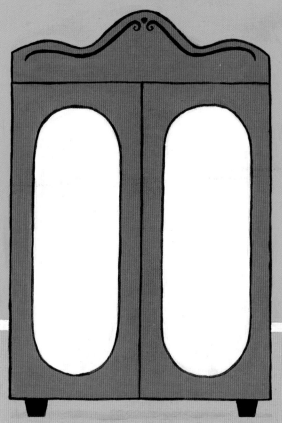

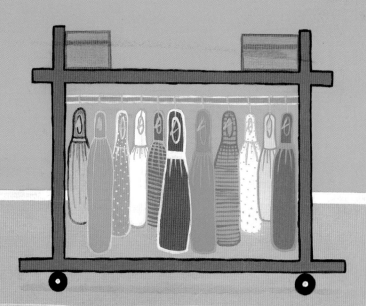

Holiday House New York

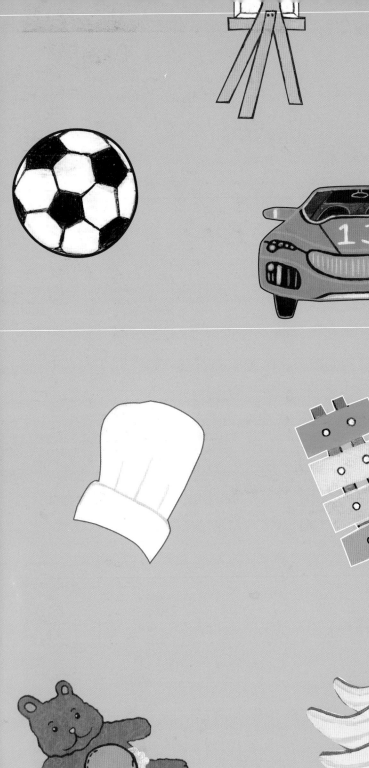

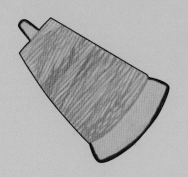

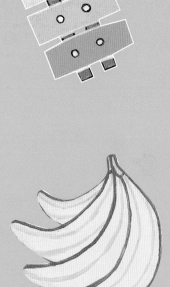

PREFACE

Sometime in winter 1997, Kay Read began looking for someone to help her take on this project. Lacking graduate students in her own institution, DePaul University (which focuses on undergraduate teaching), she began inquiring around hoping to find someone somewhere else. One of the people to whom she sent an email message was her own son, Jason González, who, at the time, was finishing up his master's thesis in Maya archaeology at Southern Illinois University (SIU) at Carbondale. Describing the project, she then asked if he knew of a graduate student who might be interested in helping out. A single little line was fired back almost instantly: "I'm a graduate student." And so began a rather fruitful mother-son collaboration, particularly good because, although both of us have traveled extensively and often to Mesoamerica, each of us focuses on different areas.

Kay's training is in art education, history of religions, and ethnohistory, with a special, although not exclusive, focus on the pre-Conquest Mexica (Aztecs). Jason has taught introductory courses at SIU and is trained in the archaeological branch of anthropology, focusing primarily (although again, not exclusively) on the pre-Conquest Maya. We split up the work according to our strengths. Kay has done the bulk of the writing (although certainly not all); Jason has used his computer skills to set up the data, graphic, and long-distance communication programs necessary to the project (because we live six hours apart, and his mother is a computer klutz); and we both have worked on the research. Since that fateful email message, Kay has continued teaching in DePaul's Religious Studies Department; but Jason completed his master's, moved on to the Ph.D. program, and then entered the dissertation stage. We're both really happy this volume is finished, and we have appreciated the chance to delve into mythological topics drawn from such a broad scope of places and times. We also have found working together fun (except for those moments when, as with all families, we drove each other a little nuts). The work, however interesting, has also proven extraordinarily daunting because of its broad scope, covering both a wide geographic area and an enormous time span.

The *Handbook of Mesoamerican Mythology* is meant to serve as a resource introducing teachers, students, and anyone else interested in Mesoamerica to its mythology. The geographic area includes what now is roughly known as Mexico and Central America. In this volume, we have focused primarily on the Mexican Highland and Maya areas, with small forays into Oaxaca and other miscellaneous locations. This was determined partly by the importance of the Mexicans and the Maya to Mesoamerican history, the practical need to limit our scope, and the reality of the kinds of studies available to us. If truth be known, scholars have tended to lavish these two areas (especially the Maya) with a wealth of studies, too often leaving the others underexamined. Our time span begins in the Paleoindian era and moves all the way up to the present—about 25,000 years or more of existence. Our primary focus has been on good stories wherever we could find them: implied in material remains and archaeological artifacts; told on friezes, through sculptures, and in pictures; sung, chanted, related, and expounded in words; retold by travelers, historians, archaeologists, linguists, and ethnographers; or reported by television and newspapers. After all, storytelling constitutes the core activity of myth making.

We have not attempted an exhaustive or deeply analytical study. That would have been both impossible given the project's scope and inappropriate to the readers we hope most to reach. This means we did not make any attempt to delineate conclusively the historical development of the various mythic traditions we address, the diffusion of mythic ideas from one group of people to another, or those mythic traditions that originated in Europe from those exclusively considered native. Such issues are more appropriately addressed in highly detailed, tightly focused studies, which are much better accomplished if they concentrate on a smaller scale and more limited area than that represented by our study.

Instead, our emphasis has been a largely synthetic one, searching for broadly shared themes, loose historical continuities and discontinuities, and that which at least appears mythically similar or distinctive. For this, we are grateful for the hundreds of careful, detailed studies other people have done and upon which we could rely. Of course, not all may agree with the broad strokes with which we paint particular areas and themes. Those may be honest disagreements, representing different but supportable positions, or they may simply be due to our own inadequacies (for which we apologize ahead of time). Moreover, because of the project's breadth, a host of topics have been left unexplored in any depth. Time and time again, we made suggestions or took sides on an issue that could bear more study, including, for example, those mythic continuities and discontinuities that we did happen to at least note. Therefore, we hope the volume serves to encourage more study.

Not the least of other issues that could use more work is the lack of numerous studies outside the Mexican Highlands and Maya areas, both ancient and contemporary. Maya studies, especially, seems to be taking over, and this includes everything from scholarly research to the production of videos and web sites. One might ask why this is so. Is it possible that the field might perhaps be subtly continuing old stereotypes? Until recently, the whole Mesoamerican area was considered "primitive" and therefore incapable of high civilization; it was characterized as nothing more significant than curiously exotic. As late as the third quarter of the twentieth century, scholars argued over whether the Mesoamericans built true cities, a debate that has been brought to a resounding conclusion with the findings that Tenochtitlan held a population of 200,000 or more and that the Maya ceremonial centers also supported high population densities. Moreover, all major centers were structured by highly complex cultural, social, economic, and political patterns. To be on the safe side, we have chosen to use the label "urban-center," but perhaps our definition of "city" needs rethinking. The question we pose is: Does the old primitive label continue to explain the lack of exploration in other, less historically central areas? Do people still think on some level that only the heirs of great centers of civilization deserve deep consideration; that if a community never had any huge pyramids, it's not interesting?

The old primitive label also traditionally split into two contradictory images: either the exotic primitive others were envisioned as brutal and uneducated savages or they were noble folk who retained their inherent human dignity and natural ties to earthly harmony. One might argue that the unfortunate pre-Conquest Mexican Highlanders (especially the Aztecs) received the first image from their interpreters, while the slightly more lucky ancient Maya received the second. Again until the twentieth century's third quarter, it was thought that the Aztecs brutally sacrificed just about everyone in sight, while the peaceful Maya did little else than stare at the sky and create mysterious religious links with all of nature. The Aztecs became hierarchical, urban theocrats, rigidly lording it over all of Mesoamerica, while the Maya were turned into spiritual stargazers, priestly theologians interested only in nature's cycles. Now it is known that this picture simply was not true.

Ancient and contemporary Mexicans and Mayans share more than people used to think. They are both part of a single cultural heritage that has included war and alliance formation; complicated hierarchical and nonhierarchical social relationships; extraordinary sky gazing and scientific and technological developments; complex theologies concerning time and space and the nature of life and death; and deeply embedded sacrificial practices. Yes, the ancient Maya were just as committed as the Aztecs to bloodletting and killing all sorts of plants, animals, and sometimes humans in order to keep the world going properly. This sacrificial tradition reaches back to the Preclassic, predating the Aztecs by a couple of thousand years at least, and forward to the present in well-established but less violent ritual traditions that now often intertwine with Christian sacrificial practices. And examples of large and small ecological disasters can be found among both groups; they (as do humans everywhere) sometimes made and make mistakes where nature is concerned. Does that old rather unfair and unhelpful way of contrasting warlike, savage Aztecs to peaceful, intellectual Maya continue to encourage the currently huge interest in Maya studies, while discouraging a similar interest in the Mexicans? Do we still see the Maya as romantically spiritual and the Mexicans as riddled with rigid religious institutions; have the first become a model for what modern interpreters wish we were, and the second for what we wish we weren't? The authors of this volume hope not.

Another issue that could use more exploration is what some call the "s" word—syncretism. This is the idea that when people mix, their ideas mix. How this clearly common human tendency occurs actually is a highly contested question. We've not attempted to explain how mythic themes move among people, why they change in the ways that they do, or why they retain their continuities with past themes; we've only noted on occasion that these things happen. In some ways, one even could argue that syncretism is an artificial issue. After all, creative, intelligent people all over the world have been exchanging ideas for millennia; ideas rapidly flow among various folk of often enormously different backgrounds, most of whom stubbornly insist on recasting their newly borrowed ideas in their own unique ways and according to their own particular experiences. The sixteenth-century indigenous folk are not really any different on this issue from the Catholic priests who sought their conversion. Each understood the other's tradition from their own perspective, and each altered the other's perspective in significant ways when they re-explained it. Of course, one cannot forget that this was not just a simple encounter between strangers seeking to comprehend each other. One acted to physically and spiritually conquer the other, while the other acted to resist or at least survive both–a hard, usually nasty reality that has continued to shape Mesoamerican mythology for five centuries.

For students of Mesoamerican mythology, this means that we must enter into our studies with a healthy dose of suspicion about those who speak with apparent authority. Everyone's authority (real or assumed) flows at least in part from our own presumptions about a world that others may not share. When a Spaniard explains the Mexica cosmos as layered in thirteen levels reaching up to the source of all existence, one needs to pay close attention to his words that also say the highest deity is like God and the first cause of all, for it sounds suspiciously Christian. Were those thirteen layers really so vertically arranged; was the highest really the first cause? Just because a Nahuatl speaker called the Virgin

Mary "Tonantzin" or "Our Holy Mother" does not mean necessarily that a pre-Christian goddess called Tonantzin existed on the same site before the Virgin; rather the devout simply may have been addressing the new Christian deity in a reverential manner, which continued in part an indigenous form of practice.

The folk or *el Pueblo* have been the greatest contributors to this volume, for we have focused largely on popular mythology. But occasionally, other kinds of myths creep in, those created by intellectuals, scholars, the educated, the well-off, and the powerful. By including such myths, we hope again to break down the dichotomies encouraged by those old primitive categories. All humans make myths, not just those exotics who live a simple spiritual life close to the land; and not all myths are orally related, for many appear first in written form. Much of contemporary mythology about Quetzalcoatl, for example, rests on academic and intellectual written traditions stretching back to the Conquest. And the mythological stories surrounding the historical veracity of the Virgin of Guadalupe have intertwined oral and folk traditions with written, scholarly, and national ones. It would have been both impossible and dishonest to suggest that true mythology appears only in oral form, and never from the mouths of the highly educated. We the authors also have our myths, and we must apologize when, unknowingly, our unexamined ones get in the way of our comprehension of other people's myths. That is the other daunting aspect of this project: how to explain accurately, with some insight and empathy, myths that often seem completely foreign to us.

In the first chapter of this volume we explore myth itself as a general topic, explaining the definition of myth we used to structure the whole project. Since mythology is the topic, it seemed only fair to explain where we're coming from. Throughout this and other chapters, we occasionally provided pronunciation guides to foreign words. These guides do not necessarily use professional linguistic style, which might not be understood by the average lay reader. Moreover, while Kay reads and translates classical Nahuatl and both of us read and speak Spanish, neither of us speaks the hundreds of other indigenous languages of Mesoamerica; this made providing correct pronunciation a challenge and, although we hope not, a mistake or two may have snuck in. The first chapter also offers a quick geographical and historical survey of Mesoamerica from the Paleoindian era to the present and a discussion of some of the challenges and possibilities that structure Mesoamerican studies. In the second chapter we examine history and time itself from a Mesoamerican standpoint, for while the project often assumes a certain historically timed perspective, it is important to realize that numerous Mesoamericans do not share that perspective. We use a very different calendar charting the course of change from the one many, many Mesoamericans have used and continue to use today. The third chapter is an alphabetized collection of selected entries on a variety of ancient and contemporary Mesoamerican deities and other powerful beings. The collection, like the entire project, is not exhaustive. We have tried to include those beings we consider particularly important for one reason or another, but some entries are a bit more idiosyncratic, deities or beings we simply found interesting for some reason. Following these three chapters are an annotated bibliography of selected print and nonprint resources and a glossary, aimed at the uninitiated reader or teacher looking for helpful study aids. Finally, we hope the list of references and the index will help both the uninitiated and initiated to pursue further studies. It was impossible in the encyclopedic format of Chapter 3 to cite every source that helped us structure each entry. Therefore, at the end of each, we list a few key sources that the lay reader will find useful; the rest can be found in the references list.

As always, numerous folk need our thanks for their help in completing this volume, for such projects often take on an air of cooperative teamwork rather than individual accomplishment. Both of us greatly appreciate the friendly services of David Goldstein, without whose excellent research skills this thing might not have been completed. Ceceley Fishman hunted up books and articles, tracked down and reviewed videos (which section she also wrote), sorted through web sites, and cheerfully relieved Kay of such deadly activities as photocopying copious course readings, which gave her a minute or two to actually write. Kay admits that she might have gone quite bananas without both David and Ceceley. Kay also wants to thank her old teacher, Alfredo López Austin, who told her many years ago that she ought to explore more contemporary mythology; his words came instantly to mind when she was asked to do so for this project. Our spouses, Ned Read and Elizabeth Fuller-González, need our thanks for their patience with our unfortunately familiar and probably genetic displays of nerves. We also appreciate Elizabeth for filling in for Jason one spring when he had to take off to Guatemala for an extended period of fieldwork. Grandma Matilda Schwalbach provided support for this "meeting of 'great' minds," and a wonderful quiet hideaway in which to work uninterrupted. Finally, we wish to thank ABC-CLIO for their generous monetary, professional, and overall support of the project, especially Todd Hallman (who has to be the most patient editor we know), Susan McRory (for efficiently handling many last-minute questions and problems), and Liz Kincaid (for helping with our overly enthusiastic reaction toward the illustrations and all resultant problems).

Several excellent resources also need to be noted, both personal and printed. Laura Grillo read and responded helpfully to our definition of myth; Anna Peterson read all of Chapter One and made numerous helpful suggestions especially in the area of contemporary Mesoamerican religious, political, and economic history; and our son-brother Ian Read helped correct and update the final version of the sections on Central American political history. James Halstead kindly read portions, helping us with Church history and technical aspects concerning official Church doctrine. The many excerpts on the Cakchiquel Maya of Panajachel come from an unpublished manuscript, "The World of the Panajachel as Told by its Maya People in 1936 and 1937" by the late Sol Tax. The Native American Educational Services (Chicago) kindly gave us permission to use this absolutely wonderful material. James Brady generously sent us a huge list of sources on caves gathered for his doctoral dissertation, "An Investigation of Maya Ritual Cave Use with Special Reference to Naj Tunich, Peten, Guatemala" (University of California, Los Angeles, 1989). Nicholas Hopkins considerately sent a copy of a paper on Tila, Chiapas, and stories of the Black-Christ that he and Kathryn Josserand presented at the University of Pennsylvania. Andy Hofling generously opened his personal library to us and pointed us in many different directions in our search for various stories. Alan Sandstrom, completely out of the blue, offered us the use of his unpublished but translated transcriptions of contemporary Nahua myths gathered in the course of his own research, asking only to be acknowledged. We can't thank him enough for this rich, invaluable resource. And Max Harris sent us several articles on contemporary folk dances, without which a number of entries would have been far less interesting. Kay would like to thank in particular her Hispanic students in Religions of Native North America (Winter, 1998) who told her some great stories about La Llorona and even gave her a wonderful child's mystery book about La Llorona. Some of the contemporary Nahua cosmological material is drawn partially from Timothy Knab's novel *A War of Witches: A Journey in the Underworld of the Contemporary Aztecs* (HarperCollins, 1995). This material goes unattested in that publication, but is based on his ethnographic work in a Nahua village. A number of delightful conversations Kay held with Tim in Doris Heyden's Mexico City kitchen in summer 1997 confirmed and elaborated on that intricate cosmic vision (the chili rellenos Tim taught Kay to make were darn good too). Doris herself needs to be thanked, for Kay began work on the volume that summer while staying in her middle bedroom, happily raiding her extensive library, and running ideas by this honored grandmother of Mesoamerican mythology.

Kay Read

Jason González

August 2000

"The Bump," Three Lakes, WI

1

INTRODUCTION

Climbing the stairs, I emerged from the bustling, crammed subway station into the subdued light of a summer day in Mexico City's rainy season. The day before at this particular underground stop, a shrine had been dedicated to the Virgencita (Veer'-hen-seeta), the "Little Virgin" (Figure 1). The month before, she had made herself known through a simple water spot that took her shape on the concrete floor of the Hidalgo Metro stop, one of the busiest subway stations in the city's center. But after hundreds of worshipers from all over Mexico so jammed the already crowded station that it became almost impossible to use it for daily travel, the government and the Catholic Church both agreed to create the shrine at a station entrance adjacent to a nearly 500-year-old colonial church. The cement block containing her damp image was removed from the station's floor, placed behind glass, and mounted on the wall of a small arched nook tiled in bright blue, the Virgin's color. Thousands attended the dedication ceremony, ranging from prosperous men and women in business dress to poor folk from Oaxaca (Wa-ha´-ka) dressed in traditional clothing. A government representative spoke at the colorful affair, which was broadcast live on television, and a representative of the Church carefully noted how important the Virgin was to people's faith, without committing either himself or the Church to a genuine miracle. A band even played the appropriate tunes.

As I emerged wondering whether I had found the right entrance, I immediately discovered my way blocked by a long line of quiet worshipers stretching down the street and out of sight. An official stood at the shrine, gently making sure that people took their turn and that no one from the small group crowding around the shrine's front became too pushy. One young man eagerly leaned his camera's telephoto lens as close to the image as he could. Many in the line held an offering of a single rose bought from a woman who had been selling her flowers for years at that same entrance. A couple with two young children waited patiently in the line as it slowly inched toward the shrine. Two peacefully pleased nuns crossed themselves as they left the Virgin's presence.

Figure 1. Shrine of the Virgin of the Metro, Mexico City, 1998 (Kay A. Read)

Known as Guadalupe, the Virgin first appeared here in 1519, enshrined on a banner carried before the small army of Mexico's Spanish conqueror Fernando (Hernán) Cortés. And ever since 1531, when the peasant Juan Diego encountered Guadalupe dressed in her rose-covered blue cape, many Mexicans swear that she has continued to make her presence clear to all those in need whether they be statesmen, warriors, or peasants. In the early twentieth century, Guadalupe led the Mexican revolutionaries (Turner 1974, 105–106, 151–152). And in the summer of 1997, she chose the crowds of a subway station. At the time, the country was floundering in financial crisis. People were suffering, many had failing businesses, and many could not provide an adequate living for themselves or their families. Surely they and the country needed her help as had others many times before in the 500 years since the Conquest.

The Virgin is not the only powerful mythological female in Mesoamerica, for she has sisters in pre-Conquest times who also were mothers, although those maternal figures tended to take somewhat different forms. The Virgin first appeared to a man named Juan Diego on a hill called Tepeyac (Te-pay-yak), which lay just north of Mexico City. The site earlier had been consecrated to an ancient Mexica (Me-shee´-ka) or Aztec[1] deity named Tonantzin (To-nant´-zin), which means "Our Honorable Mother" in Nahuatl (Nah´-wat), the Mexica's language. Thus two honorable mothers, one from the New World and one from the Old, had occupied the same place of worship. Another fifteenth-century Mexica goddess, named Cihuacoatl (See-wa-ko´-wat), or "Snake Woman," was a powerful adviser for mothers-to-be; she also lent her powers to those tilling the land and going to war. Cihuacoatl dressed in the eagle feathers and jaguar blouse of warriors. Both birthing mothers and warriors invoked her presence. Even the second highest political leader in the Mexica domain took Cihuacoatl's name to indicate his advisory power for both agricultural matters and war. He dressed in her garb for high state rituals (*Codex Borbonicus* 1974, fols. 26, 28).

Ancient, pre-Conquest mothers could hold quite a few powers. In the ninth century, the Maya queen, Lady Zak Kuk (Zak-kook´), took office in order to divert the rule of Palenque (Pa-leng´-kay) (a site in today's Chiapas, Mexico) from another genealogical line to her own. Tracing her lineage back to an even older group called the Olmec (Ol´-mek) and to a great goddess archaeologists have fondly named "Lady Beastie," Lady Zak Kuk reigned 60 years before passing the throne to her son Pacal (Pa-kal´). This was a lengthy genealogy, for Lady Beastie was said to have lived at the beginning of time, and the Olmec civilization had died 1,000 years before Lady Zak Kuk and her son even breathed the jungle's air (Schele and Friedel 1990, 221–223).

Although all these potent ladies share motherhood and rely on mythological events for their various extraordinary powers, they have distinctive characters. Lady Zak Kuk and the high political leader who took Cihuacoatl's name were flesh-and-blood figures, whereas others, such as the goddess Cihuacoatl and Guadalupe, are less tangible. For some mythological figures (human or godly), motherhood is the primary power; for others, the ability to bear children is less important than powers in war, state affairs, or agriculture. As evidenced by the commonalities among the goddesses of various Mesoamerican peoples, many myths have been shared throughout time; yet in each era, people also have done things in their own way. Carefully guarded continuity coexists with creative invention in Mesoamerican mythology. And like the myths of these ladies, all Mesoamerican myths combine events that actually happened with events that probably never occurred but that nevertheless are equally important because of their symbolic and metaphorical messages.

This book surveys a wide variety of Mesoamerican myths and mythic beings, primarily focusing on myths of indigenous groups and of the common folk—in other words, those whom Latin Americans refer to as *el pueblo* (el pweb'-lo), "the people." In exploring this rich Mesoamerican world of mythological and metaphorical invention, we first define the nature of myth itself and then discuss the Mesoamericans who made the myths, their worldviews, and their history. This introductory chapter to Mesoamerican mythology is followed by a mythological timeline (Chapter 2) and by an alphabetical presentation of major deities and other powerful beings (Chapter 3). For those wishing further information, Chapter 4 offers an annotated selection of printed resources, and Chapter 5, a selection of films and videos. A glossary can be found at the end of the book. The first time they are introduced, phonetic spellings accompany most foreign names.

MYTHS AND THE REAL WORLD

Like all mythology, Mesoamerican myths cannot be defined simply as false stories, as in "Oh, that's just a myth." When people make such a statement, they usually mean that a particular belief is untrue—for example, the beliefs that toads cause warts, and as Huckleberry Finn thought, that the right incantation said over a dead cat at midnight in a graveyard will get rid of those offending bumps. That definition looks down its nose at old wives' tales, folk stories, and magical rituals because they are not considered either effective or true. But sometimes old wives were smarter than we think, or we hold too narrow a view of truth, or both.

Like myths around the world, Mesoamerican myths are actually true stories, because they describe either explicitly or metaphorically the way people think the actual world really is. But sometimes they describe the actual world in terms that we are not used to, using unusual analogies to model what is true—fantastic creatures doing strange things to impart true messages, or ordinary people acting in extraordinary ways. But in spite of fantastical creatures and extraordinary events, myths are never very far from the actual world. A true story (in that the events really did happen) might illustrate how myth is also true. This story was told in a beginning class in Religious Studies by a student in her first quarter at college.[2]

When I was very little, I lived on a farm way out in the country. My family was big, so there were always lots of people around, but there were no other children for me to play with, and I got very lonely. So I made up an imaginary friend named Zooma. Zooma was a man who wore a shirt like the repairmen in the TV advertisements for the utility company; it was a grey shirt with two stripes down one side, one yellow and one white. He could climb tall poles just like the repairmen, and was very friendly and helpful. He liked to play every game I wanted to play and he went everywhere with me. At breakfast every day, my Grandfather would ask me, "How is Zooma?" And I would tell him what we had done together.

One day some older cousins came to visit and they made fun of Zooma. They said he wasn't really real and that I was stupid to talk to some imaginary man. I was really hurt at being called a baby, so I killed Zooma. I threw him into the pond. When Grandpa asked how come he hadn't heard about Zooma lately, I told him how I had killed him. Grandpa said that wasn't very nice and he was sorry Zooma was gone. He said, "Why don't you bring him back?" And I said, "You can't bring back someone who's dead!" I felt really sad and guilty then.

Of course, even from the beginning, I knew Zooma wasn't real and that all my play with him was imaginary and my conversations with Grandpa were about something I had made up. It's not that I was stupid. I knew that I hadn't really killed anybody, because I knew he never existed. Still, I really felt like I really had killed him, and I really did feel very guilty and sad about doing that. Zooma was imaginary, but my feelings were not. Besides, he was part of my relationship with my Grandpa, and when I killed him, that part of our relationship was gone, because Grandpa never asked me about Zooma again.

Of course Zooma wasn't real in the sense that this little girl and her grandfather could touch him. But he was real in other ways. First, Zooma came from a true need: the little girl's loneliness and her desire for a friend. Second, he was based on things in the actual world: Television advertisements of utility repairmen who climb poles in grey shirts with two stripes really did exist. Third, Zooma helped build a close relationship between her and a very tangible friend, her grandfather. Fourth, her cousins really had been mean, but they also had spoken some truth. Maybe she hadn't been stupid, but Zooma really was imaginary, and even she knew it. Fifth, the pond really did exist, and someone could drown in it if they fell in—a warning she must have heard a billion times. And finally, the dead really can't be revived—at least, not in the adult world she knew. No wonder she felt real guilt and remorse, not only for her lost friend but for how her world had changed after his death. Even though it was because of him that she had been called a baby, Zooma really did cause her to grow up a little. This true story about an actual little girl's really real imaginary friend points out how myths function metaphorically. Zooma was a mythic being; he was a metaphor, an analogy, an imaginative model for a tangible friend, without being tangible himself. As such, he helped build a tangible friendship between the child and her grandfather, and allowed her to feel actual feelings of guilt and remorse.

Like the personally mythic Zooma, all myths (whether individual or communal) act in and on the tangible world metaphorically. They are at least partially based on actual things without being tangibly real themselves. They express and discuss actual issues and teach real things, even if all the players and events are imaginary. Myths do this because even though actual things happen to us every day of our lives, in order to act at all, we must somehow understand those things and make sense of them. Warts can appear and disappear for no apparent reason, and nocturnal graveyards are scary; little girls on farms really may live in a family with no other children; financial crises hurt both families and individuals; people get conquered; mothers give birth; and pre-Conquest statesmen and rulers run their governments. All that may be tangibly true, but one still needs to understand why and how these things happen and what that means for how one acts now; one must *interpret* events.

The metaphors in myths help us imagine the analogies needed to interpret life's actualities. And by so doing, we can take action to sustain or change them. Young boys can test their courage in graveyards at midnight while trying to get rid of their warts; small girls can gain a little wisdom; people in financial need can find the support to keep going; mothers can gain the courage and knowledge needed to give birth; and statesmen and rulers can devise models for successful rule. Because myths are based on the tangible world, they help us act in that world by allowing us to imaginatively discover the theories by which we can shape our actions.

Mesoamerican myths, like other myths, are true because (a) they describe the tangible world; (b) they explain that tangible world in human terms that make sense to the people telling the stories; (c) by interpreting the tangible world in a humanly meaningful way, they educate, provide guides, offer justification, and give the impetus for real action in the tangible world; and (d) by causing real action, they act back on that tangible world in ways that sometimes confirm the world as it is and at other times transform it by creating new mythic models capable of stimulating new action. Anything that can do these four things is a myth.

Myths come in a wide variety of categories. Zooma was a personal myth, a true story holding special meaning for just one person. But myths also can be communal or social, shared by many people. They can reflect the worldviews of all societal levels, from the privileged to those with fewer advantages. Families have myths, as do clubs, associations, institutions, neighborhoods, cities, and countries. Stories of a school's great football victories are part of its own particular institutional mythology. The legends of George Washington crossing the Potomac River to attack the British and of Father Hidalgo (Ee-dal´-go) crying from his church doors that the Spanish government in Mexico should be overthrown have mythic qualities. They are stories based in fact, which have been embellished by many artists and storytellers because of their heavy symbolic meaning. Often these different categories of myths mesh together in a single context: Medical doctors may find the Virgin of Guadalupe helpful in coping daily with illness and death, tales of a particular medical school's achievements may help its students strive for success in their own lives; and they may learn from the myth of Hidalgo the importance of relieving all human suffering, no matter the sufferer's social class.

Myths also come in many shapes and sizes. Traditionally myths take the form of verbal narratives or stories, tales, and legends. But mythic themes and stories can be imaged, drawn in pictures, carved in stone, embodied by buildings, and "painted" in verse. This is particularly true for Mesoamerica, where stories often have been sung and chanted. In pre-Hispanic times, songsters of myth used books of painted pictures as an integral part of their performances. Many archaeological ruins and ancient sculptures depict mythic themes and stories; the Sun Stone shows among other things the story of the Mexica Five Ages, and ancient temples often show the mythic relationships among the sun, the underworld, and earthly rulers. Mythic themes also can appear in places we don't often think of as mythic, such as theological treatises or the homilies told in church, which refer to beliefs about truth and God. For the thoughts and reasoning therein are based on mythically true stories, such as the sacrifice of Christ, or God's creation of the world. Hence the great Salvadoran martyr Archbishop Oscar Romero moved people to continue resisting oppression, giving them strength in the direst of times with his homilies, because he drew on Biblical myths about the dignity of the downtrodden, liberation, and Christ's own death and resurrection. From the earliest times to the present, Mesoamericans have told myths in many forms and in many styles.

THE MESOAMERICAN MYTHMAKERS

Who Are the Mesoamericans?

The Virgin and her pre-Conquest sisters, Hidalgo, and Archbishop Romero resided (and in some ways still reside) in an area that extends, roughly speaking, from northern Mexico to Nicaragua. In addition to most of Mexico and a part of Nicaragua, this area includes Belize, Guatemala, El Salvador, Honduras, and a bit of Costa Rica (Map 1). Mesoamerican influence also extended to the southwestern

United States at times (Adams 1991, 13–14; Miller and Taube 1993, 9). These boundaries were established by ancient civilizations that predated the Spanish by many thousands of years; in recent times, the independent states have somewhat expanded these territories. Although many different people lived in ancient Mesoamerica, four civilizations were particularly important (Miller and Taube 1993, 10): the Olmec (ca. 1500–1 B.C.), Oaxaca (ca. 600 B.C.–A.D. 521), the Maya (ca. 1500 B.C.–A.D. 1521, and the Central Mexicans (ca. 900 B.C.–A.D. 1521) (see Map 2). The Olmec occupied the Gulf region—today's Veracruz and Tabasco. On Mesoamerica's southern border, near the Pacific coast, lies the mountain valley of Oaxaca. The ancient Maya built their villages and cities primarily in what are now the southern Mexican states of Tabasco, Campeche, Yucatán, Quintana Roo, and Chiapas and the countries of Belize, Guatemala, El Salvador, Honduras, Nicaragua, and Costa Rica. Central Mexicans resided in the high plateaus in and around modern Mexico City. The Mexica (ca. 1350–1521) now are the best known group, although the people living before them in the great city of Teotihuacan (Tay-oh-tee-wa´-kan) (ca. 200 B.C.–650 or A.D. 750) held the farthest-reaching power of anyone in all of pre-Hispanic Mesoamerica; their influence extended all the way from northern Mexico to Guatemala.

Mesoamerica has an extraordinarily diverse geography and climate, ranging from deserts and semiarid zones to mountainous and tropical regions (Map 3). A rugged mountain chain runs along the Pacific side, from Baja California to Nicaragua; another chain borders the eastern, Gulf side. The mountains along the Pacific coast and in the central areas are punctuated by volcanoes, some of which are still active. In the year before the appearance of the Virgin of the Metro, for example, the volcano Popocatepetl (Po-po-ka-te´-pet) was smoking and occasionally blowing ashes over Mexico City. The people living in the village nearest the summit regularly performed rituals to calm the volcano. Earthquakes are also a reality of life in the region. Major temblors have occurred here (most recently, in 1985), and minor shocks are commonplace.

Traveling from the north of Mesoamerica to the southeast, one first encounters a formidable desert lying between the Pacific and the Gulf mountain ranges. From early times until only recently, this desert prevented the growth of complex civilizations in the area; for this reason, it is not a site of Mesoamerican culture, although the mountains bordering it are. Below this desert, large, snowcapped mountains and volcanoes surround the semiarid Basin of Mexico, where Mexico City lies at an altitude of about 8,000 feet. Descending and moving southward from there, one passes through a variety of ecological niches at various altitudes; the thermometer rises as one drops lower. The central and southern coastal areas of both the Gulf and the Pacific Ocean enjoy a tropical climate. In the north of southern Mexico lies the flat Yucatán Peninsula. Its limestone base is clothed in

Map 1 - Modern Nations of Mesoamerica

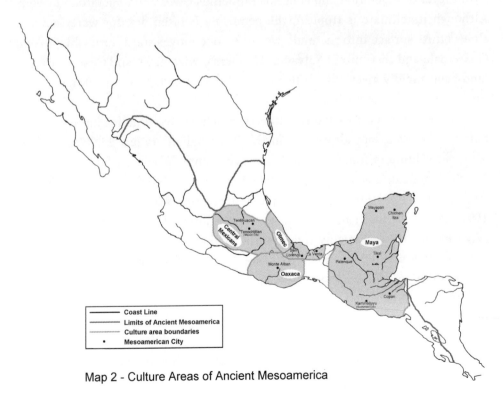

Map 2 - Culture Areas of Ancient Mesoamerica

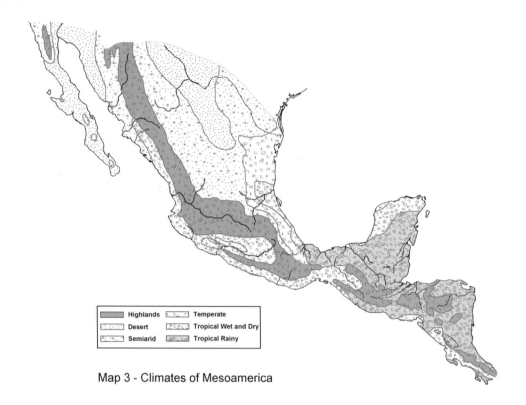

Map 3 - Climates of Mesoamerica

a thin layer of vegetation and conceals numerous caves and underground rivers. Although its climate is tropical, the peninsula is often dry, for water quickly slides off its surface into the underworld. As one moves south into Chiapas and Guatemala and east into El Salvador, Honduras, Nicaragua, and Costa Rica, the landscape rapidly rises into hills, which become mountains pockmarked by caves and covered by lush rain forests.

In spite of its jungles and rain forests, much of Mesoamerica has a semiarid climate. This was not always so. In the Paleo-Indian era (ca. 25,000 B.C.–7000 B.C.), early hunters found a cool, moist environment caused by the receding North American glaciers. The climate had become harsher and drier by the Archaic era (7000–1500 B.C.), when plant cultivation was in its infancy (Adams 1991, 25–45). At that time, two major seasons alternated much as they do now (Vivó Escoto 1964). Roughly five months of the year (June–October) are rainy, and the other seven (November–May) are dry. June, July, and early August bring gentle afternoon showers—the best rains for agriculture—almost daily. In late August, September, and October, thunderstorms appear, accompanied by high winds; these are the residue of the hurricane season occurring on the coastal areas. March, April, and May are driest, characterized by frontal winds that often bring dust storms. As we will see, these geographic and climatic conditions are frequent mythological themes.

Mesoamerican people are as diverse as their many geographic and climatic conditions, and cultural areas are often contiguous with particular geographic regions. Like other Native Americans, Mesoamerica's earliest ancestors probably began migrating from Asia around 30,000 to 40,000 years ago. They first traveled across the Bering Strait, where today just 50 miles separate Asia from Alaska. Back then, however, the earth was locked in an ice age that froze so much water that the oceans dropped up to 300 feet below their present levels, offering these early Asiatic peoples a land bridge of some 1,500 miles. Slowly they worked their way down the American continent to Mesoamerica over many thousands of years. Evidence indicates that nomadic hunters and gatherers inhabited the southern Basin of Mexico about 25,000 years ago. Both of these dates, however, may be overly conservative, and humans may have been roaming Mesoamerica's landscape even earlier. The skeletal remains of the earliest known humans in the area show a body structure much like that of present-day Indians; if dressed in modern clothing, these ancestors would go unnoticed on the streets of Mexico City today (Adams 1991, 29).

Mesoamericans did and do speak an enormous variety of languages. Spanish is now Mesoamerica's official language, but many people speak other tongues as well. For example, there are seven main branches of the Maya family of languages alone, each containing its own variants, many of which are unintelligible to speakers of another variant. A number of varieties of Nahuatl are spoken today in the central region of Mexico, and Oaxaca claims its own particular family of languages. All of these living languages also were spoken in pre-Conquest times, indicating strong forces of continuity at work in spite of the diversity. When appropriate, we will mark this diversity by noting in parentheses the language group or cultural name of the people to whom a mythic tradition belongs.

Beginning with the Conquest, Mesoamerica's mix of people became as varied as one can imagine. Following closely on the heels of the Spanish conquistadores, many others arrived: Dominican, Franciscan, Augustinian, and Jesuit clergy as well as the requisite governmental authorities and sundry opportunists, explorers, and adventurers. By the second half of the sixteenth century, not only had people of Spanish blood been born in New Spain but Indian and Spanish people had intermarried, and Black and Jewish people had joined the mix. Now this interracial and interethnic stew has become even more complex with the addition of many Europeans, Asians, and others from every corner of the world. These people have spread throughout Mesoamerica. As is true elsewhere, the greatest ethnic heterogeneity is found in the cities. And like any other major city in the world, Mexico City experiences all the joys and tensions of such enormous diversity.

How Do We Know about Mesoamericans?

With the introduction of European-style writing in the sixteenth century and the more recent advent of radio, television, video, and the WorldWide Web, numerous resources exist to tell us about Mesoamericans living since the Conquest. But how do we know anything at all about the many ancient peoples living before the Conquest?[3] Unfortunately, the Spanish conquerors destroyed great quantities of indigenous books, buildings, and sculptures. This makes learning about pre-Conquest Mesoamericans very difficult indeed; nevertheless, it is not impossible. One very rich source is archaeological ruins. Another is a few pre-Conquest books written in a pictorial form, which were lucky enough to escape destruction. A wealth of materials collected and recorded by the Spanish conquerors also remains. And numerous post-Conquest materials exist that can be used as analogies for understanding pre-Conquest peoples as well as peoples living after the Conquest. Of course, the closer one gets in time to the present, the easier it becomes. The most recent mythology often appears in newspapers, magazines, movies, and books, and on television. All of these sources report stories told in churches, on buses, around kitchen tables, or in bars. Myths were told like this in pre-Conquest times too, wherever people gathered: at rituals, on the road, around hearth fires, and in plazas.

Some of the best resources on pre-Conquest peoples are archaeological artifacts, such as buildings and urban plans, or other material cultural artifacts, such as pottery and sculpture. Archaeological evidence includes the material remains where Mesoamericans lived, the temples and pyramids where people participated in rituals, the roads where people walked, and the houses where people gathered around the hearths to tell their stories and myths. Unfortunately, the mere viewing, excavating, or reconstructing of this often impressive and beautiful architecture does not necessarily convey the content of ancient myths and stories. Sometimes one is lucky enough to find a written record in stone or clay, such as the stone stelae or columns at Classic Maya sites, which contain royal histories carved in Maya script. Usually, however, one must use other sources—written documents, oral histories, or ethnographic studies of living peoples—to help one interpret the meaning of archaeological remains. If a frieze on a building or a painting on a pot shows figures similar to those appearing in myths from other sources, then one might theorize that the figures are related to these stories, and take an educated guess as to their meaning. Or if a building is found to mark the solstices, then written and oral myths or histories that tell about solstices might help one understand why the builders were marking those particular celestial events.

Sculpture is an important source of archaeological information on mythology. Like people all over the globe, Mesoamericans permanently recorded mythic themes by incorporating them into architectural and self-standing stone sculptures, figurines, and a variety of other sculpted forms. Some of these sculptures were even incorporated into the stories and rituals, thereby structuring how new generations performed, retold, and remembered these myths. Mesoamericans created sculptures of a wide variety of forms and types. For example, a gigantic Sun Stone tells the story of the Mexica five ages. Wall murals found at Teotihuacan depict various stories and myths of individuals and deities; although we know very little about these personages, we can surmise their significance, based on later, written and pictographic texts. In a Preclassic temple at the Maya site of Cerros (Ser´-ros), the shape of the structure and the sculptured masks on its facade are believed to depict the universe itself (Figure 2). Some scholars believe Maya rulers used the temple as a ritual stage to reenact their travels through the Maya mythic world. And at Monte Albán (Mon´tay Al-ban´) in the Oaxaca valley, carefully constructed tombs of Zapotec (Za-po-tek´) rulers display painted murals showing supernatural scenes that might have been of special importance to the people who now rest there. Through the interpretation of artifacts such as sculptural art, we can to some extent rebuild the myths of pre-Conquest peoples.

Figure 2. A Preclassic temple at the Maya site of Cerros; the temple's shape and sculptured masks on its facade depict the Maya universe. (Kimbell Art Museum)

Figure 3. A Classic pottery vessel that depicts a Maya cosmic being; it was probably used in ritual ceremonies and feasting to offer food to deities. (Trustees for Harvard University. Slide 5-089-0055)

Another artistic medium that archaeologists frequently encounter in excavations is that of painted and decorated pottery. Traditionally, different Mesoamerican groups used pottery in ritual ceremonies and feasts during which food was offered to deities, various cosmic beings, and the ritual celebrants (Figure 3). Often they placed food offerings in specially made pottery, plates, bowls, or vases depicting mythic stories and deities. Among the Classic Maya, archaeologists and art historians have identified various scenes on Classic period pottery from the Colonial period K'iche' (Kee-chay')myth known as the Popol Vuh. Other Maya pottery shows scenes from a variety of different stories that we are just beginning to understand. In the Templo Mayor at Tenochtitlan (Te-noch-teet'-lan), archaeologists found incised burial urns portraying Mexica gods. And in one Monte Albán tomb, archaeologists discovered over the tomb's entrance funeral urns modeled into the shapes of Zapotec gods.

Sculpture and pottery are not the only artifacts on which archaeologists find mythic art: Mesoamericans also inscribed their stories on stones, bone, shell, jade, and obsidian. In sum, the only cultural objects that researchers have uncovered among archaeological ruins are those that withstood time and the natural elements and that were not found and taken away or destroyed by the Spanish or by modern-day looters. Soft materials such as cloth fibers or paper generally do not last, and foodstuffs and plant matter are only rarely found. Likewise, stories that were preserved only by their retelling or reenactment in ritual events have not survived the deaths of the people who perpetuated them. The interpretation of cultural artifacts that were removed from their original settings by unknown individuals (Spanish conquerors or looters) is very difficult, for an object's context tells much about its significance. For example, a bowl found in a kitchen area would have had very different uses from a bowl found on an altar or in a grave. Due to factors such as these, the archaeological record is indeed very incomplete. Fortunately, archaeological artifacts are not the only available resource. Much else has been preserved that can be explored in conjunction with material remains.

Pre-Conquest books called codices, for example, also exist (Figure 4). But because so many indigenous cultural artifacts were destroyed by the Spanish, only seventeen codices remain, fifteen of which are known to predate the Colonial era, and two of which originated either before the Conquest or very soon after.[4] Originally, these ancient books consisted of pictographs, sometimes including phonetic elements, that were painted on paper made from either bark or deerskin and folded accordion style, like a screen.[5] Their contents range from the complex Mesoamerican calendrical systems to genealogies, town histories, and descriptions of rituals. Sometimes the contents were acted out ritually, accompanied by oral recitations. Presently, close analytical studies are under way with the goal of decoding these complex texts.

The Spanish conquerors were at once repulsed and fascinated by the cultures they encountered in Mesoamerica, leading them to collect large quantities of information and to record copious impressions of the conquered natives. Military, religious, and governmental officials wrote accounts of "New Spain," gathered texts in the indigenous languages, and commissioned screen-fold codices from native artists. Native and mestizo authors, trained in Spanish schools, wrote books about their fast-disappearing traditions. Of the first group, for example, Cortés left his letters (Cortés 1986), and Bernal Díaz del Castillo (Ber-nal´ Dee´-az del Kas-tee´-yo), an officer serving under Cortés, wrote an account of the Conquest (Díaz 1956). Antonio de Mendoza (An-tone´-ee-oh day Men-do´-za), New Spain's first viceroy, commissioned a codex describing the history of the Mexica, the tribute they extracted from their vassals, and some of their daily

Figure 4. A Pre-Conquest book called a codex (The Codex Fejéváry-Mayor, Art Resource)

practices (Mendoza 1992). Father Diego Durán (Dee-ay´-go Doo-ran´) wrote an entertaining Mexica history based on a number of native histories that have since been lost (Durán 1971, 1994). The Franciscan Fathers André Olmos (Andray´ Ol´-mos) and Bernardino de Sahagún (Bare-nar-dee´-no day Sa-ha-goon´), sometimes collaborating, interviewed numerous natives from various walks of life. Olmos's collection from these interviews (see Maxwell and Hanson, 1992) is unfortunately largely lost, but Sahagún compiled a twelve-volume encyclopedia using his and Olmos's material (Sahagún 1953–1982). Written in Nahuatl and accompanied by loose and highly interpretive Spanish translations, this source is one of the most valuable. Father Diego de Landa (Dee-ay´-go day Lan´-dah) recorded what he understood about the Maya living in the Yucatán (Landa 1941, 1975). Others recorded in the original language the Maya books of the Chilam Balam (Chee-lam´ Ba-lam´), native-style histories based on indigenous calendars.

And in the sixteenth century, an unknown native songster recited the beautiful Maya myth the Popol Vuh (Poe´-pull Voo) to a priest, who wrote it down (Popol Vuh 1985). Of the second group, the indigenous authors Fernando de Alva Ixtlil-xochitl (Fare-nan´-doe day Al´-vah Isht-lil-shó-cheet), Hernando Alvarado Tezozomoc (Air-nan´-doe Al-va-rah´-do Te-zo-zó-mok), and the mestizo Diego Muñoz Camargo (Dee-ay´-go Moon´yoz Ca-mar´-go) wrote European-style histories glorifying their respective Central Mexican cities (Ixtlilxochitl 1985; Tezozomoc 1980, 1992) (Muñoz Camargo 1984).

Near the end of the Colonial period, in the late eighteenth century, travelers returning from Mesoamerica to their homes in Europe and the United States stimulated a renewed interest in the region. These cultural tourists also left behind a variety of sources that teach us much about archaeological sites and indigenous peoples. An English nobleman, Lord Kingsborough, used up all of his personal financial resources on collecting and reproducing beautiful hand-colored copies of many of the early codices, and eventually died in a debtors' prison in Britain. In the nineteenth century, New York lawyer John Lloyd Stephens and English architect Frederick Catherwood explored the Maya lowlands together. Catherwood's extraordinary drawings of many hitherto unrecorded ruins and Stephens's lively descriptions of what they encountered were best-sellers in their day and remain superb resources today (Stephens 1841) (Figure 5).

The twentieth century has seen both the growth of ethnographic studies and an integration of various disciplinary approaches to Mesoamerican studies. A wealth of fine studies of indigenous and other peoples exist—far too many to list here. Such studies not only help us understand how some current peoples live but also can provide insight into how pre-Conquest peoples might have lived; for although many changes have occurred in Mesoamerica's long history, much continuity also exists. The husband-and-wife team of Barbara and Dennis Tedlock, for example, have worked with a living K'iche' Maya daykeeper, Andrés Xiloj (An-drays´ Shee-loh´). This gentleman knows both an ancient calendrical system and the legend of the Popol Vuh, which he tells much as it was recorded in the sixteenth century by his unknown predecessor. Xiloj helped Dennis Tedlock translate this long and fascinating legend from K'iche' into English. Scenes from this same myth also appear on Maya pottery from the ninth century, testifying to this myth's great age. Although ancient Mesoamerica will probably never be completely understood because of its complexity and an often maddening lack of resources, the indication of continuity in a particular myth over the centuries makes the job a little easier. And recent collaboration among Mesoamericans like Xiloj and others from around the world—ethnographers, linguists, archaeologists, and historians who study both art works and written texts—has greatly enhanced our knowledge.

Figure 5. A drawing by Frederick Catherwood of the pyramid called El Castillo from the site of Chichén Itzá in Yucatán, Mexico (see also Figure 19) (Dover Pictorial Archive)

The Mythmakers' Worldviews

If one wanders through almost any of Mexico's crowded and bustling markets today, one can purchase plates, velvet wall hangings, T-shirts, key chains, wallets, and even shoes with an image of the Sun Stone adorning their surfaces (Figure 6). This now famous image was created by the Mexica, probably in the fifteenth century—less than 100 years before the Conquest. Sometimes incorrectly called the Calendar Stone (for it does not depict a calendar), it is really an elaborate example of a solar disk, a common ancient Mesoamerican symbol often associated with rulership.

By exploring the images blanketing the surface of this phenomenally complex and fascinating sculpture, we can gain some insight into the pre-Conquest cosmos, much of which persists today in indigenous and popular religion. The Sun Stone represented a cosmic topography that spoke simultaneously of four religious themes: (1) the world's space; (2) its power-filled inhabitants; (3) the calendrically structured form of transformative time that charted its indigenous history; and (4) the sacrifice that kept the cosmos's beings alive and functioning (Read 1997b, 824).

First, the cosmic topography appears on the stone's surface, where arrow-like solar rays map the cardinal and intercardinal directions, a sky band and two

Figure 6. The Postclassic Mexican Sun Stone (Drawing by Kay A. Read)

fire-snakes encircling the stone's outer edge depict the celestial realms of this cosmos, and jaguar-paw mouths framing the central face mark the terrestrial realms. Second, various power-filled beings inhabit this topography, from the little deities poking their heads out from between the fire-snakes' ferocious jaws, to precious stones of jade, the underworld's jaguars, and the godly face staring out from the center. Third, these beings change and transform according to a particular schedule controlled by a complex calendar. A ring depicting the twenty days founding the Mexica calendrical system joins the stone's celestial and terrestrial realms. And surrounding the central face and jaguar paws lie the emblems of the four ages or "suns" that predated the Fifth Sun, during which the Mexica lived. Each of these four ages was transformed into the next at the appropriate calendrical moment. Fourth, that enigmatic face sits in the dead center of a bull's-eye. Some believe it to be the daytime sun; some, the nighttime sun; and others, both. But all agree that a tongue, which is simultaneously a sacrificial blade, emerges from its toothy mouth as though panting in thirst and hunger for blood and flesh.

These same four themes—cosmic topography, power-filled inhabitants, calendrically determined transformation, and sacrifice—structured much of Mesoamerican life from the Preclassic era (2000 B.C.–A.D. 250), if not before, to the eve of the Spanish Conquest (A.D. 1521). And they have continued in sometimes altered form from the Conquest to the present. Christianity, of course, has played a major role since Fernando Cortés overtook the Mexica capital of Tenochtitlan in the sixteenth century, but traditional ideas of space, powers, transformation, and sacrifice have continued as sometimes subtle and sometimes not-so-subtle parts of what is particularly Mesoamerican in Christianity. And with Christianity came new mythic themes and ideas, which enriched the delicious stew pot of Mesoamerican religiosity.

Cosmic Topography

Traditionally, Mesoamericans live in worlds shaped by mythological visions.[6] These land- and skyscapes are always local in character. Particular mountains, caves, springs, and other terrestrial features define a town's landscape; and the sun, moon, and other celestial bodies create its outermost boundaries by moving along its particular horizon. Such particularity means that each human settlement is formed by its own unique cosmology. Nevertheless, almost all communities have shared certain larger visions, some apparently enduring for thousands of years. Each community enjoys its own version of these visions. One might imagine a grand world extending from the Gulf's eastern horizon to the Pacific's western horizon; northward and southward rise great mountains. Yet this great cosmic landscape contains many smaller ones, each belonging to a specific village, town, or city: each distinctive, yet similar.

Think of these cosmic topographies as containers, metaphoric terrariums in which move gods, other powerful beings, and people living out their lives. Inside these great houses, they eat, defecate, sleep, make love, work, wage war, and play tricks. All life is held within their boundaries. Like the water and gases cycling through a terrarium's space, water, beings, and many various powers flow throughout. And like a terrarium's plants, beings sprout, grow, blossom, die, and rot to nourish beings to come. Life forms continually cycle through this terrarium-house, disappearing only to appear in new forms. In precontact times, as beings moved round and round these containers, living and dying as they moved, each topographic container moved toward its own death, for each also was considered a living being that eventually must die.

Most cosmic houses are squared-off and divided into quadrants; often laid out horizontally like a four-petaled flower whose topside sometimes is called Earth's Surface (Figure 7). The precontact Mixtec depicted this schema in the Codex Fejérváry-Mayer (Figure 4), and the present-day Nahua (Na´-wa) of San Martín use a similar image to describe the underworld, which they call *Tlalocan*. The cardinal and intercardinal directions mark the flower's sides and corners. Each quarter is associated with a particular color, and often with a particular mountain. In many depictions, a great tree sprouts from each quadrant, with a bird perching atop its branches. Particular gods also claim governance over each quarter. Sometimes appropriately colored rain gods send their moist offerings from each; at other times, sets of gods that some call Bacabs (ba-kabs´, Yucatec Maya) and some others call Tlaloques (tla-lo´-kays, Nahua) hold each quarter erect. A powerful center point punctuates this terrestrial flower, and may act as its greenstone heart. Sometimes this center point demands sacrifice to keep the cosmos living. A watery, celestial, upper world arches over Earth's Surface; below extends a dank and rotting underworld. The sun travels through the upper world's waters during the day, and at night, when the moon and stars have taken its place above, through the underworld's caverns.

These cosmic containers were believed to have been created by various deities, who "spread" them out in the same way one pats out tortillas. Surrounding celestial waters "spread" as water spreads in a pan. In the precontact Nahua story of the five suns, each age was "patted out" and "divided" into its proper portions. Today, the Nahua of San Miguel Tzinacapan (San Mee-gel´ Tsee-na-ka´-pan) describe Earth's Surface as a *comal*, the flat pan that Mexicans use for roasting tortillas. The sun traveling above it produces corn with its heat; the sun beneath the comal, in the underworld, is the hearth fire that cooks tortillas made from that corn. And for the Cakchiquel (Kak-chee-kel´) Maya of Panajachel (Pa-na-ha-chel´), the watery sea spreads out to the horizon until it joins with the sky.

The horizontal quartering of precontact topographies seems fairly clear, but there is less agreement about the structure of the vertical plane. Many scholars have described precontact cosmoses as having consisted of either thirteen or nine celestial layers extending upward from the earth's surface and nine terrestrial layers extending downward. Unfortunately, the pre-Hispanic evidence for such hypotheses is slim. Among Nahua sources, for example, this interpretation is drawn from two main postcontact resources: (1) several lists (recorded mostly in Spanish) that enumerate different sets of "sky-waters" (*ilhuicatl*) and "lands-of-the-dead" (*mictlan*), which bear no reference to any topographical locations; and (2) a single pictorial codex (commissioned by the Spanish) that arranges one

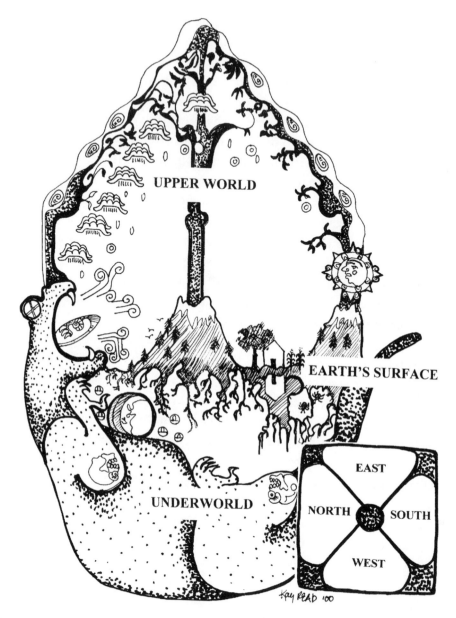

Figure 7. An imaginative rendering of a Mesoamerican mythological cosmos, portraying the upper world, earth's surface, and the underworld as well as the four cardinal directions (Drawing by Kay A. Read)

such set in vertical layers. Its Spanish commentator calls the sky-waters and lands-of-the-dead "heavens" and "hells" and makes explicit comparisons to a medieval cosmology similar to that described by Dante in *The Inferno*. One might ask whether this vertical arrangement of sky-waters and lands-of-death is not the result of Spanish misconceptions attempting to bridge two very different cultures. Today, however, contemporary Maya myths exist that describe the thirteen levels as moving seven up and six down like the sides of a pyramid.

The underworld is the place of death and of rot, a dank reverse of the dry, living surface of earth. The subterranean Land of Death for the sixteenth-century Nahua was walled by water and contained no smoke holes. Yellow dogs carried the dead on their backs across the "the place of nine waters" (also called *Tlalocan*, or the Rain God's Land); there in the Land of Death they "completely disappeared."[7] Today's K'iche' Maya also describe the underworld as a fetid place honeycombed with mountainous chasms and watery channels bearing such names as Pus River and Blood River. It is peopled by unpleasant characters like Seven Death, Blood Gatherer, Pus Master, Skull Scepter, and Trash Master. In the 1930s, the Cakchiquel Maya of Panajachel said that the devil lived inside a hill and lured people to his house, to eat. When he needed laborers, he either bribed weak souls to work for him or he asked God for them; at such times, sickness arose everywhere. Today, among the San Miguel Tzinacapan Nahua, the underworld mirrors the upper, with upside-down villages, and mountains just like those above. The Tzinacapan say that in Mexico City, skyscrapers descend as far into the earth as they ascend above its surface.

Although these trees and mountains are stationary, other living things have the capacity to move through these topographies. Some beings follow predetermined paths; others travel more freely. Like traders carrying bundles of goods, the sixteenth-century Nahua sun and moon bore their burdens of time along paths through the sky and underworld, just as the stars and Venus bore time along ancient, precontact roadways. Running water coursed through this entire Nahua land- and skyscape. Mountains, like pots, held the water that was released by Tlaloc (Tla´-lok, Rain God) or the goddess Chalchiuhtlicue (Chalchee-oot-li´-kway) in the form of rain or rivers. Water came from the sea via underground rivers to the mountains, changing from salt to fresh as it moved into the land. Thence it burst forth in lakes, springs, streams, and rivers, thereafter to return to the sea, where it formed the celestial walls. Deities and numerous other beings including birds, animals, and people were not confined to certain roadways, and had more freedom.

Temples and churches often mirror these cosmic topographies. Tenochtitlan, the huge Mexica (Nahua) fourteenth-to-sixteenth-century urban center, where the Templo Mayor (Temp´low Mai-yor´, Great Temple) stood, also was apportioned into four quarters, with the main, ritual district in its exact center. As a symbolic mountain, the Great Temple hid the underworld in its many buried caches. These were filled with the sacrificial bodies of all manner of celestial and terrestrial animals; the mountain-dwelling Tlaloc (the Rain God) also was liberally represented.

Many contemporary communities interweave indigenous and Christian elements, creating a new religious tradition. Sacred mountains and water holes mark San Juan Chamula's (San Hwan Cha-moo-lah´) Tzotzil (Tsot-zeel´) landscape. Its church door faces west, and its altar is on the east side. Outside the church, the ritual space is divided in two; on the north is the area of the rainy agricultural season, and on the south, that of dry dormancy. The western, feminine side is where the Christ-Sun descends into the underworld; the eastern, masculine side is where the Christ-Sun rises again.

Whereas some view the underworld as hell and the sky as heaven, others view the under- and upper worlds as equally filled with beneficial or dangerous potentialities. In San Martín (Nahua) the four quarters of the underworld boast mythic roots going back hundreds of years, to the great Classic city of Teotihuacan, and before. Healers and witches travel through its labyrinthine topography to seek help from its powerful inhabitants. But since the Conquest, the upper world has become the home of God, Jesus Christ, Mary, and a host of saints, all of whom can also help or hinder healers and witches in their efforts to meet the challenges of life on Earth's Surface.

In sum, Mesoamerican topographies have both changed and endured through time. With the coming of the Spanish, new themes were introduced; in many places, these themes blended with indigenous perceptions in the most wonderfully complex ways. And along with that blending, a phenomenally multifaceted portrait of Mesoamerican mythology emerged, which has continued to shape and reshape itself up to the present.

Power-filled Inhabitants

Many diverse beings inhabit the traditional topographies.[8] Everything and anything can be animated by a huge variety of powers, whether these beings move on their own accord or not. Mountains, caves, lakes, rivers, and oceans, and the humans, animals, birds, insects, fish, rocks, trees, flowers, and plants that live on, above, and in them, all have the potentiality for life. Because they have the living powers to do so, even the sun, moon, stars, and planets traverse the sky's pathways as though on a journey. Therefore, categories like "animate" and "inanimate" don't really apply to this universe, for all things are in some sense animate. Among the ancient Mexica (Nahua), for example, there were no inanimate things. Instead, the Mexica distinguished between beings that could move on their own, as could people, animals, and various spirits and deities, and those that had to be moved by others, like rocks, corn, and trees, which were rooted to particular spots. Each being had its appropriate path to follow or place to occupy. And each, because it was alive, was born, changed as it went through life eating its appropriate food, and died when its life span had been appropriately completed.

In Mesoamerica, one interacts with various beings on a daily basis; with some, periodically; and with others, only through special rituals (Read 1997b, 825). Forests and deserts might be filled with spirits that can trip one up—or do worse—as one traverses them. In ancient Nahua times, a two-headed deer turned into two beautiful women. One of them seduced a hunter and then ate him. The other chased his brother through the wilderness until she was trapped on a cactus and shot with arrows by some powerful female goddesses of the sky. To keep a tree from falling on him, a Colonial-era Nahua woodcutter might ask it not to "eat him" before he forcibly moved it from its otherwise appropriate spot. A beautiful female spirit lives today in the jungles of El Salvador who is ready to seduce and then kill unsuspecting men with her enormous teeth. In San Martín (Nahua) one might encounter deceased ancestors and neighbors, witches, gods, saints, or even the devil in dreams. Some of these might try to kill one; others are less nasty, and some may even be of help.

In precontact times, good ancestral names had powers to shape a child's personality. And shortly after birth, a baby ritually acquired a calendrical name that gave it both good and bad powers. A girl born during a certain week might carry the powers of the goddess Xochiquetzal (Show-chee-ket´-zal) and so be destined to become a great weaver if she behaved properly. If not, she would fall into bad ways. One young boy of royal Mexica (Nahua) lineage hoped to become a ruler, but only if he could overcome the powers of the day upon which he was first named, for those powers could push him toward indecisiveness or cowardice. For some rulers, part of their right to govern was based on the powers of their mothers, who handed these powers on to their sons when they were installed. Names and royal blood were important because the energies flowing through ancestral lineages bore especially effective powers for governance (lineages and patron deities). And in state ceremonies, Maya rulers drew their own blood in order to offer its life-giving powers to various cosmic beings, including the sun. Among the Nahua in San Miguel Tzinacapan today, marigolds are believed to have powers that link people with the sun. Like their ancient ancestors, the Tzinacapan Nahua believe the flowers bear an internal heat and the force of life because their seeds are mature when the flower is still alive. The bright yellow flowers also represent the hearts of the deceased, and people decorate with marigolds on the Day of the Dead, when the living welcome the dead back to share a feast with them.

Since they believed that everything was alive, ancient Mesoamericans understood the world in particular ways. Before the Conquest, observations of such things as astronomical events and the way a body fell sick and was healed were just as keen among Mesoamericans as in European science during the same era. In fact, Mesoamericans were ahead in some areas. The mathematical concept of zero was understood there before it was in Europe, and Cortés quickly learned that Mesoamerican healers were better at setting the bones of his injured conquistadores than his own medical personnel. But their keen and often accurate observations were and still are performed from a very different vantage point. As Clara Sue Kidwell has noted, Native American science is often based on the idea that all things have wills that must be accounted for if one is to control a situation effectively. So unlike European scientists, indigenous Mesoamerican scientists may not look for the general laws that govern the natural world but for the wills of the beings inhabiting that world (Kidwell 1992, 396). The sun follows a certain path throughout the years not because it is a law but because the sun's will or inborn nature is such that it is appropriately suited to this particular path.

Calendrically Determined Transformation

Because all things have the capacity for life, transformation characterizes all of cosmic reality just as it does all of everyday life (Read 1997b, 825; 1998, 38–39, 84–88). One is not the same as one was when one was born a screaming, red-faced baby. Nor is one the same as one will be when one dies a stooped and wrinkled old woman or man. Nor does one's personality stay the same throughout life; the baby is not the young woman or man, who is not a mature adult with children and grandchildren of her or his own; nor are they the aged for whom others care. Change is a part of ordinary life. And in a cosmos in which all things live, all things are transformed from one life stage to the next, until death causes their powers to change yet again.

A cosmic reality based on transformation also means there is no difference between time and space, for no space can exist that is not timed by its own life span. All things, because they are alive, are born into a particular space; they grow, age, die, and decay through time in a particular space, which also grows, ages, and dies. A baby through time becomes an adult and then an old person in particular places at appropriate times. The tree begins as a young shoot only to grow old and wither away; at its death, its powers pass on to others. Even the living mountains change. They may wear down slowly, or they may suddenly blow out lava and hot ash, irrevocably and quickly changing the landscape and the lives of all who live there. All beings hold within their bodily spaces a living clock that times their living transformations.

Many mythic metaphors express this reality of transformation. Mexica corn grew from seed into a plant, eating the underworld's rotting loam. People then ate corn's mature fruit, digested it, and used their excrement, which came from eating the corn, to fertilize new corn. In the Popol Vuh, when two Maya Hero Twins sacrificed themselves in the underworld, two corn plants that had been growing in their mother and grandmother's house above, on Earth's Surface, died. The boys' bones were ground like cornmeal, from which the twins regenerated themselves in new forms; first, they became fishermen, and later, elderly magicians. At that same moment, their corn above ground grew again. Eventually, the twins rose, transformed into the sun and the moon. Many Mesoamericans believe that because people were created from corn at the beginning of the Fifth Age, they are spiritually the same; and many ancient rulers, like the Maya hero twins, shared the powers of corn and of the sun. In contemporary San Martín (Nahua), healers and witches can shape-shift, turning into the creatures whose powers they share—such as opossums, owls, mice, or even horrible monsters.

"Nothing is forever" in this precontact world of "fleeting moments," where even "jade shatters" and one journeys through life for "just a short time" (Read 1998, 113–114). These words attributed to the fifteenth-century poet Nezahualcoyotl (Neza-wal-koy´-ot), accurately describe the timed impermanence of Mesoamerican existence. In Nezahualcoyotl's time, a living being, whether moving or rooted to a spot, underwent transformative growth and death according to its appropriate life schedule. Even suns' lives were timed. Many saw themselves inhabiting a short-lived fifth sun that had been preceded by four earlier suns. After a set period, each sun found itself changed into the next sun by means of some sort of violent destruction. Numerous variations of sun-age myths appear across Mesoamerica. Some postcontact communities tell stories that include Jesus, Mary, and various saints; others tell about only more ancient deities who do quite different things. Sometimes four sun-ages appear, sometimes five; and the colors associated with the cosmos's quadrants may vary or may not even be mentioned.

"This is the beginning, the Ancient Word, here in this place called K'iche'." And so begins the Popol Vuh intoned by a contemporary Maya daykeeper, or diviner. In the beginning, only gods existed: Plumed Serpent and Heart-of-Sky "who came as three" (Popol Vuh 1985, 73). They made the earth to rise, and then created the first age of animals, causing them to talk each to each, within each kind. But the animals could not say their creators' names, so they were eaten. The gods tried again. In the second age, they molded people from mud, but their efforts were not good. The clay people were lopsided, stupid, and fell apart. They didn't work, so the gods destroyed them. In order to get it right in the third age, the gods first asked Xpiyacoc (Shpee-ya-kok´) and Xmucane (Shmoo-ka-nay´) to count the days and cast lots with corn kernels. Then they created wooden manikins; but these fleshless beings had no hearts and minds, and no memory of their creators. So Heart-of-Sky killed them with a great flood of resin raining down upon them, the animals tore them apart, and even the manikins' own grinding stones and griddles pulverized them. After the Hero Twins balanced life with death and put the fourth age in order, proper humans were finally shaped. Xmucane ground corn for their flesh with water for their blood, and the gods molded the first four couples by means of these "sacrificial" acts.

The Nahua version from the Codex Chimalpopoca (Chee-mal-po-po´-ka) is quite different. This tale was told to a Spanish-employed recorder on 22 May 1558: The first sun-age was called 4-Jaguar, the food was 7-Grass, and the age stretched out for 676 years; jaguars ate this age. The second age was called 4-Wind. Its beings turned themselves into monkeys whose houses were trees and who ate 12-Snake. This age lasted 364 years, until wind blew it away. The third age was called 4-Rainstorm. Its beings turned into turkeys and ate 7-Knife. This age stretched out for 312 years, when Fire Rain burned it up. The fourth age was called 4-Water. The beings of this age ate 4-Flower. This age stretched out for 676 years, until a flood destroyed it. The current, fifth age is called 4-Movement because it moves along a path; the old, wise ones say that earthquake and famine will destroy it and we will all perish.

As in the Popol Vuh, multiple transformative destructions created the world as one knows it. But in the Chimalpopoca's story, each sun's life span is carefully counted out. Each contains its own unique inhabitants who live in unique houses and eat their own food (although no one knows what these foods were). Each sun draws its name from the manner of its destruction. And instead of four ages, there are five. Unlike the Popol Vuh, no moral message appears in this apparently simple recounting of events. This is a calendrical text, not an ethical one, for the arithmetic mirrors the math used to count time. Multiples of 26 count out each sun's time span, and five ages are conflated into four of 676 years by joining the counts of the second and third suns. A Maya daykeeper's divination board is divided just like this, with four parts of 676 counts—one for each of earth's quarters.

Calendrical patterns structured all these various transformations. The tale of the Nahua five suns and the Popol Vuh both are filled with obscure and sometimes hidden calendrical references. They describe not only how the world came to be but also how one calculates its existence according to the motions of particular celestial beings along their appropriate paths. The importance of calendrical calculations cannot be overstated; they are extraordinarily ancient and have permeated all aspects of life for centuries, continuing even today. Not only do things change and metamorphose according to some calendar, but much of daily life was and still can be ruled by calendrical calculations. In ancient times, one did almost nothing important without first figuring out its calendrical meaning. Calendars are even believed to control life's boundaries, for all the diverse beings living in the cosmoses live for particular spans of time that can be calculated calendrically. Even the earthquakes that would end the Mexica (Nahua) cosmos would not come until the Fifth Sun's calendrically calculated life was finished.

Today, calendars are still used to calculate the appropriate times for baptisms, marriages, trips, important business deals, and burials, although much of the complex ancient system has disappeared. The calendrical cycles, especially those governing state rites, were mostly (although not entirely) abolished under Spanish rule because of their political and religious import. Agricultural and divinatory calendars used by healers and daykeepers in remote villages escaped the Spanish because it was easier to hide them from the conquerors' eyes. Complex cycles of church festivals such as saints' days today govern much of religious life in both towns and villages. In El Salvador, this cycle may even replicate the old indigenous state festival calendar that the Spanish thought they were abolishing. And in the Maya area, service to the Catholic church follows the same indigenous calendrical patterns that governed service to the ancient temples. In the sixteenth century, the Spanish did not see such service patterns as religious but as secular; therefore, they did not expend much energy on trying to stamp them out. The indigenous participants at the time, however, probably had a more mythic view of the practice. They continued to serve the cosmos's beings as they had always done; only now some names had changed and new beings had been added.

Sacrifice

In ancient times, sacrifices nourished the living beings of the cosmos, thereby bringing about and controlling transformations (Read 1997b, 826; 1998, 123–155). Many know about the Mexica (Nahua) high state rites in which hearts were cut from the chests of warriors and offered to the sun. Certainly Hollywood and other popular media have made much of these particular rites, but most rites were not nearly as dramatic or gory as Hollywood depicts them. Few know the full variety and complexity of sacrificial practices, the extent of their integration into daily life, or that most offerings were not humans but rather animals, birds, or plants. Ritual blood-letting was one of the most common and widespread practices; small quantities of blood were offered on numerous ritual occasions, from the simple naming ceremonies of Nahua newborns to the high state ceremonies of Maya rulers. Human blood was not always used. The first corn tortilla eaten at dawn was seen as a sacrifice to the sun. Quails, jaguars, crocodiles, ducks, fish, snakes, salamanders, and amaranth cakes also found their way into sacrificial rituals. In fact, just about anything edible might be considered an appropriate sacrifice, although which food would depend on the culinary requirements of the ritual circumstances. The dedication of a new temple often required the blood of warriors captured from enemy cities. But simple amaranth cakes shaped like a god could serve the same purpose in politically less important circumstances.

Sacrificial techniques also varied widely. Extreme forms of human sacrifice included heart extraction, decapitation, drowning, and shooting with arrows. Rituals involved both willing and unwilling participants, from any segment of society—again, depending on the circumstances. Females and males of all ages were sacrificed; sometimes they were foreigners, but often not. The foci of all these rituals were equally diverse; sacrifice was associated with war as well as with the agricultural cycle, and appropriate sacrifices were offered to celestial recipients like the sun, terrestrial ones like the Earth Monster, or those in the underworld who were in need of sustenance. In ancient times, sacrifice permeated all existence from one's daily tortillas to birth and warfare, and it was performed in many ways for many reasons.

Many also are not aware of sacrifice's antiquity in Mesoamerica. Only a short time ago, it was thought that human sacrifice was primarily the invention of the Mexica or Aztecs in the late Postclassic era (ca. 1200–A.D. 1521). But as more and more archaeological data came to light, it became clear that sacrifice had an extremely long history throughout the area. Not only did Mexica priests cut the hearts out of warriors; Maya rulers waged wars after which their human booty was dispatched in similar sacrificial rituals. The sacrificial remains of 32 young men have been found in the foundations of a plaza in a small town in Belize, dating back to the late Preclassic era (ca. 400 B.C.–A.D. 250).

The tremendous diversity of sacrificial rites and their occasionally impressive drama has resulted in a large number of scholarly theories. For perhaps obvious reasons, sixteenth-century Spanish observers tended to overemphasize sacrifice's frequency and violence. Their explanations varied. Some explained indigenous sacrificial rituals as misguided practices originating with the devil; some likened indigenous sacrifice to Christian penance; others saw it as mere superstition. Each explanation depended on the author's own background and on the context and nature of the specific rite in question. Modern explanations have varied even more. Some scholars have viewed Mesoamerican sacrifice as merely one stage in a lengthy evolutionary process. Others, focusing on its environmental, biological, political, social, or psychological functions, have suggested a number of different theories: Sacrifice may have served as a means of population control, as a necessary means of providing protein to supplement people's daily diet, as a way for the elite to maintain power, or as a practice aiding political expansion.

In trying to uncover the religious logic that structures these rituals, others have focused primarily on sacrifice as a coherent system of beliefs. Many of this group of scholars agree that precontact sacrifice involved the ritual sharing of a variety of plant, animal, and human comestibles; sacrifice was a way to feed the many living beings of the universe. Most also believe that sacrifice included some kind of exchange between human and nonhuman entities; such exchanges nourished the cosmos's inhabitants and maintained them in an ordered state of existence. The logic here was simple: If one wanted the cosmic beings to provide food, one had to feed the cosmic beings in return.

A number of scholars have noted the close sacrificial bond between death and destruction and life and creation, a bond that also correlates with concepts of transformation. A close bond exists between eating and transformation in several ways. One must eat to live; eating nourishes life's transformations. If one does not eat, one will die, and the transformation of death will occur. And in order to eat, one must kill something else, transforming that thing into food that is digested and then excreted in a different form. In other words, eating things and thereby destroying them creates new things. Just as the ancient transformative realities saw no difference between time and space, so too those hungry beings saw no difference between life and death or creation and destruction, for one cannot occur without the other.

Some theories of sacrifice do not account for the phenomenon generally but focus almost exclusively on those stupendous high state rituals. None adequately explains this complex, widespread, and ancient phenomenon. For the purposes of understanding the bulk of Mesoamerican mythology, it is probably most helpful to view sacrifice as a transformative exchange that nourishes and maintains the many living beings inhabiting the various Mesoamerican cosmoses. Sacrifice creatively transformed the things of the ancient Mesoamerican world by destructively feeding some beings to other beings. This sustenance allowed gods, spirits, people, animals, plants, and mountains to grow and transform. Rituals following a carefully calculated calendrical system gave order to this transformative process of eating, for they regulated when, where, and why sacrificial transformation should take place. Ancient Mesoamerican beings needed to eat on time if transformation was to be controlled.

With the Spanish, a new kind of sacrifice entered Mesoamerica: the one-time sacrifice of Jesus Christ. For the Europeans steeped in this sacrificial tradition, traditional Mesoamerican practices seemed at once familiar and strange. For some, the killing of humans perverted God's will. One was not supposed to really kill someone and then eat his or her flesh. Sacrifice was to be a symbolic act; God acted through bread and wine, not through actual bodies. Hence, in spite of all the violent bloodshed allowed in their own political wars of conquest, the Spanish considered native rituals of human sacrifice an abomination. But some of the Spanish observers found other forms of sacrifice more understandable because they paralleled their own medieval practices of penance. They seemed to admire them even though the natives directed these apparently penitential practices at the wrong gods, for at least they showed the seriousness of their piety. Like Europeans who willingly chose to suffer in order to demonstrate their intense devotion to God, these natives also were willing to suffer for their gods. Nevertheless, the Spanish promptly outlawed all forms of formal sacrifice addressed to native gods. Only the Christian god could receive offerings, and these must be appropriate to Christian penitential practices.

Still, some traditional sacrificial practices persisted. Sometimes ancient practices were transformed into penitential Christian practices, and sometimes they remained very much the same, only quietly performed out of the sight of the wrong eyes. Today, the ritual sacrifice of chickens and other animals is a common practice. Scattered, infrequent reports and rumors of human sacrifice have continued even up to the present, although the reporters of these tales rarely are able to document and prove them. In the 1930s, in San Martín (Nahua), it is reported that a man was hung from a cross in front of the village church to end a violent feud among the village's healers, witches, and landowners.

MESOAMERICAN CULTURAL HISTORY

Four cultures have played especially important roles in Mesoamerica's history: the Olmec (ca. 2250–300 B.C.); Oaxaca (ca. 1400 B.C.–present); the Mexican highland peoples (ca. 1200 B.C.–present); and the Maya (ca. 400 B.C.–present) (see timeline opposite). Two, the Olmec and the peoples of the Mexican highlands, have exercised influence and sometimes even considerable power over great geographic expanses of Mesoamerica. The Maya and those living in Oaxaca have been somewhat less powerful in the grand scheme of things but nevertheless have made major cultural contributions to Mesoamerican life. Each of these four cultures developed its own distinctive characteristics, yet all have shared a great deal culturally and mythologically over the centuries.

Focusing on these four Mesoamerican cultures, we can distinguish seven historical periods: (1) the Paleo-Indian (ca. 25,000 B.P.–7,000 B.C.); (2) the Archaic (ca. 7,000–2,000 B.C.); (3) the Preclassic (ca. 2000 B.C.–A.D. 250); (4) the Classic (ca. A.D. 250–900/1000); (5) the Postclassic (ca. A.D. 900/1000–1521); (6) the Spanish Conquest and Colonization of Mesoamerica (A.D.1521–1808); and (7)

Timeline of Mesoamerican Culture Areas

	23000 B.C.	7000 B.C.	2000 B.C.	A.D. 250	A.D. 1000	A.D. 1521	A.D. 1808	Today
	Paleoindian	Archaic	Preclassic	Classic	Postclassic	Spanish Conquest and Colonialism	Independence	
	Mythic Beginning of Time							

Central Mexican
5048 B.C.; 1185 B.C.

Teotihuacan zenith ~500 A.D. Toltec Diaspora ~1000 A.D. Tenochtitlan zenith 1519 Grito de Hidalgo 1810

Maya
3113 B.C.

Loltun Cave Palenque zenith ~700 A.D. Chichen Itza founded ~900 A.D. Zapatista Rebellion 1994

Oaxaca
??

Monte Alban founded ~500 B.C.

Olmec
??

La Venta founded ~1200 B.C.

Spanish Conquest 1521 Peasant Rebellions 1531–1801 Mexican Independence 1821 Mexican Revolution 1910–1920

CHRONOLOGY OF MESOAMERICAN HISTORY

CULTURE AREA	SPANS OF EXISTENCE
Olmec	2250–300 B.C.
Oaxaca	1400 B.C.–Present
Mexican Highlands	1200 B.C.–Present
Maya	400 B.C.–Present

TIME PERIOD	KEY EVENTS	DATES
Paleo-Indian	Tequixquiac, bone of dog	23,000–7000 B.C.
Archaic	Loltún Cave	7000–2000 B.C.
Preclassic		2000 B.C.–A.D. 250
	La Victoria/cultivation of corn	~1500 B.C.
	Valley of Oaxaca	~500 B.C.–A.D. 200
	Monte Albán	
	Earliest divinatory calendar dates	
	Olmec	~2250–300 B.C.
	San Lorenzo	zenith ~1200–900 B.C.
	La Venta	1200–400 B.C.
	Valley of Mexico	6000 B.C.–Present
	Tlatilco	1200–400/300 B.C.
	Cuicuilco/earliest solar date	679 B.C.
	Cuicuilco's round pyramid	400 B.C.
	Volcanic eruption	150 B.C.
	Teotihuacan rises	100 B.C.–A.D. 250
Classic		A.D. 250–1000
Early Classic		A.D. 250–600
	Teotihuacan rises and collapses	100 B.C.–A.D. 650/750
	Pyramids of Sun and Moon	A.D. 150
	Collapse	A.D. 650–750
	Monte Albán	zenith ~A.D. 250–700
Late Classic		A.D. 600–900/1000
	Palenque	zenith ~A.D. 600–700
	Lord Pacal	A.D. 615–83
	Lord Chan Bahlum	A.D. 684–702
	Fall of Classic Maya	A.D. 900/1000
Postclassic		A.D. 900/1000–1521
Early Postclassic		A.D. 900–1200
	Toltecs	A.D. 900/1000–Present
	Chichén Itzá	~A.D. 900–1200
Late Postclassic		~A.D. 1200–1521
	Tenochtitlan	~A.D. 1350–1521
	Spanish begin exploration and conquest	
	Columbus finds Caribbean Islands	12 October 1492
	Cortés lands on Veracruz Coast	8 November 1519
	Fall of Tenochtitlan	August 1521
Spanish Conquest and Colonization		1521–1808
	Encomienda system	1521–1550

TIME PERIOD	KEY EVENTS	DATES
	Approximately 90% indigenous depopulation	by 1600
	Peasant rebellions	1531–1801
	Spanish pressure to take over cofradías	1759
Independence to the Present		1808–2000
	Napoleon occupies Spain	1808
	Grito de Hidalgo	16 September 1810
	Mexican independence	27 September 1821
	Central American Federation	1823–1838
	Cinco de Mayo: Mexicans temporarily resist invading French forces	5 May 1862
	Independence from France	1867
	Protestant missions in Central America	~1900
	Porfirio Díaz	1877–1911
	Mexican Revolution/ Emiliano Zapata	~1910–1920
	U.S. involvement begins in Nicaragua	1909
	Rebels organized under Sandino	1928–1933
	La Matanza/Farabundo Martí	1932
	Augusto César Sandino assassinated	1934
	Guatemalan Revolution	1944
	Overthrow of Arbenz in Guatemala	1954
	Beginning growth of Evangelical Protestantism in Central America	~1960
	Second Vatican Council/Roots of progressive Catholicism	1962–1965
	Nicaraguan Civil War/Sandinistas	1978–1979
	Oscar Romero assassinated	24 March 1980
	Salvadoran Civil War and rise of Farabundo Martí Liberation Front	~1980–1992
	Zapatista rebellion	1 January 1994–Present

Independence to the Present (1808–A.D. 2000). For each period (see timeline and chronology on pp. 33–35), we discuss one or two exemplary sites or myths in order to give the reader an inkling of what it was like to live then. The cultural development of Mesoamerica is the subject of this chapter, which touches only briefly on the development of central mythological themes, symbols, places, events, and figures. Indigenous approaches to time and history are presented in the next chapter.

1. The Paleo-Indian (ca. 25,000 B.C.–7000 B.C.)

Human life in Mesoamerica dates back at least 20,000 to 25,000 years. Some scholars believe it may stretch back even further—from at least 40,000 to 250,000 years; but the extremely early dates come from insecure dating techniques and, therefore, are uncertain. Most scholars agree that until new information is brought to light, 25,000 years is the best estimate.

During the Paleo-Indian era, nomads traveled through a moist, cool landscape, hunting the many game animals roaming the earth's rich surface. They usually bagged small animals, but sometimes people got lucky and caught a stag, a bear, or even a mammoth elephant. Little is known about these early wanderers' mythology because little remains to tell us much at all about any aspect of their lives. But we do know that they were thinking about their world, because at least one small bone carving of a dog-like animal remains from the site of Tequixquiac (Tay-keesh´-kee-yak), in the Basin of Mexico. This little figure may actually date back as far as 40,000 years ago, because it was found at the bottom of a Pleistocene lake. Simple stone scrapers and splinters of mammoth bone at Tequixquiac suggest that people did indeed get lucky at the hunt, and that they stayed here at least long enough to butcher the large beast and maybe to scrape and prepare its substantial hide.

We don't know for sure whether the little bone carving portrayed a mythological figure or simply that of a familiar animal such as a dog, wolf, or coyote. A lack of material remains does not necessarily mean that other kinds of cultural and religious activities were not very well developed. A rich oral tradition may have preserved complex mythological worlds; but of course, this could not have been preserved by the few material remains left us. In other words, there is no way for us to know what religious life was really like. We do know, however, that coyotes and various dogs appear all the way from early times up to the present as both great and minor mythological figures. Perhaps they were important in these earliest of times too. But we can only imagine.

2. The Archaic (ca. 7000–2000 B.C.)

The Archaic period ushered in a warmer climate, a weather pattern very similar to today's (Vivó Escoto 1964). With this new weather pattern came a more settled life. A number of game animals from the Paleo-Indian era disappeared, and others changed their habitats because of the climatic changes. This encouraged people to develop more diverse means of subsistence, including not only hunting and gathering but also agriculture. Except for deer, at first hunters found themselves relying almost exclusively on smaller game—such as opossums, rabbits, gophers, or lizards—and on the plants they gathered. In fact, they probably ate just about anything that walked, crawled, climbed, flew, or swam, as well as any plant that provided sustenance. Some plants, however, were more desired, perhaps because of their abundance, their superior ability to nourish, or their taste. In time, consistent patterns of gathering slowly helped people learn to cultivate certain plants, and encouraged them to remain in the same areas for entire rainy seasons, when the plants were at their best. And as life gradually became more settled, folk began to live in pit houses for at least part of the year. These dwellings were partly dug into the ground, with walls and roofs constructed of wood, reeds, or thatch arching over their cellar-like foundations.

While living this semisedentary life, Archaic folk developed corn from a couple of varieties of wild grasses. Although corn later became one of Mesoamerica's most important mythological symbols, during these very early periods it was not a very important part of the diet. The early corn was very hard and difficult to chew; it took several thousand years of cultivation and development before it tasted good enough to constitute so much as even one quarter of people's diets. It also took several thousand years before people settled down to live in just one place the year around, to concentrate on farming. Yet even with permanently settled lives, a complicated subsistence pattern continued; hunting, fishing, and gathering of wild fruits and vegetables remained as important as agriculture in village life. And as is true of corn and squash (another early plant), hunting and the game one hunted later became important mythological symbols.

At this time, people also began occupying the magnificent caves at Loltún in the Yucatán. Caves held an important place in Mesoamerican mythology. Pocketed by caverns draped with stalactites and stalagmites and crisscrossed by underground rivers, Loltún looked like the moist, dark underworld described centuries later in the Maya tale of the Popol Vuh. People used this cave for hundreds and hundreds of years, and not only for shelter: It seems likely that some of its hidden nooks and watery crannies were the sites of early Mesoamerican rituals. One can still see at Loltún and in other caverns of the area the ancient sinkholes carved out by water rushing through the Yucatán's limestone base, and the bright, crystal clear, blue-green underground pools that are home to exotic species of blind fish. These many shadowy, hidden places have not only sheltered people, fish, bats, and other earthly creatures but also a multitude of gods and powerful beings for millennia.

3. The Preclassic Period (ca. 2000 B.C.–A.D. 250)

The early Preclassic (ca. 2000–900 B.C.) ushered in both a much warmer climate and the development of larger villages and towns. Along with these came a more complex material culture, which occasionally displayed mythological themes that survived through pre-Conquest times, and in some cases, even into the present. Life was rich in communities like La Victoria, which lay in the estuaries of the Pacific Coast. The people of this coastal town feasted on oysters, marsh clams, turtles, and crabs. And at other coastal towns, they enjoyed fish, turtles, iguanas, snakes, various amphibians, a variety of birds, shrimp, and mammals such as deer and racoons, which were hunted seasonally. Villagers also cultivated corn, so that by 1500 B.C. it had begun to take its proper place in Mesoamerican life. Corn now constituted one half of the villagers' diets.

Long-distance contact may have been made by the people of La Victoria with people living as far away as South America, as suggested by certain stylistic commonalities in pottery style. This contact may have been made by boats along the coast, or through overland trade. Or such contact may have come indirectly, as goods were passed from group to group. And as in other villages of the early Preclassic, La Victoria's people did not use pit houses but instead built their dwellings on slightly raised platforms, which kept them above the earth's surface and nicely dry. Moreover, the early Preclassic people at La Victoria and elsewhere raised small temple mounds. For the first time, patterns of architecture developed that were to be repeated for thousands of years to come. Mesoamericans constructed numerous magnificent temple mounds before the Conquest, and many still use house mounds in tropical Mesoamerica.

The Preclassic period gives us the first clear indications of religious life in the material culture. People not only raised small temples to honor gods or other powerful beings (Figure 8), but clearly they were also thinking a great deal about what happens after death. In Preclassic villages throughout Mesoamerica, people sometimes buried their dead in the platforms upon which they erected their houses. Some of the dead were laid out and buried with a few grave goods; others were curled into fetal positions, inside large ceramic jars. Those buried in the platforms under the houses must have had great significance for the people moving through their daily affairs in the homes above. It is possible that these individuals had been particularly important in family and village life; perhaps their heirs wanted to preserve their memory by having them close at hand. Or it may have been more than a matter of mere sentimental memories; during later times, objects (especially bones) were believed to hold various powers that had the ability to affect and alter life on earth's surface. Maybe these buried ancestors held powers that were much needed by the family above.

Figure 8. An early Preclassic temple and mound from Cuello, Belize (N.D.C. Hammond. 1991. Cuello: An Early Maya Community in Belize. *Cambridge: Cambridge University Press, p. 103)*

The Preclassic also saw the rise of the first great urban civilizations. People in the valley of Oaxaca (ca 500 B.C.–A.D. 200), for example, began to level off the Monte Albán ridge in order to shape it into a series of grand plazas around which large buildings could be arranged (Adams 1991, 235–243). The buildings around these plazas included an astronomical observatory and various platforms supporting temples with thatched roofs. Elaborate tombs were erected there to house the remains of prominent people and their slaves and retainers. One of the earliest known examples of calendrics lies in one of these tombs; glyphs from the 260-day divinatory calendar grace the murals of Tomb 72, and urns bear the names of people based on calendrical dates. Monte Albán rose to prominence during the Preclassic period, expanding beyond its original area. This probably explains why war was a well-known activity. A series of famous friezes, now popularly referred to as the *danzantes,* or dancers, appear set into the wall of one of the platforms in the main plaza (Figure 9). These friezes most likely portray war captives who were being tortured.

The Olmec (ca. 2250–300 B.C.), however, are perhaps better known and certainly more influential; many consider them forerunners of all Mesoamerican civilizations (Diehl 1996, 29–33). The so-called Olmec heartland was located on the Gulf of Mexico, in what are now the states of Veracruz and Tabasco; but at their height, Olmec contact and influence spread from the Basin of Mexico, where Mexico City lies today, all the way south to today's El Salvador, Honduras, and western Nicaragua. At one time it was supposed that the heartland was the true center from which all cultural patterns were disseminated. Now, however, scholars recognize that many of its so-called colonies throughout Mesoamerica look more like urban civilizations in their own right and may not

Figure 9. A carved monument called a Danzante, from the Preclassic site of Monte Albán, depicting the lifeless figure of a dead and tortured war captive (Kay A. Read)

have been true colonies at all (Neiderberger 1996, 85–86, 92–93). It's currently thought that the Olmec era was more likely characterized by complex trading patterns among many centers that helped spread cultural patterns along with obsidian, jade, pottery, and other goods.

In its earliest phases, the Olmec heartland was dotted by small villages and towns whose inhabitants occupied the well-drained river levees and mangrove swamps. Like that of other villages in coastal areas, the environment here provided the Olmec with a rich array of foods. They planted corn and beans in small clearings in the high jungle; gathered wild palm nuts and other plant foods; and captured fish, turtles, clams, and other aquatic life. By 1200 B.C., urban centers began to rise that were too large to call villages. The social life in these centers was much more stratified than that in the smaller, more egalitarian villages. A number of centers existed during this time, including San Lorenzo, La Venta, Laguna de los Cerros, Las Limas, and Tres Zapotes (although this last center may have arisen after the demise of true Olmec culture). La Venta, Laguna de los Cerros, and Las Limas may have been the larger and more important centers in Olmec times; however, San Lorenzo is probably the best known to people today.

San Lorenzo was occupied and abandoned repeatedly in its 2,500 years of existence, but its cultural and political zenith was attained around 1200–900 B.C. (Adams 1991, 55–59; Cyphers 1996, 61–71). The city was located in the highest area in the region, where it would be safe from the flooding of the rivers flowing on all sides. This strategic position allowed the inhabitants to control communications, transportation, and trade in the area. By 1200 B.C., San Lorenzo was the main center of the region, with a royal family and various elites, and crafts people, farmers, fishers, and hunters. The immediate center's population was only about 1,000, but there was probably a population in the tens of thousands in the surrounding areas. This scattered urban pattern remained typical in this and the Maya areas until the Conquest. Traditionally, cities in southern Mesoamerica have tended not to have massive populations concentrated at their centers, instead reserving them for a small group of elites and their retainers. The rest of the population usually spread out in the surrounding areas, in house mound clusters, which were probably inhabited by large extended families or small communities of extended families.

Figure 10. An Olmec head monument from the Preclassic site of San Lorenzo, now in el Museo de Antropología de la Universidad Veracruzana in Xalapa, Veracruz, Mexico (Elizabeth L. Fuller)

San Lorenzo is best known for its massive sculptures of giant heads (Figure 10) and other figures carved out of the grey volcanic stone transported from the Tuxtla mountains some distance away. Among a variety of subjects (many of them human), ten giant sculptures portray San Lorenzo's rulers, providing some of the first evidence for the mythological importance of key governmental leaders. Later, the ritual and mythological importance of key governmental figures becomes even clearer, especially among the Maya. The Olmec probably used many of these sculptures ritually, to recreate mythological scenes, moving them around when needed. Perhaps because the stone was so difficult to get, old sculptures were sometimes recycled into new carvings. San Lorenzo's plateau also may have been the site of Mesoamerica's first mythic mountain, a temple mound gone extravagant. Some feel it was shaped like a bird, but others think the mound is now too eroded to tell. Between 900 and 400 B.C., San Lorenzo's importance waned considerably, for reasons as yet not understood. The possibilities range from internal revolt or external invasion to volcanic activity in the Tuxtla mountains, which altered the ecological balance in the area.

Figure 11. Altar 4 from the Preclassic site of La Venta, Veracruz, Mexico, depicting what is probably a ruler emerging from a cave (Kay A. Read)

Olmec occupation of La Venta, another important center, extended from 1200 to 400 B.C., with its apogee occurring around 600 to 400 B.C. (Adams 1991, 59–62; Lauck 1996, 73–81). The original site was large, covering more than 200 hectares (ca. 80 acres). Its central architectural feature is the Great Mound or Pyramid—another mythical mountain. Built atop a platform, the mound is more than 30 meters high, and one can view a panorama of 360 degrees from its summit. Many of the mythic themes of rulership and their relationship to ancestors and caves appear at this site, expressed by a wide variety of stunning sculptures large and small, carved in volcanic stone, jade, and serpentine. As at San Lorenzo, sculptors at La Venta carved great heads; one famous sculpture shows what is probably a ruler emerging from a cave. He appears to be tied to what may be his heirs, by ancestral ropes (Figure 11). This large, square sculpture may have been a throne. If so, the ruler would have sat above his ancestral cave upon a mat woven of reeds, cushioned by jaguar pelts. The giant heads at both sites may even have been carved from thrones such as this one.

Olmec contact and influence extended well beyond the heartland. From 1200 to 700/600 B.C., regional centers in the Basin of Mexico, for example, show strong Olmec presence (Adams 1991, 75–76; Niederberger 1996, 83–93). The Basin of Mexico in the Mexican highlands filled a rich mountain park at an elevation of about 7,200 feet or approximately 2,200 meters. Much of the water in the basin was saline, but the lower ends and some other area lakes were spring fed, offering an abundance of wetland flora and fauna. Ducks, fish, various reptiles, and amphibians such as frogs and salamanders probably were included in the local diet along with corn and other domesticated plants. People living here in the Preclassic era may even have eaten the protein-rich algae, which the Mexica (Nahua) are known to have consumed in this same area some 2,500 years later. As was true elsewhere, civilization had been developing in the region for many millennia, dating back at least to 6000 B.C. By 1200 B.C., the basin supported a culture as complex and sophisticated as that of the Olmec heartland. The Mexican highlands' relationship to the heartland is not completely understood, but it is clear that the peoples of the Basin of Mexico were trading with folk all over Mesoamerica.

Tlatilco (Tla-teel'-ko) served as one of the area's most important centers. Probably a most impressive city, Tlatilco was built on an island in a freshwater lake, as was the Mexica capital Tenochtitlan. Preclassic travelers must have been able to see Tlatilco from miles around. Unfortunately, in the twentieth century, highway construction, the erection of multistoried buildings, and clay excavation for brick manufacturing have destroyed much of Tlatilco's remains, leaving the site in very poor condition. Because so much has been lost, the reconstruction of the city's history is difficult. Nevertheless, a number of significant burial sites have been preserved, which reflect the center's stratified and complex society. Women and children as well as men were buried with considerable grave goods, indicating their importance. Many small ceramic and jade items display the rich mythological landscape of Olmec culture, including images of life and death, human-feline figures, beautiful women, and a variety of birds and other animals. Some of the objects even depict what was perhaps a very early form of pictographic writing.

By 400–300 B.C., Olmec culture had largely ceased to exist. San Lorenzo and La Venta had been abandoned by this time, and the peoples of Tlatilco in their waning years were no longer engaged with Olmec culture (Adams 1991, 107–111; Diehl 1996, 29–33). In the southern end of the Basin of Mexico, a new center had begun its rise to power. Cuicuilco (Kwee-kweel'-ko), a center of about 20,000 people, erected one of Mesoamerica's first round pyramids in about 400 B.C. At this time the town seemed destined for expansion (Figure 12). Previously the center had enjoyed some sort of relationship with the Olmec, and the original calendar round may have begun here on the summer solstice in 739 B.C. The earliest known recorded date, 679 B.C., also comes from this site (Edmonson 1988, x, 20). At the time when Cuicuilco was growing and building its pyramids, six small communities just to the north in the valley of Teotihuacan had just begun to build public architecture (Adams 1991, 109). Interestingly, these building projects were accompanied by a retreat of most communities to defensible

Figure 12. The round pyramid of Preclassic Cuicuilco (David Schavelzon. 1983. La Piramide de Cuicuilco. *Mexico City: Fondo de Cultura Economica, p. 35)*

positions on the hills above the prime farmlands. Competition must have been fairly fierce to force people into places not convenient to their fields; and if the competition was with Cuicuilco, that center seemed to be largely winning. But in 150 B.C. an event happened that altered the course of history in the Basin and perhaps even in all of Mesoamerica: A volcano erupted, completely destroying Cuicuilco and covering the surrounding area with lava. The National University of Mexico now rests atop this enormous lava flow. This disaster effectively cut Cuicuilco out of all competition, and its refugees probably migrated north to the six small towns in the valley of Teotihuacan.

These refugees from Cuicuilco's volcanic disaster may very well have helped give structure to what was to become perhaps the greatest of all Mesoamerican pre-Conquest centers, Teotihuacan (Matos Moctezuma 1990, 19). Such impressive volcanic activity may also explain the frequent appearance of pottery representations of an old fire god at Teotihuacan. By 100 B.C., the six towns had become two towns with a combined population of about 5000. By A.D. 100, the two towns had disappeared, and in their place stood a single great city, Teotihuacan, the population of which had climbed to about 60,000. Teotihuacan's inhabitants began building some of the center's most magnificent architecture; and by A.D. 150, the great Pyramids of the Sun and Moon had been erected, paving the way for the city's rise to fame in the Classic era as the post powerful center in ancient Mesoamerica.

4. The Classic Period (ca. A.D. 250–900/1000)

By A.D. 600, the urban center of Teotihuacan had reached a population of 150,000–200,000; probably larger than any other city in the entire world at the time. At present, many Mexicans call Teotihuacan simply *las Pirámides* or "the Pyramids." But the fifteenth-century Mexica (Nahua) gave it its proper name several centuries after it had collapsed and lay largely in ruins. The name *Teotihuacan* means "the place where the gods were created"; the Mexica visited this powerful site on a regular basis to perform sacrificial rituals on the decaying temple platforms. They thought the city's huge pyramids were the work of giants. No one knows who exactly lived there or what language they spoke, but we do know the city's inhabitants were of average stature. Probably one could have heard on its streets the syllables of numerous tongues, for many different peoples visited its markets and admired its awesome architecture. Some inhabitants even migrated from other parts, far outside the Basin of Mexico, living in tightly packed *barrios*, or neighborhoods within the city's boundaries. People from Oaxaca occupied one such barrio.

In the centuries leading up to A.D. 600, Teotihuacan became a diverse and sophisticated center, with tremendous power and influence throughout all of Mesoamerica. The city probably set patterns for urban structures and relations over a wide area of Mesoamerica. Its peoples traded with folk from as far away as both the Gulf and Pacific coasts and present-day Honduras. They sought obsidian, shells, and sting ray spines for use in various rituals; feathers to be woven into elite and ritual clothing; cacao (Mesoamericans invented chocolate); and cotton, salt, and grinding stones for their everyday needs. Some of these goods probably were gained solely through trade, whereas others arrived by tributary agreements, for Teotihuacan appears to have had a large amount of control over certain other urban centers, such as Kaminaljuyu and Tikal (both in present-day Guatemala). It used to be thought that this control was largely economic, but it's now fairly certain that the Teotihuacanos also waged war, although how much and with whom is not yet clear. The maintenance of their extensive trading

Figure 13. The Pyramid of the Moon at the Classic site of Teotihuacan at the northern end of the Avenue of the Dead, repeating the shape of the mountain behind it (Kay A. Read)

activities would have demanded military activity. Recent iconographic studies of some of the many beautiful murals and friezes decorating the city's buildings also indicate the importance of war.

Teotihuacan's urban pattern replicates its people's unique version of the Mesoamerican cosmos. Oriented 15°25′ east of north in order to align its buildings with the motions of the sun and the Pleiades, its grid pattern spreads out around a roughly north-south street now dubbed the "Avenue of the Dead." The Teotihuacan engineers diverted a river to intersect this avenue at right angles, thereby creating two major sectors, one in the north and another in the south. The Pyramid of the Moon (also a Mexica name) crowns the northern end of the avenue, repeating the shape of the mountain behind it (Figure 13). About halfway down this sector's eastern side, the Pyramid of the Sun rises majestically to the sky (Figure 14). Directly beneath the pyramid's center lies a cave that once held a spring, whose waters may have been channeled to the outside at one time. The cave contains four chambers, like a four-petaled flower. In the early 1900s the great Mexican archaeologist Leopoldo Batres (Lay-o-pol′-do Ba′trays) is said to have located sacrificial burials of children at the four corners of each of the pyramid's levels (Heyden 1975). In the southern sector, on the avenue's eastern side, stands a structure called the Ciudadela. Within it rises a somewhat more modest temple, called the Temple of the Feathered Serpent (Figure 15) because of the many feathered serpent sculptures gracing its four sides. Also decorated with various images of seashells, this monument holds the bodies of around 200 sacrificial offerings of what were most likely war captives. The west side of the southern sector was the site of Teotihuacan's bustling marketplace.

We do not know the languages spoken, much less the mythological stories told, on Teotihuacan's streets; nevertheless, these buildings speak of mythological themes through their images (Heyden 1975; López Austin et al. 1991; Pasztory 1992; Sugiyama 1993). The city's astronomical orientations mark the upper world. The Mesoamerican calendar can be found quite literally in the fundamental building blocks of the city's structures, for the measurements of its major streets and buildings, not to mention the building-stones, were based on classic calendrical calculations. Teotihuacan's builders used the numbers by which they tracked the motions of the sun and stars as the basis for their urban plan.

And as it does in many Mesoamerican cosmic conceptions, water flowed through all

Figure 14. The Pyramid of the Sun at the Classic site of Teotihuacan (Kay A. Read)

levels of the city. Teotihuacan's pyramids may have been symbolic mountains enclosing their watery contents. The underworld can be found beneath the Pyramid of the Sun, with its cavern divided into four quarters, like Earth's Surface; and children appear to have been sacrificed to this all-important source of water, just as they were in later Mexica times. In the fifteenth and sixteenth centuries, two Mexica children were sacrificed each spring at the height of the dry season, just before the rainy season was due. As were these Mexica children, perhaps the Teotihuacano children also gave their lives so that the rain gods would have sufficient sustenance to release much-needed water. In some of the many murals at Teotihuacan, a storm deity appears who shares the Mexica rain god's (Tlaloc's) imagery. And at the Temple of the Feathered Serpent, the sea's waters and the warriors' sacrificial blood appear to have been equated in some way. Perhaps the blood of warriors was believed to slake the thirst of the gods, just as the sea provided water to the parched earth. This temple may be a re-creation in imagery of

Figure 15. Temple of the Feathered Serpent at the Classic site of Teotihuacan (Kay A. Read)

the creation of the cosmos and the importance of sacrifice and war to its fertility. The Pyramid of the Sun seems to mirror the underworld and evoke its need for sacrifice, tying it also to the local myth of human origins. For in many Mesoamerican myths, humans first emerged from underground caves; in Olmec sculpture for example, the Olmec ruler emerged from the underworld at La Venta.

Between A.D. 650 and 750, Teotihuacan collapsed, never to rise again. The reasons for its demise, as is true of many other Mesoamerican urban centers, are probably multiple and complex, including a variety of environmental factors such as climatic changes, soil exhaustion, deforestation, and erosion as well as political factors such as rivalry among factions contending for power. By A.D. 600, the city had already begun to pull out of its foreign interests, apparently unable to maintain them. At this time, someone probably sacked and looted the city. Much of the evidence of this destruction has the character of an inside job: The looters clearly knew the exact locations of well-hidden caches of valuables. By A.D. 900, the population of the valley of Teotihuacan was only 30,000. The city's fall initiated a domino effect on other areas of Mesoamerica. On the one hand, its pulling away from foreign interests in A.D. 600 precipitated its loss of power in a number of areas, such as Monte Albán, in Oaxaca. On the other hand, the declining power of Teotihuacan created a space within which certain lesser

Figure 16. The main plaza at the Classic site of Monte Albán, Oaxaca (James A. Schwalbach)

urban centers, such as Palenque, could grow and expand in the latter part of the Classic era.

Monte Albán and Teotihuacan reached their zeniths during the same period, in ca. 250 to 700 (Figure 16), and Teotihuacan's influence is clear in some of Monte Albán's elaborate murals, ceramics, and architectural features (Adams 1991, 243–252). Probably inhabited by the Zapotec, the city of Monte Albán grew tremendously during this period, spreading outward in the Oaxaca valley. More than two thousand terraces occupied the slopes of the main ridge, and many small ravines were dammed for water; the whole area was probably dotted with small ponds and houses. The main center along the ridge top, shaped on a north-south axis, boasted two large platforms on the ends of the main plaza and many pyramid-temples, palaces, patios, tombs (no less than 170!), an old observatory, and a newer ball court and residential building. People moved some of the old sculptures created during the pre-Classic period, including some of the *danzantes* friezes, in order to reuse them in new settings, and new stelae and sculptures appeared. The gods depicted in art at Monte Albán often replicated those of Teotihuacan, including rain and maize gods and the feathered serpent. A bat god appears to have played an important role, and an opossum god also apparently dwelt at Monte Albán. The tombs also display murals hinting at rituals. Above Tomb 103, a fascinating group of figurines offers us a glimpse of one such rite: The mask of a dead man rests on a tiny pyramid, which is surrounded by an orchestra and five priests, while another priest sports the old fire god's garb. We may be witnessing a memorial service for the inhabitant of the tomb below. With the decline of Teotihuacan, the greatness of Monte Albán also began to recede; and by A.D. 700, the rulers had abandoned the center, leaving their dead ancestors alone.

In contrast to Monte Albán, the Maya city of Palenque (seventh and eighth centuries A.D.) began to grow in the latter half of the Classic period, after Teotihuacan's fall. Like Teotihuacan's, this city's layout is instructive of things mythological. Embracing the sides of mountain ridges covered by dense tropical forests, Palenque dominated the southwestern region of the Classic Maya—what is now Chiapas, Mexico (Read 1995, 351–384). The brightly colored, many-staired Temple of the Cross was constructed on the city's northeastern side, its stone structure covered with intricately carved friezes and capped by a tall decoration called a roof comb. Two shorter temples, those of the Sun and of the Foliated Cross, faced each other across the patio on the Temple of the Cross's southeastern and northwestern sides. Downslope a bit and across a small stream, the magnificent Temple of Inscriptions rose, hugging the opposite ridge (Figure 17). Its wide, steep frontal staircase faced slightly east of north. A second, hidden set of stairs led down into the depths of the structure, to the crypt of Lord Pacal, ruler of Palenque (A.D. 615–683). The intricate carving on Pacal's stone sarcophagus depicts the ruler descending the tree that holds up the cosmos's western side. He has just died and now is entering the fleshless, toothy, bony jaws of the underworld monster. Pacal's son and successor Chan Bahlum (Chan Bah-loom´, ruled A.D. 684–702) built the other three temples. These four temples coordinate specific celestial motions with Pacal's death and Chan Bahlum's accession.

At the winter solstice, the sun rose behind the ridge in back of the Temple of the Foliated Cross, illuminating the Temple of the Sun with its beams. Inscriptions and carved images associate the temple with war, captive decapitation, rites of dynastic lineage, and an event that probably designated the six-year-old Chan Bahlum as heir apparent (Carlson 1976, 111). During the solstice, the sun set directly behind the Temple of Inscriptions, marking with its motions the hidden stairs leading to Pacal's tomb. As the sun dipped behind the ridge behind this temple, a beam of light passing to the right of a column in the Temple of the Cross would have highlighted a carved panel depicting God L, a major figure in the underworld. This panel pictures Pacal standing in the west and handing the scepter of rulership to his son, Chan Bahlum (Carlson 1976, 108–111). At their death, Palenque's rulers passed into the underworld as did the setting sun. And at that very moment, a new sun/ruler arose from the underworld. The reasons for Olmec rulers' emergence from the underworld are not entirely clear; but

Figure 17. The Temple of Inscriptions at the Classic site of Palenque (Kay A. Read)

Palenque's rulers appear to have done so because in life they had been equated with the sun, which traveled across the sky in the daytime, and in death, with the sun traveling through the underworld at night. And at the time of year when the days were shortest and the nights longest, as the winter sun paused before beginning its transformation into the summer sun, the dead Sun-Lord Pacal passed his power to the new, living Sun-Lord Chan Bahlum.

The Classic period came to an end between A.D. 900 and 1000. For many years, scholars considered the collapse of the Maya urban centers relatively rapid and mysterious. In fact, neither adjective describes the situation very accurately. Now most believe that Teotihuacan's decline sowed the seeds for the Classic Maya cities' collapse back in A.D. 600. After that point, some centers gained and some lost, but none influenced Mesoamerica to the degree that Teotihuacan had. Toward the end of the Classic era, Maya centers began markedly to decline, at differing rates and for different reasons that included: natural disasters such as earthquakes, hurricanes, and disease; ecological disasters such as the overuse of the land, and soil erosion; the economic isolation of some areas due to changing trade conditions; and sociopolitical reasons such as civil war, raiding among cities, invasion by non-Maya forces, and perhaps the inability of some of the aristocracy to adapt adequately to changing times. Although scholars are only beginning to unravel the complexities of these intertwined factors, it is clear that the ending of the Classic era and the beginning of the Postclassic was a time of great change for everyone, on almost all fronts.

*Figure 18. A circular structure called the Caracol at the Postclassic site of Chichén Itzá
(Elizabeth L. Fuller)*

5. The Postclassic Period (ca. A.D. 900/1000–1521)

The beginning of the Postclassic period saw numerous changes, for people were
on the move throughout Mesoamerica. Various Maya groups traveled from the
Gulf coast to present-day Honduras, up into the Mexican highlands, and along
the coasts of the Yucatán, forging new trading patterns. In fact, coastal trading
patterns increased considerably, perhaps even replacing some of the old inland
trade networks that had linked the Classic Maya cities. This change in trading
patterns may even have contributed to the decline of some Classic cities. Other
Maya groups from the Yucatán traveled south into the Maya highlands. And
groups from the Mexican highlands traveled into the Yucatán, the Maya highlands, and even as far as present-day El Salvador. Centers such as Cacaxtla (Ka-
kasht´-la) and Xochicalco (Sho-chee-kal´-ko) in the Mexican highlands proudly
displayed murals and friezes on Mexican themes, in Maya artistic styles. In contrast, Chichén Itzá (Chee-chen´ Eet-za´) in the northern Yucatán displayed friezes
and architectural decorations on Maya themes, in the Mexican style. This was a
period of regionalization in which no one center or group held power throughout
Mesoamerica. Chichén Itzá, however, was one of the more important centers,
with close links to the new coastal trade.

Traditionally, scholars have divided the history of human occupation at

Figure 19. The pyramid called El Castillo at the Postclassic site of Chichén Itzá (see Figure 5) (Kay A. Read)

Chichén Itzá (ca. A.D. 900–1200)[9] into two periods, each associated with a different sector of the city. The earlier sector belongs to the Puuc (Pook) Maya who lived in the area, and the later, to the Toltecs (Tol´-teks); the first is seen as more Maya, and the latter, as more Mexican. The earlier, Puuc architecture (Figure 18) shares its style with a number of other centers in the immediate region, but the later, Toltec architecture (Figure 19) is clearly related closely to general Mexican highlands architectural styles, some of it apparently even copied directly from buildings at the Mexican highland city of Tula (Too´-la). Many scholars think that a group whom the Maya called the *Itzá* came to the city from Tula.

One well-known myth suggests that Chichén was invaded by a great Toltec leader named the Feathered Serpent—Quetzalcoatl (Ket-zal-ko´-wat, "Feathered Serpent") in Nahuatl, or Kukulcan (Koo-kool-kan´) in Yucatec Maya—who wrested control from its indigenous occupants, the Itzá. Some scholars have pieced together this story from a variety of post-Conquest Mexican and Maya histories (e.g., see Coe 1987, 131–134). They say that political enemies of a ruler named Quetzalcoatl tricked him and then ousted him from Tula, after which he traveled to the Yucatán, capturing Chichén Itzá, where he was named Kukulcan by the Maya. Some say, therefore, that it was the Toltecs who built the impressive Mexican highlands–style buildings. Unfortunately, this version of Chichén's history may be as much the making of a scholarly myth as one of indigenous origin—a rather creative piecing together of scattered textual fragments. The problems with the story's veracity are fourfold. Firstly, the fragmented texts from which this story is drawn are not necessarily connected with each other; secondly, each can be interpreted in a variety of ways differing from this interpretation.[10] Third, if the source was Tula, why are the buildings at Chichén so much better constructed? Usually, copies are inferior to the original. Fourth, although the architectural styles in Chichén's two sectors differ radically, neither is purely one style or another. The Mexican-style buildings display a number of Maya themes, and the Maya-style include some Mexican themes.

New archaeological evidence suggests instead that the city was founded by the Itzá and formed a single, unified entity at the beginning (Henderson 1997, 213, 284 n. 17). Chichén's leaders may have used public architecture to express its increasingly cosmopolitan character, rather than to represent two different peoples. As in cities today in which a number of styles flourish simultaneously, each representing a different group or function, Chichén's distinctive sectors may have existed at the same time, each intended for different purposes. Today's governmental buildings patterned after the ancient Greeks aren't built by Greeks; they merely indicate ideals of government based on current interpretations of Greek governance. In other words, our ideas of classical Greece serve as a mythological model for contemporary governance. Likewise, the buildings at Chichén may represent Maya interpretations of Toltec ideals. Chichén's inhabitants may have had direct links with the Toltecs, perhaps even hiring architects from Tula for a grandiose urban renewal project. We don't really know. But the mere fact that Chichén's buildings look like Tula's is insufficient evidence on which to conclude that Toltecs invaded the city and put up those buildings.

The mythological figure of the Feathered Serpent appears to have been very important at Chichén. His image appears everywhere and in many guises, from feathered snake columns at the Temple of the Warriors (Figure 20) to small heads depicting the Feathered Serpent, mounted on a Puuc-style observatory. Like its many counterparts elsewhere in Mesoamerica, this round observatory tracked the sun's motions and those of Venus (Aveni 1980, 258–269), which as the morning star was often associated mythologically with the Feathered Serpent. Certainly the most impressive display of the great serpent occurs at the spring equinox. Then the setting sun slants its rays across the city to strike the balustrades of the Castillo (Kas-tee´-yo). The shadows coming from this play of light give the appearance of an undulating snake making its way down the pyramid's steps. Although the original inhabitants of Chichén are now gone, new people find this annual mythological display impossible to resist. Today, thousands of people travel to this grand archaeological site each year at the equinox: some just to witness the spectacle, others to perform their own rituals focusing on the great sky-serpent's descent. Kukulkan lives on, although in somewhat different form.

Around A.D. 1350,[11] Tenochtitlan was founded on an island in Lake Texcoco (Tesh-ko´-ko), in the Basin of Mexico (Figure 21). Built near the Preclassic Olmec site of Cuicuilco and the great Classic center of Teotihuacan, Tenochtitlan was to become the capital of the Mexica (Aztec, Nahua) empire and the last great urban center of pre-Hispanic Mesoamerica. At first it was no more than a small town whose inhabitants lived under the heavy thumb of a neighboring center. However, by the time Cortés entered Tenochtitlan in 1519, the population had grown to around 200,000. Not as influential as Teotihuacan had been, the city nevertheless claimed tremendous military and economic power over a huge region extending from the Gulf of Mexico to the Pacific Ocean, and from the modern Mexican states of Quere-

Figure 20. The Feathered Serpent columns from the Temple of Warriors at the Postclassic site of Chichén Itzá (Kay A. Read)

taro, Hidalgo, Veracruz, and Chiapas to the southeastern borders of Guatemala. Although at this time the Mexica had not yet subdued several major areas within their borders, their ruler Chief Speaker Motecuhzoma II (Mo-te-kuh-zo´-ma) was pursuing the conquest of those regions with an intensity likely to bring him eventual success in some measure (Townsend 1992, 106, 173–191).

Tenochtitlan was a sight to behold for Cortés and his small army (Figure 22). The city was situated in a lush basin surrounded by mountain ranges stretching out for miles and miles. In a fascinating account of the conquest, one of Cortés's officers, Bernal Díaz del Castillo, described what he saw from the top of the Templo Mayor (Great Temple) in the center of the city:

Figure 21. The frontispiece of the Codex Mendoza *depicting the founding of Tenochtitlan (Bodleian Library)*

That huge and cursed temple stood so high that from it one could see over everything very well, and we saw the three causeways which led into Mexico, . . . and we saw the fresh water that comes from Chapultepec [Cha-pool-te´-pek] which supplies the city, and we saw the bridges on the three causeways which were built at certain distances apart through which the water of the lake flowed in and out from one side to the other, and we beheld

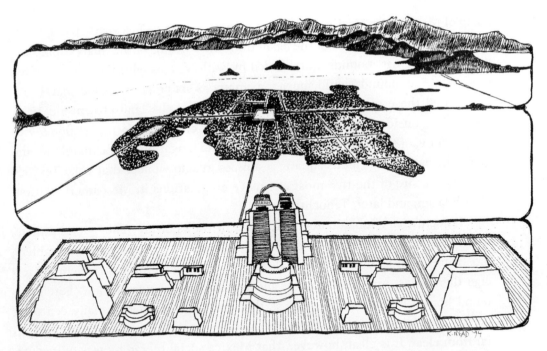

Figure 22. The Postclassic urban center of Tenochtitlan and its ritual center (drawing by Kay A. Read)

on that great lake a great multitude of canoes, some coming with supplies of food and others returning loaded with cargoes of merchandise; and we saw that from every house of that great city and of all the other cities that were built in the water it was impossible to pass from house to house, except by drawbridges . . . or in canoes; and we saw in those cities Cues [temples] and oratories like towers and fortresses and all gleaming white, and it was a wonderful thing to behold; then the houses with flat roofs, and on the causeways other small towers and oratories that were like fortresses.

. . . We turned to look at the great market place and the crowds of people that were in it, some buying, others selling, so that the murmur and hum of their voices and words that they used could be heard more than a league off. Some of the soldiers among us who had been in many parts of the world, in Constantinople, and all over Italy, and in Rome, said that so large a market place and so full of people, and so well regulated and arranged, they had never beheld before (Díaz del Castillo 1956, 218–219).

The great causeways Díaz describes connected this amazing city to the mainland. Farm fields called *chinampas* (chee-nam´-pas) ringed the urban island. This extremely efficient and intensive form of agriculture was first used in Maya and Olmec areas during the Preclassic period; the wetlands environment of the

Basin of Mexico was ideally suited to chinampa farming. On a yearly basis, farmers dredged up the rich soil of the basin from the bottoms of the many canals and piled it onto great mounds. Surrounded by willow trees whose roots prevented erosion, these mounds could support as many as six crops in a good year; farmers rotated these crops to maintain the fertility of the land (Townsend 1992, 166–173). Considering the high productivity of chinampa farming, along with the terracing of the mountainsides and the use of irrigation on the mainland, and given the basin's enormous aquatic resources, it's no wonder that Lake Texcoco became the site of the two most extensive civilizations in Mesoamerica—first, Teotihuacan, and later, Tenochtitlan.

Tenochtitlan's inhabitants came from all walks of life: They were farmers, traders, craftspeople, vendors, doctors, midwives, ritual specialists, gamblers, prostitutes, and so on. Elite officials served in the government, welcomed foreign dignitaries, mustered armies, and presided over courts of law. Foreigners found homes in the city as well, as they had in Teotihuacan many centuries before. Two basic social groups occupied Tenochtitlan, but their relationship is far from clear. It is clear, however, that Mexica social hierarchy was quite complex and that the elite class, called *pipiltin* (pee-peel´-tin), did not have an overarching control over the commoners, who were called *macehualtin* (ma-say-wal´-tin).[12] Not all elites had power, for some worked for other, more influential elite employers; at the same time, some nonelite merchants could wield a great deal of influence, and under certain circumstances, even elites shared the status of commoners. Moreover, two different schools educated the city's young men, who enjoyed upward social mobility if they showed talent either in school or at war. Social group membership appears to have been closely linked to a mythological ancestry. Tenochtitlan was divided into four quarters. In the middle of each quadrant stood a small temple housing the patron god, the ancestral progenitor of the quarter's inhabitants. Whether linked by blood ties or not, all of the inhabitants of each sector were seen as genealogically related and could trace their mythic heritage back to the city's patron god, the deity that gave life, power, and direction to their existence: Huitzilopochtli (Weet-zee-lo-pocht´-lee), the Mexica war god.

A huge ritual district sat at the crossroads in the center of Tenochtitlan. The Templo Mayor, from which Díaz surveyed the city's bustling scene, dominated both the city and this ritual district. Two sets of stairs mounted its western facade, each leading to a small house at the top, belonging to a god. The northern building housed Tlaloc, the rain god. Sacrificial hearts were placed in the bowl held ready by the hands of a stone figure called a *chacmool* (chak-mool´), which was positioned in front of Tlaloc's house (Figure 23). If rain was to come, the rain gods who released it from the mountains that held it had to be fed, for everything

Figure 23. A Chacmool that sat in front of the Postclassic site of the Templo Mayor, Tenochtitlan (Kay A. Read, Museo del Templo Mayor, Mexico City)

was alive in this cosmos. As had the people at Chichén Itzá, the Mexica copied their chacmool from the Toltec one that stood at Tula. The southern building housed Huitzilopochtli. When warrior sacrifices were made in front of this temple, the bodies were decapitated, dismembered, and flung down the steps toward the large, round panel at its base. This panel depicted the conquest and sacrifice of Coyolxauhqui (Ko-yol-shauw´-kee), the sister of Huitzilopochtli. Mexica rulers were genealogically related both to the Toltecs and to Huitzilopochtli.

This great cosmic temple-mountain marked the two seasons that the sun carried on its back as it journeyed along its annual path. The northern house marked summer's rainy season, when the sun rose from behind the northern half of the eastern mountain range. The space between the two houses marked the year's two middle points, the equinoxes. And the southern house marked the sun's rising from behind the southern half of the eastern mountain range, in winter's dry season. When the sun was in Tlaloc's house, the time had come to plant crops and tend the fields. But when the sun moved to Huitzilopochtli's house, the season of war had arrived. The fields of war were considered a plentiful source for harvesting the human sacrificial offerings needed to sustain various nonhuman beings in the cosmos. Summer was a time to concentrate on feeding humans; winter, a time to feed other important beings. Of course war had more purposes than feeding various gods and other beings. It also served to expand or consolidate the Mexica domain. But the growing of crops was so important that Mexica rulers deemed it wise to direct their energies toward the agricultural fields in the summer and not toward the fields of war; to do otherwise was considered foolish. As one ruler told his three sons and possible heirs to the throne:

> And especially take care of the ridge, of the ditch. Plant and sow in the field. . . . If you dedicate yourself only to nobility, if you do not plant in the ridges, in the ditches, what will you give anyone to eat? What will you eat? What will you drink? Where have I seen nobility [help] anyone rise from bed or go to sleep?[13] Sustenance [to eat and drink] is life; most truly it is said: [by it] one rules, one governs, one conquers. Where have I seen an empty-gutted one [one with no intestines], a non-eater, who rules, who governs?[14]

But within just a few years, Mexica (indeed, all Mesoamerican) nobility would be almost eradicated by the very visitors who had found Tenochtitlan so amazing—the people who called the Templo Mayor "cursed." They razed the city's magnificent buildings to the ground, using the stones as foundations for new buildings and the rubble to fill in Tenochtitlan's canals. In just a short time, a completely different city stood in its place—one built on a grid pattern, not on the four cardinal directions of the cosmos. Spanish governmental buildings rose where Motecuhzoma's palace once stood. And the central ritual district housed a large cathedral marking the heavens and celebrating the single sacrifice of Christ rather than a temple marking the sun's journey along the horizon and the sacrificial sustenance of a multitude of human, nonhuman, and cosmic beings (Figure 24). For no longer did those in power view the sun and all other things as alive and in need of food. A radical change was taking place.

6. The Spanish Conquest and Colonization of Mesoamerica (1521–1808)

On 3 August 1492 Christopher Columbus set sail from Palos, Spain, in search of a quick western route to the vast trading riches of the Indies, which at the time included much of India and Asia (Figure 25). Believing that China lay a mere 5,000 nautical miles to the west, he expected to sail first to the Canary Islands off the coast of Africa, and from there only 2,400 nautical miles more to the easternmost islands of Japan. There he meant to establish a trading town. Of course, this never happened. Many more miles later than expected, on 12 October 1492, Columbus

Figure 24. The main Catholic Cathedral in Mexico City with the ruins of the Templo Mayor in the foreground (Kay A. Read)

found himself not on the shores of Japan but on those of a Caribbean island probably populated by the Taino people. Two decades later the Europeans realized their mistake; but by then the word *Indians*, which they had used to describe the local inhabitants of what they had thought were the Indies, had become habitual, and it would remain so for centuries. Because the first Indians the Spanish saw were village farmers who wore little clothing in their hot climate, all Indians henceforth were viewed as simple primitives, even after Cortés encountered the impressive expanses of the Mexica empire. European cartographers named this territory *America*, after Italian navigator Amerigo Vespucci, whose accounts of his travels to this "New World" were widely read throughout Europe.

A new myth had been born that was to endure for at least the next five centuries. Of course, this was a European myth, not a Mesoamerican one. The land was not new to the people who had been its discoverers 24,000 years or more before, none of whom called themselves Indian or their various lands America, and none of whom viewed themselves as uncivilized. Nor should they have. A culture with the sophistication and antiquity of Mesoamerica certainly was not primitive. Tenochtitlan rivaled any European city of the time in both size and complexity; and Mesoamericans were skilled mathematicians, astronomers, doctors, and artists, sometimes surpassing European abilities in those areas. This

Figure 25. A sixteenth-century painting of Columbus and his ships in first contact with the New World (Library of Congress)

was not a case of a civilized nation overcoming a few primitive people but of one complex civilization confronting another in what was eventually to become an enduring battle over whose way of life had the right to exist. Because of the power of myth to create reality, the European names stuck, along with the assumptions behind them. After all, the new myths were certainly convenient and effective foundations for conquest. They have continued to serve as useful legitimating tools for those in power up to the present, often at the expense of the indigenous populations at whom these myths were and sometimes still are directed.

On Holy Thursday in 1519, Cortés and about 600 men landed on the coast of Veracruz. From there they began a march inland to Tenochtitlan, the center of the Mexica ruler Motecuhzoma II.[15] On 8 November 1519, Cortés and his forces entered Tenochtitlan as guests of Lord Motecuhzoma. Almost two years later, in August 1521, Motecuhzoma II was dead and the current ruler Cuauhtemoc (Kwaw-te´-mok) had surrendered to the Spanish invaders. The battle had not really been as easy as many historical myths suggest. The Conquest came at great cost and absorbed many resources: help from thousands of Indian warriors opposed to the Mexica, brought in by alliances that often were arranged by an Indian woman named Malinche (Ma-lin´-chay) or Doña Marina (Don´-ya Ma-ree´-na); severe losses to the Spanish when they retreated from heavy fighting in Tenochtitlan in June 1520, during a night they called *La Noche Triste* ("The Sad Night"), following an intensive, three-month siege of the city; and finally, the hugely debilitating effects on the Mexica of smallpox, a new disease from Europe against which the indigenous people had no natural resistance. Cortés also had had to destroy his ships in order to prevent some of his own men from leaving for home before the march on Tenochtitlan (he later salvaged the iron fittings to make new boats with which to attack the island stronghold). It had taken nearly two years, thousands of Indian allies, enormous struggles, and a major epidemic to defeat the Mexica (Figure 26).

Once in power, the Spanish put into effect vast changes in the land they now called New Spain.[16] The conquistadores received rewards for their work from Cortés in the form of tribute and land grants. The *encomienda* (en-kom-ee-en´-da) system also allowed the Spanish conquerors to acquire grants of people in return for their education in the Christian faith and supposed protection. The conquerors often abused these privileges and doled out extremely harsh treatment to their Indian laborers in spite of orders from the Spanish government not to do so. Around midcentury, the Spanish government took more control over colonial affairs and freed the Indians, making them citizens of Spain, and instituting policies of protection that helped somewhat to alleviate abuses. Still, by the end of the sixteenth century, some estimate that the depopulation rate among Indians was close to 90 percent, due to repeated smallpox epidemics, harsh labor practices, maltreatment, and the enforced separation of male from female laborers, which contributed to a lower birthrate.

The vast economic inequities begun with the encomienda system in the early part of the sixteenth century were furthered by the growth of haciendas (ah-see-en´-das), a system particularly suited to the world's economic conditions in the seventeenth and eighteenth centuries (Cosío Villegas, Bernal, et al. 1995, 57–58). Huge ranches and farms swallowed up large expanses of Indian lands. The loss of their land forced Indians into labor on the ranches, in mines, or in the cities, creating a dependence among them on goods produced by others. Laborers on the ranches and mines found themselves paid so little that they had to go into debt to the owners, who sold the laborers basic goods for more than they earned. This assured that they could not leave their employers. Those in the cities could find themselves working alongside black slaves and prisoners in

Figure 26. An indigenous illustration of the Conquest of Mexico (Lienzo de Tlaxcala, pl. 42, Museo Nacional de Antropología, Mexico City)

factories, where supported by harsh labor laws the exploitation was even worse than in the countryside. By 1800, Mexico had become one of the richest countries in the world; but although it had tremendous wealth, vast numbers of extremely poor people lived there in misery. Sixty percent of the population was still Indian; 20 percent was mestizo (mes-tee´-zo, of mixed European and Indian heritage); blacks and mulattoes (of mixed European and black heritage) remained a very small percentage; and Creoles (poor immigrants from Spain) constituted 16 percent. The Creoles slowly developed into a small middle class. More than 80 percent of the population lived in severe poverty, and the top 4 percent held the major part of the wealth.

It is no wonder, then, that the poor frequently rebelled against their harsh conditions, especially since the majority of poor people lived in isolated areas that had not yet been fully conquered. Between 1531 and 1801, various indigenous peoples rose against Spanish rule more than 38 times (Castro 1996, 124–125). The specific reasons for rebellion varied. Some wanted to destroy the Spanish, expel everything Spanish (even their chickens, cats, and dogs), and effect a complete return to what in most respects had become a mythic pre-Conquest past. Others viewed such a return as impossible and appropriated particular European cultural innovations as marks of a better form of liberty: Such things as cattle husbandry and mining techniques might be seen as new and useful tools, in the hands of Indians. Other movements sought greater equality and did not necessarily seek to expel the Spanish. Much could be and was accepted by indigenous populations, even in rebellion. In the insurrection of Canek (Kanek', Maya), in 1761, it was thought that warriors who died in combat would be resurrected, like Christ; and in other uprisings, rebels celebrated masses with tortillas and pulque (a fermented drink made from the agave cactus). In 1712, the Tzeltales (Tsel-ta´-lays, Maya) created a theocracy for a short time, modeled on the Spanish hierarchy, with native bishops, vicars, and a royal superior court. The Indians called themselves "Spanish," and the vanquished Spanish, "Indians"; "Indian" women were required to marry the "Spanish" victors and work in their households. Other indigenous rebels hoped for a major, cleansing catastrophe and the arrival of a new era. Some of these millenarian movements sought the return of the creator of the sky and earth, Lord Motecuhzoma. Saints, including the Virgin of Guadalupe, led still other insurrections. Toward the end of the Colonial period, many Indians thought they had the help of the King of Spain. After all, was not he the great protector of the people, the symbol of good, whose picture was so proudly hung in schools, government buildings, and churches? It could not be he who was the root of their problems but only corrupt leaders closer to home.

If the political conquest of the indigenous populations of New Spain was not complete, neither was their spiritual conquest (Figure 27). Conversions to Christianity occurred so rapidly that their superficiality was unavoidable. The first Catholic fathers sometimes performed mass conversions of thousands of Indians at a time. Moreover, these conversions took place under conditions of defeat; and when defeat had occurred in pre-Conquest times, the people believed that their own patron god was defeated by the victor's god but nonetheless continued to exist. In Tenochtitlan's ritual district stood a kind of jail, in which dwelt the many patron gods whom Huitzilopochtli had defeated. Hence, Mesoamericans may very well have seen Jesus as the victor over their now defeated but still living gods. Later their gods rose again in rebellion; or as more time passed, Jesus,

Figure 27. The Catholic Cathedral in the town of Mitla, Oaxaca, with the earlier pre-Conquest temple seen directly beneath the foundation (Jason J. González)

Mary, and the saints joined with ancient gods in an enlarged and even more complex cosmos. The result was not a simple overlay of Christianity on indigenous traditions or even a mixture of the two but the creation of many new, theologically complicated religions forming continuities with both Catholicism and the ancient traditions (Ángeles Romero 1996, 226). A variety of religious forms arose in the different regions: Earthly landmarks now might house local deities as well as saints; the devil set up housekeeping inside particular mountains; and the old deities inhabited the underworld, whereas the saints inhabited the sky. In some places, saints took over for the patron gods as the heads of ancestral lines. The old traditions were not completely lost, nor was Christianity totally rejected; instead, each enriched the other. Today, many villagers still bless the four quarters when they grill the first tortilla, watch out for scary beings inhabiting woods and rivers, nourish various "souls" (a Christian concept)[17] with sacrifices of chickens, and attend church on Sundays. Some people view these activities as mutually contradictory; others consider them a unified tradition. When these folk-Christian religious traditions of *el pueblo* clearly claim allegiance with Catholicism, current scholarship generally views them as part of the "Popular" or "People's Church" (*Iglesia Popular*), and recognizes that they may be severely at odds politically and theologically with the Church hierarchy and its approved doctrines.

As with everything in Mesoamerica, continuity and invention were intertwined—in social and group activities as well as in personal actions. People served the church now in the same socially patterned ways in which they had served the temple. This service translated into indigenous understandings of communal property as well (Ángeles Romero 1996, 225–231; Castro 1996, 109–110). Traditionally, property had always been held communally and work done cooperatively. So in post-Conquest times, groups called *cofradías* (ko-fra-dee´-as) developed. Those who served the church also guarded a chest or *cofra* in which were kept cash; records of which lands, produce, and cattle herds were communal; and records of who produced and maintained them. These groups fulfilled the role of governing bodies in villages, towns, and city neighborhoods. But in 1759, the Spanish king Charles III began to pressure the groups to move their assets to federal banks so that the government might gain greater control over money and power in local communities. This pressure, coupled with a famine in 1756 and with other forces, helped move New Spain toward revolution and a bid for independence. And in 1808, events in Europe helped make independence a reality.

7. Independence to the Present (1808–2000)

The occupation of Spain by Napoleon in 1808 weakened the Spanish hold on the Americas.[18] By this time, many Creoles had gained a modern education, having been trained by Jesuit priests in humanist philosophy, and some had begun to move into the wealthiest social strata. Inspired by the successful revolutions in the United States (1776) and France (1789), they argued strongly for independence and played a major role in mobilizing local forces against Spain. Conservatives remained loyal to Spain, but their voices were overcome by the more vociferous liberals who deeply resented Spanish intrusion into community affairs, taxes, and trade restrictions, and who wanted to be masters in their own houses. On Sunday morning, 16 September 1810, the Jesuit-trained Father Miguel Hidalgo y Costilla freed the prisoners in his village of Dolores, Mexico, and locked up the Spanish authorities. Calling his parishioners to mass, the elderly priest urged them to join with him in overthrowing the bad government (Figure 28). Within days, his 600 followers had swelled to 100,000 workers from the mines and haciendas; and when the Bishop excommunicated him, his followers forced the cathedral council to lift the ban. This outcry, or *grito de*

Figure 28. A mural painting by Juan O'Gorman depicting Hidalgo crying from the church steps, surrounded by his followers (Corbis-Bettmann)

Hidalgo, launched the revolution. Mexico officially gained its independence on 27 September 1821, just twelve days after the other Central American countries had declared their independence. From 1822 to 1823, what are now the countries of Costa Rica, El Salvador, Guatemala, Honduras, and Nicaragua were legally parts of Mexico.[19] But in 1823, they broke ranks with Mexico and formed the Central American Federation, which lasted until 1838, when it broke into the five countries we know today.

Inequities between the haves and the have-nots continued into the nineteenth and twentieth centuries, exacerbated by almost continual political conflicts. Throughout the nineteenth century, liberals and conservatives fought each other politically and militarily in both Central America and Mexico; frequent coups, military dictatorships, unstable political alliances, and continuing indigenous uprisings defined the entire region. These constant political tensions undermined the economy, causing suffering especially among the poor. Moreover, the United States and European powers repeatedly inserted themselves into

Mesoamerican political and economic affairs. War with the United States resulted in Mexico's loss of its northernmost lands.[20] France, under Napoleon III, seized power for a brief period, placing the young, romantic Hapsburg prince Maximilian and his beautiful Belgian wife Carlotta in power. But pressure from the United States and fear of war in Europe weakened France's hold. On 5 May 1862, Mexican defenders drove the invading French back (a victory that is still celebrated today in Cinco de Mayo festivities); and in 1867, Benito Juarez executed Maximilian and rode victorious into Mexico City. Carlotta, who had returned to France to plead unsuccessfully for Napoleon's support, went insane from worry and grief. The Mexican chaos was temporarily stanched in 1877, when Porfirio Díaz took control of the country by force, asserting an extremely efficient rule that lasted 30 years. As Mexico began to attract foreign capital, its economy gradually improved.

By the late nineteenth century, coffee had been introduced into Central America and southern Mexico, and it soon became a major product of those regions. Euro-U.S. powers increasingly sought to control coffee and fruit growing interests as well as mining and oil concerns in all Mesoamerican countries. External powers also funded and promoted the shipping enterprises needed to export those products, by building railroads and lobbying for canals. By the early twentieth century, the United States had become the dominant player in these politico-economic battles, and Porfirian Mexico (which benefited economically from U.S. interests) was a model of peaceful development for the region.

As in earlier periods, however, only a minority enjoyed Mexico's great wealth under the Porfirian regime, and Indians lost more and more of their lands to big investors. To make matters worse, Díaz suggested the possibility of free, democratic elections toward the end of his reign, but then did not follow through with that suggestion. The poor economic conditions for most Mexicans, and the younger generation's resentment of Porfirian autocracy, resulted in revolution and the ousting of the 80-year-old Díaz in 1911. Led by the mythic Virgin of Guadalupe, and in part by the Indian guerrilla rebel leader Emiliano Zapata (d. 1919; see Figure 29), the revolution ended in 1920, after a decade of intense fighting. A lasting stability was finally established nine years later with the institutionalization of political rule under the leadership of what is now called the Institutional Revolutionary Party (PRI).[21] But almost two decades of considerable chaos had left the economy a shambles. Working against strong opposition from landowners and foreign investors, Álvaro Obregón, the first Mexican president (1920–1924, before the PRI), and President Lázaro Cárdenas (1934–1940, after the creation of the PRI) instituted limited social and land reforms that addressed some of the inequities, but these efforts did not radically alter the situation.

Throughout most of the twentieth century, Central American countries remained under the control of military dictators supported by small classes of

Figure 29. Emiliano Zapata—detail of a mural by Diego Rivera in Cuernavaca, Mexico (Archivo Iconografico, S.A./Corbis)

very wealthy landowners who cooperated with the heavy presence of the United States. This foreign presence was largely economic, but it was sometimes supported by direct political and military intervention. For most of the century, from the 1920s to the years of Ronald Reagan's presidency (1981–1989), much of U.S. involvement centered on sometimes real but just as often imagined fears of Communist influence in Central America. Harsh economic sanctions were placed on governments that were not sympathetic to U.S. interests, whereas sympathetic governments received tremendous amounts of foreign aid, including military support. None of this did anything to help the huge numbers of poor living in these countries; instead, the foreign presence often exacerbated already poor living conditions. Because social inequities were not adequately addressed, civil wars broke out in Nicaragua, Guatemala, and El Salvador in the late 1970s and early 1980s.

U.S. involvement in Nicaragua was particularly marked in the early part of the century. In 1909, the United States sided with rebels to drive a ruler from power who was not cooperating with U.S. interests in building a canal from the Atlantic to the Pacific. Marines were sent to Nicaragua in 1911 to protect U.S. interests and supervise elections, and a Marine force remained there almost continuously until 1933. These early incursions into the government's operations were resisted by rebels led by Augusto César Sandino, who was later assassinated by U.S.-trained Nicaraguan troops. In the 1970s, widespread protests against the forty-year-old rule of Anastasio Somoza began to build. Somoza had been sympathetic to U.S. economic interests and had done little to relieve the social and economic inequities. By 1978, the tensions had grown into civil war, and by 1979, the rebel guerrillas, including a group called the Sandinistas (named after Sandino), had won the war. The new government headed by the Sandinistas undertook many reforms designed to help the poor and improve the economy, but recovery was slow. In the 1980s, rebels called the contras sided with old Somoza forces in stepping up antigovernment attack, and in 1983, they launched an all-out war. President Reagan claimed that the Sandinista government was communist, and awarded U.S. support to the contras, ordering mines to be placed in Nicaraguan harbors and slapping an embargo on the country. Short-lived negotiations between the two sides fizzled and fighting resumed in 1989, only to cease after an anti-Sandinista president was elected. Since then the Sandinistas continue to influence politics in the country, although they have not been able to recapture the presidency.

In El Salvador, the United States backed the government during a twelve-year civil war in the 1980s. Here too, the roots of war lay in longstanding economic inequities that governmental policies had exacerbated. As elsewhere in the early 1900s, coffee had been introduced into El Salvador. This precipitated reforms in 1908 that removed many lands from peasant farmers and placed them in the hands of a small but wealthy minority. A system was set up very similar to the hacienda system of the previous two centuries, and by the 1920s, governmental and Church pressures successfully had eradicated the cofradías. In the early 1930s, the world plunged into economic depression. The poor suffered most because they had the least to begin with and governmental policies failed to support them. Economic suffering, the overthrow of a reformist leader, and the events of the preceding two decades had caused enormous resentment toward the government. As a result, in 1932 the communist trade unionist Farabundo Martí led peasants against the government of President Maximiliano Martínez, demanding reforms. The response was a massacre now called *La Matanza* (La Ma-tan´-za, "the Slaughter"), which killed an estimated 10,000 to 30,000 people, most of them peasants. In its aftermath, all overtly indigenous cultural patterns were outlawed; one could be killed for merely speaking Pipíl (Pee-peel´, a dialect of Nahua), for wearing native dress, or for producing indigenous crafts.

La Matanza and Martí's name became rallying cries for civil war in the 1980s. The war ended with a United Nations brokered peace accord in 1992. As in other Central American countries, enormous economic and social inequities underlay the Salvadoran civil war. Before the war, 1 percent of the population held 70 percent of the land, and 8 percent of the population received 50 percent of the national income, whereas 20 percent owned no land and received only 2 percent of the national income. Moreover, 70 percent lived in absolute poverty, mostly working on hacienda-like plantations; their wages could not provide enough food to meet even minimum health requirements. In the 1970s, when the world entered a major economic recession, many faced starvation on a daily basis. Peaceful demonstrations were countered by massacres, and by 1980, the

Figure 30. FMLN (Farabundo Martí National Liberation Front) painted on the side of what was left of a bombed bridge in El Salvador (Kay A. Read)

peasants were engaging in guerrilla warfare (Figure 30). Although great numbers of peasants who joined the rebel forces of the Farabundo Martí National Liberation Front (FMLN) did not even know what communism was, much less adhere to it, the Reagan government supported the Salvadoran government, accusing the rebels of being communist-inspired and -controlled.[22] Hundreds of millions of dollars flowed into the country from the United States, and they trained Salvadoran military personnel in Honduras and the United States. While wealthy Salvadoran landowners set up extra houses and large bank accounts in places like Miami, massive numbers of refugees fled the country to Nicaragua and Honduras. Others came legally and illegally to the United States. Most were fleeing death squads that systematically tortured and murdered anyone speaking out against the government, as well as other abuses of human rights (such as massacres of whole villages).

After the demise of the Soviet Union and its communist satellite nations, U.S. interest in El Salvador waned, causing the withdrawal of U.S. support from the Salvadoran government. The FMLN fought government forces to a stalemate, leaving the country in disarray. The war had claimed some 70,000 lives, in a country about the size of Massachusetts. From 1992 to 1995, the United Nations oversaw a moderately successful reconstruction that sought to accomplish necessary, substantive reforms. More recently, new industries and economic policies based on free trade appear to be changing conditions in El Salvador. But the country still faces high unemployment, and the gap between the rich and poor is growing again. El Salvador is far from healed, and many remain suspicious that the new policies are only a repeat of policies of earlier centuries, benefiting foreigners and small groups of the wealthy elite while leaving the vast majority of the population in a state of exploitation and poverty.

Guatemala, the home of many Maya groups, has experienced the same social and economic problems as Nicaragua and El Salvador, and is no stranger to civil war. As elsewhere, private owners gained control of peasant lands, turning them to coffee and fruit production, thereby forcing landless peasants to work in hacienda-like conditions. In 1951, the reform government of Jacobo Arbenz Gúzman began taking over much land that was owned privately by a small minority, in order to redistribute it to landless peasants. These lands included large areas owned by the United Fruit Company, which maintained close ties to business interests in the United States. The U.S. government, fearing communism, supported a rebel attack against Gúzman, forcing him to retire. After a decade of chaos and military rule, civilian rule was restored under Julio César Méndez Montenegro in 1966. But violence grew during his regime, with terrorist raids killing many. By the late 1970s, the violence had become widespread. Antigovernment groups included many poor Indians and peasants who like the Salvadoran and Nicaraguan rebels sought a better quality of life. As tensions mounted, many Indians fled deep into the Guatemalan mountains, to Mexico, and to the United States. In 1996, the Guatemalans finally signed a peace agreement, ending some thirty years of violence.

As elsewhere, conditions in Mexico had always adversely affected the poor, but they increasingly were affecting the nascent middle class, as the poor became poorer. In the early 1960s, 10 percent of the population received almost 50 percent of the national income, and 40 percent of the population, barely 14 percent. By 1977, 10 percent of the middle class had become poor, and the poor were receiving less (Cosío Villegas, Bernal, et al. 1995, 154); economically based class distinctions were becoming more marked. The Mexican economy, by the early 1980s, was on the verge of collapse due to a decline in the oil market. Severe austerity measures were imposed, including a devaluation of the peso that left many middle-class and poor people destitute and many others living on the edge. Moreover, corruption at the highest levels of the Mexican government had increased dramatically since World War II.

It was in this environment that a new mythic political figure was born. Shortly after the institution of the North American Free Trade Agreement (NAFTA), it became painfully clear that President Carlos Salinas de Gotari (who had assumed office in 1988, after elections that were rumored to have been fixed) was implicated in major economic scandals. His brother Raul had been jailed for amassing huge sums of money from drug racketeering. Accused of stealing the equivalent of billions of dollars from Mexico and placing them out of reach in foreign banks, Carlos Salinas eventually was forced into exile. He quickly became the mythic cause of all of Mexico's economic woes. Dolls, masks, and T-shirts mocking him appeared overnight in the markets, and street dances and plays satirized him as the latest symbol of the decadent and exploitative rich.

Given the enduring poor economic conditions throughout Mesoamerica, it is not surprising that indigenous and peasant rebellions continued throughout the nineteenth and twentieth centuries. From 1847 to 1855, Maya Indians in the Yucatán rebelled in response to racism, the destruction of communal life by governmental attempts to disband cofradías and take over communally owned lands, and other forms of exploitation, such as hacienda-type working conditions (Bracamonte y Sosa 1994, 109–159). One also can count the 1932 rebellion in El Salvador as a peasant rebellion. And most recently, on 1 January 1994, just a few hours after NAFTA went into effect, largely indigenous populations revolted in Chiapas, Mexico. They called themselves Zapatistas in honor of Emiliano Zapata, the fabled revolutionary reformer. Mexico's economic austerities in the 1980s had caused much suffering to many of Chiapas's poor; and like many post–civil war Central Americans, the rebels felt that NAFTA was a return to the old, unfair policies of the past, dressed in new clothing. The revolt used NAFTA as a symbol of centuries-old racism and economic and social injustices. Far less violent than many other revolts, it lasted only a short time before the sides began negotiations, which predictably brought little result. The rebels' restraint might in part have resulted from a skillful use of computerized technologies to quickly communicate with supporters all over the world, and from the fact that Mexico could ill afford adverse publicity that would discourage the foreign investment that people hoped NAFTA would bring. The rebellion's mysterious poet-leader, subcommander Marcos, and his partner Ramona, have become folk heroes in Mexico (Figure 31), representing a mythological opposition to Carlos Salinas. As of summer 2000, the political environment had altered in Mexico. For the first time since the creation of PRI in 1929, a non-PRI candidate was elected for presidency; free elections in Chiapas offered the possibility for change through less violent means. Substantive reforms, however, had not yet occurred and deep-set tensions were building in other parts of the country.

The recent popularity of mythic figures like Carlos Salinas and the Zapatista leaders mirrors a rise in respect for those who have suffered at the hands of the influential, for the concerns of el pueblo. Included in these many and diverse peoples are the indigenous groups. Events like the 1992 Quincentennial celebrations of Columbus's discovery of America, which were followed by the Year of the Indigenous sponsored by the United Nations, fostered new mythic attitudes toward indigenous peoples in Mesoamerica. Only a short time ago, for example,

Figure 31. Subcomandante Marcos (left) and Comandante Moises of the Zapatista army at a press conference in La Realidad, Chiapas, August 1996 (AP Foto/Jorge Nunez)

many claimed that Catholicism had entirely replaced traditional religions. Now, new voices, not the least of which are those belonging to indigenous peoples themselves, offer very different visions. Catholicism may have been the most influential religious tradition in Mesoamerica since the Conquest, but neither the indigenous nor their mythic traditions simply rolled over and died when the conquistadors marched into Tenochtitlan.

Moreover, the increased emphasis on the concerns of the poor expressed by the Second Vatican Council (1962–1965) helped Catholics focus on the problems of ordinary people (Peterson and Williams 1996; Peterson 1997). Prior to this time, the Catholic Church in Mesoamerica tended to side with the influential and well-to-do, especially in Central American countries such as Nicaragua, El Salvador, Guatemala, and the adjacent states of Mexico. Thus, these areas felt the influence of reform movements inspired by post-Vatican II, progressive Catholicism more than some others. Progressive Catholicism took the Council's preferential option for the poor very seriously. Largely independent Catholic religious orders—often viewed as subversive by local church factions that sided with the upper classes and opposing governmental forces[23]—sponsored programs that combined spiritual formation and community building with training in literacy and in political affairs. Drawing their strength and resolve from biblical myths such as Exodus and stories of Christ's life, many common folk soon made their desire for liberation from suffering heard by their active participation in peaceful or in violent protests. No longer did they think that their rewards must wait until heaven; now their religion allowed them to believe that Christ himself had fought for an end to earthly injustice and suffering. And in their view, like Christ and the early Christians, they did not openly seek martyrdom, but they were willing to accept it if that is what it took to improve their lot (Peterson 1997, 79–80, 83, 85–88, 174).The most famous martyr of all was not a peasant but Oscar Romero, archbishop of El Salvador. Assassinated by a pro-government death squad while saying mass on 24 March 1980, Romero was a strong and effective spokesman for the poor. Since his death, grateful Catholics have attributed numerous miracles to him, and the Church is considering him for sainthood.

Now, however, one can no longer say that all countries are exclusively Catholic. The rapid growth of evangelical Protestantism since the 1960s indicates important changes in Mesoamerica's religious character. Mainline and evangelical Protestants primarily from the United States began missions in the region at the end of the nineteenth and beginning of the twentieth centuries; at the time, they exerted only a very small influence. But in the 1970s, evangelical movements gained enormous momentum, drawing many new converts, especially in Central American countries such as Guatemala. Some postulate that evangelical Protestantism has had less success in Mexico because of the popular view there that Protestantism supports the economic policies of the United States, and because of the Virgin of Guadalupe's past mythic support for revolutionary reform and her close mythic association with Mexican national identity (In conversation, Peterson 1998). In Mexico, even nominal Catholics may not be eager to convert to another tradition, because they cannot abandon their Virgencita.

And so life in Mesoamerica continues to change and be transformed in ways that sometimes repeat the past and sometimes produce entirely new creations. Myths also are changing along with everything else. But, the historical view presented in this chapter is not necessarily the one many Mesoamericans would describe. Mythical time does not always march forward in such a neat, straight line; it can curve back or twist inward on itself, destroying any sense of linear momentum. Dates may be important, but for different reasons, just as reality may be based on somewhat different premises. We turn now to an exploration of history from a more mythic viewpoint.

NOTES

1. According to the sixteenth-century historian Fray Diego Durán, the Mexica were first called the Aztecs because they came from a place called Aztlan. Later they were called Mecitin, or Mexicans, after their leader, whose name was Meci—a name that seemed to stick so well that even Tenochtitlan was renamed Mexico City by the Spanish, and the

country, Mexico (Durán 1994, 21). Since the word *Aztecs* is a nineteenth-century revival that refers imprecisely to a variety of peoples who weren't even Mexicans, *Mexica* has been the preferred term in more recent times.

2. My thanks to Nora Carrol, who told me this story and gave me permission to use it (even though I changed it a little because I could not remember it exactly).

3. See Adams (1991, 3–9) for an excellent survey of many of the main resources on ancient Mesoamerica. See Keen (1971) for resources on central Mexicans.

4. Four pre-Conquest Maya pictorial codices have survived, as have five Mixtec from western Oaxaca and six others from a disputed area (probably southern Puebla, western Oaxaca, or the Gulf coast). The *tonalpohuallies*, or divinatory calendars, of the *Codex Borbonicus* and the *Codex Aubin* are both probably very early post-Conquest texts done in fairly authentic pre-Conquest style (see Robertson 1959; Wauchope 1964–1976, vol. 14, pt. 3).

5. The Mesoamerican pictographic writing often used rebuses, in which a picture is used to represent the sound of a spoken word. Many readers will have seen (perhaps in their childhood) a rebus—for example, a picture of an eye being used to indicate the sound for "i" or the word *I*.

6. See Read (1998, 137–144) for a description of Mexica topography.

7. Translation by Kay Read and Jane Rosenthal from the Nahuatl in Sahagún (1953–1982, bk. 3, pt. 4, 41–46).

8. See Read (1998, 144–151, 157–161) for a description of Mexica cosmic beings.

9. John Henderson (1997, 213) suggests a different set of dates for Chichén Itzá: the Terminal Classic era, or ca. A.D. 800–1000.

10. Others suggest that some of these myths represent the motions of the star Venus (e.g., Aveni 1980, 261–262).

11. 1350 is an estimated date. The dates suggested in various sources for Tenochtitlan's founding range from 1140 to 1372. The earliest dates (all of which come from a single source) are probably off, and the rest cluster around 1350.

12. This suggestion comes from Frederick Hicks (in conversation, November 1997).

13. The father is asking the sons how they expect the fact of their nobility to sustain them.

14. Translation by Kay Read from the Nahuatl found in Sahagún (1953–1982, bk. 6, pt. 7, 90–91).

15. See Díaz del Castillo (1956) for an account of the Conquest.

16. The following has been drawn from Cosío Villegas, Bernal, et al. (1974); and Liss (1975).

17. For Nahua speakers, the idea that beings should have souls was such a foreign concept that a Spanish word *(anima)* was borrowed to describe the soul. In pre-Conquest times, beings appear to have had multiple centers in their bodies that contained a variety of animating forces able to do different things. These forces could continue after death by migrating into other bodies or to various places. But nowhere does any one force exactly match Christian beliefs in a single soul that outlasts the body. See López Austin (1988a, 203–236), and Read (1998a, 111–112, 114–115, 159, 202, 206, 208).

18. See Cosío Villegas, Bernal, et al. (1974) for a good summary of Mexican history.

19. New Spain was divided into two major sectors. Ruled from Guatemala City, the first included what are now Guatemala, Honduras, Nicaragua, El Salvador, Costa Rica, and Panama. Controlled from Mexico City, the second included what are now Mexico, California, the southwestern states of the United States, and Texas. Belize had been brought under implicit British control over a period 150 years after shipwrecked British sailors established a colony there in 1638. By 1821, it was more British than Spanish. In 1862, Britain formally declared the area the Colony of British Honduras, and it gained independence in 1981.

20. California, the southwestern states, and Texas were acquired by the United States, and the current boundaries were established in 1848, as a result of the Mexican War.

21. In 1929, at its establishment, the party was named the National Revolutionary Party. In 1938, it was restructured and given the name Party of the Mexican Revolution. Another restructuring in 1946 resulted in the present name.

22. Although some (though not all) FMLN leaders were socialists, the majority of rank-and-file members were peasants seeking concrete economic gains and greater access to political processes.

23. The accusation of subversive activities made against various progressive clerics and religious lay workers at times had consequences as serious as torture and death.

MYTHIC TIMELINES

Mythic timelines are based in both tangible and intangible worlds. On the one hand, the idea of time is founded on actual human experiences of tangible change. After all, we all experience a great deal of unavoidable transformation from birth to death. As babies we are not the same as when we are children; and as children, we are not exactly like what we will be as young adults. We change when we marry and have children of our own, and again when we reach the age at which our children care for us. People experience change on a daily basis: This year's summer is different from last year's, yesterday was different from today, and morning is different from night. Flowers grow from seeds; eventually they wither and die, and new ones take their place. Change is a simple fact of life. And it often seems to occur in a moving line of moment-like events, one leading to the next, with past events slipping away as present ones replace them. Many say that these kinds of common experiences characterize time; they are what time is made of.

On the other hand, from a somewhat less tangible position, time can be much more than a mere march from one moment to the next. For although life's changes seem to occur sequentially, moving from beginning to end, mythically people do not always view change that simply. While one's life progresses from one's beginning in birth to one's end in death, one encounters mythic moments along the way—moments in which one can pick up part of the past and make it present. Many families tell mythic stories about what particular individuals did in the past, helping shape their own familial image as well as that of the individuals in question. Stories about a grandparent who fought heroically in a war lend a treasured aura both to grandpa and his family; or stories about a child who early on proved particularly talented in music help mold the child's personality and future career as well as express familial pride and the value the family places on music.

Even history contains many mythic elements, although more than any other kind of time it seems to speak about moving from some objectively true past to the present. But histories are never simple, unobjective recordings of past events; they tend to be particular to the people who tell them. The mythic elements in historical narrations reflect ideals and help people recapture past moments, making them present once again. People pick and choose events they wish to remember, often elaborating on or sometimes even altering them to fit the story they want to tell. In its official history, a nation may count its independence as its birth, and then mark all those past events up to the present that its influential people deem important. But the less influential may tell an unofficial counterversion of the same nation's history, focusing on events the influential would be happy to forget. Each individual also can tell his or her own personal history from a particular standpoint, or a family may trace its historical lineage back to a particularly important founding figure, leaving past mistakes or family skeletons quietly locked in the closet. This careful scripting of history helps people to create ideal models for the present, for what they wish life would or would not be like. And by so doing, they may even successfully shape the future according to those ideals.

Mesoamericans often use the past in these ways, and like others, they frequently participate in rituals drawing on mythic models gleaned from the past. They even sometimes hope with luck to use the past together with the present to mold the future by means of both their ordinary and ritualized actions. As for many around the world, modern astrology is one way for Mesoamericans to account for the present and future. One's daily horoscope is based on one's birth and the convergences of the stars, but its outcome may depend on how one acts on the astrologer's advice. Similarly, prophetic and other types of rituals based on specifically Mesoamerican calendrical systems draw on influences such as one's ritual naming day at birth, one's ancestry, one's dreams, the convergences of heavenly objects and particular calendrical counts, and one's own actions. As with modern astrology, people often hope to use this information to act effectively, sometimes altering future events such as travel or career plans, marriage, or business deals. Mesoamericans also have used past events not only to effect the future but sometimes to predict their own demise as individuals or as a people. Throughout one's lifetime, change may proceed from beginning to end, but before one reaches the finish line, one will momentarily bring the past into the present many times—whether in the form of memories, dreams, the circumstances of one's birth, or one's familial or national histories. In this way, the past both prefigures and shapes one's future life and events. Later, we will explore in more detail how Mesoamerican rituals and mythic histories could bring forth the past into the present and predict the future. But first, two indigenous mythic histories need to be told, for it is through such stories that Mesoamericans organize and express their ideas about time. Because of this, these historical tales can offer us good insight into Mesoamerican temporal concepts.

TWO MYTHIC HISTORIES: K'ICHE' AND NAHUA

Many indigenous Mesoamerican histories follow a particular pattern: (1) The present world is created after three or four other ages have lived and died. The gods, who already exist, both shape each age and participate in its destruction. (2) Events performed by nonhuman beings and gods create the important things of the present age, such as the sun, moon, and food. (3) Then the gods create human beings. (4) The story moves on to tell of the migratory travels and settling down of a particular group, usually those to whom the story belongs. Finally, (5) the history is given of the group's royal lineage—who its rulers were and what they did. The K'iche' Maya Popol Vuh provides us with a wonderful resource because it presents these five elements in great detail. The situation is somewhat more difficult for the Nahua because no one source offers all these elements with the same richness and depth as the Popol Vuh, although the "Legend of the Suns" (Codex Chimalpopoca 1992b, 141–162) offers quite a bit. In the following narrative, we have summarized the stories of both the Popol Vuh and the "Legend of the Suns"; in the case of the latter, we have supplemented the story with tales from other sources.

K'iche' Maya History

The epic legend of the Popol Vuh begins with these words:[1]

This is the beginning of the ancient word, here in this place called Quiché.[2] Here we shall inscribe, we shall implant the Ancient Word, the potential and source for everything done in the citadel of Quiché, in the nation of Quiché people.

And here we shall take up the demonstration, revelation, and account of how things were put in shadow and brought to light

by the Maker, Modeler, named Bearer, Begetter,
Hunahpu [Hoon-ah-poo'] Possum, Hunahpu Coyote,[3]
Great White Peccary, Tapir,
Sovereign Plumed Serpent,
Heart of the Lake, Heart of the Sea,
Maker of the Blue-Green Plate,
Maker of the Blue-Green Bowl,[4]

as they are called, also named, also described as

the midwife, matchmaker
named Xpiyacoc [Shpee-ya-kok'], Xmucane [Shmoo-ka-nay'],

defender, protector,
twice a midwife, twice a matchmaker,

as is said in the words of Quiché. They accounted for everything—and did it, too—as enlightened beings, in enlightened words. We shall write about this now amid the preaching of God, in Christendom now.[5] We shall bring it out because there is no longer a place to see it, a Council Book,

a place to see "The Light that Came from Across the Sea,"'
the account of "Our Place in the Shadows,"
a place to see "The Dawn of Life,"

as it is called. There is the original book and ancient writing, but he who reads and ponders it hides his face. It takes a long performance and account to complete the emergence of all the sky-earth:

The fourfold siding, fourfold cornering,
measuring, fourfold staking,
halving the cord, stretching the cord
in the sky, on the earth,
the four sides, the four corners,[6]

as it is said,

By Maker, Modeler,
mother-father of life, of humankind,
giver of breath, giver of heart,
bearer, upbringer in the light that lasts
of those born in the light, begotten in the light;
worrier, knower of everything, whatever there is:
sky-earth, lake-sea.

After this preamble, the storyteller goes on to retell this long, ancient tale, beginning at the beginning, with the creation of the four ages, and ending at the end, with the coming of the K'iche' lords.

1. The First Three Ages.

At first only the sky and sea existed. The great knowers all enclosed in a sea of bright blue-green quetzal feathers and called Plumed Serpent—the Maker and Modeler, the Bearers and Begetters—met with the three Thunderbolts, also called Heart of Sky.

Figure 32. A Classic Maya vase portraying a mythic story or event with animals from the Popol Vuh (Justin Kerr Archives, File no. 3413)

"How should it be sown, how should it dawn? Who is to be the provider, nurturer?" the gods all asked (Popol Vuh 1985, 73).

They decided that earth must first be emptied of water so that humans would have a place to work. For without humans, no one would exist to sing out bright praises for the gods' work and designs. And so by simply calling its name, the gods caused earth to rise up through the water, instantly covered with mountains, trees, and rivers.

Age One: Once this was done, the gods created animals to inhabit the earth. The animals could multiply, but unfortunately they all spoke to each other only according to their own kind. They hummed, buzzed, chirped, cackled, snorted, barked, and whined (Figure 32).

"'Talk, speak out. Don't moan, don't cry out. . . . Name now our names, praise us. We are your mother, we are your father. Speak now,'" the gods all said to the animals (Popol Vuh 1985, 78).

But the animals only kept squawking, chattering, and howling.

"'This hasn't turned out well,'" the gods said (79).

So they told the animals that they would simply have to be transformed, that it would be their place to be of service to others by becoming their food. And so the animals were killed and eaten.

Age Two: The gods tried again. They had to work fast because the time of planting was drawing near. This time they tried with mud, but the body they made did not look so good. It kept going soft, crumbling, and falling apart. Its head wouldn't turn, and its face was lopsided and twisted. It could talk only nonsense. It could not walk or procreate. So they just let it dwindle away, finally taking it apart completely; they let it become just a "thought" (80).

Figure 33. A Postclassic probable Maya daykeeper throwing lots with corn (Museo de América/Art Resource)

Age Three: Then the gods summoned Xpiyacoc and Xmucane, Hunahpu Possum and Hunahpu Coyote, and other daykeepers. They asked them to count the days, to count the lots, to throw the corn kernels in order to see how it was to be done (Figure 33).[7] The daykeepers told them to make wooden manikins. This the gods did. The man they carved of coral tree wood, and the woman, of reeds. The manikins could walk, talk, and multiply. But there was nothing in their hearts or minds; they had no memory of their creators, the gods. They became the first of many peoples here on earth's face, but they accomplished nothing. So Heart of Sky created a great flood of resin to destroy them. Then various beasts and beings gouged out their eyes, snapped off their heads, crunched their flesh, and tore them open. Even their dogs went after them because the manikins never fed them enough. They were smashed and pulverized because of their incompetence. It is said now that monkeys are made of wood and look like humans, but they are really a warning that we people must have a heart.

2. The Hero Twins and 7-Macaw

Once the three ages were completed, preparations for the fourth and present age became possible. This story, however, does not begin at the beginning; instead, it appears to begin with a story plucked out of the middle of a longer tale about the birth and feats of the twin boy heroes Hunahpu (Hunter) and Xbalanque (Sh-ba-lan-kay', meaning Jaguar Deer). This particular story begins after the Hero Twins are already beyond childhood. Holding special powers, they defeat 7-Macaw, an overly prideful ruler who claims to be the sun. First they break his jaw by shooting it with a blowgun; then, enlisting the help of an old grandfather and healer, they "cure" this bird-lord by plucking out his bejeweled eyes and teeth, after which he loses his luster and, along with his wife, dies. Again using trickery, the Twins also defeat Seven Macaw's sons: Zipacna (Zee-pak-na'), who claimed to have created the mountains, and Earthquake, who said he could scatter them. Both are buried now, one under a mountain and the other in the earth. The Twins defeated these three because of their self-glorification and false claims.

3. Exploits in the Underworld

Now the tale turns back to the past, to the time of the Twins' father 1-Hunter and their uncle 7-Hunter. Also twins, 1-Hunter and 7-Hunter were born of the old couple who threw lots before the Third Age, Xpiyacoc and Xmucane. The lords of the underworld—1-Death, 7-Death, Pus Master, Bone Scepter, Jaundice Master, Bloody Claws, and so on—summoned the Twins to play ball. They endured several tests, only to be defeated and sacrificed by the lords, who buried them in the ball court and hung One Hunter's head in a calabash tree (Figure 34). A daughter of one of the lords, an innocent young maiden named Blood Woman, went to the magical tree to pick its fruit, not wanting its sweetness to go to waste. But the skull of One Hunter spoke to her:

"'You don't want it,'" he said.

"'I do want it.'"

"'Very well. Stretch out your right hand here, so I can see it,'" said the skull (114).

She did, and the skull spit a bit of saliva into her palm, which promptly disappeared. The skull told her:

"It is just a sign I have given you, my saliva, my spittle. This, my head, has nothing on it—just bone, nothing of meat. It's just the same with the head of a great lord: it's just flesh that makes his face look good. And when he dies, people get frightened by his bones. After that, his son is like his saliva, his spittle, in his being, whether it be the son of a lord or the son of a craftsman, an orator. The father does not disappear, but goes being fulfilled. Neither dimmed nor destroyed . . . he will leave his daughters and sons. So it is that I have done likewise through you" (114–115).

Upon learning that Blood Woman is pregnant, her enraged father tries to sacrifice her. But with the help of some owls, Blood Woman escapes to the upper world. She goes to the house of her mother-in-law Xmucane and her twin brothers-in-law. Xmucane does not believe her story any more than her father did. But when Blood Woman prays to the goddesses of the field, she proves her unborn sons' heritage by bringing the old woman a huge bag full of corn gathered from just one measly stalk. The babes are born, and even though their uncles try to

Figure 34. A Mesoamerican ballcourt at the Classic site of Monte Albán, Oaxaca (Elizabeth L. Fuller)

kill them by placing them first on an anthill and then on some brambles, the infants not only survive the ordeals but sleep peacefully through them. When the boys grow older, they get their revenge by enticing their uncles to the top of a tree, where they turn them into monkeys.

As young adults, the Twins decide to become farmers, but this turns out to be a bad career choice. Every day they plant corn (Figure 35), which magically matures by evening, but animals eat it in the night. Finally they catch a rat, who—after they singe his tail, try to choke him, and promise him food—tells them that they are meant to be ball players like their fathers (Figure 36). He helps them get their ball playing equipment down from the rafters where their grandmother had hidden it. As his reward, the rat receives many seeds and kernels, as well as the household garbage.

But as had their fathers, the boys disturb the underworld lords by playing ball over their heads; so the lords summon the Twins below. This worries both their mother and grandmother, for this is how their father and uncle had died. In an effort to stall their leave-taking, Grandmother sends the summons with a tiny, slow-moving louse. But Louse is eaten by Toad, who is eaten by Snake, who is eaten by Falcon, who flies swiftly to the ball field with the message in his belly. There Falcon vomits up Snake, who vomits Toad, who just sits there and drools. So the boys squash Toad's rear end and pry open his mouth, where they find Louse stuck in his teeth. Louse tells the boys that they must go to Xibalba (Shee-

Figure 35. A farm field, or "milpa," with corn, beans, and squash (Carmen C. Arendt)

Figure 36. A Classic depiction of the Hero Twins as Ballplayers (Israel Museum, Jerusalem)

bal-ba'), the underworld, to test themselves against the lords there. To assuage their mother's and grandmother's worry, they each plant a corn seed in the middle of their house. If they die, the plants will die; if they live, so will the plants.

In Xibalba, the lords cannot trick the Twins into defeat as easily as they had their father and uncle (Figure 37). After passing a few minor tests, the Twins are sent to six different houses to spend six successive nights in various trials. In the Dark House, they trick the lords into thinking they are smoking a single cigar all night without burning it, by "lighting" it with a firefly. In the Razor House, the boys give the great chopping knives who dwell there the flesh of all the animals

Figure 37. A Classic depiction of the Hero Twins in Xibalba (Justin Kerr Archives, File 1742)

to eat so that the knives will not chop them up. In the Cold House, they shut out the drafts and hail, making it warm. In the Jaguar House, they give the ferocious cats bones to eat, thereby saving their own skins; in the Fire House, the Twins merely simmer, they don't boil to death. But Hunahpu meets his match in the Bat House. There a bat chops off his head, which is taken to the ball court to become the ball. All the animals come to help Hunahpu, who is lying helpless in the Bat House. Each brings his own kind of food; Coati brings a pumpkin. While Possum holds back the dawn by painting it with red and blue streaks,[8] they fashion a fake head from the pumpkin for Hunahpu. Then the boys go to play ball with the lords. At a good moment, Rabbit diverts the lords' attention; he rolls off like a ball, making them chase him. Quickly the Twins make a switch. Placing Hunahpu's proper head back on his shoulders, they turn the pumpkin into a ball. The game begins again, but this time Xbalanque rapidly ends it by kicking the "ball" and smashing it to pieces, releasing its seeds. With this, Hunahpu and Xbalanque defeat the lords of death and disease.

But they have not yet really won. The lords hope to trick the Twins into falling into a big fire, but the Twins thwart the lords by willingly leaping to their death in the conflagration. An aged seer who is secretly working for the Twins advises the lords to grind the boys' bones and sprinkle them on the river. As a result, on the fifth day, the Twins reappear as catfish; and on the sixth day, they appear as two old vagabonds. Of course these are no ordinary vagabonds but magnificent entertainers who can dance many dances, burn houses down and make them reappear, and bring sacrificed dogs and people back to life. After the boys sacrifice themselves and return to life, Lords 1-Death and 7-Death become caught up in the magical dance and shout:

"Do it to us! Sacrifice us! Sacrifice both of us!" (Popol Vuh 1985, 153).

The Twins sacrifice the two lords but do not bring them back to life. Upon seeing this, all of the other lords immediately surrender, and the boys reveal their true identity. Instead of killing the remaining lords, the boys tell them that as inciters of evil, the lords of the underworld henceforth can feed on only the creatures of meadows and clearings, and not on humans;[9] and that only the guilty and violent will come to them. Next the Twins go to the Place of Ballgame Sacrifice, where their father still lies. There they try to put him back together again; but they only partially succeed, because he cannot remember all the names of his body parts. So they leave him there as he is, promising him that he will be the first to be consulted and worshiped, thereby somewhat comforting him. Then, ascending into the sky, one twin becomes the sun, and the other, the moon.

4. The Creation of People, and Their Migrations

After the Hero Twins rise as the sun and moon, the cosmos is now ready for the fourth and present age. And with the promise of the first dawning, the gods' thoughts on how to make proper humans now appear clearly. Fox, coyote, parrot, and crow bring them white and yellow corn, along with the news that the mountain at Broken Place, Bitter Water Place holds all manner of sustenance: corn, cacao, zapotes, anonas, jocotes, and nances, all sweet and delicious. All of the edible fruits, great and small, are there.

Xmucane then grinds the white and yellow corn. The gods model human flesh, arms and legs from the cornmeal. Water becomes human blood, and the water in which Xmucane rinsed her hands becomes human fat. The first humans are not born of any woman but by the sacrifice and genius alone of Builder, Sculptor, Bearer, and Begetter. These new human creatures, made of the food that will sustain them, are the final and most successful creation. They talk in words, look and listen, walk and work; and most importantly, they praise and thank the gods for having been created by them. Yet all is not quite right. These first humans can see with such intensity that their knowledge is perfect, they understand everything, they understand too much, as much as the gods themselves. So the gods dim their eyes as a mirror's face is dimmed when one breathes upon it, taking back some of their knowledge. Now humans can only see things nearby, not those far away.

First the gods mold four men, and then they shape their four wives. Thus the first human pairs are created: Jaguar Quitze (Keet-zay') and Celebrated Seahouse, Jaguar Night and Prawn House, Mahucutah (Mah-hoo-koo-tah') and

Hummingbird House, and True Jaguar and Macaw House. Lots of people come about then, many lineages are created, black and white, of many faces and languages. Each can trace itself to one of the first four men; the K'iche' trace their lineage to Mahucutah. All these people stand around at the edge of the sky, watching for the first sunrise. While waiting at this place called Tollan (Tol'-lan),[10] a place of seven caves, each lineage receives its own language and gods. Among others, the K'iche' receive Tohil (Toh-heel'), a great god of fire who is worshiped by others as well. Then, dressed in nothing but animal skins, they all leave and begin migrating to their various homelands; along the way, they create shrines for their gods, whom they pack on their backs. And all this time they await the sun's rising. Finally, like a person, the sun shows its face, which is so hot that it dries out the soggy earth. Then the first sacrifices to Tohil begin. After several other adventures, the first four men come to the time of their deaths. Knowing this, they leave instructions for their wives and sons, telling them to press on to their true homelands.

5. More Migrations, and the Coming of the K'iche' Lords

Remembering the words of their fathers, they move eastward, toward their fathers' birthplace. The only son of Mahucutah, Coacutec (Kwa-koo'-tek), leads the K'iche'. They visit many places on their travels. At one, the lord of Nacxit, keeper of the royal mat, bestows upon them the signs of lordship, such as a canopy and throne, bone flute, jaguar's paw, nosepiece, and parrot and heron feathers. As the groups travel, they carry these things along with the writings about Tollan. The first four women die, but the four groups continue traveling. Eventually they become so numerous that each group splits into various lines. The K'iche' split into four lines that multiply, becoming great, with numerous lords. Lord Plumed Serpent, of the fourth generation, is particularly great, able to go up into the sky and down into Xibalba. At other times he transforms himself into a great jaguar, a serpent, an eagle, or a pool of blood. Bit by bit, the K'iche' lords take lands from others whom they have conquered, erect houses for their gods, and create lovely things from jade, metal, and feathers. Now there have been fourteen generations of K'iche' lords living in K'iche'; the Spanish appeared during the twelfth. At that time Tonatiuh, or Pedro de Alvarado (Pay'-dro day Al-va-ra'-do) arrived.[11] Now K'iche' is called Santa Cruz (San'-ta Kroos).

Nahua History

The Mexica Nahua also tell a tale beginning with the creation of the cosmos in a series of ages and ending with the coming of their lords. Most of this story is preserved in the "Legend of the Suns."[12] Although the latter lacks the richness of the Popol Vuh, several other texts offer more detailed variations of the individual stories.[13] The legend, which the teller relates on 22 May 1558, begins with what may seem to many readers an odd little tale. This now unknown songster first explains: "They divided the earth into one portion each. . . . Thus it is known how all things originated. Everything existed as the Sun's time and place for 2,513 years."[14] The Narrator then goes on to tell about four different ages that were created before the present one.

1. The First Four Ages

Age One, whose name was 4-Jaguar, lasted 676 years before Jaguars ate it up in the year 1-Reed, on the day 4-Jaguar. Its inhabitants ate 7-Grass for their food. We are not told much more about this age, nor are we told what kind of food 7-Grass was. 7-Grass is a date in the Mexica calendar; since the ancient Mesoamericans often used calendrical dates for names, this phrase could have referred to any number of things. It could have been, of course, something they actually ate (which is now called something else), or it could have been the name of a god. That particular day might have carried special powers rather as astrological signs carry powers, so that its "food" is mythically real but not actually so. Or 7-Grass could have been referring to a specific period of time that was passing—hence, being "eaten" metaphorically. We really don't know. But we are told that when the man-eating jaguars ate this age, people turned themselves into monkeys to escape into the second age. The next three ages all follow the same pattern: Each disappears in a particular year, has a name based on the day and manner of its own destruction, and has inhabitants who eat something with a calendrical date for a name. Probably each age had a house too, because in the second age, the monkeys' houses are mentioned. Our problem is that the ancient songster may have offered his or her Spanish interrogator a highly abridged version, and this is all we're left with now.[15]

The second age, named 4-Wind, existed only 364 years before it was blown away by the wind in the year 1-Knife, on the day 4-Wind. The wind was so strong that it blew away the monkeys' tree houses too. During this age, the monkeys ate something called 12-Snake, and turned themselves into turkeys to escape the wind. The third age, 4-Rainstorm, existed only 312 years before a great volcanic rainstorm of fire burned everything up. Like the second, this age also disappeared in the year 1-Knife, but on the day 4-Rainstorm. During this age, the turkeys ate 7-Knife, and turned themselves into nobles when their age was destroyed. The fourth age, 4-Water, existed for 676 years before being destroyed by a huge flood in the year 1-House, on the day 4-Water. During this age, the nobles ate 4-Flower, and turned themselves into fish to escape certain death when the flood poured in. Then water spread out for another 52 years, while the gods rearranged the cosmos into four parts.

Unlike the Popol Vuh, this curious little story's main concern lies less with the nature of various beings, than with counting out time's passing as things disappear or transform themselves. The Popol Vuh made it clear that proper human beings were to have a heart and mind capable of praising their creators but not so great as to compete with them. No such moral message exists in the Nahua version, which contains only objective observations voiced mythologically. Because the Mexica lived in the fifth of five ages, how and when each age would end was of great concern, for it indicated when their own age's end would come due. Each age is only very briefly described, but at the same time, quite carefully counted out. The significance of this story lies in its calculation of how long each age lasted and how its destruction transformed it into something else; it describes the mathematics that structure the cosmos. Like the people at Teotihuacan, who built their city's buildings according to math based on celestial patterns, the Mexica also lived in a world built on celestial calculations.

2. First Couple[16]

Once the cosmos had been laid out in four parts, it came time to create the fifth age and the beings who would inhabit it. As in the Popol Vuh, the creation of humans does not occur after just one try. The first attempt goes like this:

The great god, Titlacahuan,[17] called to the first couple, Tata [Tah'-ta] and Nene [Nen'-nay], and asked,

"Children, do you want anything more?"

"Make a very big hole in a cypress tree[18] and put us in it when the vigil begins and the sky falls." This he did. And when he was finished he told them,

"You will have one cob of corn each to eat. When you have finished all the kernels, then you will see that the water is all gone and that your cypress trunk has stopped rocking."

When the corn was gone and the cypress trunk had stopped rocking, Tata and Nene emerged and found that they were saved. Using a drill to start a fire in some small sticks, they roasted a few fish. But this was not appreciated by the gods because it smoked up the sky, making it black. Titlacahuan-Tezcatlipoca [Teet-la-ka'-wan/Tez-kat-lee-po'-ka] bawled them out for their error. He then cut their heads off at their necks and sewed them back onto their buttocks. This turned them into dogs, the first ancestors of all those living in the Fifth Sun.

The sky was smoked by these dogs in the year 1-Rabbit. Afterward, it was dark for 25 years. Then [in the 26th year], which was called 2-Reed, Tezcatlipoca lit the fire drill and smoked the sky once more.

As with the early attempts of the Maya gods to make people, this trial was not entirely successful. But the gods' next attempt worked out a bit better.

3. Creation of People[19]

And then the gods consulted among themselves. "Who will be the ones to settle there?" they asked. "The sky has been spread out, the earth lord has been spread out. Oh gods, who will settle there?" [All the gods including] Quetzalcoatl and Titlacahuan were not happy.[20]

Then Quetzalcoatl went to Mictlan [Mict'-lan] (Land of the Dead). Upon arriving, [he met] Mictlanteuctli [Mict-lan-tay-ooct'-lee] and Mictlancihuatl [Mict-lan-see'-wat] (the Lord and Lady of Death). He said, indeed he [spoke] like so:

"I have come for the precious greenstone bones that you are guarding. I have come to take them away."

"What will you do with them, Quetzalcoatl?" [Mictlanteuctli] asked.

He answered once again, indeed he [spoke] like so: "The gods are unhappy; who will settle there on earth?"

Mictlanteuctli again responded, "Oh, very well! Blow my conch-shell horn and encircle my precious enclosure four times. And may the shell horn not have holes."

Immediately [Quetzalcoatl] summoned worms who drilled holes in it. Then bumblebees and honeybees entered it. When he blew it, Mictlanteuctli heard it.

"Oh, very well! Take them!" Mictlanteuctli once again replied. Right away Mictlanteuctli said to his messengers, the Micteca (the People of the Land of the Dead), "Gods, tell him that he has to leave them here!"

Quetzalcoatl responded, "No, I'm taking them once and for all!"

Just then Quetzalcoatl's *nahualli* [na-wal'-lee][21] spoke to him. "You tell him that you have left them." So [Quetzalcoatl] said to [Mictlanteuctli], he called out to him, "I've left them!"

Quickly rising, Quetzalcoatl took the precious greenstone bones. A man's lay in one place and a woman's in another. Immediately, Quetzalcoatl gathered them up, wrapped them up, and carried them off.

Once again Mictlanteuctli said to his messengers, "Gods! Quetzalcoatl is actually taking the greenstone bones! Gods! Quickly, make a pit!" They wanted to make him fall down.

He fell right into that pit, he whacked himself and the quails startled him. He passed out from that fall, spilling all the greenstone bones. The quails chewed them; they ground them to bits.

Then, Quetzalcoatl was revived. He howled out, he said to his *nahualli*, "My *nahualli*, how will they be?"

He told him how it would be: "Really, he messed things up. However it actually goes, is how it goes."22

Then [Quetzalcoatl] gathered them up, he picked them up and wrapped them. Like so, he carried them to Tamoanchan. When he delivered them, the [goddess] named Quilachtli [Kee-lacht'-lee] who is called Cihuacoatl here,23 ground them and bathed them in a greenstone bowl. Quetzalcoatl bled his member on them. Then all the gods in that place gave them merit. . . .24

And then they said it: "The gods and commoners were born because they gave us merit."

4. Creation of Corn25

After the commoners were created, the gods wondered what they would eat. The ant went and got a kernel of corn from inside the Mountain of Produce.26

Meeting this ant, Quetzalcoatl asked him, "Tell me where you mean to take that corn you are carrying." But the ant didn't really want to tell him. So Quetzalcoatl questioned him very firmly, and eventually the ant gave in. "Over there," he said.

Instantly Quetzalcoatl turned himself into a black ant and followed the red ant, helping him to carry the corn.

He carried the corn to Tamoanchan. It is there that the gods chew it up and place it on our lips. In this manner, we [who live now] grew strong.

The gods asked, "What will we do with this Mountain of Produce?" Quetzalcoatl wanted to carry it on his back. He tied it up and tried, but he couldn't do it.

So Oxomoco [Oh-sho-mo'-ko] and Cipactonal [See-pak-to'-nal] cast fortunes with corn (Figure 38). They also cast fortunes of the day.27 They said, "Nanahuatl [Nah-Na'-wat] will be the one who strikes open the Mountain of Produce."28 They knew this because they had "opened up" the fortune.29

Immediately, the Tlaloques [the fierce rain and lightning gods of the mountains] piled up: the green Tlaloques, the white Tlaloques, the yellow Tlaloques, and the red Tlaloques.30 Instantly Nanahuatl struck the mountain and the Tlaloques snatched out all the food—the white, black, yellow, and red corn, beans, chia, and amaranth, all of it they snatched away.

5. Creation of the Fifth Sun31

Now the earth's surface has been prepared, and both people and their food exist. All that is missing is the dawning of the fifth age. The story goes like this:

Figure 38. Oxomoco and Cipactonal casting lots with corn (Codex Borbonicus, *fol. 21,* Museo de América/Art Resource)

I.

Here it is, the story in which it is told how the
little rabbit is stretched out on
the Moon's face.
The Moon, it is said, was played with like so:
Like so they whipped his face,
Like so they beat his face,
Like so they wrecked his face,
Like so they killed his face,
The gods did all this.
When later he came out, he was spread out flat.

II.

It is said that:

When it was still the dark-place time,
When there was not yet warmth,
When there was not yet day,
They met together,
They all consulted together,
The gods did all this at Teotihuacan.

They said it, they took counsel:
"Please come here, oh Gods!
Who will carry it?[32]
Who will bear it:
The warming,
The dawning?"[33]
And then, like so:
He says it,
He steps forth,
He makes it clear,
Tecuiçiztecatl [Te-kwi-seez-tay'-kat] did all this.
He said it: "Oh Gods! Indeed I, I will be the one!"

Yet a second time, the gods said it:
"Who will be another one?"
Like so, then,
They, altogether, look at each other,
They look closely at each other.
They take counsel with each other.
"How will this thing be there?
How will we do it then?"

No one was daring.
No other would step forth there.
All men were frightened.
They were turning tail.
And still, not even one man would present himself there.
There, in the company of all,
Nanahuatzin was listening to what was being said.
Like so, the gods called to him there.
They took counsel.
"You! You will be it, Nanahuatzin [Na-na-wat'-zin]!"

Quickly he responded to their rallying cry.
He accepted it with pleasure.
He said to them:

"Indeed, this is good, oh Gods!
You have done me a great favor!"

III.
Like so, then,
They set forth,
Preparing themselves to celebrate the rituals.
They fasted for four days,
The two of them together,
Tecuiçiztecatl [and Nanahuatzin].

Also then,
The fire was set in order,
Burning there in the fire pit,
They call that fire pit[34] the "God Oven."

And he, Tecuiçiztecatl,
He was preparing himself with very precious things:
His ritual branches were of quetzal feathers,
His grass heart was woven of gold,
His spine was of greenstone,
Likewise,
The bloodletting,
Blood-covering instrument was of coral,
And, his incense was copal, a very fine copal.
As for Nanahuatzin,
His ritual branches were made only of
green grass and green reeds,
Tied in three bundles,
Bound bundles of nine each, three in all.
And his grass ball was woven only of pine needles,[35]
And his bloodletting spine was only a maguey thorn.
He was bloodying them well with his own blood.
And his incense consisted of only scabs that he was twisting off.

For those two,
For each one,
Their mountain was made.
There, where for four nights,
They had been ritually celebrating,
It is said that now there are pyramid-mountains:
His pyramid, the Sun's;
His pyramid, the Moon's.

When they had completed
four nights of ritual celebration,
They hurled them down,
They dashed them down,
Their ritual branches,
Everything with which they had celebrated.

This was done:
When it was their lifting up.
When it was just getting dark.
They would serve as slaves,
They would create gods.

And when midnight arrives,
They arrange them,
They adorn them,
They prepare them.

To Tecuiçiztecatl, they gave
His tall, round egret headdress and his vest.
But to Nanahuatzin, they gave only paper.
Like so:
They braided his hair,
They bound his head with its name,[36]
His paper hair,
His paper robes and
His paper loincloth.

And, when midnight arrived,
All the gods made a procession around the fire pit,
They spread out around it.
They praised it as the "God Oven."[37]
The fire burned there for four days.

The gods lined up on both sides.
And Nanahuatzin and Tecuiçiztecatl
were placed in the middle.
They stood up very straight.
These two together were called,
Nanahuatzin and Tecuiçiztecatl.
They faced each other.
They stood facing each other,
At the fire pit.

IV.
Then the gods spoke.
They shouted at Tecuiçiztecatl:
"Oh do it, Tecuiçiztecatl!
Fall down!
Hurl yourself into the fire!"

Like so, then,
He is now going!
He will throw himself into the fire!

The fire became a heated thing,
A thing not to be faced.
A thing not to be tolerated.
A thing not to be suffered.
The fireplace was burning well.
The fire was going well.
The fire was in good order.
Because of this, he was growing frightened.
He stops!
He retreats!
He turns back!
Once again he goes, but:
He struggles!
He tries his hardest to throw
himself into the fire!

But he dares not to approach that heat!
He retreats!
He turns tail!
He cannot do it!
Four times, four times.
He tries to do it.
But it was not possible to throw
himself into the fire.
Nevertheless, he persisted four times.
And he drew back four times.

Like so, then, they called to Nanahuatzin there.
The gods called to him:
"You!
Quickly, you!
Oh Nanahuatzin, on with it!"

Nanahuatzin was the only one who dared.
He completed it.
His heart strengthened him.[38]
He closed his eyes, but not because he was afraid.
He did not stop.
He did not turn back.
He did not retreat.
He simply threw himself down.
He hurled himself into the fire.
Like so it goes well!

Like so, then, he burns.
He blossoms.
His flesh sizzles.
And when Tecuiçiztecatl saw him burning,
He hurled himself after him.
And they say,
It is said that,
Then an eagle also rose out of the fire after them.
He threw himself into the fire.
He hurled himself into the fire.
The eagle is arranged well everywhere because of this.
His feathers are darkened.
They are smoky.
But the jaguar was last.
Then the fire was no longer very well arranged.
He fell.
Like so,
He was barely burned,
He was burned just a little,
He burned here and there.
The jaguar was not arranged completely.
Because of this:
He was painted.
He was sprinkled with black soot.
He was spattered with black soot.

It is said that because of those things:
The traditional words spread out there,
They were considered there.
In this way,
He who was brave was named.
"Eagle-Jaguar" was his name.

That one, the eagle, came first.

It is said,

They say that:

This is because he went first into the fire.

But the jaguar is only last.

Therefore they say it [as one word]:

"Eagle-Jaguar."

Because of these things, the jaguar fell into the fireplace afterwards.

V.

When, in this way,

The two had both thrown themselves in the fire,

When they had burned,

Then the gods sat waiting to learn

from where Nanahuatzin would emerge.

He was the first to fall into the fire,

So he would be the first to shine,

Like so, he would light up first.

For a long time they stretched out there,

They sat waiting.

The gods stretched out there.

Then, like so, it begins.

Everywhere it becomes red,

Everywhere was surrounded,

The lighting of dawn,

The reddening of dawn.[39]

Hence, it is said that the gods knelt down.

Like so, they will wait

For the place from which the sun will emerge.

It was done.

They would look for it everywhere.

They keep on turning around.

Nowhere were they well united.

Their traditional words,

Their oration:

Nothing which they said was good.

Some thought he would emerge

from the Place of the Dead.

They spread themselves out to look there.

Some thought the Place of Women,

Some thought the Place of Thorns,[40]

They expected this because
Dawn's reddening encircled everything.
And some did well,
They spread out to look for him at the Place of Light.[41]
They said it:
"Already he is way over there,
Already he is there,
The sun will be emerging!"

Their words were very true,
Those words belonging to
Those who waited there,
Those who pointed there. . . .

And when the sun was emerging, he was spreading like red dye[42]
He was spreading in an undulating way.[43]
He could not be faced.
He dazzled a great deal.
He shines a lot,
He shimmers.
His shimmering rays were coming from everywhere.
He arose.
His warm rays entered everywhere.

And afterwards,
Tecuiçiztecatl came to emerge
from the Place of Light.
He could only follow him,
He came to be spread out like the sun.
As they fell into the fireplace,
So too did they come out.
In this way, they followed each other.

VI.
They say that the gods talk over many things.
They discuss and discuss it.
[The suns'] appearances were just alike.
Thus they were shining when seen by the gods.
Just alike were [the suns'] appearances.

Then once again it was discussed over and over.
[The gods] said: "How will these two [suns] be, oh Gods?
Will both of them follow the same road?

Will both of them shine in the same way?"
And the gods all gave their opinion.
They said it:
"Like so it will be, this thing.
Like so it will be done."

Then like so, a person fled from the gods.
Like so, he beat Tecuiçiztecatl in the face with a rabbit.[44]
Thus, they wrecked his face.
Thus, they killed his face.
In this way now,
Like so, he appears.

Right then, like this:
When they were both spread out,
It was still not possible for them to move.
They still did not follow their paths.
They were only spread out.
They were only spread out on the edge.[45]

Like so, once again, the gods say it:
"How will we live?
The sun does not move.
Will we live a life mixed up with the commoners?[46]

This one, the sun:
May he go on.
May he be revived [or born].
May we all die!"
Then, like so, that one, Ehecatl, did his work.
Right away he kills the gods.

But they say that Xolotl [Sho'-lot] did not want to die [Figure 39].
He tells the gods: "Let me not die, oh Gods!"
For this reason,
He was crying a great deal.
His eyes were very swollen.

His eyelids were very swollen.
Right then Death quickly comes forward,
Xolotl fled to the field of young corn, diving into it.
There he transformed himself into something else.

He turned himself into the
young maize with two
stalks.
This is called "Xolotl of the
Field."

But he was seen there in the
field of young corn.
Once again, Death quickly
comes forward,
Again he entered the
maguey field.
Like so he turned himself
into the double maguey.

Its name is "Maguey Xolotl."
Right away once again, he
was seen.
Again he entered the water
place.
He turned himself into the
"Water-Xolotl."⁴⁷
Right away, there they went to seize him.
In this way, they killed him.

*Figure 39. Xolotl (Codex Borbonicus, fol. 19,
Museo de América/Art Resource)*

VII.
And they say that, even though all the gods died,
In truth, still he did not move.
[It was] not possible for the Sun, Tonatiuh,
To follow his path.

In this way,
Ehecatl did his work.
Ehecatl stood up straight.
He grew extremely strong.
He ran and blew lightly.
Instantly, he moved [the sun].
Like so, he follows his path.

And when [the sun] was following his path,
The moon was left behind.
When the sun was going to go into his entrance again,⁴⁸
Like so, the moon came forth.

In this way, they exchanged with each other.
They separated from each other.
In this way, the sun emerges once,
He takes one whole day.
And the moon shoulders his work for one whole night.
He shoulders his work for one night.

Like so, he appears there.
It is said that, certainly,
He, the moon, Tecuiçiztecatl,
Would have been the sun
If he had fallen into the fire first.
Because, indeed, he offered himself first.
With all precious things,
He celebrated the rituals.

Here it ends, this thing:
The tale,
The ancient fable,
In this way, they used to tell it,
The old ones whose charge it was.

6. Birth of Huitzilopochtli[49]

Now that the fifth age has begun, the patron god of this age's inhabitants, the Mexica, can be born.

On the top of Snake Mountain, Coatlicue [Ko-wat-lee'-kway] (Snake Skirt) was performing her rituals by carefully sweeping up, keeping the mountain tidy [Figure 40]. As she swept, some feathers dropped from above. She picked them up and placed them in her clothing near her waist. But when she had finished sweeping and reached for them, the feathers had disappeared. It was in this manner that she became pregnant.

When her daughter Coyolxauhqui and her four hundred sons from the south found out about this mysterious pregnancy, they became very angry and wrathful, accusing their mother of having gravely dishonored them. Calling her wicked, they determined to kill her.

This really frightened the poor woman, who had done nothing more than ritually sweep the mountain. But her unborn child, Huitzilopochtli, spoke to her from her womb, comforting her, "Do not fear, I already know what I am going to do about this!"

Coyolxauhqui led her brothers in the attack. But a traitor warned Huitzilopochtli about their plans. He told him about every movement Coyolxauhqui and

Figure 40. Statue of Coatlicue (Museo Nacional de Antropología de Mexico, Mexico City)

her army made, about each place they passed on their way to Snake Mountain.

Just as this fearsome army with Coyolxauhqui in the lead scaled the heights of Snake Mountain, Huitzilopochtli was born. He was magnificently arrayed! He carried his magical shield, his darts and dart thrower. His faced was painted with diagonal stripes and his upper arms and thighs were striped blue. Feathers were pasted on his forehead and ears. The sole of his one thin left foot also was coated with feathers.[50]

Suddenly, the turquoise snake burst into fire. Commanding it, Huitzilopochtli pierced Coyolxauhqui and then quickly chopped off her head. Her body fell over the edge of Snake Mountain and crashed to the ground, breaking apart as it fell; her legs and her arms each came off.

Then Huitzilopochtli charged his 400 brothers. He plunged after them, scattering them from the top of the mountain. He chased them down and around the mountain four times. He made them turn tail. He destroyed them well, he completely enveloped them in clouds and thoroughly finished them off with smoke.[51]

Even after all that he continued to chase them. They cried out piteously to him, "Please, let this be enough!" But he continued after them, and only a few escaped back to the south, whence they had come.

7. Migration

The time had come for Huitzilopochtli to lead his people on their travels in search of their homeland. Fray Diego Durán tells the following story. The seven peoples of the Valley of Mexico all originated in the Place of Seven Caves, or

Chicomoztoc (Chee-ko-moz'-tok). One by one, each group exited their subterranean home to migrate to the valley. The Mexica were the seventh and last to leave, led by their patron god Huitzilopochtli, whom they carried hidden in a bundle on their backs. They were called Mexicans in honor of Meci (Me'-see), a priestly lord who led them forth. They also called the Place of Seven Caves Aztlan (Azt'-lan). In this delightful land, people lacked nothing; they lived in leisure there and never grew old. Aztlan was a place of beautiful lagoons filled with reeds and all manner of waterfowl and fish. But once the Mexica left there, life became very hard. The stones became sharp, wounding them; the bushes became prickly and the trees thorny. Everything turned against them, and they no longer could remember how to return to this beautiful place. Along the way, the Mexica stayed in many places. At one time, the Mexica were related to the people of Malinalco (Ma-lee-nal'-ko), just west of the Valley of Mexico. But Huitzilopochtli had a falling-out with his sister Malinalxochitl (Ma-lee-nal-sho'-cheet):[52]

This woman was very beautiful, had a charming disposition and was so intelligent that she became skilled in the magical arts. She was very cunning, however, and did harm to the people, causing them great fear. They suffered her presence and gave her respect only because she was the sister of Huitzilopochtli. [Eventually, however, things became so bad that] they decided to ask their god to rid them of her for everyone's sake.

In the usual manner, the priests consulted Huitzilopochtli through dreaming[53] and passed on these revelations to the people:

"Your god sees your affliction. He says that his sister, with her cunning ways and bad talk, endangers you. He is disturbed and very angry to see the powers she has acquired by illicit means. She has power over fierce and dangerous beasts. She kills all who anger her by magically sending snakes, scorpions, centipedes, or deadly spiders to bite them."

"Since she is so dangerous, and since your god loves you so much and has no wish to bewitch or harm you, he says you should leave her. After she has fallen asleep, you should depart, leaving no one behind to tell her the way."

So all of those who were not Malinalxochitl's followers went away. They abandoned her and her attendants while they slept.

Malinalxochitl, not being able to follow the departed Mexicans because she did not know where they had gone, went on to found the town of Malinalco. There she bore a son she named Copil [Ko'-peel]. When Copil was old enough, she told him the story of how she was so cruelly abandoned by the followers of her brother, Huitzilopochtli. Her son was moved by his mother's tears, and his heart was so filled with wrath that he promised to seek revenge.

Seeing Copil's determination, she helped him to prepare by inciting all the nations against the Mexicans and teaching Copil her own wicked tricks and sorcery.

While the Mexicans camped at Chapultepec,[54] Copil set out, passing from town to town, turning many hearts against the Mexicans and inciting the nations to destroy them with their most fiendish skills and cunning.

But events came out exactly opposite to what Copil had hoped. His uncle, Huitzilopochtli, learned of Copil's bad intentions and warned the Mexicans. He told them that before Copil had a chance to surround their hill, they must take him by surprise, kill him, and give his heart to him, their god.

Shouldering their idol [Huitzilopochtli], the Mexicans successfully stalked and slayed Copil. But when the Mexican priest presented the captured heart to Huitzilopochtli, he was told to cast it as far as he could into Lake Texcoco. It is said that the heart landed in a place . . . where a prickly pear cactus sprouted out of it. It is in that same spot that Mexico City [Tenochtitlan] was later built. It also is said that hot water began to gush forth from the place in which Copil was killed. These springs are now called . . . "Water of Copil."

After visiting many more places and fighting a few battles, the Mexica settle down on land owned by the people of Colhuacan (Ko-wah'-kan).[55] The land is very poor and filled with venomous snakes. But the Mexica solve the problem by eating the snakes, and live there in peace and contentment. The lord of Colhuacan had been so sure that the snakes would kill them, he is disturbed by this turn of events, and just a little bit frightened of the Mexica. So when they request permission to trade in the city, he feels obliged to grant their wish. They even intermarry with the city's people. But Huitzilopochtli views Colhuacan as his enemy and determines that they should depart from this place in a manner that would be anything but peaceful. He instructs the Mexica to ask for one of the lord's daughters to serve Huitzilopochtli as a living goddess, to which the ruler agrees. But as soon as the maiden comes to the Mexica, they sacrifice her, and then invite her father to a festival in her honor. After the lord and his entourage had received their fine hospitality, the Mexica invite him into an inner chamber to view their god Huitzilopochtli and his goddess Toci (To'-see), his daughter. When to his horror he sees a Mexica youth dressed in his daughter's flayed skin sitting next to Huitzilopochtli, he flies into a rage and calls for vengeance. The people of Colhuacan chase the Mexica out of the city and into the marshes of Lake Texcoco.

This is actually good fortune in disguise, for after a bit of soggy wandering, the Mexica finally find their true homeland on an island in the middle of the lake. Huitzilopochtli tells them to search for the signs that will tell them where to build Tenochtitlan. First, they find a spring out of which runs one stream of water as red as blood, and another bright blue and extraordinarily thick. Soon after, they discover a prickly pear cactus, on which stands a magnificent eagle basking in the bright sun; in his talons he grasps a very fine bird (Figure 41).[56] This was the sign. It was here that they built their city of Tenochtitlan and elected their first ruler, Acamapichtli (A-ka-ma-peecht'-lee). The city and its people enjoyed a very long and successful history, with many rulers who performed many astounding feats.

8. Return to Aztlan
But all good things must come to an end. And the Mexica know this. One of their greatest rulers, Motecuhzoma I, in the midst of his successes, received a warning to this effect:[57]

After the king, Motecuhzuma I, had established himself in his office and was very rich and well off, he wanted to find the home of his ancestors. He had heard that Huitzilopochtli's mother, Coatlicue, was still alive and living there. Since he wanted to find her and give her a

Figure 41. The Eagle and Cactus (Codex Mendoza, frontispiece, Bodleian Library)

fine present, he called his associate, Tlacaellel [Tla-ka-e'-lel]. Tlacaellel told him that he would need many priest-shamans, because according to history, this Place of Seven Caves was very well hidden by huge rock roses, thorny and tangled plants, and lagoons with thick reed beds. Moreover, it was a place inhabited by their fathers and grandfathers who were described not only as agreeable and delightful but also as very vicious.

So Motecuhzuma gathered a quantity of mantles, women's clothing, rich rocks, precious jewels, much cocoa, the aromatic *teonacaztli* [Tay-o-na-kazt'-lee] plant,[58] cotton, flowers of the vanilla plant, and the biggest, most beautiful, and finest feathers he could find. He sent his priest-shamans off with these gifts, to look for Aztlan. When they arrived at the hill called Coatepec in the province of Tula, they drew circles around themselves and anointed their bodies with salves so they might call down the gods and be changed into birds and fierce beasts, into lions and tigers and terrible cats. In these forms, they arrived on the banks of the place of their ancestors. There they changed themselves back into human beings.

A number of people of the earth were there, fishing from their canoes and farming. Upon encountering them, these strange people of the earth asked in the Mexica-Tenochca's own language what the newcomers were doing there.

"Sirs, we are from Mexico and we have been sent by our lords to look for the place of our ancestors."

"Whom do you worship?"

"We worship the great Huitzilopochtli. The great Motecuhzuma and his associate, Tlacaellel, have sent us to search for the mother of Huitzilopochtli, whose name is Coatlicue, and for the place of our ancestors which is called Chicomoztoc (Place of Seven Caves). We have presents for her, if she still lives, and if not, for the fathers and tutors who served her." The people told the Mexicans to wait and then went to the tutor of Huitzilopochtli's mother.

"O venerable sir, some people have arrived at the shore who say they are Mexicans sent by a great lord called Motecuhzuma and another called Tlacaellel. They say they have gifts for the mother of their god, Huitzilopochtli, and that they have been sent to present them to her personally."

The ancient one replied, "It is good they have come. Go back and bring them here."

So in canoes they were brought to the island. There they went to the foot of the hill of Colhuacan, where the house of the ancient one stood. It is said that in the middle of the top of this hill there was a tiny, sandy spot that could not be mounted because it was so soft and so deep.

"O venerable aged one and sir, here we have arrived, your servants, at the place where your word is obeyed and the desires of your mouth are revered."

"It is good you have come, my children. Who has sent you?"

"We have been sent by Motecuhzuma and his associate, Tlacaellel, whose other name is Cihuacoatl."

"Who is this Motecuhzuma and who is Tlacaellel? No one by those names left here. . . . [S]even went out as leaders of each . . . neighborhood. Four marvelous tutors of Huitzilopochtli also left here . . . and two others."

"Sir, we must confess that we do not know these gentlemen. We have never seen them. We have only a memory of them, for they have died. I have heard them mentioned."

The ancient one was amazed. "O lord of the born! What killed them? Why are all of us whom they left behind still living? Why has none died? Who are those that live now?"

"We are their grandsons."

"Who then is now the father and tutor of Huitzilopochtli?"

"A great priest whose name is Cuauhcoatl [Kwaw-ko'-wat]."

"Have you spoken with Huitzilopochtli?" the ancient one asked.

"No, we were sent by our king and his associate."

"When will Huitzilopochtli return? He told his mother that he would, and the poor woman spends each day waiting and crying with no one to console her."

"We only have been sent by our lords. But we have a present for the great lady, and we would like to give it to her and bring her our greetings. We want to bring her the loot and riches that her son enjoys."

"All right then, get it and follow me." And he moved off with such great agility that they had difficulty in keeping up with him.

When they reached the sandy place at the top of the hill, the Mexicans sank into it, first to their knees and then to their waists, as they struggled forward. Finally, they could not move.

The old one returned to where they were stuck and asked, "What have you been doing, Mexicans? How have you made yourselves so heavy? What do you eat there in your country?"

"We eat the food that is grown there and we drink cocoa."

"These foods have made you heavy. They do not allow you to visit the place of your fathers and they have resulted in death. And these riches that you carry, we don't use them here. We are poor and simple folk. Now, give them to me and wait while I go and see if the lady of this house, the mother of Huitzilopochtli, will see you." He took their ample gifts, carrying them on his shoulders as though they were no more than a tiny straw, and climbed the hill with ease.

When he returned, they were able to continue to the top because they were no longer weighed down by all their goods. There Coatlicue appeared. She was a lady of great age, her face was blackened, and she was as ugly and dirty as one could imagine. Crying bitterly, she said, "It is good that you have come, my children."

Full of fear and trembling, they replied, "Great and powerful lady, we have been sent by our lords and your servants, the king, Motecuhzuma, and his associate, Tlacaellel Cihuacoatl, to search for the place where our ancestors lived. We bring you kisses for your hands. Motecuhzuma is not the first king. . . . [He] is the fifth, and remains in your service.

"The four previous kings have suffered much hardship, hunger, and work. They paid tribute to other provinces, but now they have their own city and are prosperous and free. They have opened roads to the seacoast and all of the earth. And now Mexico is the lord and prince, the head and queen of all the cities. They have discovered mines of gold and silver and of precious rocks, and they have found the house of rich feathers. And as you can see, we have been sent with these things, which are the goods and riches of your marvelous son, Huitzilopochtli, who is brave and strong with a good head and heart, the lord of the born and of the day and the night. And with these gifts, we have completed our mission."

Her weeping somewhat assuaged, she replied, "I congratulate you, my children. I greet you, my children. Tell me, are those who left with my son still living?"

"Madam, they are not of this world any longer. They are dead, and we did not know them. We only have them in our memory."

Her weeping returned. "What killed them? Here all their companions are still living! And tell me, children, this that you carry, is it food?"

"Madam, it is eaten and it is drunk. The cocoa is drunk, and the rest of it is mixed with it and, at times, eaten."

"You have become attached to it, my children, and this is the reason you could not climb up here. But tell me, my children, is the clothing of my son the same as these rich, feathered mantles?"

"Yes, Madam. They are crafted elegantly and are richly arrayed, for he is the lord of us all."

"This is very good, my children. My heart is at peace. But I tell you, I am in much sorrow because it is difficult to be without him. Look at me now, a penitent who fasts for your cause. He told me when he left:

"'Dear Mother, I will be gone only as long as it takes me to establish the seven *barrios* [neighborhoods] in the places that have been promised them so that they can live on and populate this earth. And then I will return. The assigned years of my migration will expire after I have waged war against all the provinces, cities, villages, and hamlets and have placed them in my service. But then I will lose them to strangers in the same order that I won them, and I will be expelled from this earth.

"I will return after that, because those whom I have subjected with my sword and shield will turn against me, and I will be turned on my head, and my weapons will be thrown on the ground. Whereupon, Mother dear, I will return to your lap. But until then, do not feel sorrow. Give me two pairs of sandals, one to go with and one to come back with; four sandals, two with which to leave and two with which to return."

"I congratulated him and told him that he should not linger so that the time would be completed and he could return. But I think he must be happy there, for he does not remember the sadness of his mother. So tell him that his period is now completed and it is time for him to come home. To help him remember his mother, please give him this mantle and loincloth made of maguey fiber."

They took the mantle and loincloth and descended the hill. When they had arrived at its skirt, she called to them:

"Wait a minute and see how, in this land, no one grows old! Watch my old tutor!"

The ancient one descended the hill; the lower he got, the younger he became. Then he turned to ascend. And as he climbed, he grew older.

"This is how we live here, my children," he said. "And this is how your ancestors lived. No one dies here. We can rejuvenate ourselves whenever we want. Now look, your problems have been caused by the cocoa you drink and the food you eat. They corrupt you and rot you. And these rich clothes and feathers, they ruin you. But because you cannot take this manner of attire back with you, come and take from what we have to offer."

And he offered them all the wonderful game and fruits of the earth that grew in that place. Then he gave them two mantles and loincloths of maguey, one each for their king, Motecuhzuma, and his associate, Tlacaellel. Telling them please to forgive them, for they had nothing better to offer, he left.

They took their presents, drew their circles around themselves, and turned into the same animals as those they had come as. When they arrived at Coatepec, they turned themselves back into human beings. Twenty members, one-third of their party, had been decimated. Some said that the fierce beasts and birds that they had encountered had eaten them.

They returned to Mexico and told their story to Motecuhzuma, giving him the gifts. They told him how Coatlicue awaited the return of her son, how his time would be completed when all the towns that he had conquered were lost again in the same order.

Motecuhzuma then called Tlacaellel and related the whole story to him; about the abundance of Aztlan and how their own food and things weighed them down, corrupted them, causing death. Crying because they were remembering the ancestors and wanted very much to see this place, they told those who had gone on the mission to rest and then gave them the gifts that they had brought back. Finally, they gave the mantle and loincloth of maguey to Huitzilopochtli because his mother had sent it to him.

9. Destruction of the Fifth Age

Just as the four previous ages had come to an end and the reign of the Mexica was foredoomed, so too will the fifth age end. When its time is up, it will end, in this way:[59]

Like so is the Fifth Sun.
Four Movement is its day sign.
It is called Moving-Sun because
It moved,
It follows a path.
The old ones say that,
On Four Movement, it will be done like so.
The earth will quake.
They will be hungry.
Like so, we will perish.

MYTHOLOGICAL TIME

These two indigenous histories are very different from the history of Mesoamerica presented in Chapter One. Even if we had begun that history with the creation of the cosmos, as these began, they still would have been different. Not only are their main actors gods, animals, and humans with some pretty unusual powers (all in true mythic style), but in addition, time in these stories does not simply march onward. True, time moves in a kind of line; but it also sometimes both doubles back on itself and springs forward. Under the names Hunahpu Possum and Hunahpu Coyote, the Maya twin heroes appear at the beginning of time as two of the daykeepers who cast lots to see how people should be made; yet they are not even born yet, for that doesn't happen until the next age. Also before they are born, they destroy Zipacna and his two sons. In the Nahua myth, each age (including the present) will self-destruct according to a cosmic mathematical plan; and the Mexica magicians will return to the place of their origin in Aztlan, only to find out about their own future demise. Moreover, in that strange place of Aztlan, the normal aging processes do not operate; one can become young or old simply by running down and up a hill. How can what hasn't yet happened act in the present, transforming it? How can one know what is to come before it gets there? And how can one manipulate time, making it move backward and forward at will? A Euro-American historical timeline would never operate like this.

But time for indigenous Mesoamericans is not always like Euro-American time.[60] Euro-Americans base their calendar on only one celestial object, the sun; therefore they count the moments linearly, like beads on a rope. The sun was born a long time ago and will die many years from now; in the meantime, our lives tick onward like the hands of a clock, never turning back. But Mesoamerican calendrics are not based on just one but on many calendar rounds and on numerous celestial cycles, all moving according to their own paths. These all operate simultaneously, creating a very complex system. Moments do not line up like beads on a rope; instead, time is more like the rope itself, in which many fibers of differing lengths spin together. Now some fibers overlap and others do not; now others overlap that before had not.

As though one is weaving all the same points together into a coil of rope, rituals collapse many past and future moments (or fibers) into one moment (or rope section). By so doing, they bring all those moments' powers to bear on the present. This binding creates a unique meshing of many moments, just as a single binding of many points on a rope's coil ties together a number of unique sets of fibers. The present moment, which contains many past and future ones, is identical to no other moment that ever existed or will exist, just as a particular group of bound fibers on a coiled rope contains different fibers from other groups that could be bound. In this way, present moments reach backward and forward simultaneously, picking up all the powers of specific years, deities, days of times past and future. By manipulating different calendrical bindings, one can control the present, shape the future, and even reshape the past.

Thus, because these different moments could in fact converge, the Hero Twins could exist both at the beginning of time, helping to create some of the first beings, and still be newborns long after that creation was completed. As their father One Hunter told their mother Blood Woman, "The father does not disappear, but goes being fulfilled. Neither dimmed nor destroyed." One lives on in one's heirs, but this was more than simply a father's heritage carried on in his sons. Just before rising as the sun and the moon, the Twins also partially put their father back together again—not quite the same as he was before, but almost. Most importantly, he could still talk to them, just as he had to his daughter-in-law years before. The Twins' dead father was different from how he had been before, but he was not really dead; and even though he had been transformed, he also transformed the present, and was promised a future of continuing to do so. Transformation or change creates new things out of old things, and some of the old continues to live actively in the new. The father simultaneously lives in his sons, alongside his sons, and for them, long after he has died. The past still lives in, along with, and for the present.

Time's Purpose

Calendars help control the transformative change that is a natural part of life, because each moment holds particular powers able to shape and mold tangible events. By combining and recombining various moments, people can create new

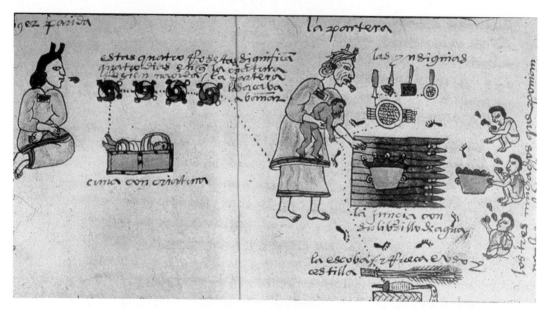

Figure 42. A midwife naming a newborn (Codex Mendoza, *fol. 57, Bodleian Library*)

moments that will prove propitious for certain activities. Conversely, some combinations are unlucky for certain things, and are avoided. The points in life when change occurs are linked to the calendrical system through rituals, which are timed to coincide with the most effective moments for their success. Thus, calendars help shape everything from the changes a new birth brings upon a family to the transformation of a dead leader's power into that of a new leader. Calendrical rituals exist for successful planting and harvest, marriage, travel, business transactions, waging of battles, and conduct of diplomatic missions. In ancient times, people's personal identities were partially formed by temporal calculations, for a calendrical name given at birth gave a child positive and negative traits (Figure 42). These traits became part of a person's personality and destiny, along with the effects of other life-changing calendrical rituals, other names (a person could have many), actions of the gods on a person, that person's own deeds, and his/her physical constitution—all of these, if properly controlled, came into existence at positively charged moments. Their sum total was called one's *merits*.[61] And because time changes, so too did one's merits.

Histories usually were tied directly to the elite classes and could be manipulated calendrically to create more favorable stories. However, when a particular city was conquered by another, these historical stories and the calendars on which they were based often ceased to function. Such was the case with the Classic Maya. Their elites used a particular calendar called the Long Count to tell their histories; this calendar was not used for any other purpose, and only those in control had the right to use it (Figure 43). Extremely accurate, the Long

Count could pinpoint events to the day within a several-thousand-year span. Maya elites used the count to shape their future and remain in control. But when the Classic Maya cities disappeared, so too did the Long Count, for no powerful rulers existed any longer to use it. Although the Maya were the only people who used the Long Count, other groups used a variety of calendrical systems for similar purposes. The Mexica rewrote their history in order to manipulate the calendar's powers to their benefit. Given the transformative powers possessed by particular dates, this was more than a mere reworking of self-image (although that was important too); by changing how they coordinated historical and celestial events, the Mexica believed they could literally change their past, present, and future, because the past always prefigures current and future events. It both foretells and shapes what is to come; and what is happening now happens because of what happened earlier.

Time's Workings

At one time, mathematics structured almost everything in Mesoamerica; and even today, calendrical concerns govern much of daily life, especially in villages and the countryside. Since indigenous calendars are neither simple nor all the same, we won't go into much detail here, but a small glimpse into how three or four cycles mesh might prove helpful to understanding how moments in the past, present, and future can converge. All Mesoamerican calendars are based on a running count of twenty days. Each day is named for and bears the powers of a particular deity (calendar dieties). The basic calendar was and still is the divinatory calendar, called the Tzolkin (Tsol-kin') in Yucatec Maya and the Tonalpohualli (To-nal-po-wal'-lee) in Nahuatl. Its age is very long and its origin quite obscure; possibilities range from a lunar cycle to a baby's gestation period, or the length of the rainy

Figure 43. A Maya Long Count date from the Temple of the Sun, Palenque, Chiapas, Mexico (drawing by Jason González, from frontispiece by Frederick Catherwood in Stephens, 1841)

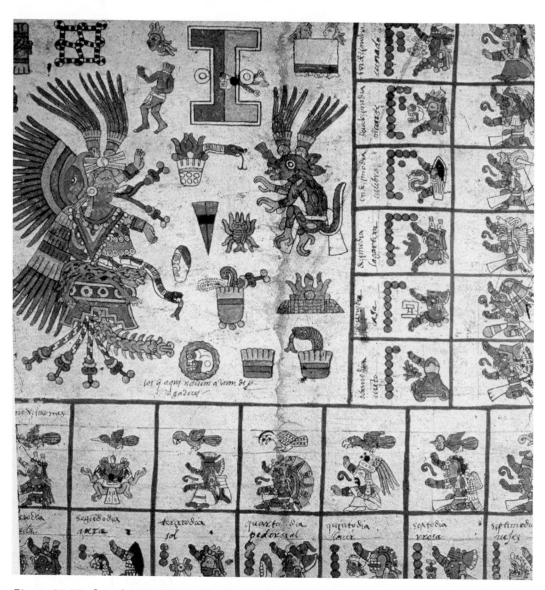

Figure 44. Week 18 from a Mexica Tonalpohualli (divinatory calendar) (Codex Borbonicus, fol. 19, Museo de América/Art Resource)

season to the period between zenith passages of the sun. People use the divinatory calendar for prophesying individual and communal events. This is the calendar one consults if one wants to know when to name one's baby, marry, or make a business deal: 260 days long, the round consists of 20 "weeks" of 13 days each (20 X 13 = 260). The basic 20-day count (each day indicated by a deity) lines up with each week's count of 1 to 13 (marked by dots). The Mexica version of this looked something like this (see Table 2.1 and Figure 44 and Table 2.1).

Another basic round is the solar calendar, called the Haab (Hahb) in Yucatec and the Xiuhmolpilli (Shee-ooh-mol-pee'-lee) in Nahuatl. In ancient times, this

TABLE 2.1. THE ROTATION OF TWENTY DAY SIGNS AND THIRTEEN *TRECENA* DAYS IN THE *TONALPOHUALLI*

Day-Signs	Dots, Thirteen Days of each *Trecena*
1. Crocodile	1 dot, *Trecena 1*
2. Wind	2 dots
3. House	3 dots
4. Lizard	4 dots
5. Snake	5 dots
6. Death	6 dots
7. Deer	7 dots
8. Rabbit	8 dots
9. Water	9 dots
10. Dog	10 dots
11. Monkey	11 dots
12. Grass	12 dots
13. Reed	13 dots
14. Jaguar	1 dot, *Trecena 2*
15. Eagle	2 dots
16. Vulture	3 dots
17. Movement	4 dots
18. Knife	5 dots
19. Rain	6 dots
20. Flower	7 dots
1. Crocodile, etc.	8 dots, etc.

calendar controlled the yearly agricultural cycle and was often used for high state rites; today local communities still use it to govern their civic events. It consists of 18 "months" of one 20-day round each, plus a period of 5 days generally considered dangerous; in pre-Conquest times, those five days were not even officially marked ([18 X 20] = 360 + 5 = 365). Every fifth name of the 20-day round was also a solar year name. For the Mexica, these were House, Rabbit, Reed, and Knife (underlined in Table 2.1 above). The mathematics of the system assured that every 365 days, the year would end on one of these days, and each of these four days would appear in succession every four years. Like the weeks in the divinatory calendar, this count went up to 13, and then started again with 1. In the Mexican Highlands, a 52-year round was counted out using this system, with each count of 13 being aligned with one of the 4 cardinal directions (4 X 13 = 52). For the Mexica this worked like so (see Table 2.2 and Figure 45).

The Mexica divinatory and solar rounds ended on the same day every 52 years. At that very same moment, the Pleiades reappeared in the sky after having disappeared for six weeks, and the sun rested at its nadir. Moreover, this happened in November, when the rainy season of agriculture ended and war's dry season began. At this power-laden conjunction of several celestial and seasonal moments, a ceremony took place in which a new sun was given birth, for it was said that the

TABLE 2.2. THE 52-YEAR CYCLE OF THE *XIUHMOLPILLI*

Southern Quarter Dots-Year Sign	Eastern Quarter Dots-Year Sign	Northern Quarter Dots-Year Sign	Western Quarter Dots-Year Sign
1-Rabbit	1-Reed	1-Knife	1-House
2-Reed	2-Knife	2-House	2-Rabbit
3-Knife	3-House	3-Rabbit	3-Reed
4-House	4-Rabbit	4-Reed	4-Knife
5-Rabbit	5-Reed	5-Knife	5-House
6-Reed	6-Knife	6-House	6-Rabbit
7-Knife	7-House	7-Rabbit	7-Reed
8-House	8-Rabbit	8-Reed	8-Knife
9-Rabbit	9-Reed	9-Knife	9-House
10-Reed	10-Knife	10-House	10-Rabbit
11-Knife	11-House	11-Rabbit	11-Reed
12-House	12-Rabbit	12-Reed	12-Knife
13-Rabbit	13-Reed	13-Knife	13-House

Note: Read each column down, beginning with the southern quarter (on the left), move right to the eastern quarter, then the northern quarter, and end with the Western quarter. This cycle repeats every fifty-two years.

life of a sun lasted only fifty-two years. This ceremony, called the Binding of the Years, or the New Fire Ceremony, took place on a hill overlooking Tenochtitlan (Figure 46). All fires in the entire domain were snuffed out, houses swept clean, and old clothing and household goods thrown away. At midnight, a specially trained priest cut out the heart of a distinguished war captive (a man, probably 52 years old), and then sparked a fire in his chest cavity. His heart was fed to the fire, which also consumed his entire body. If the fire was not successfully lighted, creatures of the night would descend and eat up the age; but if it was, a new sun would rise. Because the years had been properly bound, like the Hero Twins containing something of their father One Hunter, this new sun would contain something of the old sun but would still be a different entity. And like the Hero Twins, Nanahuatzin, and Tecuiçiztecatl, this new sun had risen out of the ashes.

In the Nahua five mythic ages, time spans also were calculated on the 52-year cycle: 13 X 52 = 676 years, the length of the first and fourth ages; 312 + 364 = 676, the length of ages two and three combined. Remember that in the Nahua myth ages two and three both ended on the same year, 1-Knife. Like the two suns in the myth about the birth of the fifth age, they were named the same and so were considered the same. While this was inappropriate to the creation of the fifth age, which needed only one sun at a time, here it was appropriate because the two ages needed to be made the same. Mathematically joining them left 676 years for the fifth age to live—years that otherwise would have been used by a previous age. By juggling numbers in this way, those skilled in calendrics could manipulate the calendars to create their own realities. If four ages have already

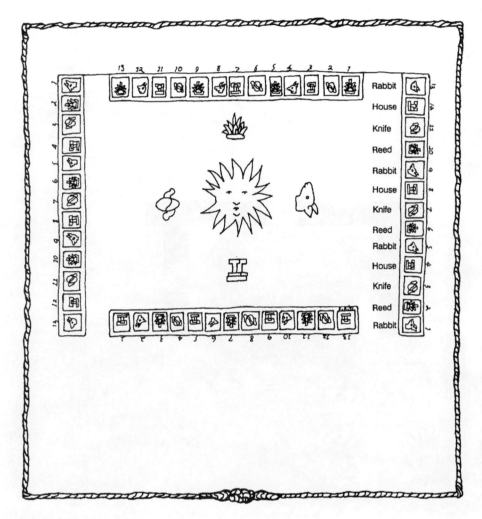

Figure 45. The Mexica fifty-two-year round (drawing by Kay A. Read from the Codex Aubin)

occurred, then simply take two past ages and bind them together; join the two in order to create room for a future, fifth age that now needs to be made present.

This is what Mesoamerican calendrics were and are all about: the chance to manipulate life's events by coordinating them with the motions of celestial events governing time. Calendars provide the tools by which the many cosmic powers could and can be controlled in order to improve the quality of one's existence. Calendars are not and never were rigid mathematical systems, unyielding to any outside shaping. Not only are they guides for one's journey through life, but one can even use them to mold the very landscape over which one travels.

So while some Mesoamericans tell a story of time that begins at the beginning and builds moment by moment to the present, others tell a story of time

Figure 46. Binding-of-the-Years or the New Fire Ceremony (Codex Borbonicus, fol. 34, Museo de América/Art Resource)

that presents a more complex picture. In the indigenous timeline, the present can pick up moments from the past and make them real again; time also can join past and present moments with the future, binding all three together. Thus is life controlled and transformed at the very same time as it moves forward, carrying one from birth to death. The past predicts and even molds what is to come; and present events happen because of what happened in the past.

NOTES

1. I base my retelling of this story on the Popol Vuh translated and annotated by Dennis Tedlock (1985, 71–72).

2. *Quiché* is an alternate spelling of *K'iche'*. Depending on the circumstances, this word might refer to the people, their language, their homeland, or all three.

3. Hunahpu Possum and Hunahpu Coyote are names for the Hero Twins who, in the form of vagabond dancers and magicians, later defeat the lords of the underworld (*Popol Vuh* 1985, 342).

4. The Maya creator gods are many.

5. The original text, which was translated by Dennis Tedlock with the help of K'iche' day-keeper Andrés Xiloj, was first recorded in the mid-sixteenth century *(Popol Vuh* 1985, 28). Xiloj knew this same tale very well and told it almost the same as it had been told 400 years before.

6. The storyteller is describing the measuring-out of the horizontal and vertical dimensions of the cosmos's four quarters as one might measure out a house under construction.

7. Modern daykeepers like Andrés Xiloj cast lots using corn kernels and pieces of coral, rather like some people use dice or cards to judge fate. This is done by coordinating the count of kernels as they fall with the count of days in a calendar called the divinatory cycle. Ideally, the best divinations are believed to be those performed by a male and female pair working together (*Popol Vuh* 1985, 370).

8. Because of Possum, the dawn now is streaked with red and blue.

9. According to Tedlock, this means that the lords of the underworld will be denied human sacrifices (*Popol Vuh* 1985, 293).

10. Tollan—or in an alternate spelling, Tula—is the home of the ancient ancestors in many Mesoamerican mythic traditions. Mexica myths indicate that the Toltecs, or people of Tollan, may have lived at an actual city called Tula. More likely, however, the Toltecs were mythical, and more intangible than tangible.

11. *Tonatiuh* is a Nahuatl word meaning "sun." This was the name the Nahua of the Mexican Highlands gave Pedro de Alvarado, one of Hernan Cortés's main men (*Popol Vuh* 1985, 366).

12. For a full English translation (by John Bierhorst) of the "Legend of the Suns," see *Codex Chimalpopoca* (1992b).

13. Most of the Nahua stories included here appear in Read (1998, 48–84), in either the same form or an expanded form. We have taken the liberty of eliminating some of the more technical information and have included phonetic spellings for foreign words. Some stories are translated in full, and others are retellings. All translations from the original Nahuatl were done by Kay A. Read and Jane Rosenthal.

14. Summary based on Read (1998, 67). Original translation by Kay A. Read and Jane Rosenthal (*Codex Chimalpopoca* 1992a, 87).

15. Many other versions of this tale of five ages exist, some of which are a bit more detailed than this one. See Moreno de los Arcos (1967) for a discussion of these versions.

16. From Read (1998, 70), retold from the Nahuatl in the *Codex Chimalpopoca* (1992a, 88).

17. This is one of the many names of the god Tezcatlipoca, a major deity who was sometimes paired with Quetzalcoatl and sometimes identified as the Mexica god Huitzilopochtli.

18. The cypress tree, or *ahuehuetl*, can grow to an enormous height and live hundreds of years. In Mesoamerican myth, the tree is a symbol of rulership.

19. Read (1998, 71–72), retold from the Nahuatl in *Codex Chimalpopoca* (1992a, 88–89).

20. Like those of the Maya, the Nahua creator gods are many.

21. *Nahualli* can mean a lot of things. Often it means "magician" (or shaman or medicine person), or the transfiguration of that magician into some other form. In this passage, *nahualli* also means an extra spirit that can act independently of the magician himself.

22. He's saying "que será, será," or "whatever will be, will be."

23. This bit of added information indicates that the narrator was from out of town.

24. Merit is the sum total of one's powers received through birth, various rituals, circumstances determined by the gods, and as the result of one's own actions (Read 1998, 114–116, 254 n97).

25. Read (1998, 73), retold from the Nahuatl in the *Codex Chimalpopoca* (1992a, 89–90).

26. Like the K'iche' Maya, the Nahua told stories about a mythic mountain filled with good things to eat.

27. Oxomoco and Cipactonal, like Xpiyacoc and Xmucane in the *Popol Vuh*, are daykeepers who use corn kernels to throw lots.

28. In modern versions of this Nahua myth told by the Nahua of Yaonahuac and Huitzilan, Nanahuatl is lightning, and he strikes the mountain with his head, cracking it open (Taggert 1983, 88–92).

29. "To cast fortunes" also means "to open something," which implies that the future can be opened.

30. There were four sets of Tlaloques, one for each cardinal direction.

31. Read (1998, 49–58). Translation by Kay A. Read and Jane Rosenthal from the *Florentine Codex* 1953–1982, bk. 7, pt. 8, chap. 2:3–9, app. 42–58.

32. They are asking who will govern this age ("to carry" also means "to govern"). Many metaphors describe the ruler as governing the city by carrying it on his back as one might carry a child.

33. The burden to be borne will be time itself, and the sun and the moon will be the bearers because they are the ones governing these periods.

34. This fire pit is a cooking fire in which three stones were used, as they still are today in many parts of Mesoamerica, to support cooking vessels.

35. Balls, usually woven of grass, were used to catch blood flowing out during bloodletting ceremonies.

36. A headdress bore on it the image, or name, of a particular god. As with all names, this image was imbued with that god's power. Hence the name belonged to the god and not to Nanahuatzin.

37. "Praising" also means the ritual summoning of gods and various powers.

38. This passage probably means that because Nanahuatzin has a good heart, he has the power to do the deed he needs to do; his merit is of a good variety.

39. In Nahuatl, this first phrase describes the lighting of a house (the cosmos was thought of as house in which people lived). The second describes dawn's first rosy rays as doves the color of burning embers, perhaps the embers of the fire from which the new sun has just emerged.

40. These are the cardinal directions, described in a counterclockwise order, beginning with the north (the Place of the Dead) and moving to the west (the Place of Women) and then to the south (the Place of Thorns).

41. This, as one might expect, is the east.

42. The dawn is metaphorically a red sacrifice, and *dye* also refers to blood.

43. "Spreading in an undulating way" is a rich metaphor for the growing light of dawn. The sun's rosy hues are twisting and bending like red dye or sacrificial blood spreading out in a body of water. Since the walls of the cosmos were made of water, this seems particularly fitting.

44. If one looks carefully, one can see a rabbit on the moon rather than a face. Viewed from the United States the rabbit is crawling up the left side, but seen from Mesoamerica he runs along the bottom just as he should.

45. In other words, they spread on the earth's eastern horizon or edge.

46. Gods and people are not supposed to be living together on the same level, as that would literally mess things up.

47. The *axolotl*, or salamander, is not really a fully developed salamander but is still in the larval stage. This particular variety is known as the mole salamander (*ambystoma talpoideum*) in the United States. But in Mexico, it never loses its gills, and remains fully aquatic. The creature looks like a full-grown salamander, apart from the huge, feathery gills on each side of its head.

48. The sun's daily path (ending in the west) is established and he will now continue to set there. From now on, he will enter the earth each night and travel through the underground before emerging again in the east.

49. Read (1998, 75), retold from the Nahuatl in the Florentine Codex (bk. 3, pt. 4, chap. 1:1–5).

50. Huitzilopochtli, like his close counterpart Tezcatlipoca, often is depicted with one small or oddly shaped foot.

51. This imagery depicts a powerful mountain storm, with Huitzilopochtli wielding a comet or lightning-like weapon and throwing up huge storm clouds to defeat his enemies.

52. Read (1998, 76–77), retold from Durán (1994, 24–25, 31–33).

53. Dreaming is probably analogous to the longstanding tradition of vision questing among North American native peoples, in which youths who are coming of age seek visions by "dreaming." These visions might be thought of as extrasensory visual experiences by Westerners. They are acquired through a wide variety of ritual practices. In ancient Mesoamerica, sometimes visions were induced by fasting, bloodletting, dancing, or the use of hallucinogenic drugs.

54. Chapultepec was situated on a rocky outcropping on the shore of Lake Texcoco, just to the west of Tenochtitlan—the site of today's Chapultepec park and zoo, in Mexico

City. In pre-Conquest times, the site included a magnificent garden. Then springs flowed from the rocks, and Mexica rulers visited there.

55. This summary is based on Durán (1994, 34–57).

56. The text says that the eagle grasped a bird, but the picture in Durán shows a snake in the great bird's grip (ibid., plate 6). One must remember that Durán was a Spaniard retelling Nahua stories and didn't always get things right (although he didn't always get them wrong, either). The current Mexican flag depicts the image in Durán's picture. This picture from the *Codex Mendoza* shows nothing in the eagle's grasp.

57. Read (1998, 78–82), retold from Durán (1994, 212–222).

58. This is a beautiful plant with yellow flowers and a lovely aroma that was used to perfume cocoa when it was made into a drink.

59. Read (1998, 83–84). Translation by Kay A. Read and Jane Rosenthal from the Nahuatl in the "Anales de Cuauhtitlan," one of two other texts contained along with "The Legend of the Suns" in the *Codex Chimalpopoca* (1992a, 5).

60. See Read (1997a, 821–824; 1998, 211–235) for more information on Mesoamerican time and calendrics.

61. The Nahua word for this is *mahceua*. Read (1998, 114–116, 151, 185, 203, 246 n19, 264 n1).

DEITIES, THEMES, AND CONCEPTS

ACAMAPICHTLI, LORD

Time period: Postclassic

Cultural group: Nahua-Mexica

Lord Acamapichtli (A-ka-ma-peecht´-lee) was the first Chief Speaker of the Mexica or Aztecs (Nahua; ruled ca. 1369–1403), and mythically represents the origins of Mexica greatness. He and his reign symbolize the official beginning of the Mexica as an independent political entity, for without its own royal lineage, a city could not aspire to any real power. Acamapichtli's father was a Colhua nobleman, his mother the daughter of a Mexica ruler, and he married a Colhua noblewoman. Through this Colhua heritage, he linked the Mexica royal line with that of the fabled Toltecs and their patron deity Quetzalcoatl, whose ancestry gave them a civilizing legitimacy. And he acted as the "likeness" of the Mexica patron deity Huitzilopochtli, who was closely associated with the great god Tezcatlipoca. This first ruler therefore embodied two of the most powerful deities in the Nahua cosmos, Quetzalcoatl and Tezcatlipoca, and thus served as a harbinger of the Mexica's later power.

For years the Mexica remained too weak to throw off the control of neighboring city Azcapotzalco, whose territory they occupied. It is told how, during Acamapichtli's reign, the Azcapotzalco ruler Tezozomoc demanded the Mexica pay a seemingly impossible tribute for this privilege: a floating raft sown with maize, chiles, beans, squash, and amaranth. They succeeded in this task with the magical help of Huitzilopochtli. Then Tezozomoc raised his demands, this time requiring that duck and heron chicks hatch from their eggs the moment another garden-raft floated into Azcapotzalco. Again Huitzilopochtli helped, this time predicting the future demise of Azcapotzalco. Impressed with their ability to accomplish the impossible, Tezozomoc declared that the Mexica were the chosen people of their god and some day would rule over all other nations, a prophecy that came largely true.

See also Huitzilopochtli; Quetzalcoatl; Tezcatlipoca

Suggested reading:

Codex Mendoza. 1997. As reproduced in the *Essential Codex Mendoza.*
    Commentary and edited by Frances Berdan and Patricia Rieff Anawalt.
    Berkeley: University of California Press.
Durán, Fray Diego. 1994. *The History of the Indies of New Spain.* Trans. Doris
    Heyden. Norman: University of Oklahoma Press.
Townsend, Richard Frazer. 1992. *The Aztecs.* London: Thames and Hudson.

AHUITZOTL, LORD

Time period: Postclassic

Cultural group: Nahua-Mexica

As the eighth Chief Speaker of the Mexica or Aztecs (Nahua, ruled ca. 1486–1502), Lord Ahuitzotl (A-weet´-zot) expanded the Mexica or Aztec domain tremendously and consolidated their power at a time of potential weakness. He was the third son of Lord Motecuhzoma I (Ilhuicamina), the fifth Chief Speaker (ruled ca. 1441–1469), and he sired the last true Chief Speaker, Cuauhtemoc (ruled ca.1520–1524), whom the Spanish captured and executed. Ahuitzotl, with his energy of youth and great capabilities, symbolizes the return of Mexica power. At the same time, he represents the limitations of all people, including rulers.

When Chief Speaker Tizoc died from poisoning after a short and rather ineffectual rule (ca. 1481–1486), political wolves in the form of Tenochtitlan's neighbors were barking at Mexica doorways. The Mexica desperately needed a strong ruler; Ahuitzotl, a high-ranking military leader, proved to be their man.

Stories surrounding Ahuitzotl often stress his youth, skills, energy, strength, and audacity. Fray Diego Durán tells a magical tale of his election, in which he is not an experienced military leader, but a mere youth, one who requires training from the Tlacaellel, a leader often ruling in partnership with the Chief Speaker. Ahuitzotl is so young that, upon election, the electors fetch him from school. Yet, he comports himself with the maturity of an elder, and although inexperienced, returns victorious from his first war. The Mexica became so strong they could secretly invite their enemies to the celebration of the rebuilding of their main temple, and shower them with extravagant gifts. Durán also claims that Ahuitzotl sacrificed 80,400 war captives at this celebration, in spite of the impossibility of both doing this in the manner Durán describes, and that disposing of that many bodies would have caused serious environmental damage. These myths' exaggerations stress Ahuitzotl's strength, ability, and wealth, as well as Mexica power and ruthlessness, and the invincibility of their patron god Huitzilopochtli.

Yet Ahuitzotl's own invincibility went only so far. In another story, against the advice of his counselors, he murders the magician-ruler of Coyoacan because

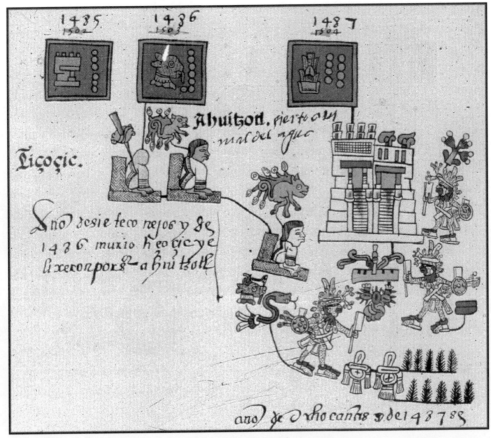

Figure 47. Ahuitzotl's sacrifice at the Templo Mayor (Codex Telleriano Remonsis, *fol. 39, Bibliotheque Nationale/Art Resource*)

he wants the control of his spring. Ahuitzotl builds an aqueduct and brings the water to Tenochtitlan, only to flood the city forty days later. His counselors bade him to stop the flow and make offerings to the water goddess Chalchiuhtlicue, who was clearly offended by the ruler's death. Ahuitzotl also died unnaturally young from a strange disease perhaps brought on by poison, an event reminiscent of his predecessor's death. The moral is that both the incompetent and arrogant will fall, and even the strong can die.

> **See also** Chalchiuhtlicue; Cuauhtemoc, Lord; Motecuhzoma I, Lord; Tizoc, Lord; Tlacaellel
>
> **Suggested reading:**
>
> *Codex Mendoza.* 1997. As reproduced in the *Essential Codex Mendoza.* Commentary and edited by Frances Berdan and Patricia Rieff Anawalt. Berkeley: University of California Press.
>
> Durán, Fray Diego. 1994. *The History of the Indies of New Spain.* Trans. Doris Heyden. Norman: University of Oklahoma Press.
>
> Townsend, Richard Frazer. 1992. *The Aztecs.* London: Thames and Hudson.

AJITZ C'OXOL

Time period: Contemporary

Cultural group: Tzutuhil Maya

Ajitz C'oxol (A-heets' K-h-o-shol') also goes by the names K'ek Co'xol and Huitzil. A myth from the town of Tzutuhil San Jose la Laguna describes him as a red witch of the K'iche' King Tecun Uman. He had a red face like a devil and lived in a nearby hill called Paquixquil. San Jose used to be a wealthy place where one had only to lift up a stone to find gold, and everyone was contented. However, when Ajitz arrived he berated the Tzutuhiles, calling them dead fish and crab eaters and poor excuses for men. After many years of this abuse, the Tzutuhiles got tired of it. One day, all the witches and *nahuales* gathered and changed into animals that flew or had four legs. The flying animals caught Ajitz and dropped him over a large stone, where the four-legged ones tore into him; but Ajitz was very strong, and they could not kill him. After the animals had repeated this punishment a number of times, Ajitz repented; he finally left them, cursing the people of San Jose to eternal poverty and taking their wealth with him to the town of Santa Clara.

> **See also** Nahual
>
> **Suggested reading:**
>
> Sexton, James D. 1992. *Mayan Folktales: Folklore from Lake Atitlan, Guatemala.* New York: Anchor Books, Doubleday.

BACABS

Time period: Postclassic–Contemporary

Cultural group: Yucatec Maya

These four Maya deities hold up the heavens; in fact, a creator god placed these skybearers at the four corners of the universe for this very purpose. Because each stands at one of the four cardinal directions, each claims a specific color and particular years of influence in the Maya calendar that are symbolically linked to that direction. The eastern Bacab (Ba-kab') claims the color red, Kan years, and the name Hobnil; the northern Bacab, the color white, Muluc years, and the name Can Tzicnal; the western Bacab, the color black, Ix years, and the name Zac Cimi; the southern Bacab, the color yellow, Cauac years, and the name Hozanek. In Yucatec Maya cosmology the Bacabs also control the rain and wind and often serve as patrons of beekeeping and divination.

According to the sixteenth-century historian Diego de Landa and the Chilam Balam de Chumayel (a mythic history from the town of Chumayel), the Yucatec creator deity Hunab Ku created the Bacabs when the gods made the universe in the third and previous age. A great deluge destroyed that age. These four brothers escaped, received new names, and once again took up their places at the four quarters of the cosmos when the gods created the fourth and present age. Landa tells us that each Bacab received "one of the four dominical letters [the four days on which a new year could start]. They also indicated the miseries or happy events which they said must occur the year of each one of them" (Landa 1941, 144–145). According to the Chilam Balam de Tizimin (a mythic history from the town of Tizimin): "The Bacabs planted five trees. They stretched out the earth, planted a red Imix in the east, a white Imix in the north, a black Imix in the west, a yellow Imix in the south, and a green Imix in the center of the country" (Makemson 1951, 23).

These four brothers appear relatively late in Maya history. Scholars have identified Postclassic sculpture at the site of Chichén Itzá as the Bacabs. There they appear with their

Figure 48. Two Bacabs with their hands in the air holding up the universe (Thompson, J. E. S., Peabody Museum of American Archaeology and Ethnology)

hands outstretched above them. Bacabs also appear in two Postclassic documents, the Madrid and Dresden Codices, which contain divination almanacs. We also know stories of the Bacabs from historical documents such as Landa's *Relaciónes*, the Chilam Balam de Chumayel, and Tizimin. In the modern era, people living at Chan Kom in the state of Yucatán, near the ancient Maya ruins of Chichén Itzá, continue to make ritual offerings to the Bacabs, hoping for more rain and better crops.

Much of our understanding of the Bacabs comes from stories found in Landa's descriptions and the various Chilam Balams. Throughout the colonial period and into the modern era, the stories and myths of the Bacabs have metamorphosed. At some point in history they became joined with the figure of Chac, a Maya rain god with an extraordinarily long mythic history. The Yucatec

Maya of Chan Kom believe in four Chacs, each associated with one of the four corners of the universe, and each having a cardinal direction and color. Besides their task of bearing up the sky, these Chacs/Bacabs of Chan Kom bring rain. However, their duties as patrons of beekeeping have changed. For at Chan Kom, different deities, the Balams, maintain bees; they also stand at the four quarters, along with the Chacs/Bacabs. Like many other deities, the Bacabs are important in divination ceremonies for both ancient Maya and modern Maya. One might approach the Bacabs with questions about future rain or wind, or maybe the health of one's beehive. In response the skybearers might foretell what is to come or might help with one's needs.

> **See also** Chac and the Chacs; Earth, Agricultural, and Hunting Deities; Hunab Ku; Rain and Water Deities; Tlaloc and the Tlaloques
>
> **Suggested reading:**
>
> Landa, Diego de. 1978. *Yucatan before and after the Conquest.* Trans. William Gates. New York: Dover.
>
> Roys, Ralph L. 1965. *Ritual of the Bacabs: A Book of Maya Encantations.* Norman: University of Oklahoma Press.
>
> Thompson, John Eric Sydney. 1970b. *Maya History and Religion.* Norman: University of Oklahoma Press.

BATS

Time period: Classic–Contemporary

Cultural group: Mesoamerica

Bats mark the Underworld, death, rottenness, and destruction in Mesoamerican mythology, perhaps because these creatures travel the sky by night and hide in caves by day. In many although not all myths, bats also are associated with male sexuality; and as blood-sucking beasts, they sometimes serve as mythic agents of sacrifice. Not all bats suck blood, of course: 118 of the 120 species inhabiting Mesoamerica suck only the nectar of flowers or eat fruit and insects, and only two tropical species of vampire bats (Desmodontinae) suck blood.

Classic Maya ceramists often pictured bats as pop-eyed males, associated with human skulls and bones. In the Postclassic era, Central Mexicans sometimes depicted bats sporting snouts that resembled sacrificial knives and carrying severed human heads. In some representations, the starry eyes of the night sky decorated their wings; and occasionally they appeared alongside other dangerous nocturnal beasts, such as scorpions and owls. Among the Postclassic Zapotec, depictions of bats appeared frequently with funerary goods and bore some characteristics of the Jaguar, another figure of night and the Underworld. An impressive, life-size ceramic bat-man has been unearthed from the Templo Mayor in the center of the Mexica capital of Tenochtitlan. This god of death has a human body, but his clawed feet and hands are those of a bat. His bulging, humanoid eyes peer menacingly from a bat-like head, reminding one of the Zapotec images. Huge fangs protrude from his gaping mouth, and his mouse-ears are incongruously large. This is not a beast one would want to meet in the dead of night. In contrast, contemporary representations of bats bear a much less threatening character, although some still associate bats with death and the Underworld.

The Hero Twins of the K'iche' Maya Popol Vuh came up against the cunning and destructiveness of bats in their contest with the gods of the Underworld. In their last house of trials, the House of Bats, the boys hid in their blow-guns to prevent themselves from being decapitated by the monstrous snatch-bats with snouts like knives. All night the creatures flew around them, screeching as they rushed through the night air. Then the wily beasts stood very still for awhile, tricking the boys into thinking that dawn finally had come. Hunahpu peeked out from his blow-gun to see if light was coming. Instantly a bat swooped down and plucked off his head almost as though it were a piece of fruit hanging from a tree. Hunahpu's head rolled off to the ball court, to serve as the ball for the gods' next game. Xbalanque, with the help of Opossum and the other animals, fashioned a makeshift head for Hunahpu from a pumpkin. Only then could the boys continue their task of unseating the Lords of Death.

An ancient Nahua story says that the first bat was born when Quetzalcoatl's semen dripped onto a rock while he was washing. The gods sent the bat to bite out the vulva of the young goddess Xochiquetzal, from which they grew nasty-smelling flowers to present to Mictlantecuhtli, lord of the Underworld Land of Death. In some stories, Xochiquetzal appeared as the Sun's wife, so this odd little tale may refer to celestial and terrestrial journeys. Quetzalcoatl, as the morning star that heralds the rising sun, inadvertently had spawned an Underworld servant, who through a sacrificial act forced upon the Sun's wife, created the fruits of the rotting, foul-smelling Land of Death. Like the Hero Twins, the Sun would travel through that same nasty underworld every evening, abandoning the pleasant upper world to the creatures of the night.

Death continues as a theme in contemporary myths about bats. In the 1930s, the Cakchiquel Maya said that the bat was the Devil's cook. Every night she went out from the Hill, or the Devil's Underworld home, to collect blood from animals, which she then brought back to make into delicious dishes for her boss. Dead sinners spent time laboring for the Devil to pay off their debts before going to heaven, so perhaps the bat too was a sinner.

A contemporary story from Oaxaca is more benign. Oaxacans say that one day the bat complained to God that he was cold, although in truth he was jealous of all the birds' fine plumage. God reluctantly asked each bird to donate one feather to keep the bat warm. Because of all these feathers from so many different birds, the bat became the most beautiful flying creature around; he spread color through the sky both day and night, and he could even create a rainbow. As a result, he became insufferably proud. Fed up with the bat's arrogance, the birds flew up to heaven to have a little talk with God, who then summoned the bat so that he might see all of the wonderful things he was doing on earth. As the bat performed his marvelous feats, his feathers fell out one by one, leaving him exactly as he was before. And to this day, the bat remains so ashamed of his ugly body that he comes out only at night, when he flies rapidly back and forth, looking for his lost feathers.

> **See also** Hero Twins; Opossums; Quetzalcoatl; Sun; Underworld and Caves, Deities of the
>
> **Suggested reading:**
>
> Henestrosa, Andres. 1994. "The Bat." Pp. 33–37 in *Myth and Magic: Oaxaca Past and Present.* Palo Alto: Palo Alto Cultural Center.
>
> Tedlock, Dennis, trans. 1985. *Popul Vuh: The Definitive Edition of the Mayan Book of the Dawn of Life and the Glories of Gods and Kings.* New York: Simon and Schuster.

BLOOD WOMAN

Time period: Postclassic–Contemporary

Cultural group: K'iche' Maya

Blood Woman (Xquic, or Little Blood) appears in the Popol Vuh legends as an underworld maiden, the daughter of Blood Gatherer, one of the death lords. Having been impregnated with the Hero Twins Hunahpu and Xbalanque, Blood Woman secretly migrated to Earth's surface so that her sons could carry out their destiny: the destruction of her own male relatives, the lords of death, and the creation of the world as we know it.

Blood Woman's pregnancy was miraculous, as she remained a virgin even after conception: According to myth, she was impregnated by the calabash head of Hun Hunahpu. After the Twin's father and uncle were sacrificed, the Xibalba lords placed Hun Hunahpu's head in a barren tree as a victory trophy. Immediately, this tree burst into new leaf, blossomed, and became laden with calabash gourds, one of which was Hun Hunahpu's head. One day Blood Woman heard of this magical tree, and even though her father warned her away from it, she had to see it for herself. Just as she was about to pick the tree's fruit, Hun Hunahpu's calabash head talked to her, telling her that she did not really want to take it. He then spit into her hand as a sign of what was to come. His spittle caused Blood Woman to become pregnant.

Her pregnancy angered her father and the Xibalba lords, who did not believe that she could have conceived without knowing a man. They demanded that Blood Gatherer discover who the father was; if Blood Woman refused to divulge his identity, then her father was to sacrifice her. Although she was visibly pregnant, Blood Woman insisted that she had not lain with any man. Her father then ordered the Death Lord's messenger owls to kill her and to bring her heart back to him in a bowl. But Blood Woman convinced the owls instead to bring back the sap of the croton tree, which was shaped like a heart and bled red liquid as a real heart would. Seeing the fake heart, the Xibalba lords believed her dead, and she was able to escape to the world above.

> **See also** Hero Twins; 1-Death and 7-Death; Sky Deities and Beings; Underworld and Caves, Deities of the
>
> **Suggested reading:**
>
> Tedlock, Dennis, trans. 1985. *Popol Vuh: The Definitive Edition of the Mayan Book of the Dawn of Life and the Glories of Gods and Kings.* New York: Simon and Schuster.

CALENDAR DEITIES

Time period: Prehistoric–Contemporary

Cultural group: Mesoamerica

Each day, week, month, and year—each calendrical count—holds particular powers and so is considered a deity with special capacities and characteristics, both negative and positive. Dates can serve as patrons for people born on their day, month, and year, as well as hold prophetic powers over human and cosmic events. What may be the earliest recorded date, 679 B.C., came from Cuicuilco in the Valley of Mexico. Of course we do not know for sure if this date was also a deity at that time, but we know that calendrical dates operated as such by the time of the Conquest. Then documents such as Landa's *Relaciones de las Cosas* and Sahagún's *Florentine Codex* describe the nature of many of the calendar deities. Today, similar ideas about the calendar deities continue among indigenous groups in many parts of Mesoamerica, although each may have its own distinctive calendar and names for their deities.

Calendar deities have a great deal to do with dreaming and prophecy. Because of them past, present, and future moments can relate to each other, and sometimes even collapse into each other. Hence once an event is placed into the calendar, earlier events are seen to have prefigured it, while the event itself becomes a prophecy of future happenings. Ancient Nahuatl speakers began and ended migrations, and founded cities on the year 1-Knife, for that year marked foundational moments for Mexica history. In 1695, the Itzá Maya sent word to the Spanish that they were ready for conversion to Christianity because, according to the count of their calendar deities, this was the same year the Spanish had conquered them; first the physical conquest, then the spiritual conquest, each governed by the same calendrical powers. On a more personal level, traders consulted the calendar deities with the help of diviners to know when to travel, and warriors to know when to go to battle. Families even named babies on days propitious to the future development of their character.

The ancient Mexica, for example, said the day 1-Death held largely good powers. The great war god Tezcatlipoca received honor then, and people sacrificed quail and made other offerings to him on their home altars and the altars of the city's district temples. But, if people failed to show Tezcatlipoca honor, then he could turn on them, withdrawing his favors. A child born on this day would prosper, and those wishing him dead would die instead. If that child failed to perform the requisite rituals for Tezcatlipoca, however, the child would harm the god's day sign, receiving harm in return. Slaves also claimed 1-Death as their sign, and received very fine treatment on this day. If one did not properly honor the slaves on this day, then one would be covered with pustules and sores, struck and beaten like a slave, and chased from place to place, never to settle down.

The contemporary K'iche' Maya use certain phrases like "at dawn," "opening," "to blame," "conceal," "lie," or "trick" to help them remember the qualities of the day-lord Foredawn. On Foredawn, one performs rituals such as the opening rites for new priest-shaman students. Young men and their families also mark the beginning of planning for his marriage with rituals, and begin negotiations with the young girl's family on Foredawn. A child born on Foredawn will be wealthy and verbally skillful but also possibly a liar, cheat, or complainer. The babe will be blessed with an extra body-soul called lightening, which will enable him/her to talk directly with animals, plants, and other powerful beings. Because of such attributes of his/her nahual, or character, the child may grow up to be a priest-shaman, community elder, or perhaps a marriage spokesman.

Dennis Tedlock, a contemporary anthropologist from the United States, reports that once he had trained as a K'iche' daykeeper skilled in interpreting the calendar, he could not help but use it to seek the meaning of his daily events, even when living in the United States. He now spontaneously feels the "sheet lightning" a daykeeper feels, slight twinges like small electric shocks that produce invisible spasms and stir his blood. Combined with his dreams and the portents of particular calendar deities, these twinges relay important information to him about future events. Thus by studying with Maya teachers, he learned to live by both a Western calendar and the invisible powers behind it that the many Maya calendrical deities govern.

See also Fifth Sun; Nahual; Tezcatlipoca
Suggested reading:
Edmonson, Munro S. 1988. *The Book of the Year: Middle American Calendrical Systems.* Salt Lake City: University of Utah Press.
Sahagún, Fray Bernardino de. 1953–1982. *The Florentine Codex: A General*

History of the Things of New Spain. Books IV, V. Trans. Arthur J. O. Anderson, and Charles E. Dibble. 12 books, 13 parts. Monographs of the School of American Research no. 14. Santa Fe: School of American Research; Salt Lake City: University of Utah Press.

Tedlock, Barbara. 1982. *Time and the Highland Maya.* Albuquerque: University of New Mexico Press.

Tedlock, Dennis. 1990. *Days from a Dream Almanac.* Urbana: University of Illinois Press.

CANEK

Time period: Classic–Modern

Cultural group: Maya

Canek (Kan-ek´) served as the name for both an ancient form of pre-Conquest Itzá Maya rulership and a post-Conquest culture hero who was to save the Itzá from their conquerors. In ancient times, the name stood more for an ancestral lineage and office of rulership than any one particular person; in Colonial times, however, a mythic royal figure called Canek repeatedly and miraculously reappeared to lead the Itzá in revolt against their oppressors. These salvific reappearances were based on predictions made in the Chilam Balams (native mythic histories), which described an ancient, deceased Maya ruler called Canek as returning to life in order to drive foreigners out of Maya Lands. Thus, through time, this culture hero transformed from a form of governance, to a messianic rallying cry of numerous Maya colonial uprisings; moreover, the mythic Canek remains a symbol of hope for many today.

Shortly after the conquest of the Mexican Highlands, Hernán Cortés traveled with his conquistadors through the Itzá lands on his way to what now is Honduras. Although the Itzá, at an earlier time, had lived in northern Yucatán in the area of Chichén Itzá, by the time of Cortés's travels, they had migrated to the central Petén in the southern lowlands of Guatemala. Spanish reports from that trip and the reports of others who followed indicate that the Itzá called their rulers Canek (or Can Ek). Apparently, conquest of the Itzá did not come easy, for every twenty years or so, a person called Canek would meet with Spanish officials or priests either to express Itzá defiance of the Spanish or discuss an alliance with them. In fact, the Spanish did not fully conquer them until 1695, making the Itzá the last of all Maya groups to give up their independence. Only after their conquest did the figure of Canek take on messianic import, when he became a reborn ancient Maya ruler.

The pre-Conquest name Canek served both as a title and lineage marker. Given common indigenous perspectives on death and ancestry, a living pre-Hispanic Canek may have inherited portions of the previous, deceased Canek's powers, which he carried in his own physical body. If this were so, he would have received his ancestors' powers, just as he inherited his nose or mouth from them. In some sense, then, the old Caneks might have been reborn at least partially in the body of the current Canek. They both looked similar and could accomplish similar things, so they were similar (even almost the same) beings. This idea may have helped form the messianic image that Canek acquired after the conquest of the Itzá, for such an idea probably meshed nicely with Christian concepts of rebirth.

With conquest came oppression and a longing for lost freedoms. The Itzá's long political resistance to the Spanish now transformed into a new mythic resistance that continued to fuel further political resistance up to the twentieth century. Moreover, Canek-inspired rebellions were not confined to the Itzá alone. More than one Maya prophet or would-be rebel leader adopted the name Canek to evoke popular support. In these prophetic leaders, a deceased ancient ruler called Canek was said to have been reborn in a manner reminiscent of both the pre-Conquest ideas of ancestry and Christ's own rebirth.

In 1761, rebels subscribing to the prophecy set down in the Chilam Balams anticipated the imminent return of the Itzá king of the royal lineage of Canek to rescue them from their Spanish oppressors. Their Maya leader assumed the name of the prophet Jacinto Canek, and in an attempt to make the prophecy come true, he and his followers tried to drive the whites into the sea. However, the Spanish squelched Canek's uprising and he was publicly drawn, quartered, and burned in the plaza of Mérida. From that time forward, "Jacinto Canek" became the rallying cry of Yucatec Maya rebellions and separatist movements. The latter flowered most notably in the Caste Wars, which began in 1848 and lasted until the twentieth century.

The Caste Wars were a series of semisuccessful rebellions by the Yucatec Maya against the Mexican government. Although rebels forced the government to allow them autonomy in their villages and personal lives, they were unsuccessful in gaining true independence, and the rebellion eventually was crushed by the Mexican military. By the beginning of the twentieth century, the government had forced the various Maya villages in the state of Quintana Roo, where the Caste Wars were centered, back into the national political system.

In more recent years, modern Mexican authors have created new myths about this hero figure. For example, Ermilo Abreu Gómez, in a small collection of short stories titled *Canek: History and Legend of a Maya Hero*, tells about the friendship of a Creole boy and a Maya boy named Jacinto Canek, growing up together on a henequen plantation just before the Caste Wars. Because of this book and other stories, *Canek* continues to be a powerful name among the Maya, symbolizing unity, resistance, and cultural independence.

See also Ahuitzotl, Lord; Christ; Motecuhzoma I, Lord; Motecuhzoma II, Lord; Pacal

Suggested reading:

Abreu Gómez, Ermilo. 1979. *Canek: History and Legend of a Maya Hero.* Trans. Mario L. Davila and Carter Wilson. Berkeley: University of California Press (English ed. of *Canek* [Mexico City: Ediciones Canek, 1940]).

Carmack, Robert M., Janine Gasco, and Gary H. Gossen. 1996. *The Legacy of Mesoamerica: History and Culture of a Native American Civilization.* Upper Saddle River, NJ: Prentice-Hall.

Jones, Grant Drummond. 1989. *Maya Resistance to Spanish Rule: Time and History on a Colonial Frontier.* Albuquerque: University of New Mexico Press.

CHAC AND THE CHACS

Time period: Preclassic–Contemporary

Cultural group: Lowland Maya

This Maya deity of rain and lightning served as a patron or protector of warriors, sacrificers, and fisherman; and because of his close association with water, he was also the patron deity of agriculture. He possessed a long, pendulous nose ending in a curl; a scroll design under each eye; and a mouth sometimes depicted as lacking teeth. Chac (Chak) appears both singly and as a set of four gods, one for each cardinal direction. Each of the four aspects bore a different name and color: Chac Xib Chac was the red Chac of the East; Sac Xib Chac, the white Chac of the North; Ek Xib Chac, the black Chac of the West; and Kan Xib Chac, the yellow Chac of the South. Because both the Bacabs and the Chacs were associated with the four colors and the four cardinal directions, one might assume that their present close connection always existed. However, in ancient times, it did not; Bacabs served as skybearers, whereas Chacs served as gods of lightning. Only in more recent times have the Bacabs and Chacs merged into more general rain deities under the name *Chacs* or *Chaacs*.

In Postclassic codices or ritual almanacs, Chac is found wielding serpents, axes, and conch shells to create rain, lightning, and thunder. These books often identified him as the patron of fishing, where he used lightning to kill and catch fish. Chac taught agriculture and breadmaking to humans, and ruled over the farm fields and crops. Perhaps Chac figured so prominently in these divinatory almanacs because farmers needed to predict the appropriate times for their ritual and agricultural activities.

The Chacs' importance centers primarily around concepts of rain and water. They make the water fall from the sky, beginning in the east as they move through the heavens, and tip their conch shells filled with rainwater. According to early myths, one could see Chac also on earth: in streams, waterfalls, or cenotes. Many stories describe Chac as central to Maya farming activities. The colonial Maya credited him with breaking open a rock and retrieving the first maize plant. Another story, from the Chol Maya, tells how Chac once stood above the water after it had rained. He asked his servant to fetch a cloth from his wife. However, when the servant looked around, he saw only toads—Chac's wife's children—and not Chac's wife. After much searching, he finally found Chac's wife, and she gave him some cotton. However, the cotton was really a cloud, which rose above the earth, taking the rain back up to heaven, where it might again fall to water the earth.

Maya perceptions of Chac have changed over time. Even though we do not know the prehistoric Maya myths and stories of Chac, prehistoric pictures suggest what those stories might have been. Early images of Chac depict him in close association with water symbols, as do images dating from the Colonial and modern periods. They show no fourfold configurations, with a different Chac for each cardinal direction. At this time, a fourfold manifestation was more typical of Tlaloc, a similar rain deity belonging to the Nahua of Central Mexico, whose culture was influential during the Postclassic era. The Maya Chac may have borrowed Tlaloc's cardinal directionality.

Chac is one of a few Maya deities with a particularly long history. His image appears on Preclassic sculpture at the Maya site of Izapa, and reappears in Maya art and sculpture throughout the Classic period among the lowland Maya. Later, in the Postclassic period, we know Chac existed as a mythical figure because of the glyphic texts and pictures in the Maya codices describing him. It was during this time that he may have gained his fourfold character. Today, myths and stories of Chac and the four Chacs continue to circulate among the Maya.

> **See also** Bacabs; Chalchiuhtlicue; Earth, Agricultural, and Hunting Deities; Rain and Water Deities; Tlaloc and the Tlaloques
>
> **Suggested readings:**
>
> Freidel, David, Linda Schele, and Joy Parker. 1993. *Maya Cosmos: Three Thousand Years on the Shaman's Path*. New York: William Morrow.
>
> Taube, Karl. 1992. *The Major Gods of Ancient Yucatan*. Washington, DC: Dumbarton Oaks Research Library and Collection.
>
> Thompson, John Eric Sydney. 1970b. *Maya History and Religion*. Norman: University of Oklahoma Press.

CHALCHIUHTLICUE

Time period: Postclassic–Contemporary

Cultural group: Nahua, Central Mexico

Chalchiuhtlicue (Chal-chee-oot-lee´-kway) governed the waters of the ocean, rivers, springs, and lakes; and she cleansed and protected newborn children and cured the ill. Like her husband, brothers, or children Tlaloc and the Tlaloques,

*Figure 49. Chalchiuhtlicue (*Codex Borbonicus, *fol. 5, Museo de América/Art Resource)*

she lived in mountains, releasing her waters when appropriate; and as with all rain and water deities, Chalchiuhtlicue served an extraordinarily important role for the Postclassic Nahua of Central Mexico; Fray Diego Durán, the sixteenth century historian, says that she was "universally revered" (1971, 261). Today's water sirens and goddesses living in local rivers, lakes, and mountains such as Malinche share a number of traits with Chalchiuhtlicue.

Her relationship with Tlaloc and the Tlaloques varies with the mythic source. Some myths call Chalchiuhtlicue Tlaloc's wife, others the elder sister of Tlaloc and the Tlaloques, and still others their mother. Like them, she resided inside the mountains. From these cavernous pots she released various ground waters, both positive and negative. She could send calm water, which heaved to and fro, gently splashing and spattering the shore or, if there was no wind, spread very quietly. But her waters could also become restless, tossing and crashing, overturning boats and drowning people.

Like her various waters, Chalchiuhtlicue appeared in both positive and negative forms. She could provide the waters necessary for growing crops, in which case, she associated with a young virgin the corn goddess Xilonen; or if she chose to withhold her moist bounty, drying the earth and killing the crops, then she associated with the slavering snake goddess Chicomecoatl. Like many water deities, Chalchiuhtlicue often appeared with Quetzalcoatl who, as the wind, moved the waters. Certainly the wind helped churn the waters into a dangerous place for boaters, but Chalchiuhtlicue also could act alone, stirring herself up into whirlpools and great waves that dangerously swallowed or rocked hapless vessels. On Lake Texcoco in the Valley of Mexico, these phenomena probably were due to unstable geological conditions underlying the basin, which sometimes produced fissures and earthquakes.

Two children were sacrificed to the rain deities, including Chalchiuhtlicue, at the height of the dry season just before the rains were due. It was felt that the gods—as living entities—needed nourishment if they were to produce rain at the appropriate time. Moreover, this was a debt payment, for people owed their lives to the rain gods, without whom all would die of thirst. Drought loomed as an ever-present danger for the entire cosmos. Therefore, on the same day that a six or seven year-old boy was sacrificed to Tlaloc on his mountain just east of Tenochtitlan, the Mexica sacrificed a young girl to Chalchiuhtlicue in Lake Texcoco at Pantitlan, where a whirlpool sometimes suddenly engulfed boaters. They say that Motecuhzoma II's lost treasure, which disappeared during the Conquest, still lies buried at Pantitlan.

As the patroness of birth, Chalchiuhtlicue cleansed newborns of harmful things like disease. At a baby's birth, the midwife quietly said: "Our Lady Chalchiuhtlicue, Chalchiuhtlatonac, the tail feather, the wind feather has arrived. Receive him/her" (Sahagún 1953–82, bk. VI, 176–77). She then gently immersed the child into Chalchiuhtlicue's blue and yellow waters, telling it to descend and be cleansed. When she had swaddled the babe, and placed a jade strand around its neck, the midwife told the child that it had come to a difficult life of many sorrows. In a few days when the child was named, the midwife placed a bit of water in its mouth to cleanse its insides. If it was a boy, he received the implements of war; if a girl, the tools for weaving. The midwife then told the babe that Chalchiuhtlicue continually watches over it, washing harm away with her waters.

Indeed Chalchiuhtlicue's waters washed much harm away. Not only new mothers and their babes bathed in her preciousness, the ill also washed in Chalchiuhtlicue's gifts; and all left offerings of small jade figurines of frogs, fish, ducks, crabs, and turtles in springs and rivers. Today's many water sirens share a great deal with Chalchiuhtlicue. They too reside in rivers, springs, lakes, and mountains. They too can protect the young, wash disease away, and make crops grow and can either release or withhold their bounty from earth's inhabitants, depending on how one treats them.

See also Bacabs; Chac and the Chacs; Earth, Agricultural and Hunting Deities; Malinche; Motecuhzoma II (Xocoyotzin, Lord); Quetzalcoatl; Rain and Water Deities; Tlaloc and the Tlaloques; Underworld and Caves, Deities of the

Suggested reading:

Durán, Fray Diego. 1994. *The History of the Indies of New Spain.* Trans. Doris Heyden. Norman: University of Oklahoma Press.

Sahagún, Fray Bernardino de. 1953–1982. *The Florentine Codex: A General History of the Things of New Spain.* Trans. Arthur J. O. Anderson, and Charles E. Dibble. 12 books, 13 parts. Monographs of the School of American Research, No. 14. Santa Fe: School of American Research; Salt Lake City: University of Utah Press.

CHRIST

Time period: Colonial–Contemporary

Cultural group: Mesoamerica

The traditional Christ, with a bit of a local twist, is easily recognized in Mesoamerican Christian stories, but in other "unofficial" tales, Christ bears little resemblance to the more "official" or orthodox representations. In early Colonial times, Christ and his Cross became the first two and most widespread indigenous saints. Like other Mesoamerican Catholic saints in the unofficial, Popular Church, Christ and the Cross appear to the faithful in concrete forms, such as statues; serve as the patrons of particular localities; establish landholdings; and give communities their identities. Representations of the sacrifice and the resurrection of Christ often contain distinctly indigenous symbolism. Christ's most common Mesoamerican persona is the Sun, who fights darkness and provides light. Because Christ and the Sun also helped create the world and many of the things in it, in some myths the Christ-Sun appears to have taken over the tasks of the ancient Hero Twins in the Popol Vuh. Christ and his Cross heal the sick, protect those in danger, affirm the worth of traditional life, and support peasants fighting against vast inequities.

Indigenous peoples of the Colonial era understood the Cross, Christ, and his story in their own particular ways. They embraced both the Cross and Christ as repositories of sacred power, capable of performing miracles of all kinds. Then, as now, the Cross itself was personified: It could answer the faithful's pleas by taking action or by speaking to them; and it sometimes appeared draped in a traditional skirt and petticoat. Crosses marked Colonial plots of land, claiming them for particular families or communities. Stories even told of how people could die if they objected to a cross being located on a parcel of land; if the Cross wanted to be there, then so it must. Generally speaking, Colonial human souls went to God and Jesus in Heaven, but people's lands remained on earth in the care of the Cross and other patron saints. Among the Maya, Christ's Cross became the living World Tree standing in the center of the world. Early Christian travelers made the reverse analogy: For them, because of its visual similarity, the Maya World Tree was a manifestation of the Christian Cross, evidence of the universal presence of Christ.

Creative interpretations of the Christ story take many forms in Mesoamerica. Christ's relationship with Mother Mary and God the Father could follow distinctly indigenous family patterns. As a Nahua mother, the Colonial-era Mary did not want her son to leave her; but his father God said he must, and the ancestral prophecy declared that he would. Caught between opposing familial duties, Jesus decided to follow his prophetic destiny in spite of his mother's distress (Burkhart 1996, 89–95). The Colonial-era Christ was a distinctive saintly figure, completely separate from the other members of the Holy Trinity. Even today, the Trinity is understood by some Mesoamericans as three separate brothers whose names are Father, Jesus, and Spirit.

The Spanish brought with them scenes of Christ's harrowing in Hell, in which Hell was pictured as a great monster with a large, open, toothy mouth. This very European bestial figure naturally became the mouth of the indigenous Underworld; and Christ, upon his death and entombment, passed through that world just as the Sun, rulers, and the Hero Twins had in ancient times. Louise Burkhart tells us that in Spanish-Christian terms, Christ traveled to the Underworld to redeem Adam and Eve and others lost in limbo; but for the colonial Nahua, the lost became the ancestors who prophesied his sacrifice and transformation into the Sun. In one sixteenth-century tale, it was Quetzalcoatl rather than Christ who lay in a stone sepulcher while he traveled through the Underworld, before rising as the Morning Star—a reasonable act for a deity who had often followed the ancient Sun on its path. The Nahua were not alone in identifying Christ's death with ancient prophecy or in linking him to the Feathered Serpent: The Maya Chilam Balam of Chumayel predicted Christ's appearance in association with the return of Kukulkan at Chichén Itzá on the date Katun 4 Ahau.

The Sun-Christ, a common figure throughout Mesoamerica, fights the forces of darkness and evil that take on the forms of night, devils, and people who lived in a bygone age. The colonial Nahua called the nails pinning Christ to the Cross his blood-letting thorns, and said that his sacrificial death brought the world into a new and peaceful age, much as sacrifice caused the transformation of previous ancient sun-ages.

A twist on the Sun-Christ story comes from Chiapas, where the members of the Trinity are three brothers. The elder is named God and the middle one Jesus; but the youngest, named K'osh, proves the most clever of the three. K'osh turns his elder brother God into a pig by placing a tortilla on his nose. The middle brother Jesus runs off into the forest after becoming a wild boar. In the end, K'osh becomes the sun and his elder pig-brother becomes the moon because he cannot walk as well.

More commonly in such tales, Jesus is transformed into the Sun. The Kanhobal Maya say that when Christ died on the Cross, he climbed into Heaven on a golden ladder so that he could shine down upon earth. The Jacalteca Maya say that when Christ arose, the sun became real, and the Spaniards fled into caves and under the water, where they all eventually died. According to the Tzeltal Maya, during the Third Creation (or third age), Christ offered to become the sun because Lucifer the Devil could not give enough light or warmth (after all, he lived in the dark, damp Underworld); Christ ascended into the sky to become the sun, while his mother Mary became the moon. Yet they also say that Grandmother Moon fights the Sun during an eclipse because she wants things to stay the same; she does not want Lord Sun to become angry and kill all of the people who have done wrong. For this reason, the people say that she bears their sins. According to the Nahua, various birds betrayed Christ to a group of nasty policemen before his death and resurrection. Not surprisingly, the miscreants were roosters, doves, and other birds that typically herald the dawn with their singing.

Christ also acts as a creator of the current world and many of the things in it. The Mam Maya say that in the Third Creation, St. Joseph made a perfectly flat earth; and then, because it was very dark, he created the sun and moon. Jesus was born to the Blessed Virgin Mary and grew to full size in just four days. He told his father: "Do not be troubled, for I am going to make another world, and you will be able to help me." Then Jesus made mountains, valleys, canyons, and rivers; he even made the moon less bright than the sun so that people could sleep at night. But in a Tzeltal version of the story, Christ unfortunately also created three Ladino couples to lord it over the Indian workers.

In the Maya area, Christ often appears as a pair of brothers who act like the ancient creator pair, the Hero Twins; and two infant boys appear in many Maya Christmas creches. In San Miguel Acatán, Jesus convinced his elder brothers to climb a tree that just kept getting taller and taller as they climbed; they became monkeys, just like the Hero Twins. But unlike in the Popol Vuh, here Jesus also stripped bark from the tree and used it to form a lake at its base. According to Linda Schele, every February, in Chamula's New Year's celebrations, the Sun-Christ confronts the forces of darkness in the form of monkeys who belong to the previous age or world. Following the Path of God or the Sun's path across the sky, the Jesus-Gods overcome the monkey-gods of the age before them. Evoking the Hero Twins' self-sacrifice by fire, which enabled them eventually to become the sun and the moon, the individuals playing the Sun-Christ's part in these celebrations race across a road strewn with burning thatch (Friedel, Schele, and Parker 1993, 120, 290–292, 331–334). K'osh, the clever younger brother of the Trinity in Chiapas, repeatedly burned his field to clear it, only to find every time that it had grown back the very next day; the same occurred to the Hero Twins before they realized they were meant to be ballplayers and not farmers. One day, K'osh picked up his flame, and instead of going to his field, he went to where the day meets the heaven; similarly, the Hero Twins eventually went to the east, where they rose as the sun and moon.

Christ is not always so inept a farmer; indeed, he often produces material things, agricultural and otherwise. In Santo Tomás Chichicastenango, they say that when Jesus was crucified, he turned around, and white, yellow, and black corn sprouted from his bare back. In another story from Chiapas, Jesus and Mary couldn't get corn to grow because the Devil's children watched over it. So they tricked the Devil by throwing a party, enticing him in with good music and dance. Mary got the Devil drunk, distracting him while Jesus sneaked off to their field. There, making the sign of the Cross, he killed all the Devil's children and seized control of the land. And, so it is true that we are Christ's children, and that people say liquor is one half God and one half the Devil. In yet another story, the Tzeltal say that liquor came from Santa Lucia's bath water, which Christ gave to the community; but in another version, liquor comes from Christ's own bath water. Even dirty saintly water can hold impressive powers. Among some Nahua, Christ also is responsible for the various winds, which, like liquor, are both good and bad. These winds are people who, because they put their hands on Christ, are now condemned to live in some unpleasant place such as a cave or ravine. For some, the entombed Christ—perhaps because he travels through the Underworld—carries the powers of the fertile rain god Tlaloc.

Christ's suffering at the hands of the Romans parallels the suffering of peasants at the hands of Ladino or White oppressors in some regions, making Christ a symbol and source of power for resistance. During El Salvador's civil war in the 1980s, Jesus was seen as an ordinary person with a weather-beaten face; one who, like the peasants, sweated as he toiled. The martyrs who died in the war repeated Christ's sacrifice, and Christ was resurrected in every martyr's death.

Some Mesoamerican Christs are Black, which may be a result of Latin America's African heritage; there also were and still are dark-faced Indian Christs. At Tila in Chiapas, a white Christ appeared three times when the villagers were building their church. Each time he told them that the spot upon which they were erecting the building was bad for some reason, either because it was too wet or had too many ants. In the end they followed his advice, erecting the town and its church on top of a mountain. But during the rebellion of 1712, Christ fled from people who were looting his churchly home, taking refuge in a cave across the valley. Eventually he reappeared on his own accord back in the church, but he had returned black! Meanwhile, a stalagmite resembling Christ was left behind in the cave. Later, this same Christ miraculously lightened himself to mulatto tones, preempting a priest's threat to paint him even lighter. Like the Cross and other Mesoamerican saints, Christ often represents his particular people and locality very well. Moreover, he can transform to meet local needs—sometimes by means of violent sacrifice, and sometimes in gentler ways.

> *See also* Feathered Serpents; Hero Twins; Kukulkan; Quetzalcoatl; Saints; Sun; Underworld and Caves, Deities of the
>
> *Suggested reading:*

Bricker, Victoria Reifler. 1981. *The Indian Christ, The Indian King.* Austin: University of Texas Press.

Burkhart, Louise M. 1996. *Holy Wednesday: A Nahua Drama from Early Colonial Mexico.* Philadelphia: University of Pennsylvania Press.

Friedel, David, Linda Schele, and Joy Parker. 1993. *Maya Cosmos: Three Thousand Years on the Shaman's Path.* New York: William Morrow.

Nash, June. 1985. *In the Eyes of the Ancestors: Belief and Behavior in a Mayan Community.* 2nd ed. Prospect Heights, IL: Waveland Press.

Thompson, John Eric Sydney. 1970. *Maya History and Religion.* Norman: University of Oklahoma Press.

CIHUACOATL

Time period: Postclassic

Cultural group: Nahua, Central Mexico

The goddess Cihuacoatl (See-wa-ko´-wat), or Snake Woman, appeared in many places and took on many guises. She was a powerful woman warrior whose battlefield resided in the sky; a patroness of agriculture who dwelt on the earth's surface, and an inhabitant of the underworld. Some cities, including the Mexica city Tenochtitlan, claimed her as their primary matron, watching after the city's household. As a warrior, she often played the role of a supreme strategist both on military battlefields and those of childbirth. And, she appeared as a harbinger of death, wailing out bad omens in the night.

Sometimes known as Quilaztli, Cihuacoatl both watched over the agricultural fields and helped create human beings. She did this in the same way one would make corn tortillas. The god Quetzalcoatl retrieved some jumbled up bones from the land of the dead, and brought them to Cihuacoatl in the women's house by the western tree or the cosmos's western quadrant. Taking them, she ground them like corn kernels, wetting them with blood from Quetzalcoatl's

Figure 50. Cihuacoatl (drawing by Kay A. Read from the Florentine Codex, *bk. 1, no. 6)*

member. Thus ancient Nahua people were made of godly corn and sacrificial blood.

Cihuacoatl served as the patroness of midwives, so women invoked her powers to help them through the battle of birth. Midwives called on her especially for difficult births, exhorting their charges to have the courage of Cihuacoatl, and using her powers to carefully plan the strategy required for a successful campaign. If the woman unfortunately died, she turned into one of the Eagle Women or honorable women warriors who, each noonday, captured the sun from dead male warriors. These women took the sun to their house in the west, where the People of the Dead captured it at dusk, they kept it until dawn when the male warriors recaptured it. If the woman lived, she could receive much fortune from Cihuacoatl, perhaps even the capture of twins who were said to have come from her.

Because of Cihuacoatl's powers at war, young male warriors tried to capture the middle fingers and hair from the bodies of women who had died in childbirth; they attached these potent trophies to their shields to make them valiant and paralyze the feet of their opponents. Cihuacoatl wore the eagle plumes of the great warrior god, Mixcoatl. She carried a shield of eagle plumes and wielded a weaving batten like a weapon. The Tlacaellel, a governor of Tenochtitlan who could hold as much power as the ruler, dressed in her clothes for ceremonies, and thus acquired her skills at war to use for his city's gain.

She also could bring bad news about death and destruction. Usually she wore her hair up in the manner of a matron, but sometimes she wore her hair loose, dirty and tangled in the manner of a woman in mourning. At these times, she also wore the jawbone of the death deities and the underworld, and lived in a dark house in which all the gods were kept. Dressed thus, she could appear at night crying out warnings for all to hear. Cihuacoatl delivered such a warning twice to the Mexica before the Conquest. Then she wailed: "Dear children, soon I am going to abandon you! We are going to leave you" In this guise she is a forerunner of La Llorona, the woman who at present still cries out in the night.

See also La Llorona; Quetzalcoatl; Tlacaellel

Suggested reading:

Durán, Fray Diego. 1994. *The History of the Indies of New Spain.* Trans. Doris Heyden. Norman: University of Oklahoma Press.

Read, Kay A. 2000. "More than Earth: Cihuacoatl as Female Warrior, Male Matron, and Inside Ruler." Pp. 51–67 in *Goddesses and Sovereignty.* Ed. Elisabeth Benard and Beverly Moon. New York: Oxford University Press.

Sahagún, Fray Bernardino de. 1953–1982. *The Florentine Codex: A General History of the Things of New Spain.* Trans. Arthur J. O. Anderson, and Charles E. Dibble. 12 books, 13 parts. Monographs of the School of American Research, No. 14. Santa Fe: School of American Research; Salt Lake City: University of Utah Press.

CIZIN

Time period: Classic–Contemporary

Cultural group: Maya

Cizin (See-zeen′), also known as Yum Cimil, is the principal lord of the Yucatec Maya underworld and presides over the deceased. He has been depicted throughout Maya history, to the present day, as a skeletal figure with a prominent skull and disembodied eyeballs hanging in his hair or around his neck. By means of this imagery, the Classic and Postclassic Maya art suggests Cizin's close association with putrescence and filth. According to a Lacandon Maya myth, after a person dies, Cizin burns the soul on its mouth and its anus. When the soul complains, Cizin drenches the soul in ice water, causing further protests, which causes Cizin to burn the soul again, and so on, until the soul disintegrates from this cycle of hot and cold. Cizin has counterparts throughout Mesoamerica. Among the Highland K'iche' a similar figure, called Hun Came (1-Death), is found in the Popol Vuh; and among the Mexica, Mictlanteuctli mirrors Cizin.

See also Devil; Mictlanteuctli; 1-Death and 7-Death; Underworld and Caves, Deities of the

Suggested reading:

Taube, Karl. 1992. *The Major Gods of Ancient Yucatan.* Washington, DC: Dumbarton Oaks Research Library and Collection.

Thompson, John Eric Sydney. 1970. *Maya History and Religion.* Norman: University of Oklahoma Press.

COATLICUE

Time period: Postclassic–Contemporary

Cultural group: Mexica, Central Mexico

Coatlicue (Ko-wat-lee'-kway) or Snake Skirt was the mother of the sixteenth-century Mexica patron and warrior god Huitzilopochtli, and his sister and rival Coyolxauhqui. Coatlicue's symbolic associations included agricultural fertility, war, and governance; and she probably was a warrior woman who, like Cihuacoatl, warned the Mexica of their eventual demise. Today, as some reinterpret the early sixteenth century indigenous myths, she has become a representative of fierce feminine strength and the dark power of the unconscious.

Coatlicue was celebrated (along with other deities) in two pre-Hispanic Mexica rituals. The first, a spring ritual called Tozozontli, occurred when the rains began to fall heavily. It ended an earlier ritual in which sacrificial offerings were flayed, and it celebrated the first fruits of the season. Among other things during this ritual, the flayed skins were placed in a cave, bones of dead war captives received special attention, and it was believed that the ritual cured the sick. During the second, an autumn ritual focused on hunting called Quecholli, a woman impersonating Coatlicue was sacrificed. These two rituals suggest that agricultural and hunting fertility along with sacrifice and war may play roles in Coatlicue's symbolism.

Her mythic imagery highlights primarily themes of sacrifice, war, and governance. Here, Coatlicue represents the maternal source of Mexica heritage and power gained through war. It is said that one day a ball of feathers floated down from the skies above while Coatlicue swept the top of Snake Mountain. Picking up this ball, she tucked it into the belt of her skirt; this act impregnated her with Huitzilopochtli. Accusing her mother of incorrect behavior (for proper babies do not drop from the sky), the enraged Coyolxauhqui led her 400 brothers, the Centzonuitznaua, against her. But just as they approached the top of Snake Mountain, Huitzilopochtli spoke from the womb, telling his mother that she shouldn't worry because he would vanquish her attackers. Indeed, at the last moment and dressed in full battle array, he sprang from her womb, slaying his sister and routing his brothers.

In a counter myth, Coatlicue warned the Mexica of their eventual demise. In this tale, which happened when the Mexica were rising to power, she was waiting in her home Aztlan or Chicomoztoc (The Place of Seven Caves) for her son Huitzilopochtli to return. The great Mexica ruler Motecuhzoma I (ruled ca. 1440–1469) sent sixty magicians to visit her, for Aztlan was the Mexica place of origin. There the magicians met Coatlicue's aged tutor who agreed to take them to her, but they were unable to climb a tall, sandy hill to meet her because they were too heavily laden with gifts. So, the ancient tutor picked up their burdens and ran up the hill as though carrying no more than a few straws. On top, they found Coatlicue weeping because she missed Huitzilopochtli. Asking after those Mexica ancestors who originally had left Aztlan many years before, she was shocked to learn of their deaths, for people in Aztlan do not die. Moreover, she told them that the reason they could not carry their own burdens was because they had grown too heavy from all their rich foods and beautiful clothing. She then said that Huitzilopochtli would lose all the cities he had conquered for the Mexica in the same order that he had won them. Only then would he return to his mother's side, abandoning the Mexica to their fate. She gave the magicians two simple grass capes and two pairs of sandals to encourage her son to return. The returning magicians gave them to Motecuhzoma and Tlacaellel, who placed them on Huitzilopochtli's shrine; both leaders were greatly saddened by Coatlicue's strong admonitions, and her grim prediction.

A Mexica sculpture of Coatlicue depicts her as an aging warrior woman (Figure 40). Perhaps a column supporting the roof of a temple, this massive structure portrays a woman dressed in a warrior's skirt of netted rattlesnakes. She has been decapitated; sprouting from her neck, two coral snakes face each other, together forming a new fearsome face. Snakes also form her arms and hands, and another snake coils between her feathered legs. She wears a necklace of hands and hearts with a skull medallion. Her limbs sport signs of the underworld and, on the bottom of her taloned feet, where nobody can see it, the toadlike underworld monster spreads its legs and open maw. Here one envisions the horrors of war, sacrifice, and death. One might read this as representing the entire cosmos, as have some; or one might see it as the power of the Mexica to overtake their enemies, for they often portrayed the conquered as warrior women. Or one might even see the reverse, the threat of its temporarily conquered enemies waiting for revenge. After all, some day Huitzilopochtli will abandon the Mexica to their fate, and go home to his mother Coatlicue.

Primarily a Mexica deity, Coatlicue nevertheless was known by others. In Tlaxcala, she sometimes took the place of another mythic female warrior and chief named Chimalman, whom the great male warrior Mixcoatl was unable to kill because this clever woman moved too quickly. Eventually grabbing her, he forcibly impregnated her; from this union, came the god Quetzalcoatl.

In more recent times, the Coatlicue sculpture has served as a philosophical and poetic starting point for women struggling to comes to terms with the modern world. Here she represents the force women can have, and the dark, hidden underside of one's subconscious. Gloria Anzaldúa has said that by delving deep into her own Coatlicue consciousness and being cradled in the earth mother's arms, she can confront her own fears and make the leap into the dark unknown. There like a seed in the underground, she is regenerated, and slowly becomes able to straddle the various borders of her own ancient-modern, patriarchal-feminist, and southern-northern Hispanic heritage. By confronting herself in Coatlicue's eyes, she becomes whole.

> ***See also*** Blood Woman; Coyolxauhqui; Earth, Agricultural, and Hunting Deities; Huitzilopochtli; Motecuhzoma I, Lord; Quetzalcoatl; Tlacaellel; Underworld and Caves, Deities of the
>
> ***Suggested reading:***

Anzaldúa, Gloria. 1987. *Borderlands/La Frontera: The New Mestiza.* San Francisco: Aunt Lute Books.

Durán, Fray Diego. 1994. *The History of the Indies of New Spain.* Trans. Doris Heyden. Norman: University of Oklahoma Press.

Sahagún, Fray Bernardino de. 1953–1982. *The Florentine Codex: A General History of the Things of New Spain.* Trans. Arthur J. O. Anderson, and Charles E. Dibble. Monographs of the School of American Research no. 14. Santa Fe: School of American Research; Salt Lake City: University of Utah Press.

CORTÉS, FERNANDO (HERNÁN)

Time period: Conquest–Contemporary

Cultural group: Mesoamerica

Fernando (Hernán) Cortés (Kor-tez´, Fer-nan´-doe [Her-nan´]) became the first European to establish colonial power in Mesoamerica, conquering the Mexica in 1521, in the name of Spain. He was reputedly a highly skilled and creative leader, with an extraordinary ability to adapt to changing conditions in an alien land. A bit greedy and unwilling to brook any competition, he nevertheless operated by clear (although sometimes brutal) ethical standards common to sixteenth-century European warfare. Against the wishes of his monarch, Cortés perpetuated the terribly ruthless encomienda system, thereby richly rewarding both himself and his men for risking their lives. Cortés also supported his own offspring, whether Spanish or mestizo, in high style.

The Cortés of popular myth is an amorphous character, representing different things to different people at different times. This one man has come to symbolize both the civilizing and the brutalizing effects of the Conquest in folk and literary traditions. Conquest mythology describes his uncanny military and leadership powers. With shipwrecked sailor Jerónimo de Águilar and a native woman known as Malinche acting as his translators and advisers, Cortés manipulated the desires and fears of various indigenous groups to further his goals. He also managed to turn opposing Spanish forces to his side. In the end, after much effort and many reversals verging on defeat, Cortés, his men and supporters, and his many Indian allies subdued the Mexica, opening the way for tremendous, jarring shifts in Mesoamerican world realities. Myths expressed the fears these shifts produced in the indigenous people. Various stories suggest that the Mexica leader Motecuhzoma II found Cortés both puzzling and unsettling. Some sources describe Motecuhzoma repeatedly testing Cortés: Was he the returning Quetzalcoatl, or not? Given that he would not partake of human sacrificial blood, could he be trusted? Was the demise of the Mexica close at hand, and if so, could Cortés help Motecuhzoma escape to the underworld? Whether these stories have a basis in fact is unclear. Other stories describe many Mesoamericans as less intimidated, some even taking advantage of the Spaniards' presence, allying with them in order to advance their own causes.

Stories about Cortés often suggest that the Conquest was inevitable. Early on, some indigenous people might have viewed Cortés as a model conqueror. Susan Gillespie (1989, 226–230) suggests that the Indians saw him as the next ruler, a kind of boundary figure whose time had come to replace the old line of Motecuhzoma–a perspective reflected today in a number of folk dances. Indeed, at least one indigenous informant said Cortés had acquired a Tlacochcalcatl, or native judge, in Cempoala, and noted that a native woman had brought him to Mexico. Others believed that Cortés was a reincarnation of Quetzalcoatl—a sort of sixteenth-century Moses ushering in a New Israel. Literary sources often have painted Cortés as the bringer of Christianity and/or European technological superiority, as though the Conquest were ordained by God or scientific progress. A number of histories have suggested that the superstitious Indians fell down in awe before the Spaniards' strange horses and powerful weaponry—their authors having forgotten how long the Conquest actually took, the thousands of native allies assisting the Spaniards, the numbers of Mexica claimed by smallpox, and how close the Spaniards came to defeat. These histories, many of them quite recent, frequently have stressed Cortés's early mythological link to Quetzalcoatl, without noting how Cortés's own grasping behavior quickly dispelled that honorable connection.

Positive images of Cortés also developed among his native allies, for whom his name quickly came to symbolize New World nobility. Cortés sponsored numerous native leaders, who as a gesture of gratitude gave his name to their sons at baptism; this quickly made *Cortés* the most common Indian noble surname in colonial New Spain. And within 150 to 200 years after the Conquest, traditional lordly rhetoric in Nahuatl had fused with Spanish titles to create a picture of a noble past. For example, a group of local Chalcan officials argued for land entitlement by prefacing their request with the phrase: "Cortés don Luis de Velasco Marqués brought us the true faith." They then argued that this gentleman of lengthy title had ordered them to build a church, for which purpose they needed land (Lockhart 1992, 123, 412).

In 1539, a sumptuous play was performed in Mexico City called the *Conquest of Rhodes*, in which Cortés probably played himself successfully leading a troop of Christians against an infidel army of Moors. But not all accounts describe Cortés so positively. Later that same year, a play in Tlaxcala entitled the *Conquest of Jerusalem* reversed this image, placing a fictitious Cortés and his second-in-command Pedro de Alvarado at the head of the Moorish army instead! A troop of Indians soundly defeated the Moors, expressing in theatrical disguise the conquered peoples' resentment. Less complimentary images also appear hidden in contemporary folk dances. In *La Danza de la Pluma*, performed today in Oaxaca during annual Catholic festivals, the figure of Cortés plods around with an army of very small boys, all dressed in rather boring costumes, while Motecuhzoma and his adult warriors dance magnificently, in splendid dress. At the dance's end, Cortés finds himself abandoned by his consort Marina and defeated by a resurrected Motecuhzoma. Moreover, the 1992 quincentennial celebration of Columbus's entrance into the New World raised many people's consciousness of the plight of Mesoamerican natives. Since then, Cortés's name has enjoyed far less worshipful treatment than in past eras, symbolizing the continuing Euro-American brutalization of embattled yet resistant noble indigenous traditions.

See also Malinche; Motecuhzoma II, Lord; Quetzalcoatl

Suggested reading:

Cortés, Hernán. 1986. *Letters from Mexico.* Trans. and ed. A. R. Pagden. New Haven, CT: Yale University Press.

Díaz del Castillo, Bernal. 1956. *The Discovery and Conquest of Mexico: 1517–1521.* New York: Farrar, Straus and Giroux.

Gillespie, Susan. 1989. *The Aztec Kings: The Construction of Rulership in Mexica History.* Tucson: University of Arizona Press.

Harris, Max. 1997. "The Return of Moctezuma: Oaxaca's *Danza de la Pluma* and New Mexico's *Danza de los Matachines.*" *Drama Review* 41, 1 (T153): 106–134.

Lockhart, James. 1992. *The Nahuas after the Conquest: A Social and Cultural History of the Indians of Central Mexico, Sixteenth through Eighteenth Centuries.* Stanford, CA: Stanford University Press.

Sahagún, Fray Bernardino de. 1953–1982. *The Florentine Codex: A General History of the Things of New Spain.* Trans. Arthur J. O. Anderson and Charles E. Dibble. Monographs of the School of American Research, no. 14. Santa Fe: School of American Research; Salt Lake City: University of Utah Press.

COYOLXAUHQUI

Time period: Postclassic

Cultural group: Mexica, Central Mexico

Coyolxauhqui (Koy-ol-shauw´-kee) was either the mythic sister or mother of the sixteenth-century Mexica patron and war god Huitzilopochtli. In either case, she symbolically represents the Mexica's first victorious conquest, for in both, Coy-

olxauhqui challenged Hiutzilo-
pochtli, only to be defeated. In
the first case, it is told how she
led her 400 brothers, the Centzonuitznaua, in an attack on her
mother, Coatlicue, because
Coatlicue had become pregnant
by mysterious means. But just as
Coyolxauhqui and her forces
were about to strike, Huitzilopochtli was born in full war
regalia. He immediately killed
his sister, decapitating her and
chopping off her limbs and
throwing them down the sides
of Mount Coatepec, and then he
routed his brothers.

In the second case, Huitzilopochtli took Coyolxauhqui as
his mother. At this time, the

*Figure 51. The Coyolxauhqui Stone from the Postclassic
site of Tenochtitlan (drawing by Kay A. Read)*

Mexica were living at Coatepec or Snake Mountain, for they had not yet found
their island home of Tenochtitlan. Coatepec was very beautiful, for the Mexica
had dammed a river, creating a wonderful, rich marshland full of frogs, fish, and
water birds. It was so pleasant that, when Huitzilopochtli ordered the Mexica to
leave and continue searching for their real home, Coyolxauhqui and her brothers, the Centzonuitznaua, objected, wishing instead to remain at Coatepec. This
did not sit well with Huitzilopochtli, for he did not like being told what to do.
Late that night a huge commotion arose from the ball court; and in the morning,
the Mexica found that Huitzilopochtli had decapitated Coyolxauhqui and eaten
her heart. In one version, Huitzilopochtli then became a demon of darkness and
burrowed into the ground, draining all the water from the lagoon; in another, he
ordered the Mexica to break the dam. In any case, without water, Coatepec dried
up and the Mexica were forced to continue searching for their final settlement.

A huge, impressive shield-shaped stone frieze has been unearthed from the
base of the stairs on the Huitzilopochtli side of the Templo Mayor. Coyolxauhqui spreads out on her side, wearing nothing more than a warrior's belt
knotted from a double-headed snake. Her head, arms, and legs have been
chopped off, the bones poking out from the flesh. Her hair sports balls of eagle
down; from her ear hangs the Mexica year sign; a bell graces her cheek; she bears
the marks of the underworld on her joints; and as with her mother Coatlicue, her

belt ties a skull to her back. An earlier frieze also has been found, and although she does not appear nude on this one, Huitzilopochtli's weapon, a xiuhcoatl or fire-serpent, pierces her chest.

Some have thought she is the moon, who has been vanquished by the sun; but others feel she is the goddess of the Milky Way. Even if her celestial associations are less obvious, her vanquished eagle warrior status seems clear. The Nahua called defeated cities fallen warrior women, and said they lay on the ground like shields dropped in battle, just as Coyolxauhqui now lies. In fact, warrior ritual sacrifices imitated her myths. As Huitzilopochtli had decapitated Coyolxauhqui and chopped off her limbs, flinging them down the side of Mount Coatepec, so too were war captives ritually treated. First, the captives' hearts were cut out, then they were decapitated, their limbs chopped off, and finally their bodies rolled down the steps of the temple to land on the great Coyolxauhqui stone.

Of course, as with any good myth, multiple meanings are simultaneously possible; Coyolxauhqui may have represented simultaneously the cities Tenochtitlan defeated in battle, and either the moon or stars defeated by the great sun warrior Huitzilopochtli.

> **See also** Coatlicue; Huitzilopochtli; Ix Chel; Moon; Sky Deities and Beings; Underworld and Caves, Deities of the
>
> **Suggested reading:**
>
> Codex Chimalpahin. 1997. As reproduced in *Codex Chimalpahin: Society and Politics in Mexico Tenochtitlan, Tlatelolco, Texcoco, Culhuacan, and other Nahua Altepetl in Central Mexico: The Nahuatl and Spanish Annals and Accounts Collected and Recorded by Don Domingo de San Antón Muñón Chimalpahin Quauhtlehuanitzin.* Edited and translated by Arthur J. O. Anderson and Susan Schroeder. Norman: University of Oklahoma Press.
> Durán, Fray Diego. 1994. *The History of the Indies of New Spain.* Trans. Doris Heyden. Norman: University of Oklahoma Press.
> Sahagún, Fray Bernardino de. 1953–1982. *The Florentine Codex: A General History of the Things of New Spain.* Trans. Arthur J. O. Anderson, and Charles E. Dibble. Monographs of the School of American Research, No. 14. Santa Fe: School of American Research; Salt Lake City: University of Utah Press.

CUAUHTEMOC, LORD

Time period: Postclassic

Cultural group: Nahua-Mexica

Lord Cuauhtemoc (Kwaw-teh´-mok) was the eleventh and last pre-Conquest Chief Speaker of the Mexica (ruled 1520–1524), and the son of the great Lord Ahuitzotl (ruled ca. 1486–1502). He surrendered to Fernando (Hernán) Cortés on 13 August 1521, after a year of strong resistance. Cortés hanged him in 1524.

Cuauhtemoc symbolizes the ending of Mexica hegemony and the fall of a valiant pre-Conquest indigenous life. The Spanish viewed his conquest as justified and proper; the indigenous saw it as simply tragic.

The Mexica elected Cuauhtemoc to rulership in the midst of war, after Cortés's principle captain Pedro de Alvarado massacred hundreds of Mexicans. Responding to this tragedy, the angry Mexica elected Cuitlahuac to replace Lord Motecuhzoma II (Xocoyotzin) whom they considered a traitor, and rebelled against the Spanish, expelling them from Tenochtitlan in a bloody battle. But soon after, Cuitlahuac succumbed to smallpox, and Cuauhtemoc replaced him. A strong opponent, Cuauhtemoc held the Spanish and their thousands of allies at bay, causing them considerable damage.

Most stories describe Lord Cuauhtemoc as noble, valiant, intelligent, and sometimes cunning. It is said that he fought to the death, carrying on the warring tradition of his deceased father Lord Ahuitzotl. When the Spanish attacked the city with a catapult, Cuauhtemoc dressed one of his finest warriors in his father's power-laden attire to instill bravery into his discouraged troops. Apparently Ahuitzotl's powers still held, for they won the battle.

But different authors sometimes describe him in different ways. The Spanish claim he deceived them by attacking after saying he wanted to surrender; more indigenous sources, however, say he met with his council who dissuaded him from giving in. Spanish sources say that, when Tenochtitlan fell, he tried to escape in fifty canoes laden with wives and goods, was hoodwinked into capture, and then dramatically pleaded with Cortés to kill him because he had failed. Indigenous sources say that, after discussing with his council what tribute they would offer, he went willingly to surrender to Cortés in a single canoe with only two companions. Spanish sources say he was hanged because he plotted rebellion; indigenous sources say he was falsely accused by Malinche, Cortés's influential indigenous translator. Thus Spanish historical mythology creates an image of a mostly worthy, but appropriately vanquished opponent; and indigenous sources a valorous, but tragic figure.

See also Ahuitzotl, Lord; Cortés, Fernando; Malinche; Motecuhzoma II, Lord
Suggested reading:

Díaz del Castillo, Bernal. 1956. *The Discovery and Conquest of Mexico: 1517–1521.* New York: Farrar, Straus and Giroux.

Durán, Fray Diego. 1994. *The History of the Indies of New Spain.* Trans. Doris Heyden. Norman: University of Oklahoma Press.

Sahagún, Fray Bernardino de. 1953–1982. *The Florentine Codex: A General History of the Things of New Spain.* Book XII. Trans. Arthur J. O. Anderson, and Charles E. Dibble. 12 books, 13 parts. Monographs of the School of American Research, No. 14. Santa Fe: School of American Research; Salt Lake City: University of Utah Press.

DEAD, DAY OF THE

Time period: Colonial–Contemporary

Cultural group: Mesoamerica

The dead return to visit the living on the Day of the Dead, also called *Todos Santos*, or All Saints' Day. The "day" is actually a festival beginning on 31 October and usually lasting until 2 November. Many communities extend the ritual until 8 November or longer by linking it with other rites performed throughout the year for the recently deceased. Traditionally, people welcome back the souls of the departed to family hearths with lavish meals, new clothes, and delightfully elaborate and idiosyncratic altars, or *ofrendas*, commemorating them. Families share food and drink with their relatives and neighbors. These spectacular repasts include everything from figurines and skulls made of sugar and chocolate to special breads, stews, and tamales; fresh fruits; beer and soda pop; and even junk food, depending on the tastes of both the dead and the living. An ofrenda may include pictures and portraits of the dead, important saints, or Mary and Jesus; flowers, especially marigolds; lacy paper cutouts depicting skulls and skeletons; and papier-mâché dolls of skeletons doing everything from dancing and singing to typing, cycling, or riding in cars and buses, cooking, or using the facilities. In fact, in recent years the rite has spawned a head-spinning array of public and private displays both humorous and serious, which can be made out of everything from traditional palm-frond weaving to white plastic and neon lights. Rural displays tend toward the traditional, reflecting the serious purpose of the original rites; but in cities, there are no limits to the imagination, and displays there often diverge far from the festival's personal commemorative purposes. In recent years, the festival even has begun to merge with Halloween.

Contemporary ritual use of skulls and skeletons suggests a relationship to pre-Conquest sacrificial traditions; however, the similarities are only superficial. The ancient Nahua, for example, honored the dead on a number of occasions throughout the year, not just in the fall, and skulls were not necessarily part of their celebrations. Sometimes food was offered, as it is today. Such practices are also common to many ancient folk traditions in Europe. Soul concepts, furthermore, have changed radically from pre-Conquest times to today. Ancient Mesoamericans, like many Native Americans, tended to understand a human as containing not just one sole soul but multiple "souls" or living forces that scattered upon a person's death: one went with the body's ashes (if cremated) or the bones; some remained with the deceased's names, which could be passed on; some might go with particular gods or birds and butterflies; and one went into the woods, to threaten the living. Although some of these and other pre-Conquest conceptions of death have survived to the present, often melding with Christian worldviews, the idea of a single spirit that remains intact after the body's disappearance is more Christian than indigenous. Today, souls generally are regarded as singular rather than multiple entities, as reflected in the celebration of Todos Santos.

Many of the specifics of All Saints' Day can be traced directly to Europe. The sugar figurines have predecessors in celebrations of All Saints' Day in twelfth-century Naples, and they still appear in Palermo, Sicily today. The earliest Mesoamerican sugar skulls did not appear until the nineteenth century and may have been related to an indigenous practice in the Yucatán. There the intrepid traveler John L. Stephens reported in 1843 that skulls of the dead were housed in a local church at Kabah; each bore the deceased's name on its forehead, along with a short prayer. Today one can buy sugar skulls with a space on their foreheads for the name of a deceased loved one or a living friend. Humorous skeletons appearing today may have gotten their start with the skeletons used for political satire in the early twentieth century. Before that, skeletons on carts represented the Grim Reaper in celebrations of death cults, which originally grew up in plague-infested medieval Europe; but these festivals are distinct from All Saints' Day celebrations.

Of course this does not mean that no pre-Conquest elements whatsoever survive in today's rites. The sugar figurines and skulls may have replaced earlier amaranth and honey figures frequently used in pre-Conquest rituals. The art of paper-cutting claims a centuries-long tradition; and the ancients used marigolds ritually for centuries, believing that they bore the sun's warmth and power. Today, one still finds the bright yellow-orange flowers arranged on altars and church floors as an offering, not just for the dead, but for others as well. At San Miguel Tzinacapan, marigolds sown between Saint Antoni Tixochit's Day (13 June), when the sun is said to be in the underworld, and Saint John's Day (24 June), when the sun appears in the sky, are used specifically for the Day of the Dead.

The variation among Day of the Dead rites is enormous. The rites now span all of Mesoamerica and its diaspora in the United States. Many say that if you do not honor the dead, they will return to bother you; or you might actually see the dead, and then die yourself. Typically, the souls of small children are believed to return first, sometimes as early as 30 October, followed by older children on 31 October and by adults on 1 November. Often a path of marigolds shows the dead the way to the front door, which is left open to welcome them; but those who died a violent death by murder or were drowned may be kept outside the house because they are considered dangerous. Because the returning spirits normally can only be sensed and not seen, they only absorb the food's essence, after which the family distributes the meal among grandparents, relatives, and neighbors. Some food may be brought to the cemetery, where the graves may be decorated elaborately on 2 November or some other day during the festival. In some areas, a night-long vigil takes place in the cemetery.

In the 1930s, at the cemetery in Chan Kom, which had reached its capacity, bones were dug up on the Day of Dead after two or three years in the grave. They were sprinkled with holy water and placed in cloth-lined boxes, and prayers were said over them. People then carried the boxes to their homes, and placed them on decorated tables. More prayers were said and food offered, and the celebrants drank chocolate that evening. Again holy water was sprinkled over the bones, and then they were deposited in a house in the cemetery. It is said that the bones were stored there for some time, until one day when strange sounds began coming from the building, after which people moved the bones outside.

A story from Oaxaca tells about a man whose wife had disappeared. A vulture took him to a strange church, where he recognized his wife. He followed her home and asked her where she had gone. She replied that she couldn't tell him but he should take their money and cook a turkey on All Saints' Day, and she would return to eat it with him. This he did and waited patiently, watching the door. Tiring after a while, he looked around the room, and lo and behold, he saw a great snake with a pot on its head. Afraid, he took up his machete to kill it; but as soon as he approached the creature it disappeared. Still not seeing his wife, he called the vulture and asked to visit her again. Upon arriving at the church, he asked why she hadn't come to visit him. She responded that she had been there but he had chased her away with his machete!

Today, among the Totonac, the dead who died tragically are believed to suffer punishment at the hands of the god of death. They must wander for four years, sometimes appearing at streams as voices that try to trap the living. Every morning, the dead help the sun to escape the god of death residing in the underworld; by turning into birds, butterflies, clouds, stars, and planets, they help the sun move across the sky to its death and reentry into the underworld at sundown. On the Day of the Dead, insects who eat the festival food are believed to be the dead returning for their annual visit. At Huaquechula, the altars vary with the neighborhood. Some ofrendas rise as high as 10 to 12 feet and are covered in white satin or plastic. At Iguala, one might hire actors to perform a living tableau representing scenes from the life of Christ. And in Mexico City, stores paint their windows with humorous skeletons; bakeries sell countless sugar figurines, breads, and chocolate skulls; the markets are filled with skeletons and paper-cuttings, many amusing and satirical; and businesses and local groups sponsor competitions for the best ofrendas.

Many from the United States return to Mexico for Todos Santos; others remain to celebrate in their own fashion. In Los Angeles, traditional foods are sold; ofrendas appear everywhere, decorated with both local and imported offerings; and a big parade and fiesta are held. Throughout the United States, Hispanic churches celebrate with marigolds, pictures of the deceased, and spoken remembrances of the year's dead. Museums hold exhibits, artists create elaborate displays, and many schools offer special programs. North of the border, the Day of the Dead embodies a Mexican sense of national identity and cultural pride as well as providing a chance for mourners to remember their lost loved ones. Certainly the creativity with which the dead are welcomed home is astounding both north and south of the border. The Mesoamerican festival's roots may lie largely in Europe; but after five centuries of practice, the American celebrations have developed their own wonderful character, unlike that of All Saints' celebrations anywhere else in the world.

See also Sky Deities and Beings; Underworld and Caves, Deities of the

Suggested reading:

Carmichael, Elizabeth, and Cloë Sayers. 1991. *The Skeleton at the Feast: The Day of the Dead in Mexico.* London: British Museum Press.

Furst, Jill Leslie McKeever. 1995. *The Natural History of the Soul in Ancient Mexico.* New Haven, CT: Yale University Press.

Parson, Elsie Clews. 1936. *Mitla, Town of the Souls: And Other Zapteco-Speaking Pueblos of Oaxaca, Mexico.* Chicago: University of Chicago Press.

DEER

Time period: Prehistoric–Contemporary

Cultural group: Mesoamerica

Deer are encountered throughout the Americas, both physically and in mythology. They range from northern Mexico and the southwestern United States to Central America. White-tailed deer are the most common; mule deer are found mostly in the northern regions of Mesoamerica; and the small brocket deer are found only in the tropical lowlands. Although people have hunted them for centuries, deer are not easily domesticated. The sixteenth-century historian Fray Diego de Landa reported that the Itzá Maya had domesticated deer; but these particular deer probably looked less like cows grazing in a pasture and more like Sami reindeer, roaming free until people rounded them up to count and cull them. The animal's wide-ranging habitat and general resistance to domestication, as well as the age-old traditions of hunting this game for food and clothing, may help explain the plethora and variety of mythological deer. People have had centuries to spin tales around these familiar animals, as they have around dogs. But unlike the highly sociable canine, a deer interacts with humans only from a distance, and so always remains somewhat unknown; and not knowing much can stimulate the creative imagination wonderfully. One of the twenty days in many calendars is named for the deer; and in some calendars, one of the four years bears its name. Beyond that, there seems to be little mythological homogeneity among the many deer stories, although diverse themes may randomly intersect; the subjects range from deer tails and myths of cosmic fatherhood and female sexuality to fables depicting the animals as downright silly.

The Popol Vuh says that deer have short tails because of something that happened back when the Hero Twins still thought they might like farming. Deer and other animals ate up the corn the twins had just planted, but when they tried to catch the deer by grabbing them by their tails, the tails broke off and the beasts leapt free. The present-day Tzeltal and Chol tell a tale in which the first family kept deer, peccaries, and rabbits as pets, all bound together by their tails. One day they left them alone with Grandmother, warning her that if she laughed, they would break loose. She did, and they did, leaving their tails behind them. The Chamula say that during the time of the first father and mother, the father cut off the deer's ears and tail because he was caught eating from the family's cornfield.

Deer are depicted as having been present at the beginning of time. A deer was the father of the sun and the moon; another carried the sun into the sky; and others were used or abused by the solar deity. In one contemporary story from Oaxaca, the sun and moon are described as two very bad children who, feeling ashamed that their deer stepfather is a mere animal, kill him and stuff his hide with wasps. When the twins' stepmother comes along and strikes her stuffed husband with a stick because she mistakenly thinks he is making fun of her, the wasps swarm out and sting her. She comes home very angry with the twins. To avoid punishment, the two terrible children lock her in a small sweathouse used for bathing, and there she dies. In another tale, from the Kekchi, the Lord Sun tries to win the hand of a maiden by impressing her with his hunting prowess. He shoots a deer and carries it past the girl's house. Then he skins and stuffs it, each day thereafter lugging the same dead beast past her. This impresses the girl, who thinks he is a great hunter, but her father is a little more suspicious. He tells the girl to throw some water on Sun's path the next time he parades by. Using the slippery lime water from her corn preparation, she does; Sun slips in it and falls, breaking open the fake deer. Fully exposed and embarrassed, he runs away to escape her laughter.

Sometimes deer are linked with sexual or warring powers. The contemporary Mopan and Kekchi say that the deer trampled on the Moon Goddess when he escaped from a log in which the sun and moon had imprisoned him. In the process, he split the goddess, thereby forming her vagina; hence, today the deer has cleft hooves. In an ancient Nahua story, two hunters, Mimich and Xiuhnel, chased two deer, each with a double head; but by the end of the day, the deer had worn the hunters out, so they stopped for the evening. Then two beautiful women appeared, calling the hunters to come eat and drink. Xiuhnel succumbed to one of the deer-women's enticements; but after making love, she killed him. Frightened, Mimich started a fire and ran through it. The other deer-woman followed, chasing him all night and all morning. At noon, a barrel cactus descended from the sky, and the woman fell into it and was pinned down by its spines. Mimich shot her full of arrows. Then Mimich led the Fire Lords to a goddess named Itzpapalotl. They burned her, and four great flints burst forth: blue, white, yellow, and red. Mimich took the white one because it held Itzpapalotl's spirit, which made him a great warrior (thereafter, he was called Mixcoatl). The pre-Conquest Nahua also sometimes said that the single-headed goddess and warrior-woman Cihuacoatl was named Deer of Colhuacan.

Other narrators also spun two-headed deer stories. A present-day Tzotzil tale explains that weird creatures called Charcoal Crunchers no longer exist because, way back when, a man got rid of his charcoal crunching wife. Every night, his wife's head would leave her body and bounce over to the fireplace to eat hot charcoals; sometimes, she would bounce out of the house and thud around the neighborhood. One night he rubbed salt on her empty neck, so that when she returned, she could not stick her head to her body again. Annoyed, she bounced up on his shoulder and stuck there, which caused him no end of physical and psychological discomfort. A week or so later, he convinced his wife to bounce off temporarily so that he could climb a tree to gather pine nuts for her. But then he refused to come down, and she could not bounce high enough to reach him. "Go die somewhere else!" he told her. Banging around the tree, she accidentally crashed onto the shoulder of a passing deer and stuck there. The startled deer ran off, carrying the last Charcoal Cruncher with it.

Just as the hare once lost a race with the tortoise, the supposedly swift deer sometimes loses races with other proverbial underdogs. In a contemporary Zinacatecan story, Deer is distracted by Mosquito, who keeps buzzing around, telling him what to do, and in the end Deer is worn out by Toad, who just keeps going. In a modern Nahua story, Hummingbird asks Deer to keep an eye on him. Deer follows him wherever he goes, but suddenly Hummingbird disappears. Where has he gone? Deer hears him call. Oops! There's Hummingbird, sitting on his antlers. And so the many stories spin on, explaining why the animal has such a short tail, and weaving together various tales of hunting, sex, war, two-headed beasts, stuffed deer, or just plain silliness.

See also Cihuacoatl; Dogs; Hero Twins; Moon; Sun
Suggested reading:

Codex Chimalpopoca. 1992. As reproduced in *History and Mythology of the Aztecs: The Codex Chimalpopoca.* Trans. John Bierhorst. Tucson: University of Arizona Press.

Sexton, James D. 1992. *Mayan Folktales: Folklore from Lake Atitlán, Guatemala.* New York: Doubleday.

Thompson, John Eric Sydney. 1970b. *Maya History and Religion.* Norman: University of Oklahoma Press.

DEVIL

Time period: Colonial–Contemporary

Cultural group: Mesoamerica

The Devil evolved a multifaceted, distinctively Mesoamerican personality after he migrated to the New World in the sixteenth century. At his early appearances in the friars' stories and plays, he still looked quite European, but the locals quickly claimed him as their own, and today, one often can catch only glimpses of his European ancestry. In the 500 years since the Conquest, the Devil has adopted many personae.

A contemporary Nahua tale tells of his incessant changeability. Late one night while walking home, a good Christian Nahua man found himself being harassed by the Devil. First the Devil appeared to him as an elegant gentleman dressed in a black cape and a great, flat hat; then the gentleman yanked on his hat, and it became a mariachi musician's sombrero, and his teeth grew as big as those of a horse. The musician rolled his hat up, and it became two big horns on his head; then he mounted a great black horse that struck sparks from the ground with its hooves. Finally, after the poor villager passed the church, the Devil reappeared as Pontius Pilate. Unable to take anymore, the man went home, got his machete, and attacked the nasty apparition, slicing him through a good twenty times.

While this shape-shifting, shifty character (see Nahual) rarely appears twice in the same form in all the years of his existence, his home and area of influence have remained pretty much the same. Like his European counterpart, the Mesoamerican Devil usually claims a portion of the Underworld as his domain, deals with the dead, and punishes those who step outside the boundaries of propriety; but unlike the European Devil, his Underworld home remains uniquely Mesoamerican, and he sometimes also offers sinners a route to redemption.

The Devil meant different things to the sixteenth-century Christians and their indigenous converts. For the Spanish, the Devil became a convenient way to explain the presence of evil in a world created by a completely good deity. In this worldview, the New World's pagans had perverted God's plan, having allowed themselves like ignorant children to be led astray by the Devil. Christ now offered them redemption, but only if they would let the friars lead them from their sinful ways. In his earliest appearance in a play in Tlaxcala, the Devil and three demon companions vied for people's souls (the Devil went after

Christ's). Not being too smart, the Devil, who had dressed up as a hermit, failed to hide his horns and his clawed feet and hands.

This early manifestation would have seemed somewhat familiar to the indigenous audience, as it evoked native depictions of both the ancient earth monster with its clawed feet and hands, and the nasty, skull-headed, underworld god of death. Thanks to similar, more explicit comparisons by the Spanish clerics, the Nahuatl word *tlacatecolotl*, which once meant a shaman who drew on the powers of the horned owl, today means "devil." In ancient times, the nocturnal bird of prey was believed to be an agent for the Lords of Death and to bring misfortune. Drawing on this powerful mythic association, the early friars called the great Mexica god Tezcatlipoca *tlacatecolotl*, but they never translated the word properly as Owl-man, instead telling the Mexicans that it meant "devil." And so it came to be.

Creatures of the Mesoamerican night were also creatures of the underworld and caves, and visual representations soon appeared that combined European devils with these indigenous dark, subterranean features. A popular Spanish image of Hell as a great monster from whose open, toothy mouth Christ first pulled Adam and Eve and then others in need of redemption, was painted on the walls of outdoor chapels where the newly converted came to hear priests' lectures. Although the depiction itself was a direct copy of a Spanish prototype, the native understanding of its meaning seems to have been a somewhat less exact replica. A play translated into Nahuatl by a native scholar for a celebration on Corpus Christi showed the Devil in Hell, having been imprisoned there by Christ, who thereby liberated Adam and Eve and others from Satan's servitude. However, the ancient figures whom Christ liberated became, in the indigenous mind, more than simply Adam, David, or Moses of Old Testament times; they were ancient ancestors who offered prophecies from a past era, predicting that their indigenous heirs would receive the same redemption (Burkhart 1996, 125, 244).

Medieval European theological dualism translated into a complex cosmological dualism for indigenous Christians. They quickly came to understand that the Devil stood in opposition to Christ, and that Church authorities did not like the Devil in any size, shape, or form; so the Devil took up residence on the edge of native homes. One found him and the entrances to his subterranean home in the forests far from human habitation, the pre-Conquest location for nocturnal, Underworld beings. But that did not mean that people paid him no attention. In the native world, life-giving creation cannot happen without death-producing destruction. The Devil, as the representative of death, the Underworld, and night, must continue to exist in order to give power to life, the upper world, and daylight. As Fernando Cervantes points out, in the indigenous mind it wasn't an issue of evil versus good; without the Devil, the world would swing out of whack because destruction could no longer balance out creation. Indeed, the world already had become unbalanced, for disease and death were everywhere. If devils were like the old gods, who brought disease when they were neglected or in need, then people should make sacrificial offerings to them in order to right things. Priests caught some people in the Mexican highlands imitating the crucifixion, with a chicken as sacrificial victim (Cervantes 1994, 50). Significantly, this rite occurred at midnight, when the night shifted to day, and when pre-Conquest prayers traditionally were said to Tezcatlipoca and other deities. Cervantes also reported that one indigenous man had tattooed a picture of Christ on one arm and the Devil on the other, to remind him not to worship one when he was worshiping the other (Ibid., 49–50). With the introduction of Christian deities, the Devil had been transformed into the nocturnal, Underworld counterpart of the solar-based, diurnal Christ.

The Devil thus came to be explicitly equated with various Underworld gods. In seventeenth-century Oaxaca, no less than five deities took on the Devil's characteristics: a god of death, and two apparently distinctive male and female deity pairs of disease and misfortune. In the midnight sacrifices mentioned above, part of the offerings were given to the Devil in the form of either the old Fire God or the God of Thunder (who could bring corn), and another part to the Church. In other cases, St. James was invoked as both the Devil and the God of Thunder. A whole host of native rain and water deities dwelt inside the mountains. If the Devil was the master of this subterranean realm, then he must be the one who controlled water in its many forms. Even today, some say that when lightning strikes a house it is because the Devil wants to kill the people inside.

Many of these themes find echoes in contemporary mythology. The Devil today is very human, although his powers certainly exceed those of normal people. He still lives in the underworld and plays the counterpart of Christ; causes disease and death by disrupting the status quo; and enslaves the dead, especially those who have sinned in some way (which includes just about everybody). As with the European Devil, people sometimes turn the tables by tricking him, and some even get away with it. In numerous and significant ways, however, this rich, rather wonderful trickster has grown closer to the ancient gods than to his European ancestor; for even when one might recognize a European mythic genre, the details quickly mark these stories as distinctively Mesoamerican.

The Nahua of Amatlán say that Tlacatecolotl (or an owl-man devil) is the elder brother of Toteotsij, who is God, the Sun, and Jesus all rolled into one; therefore, darkness has the upper hand. But among the Sierra Nahua, the story is a little different. The Devil got annoyed with God at this world's creation because he made crickets that chattered all night. In the process of arguing with God, he made and lost a bet that limited his rule; henceforth, when the rooster crowed at dawn, the Devil had to return to his underworld home. During labor in Tecospan, God and the Devil duke it out in the birthing room's hearth fire. If God wins the battle, the baby's *tonalli,* or shadow-soul, will be strong and win a place in Heaven; if not, it will weigh heavily, fail in earthly endeavors, and go to Hell. Disease often is attributed to the Devil or devils. When bidden, the Maya Ah Yacax will send worms and flies into people's noses. In Amatlán, a number of disease-causing devils exist. Besides Owl-man and his wife, there is also his partner who commands the spirits in the Land of the Dead; another, the brother of Death, flies like a butterfly and can attack and kill whomever he meets. Before a healer can accomplish a cure, he must use these beings to balance out the disequilibrium. Often disease-bearing devils arrive as ill winds. The Nahua of Amatlán, the Chortí and Yucatec Maya, and people of Mitla in Oaxaca all say that the Devil hides himself in whirlwinds, which make people sick.

The Cakchiquel Maya of Panajachel in the 1930s said that everything was reversed inside the Underworld home of the Devil, which they called the Hill; for example, if one drinks a lot here, one will drink nothing there. One went to the Hill either to be cleansed in its fires or, more commonly, to work hard at paying off one's debt before being admitted to Heaven. Only saints like Francis, who didn't mind poverty, could avoid involvement with the Devil; so pretty much everyone landed in the Hill at least for a time. Merchants had to work an especially long time because their debts were huge; and Ladinos never got out because they worshiped the Devil. These people did not sin in the usual small ways, for both groups clearly did not work in life but came by their wealth through their allegiance to the Dark Chief's tempting powers. When the Devil found himself short on labor, he asked God for more workers, and then there was lots of sickness. Like the pre-Conquest rain god's land of Tlalocan, the Hill had its own inner landscape, with beautiful rivers, streams, trees, plants, and birds. One entered this place through certain caves, rocks, and trees; one could even hear its dogs barking, cocks crowing, and church bells ringing if one of these windows opened up. The forest was a dangerous place, so if one heard such sounds, one had to get out fast. The Devil, that paradigmatic rich landowner, was always looking for more workers to enslave.

Various animals are associated with the Devil. The Cakchiquel said that the bat sucked blood in order to cook the Devil delicious dishes, and the mosquito gathered the Devil's wine. Throughout Mesoamerica, the Devil might appear as a jaguar, caiman, or snake that kills and eats livestock; or he might send his coyote to reward a brave hunter who managed to survive a wild bull ride across the Oaxacan landscape. But if one accepts such rewards, one is in trouble, for one will surely find oneself paying for them later with one's own backbreaking labor.

Stories abound of the Devil's attempts to trick people into his employ. He may entice a stubborn and arrogant Maya girl into marriage by sporting the two gold teeth she wanted to find in her future husband's mouth. Or the poor might be tempted by his other riches. He sometimes helps people by having them cure a king's illness that he himself has induced. The healer's fortune is made when he succeeds where doctors have failed. But if he breaks the contract, or when he dies, he will have to serve the Devil. Teofila from Oaxaca once called to the Devil, out of desperation, to help her out of her poverty. To her surprise, that night he turned up, suave, handsome, and riding a beautiful honey-colored horse. He apologized for being late and offered her a bag of money, which she wisely refused. But he said, "Are not your brother and friend coming to visit? Here is a chicken to feed them when they come." Teofila had not been expecting any guests, but they did indeed arrived; and the Devil—visible only to Teofila— slipped into the house with them to join in on the fun. This happened night after night, for the Devil had fallen in love with her. Still, she would not accept his money. He even built himself a ramshackle house in her front yard and camped out there. Slowly she weakened and became sick; finally, she confessed to the priest. He blessed her house with holy water and raised a cross in her door. The Devil then left, his shack disappeared, and Teofila lived to a ripe old age, with her children supporting her.

The Devil often appears as a rich, handsome landowner who rides a beautiful horse, and the outcome can be quite pleasant. In another Oaxacan story, one evening he came riding up on a great white horse to a tired ranch foreman snoozing peacefully on his front porch.

"Aren't you going to the fiesta in town?" he asked.

The startled foreman explained that he was not because he had worked his mule all day and she was too tired to travel the 35 leagues to town. Moreover, he would never be able to make that distance and return in time to work again the next morning.

"But it will be great fun! Come with me, my horse is very fast and we can get there in plenty of time to drink a few rounds with your friends and still return for work tomorrow morning. Anyway, it's no problem, because I too have work tomorrow. Look, I'm your friend, and here are ten pesos to prove it."

The man, after vacillating a bit, took the money and finally said yes. He thought of the fun drinking with his buddies, and he was just a little curious about this strange, obviously well-off gentleman. So off they went. In a twinkling they had covered the 35 leagues, even with a short stop to pick up some mescal. They boozed all night with the foreman's friends, and with the first streaks of dawn's light, the strange man said it was time to return. So they mounted his horse and absolutely flew back. The gentleman graciously took his leave and disappeared on his marvelous steed. Just then the foreman woke up on his own front porch, exactly where he had been the night before. Had this really happened, or was it just a dream? He reached into his shirt pocket, and there were the ten pesos! The foreman and his boss were great friends, so he told him what had happened. Both of them agreed it would be great fun if that strange man on the white horse returned, but he never did.

Sometimes a person tricks the Devil and wins. The Maya woman who wanted to marry a man with gold teeth quickly found out that she had made a big mistake. Her new husband refused to work, and kept popping into little containers like glasses of water or kettles and disappearing instead. Upon the advice of a shaman, she convinced him to pop into a gourd jar, and then slapped a lid on it, trapping him. She tossed the jar in the rubbish heap, where he sat for several days, stuck. Finally, a drunk came along and let him out, having been promised a reward. The Devil helped him become a healer by curing (you guessed it) a sick king. The story ends with the comment that some think shamans can cure better than doctors, but they're mostly drunks who are in cahoots with the Devil.

Occasionally, the stories are simply silly. In Amatlán, the crazy, sometime-saint Pedro was always getting into trouble. In his saint aspect, Pedro could revive the dead; but when his stupid shepherd assistant (acting against orders) tried to do it on his own, the Devil locked him up in a suitcase. In one story, as a mere mortal, Pedro secretly tied the tails of a bunch of devils together and then shouted "Holy Mother Mary!" They all leaped up at once, falling over each other in a great jumble. Wishing to meet his saintly namesake, Pedro went to heaven; but they didn't want him there. They slammed the door shut; having just stuck his head in, he was decapitated. His head stayed in heaven, while his body went back to the devils. Once upon a time, the Devil peed in the pulque at a dance, getting people really drunk and raucous. A young, awesome violinist whipped the dancers into a frenzy; then losing all restraint, he kidnapped a young girl. The next morning, his new wife asked him to play the violin again, but he said he couldn't because he had no instrument. So she got out her father's violin, but he still couldn't play. The devil's pee had bewitched him!

The Mesoamerican Devil often seems to express aspects of human life that are out of control, for he brings hard labor, disease, and death. He also preys on people's natural limitations by tempting and tricking them. But at the same time, the Devil occasionally offers a second chance, perhaps even a route to redemption. Admit your faults, pay your debts to him, and you too can go to Heaven. After all, if only saints could attain perfection, then only saints would be redeemed; and that was never how *el Pueblo* understood the Christian message, even back in the sixteenth century. It might be said that in this case, the Popular Church took the old theology offering them rewards after death and subtly turned it to their own advantage. The Devil belonged to them, not the priests;

and if rewards could not be enjoyed in this life (or even immediately in the next), at least imperfection could be savored now, with a chance at redemption later!

See also Bats; Christ; Rain and Water Deities; Saints; Tezcatlipoca; Underworld and Caves, Deities of the

Suggested reading:

Burkhart, Louise M. 1996. *Holy Wednesday: A Nahua Drama from Early Colonial Mexico*. Philadelphia: University of Pennsylvania Press.

Cervantes, Fernando. 1994. *The Devil in the New World: The Impact of Diabolism in New Spain*. New Haven, CT: Yale University Press.

Sandstrom, Alan. 1991. *Corn Is Our Blood: Culture and Ethnicity in a Contemporary Aztec Indian Village*. Norman: University of Oklahoma Press.

Wisdom, Charles. 1940. *The Chorti Indians of Guatemala*. Chicago: University of Chicago Press.

DOGS

Time period: Paleo-Indian–Contemporary

Cultural group: Mesoamerica

Long ago, a Paleo-Indian living at Tequixquiac in Mexico shaped a cameloid bone into a doglike creature. We don't know for sure whether the object depicts a mythological beast or a familiar animal; unfortunately, its material remains cannot tell the stories that may have been spun around it. Nevertheless, we know that dogs were one of Mesoamerica's first domesticated animals and that they have provided fodder for mythological tale-spinning for many centuries.

Like cows and sheep in Europe, dogs in Mesoamerica were considered useful farm beasts, not family pets. Many of these dogs were of hairless species, and they were often used in the hunt. The colonial Yucatec Maya even bred a barkless hunting dog. Dogs themselves also served as food: Before the Spanish Conquest, male dogs frequently were castrated and force-fed in preparation for one feast or another. Dogs also could become sacrificial offerings, especially in funerals. These various uses may explain why people often still differentiate between cosmologically important dogs and those considered common yard beasts, sometimes even giving them different names. In ancient Nahuatl, for example, the calendrical and ritual dog was always referred to as *Itzcuintli*, whereas other dogs were *Chichimeh*. The calendar also indicates dogs' great mythological age, for the tenth day of many ancient and current twenty-day counts is called "dog." Mesoamerican dogs participate in three broad mythological streams: the first, concerning the creation of people; the second, food—particularly, the discovery of maize (in which dogs sometimes overlap with coyotes, foxes, or opossums); and the third, the underworld, death, the evening star and Quetzalcoatl. Occasionally, dogs also are the butt of jokes.

Dogs date to the first periods of mythic creation. The Popol Vuh describes how dogs and turkeys killed the people of the second age because the people always beat them; those folk who escaped turned into monkeys. The Tzotzil and Tzeltal say that in the Third Creation, a white dog mated with Eve to produce Ladinos, whereas a yellow dog sired Indians. Dogs also often appear as trickster figures. When the pre-Conquest Nahua Fourth Sun disappeared in a great deluge, a man and woman called Tata and Nene

Figure 52. A dog figurine (Kay A. Read/Museo de Antropología e Historia, Puebla, Mexico)

survived inside a great cypress log. When the log stopped rocking in the water, they climbed out on a beach, caught some fish and built a fire to roast them. The fire smoked the sky, upsetting the stars Citlallatonac and Citlalicue; this, in turn angered Tezcatlipoca. He bawled the two out for making such a mess, then chopped off their heads and sewed the heads onto their rumps, thereby turning them into dogs. This is how the first cooking fire came to be. During the Fifth Sun's creation, Death hunted the Nahua dog-god Xolotl. Xolotl first eluded Death by turning into a small green maize sprout, hiding in a field; when Death found him there, he ran away and turned into the parrot-like leaves of a young maguey plant; when found again, he hid as a salamander in a pool. But there Death cornered and killed him. Thus, three important native foods were born from a dog's shape-shifting body (see Nahual).

A number of stories exist today in which a coyote or fox discovers corn; after all, dogs and their relatives are great scavengers. The Cakchiquels believe maize first grew from the entrails of a dead coyote. The K'iche' say the coyote was one of four animals to discover corn; the Mopan, Kekchi, and Pokomchi say that a fox made the discovery, although some think this fox was really an opossum. Like Xolotl's twin Quetzalcoatl, this fox met some ants carrying corn seeds back to their nests. After eating some of these seeds, Fox returned to the other animals. When he broke wind, the other animals smelled a difference, and they accused him of having found a new food, which he denied. So they followed him back into the forest, where they discovered Mesoamerica's most important form of sustenance.

Dogs roam the underworld in a number of guises. Perhaps the best known is Xolotl, who as a manifestation of Venus, teams up with the sun by following its path closely. Among the pre-Conquest Nahua, Quetzalcoatl played the role of Venus in its Morning Star phase, moving with the rising sun; his twin Xolotl played the role of Venus as the Evening Star, moving with the setting sun. A graphic depiction in the *Codex Telleriano Remensis* shows Xolotl opposite a figure called Tlachitonatiuh. In this cosmic image, the earth monster (see Earth, Agricultural, and Hunting Deities), fanged mouth gaping wide, swallows the sun. Sun, after being eaten, will travel through Earth's body at night before emerging at dawn, and Xolotl will travel with him until Quetzalcoatl takes over. A contemporary Totonac story tells how Moon, who thought he was the lover of all women and master of all, was led on a wild goose chase through the underworld by a little dog. This gave Sun enough time to escape and emerge first from the underground. Now, Moon must follow Sun. The Popol Vuh tells how the Hero Twins sacrificed a dog and then brought it back to life in order to impress 1-Death and 7-Death, the lords of the underworld. The dog was so grateful to live again that he wagged his tail.

When they die, people often go to the underworld accompanied by a dog. As early as the Preclassic, the Chupicaro buried dogs with the dead. Dogs also went with the Classic Maya to the underworld, for they appear both in tombs and in underworld scenes painted on pottery. The Maya believed the dead needed a dog to cross a body of water. Likewise, the Postclassic Nahua believed that a yellow dog waited by a body of water to carry a dead person across, after which the deceased completely disappeared. Only yellow dogs could do this; white dogs said they couldn't because they had just washed themselves, and black ones said no because they had just finished carrying themselves over. In the funeral ritual, a yellow dog was killed and cremated before the cremation of the deceased. Today, the Huitzilan say a dog takes a dead man across the water to reach the Devil's underground home; the Tarascan dog-god Uitzimengari saves the drowned by taking them to the Land of the Dead; and the Mixquic offer pictures and effigies of dogs to their deceased.

Dogs also can become the butt of jokes; after all, like Tata and Nene, one might say they were created to think with their behinds. One contemporary Nahua farce tells the tale of a grandmother and her dog-like grandson. Grandmother happens to come by a gourd full of fermented agave juice. Because she wants it all for herself, she tells the dog it is poisonous. She then goes out for a while. While she is gone, her grandson drinks the juice; becoming drunk, he thinks he's dying. Upon Grandmother's return, he tells her that thousands of dogs came and drank it, so he had to try it too. Angry, she beats him with a stick as she would a dog. Nevertheless, not all dogs or dog-like people are depicted as fools: Without dogs, people and maize might not exist, hunting might be less successful and meals more boring, the sun might not rise properly, the dead might lose their way, and some good jokes might never be told.

See also Devil; Earth, Agricultural, and Hunting Deities; Fifth Sun; Hero Twins; Nahual; 1-Death and 7-Death; Quetzalcoatl; Sky Deities and Beings; Sun; Tezcatlipoca; Underworld and Caves, Deities of the

Suggested reading:

Bricker, Victoria Reifler. 1973. *Ritual Humor in Highland Chiapas.* Austin: University of Texas Press.

Quiñones Keber, Eloise. 1995. *Codex Telleriano Remensis: Ritual, Divination, and History in a Pictorial Aztec Manuscript.* Austin: University of Texas Press.

Sahagún, Fray Bernardino de. 1953–1982. *The Florentine Codex: A General History of the Things of New Spain.* Trans. Arthur J. O. Anderson and Charles E. Dibble. Monographs of the School of American Research, no. 14. Santa Fe: School of American Research; Salt Lake City: University of Utah Press.

EARTH, AGRICULTURAL, AND HUNTING DEITIES

Time period: Preclassic–Contemporary

Cultural group: Mesoamerica

Earth's Surface, sandwiched between the skies above and the underworld below, is the space in which people live and eat, in which they grow crops and hunt animals. Like the Underworld, the Earth's Surface in much Mesoamerican mythology is divided horizontally into four parts aligned with the cardinal directions, but the precise point at which the Earth's Surface ends and the underworld begins is difficult to ascertain. This may be because the Earth's Surface generally forms either the roof of the Underworld or the skin of the Earth Monster that contains the subterranean realm. Moreover, many of the same deities who govern sustenance—rain, the crops, domestic animals, and game—move freely between Earth's Surface and the Underworld, blurring the distinctions even further. Sometimes Earth appears as a being in its own right, a forceful creature who requires care and demands respect. At other times, Earth's Surface is a landscape in which people, various animals, and other beings dwell along with powerful agricultural and hunting deities.

The mythology of Earth extends at least as far back as the Preclassic Olmec, and probably farther, although direct evidence from the earlier period is lacking. Among the Olmec, Earth was pictured as a great dragon floating on the sea, whose body sustained and nourished a vast array of plants. The Olmec also claimed a maize god with a cleft head from which corn sprouted—possibly an artful depiction of a mythological mountain in which the Olmec believed maize originated. The Classic Maya divided Earth into four quarters, one each for the four cardinal directions. Each quarter housed a great tree atop which perched a bird, and a fifth tree stood in the center. They also depicted the maize god Yum Kaax as dead and surrounded by ears of corn. This symbolic link between corn and death echoes the common bond between creation and destruction in Mesoamerican mythology. By

Figure 53. An ancient Hill of Seeds perhaps portrayed as the goddess Xochiquetzal from a mural at Teotihuacan (Kay A. Read/Museo Nacional de Antropología)

the Postclassic era, Yum Kaax had been joined by many other agricultural tales linking life with death, and creation with destruction.

The Postclassic Mixtecs continued to divide the earth into four portions: the east was that of light and the rising sun; the north, the place of the dead; the west, the dwelling of women and the setting sun; and the south, the place of thorns. In each, a pair of deities flanked the quarter's tree and bird (see Figure 4). The Nahua of this period told a story reminiscent of the Olmec dragon and the themes of life and death imaged by Yum Kaax: Seeing the great female creature called "Water-Earth Deity" (Atlalteutli) floating on the sea, Tezcatlipoca and Quetzalcoatl transformed themselves into snakes. One grabbed her right foot and left arm, and the other grabbed her left foot and right arm; and together they pulled on her until she was torn in two. One half produced the sky, and the other, the Earth. From her hair and hide came the trees, flowers, and plants. From her eyes and nostrils came springs and caves, and from her mouth came the valleys and mountains. But she cried out from this simultaneously destructive and creative act, and would not be quieted until fed human hearts; and she could not produce fruit unless watered with human blood. So, for people to continue eating the fruits of Earth, they must in turn feed her body with something from their own bodies. This respect was marked by ritual sacrifices that fed the earth with human hearts, rulers who ceremonially let their own blood to water it, and people who offered a sign of respect by taking a pinch of earth to eat before speaking to a great ruler or lord. When praying for a newborn child, the midwife called upon this great beast with the phrase "Our Mother, Our Father; Tonatiuh [Sun], Tlaltecutli [Earth-Lord]"—an apparent example of the sexual dualism so common to Mesoamerican mythology.

The Nahua also told a tale of the Mountain of Seeds, which was reminiscent of the Olmec maize-mountain god. Quetzalcoatl was the first to discover this mountain, by following a red ant into its depths, but he was not strong enough to crack it open. It took a god named Nanahuatl, who was probably lightning, to break it apart. As soon as he did this, the Tlalocs (fierce lightning and rain deities) snatched out all the food: the corn of the four directions, white, black, yellow, and red; beans; chia; and amaranth. And so, while food-filled mountains existed on earth's surface, it was the rain gods dwelling inside the mountains who governed all sustenance. Cinteotl was the Nahua maize god, comparable to Yum Kaax. A number of female deities governed corn in all its developmental phases: Cihuacoatl governed the raised fields and wetlands in the Valley of Mexico in particular; the goddess Toci was called the heart of the Earth; and the god Camaxtli served as patron of the hunt. By the seventeenth century, Oaxacans were honoring a god of lightning and rain, as well as a solar deity whose benefits were avidly sought by hunters; they also offered sacrifices of birds to a maize god and a wealthy Guardian of Grain.

Figure 54. Agricultural deity (Kay A. Read/Museo del Templo Mayor, Mexico City)

Many of these earthly themes of sustenance have survived until recent times, albeit sometimes in altered form. The Cakchiquel Maya of Panajachel in the 1930s said that when God first made the world, everything was flat, and it was too easy to travel from place to place. Afraid that people might forget him, he thought it would be better if they had it a bit harder. So God made mountains, hills, ravines, and volcanoes to make sure people would remember to pray to him. Now when people are facing a steep climb or a gorge that must be crossed, they say: "May God will that we arrive safely!"

As a deity, Earth's need for respect is clear. In Panajachel, they said that Mother Earth was like God himself, for she used her eyes and ears to judge the world. Before one did anything (bad or good), one needed to ask permission of both God and Earth by praying to them from either the patio or the crossroads. To do so, however, was a very serious act, because Earth was severe and unforgiving, and never had to be asked twice. Bad people did not last long because Earth would open up and simply swallow them. It was said that one day, a bad person from Santa Apolonia was riding his horse when, all of a sudden, a great hole opened up before him. He fell into it, and it closed over him, leaving only his hat and his horse's ears showing above ground. The tale's teller went on to say that these could be seen today because they had turned to stone. For this reason, people used to show Earth great respect. They prayed first to God to dispel any evil before they began to work the land, and then kissed a pinch of dirt before striking the Earth with any tool. She was very touchy then, and would cry out in pain when anyone hit her if not given respect first; they also risked her retaliation if they mistreated her. The Cakchiquel said that because people are made of earth, Earth knows the needs of the body; so a pinch of dirt can heal a wound caused by any earth-working tool. The Nahua of today's Amatlán, when talking about the Hill of Postejtli, whence comes all sustenance, say that Earth must be respected and that people tire her out by walking on her, but many people don't care, and make no offerings on the Hill, and even pee on it; but if one paid more respect, rain would come and the crops would do well.

These ideas of respect and judgment extend to stories about grain as well as other plants and animals of sustenance, and some even include the implements people use to prepare food. The Popol Vuh tells of the Third Age's wooden people, who had no heart or memory. They did not offer proper respect to the gods' creations. Because of this incompetence, a great resin from the sky rained upon them, and nasty beings snapped off their heads and ate their flesh. Everything complained to them: their cooking pots, griddles, grinding stones, and water jars. "Everyday you rub and rip our faces. Pain, that is all we get!" they shouted. Their dogs and turkeys asked: "Why can't you give us food? All you do is beat us for our troubles!" So they too attacked the people and smashed their faces in, scattering them. Today, this is why monkeys exist as a sign for humans; they look like people, but are made of nothing but wood and have no hearts.

Similarly, contemporary Tzutuhil Maya say that once upon a time complaints issued from many of the produce gods. Numerous people didn't pay proper respect to God for his creations, so a judgment was passed, and God threatened to end the world. But first God interviewed all the produce to learn exactly how people treated them. Corn and Beans griped bitterly, saying that their lives were full of torment. "Day and night people burn us in the fires and grind us to make corn tortillas and bean burritos, and then they chew us up and turn us into poop! Please make justice on them!" The grinding stones and griddles agreed that they too suffered from having their faces burned all the time. But then Tomatoes and Chilies told God that not all people were bad; and Squashes and Pumpkins said that, indeed, good people existed, Corn and Beans were just jealous because they received less respect. Sweet Potato agreed. The bad, disrespectful people became frightened and ran into caves to hide—whereupon God turned them into burrowing rodents and coyotes. These animals now are enemies of all who obediently till the earth.

Contemporary Nahua still tell tales about a Hill of Seeds, which sometimes contains domestic animals as well. In Amatlán, a variety of stories are told about a hill called Postejtli. In one story, the Virgin Tonantsi, or Our Honorable Mother, called the Gods of Thunder to destroy the Hill because ants kept cutting its flowers. The Hill's destruction resulted in seeds, but nobody could get them to grow. So St. John raised clouds from the sea, which watered them, causing the birth of black and yellow maize. In a second story, they say that God became annoyed because lawless men went up to the Hill to see what bad things they could do, so God decided that the Hill needed to be knocked down. He

Figure 55. A Mazahua child making tortillas (Kay A. Read)

called Woodpecker to do it, but the Hill proved too tough for Woodpecker's pecking. Then he called in old San Juan, who in spite of his age split the Hill into seven pieces with a single rumble of thunder and a bolt of lightning. The pieces burned by lightning became black maize, and those that had been white became yellow maize. This is what God had prayed for. Yet another story tells of two children who had killed their grandmother because she wouldn't let them marry each other, and who had hidden inside the Hill. Those who went looking for them knocked the Hill down, but they found that the lightning gods had burned them and they were no longer children. Now they were Seven and Five Flower, from which all of the crops sprang: black and yellow maize, beans, squash, and melons—every food that grew in the region.

Among the Chortí, the Earth God Ihp'en personifies earth, soil, plant growth, riches, and property in general. Ihp'en, both male and female, joins San Manuel with the Virgin. Ritually buried in the fields, s/he guards a family's possessions, and the union of these two brings about the birth or sprouting of their children, all cultivated plants. Maize is male, and the consort of beans. Because the male and female gods produce these comestible male and female offspring, people eat the male maize and the female beans together. Among the Mopan, Huitz-Hok, the mountain-valley god, along with Morning Star and Moon, receives prayers and offerings for good crops. In parts of highland Mexico, Malinche protects both animals and produce. But in Chan Kom in the 1930s, the Yucatec Maya said that the Balams guarded both the fields and the villages. Sometimes they had no definite form; other times they appeared as little old men wearing sombreros, sandals, and local dress. Balams behaved themselves when people offered them proper gifts and prayers; they could turn nasty if people didn't, bringing sickness to both the field and its owner. If jilted, they might even live off children's souls. If the Balams cried out during the night, then someone was going to die.

In addition to crops, Earth's Surface supports trees and shelters the animals that people hunt. Before felling a tree, a Colonial Mexica logger would respectfully ask a tree not to "eat" him. Similarly, the Yucatec Maya of Chan Kom requested permission to cut trees, and made offerings to the Kuiob Kaaxob, forest deities. Hunters of seventeenth-century Oaxaca petitioned two deities: one, the solar deity Licuicha, and another named Lexee, who protected them and sent them dreams. Today, the Itzá Maya tell a story about a hunter who went out shooting deer every day. One day he shot a very large deer, but only wounded him; the deer turned and ran off into the forest. The hunter followed his trail of blood into a great, door-like cave at the base of a hill. Inside he found a big ranch, and the wounded deer standing with a number of other deer. Among them stood an old man who was giving the animals food. The man looked at him and said:

"You are the one who shoots my animals. Now you see how you have hurt and wounded them. I have had to cure them all. Next time you shoot a deer, shoot it well, don't shoot it badly! Otherwise, you will have to come back here, and I will be waiting. All right, I will take you home now, but don't tell anyone anything about this!"

The old man told him to shut his eyes, and in an instant, the hunter found himself back outside at the base of the hill; the cave-door had disappeared. When the hunter arrived back home, his wife and children broke into joyful tears. Although he was positive he had been gone only a few hours, they told him he had been gone for three months, and they were sure he was dead!

And thus life is sustained on earth's surface, often with the help of those living below, who nourish the corn with water and the things of death, or who guard the living grain, plants, and animals so necessary to life above. If one is not careful to show the proper respect for the forces that help life continue, then one may find oneself in deep trouble, perhaps even face Death itself. After all, the living eat things that feed off the goods of the underworld; it is only fair that they should feed those subterranean forces in return, and carefully honor that relatively small terrestrial portion visible to human eyes—Earth's surface.

See also Chalchiuhtlicue; Cihuacoatl; Deer; La Llorona; Moon; Quetzalcoatl; Rain and Water Deities; Saints; Sky Deities and Beings; Sun; Tezcatlipoca; Underworld and Caves, Deities of the; Yum Kaax

Suggested reading:

Codex Chimalpopoca. 1992. As reproduced in *History and Mythology of the Aztecs: The Codex Chimalpopoca.* Trans. John Bierhorst. Tucson: University of Arizona Press.

Joralemon, Peter David. 1996. "In Search of the Olmec Cosmos: Reconstructing the World View of Mexico's First Civilization." Pp. 51–59 in Elizabeth P. Benson and Beatriz de la Fuente, eds., *Olmec Art of Ancient Mexico.* Washington, DC: National Gallery of Art.

Sexton, James D. 1992. *Mayan Folktales: Folklore from Lake Atitlán, Guatemala.* New York: Doubleday.

Tedlock, Dennis, trans. 1985. *Popol Vuh: The Definitive Edition of the Mayan Book of the Dawn of Life and the Glories of Gods and Kings.* New York: Simon and Schuster.

Read, Kay A. 1998. *Time and Sacrifice in the Aztec Cosmos.* Bloomington: Indiana University Press.

Wisdom, Charles. 1940. *The Chorti Indians of Guatemala.* Chicago: University of Chicago Press.

FEATHERED SERPENTS

Time period: Preclassic–Contemporary

Cultural group: Mesoamerica

Feathered serpents—powerful beings, combining features of the quetzal bird with those of the rattlesnake—claim a lengthy history stretching back into the Preclassic era. These zoomorphic characters often both help create the cosmos and associate closely with humans, thereby joining cosmic elements with human events. Feathered serpents appear only rarely until the Classic era, when a few begin to grace some of Teotihuacan's walls. They become a stronger theme in the Postclassic era, when they appear in an area stretching from the Mexican highlands to the Yucatán and Guatemala. Their most famous representative, the Nahua Quetzalcoatl, claims the greatest ascendancy, having been linked mythologically during the Conquest with the Spanish and with Christianity. Eventually, however, that mythology was reversed, and Quetzalcoatl now represents Mexican nationalism and its noble indigenous heritage.

Among the Preclassic Olmec, the feathered serpent appears in his most basic form, as a rattlesnake wearing feathers or a winged element on the back of his head. Overshadowed by many jaguar images, the Olmec feathered serpent's infrequent appearances suggest that he was not the most central deity. The occasional snake appearing paired with a jaguar may foreshadow the Postclassic partnership of Quetzalcoatl and Tezcatlipoca's jaguar aspect; and as did Postclassic feathered serpents, Olmec versions usually appear with humans, but this does not mean the Preclassic feathered serpent is identical to his Postclassic relative. On Monument no. 19 from La Venta, a rattlesnake wearing a feather headdress gracefully encircles a priest holding a ceremonial bag and wearing the snake's mask, its jaws framing his head. In small sculptures from Guerrero and Guatemala, coiled bird-snakes also appear framing human faces with their jaws. In still other depictions, feathered serpents and jaguars devour humans. Scholars can only make educated guesses as to what these various images mean. Priests likely dealt with ceremonies involving feathered snakes; and given the feathered serpent's later Postclassic association with ritual practices and its reputed shape-shifting capacities, perhaps the feathered serpent served some Olmec priests as their nahual. But the word for "serpent" in Maya languages also means "sky," so this figure also may have been a celestial deity.

The feathered serpent does not really become a featured figure until the Classic era, when he appears on a few of Teotihuacan's buildings. His most famous portrayal is on the walls of the Feathered Serpent Temple in the Ciudadela (see Figure 15). There his body flows through the water with shells and marine animals; his own head alternates with another imposing portrayal of an unidentified figure. This second head could represent a number of things: the rain god Tlaloc, although he bears few of Tlaloc's distinctive features; a war headdress, although it bears only a few resemblances to other headdresses; a fire-snake representing war; or a crocodile, perhaps like the Nahua Cipactli, from whom Quetzalcoatl and Tezcatlipoca formed the earth. Thus some feel that the two figures together may represent the wet and dry seasons; for in later times, Quetzalcoatl, in his wind form, was closely associated with rain and water gods, and the dry season was considered the season of war. Others suggest that the whole temple refers back to the beginning of time, when the earth was formed. What is more clear is that the temple probably was situated in a residential complex for Teotihuacan's rulers and other elite. Their deceased may have been buried in the temple, although no clear evidence of nobles' tombs has yet surfaced. A massive burial of war captives and other burials of women and children have been found inside the temple, but the only indication of a possible royal burial is an interment that was long ago thoroughly stripped by looters.

At other sites that originated at the end of the Classic and beginning of the Postclassic eras, the feathered serpent usually is displayed with important people. At the Mexican highland site of Xochicalco, a Teotihuacan-like feathered serpent snakes beneath seated rulers who appear to be Maya; likewise, he usually is depicted with elite individuals at Cacaxtla and at Chichén Itzá. Nahua tales of Quetzalcoatl suggest that his name had become a title for rulership; perhaps these sites testify to his association with elites. Quetzalcoatl also has a creator aspect, which may link rulers with cosmic responsibilities such as making sure rains arrive on schedule. A Preclassic Olmec frieze from Chalcatzingo, Morelos, shows an elite person, probably a ruler, seated inside the cave-like mouth of the earth monster. Mist and clouds come from this mouth, and rain falls on crops below. Postclassic Mexica rulers also held responsibilities for maintaining crops, assuring a good climate, and playing priestly roles in rain ceremonies; moreover, drought indicated a ruler's personal failure. Just as he did in the Preclassic, the feathered serpent in the Postclassic era joined cosmic and human events; thus, it seems likely that as a deity of both sky and waters, he was believed to endow human rulers with his special powers.

The feathered serpent comes into his own in the Postclassic era, when depictions bearing both Toltec and Maya traits appear at various sites, from the Mexican highlands to the Yucatán and Guatemala. He also emerges in stories collected just after the Conquest from those areas. By then, it's obvious he has become a complex figure with both a creative-cosmic side and a rulership association. As Gukumatz in the Popol Vuh, he cooperates with the deity Jurakan to create the first K'iché world; later, he enjoys a priestly keeper, who watches out for his ceremonial needs. Quetzalcoatl creates the Nahua world with Tezcatlipoca, helps shape the first humans, discovers corn, forms the prosperous Toltec civilization, and lends his name to its line of rulers. Fray Diego de Landa wrote that Quetzalcoatl, as Kukulcan, came from the West and founded Mayapan, a new city near Chichén Itzá in the Yucatán. He wrote that after Kukulcan returned to Mexico, he built himself a memorial on the sea at Champotón. At one time, scholars created their own tale by linking Landa's with one about Quetzalcoatl's departure from Tula in the Mexican highlands; in that story, he left because of sexual transgressions. Scholars suggested that a real person named Quetzalcoatl journeyed from Tula to the Yucatán. More recently, new archaeological evidence has cast doubt on this assumption.

With the Conquest, Quetzalcoatl enjoyed an extraordinary popularity. At first, Cortés became the returning Quetzalcoatl ready to vanquish Tezcatlipoca's Mexica, although this myth did not live for long. In the centuries that followed, however, many mythic permutations occurred in literary traditions. Quetzalcoatl became Saint Thomas evangelizing the New World; the Mexican national representative of a noble indigenous heritage; and finally, the triumph of that heritage over an imposed European culture. But by the twentieth century, the feathered serpent largely vanishes from folk traditions. Now Gukumatz appears only rarely among the K'iche', and the Lacandon say he is the large, malevolent pet snake of their principle sun deity. In a number of places, San Sebastian appears to have taken over his wind shrines; among the Nahua, various wind gods still move storm clouds as did Quetzalcoatl; and some Maya tales now attribute Quetzalcoatl's past sexual transgressions to Saint Thomas. Even where the folk feathered serpent does not survive in name, his actions are remembered.

See also Cortés, Fernando; Gukumatz; Jurakan; Kukulcan; Nahual; Quetzalcoatl; Rain and Water Deities; Saints; Sky Deities and Beings; Tezcatlipoca; Tlaloc and the Tlaloques

Suggested reading:

Codex Chimalpopoca. 1992. As reproduced in *History and Mythology of the Aztecs: The Codex Chimalpopoca.* Trans. John Bierhorst. Tucson: University of Arizona Press.

Joralemon, Peter David. 1996. "In Search of the Olmec Cosmos: Reconstructing the World View of Mexico's First Civilization." Pp. 51–59 in *Olmec Art of*

Figure 56. Jaguar from a wall mural at Teotihuacan (Kay A. Read)

Ancient Mexico, eds. Elizabeth P. Benson and Beatriz de la Fuente. Washington, DC: National Gallery of Art.

Pasztory, Esther. 1997. *Teotihuacan: An Experiment in Living*. Norman: University of Oklahoma Press.

Tedlock, Dennis, trans. 1985. *Popol Vuh: The Definitive Edition of the Mayan Book of the Dawn of Life and the Glories of Gods and Kings*. New York: Simon and Schuster.

FIFTH SUN

Time period: Postclassic

Cultural group: Nahua-Mexica

The Mexica lived in the Fifth Sun, the Nahua age of life and power. When the sun died, their life would also end. Following the demise of the fourth age, the gods created the fifth yearly calendar deity through their sacrificial activities at the great city of Teotihuacan. Two gods were chosen to sacrifice themselves, a very rich but somewhat overly proud god named Tecuiçztecatl, and a poor but very humble god named Nanahuatzin. Both performed preparatory rituals, the first with implements and attire made of gold, precious stones, and fine feathers, the second with objects made only of paper and grass. When finished preparing, they threw their goods down on the ground into great piles, thereby creating the Pyramids of the Moon and the Sun. One can still visit these pyramids just outside of Mexico City today.

Once preparations had been made, the gods called to Tecuiçiztecatl to jump into a great bonfire burning brightly there, but he could not make himself do it. Then the Gods called to Nanahuatzin, who willingly performed his duty by leaping bravely into the conflagration. This inspired Tecuiçiztecatl so much, that he gained the courage to also make the leap. Nanahuatzin rose from the fire as a well blackened eagle, but Tecuiçiztecatl arose only as a partly spotted jaguar; he had not burned as well because the fire had died down before he leapt into it. Then two suns appeared, each exactly the same, sitting on the eastern horizon. The gods solved this duplication problem by smashing one with a rabbit thereby dimming its light, but still neither orb moved. After food had been created, and all the other gods had been sacrificed, Quetzalcoatl gently blew the sun into motion. The moon with its rabbit face followed suit. Thus the Fifth Age was born. It is said that Tecuiçiztecatl would have been the sun if he had jumped into the fire first. The tale also is told that this sun will die from famine and earthquakes when it is 676 years old. Hence people call the Fifth Sun 4-Movement, for it will die by motion.

See also Calendar Deities; Moon; Quetzalcoatl; Sun

Suggested reading:

Codex Chimalpopoca. 1992b. As reproduced in *History and Mythology of the Aztecs: The Codex Chimalpopoca.* Trans. John Bierhorst. Tucson: University of Arizona Press.

Sahagún, Fray Bernardino de. 1953–1982. *The Florentine Codex: A General History of the Things of New Spain.* Trans. Arthur J. O. Anderson, and Charles E. Dibble. 12 books, 13 parts. Monographs of the School of American Research no. 14. Santa Fe: School of American Research; Salt Lake City: University of Utah Press.

GOD L

Time period: Classic–Postclassic

Cultural group: Maya

God L is a deity represented as an old man dressed in a muan bird (an owl or another raptor) headdress; often black in color, he is closely linked with the underworld. His animal counterparts are the jaguar and the muan bird, both creatures of the night and caves, which are gates to the underworld. Unfortunately, we do not know his given Maya name, so scholars have simply designated him by the letter *L*. However, because of the consistent presence of the muan bird and sky symbols in his headdress, some scholars have suggested his name may have been Muan Chan, or "Misty Sky."

The Maya often viewed God L as a deity of death and destruction and associated him with war and conflict. However, like many other Mesoamerican deities who bore multiple traits, he was not just a god of death but also one of merchants and trade, frequently appearing with riches, a merchant bundle, and a staff or spear. In addition, in many artistic renditions, God L has water, rain, and agricultural fertility associations. A common figure in Classic art and iconography, God L clearly served as an important figure in Maya myths and lore during this period. Many Classic scenes show the moon goddess taking the regalia of God L, illustrating a mythic scene from an oral story that no longer exists. By the Postclassic period, God L is a far less important deity, appearing only infrequently in art and Maya codices.

> *See also* Earth, Agricultural, and Hunting Deities; Moon; Rain and Water Deities; Sky Deities and Beings; Underworld and Caves, Deities of the
> *Suggested reading:*
> Sharer, Robert J. 1994. *The Ancient Maya.* 5th ed. Stanford, CA: Stanford University Press.

Figure 57. God L from the Dresden Codex (Museo de América/Art Resource)

Taube, Karl. 1992. *The Major Gods of Ancient Yucatan.* Washington, DC: Dumbarton Oaks Research Library.

GUADALUPE, VIRGIN OF

Time period: Colonial–Contemporary

Cultural group: Mesoamerica

Like all Mesoamerican saints, the Virgin of Guadalupe possesses a personality and powers that are unique to the particular locale; but unlike other saints, this particular representative of Mary the mother of Christ also has a national cult: Her powers are believed to be directed toward helping the nation of Mexico as much as individual communities and individuals. As a result, there are two contrasting ways of understanding Guadalupe and two different, traditional ways of interacting with her. Guadalupe invokes strong emotions, and her interpreters typically have taken either a markedly sympathetic, believing view of her or a strongly unsympathetic stance based on an entirely different worldview. People

*Figure 58. The Virgin of Guadalupe (ng.netgate.net/
~norberto/materdei.html)*

have interacted with her in two different but related ways: either as a follower of her national leadership, or as a simple worshiper with loving gratitude, hopeful supplication, and humble awe of her powers.

The historicity of the events surrounding the mythological Guadalupe remains unproven by scientific or scholarly means, but the effect of Guadalupe's myth on national and personal events is profound and undeniable. As with all powerful myths (any of the myths described in this volume), the truth and the reality of Guadalupe lie outside of the methods contemporary historians have at their disposal. Even if it could be proven that Guadalupe never existed in reality, what people actually have done with her powers in real life would remain irrefutable; both the national history and personal biographies provide ample evidence of it.

According to Guadalupe's Mexican myth, early one morning in December 1531, the Virgin miraculously appeared before a shepherd and Christian convert named Juan Diego. This apparition occurred on Tepeyac, a hill just a few miles north of the center of Mexico City, or Tenochtitlan, the traditional center of the entire Mexica domain. As did the Juan Diego at Ocotlan, Tepeyac's Juan Diego heard strains of beautiful music and a lovely lady calling to him: "Juanito, Juanito! The least of my sons, where are you going?" He told her he was going to church. She then told him that she was the "Virgin Mary, Mother of the true God," and that she wanted a church built for her right there on Tepeyac. She also promised to reward his faithfulness.

Juan Diego hurried to Mexico City to make the Virgin's request known to Bishop Zumarraga, but the good father dismissed the shepherd's story as nonsense and sent him away. Juan Diego went back to the lady at Tepeyac to explain the problem; she sent him back to the bishop, who again rebuffed him. Then he was sidetracked by his uncle who had fallen mortally ill with smallpox. On his way to find a priest to administer last rites, Juan encountered the Virgin again. She told him she had already cured his uncle. Then she directed him toward the normally dry, cactus-ridden hilltop, where he was to pick some unusually lush roses. After he had done so, she arranged the flowers carefully in his cloak, telling him to take them back to the bishop, for they were a sign. When Juan Diego opened his cloak at the cleric's house, the roses tumbled to the floor, revealing a lovely painting of the Virgin that had not been there before. The bishop carried this amazing cloak to the chapel and hung it on the wall. The next morning, he rode with Juan Diego to the latter's house, where they found his uncle in perfect health. His uncle reported that the Virgin had appeared to him the previous evening, had cured him, and had informed him that she wanted to be called "Guadalupe." The bishop was finally convinced, and had a chapel built to honor the Virgin of Guadalupe. As the story goes, the Indians had already been acquainted with this Lady for many years and called her Tonantzin, which means "Our Honorable Mother" in Nahuatl.

Such is the mythic history of Guadalupe. Scholarly historians suggest a somewhat different story. The Virgin of Guadalupe is said to have appeared first in Extremadura, Spain. A small wooden statue of her was supposed to have been hidden during the Moorish invasion, but a shepherd recovered it in the thirteenth century, and the shrine of Guadalupe eventually became a popular pilgrimage site. The name "Guadalupe" is Arabic in origin, but its meaning remains uncertain. Columbus and the conquistadores (many of whom came from Extremadura) brought the Virgin's cult with them to the New World. Indeed, she rode into Tenochtitlan emblazoned on a flag carried by Cortés's men.

The chapel at Tepeyac, dating to 1555 or 1556, originally was dedicated to the Virgin Mary. Early on it received the popular name of Guadalupe because of the similarity between the chapel's image of Mary and the one in Extremadura. Some interpreters claim that the site was the location of a pre-Conquest goddess called Tonantzin, but as many scholars have noted, the evidence for that is almost nonexistent. The sixteenth-century scholar Fray Bernardino de Sahagún did express his disapproval of the veneration of the Virgin at Tepeyac, saying that it constituted idolatry and played on the ambiguity of the name Tonantzin. He may not have been far wrong, for the Nahuatl word *tonantzin* was and still is a form of reverent address used for numerous female deities, not just one; today, people often address Mary this way. The Tepeyac site itself may or may not have been an ancient place of pre-Christian worship (we can't be sure); but in any case, the site clearly encouraged an indigenous form of piety that worried Sahagún. At about the same time, the Franciscan provincial Francisco de Bustamante also issued an intense condemnation of popular devotion to Guadalupe, claiming that her image had been painted by an Indian named Marcos. There is no clear documentary record of any physical manifestation of the Virgin of Guadalupe during the next hundred years (Poole 1997, 1536). However, others embraced her cult, if not her apparition; Jacques Lafaye has suggested that the Virgin of Guadalupe signaled the creation of a "Western Paradise" legitimizing the European hold on the New World (Lafaye 1976, 228). These arguments for or against her veneration, which often reflected tensions between the clerical orders operating in New Spain at the time, have continued in various forms to the present.

In spite of all the arguments over her, Guadalupe did not really come into her own until 1648, when Miguel Sanchez published a book apparently retelling oral tales about her because he could find no written references. He related her to the founding of Tenochtitlan, which was depicted as an eagle standing on a cactus (this image now appears on the Mexican flag; see Fig. 41). Transforming Guadalupe's Spanish image, Sanchez turned an angel at her feet into a Mexica-like cactus, and the angel's wings into eagle feathers. This transformation, combined with stories of the Virgin of Guadalupe, made the Virgin instantly appealing to the criollo population (European immigrants' children born in New Spain), who had been living betwixt and between two worlds, longing for their own legitimacy. Sanchez gave them a Virgin who combined both the Old and the New Worlds, a saintly validation of both their heritages. The next year his book was published in Nahuatl, but this edition, *Nican mopohua*, never caught on with the Indians. Guadalupe remained a largely criollo saint throughout the seventeenth century.

In the eighteenth century, and even more so in the nineteenth, devotion to Guadalupe took off as the criollos' descendants appropriated her as a mascot for their nationalist aspirations. In 1810, Hidalgo chose her as the symbol of rebellion and liberation. Of course, many Mesoamerican saints have led rebellions, but few have led one that succeeded as well as this one; Guadalupe led the Mexican people through a full-scale revolution to independence. After Independence, the ruling and intellectual classes made the Virgin an icon of Mexican identity and a unifying focus in a fragmented society; even the anticlerical Benito Juarez respected the symbolism of Guadalupe's chapel. For indigenous peoples, she also became a source of intensely personal devotion. This "Queen of Peace" and "Queen of Mexicans" requested that her devotees give themselves over to "Mary and to Jesus through Her," and do everything "by Mary, with Mary, in Mary, and for Mary" (Lafaye 1976, 287).

Anticlericism flourished among certain sectors of Mexican society in the nineteenth century. Some said Guadalupe was nothing more than a way for the power-mongering clerics to maintain control over the simple folk. The history of the tale had been questioned since the seventeenth century, but the controversy surrounding it had since become so inflamed with passions that any scholarly investigation was impossible. In this debate, two worldviews and two camps were pitted against each other—Christian mythology against humanist myths of objectivity and rationality, and those who supported the Church as a valid institution against those who saw it as an evil force that oppressed humanity. The debate became so intense that one premier historian, Joaquin Garcia Icazbalceta, abandoned his research altogether near the end of his life, too tired and discouraged to deal with the controversy swirling around his biography of Zumarraga (which omitted any mention of Guadalupe's apparition) and a subsequent letter he wrote that strongly questioned her myth's historical validity.

Although passions abated in the twentieth century, the issue of Guadalupe's historical veracity continued to be questioned. In 1922, historian Mariano Cuevas popularized the idea that *Nican mopohua* was an eyewitness account dating from the time of the apparition. However, his claim that the original document had been looted by the Americans during the Mexican-American war was discredited, and other historians continued to question the myth's historicity. In this century as in the past, Guadalupe has had her defenders and detractors, but now there is a trend toward more balanced historical treatments.

Today's devotion to the Virgin of Guadalupe remains central to Mexican national and religious life in spite of scholarly debates. A metro stop at the Basilica of Guadalupe is clearly marked on the subway heading to this northern suburb of Mexico City. The Basilica itself is a huge, ultramodern affair in which the traveler to Tepeyac can view both the cloak and a fine old painting of the Virgin. There she stands in a blue cape upon a crescent moon, with solar rays emanating from behind her. The explanation for this painting, other images of her, and Sanchez's earlier criollo adaptation can be found as easily in a biblical reference as in indigenous tradition. Revelation 12 describes an apparition of a woman clothed with the sun, the moon at her feet, and a crown of twelve stars; she was threatened by a serpent and received two wings of an eagle. Guadalupe's association with the moon also links her to some indigenous, pre-Christian lunar goddesses, and her solar rays often are painted in the ancient style. Moreover, until quite recently, pilgrims could be seen crawling on their hands and knees up to the basilica in an expression of extreme piety; some had come from miles away. Such contemporary pilgrimages echo the ancient journeys people took to various shrines throughout ancient Mesoamerica. Indigenous piety may have shaped these practices of veneration of Guadalupe.

Guadalupe seems to have special meaning for a number of contemporary Mexican-American women. Jeanette Rodriguez has reported that Guadalupe provides women with positive models of an ideal self, nurturing, strongly connected with the family and community, and self-controlled. Yolanda, one of the women Rodriguez interviewed, said that Guadalupe represented strength, hope, and optimism, and that she belonged particularly to *los latinas*. Another interviewee, Edyth, said that Guadalupe belonged to everyone, that she was a "Mexican Mother, waiting, caring, unselfish." At the same time, Rodriguez noted that negative ideas, such as the conforming child and critical parent, also resulted from her veneration (1994, 106, 109). This echoes what other feminists have said about her. For some, she represents strength and liberation; for others, subjugation—arguments that mirror those surrounding Guadalupe throughout previous centuries. The fact that Guadalupe's historicity continues to be questioned suggests the power of history itself to form mythic realities.

See also Christ; La Llorona; Malinche; Moon; Saints; Sun

Suggested reading:

Florescano, Enrique. 1994. *Memory, Myth, and Time in Mexico: From the Aztecs to Independence.* Austin: University of Texas Press.

Lafaye, Jacques. 1976. *Quetzalcoatl and Guadalupe: The Formation of Mexican National Consciousness, 1531–1813.* Chicago: University of Chicago Press.

Poole, Stafford. 1997. "Virgin of Guadalupe and Guadalupanismo." Pp. 1535–1537 in *Encyclopedia of Mexico: History, Society, and Culture,* vol. 2, ed. Michael S. Werner. Chicago: Fitzroy Dearborn.

Rodriguez, Jeanette. 1994. *Our Lady of Guadalupe: Faith and Empowerment among Mexican-American Women.* Austin: University of Texas Press.

GUKUMATZ

Time period: Postclassic–Contemporary

Cultural group: K'iche' Maya

Gukumatz (Goo-koo-mats´) is the K'iche' Maya version of the highland Mexican feathered serpent deity Quetzalcoatl, found throughout Postclassic Mesoamerica. In the K'iche' creation myths, called the Popol Vuh, Gukumatz is one of the gods who helps create the universe and the first human beings.

Gukumatz has six major symbolic representations in K'iche' myths and stories. First, he appears as a plumed serpent, for his name translates to "feathered serpent." Second, the K'iche' Maya viewed Gukumatz as an eagle. Third, some K'iche' myths recount his transformation into a jaguar. Fourth, one story records his transformation into a pool of blood. Fifth, sometimes the K'iche' represent Gukumatz as a conch shell or snail. And sixth, the K'iche' associated Gukumatz with a flute made of bones.

The Popol Vuh describes him as one of the creator deities, who threw lots to decide the fate of the people they had created, and what kind of relations these new creations would have with the gods. Gukumatz probably was borrowed either from the Toltecs of highland Mexico (Quetzalcoatl) or the Yucatec Maya (Kukulkan). The K'iche' gave him a secondary role as a creator god and blended him with other deities. In addition, some of the myths in the Popol Vuh and elsewhere indicate an association between the creator deity and a historically known ruler or individual named Lord Gukumatz. This person may have been so named because he drew some of his powers from Gukumatz.

See also Feathered Serpents; Kukulkan; Quetzalcoatl

Suggested reading:

Preuss, Mary H. 1988. *Gods of the Popol Vuh: Xmucane, Kucumatz, Tojil, and Jurakan*. Culver City, CA: Labyrinthos.

Tedlock, Dennis, trans. 1985. *Popol Vuh: The Definitive Edition of the Mayan Book of the Dawn of Life and the Glories of Gods and Kings*. New York: Simon and Schuster.

HERO TWINS (HUNAHPU AND XBALANQUE)

Time period: Classic–Contemporary

Cultural group: K'iche' Maya

Hunahpu (Hoon-ah-poo´) and Xbalanque (Sh-ba-lan-kay´), known as the Hero Twins, are the main figures in two of the five myths from the Popol Vuh, the K'iche' legend of creation. The Hero Twins are not creator deities or gods that control the fates of ordinary humans but rather trickster figures that outsmart and defeat morally questionable supernatural figures. First, they defeat those who tried to magnify themselves over the creator god Jurakan; and second, they trounce the unsavory underworld lords of Xibalba. These contests were disputes within a single family, for Hunahpu and Xbalanque share the same genealogy as the gods. These two twins are the sons of Vucub Hunahpu (Yum Kaax, or the diving god), often interpreted as a maize god, and Blood Woman, a daughter of one of the underworld deities. Moreover, they are the grandsons of Xmucane and Xpiyacoc, the Grandmother and Grandfather deities responsible for helping Jurakan create the universe and for grinding the maize from which the first humans came.

Hunahpu and Xbalanque appear primarily in the Popol Vuh's second and third sections. In the second, the Hero twins defeat three self-glorifying gods, 7-Macaw, Zipacna, and Earthquake. 7-Macaw claimed to be the sun, Zipacna claimed to have made the Earth, and Earthquake claimed to have the ability to bring down the sky and destroy the Earth. Because of their evil self-aggrandizing over the true creator deities, each was defeated by Hunahpu and Xbalanque through deceit. The third myth describes the birth of the Hero Twins; the death

*Figure 59. Hero Twins, Hunahpu and Xbalanque, talking to 1-Death, Hun Came, in Xibalba
(Justin Kerr Archives, File no. 1183)*

of their uncle and father at the hands of the lords of Xibalba, and the Hero Twins'
entrance into the underworld, where they outwitted and defeated the Xibalba
lords by tricking them into wanting to be sacrificed. After they tricked the
underworld gods, they partially resurrected their father, Vucub Hunahpu, and
rose into the sky to become the sun and the moon. Among other things, one can
see this myth as a metaphor for the cycles of the sun and moon, which also enter
the underworld at the end and the beginning of every day and reappear victorious after their travels and trials in Xibalba. In like fashion, a ruler such as Pacal,
who bears the sun's powers, enters the underworld at death, to rise as a new sun
with the next ruler.

The origins of the Popol Vuh stories and the first myths of Hunahpu and
Xbalanque remain unclear. However, among the Classic-era ruins of the lowland
Maya, archaeologists and art historians have found painted images of the Hero
Twins on pottery depicting not only scenes from the Popol Vuh but also scenes
from stories that cannot be identified because they no longer exist. Hunahpu and
Xbalanque were important to the prehistoric Classic Maya just as they are crit-
ical figures among today's K'iche' Maya, who continue to tell stories about them.

See also Blood Woman; Earth, Agricultural, and Hunting Deities; Jurakan; Moon;
Pacal; Quetzalcoatl; Sky Deities and Beings; Sun; Underworld and Caves, Deities
of the; Yum Kaax

Suggested reading:

Preuss, Mary H. 1988. *Gods of the Popol Vuh: Xmucane, Kucumatz, Tojil, and
    Jurakan.* Culver City, CA: Labyrinthos.

Sharer, Robert J. 1994. *The Ancient Maya.* 5th ed. Stanford, CA: Stanford
    University Press.

Tedlock, Dennis, trans. 1985. *Popol Vuh: The Definitive Edition of the Mayan
    Book of the Dawn of Life and the Glories of Gods and Kings.* New York:
    Simon and Schuster.

HUITZILOPOCHTLI

Time period: Postclassic

Cultural group: Nahua-Mexica

Huitzilopochtli (Weet-zee-lo-pocht´-lee) was the Mexica patron and war god. His name means "Hummingbird on the Left." Mythically, he was said to be instrumental in the creation of the cosmos; he led the Mexica to their island home of Tenochtitlan and brought both victory and defeat to the Mexica on the battlefield. In fact, his defeat meant the demise of the Mexica. He stood for cosmic creation, success in war, strong governance, and good trade. Historically, he was probably a relatively young deity, and perhaps not even a terribly central one; but in post-Conquest times he found himself elevated to a position of extreme importance by Spanish commentators who misunderstood his role in Mexica mythology.

One story of cosmic creation describes how Huitzilopochtli was one of four sons of the ancient creator couple Tonacateuctli and Tonacacihuatl; the other three brothers were the red and black Tezcatlipocas and Quetzalcoatl. It's said Huitzilopochtli was born with only bones and no flesh; and that, of the four, he was the smallest and his place lay on the cosmos' left side. After 600 years, Tonacateuctli and Tonacacihuatl told Huitzilopochtli and Quetzalcoatl to put the world in order. Together they made fire; a sun that did not shine much; the first man and woman, Oxomoco and Cipactonal; they put Mictlantecutli and his woman Mictlancihuatl (the Lord and Lady of the Land of the Dead) in the underworld; created the earth from the crocodilian creature Cipactli; and created Tlaltecutli and Chalchiuhtlicue from whom the deities of water were born.

Another story describes how he was born magically in full war regalia to the fierce goddess Coatlicue; his first act was to destroy his sister Coyolxauhqui who led her brothers, the Centzonuitznaua, against their mother on Coatepec Mountain. Still other stories tell how he led his people, the Mexica, from their island place of origin Aztlan or Chicomoztoc (Place of Seven Caves). Traveling often, they settled temporarily in many places; and after several incidences establishing his primacy, Huitzilopochtli finally led them to their proper settlement on their new island home of Tenochtitlan.

But Huitzilopochtli would not always remain victorious; his defeat meant the defeat of the Mexica. It's said that in Motecuhzoma I's time, magicians went to Aztlan only to be told that Huitzilopochtli would lose all the cities he had conquered for the Mexica in the same order he had won them. Then he would return to Aztlan, abandoning them. Before the Spanish arrived, one of Huitzilopochtli's temples burned down in an uncontrollable fire; throwing water on the flames only made them worse. This presented the Mexica with an omen of their impending demise, for the burning of a patron deity's temple was the sign of a city's defeat. Indeed, Pedro de Alvarado attacked and massacred many

Figure 60. Huitzilopochtli (Codex Magliabechiano, fol. 53r, Art Resource)

Mexica on Toxcatl, Huitzilopochtli's main feast day; this event began their disastrous war with the Spanish.

His ritual and iconographic imagery often indicated his powers of governance and war. Besides his trademark blue-green hummingbird helmet, he also sometimes wore white heron feathers that linked him to Aztlan and royal origins. Like Tezcatlipoca, he could sport a smoking mirror, a cloudy obsidian mirror, and serpent foot, all ancient Mesoamerican signs of rulership. Often he carried instruments of war: a shield, darts, and the terrible xiuhcoatl or fire-serpent. When he destroyed Coyolxauhqui and his brothers on Coatepec Mountain, he appeared as an intense storm or fire; piercing Coyolxauhqui with his lightning-like xiuhcoatl, he completely enveloped his brothers in clouds and finished them off with smoke. The Mexica dressed their dead rulers in his clothing because the governors embodied some of his powers. These powers, which the rulers received upon coronation, assured a forceful success in war and governance. Mexica rulers, furthermore, were closely linked with merchants in rituals in which Huitzilopochtli's substitute Paynal helped assure good success in battle and trade through sacrifice. As the vanguards of the expanding Mexica domain, traders could find themselves engaged in activities more violent than merely buying and selling goods.

Historically, he was probably a very young god, and may even have been a Mexica chief in their early migratory years. One tale first describes him as an image carried in a bundle on the back of the early Mexica ancestors wandering the land. This bundle looked very like the bundle dead rulers were wrapped into before their cremation. Like many Native American medicine bundles, it probably contained Huitzilopochtli's powers embodied by his image and perhaps other potent objects. Yet, at another point, the same story describes him as if he were a real person. This person may have been a chief named for the god, or a great chief who later died and became the god.

A lack of imagery indicates his youth. No great sculptures exist depicting Huitzilopochtli, and he appears in only one codex, which may actually be a picture of a ritual participant wearing his garb. Instead of fine stone, his image was made of perishable materials such as amaranth dough and wood. Moreover, only one object consistently defined Huitzilopochtli, his hummingbird helmet. One of Cortez's captains Bernal Díaz del Castillo reported that the similarity between this and the conquistador helmets convinced the Indians that the Spanish were people like them. All his other garments and decorations, however, changed with the ritual circumstances. Moreover, unlike most other patron deities, he shared the Templo Mayor in the center of Tenochtitlan with another deity, an ancient rain god called Tlaloc. The southern side housed Huitzilopochtli, while the northern side housed Tlaloc; as the year was divided between a rainy agricultural season and a dry warring season, so too the temple. Huitzilopochtli may have been the Mexica's patron, but he shared the limelight.

After the Conquest, however, Spanish commentators and others quickly elevated him to a central spot of importance. He became the principle god responsible for all past Mexica life and success. At the same time, because of his close association with war and sacrifice, the Spanish likened him to the Greco-Roman god Mars or to the Christian Devil, depending on whether the interpreter wished to idealize a lost Indian past or justify its demise. This classic-demonic divide continued into the seventeenth century. But by the early eighteenth century and up through the late twentieth, Quetzalcoatl surpassed him as the quintessential Mexica god—perhaps because, by then, people sought a more benign image of Indian origins, something Huitzilopochtli's bloody history could not provide.

See also Chalchiuhtlicue; Coatlicue; Coyolxauhqui; Devil; Motecuhzoma I, Lord; Quetzalcoatl; Rain and Water Deities; Sky Deities and Beings; Sun; Tezcatlipoca; Tlaloc and the Tlaloques

Suggested reading:

Boone, Elizabeth H. 1989. *Incarnations of the Aztec Supernatural: The Image of Huitzilopochtli in Mexico and Europe.* Philadelphia: American Philosophical Society.

Durán, Fray Diego. 1994. *The History of the Indies of New Spain.* Trans. Doris Heyden. Norman: University of Oklahoma Press.

Sahagún, Fray Bernardino de. 1953–1982. *The Florentine Codex: A General History of the Things of New Spain.* Trans. Arthur J. O. Anderson, and Charles E. Dibble. Monographs of the School of American Research no. 14. Santa Fe: School of American Research; Salt Lake City: University of Utah Press.

HUNAB KU

Time period: Colonial

Cultural group: Yucatec Maya

A mystery surrounds Hunab Ku's (Hoon-ab´ Koo) full character and importance. According to some, because he was the original creator god and father of

Itzamna, Hunab Ku was the most important Postclassic and early colonial era Maya deity. However, many early chronicles, both native and non-native, suggest that Hunab Ku and Itzamna are merely different names for the same divine individual. Different explanations are possible for this discrepancy. If he was truly the creator/father god, then his importance was quickly eclipsed by Itzamna, thus his early significance being masked. Or it could be that Hunab Ku is a colonial Maya name for the Spanish Christian God. In fact one translates Hunab Ku as "Unified God," a concept that fits the Christian God somewhat better than the many diverse deities of pre-Conquest religious traditions. Perhaps Hunab Ku represents an early step in the gradual religious conversion of the Maya, which also would explain why Hunab Ku does not appear in pre-Conquest indigenous literature or art. The colonial Maya considered Hunab Ku, the Christian God, to be the father of all and the Maya universe.

See also Christ; Itzamna; Saints

Suggested reading:

Landa, Diego de. 1978. *Yucatan before and after the Conquest.* Trans. William Gates. New York: Dover.

Morley, Sylvanus G., George W. Brainerd, and Robert J. Sharer. 1983. *The Ancient Maya.* 4th ed. Stanford, CA: Stanford University Press.

ITZAMNA

Time period: Postclassic–Colonial

Cultural group: Yucatec Maya

In some stories Itzamna (Eet-sam-na´) is said to be the son of Hunab Ku (the first god) and the husband of Ix Chel (the primary female deity). Itzamna was the greatest of all the Yucatec Maya deities. Among the Yucatec Maya in the early Colonial period, Itzamna was the god of heaven and sun, and he is described in the codices as the lord of the gods. In keeping with his great importance, he was worshiped under various names and possessed many different attributes.

Itzamna was the Yucatec god of writing and esoteric knowledge, and the god of maize, the sun, and the wind. The Yucatec Maya considered Itzamna the first priest—the one who invented writing and books, gave the names to earthly places, and divided the lands among the people. Itzamna located himself in the heavens; but in the social, earthly world he associated with rulers, scribes, and priests. His terrestrial animal and plant counterparts were the caiman (alligator), a principal bird (maybe the king vulture), the ceiba tree (kapok), and maize. As the one lord god and father of the gods, Itzamna served as the calendar patron of the day called Ahau. The Maya also associated him with sky and earth monsters, the cardinal directions and their four colors (red, white, black, and yellow), and what we call the Pleiades constellation. Later, during the Colonial era, because of Itzamna's promi-

nence and Spanish religious influence, the Maya combined Itzamna
with the Spanish Christian God.

Maya texts of the Postclassic
and Colonial periods often depicted Itzamna in priestly clothes
because of his close association
with priests and the priesthood.
Maya priests invoked him during
New Year rites, and people prayed
to him at the beginning of specific
years to avert great natural disasters. Early historical reports say
that the Maya prayed to Itzamna
at the beginning of those years
called Ix, in order to avert drought,
hot sun, famine, and thefts. The
Maya also prayed to Itzamna in
other years to fend off other disastrous predictions.

In the past, many stories
and myths existed concerning
Itzamna, the lord of the gods. Unfortunately, today very few such
stories remain. What remains are

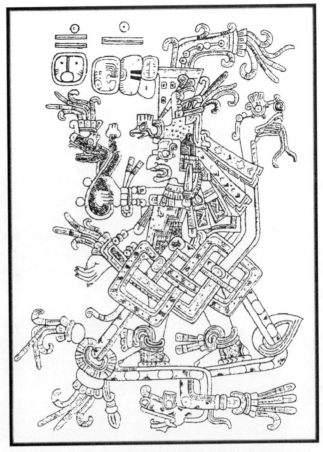

*Figure 61. Itzamna, from the Postclassic site of Santa
Rita, Corazal, Belize (Bureau of American Ethnology)*

pictures in Maya art, the descriptions of the sixteenth-century Spanish historian
Fray Diego de Landa, and the narratives from the Chilam Balams (mythic histories of various Yucatec Maya groups).

No images of Itzamna have been found dating from the late Classic period;
but after Spanish contact and during the Colonial period, Itzamna appears as a
major deity who in eclipsing all other gods is the equal of, or identical with the
Christian God. During the early Colonial and late Prehistoric periods, sculptures
of Itzamna were created for ritual purposes of worship, including human sacrifice, new year celebrations, and prophetic divinations.

The Chilam Balam of Chumayel refers to Itzamna only briefly. It states that
early in the sixteenth century, Itzamna was provoked by the coming of the Spanish Christian God; later in the same century, a group of Maya called the Itzá visited a place named Itzamna while journeying to a new home. Finally, in the
nineteenth century, stories say that Itzamna was one of the lords of the last
katun calendar cycle (a great cycle of time), which occurred at Coba in north-

eastern Yucatán. The Chilam Balam of Tizimin similarly mentions Itzamna. Unfortunately, these accounts are probably only excerpts from much longer stories, and few other written historical myths exist concerning Itzamna. Today, Itzamna is no longer encountered in Maya mythology, having been replaced with Christian stories and beliefs.

See also Christ; Hunab Ku; Ix Chel; Sky Deities and Beings; Sun

Suggested reading:

Edmonson, Munro S., ed. and trans. 1982. *The Ancient Future of the Itza: The Book of Chilam Balam of Tizimin.* Austin: University of Texas Press.

Edmonson, Munro S., trans. 1986. *Heaven Born Mérida and Its Destiny: The Book of Chilam Balam of Chumayel.* Austin: University of Texas Press.

Landa, Diego de. 1941. *Relación de las cosas de Yucatán.* Ed. and trans. Alfred M. Tozzer. Papers of the Peabody Museum. Cambridge, MA: Harvard University Press.

Sharer, Robert J. 1994. *The Ancient Maya.* 5th ed. Stanford, CA: Stanford University Press.

Taube, Karl. 1992. *The Major Gods of Ancient Yucatan.* Washington, DC: Dumbarton Oaks Research Library.

IX CHEL

Time period: Late Classic–Colonial

Cultural group: Yucatec Maya

Like many of the Maya deities, Ix Chel (Eesh-chel´) played a variety of roles that sometimes contradicted one another. In fact, much confusion exists as to who she truly was in the late Classic and Postclassic periods; her early Colonial character is clearer. Ix Chel, or "Lady Rainbow," was the female member of the creator couple (with Itzamna). She served as the patron of divination, weaving, medicine, healing, and childbirth. However, she also was associated with floods, destruction, serpents, and sometimes war. And she may have been associated with the moon. The Maya closely linked Ix Chel with the spider, which has connections to weaving, childbirth, divination, and creation. The spider, like Ix Chel, had a dual nature, being associated with childbirth and creation, and with war and destruction. Ix Chel was a complex figure with multiple aspects, varying in accordance with the situation or the time in which she was invoked.

Various reasons exist for her ties with both the creative (healing and childbirth) and the malicious (war and destruction). Among the Maya, rainbows are not harbingers of good and beauty but signs of sickness and disease. However, her name "Lady Rainbow" also indicates the other side of her personality, for sickness and disease are treated through healing and medicine, which are also in her domain. She does not bring sickness but rather serves as the curer, therefore playing a powerful role in Maya society.

A few portrayals of Ix Chel exist in late Classic art, largely in the form of small sculptures and painted pottery, which depict her as a powerful old woman, sometimes accompanied by imagery of death. In Postclassic art, her portrayals are more vivid, intertwining a variety of symbols of death and destruction with those of water, life, and weaving. In late Classic and in Postclassic art, Ix Chel often appears with jaguar aspects including fangs, a jaguar eye, clawed hands and feet, and a skirt of crossbones and other death symbols. In the Dresden codex, she is depicted as an aged female, often reddish brown in color.

Figure 62. Ix Chel (Codex Tro-cortesianus, *pl. 30b, Museo de América/Art Resource*)

By the time of Spanish contact, the Yucatec Maya worshiped Ix Chel primarily as a goddess of childbirth, divination, and weaving, as such she may have represented the aged moon. Women from the Maya lands and possibly all of Mesoamerica visited great shrines dedicated to her, which lay off the east coast of Yucatán on the islands of Cozumel and Isla de Mujeres. Ix Chel was an important deity to the Yucatec Maya, and like many Maya gods had very complex aspects as the foreteller and bringer of both life and death. But like the stories of Itzamna and other Yucatec Maya deities, myths of Ix Chel have not withstood the test of time; few, if any, are remembered and retold today.

See also Cihuacoatl; Itzamna; Moon; Rain and Water Deities

Suggested reading:

Coe, Michael D. 1977. "Supernatural Patrons of Maya Scribes and Artists." Pp. 327–347 in *Social Process in Maya Prehistory: Studies in Honour of Sir Eric Thompson*, ed. Norman D. C. Hammond. New York: Academic Press.

Landa, Diego de. 1941. *Relación de las cosas de Yucatán*. Ed. and trans. Alfred M. Tozzer. Papers of the Peabody Museum. Cambridge, MA: Harvard University Press.

Taube, Karl. 1992. *The Major Gods of Ancient Yucatan*. Washington, DC: Dumbarton Oaks Research Library.

JURAKAN

Time period: Postclassic–Contemporary

Cultural group: K'iche' Maya

One of the most important deities among the K'iche' Maya, Jurakan (Hoor-a-kan´) represents fire, water, lightning, thunder, and heavy rain. It remains unclear whether Jurakan was originally a male or female deity, for s/he at times appears as a figure with no ascribed gender. In the Popol Vuh, s/he creates the cosmos, giving reality to the universe. Jurakan also uses the Hero Twins as his/her messengers to, and instruments of change in, the terrestrial and lower worlds. It is by Jurakan's wish that the Hero Twins defeat the three deities 7-Macaw, Zipacna, and Earthquake. S/he also embodies the K'iche' Maya conceptualization of the great unifying force of the universe. The name *Jurakan* is derived from the Carib word *huracan* (hurricane); Jurakan is the hurricane, the terrifyingly unpredictable and destructive forces that bring new life and creation through the water and the wind.

> *See also* Hero Twins; Rain and Water Deities
>
> *Suggested reading:*
>
> Preuss, Mary H. 1988. *Gods of the Popol Vuh: Xmucane, Kucumatz, Tojil, and Jurakan.* Culver City, CA: Labyrinthos.
>
> Tedlock, Dennis, trans. 1985. *Popol Vuh: The Definitive Edition of the Mayan Book of the Dawn of Life and the Glories of Gods and Kings.* New York: Simon and Schuster.

KINICH AHAU

Time period: Preclassic–Colonial

Cultural group: Yucatec Maya

The name *Kinich Ahau* (Kee-nich´ A-how´), which applies to the Yucatec Maya sun god, translates as "sun-faced lord." At one time many scholars saw this figure as an individual deity, but now most believe him to be the day aspect of Itzamna, although he bears certain traits that are entirely his own. As the sun god, he was considered by some the supernatural patron of warriors and rulers, like Itzamna. Throughout Maya prehistoric art, Kinich Ahau was identified with the jaguar, decapitation, fire, rulership, and dynastic descent.

On Classic and Postclassic Maya sculpture and pottery and in Postclassic codices, one can distinguish Kinich Ahau by an aquiline nose; eyes shaped like crosses; a large square eye in profile; occasionally a beard like the rays of the sun, its curly tendrils sprouting from the corners of his mouth; a spiral protruding from his nose when viewed in profile; and most importantly, the four-petaled Maya glyph *kin* (sun).

Among the Yucatec Maya, Kinich Ahau symbolized the sun's life in its daily travels through the sky. Thus, historically, many Classic Maya rulers assumed the name, powers, and patronage of Kinich Ahau. They did this not only to evoke the protection of a strong, supernatural force; some may have believed and wanted others to believe that they were terrestrial manifestations of the sun god and that through his divine power they kept the sun moving through its natural daily cycle.

See also Itzamna; Pacal; Sky Deities and Beings; Sun

Suggested reading:

Taube, Karl. 1992. *The Major Gods of Ancient Yucatan.* Washington, DC: Dumbarton Oaks Research Library.

Thompson, John Eric Sydney. 1970b. *Maya History and Religion.* Norman: University of Oklahoma Press.

KUKULCAN

Time period: Postclassic–Contemporary

Cultural group: Yucatec Maya

Kukulcan (Koo-kool-kan´) was a mythic/historical figure related to the Mexican feathered serpent deity Quetzalcoatl. However, for the Yucatec Maya, the name refers to two figures: one is the feathered serpent deity, common throughout the Postclassic era; the other is the Yucatec ruler/priest of Chichén Itzá, a mythical/historical figure first appearing around the end of the tenth century.

Like the K'iche' Maya deity Gukumatz, Kukulcan is a feathered serpent god, introduced from highland Mexican peoples. We know little of the pre-Hispanic Kukulcan. However, we find large temples dedicated to this deity at sites throughout northern Yucatán, such as Chichén Itzá, Mayapan, and Uxmal.

According to Fray Diego de Landa, Kukulcan was a great lord of the Maya at Chichén Itzá in northern Yucatán. He is said to have arrived around the end of the tenth century from México, where he was considered a god. Kukulcan established the city of Mayapan as the central capital of the Postclassic Yucatec Maya, and he brought all of the Maya lords to this city, dividing the towns and land among them. After many years he left Mayapan in peace and friendship.

However, the Chilam Balams (mythic histories of various Maya towns) give a different view of the individual known as Kukulcan, who is said to have existed in the fifteenth century at Mayapan, not during the tenth century at Chichén Itzá. These books describe Kukulcan as a priest of the Feathered Serpent who takes over the lordship of the city after the fall of Mayapan and the sacrifice of the Chichén Itzá ruler by the Xiu Maya. Kukulcan then leads the Itzá Maya into a series of skirmishes with the Xiu Maya, in an ill-fated attempt to reestablish Chichén Itzá's control over northern Yucatán. It is unlikely that these two Kukulcans are the same person, assuming that the dates are accurate.

Perhaps after the original Kukulcan's departure, the Quetzalcoatl priests took his name as their own. In addition, scholars have noted that *Can* denotes a prominent lineage among the Itzá Maya. Perhaps *Kukul* was merely a personal name that was given to various scions of this lineage at different times.

Contemporary Yucatec Maya groups continue to tell stories of the feathered serpent. One modern Yucatec Maya story describes Kukulcan as a young boy who was born as a snake. As he grew, it became apparent that he was the feathered serpent. His older sister took care of him and fed him in a cave. However, soon he grew so large that she could no longer feed him, and he flew out of his cave into the ocean, creating an earthquake. To calm his upset sister, who wants to know if he is still alive and well, he now makes the earth shake every July. Another story, by the Lacandon Maya, gives the feathered serpent a minor role among the gods. For the Lacandon, the feathered serpent is a huge, malevolent snake who is merely a pet of the principal sun deity and creator of human beings. Kukulcan, whether the feathered serpent deity, a pet of the creator god, the source of earthquakes, or the great Mexican leader of the Itzá Maya, plays some role in the mythic history of many Maya groups.

See also Feathered Serpents; Gukumatz; Quetzalcoatl

Suggested reading:

Burns, Allan F., trans. 1983. *An Epoch of Miracles: Oral Literature of the Yucatec Maya.* Austin: University of Texas Press.

McGee, R. Jon. 1990. *Life, Ritual, and Religion among the Lacandon Maya.* Belmont, CA: Wadsworth.

Sharer, Robert J. 1994. *The Ancient Maya.* 5th ed. Stanford, CA: Stanford University Press.

Thompson, John Eric Sydney. 1970b. *Maya History and Religion.* Norman: University of Oklahoma Press.

LA LLORONA

Time period: Postclassic–Contemporary

Cultural group: Mesoamerica

Dressed all in white, La Llorona (La Yo-ro´-na) wails in the night, often lurking around water, because her children have drowned. A dangerous woman, in some stories she kills her own offspring or brings misfortune to hapless men. Apparently a relatively new figure, she possibly hides pre-Conquest roots within her mythology, although these roots now lie very deeply buried. Like Malinche, with whom she sometimes fuses, La Llorona expresses more contemporary than ancient images of women; unlike those of Malinche, who remains largely Mexican, La Llorona's tales are spun throughout Latin America.

Women wailing in the night is not a new mythological theme. La Llorona is predated by a number of pre-Conquest Nahua mythic figures who likewise cry out nightly messages. Most of these ancient women either make demands or issue warnings about impending disasters. The female earth monster Tlalteuctli wailed in the night after Quetzalcoatl and Tezcatlipoca twisted her in half to make the earth; she demanded human sacrifice in return for her own sacrificial pain. In 1452, a weeping woman appeared to a saddened Motecuhzoma I during the great drought; he, unlike his heir who bore his name, survived that disaster. Perhaps because of that past warning, Motecuhzoma II told his chieftains to watch out for weeping women, for they could foretell an impending disaster such as conquest. Indeed, the goddess Cihuacoatl cried out in the marketplace that she was going to leave the Mexica, abandoning them to their fate. The post-Conquest La Llorona may carry some of this teary tradition, although she presents a rather different picture, in which deprivation, revenge, or malice is the motive for her wailing. Similar European myths exist that might have provided precedents for the modern Llorona.

As a mother, she wails because of a number of reasons involving her dead children. In some tales, she herself has killed them: (a) out of revenge to get back at their father, who has deserted her; (b) to conceal an illegitimate birth; (c) in order to lead a life free of motherhood's responsibilities; (d) because she wants to develop a new relationship with a man and the children are in the way; (e) because she's either widowed or abandoned, and is suffering from deprivation (in this scenario, she usually kills herself too); or (f) out of some mistake. Sometimes an accident has killed her children, or some other person has murdered them. Usually her children have been drowned, so she wails out her pain by some body of water: a spring, river, lake, or ocean. In the Malinche version of this tale, La Llorona wails because Cortés has abandoned her in favor of a high-bred Spanish wife. One such modern tale interweaves Llorona-Malinche with child sacrifice and Cihuacoatl. In this one, after the ancient gods sacrifice her children in Lake Texcoco, she turns into a female demon and warns Cortés (who admits he has wronged her) that Mexicans will rise someday against the Spaniards. Contemporary ghost tales from Guanajuato say she drowned her children and so now can be heard calling from the river during storms. Other Hispanic tales paint her as a bogeyman who will get you if you are not careful. Young women on sleep-overs challenge each other to say her name three times in front of a mirror, for then she will appear. The normal response to this is: "Not me!," or "I don't think so!" La Llorona even appears in make-your-own-mystery stories for children. A number of feminists have interpreted her figure as that of a passive woman who wails because that is her only recourse in a male-dominated world.

La Llorona also can become an evil temptress bringing great misfortune to hapless men wandering in the woods. No children appear in this story line;

instead, she fuses with a number of other contemporary female demons to lure either young men about to be wed or married men into disaster. One K'iché story tells how she appears to nighttime bathers during Lent, when the moon shines brightly. Dressed in white, she leads them on, crying and singing songs. One might hear people singing at a spring, but when one arrives, no one is there. Her cold iciness can leave a person stiff and unconscious on the road. If that happens, one must pry open his mouth and pour in a bit of kerosene to revive him. She appeared before one young man as his fiancée, telling him to come bathe. But when he had stripped to his underwear, she disappeared. This frightened him so much that he returned home naked, wearing nothing but his shorts. When his real fiancée came calling, she found him lying stiff and dead upon his bed. As with the nasty woman who appears in mirrors, one never knows what might happen if one should meet La Llorona.

> *See also* Cihuacoatl; Cortés, Fernando; Guadalupe; Malinche; Motecuhzoma I, Lord; Motecuhzoma II, Lord; Quetzalcoatl; Rain and Water Deities; Tezcatlipoca
> *Suggested reading:*
> Anaya, Rudolfo A. 1984. *The Legend of La Llorona.* Berkeley, CA: Tonatiuh–Quinto Sol International.
> Arora, Shirley L. 1997. "La Llorona." Pp. 753–754 in *Encyclopedia of Mexico,* vol. 1, ed. Michael S. Werner. Chicago: Fitzroy Dearborn.
> Tedlock, Dennis. 1993. *Breath on the Mirror: Mythic Voices and Visions of the Living Maya.* San Francisco: HarperCollins.

MALINCHE

Time period: Postclassic–Contemporary

Cultural group: Mesoamerican

The historical Malinche (Ma-lin´-chay), also known as Malintzin or Doña Marina (d. 1527), served as the Indian interpreter for Fernando (Hernán) Cortés during the Conquest. Perhaps because her role in that event proved so enormous, at least seven more distinctive mythological strands have developed that reach well beyond and sometimes completely outside her original historical tale, and multiply her personality in some amazing ways.

The few resources documenting Malinche's actual life are far more scarce than the extravagant mythology surrounding her. What little one can learn from early documents suggests that she was born to Nahuatl speaking parents of high lineage, the chiefs of a small town somewhere in the modern states of Jalisco or Veracruz. Bernal Díaz del Castillo, the captain in Cortés's army who documented the Conquest, weaves a romantic tale around her, which he swears is true because he claims to have met her parents. He says that, after her father died, she was given by her mother and stepfather to people from Xicalango because her parents did not want her to succeed to the throne, preferring instead that her half brother become ruler. Díaz claims Malinche's parents faked her death by telling the townspeople that a newly deceased slave's child was Malinche. They then gave her to the Maya of Tabasco. Pre-Conquest women sometimes did become rulers, so it is possible that her stepfather sought to consolidate his political control in this manner.

Cortés received Malinche as part of a package of gifts given him by the Tabasco Maya. The twenty women who came with the package were promptly baptized, given Christian names, and parceled out to various soldiers as concubines. One linguistic theory suggests that Malinche's name might be based on the Nahuatl day-sign *malinalli* (named for a type of grass); but more likely Malinche is a Spanish reworking of Malintzin, which is probably a native Nahuatl reworking of her Spanish baptismal name Marina. Thus even her name embeds the mestizo mix that came to characterize Mexico, a theme appearing in some of her later mythic personalities.

As soon as Cortés realized Malinche could speak both Maya and Nahuatl, the language most widely understood throughout Mesoamerica, she became his translator and lover. Malinche spoke Nahuatl to either a native Nahuatl speaker or someone translating Nahuatl into the local tongue; then she translated that into Maya for Jerónimo de Águilar, a Spanish sailor who had learned to speak Maya while living shipwrecked among the Indians; and finally, Águilar translated the message into Spanish for Cortés. Eventually, Malinche learned Spanish, simplifying this three- and sometimes four-way interpretive process. She bore Cortés a favorite son named Martín; and after the Conquest, Cortés gave her away in a proper Christian marriage to Juan Jaramillo, a Nahuatl gentleman with whom she bore a daughter in 1527. Unfortunately, she died shortly after.

Far more than a translator, Malinche was extremely skilled in the very difficult art of lordly rhetoric used in the presence of notables such as rulers, and she proved a skilled negotiator on many occasions. The only way for her to have learned these skills would have been for her to have trained for court life, which lends some credence to Díaz's story. Given her high birth, it is likely that Malinche saw her loyalty to Cortés as dictated by elite indigenous patterns of marriage alliances. She probably played the role of a primary wife acquired through an alliance deal made between the Maya and Spanish. Thus she was expected to help her husband Cortés; in fact not to do so would be to break the alliance, thereby placing her former Maya stepfamily in jeopardy. Historically then, she was neither a traitor to Mexico nor victim of circumstances, but a highly intelligent woman performing an extremely fine job according to indigenous standards.

Malinche's various mythic strands, however, portray her in a number of quite different ways. Sometimes these strands intertwine with one another, and sometimes they act completely independently. The first appeared during the Conquest while Malinche was still alive; people then often viewed her as a powerful "conquistadora;" and shortly after, they saw her as helping to bring Christianity to a people led astray by pagan beliefs. Indeed, this theme still appears occasionally in contemporary folk dances reenacting the Conquest. But with national independence in the early nineteenth century, a second Malinche emerged who was described in negative terms by Spanish language literature. Mexico then needed a new and more honorable national mythology, so Malinche became the traitor to an ancient noble past. These dark images still appear today. The third and fourth Malinches emerged later in the century, at which time she had taken on Euro-American mythic models of sexuality. In these tales, she became either an insatiable, conniving woman using her sexual wiles for her own gain, or an ideal mother to her mestizo children who becomes the victim of colonization and sexual violation. In the first—like Eve—she despoiled the American paradise; in the second—like the Indians of that paradise and, later, Mother Mary—she faithfully gave Mexico its first true heirs, but was wronged by the very people she served.

Many stories portray these themes, few of which find roots in the original documents describing her life. For example, she never traveled to Spain, her two children were not the first mestizos born (only Martín was mestizo, and he was not New Spain's first), she herself raised her children (they were never stolen from her), and she did not kill herself and her children because Cortés married a noble Spanish woman. This last story line intertwines Malinche with tales of the tragic and often nasty woman La Llorona who cries in the night because her children are dead. Nevertheless, such tales serve a need to portray history in a meaningful way. A fully independent Mexico needed to reject Spain and claim its ancient past, it therefore wanted to explain how its magnificent pre-Conquest civilizations could fall to European hands. To call Malinche a traitor or fallen woman does that, although that story line doesn't give full power to Mexico's mestizo heritage. To paint her as a victim, however, explains her otherwise traitorous actions in the Conquest without rejecting the ancient ways she represents or the new heirs she produced. Recently, a fifth myth has begun to emerge; in this modern tale, Malinche becomes a strong, capable woman caught in male-dominated circumstances beyond her control. This story serves as a feminist counter to the earlier overly negative or idealized Euro-American myths about women.

Oral folk traditions have presented two more themes that have little, if anything, to do with either the historical Malinche or those later tales dominating written literatures. The sixth Malinche must have developed very early. In this tale she takes on many of the characteristics held by ancient and contemporary indigenous goddesses who control the rivers, lakes, and springs and often reside in mountains. As with these deities, frogs, various snakes, and other watery creatures sometimes appear in Malinche's ritual iconography. A volcano in Tlaxcala in the Mexican Highlands bears her name, and people living on its sides see her as the carrier of moist, agricultural fertility. Others align her with Ixtaccihuatl, the great snowcapped female volcano lying just to the west of Mount Malinche; like Ixtaccihuatl, Malinche protects animals needed for food.

The seventh and last mythic strand appears as a hidden theme of indigenous resistance in the same dances that extol the Conquest and its spiritual gifts. The public or officially spoken tales of these dances describe the victory of Cortés and Christianity over Lord Motecuhzoma II and paganism, but the dancers' unspoken actions and costumes portray a more private tale in which Motecuhzoma reappears as a returning ancestor; and Malinche—as his wife, sister, or daughter—helps him reestablish his ancient rule. In La Danza de la Pluma performed annually in Oaxaca, Malinche even becomes two figures: the wife of Motecuhzoma, dressed in resplendent native costume; and Marina the consort of Cortés, dressed in rather plain European garb. In the end, Motecuhzoma defeats Cortés, regains his rule; and Marina abandons Cortés, returning to Motecuhzoma's and Malinche's sides. Thus, her tale comes full circle. Malinche continues to uphold pre-Conquest cultural patterns, but this time patterns bearing a temporal nature and social critique.

> **See also** Cortés, Fernando; La Llorona; Motecuhzoma II, Lord; Rain and Water Deities
>
> **Suggested reading:**
>
> Anaya, Rudolfo A. 1984. *The Legend of La Llorona*. Berkeley, CA: Tonatiuh–Quinto Sol International.
>
> Díaz del Castillo, Bernal. 1956. *The Discovery and Conquest of Mexico: 1517–1521*. New York: Farrar, Straus and Giroux.
>
> Harris, Max. 1996. "Moctezuma's Daughter: The Role of La Malinche in Mesoamerican Dance." *Journal of American Folklore* 109, 432: 149–177.
>
> Karttunen, Frances. 1997. "Rethinking Malinche." In *Indian Women in Early Mexico*, ed. Susan Schroeder, Stephanie Wood, and Robert Haskett, 291–312. Norman: University of Oklahoma.

MOON

Time period: Preclassic–Contemporary

Cultural group: Mesoamerica

The Moon plays counterpoint to the Sun but also acts independently in Mesoamerican cosmology and mythology. Although the Moon's phases most define its character in mythology, its relationships with the Sun and his alter-ego Venus also shape lunar myths. In Mesoamerican cosmology, the Moon usually moves through the night sky above as the Sun moves through the Underworld;

and when the Sun moves above, the Moon dives below. The Moon frequently acts on it own in determining the timing of rainfall and of childbirth, but at many other mythic times, Moon and Sun have acted in tandem—for example, in creating the world, and in disciplining its inhabitants. The complex interweaving of astronomical, cosmological, and mythic lunar themes presents a good example of how Mesoamerican deities embody particular sets of ideas: a plethora of details assembled under a fairly limited set of related themes, which may appear in groupings or alone depending on the place and time, but which always refer to an overarching idea. In this case, that idea concerns nocturnal, wet fertility in its twin-like essence, combining life with death. The Moon's participation in both creative and destructive deeds makes it fertile. The Moon as an acting, moving being frequently appears as a female creator, sustainer, or destroyer of life; but in almost as many cases, the Moon appears as an equally creative and destructive male. Often these tales describe some sort of relationship between a female moon and a male sun; a male moon and a male sun; or occasionally, a female sun and a male moon.

The Moon's role is not nearly as obvious in the Preclassic era as the Sun's. That doesn't mean it wasn't important; it just means that we still lack good information about it. Moon's mythic Preclassic existence is implied at Izapa by the appearance on a stela of what seem to be the Hero Twins vanquishing the false sun-bird. Since in the later story of the Popol Vuh one twin eventually becomes the Sun and the other the Moon, we can hypothesize that the Moon's mythic role was well developed at this time. This may very well be true, because almost everywhere in the world, lunar calendars preceded solar ones. The earliest known calendar dates appear in the Preclassic era and pertain to the divinatory calendar, which some argue was based on lunar cycles.

The Moon comes into its own in the Classic period, when both male and female moons appear in a variety of mythological situations among the Maya. A young woman sits on a lunar crescent, holding a rabbit, which in Mesoamerica appears on the full moon's surface. In some stories it is an aged goddess; but the Classic Maya seemed to prefer the Moon in her youthful state. The very male, warrior-like, ball-playing Hero Twins also come into their own at this time. The Hero Twins play the roles of Venus, the Sun, and the Moon, thereby marking the close astronomical ties among those celestial objects: Venus travels close to the sun's rising and setting, and the crescent moon often sits near Venus. The twins not only formed the world but also provided the foundations for Maya rulership. One of the major icons of rulers, a woven mat, shows up on the neck of the lunar jaguar Hero Twin; and at Palenque, rulers traced their ancestry to a lunar goddess. Mats, jaguars, and the paired Sun and Moon signified Classic rulers' powers.

During the Postclassic era, lunar veneration flourished in the Yucatán, especially at Tulum. At this coastal center, the aged lunar goddess took precedence—perhaps because there the Moon reached the end of her cycle and disappeared neatly into the Underworld's sea-waters. Some may have called an aged lunar goddess Ix Chel. Elsewhere the youthful and aging Maya goddesses depicted the waxing and waning moons, and the new moon sometimes played the part of a monster who ate the sun (explaining the solar eclipse). In Central Mexico, a male pair resembling the Hero Twins play the role of cosmic creators. In this myth, the gods Nanahuatzin and Tecuiçiztecatl jumped into a fire. As direct results of their sacrificial act, a black eagle and spotted jaguar rose from the fire's ashes, and two suns hovered on the eastern horizon. Another god smashed a rabbit into the second sun, thereby dimming its face; and the sacrifice of all the other gods, along with Quetzalcoatl's gentle puff, got the Fifth Sun's solar and lunar objects moving on their appropriate paths. The Nahua moon goddess, as either a youthful or an aged being, is less obvious than is the Maya moon goddess, although a number of similar traits are shared by various Postclassic moon goddesses in Central Mexican mythology. The youthful, defeated warrior-woman Coyolxauhqui might have been a lunar figure, as in various Maya tradition she was beheaded on the ball court; wore coral snakes and other Underworld signs, and was either the sister or mother of Huitzilopochtli in his hummingbird form, probably linking him also with the Sun. The aged goddess Cihuacoatl shares with Maya lunar figures references to the underworld, weaving, snakes, and jaguars, as well as governance of childbirth and earthly rulership. In both these cases, however, no direct statement in the written sources confirms these goddesses' lunar nature.

With the introduction of Christianity after the Conquest, moon gods and goddesses retained their prominence in mythology, but the Virgin sometimes took over aspects of their roles. The Virgin of Guadalupe, for example, came to stand on a crescent moon, repeating the Biblical tradition that spawned her—a most convenient link between European and Mesoamerican lunar mythologies. Modern Mesoamericans, like their predecessors in pre-Conquest times, sometimes address the lunar goddess as "Our Mother" and venerate her variously as either the wife or mother of God and/or Christ.

For today's Maya, the Moon's astronomical phases have the greatest affect on lunar mythology. The Maya say that the Moon disappears at the time of the new moon for a number of reasons: The Moon is now dead, and evil reigns because her protective light is lacking; or the Moon has gone to the underworld Land of the Dead, the Rain Deities, or a well or sinkhole. The waxing moon often plays the role of a young woman, perhaps one getting ready to bear children. The Tzotzil say people are fertile during the full moon, but the K'iche' say the full moon is masculine, the nocturnal likeness of the sun. For many others, this is the time of aging, a rapprochement with death. Both the K'iche' and Cakchiquel say that rain comes at the new or full moons; indeed, in this region, rain does often fall at these times. Others link the wet and dry seasons to the moon's yearly cycles. Some K'iche' say that the moon stands upright during the dry season so that water can't escape from its crescent, but lies tipped over during the rainy season.

Given the Moon's mythological connections to precipitation, it is not surprising that agricultural cycles were traditionally linked to the moon's phases. The Cakchiquel of Panajachel in the 1930s said that the moon was governed by four phases that also affected life on earth. At the new moon, people and animals were believed to be full of blood, and plants and trees, of sap; all were considered "green," even if they were old, and all were thought particularly vulnerable to death and disease. For this reason during a new moon no one was to spill blood for any purpose, whether gelding a rooster, harvesting grain, or cutting trees. As the moon waxed, people, animals, and plants hardened little by little, making it safe to harvest and cut things during the third stage, when the moon was full. But in the moon's fourth phase, people hurried to finish these activities before the new moon returned. The Yucatec Maya, however, said that maize, beans, and squash should be planted at the full moon in May or June, and everything else during the waning moon. Among the Classic Maya, Yum Kaax was a maize god who sometimes was linked with the moon and perhaps with Venus as the morning star and the rainy season. The Classic Maya God CH was the male counterpart to today's Hunahpu of Hero Twin fame; during their adventures in the underworld, both twins rose and fell with the corn they planted in their mother's courtyard.

The Moon also can govern women's cycles, pregnancy, birth, and motherhood. The Itzá said "her moon lowers" when a woman was menstruating, and the Tzotzil described the new moon itself as menstruating. The Tzotzil also said that women were most fertile at the full moon. Many Mesoamerican women counted the months of pregnancy by lunar phases. The goddess Yohualticitl of the Nahua died in the steam bath, so she now protects new mothers who rest there. And the Chamula say that every day, the Moon feeds maize gruel to her son the Sun.

The Moon often appears in tandem with the Sun, paired as dull and bright, cold and hot, sister and brother, husband and wife (sometimes fooling around with the Sun's rival, Venus), or mother and son. In Panajachel, some said that the Moon was married to the Sun. She came out at night to watch over their children, while her husband watched over their children in the east. Others in Panajachel said that an eclipse happened because the Moon was fighting with her husband. She was angry because the Sun had not been watching his children well and correcting their bad ways. Therefore, an eclipse showed how much closer the earth was to being lost because of all the wicked people. People rushed out to beat pots and pans, making a lot of noise to show that they were helping her, that they didn't want the Sun to strike her any more. They were afraid that if the Sun killed the Moon, she would take with her whomever she could. Moreover, she caused women's periods, and shaped the unborn, so a pregnant woman never came out during an eclipse; the Sun's blows might miss their mark and land on her, deforming or even killing her child. Throughout Mesoamerica, lunar stories are many and varied, but they usually have to do with fertility in its moist, nocturnal forms, both creative—forming babies, animals, and plant—and destructive—smashing ages to create new ones.

> ***See also*** Christ; Cihuacoatl; Coyolxauhqui; Earth, Agricultural, and Hunting Deities; Fifth Sun; Guadalupe, Virgin of; Hero Twins; Huitzilopochtli; Ix Chel; Quetzalcoatl; Rain Deities; Sky Deities and Beings; Sun; Underworld and Caves, Deities of the; Yum Kaax
>
> ***Suggested reading:***
> Aveni, Anthony. 1980. *Skywatchers of Ancient Mexico.* Austin: University of Texas Press.
> Milbrath, Susan. 1999. *Star Gods of the Maya: Astronomy in Art, Folklore, and Calendars.* Austin: University of Texas Press.
> Sahagún, Fray Bernardino de. 1953–1982. *The Florentine Codex: A General History of the Things of New Spain.* Trans. Arthur J. O. Anderson and Charles E. Dibble. Monographs of the School of American Research no. 14. Santa Fe: School of American Research; Salt Lake City: University of Utah Press.
> Tedlock, Dennis, trans. 1985. *Popol Vuh: The Definitive Edition of the Mayan Book of the Dawn of Life and the Glories of Gods and Kings.* New York: Simon and Schuster.
> Thompson, John Eric Sydney. 1939. *The Moon Goddess in Middle America.* Carnegie Institution of Washington pub. no. 509, Contributions to American Anthropology and History no. 29. Washington, DC: Carnegie Institution.

MOTECUHZOMA I (ILHUICAMINA), LORD

Time period: Postclassic

Cultural group: Nahua-Mexica

Motecuhzoma Ilhuicamina (Mo-te-koo-zo´-ma Il-wee-ka-mee-na), the fifth Chief Speaker of the Mexica or Aztecs (Nahua, ruled ca. 1440–1469), symbolizes the epitome of good governance. As the first of two Motecuhzomas to rule the Mexica, Motecuhzoma I represents their first real independence and power. Histories portray him as a shrewd and wise warrior and statesman, a noble leader who properly governed his people and created good order for the quickly developing Mexica state.

Motecuhzoma I followed on the heels of Lord Itzcoatl (ruled ca. 1428–1440), who first outlined the basic shape of the Mexica domain. It fell to Motecuhzoma to fill in that outline, thereby establishing the direction of Mexica hegemony for the next four rulers. It took the Spanish, during the reign of Lord Motecuhzoma II (Xocoyotzin) (ruled ca. 1502–1520), to decisively interrupt this thrust toward widespread power.

Motecuhzoma Ilhuicamina's magical birth foretold his great destiny. One night his father, the second Chief Speaker Lord Huitzilihuitl (ruled ca. 1403–1417), dreamed that he should marry the beautiful daughter of Cuernavaca's ruler, a renowned nahualli or magician. This ruler jealously guarded his daughter Miahuaxihuitl from all suitors. All manner of wild beasts—centipede, serpents, bats, and scorpions—surrounded her palace, keeping out intruders. Huitzilihuitl sent an envoy to ask her father for her hand. But he denied the petition because the Mexica were too poor to support Miahuaxihuitl in the manner to which she was accustomed. This left Huitzilihuitl very sad, but a second dream gave him hope. He was to make a beautiful arrow from the best cane, paint it most carefully, and in its center attach a greenstone shining with many brilliant lights. Standing on the borders of Cuernavaca, he shot this arrow high into the air so that it landed in the patio of Miahuaxihuitl's palace. When the princess saw the magical arrow land, she could not help picking it up. Discovering the luminous greenstone, she placed it in her mouth. Instantly she swallowed it, and thus became pregnant with Motecuhzoma I. Later, Lord Huitzilihuitl conquered Cuernavaca and claimed his heir.

Many trials awaited Motecuhzoma Ilhuicamina, including pestilence, floods, frosts, and snow that destroyed their crops, and a four year drought that caused tragic starvation among his people. But he managed them all as well as anyone could. When prosperity finally returned, Motecuhzoma successfully resumed the expansion of his domain through trade, negotiation, and war. He improved living conditions by bringing fresh water to the city, establishing penal and social laws, and setting high standards for civic and social advancement. He also encouraged the development of a sophisticated culture secure in its history and proud of its present accomplishments. Motecuhzoma is famous for reworking the Mexica calendar and recording Mexica history, and he constructed magnificent sculptures, beautiful temples, and rich botanical gardens.

In his quest for knowledge, he sent sixty magicians to their mythical place of origin Aztlan. There the goddess Coatlicue told them that her son Huitzilopochtli, the Mexica patron god, would abandon them; he would lose all the cities he had conquered for them, and return poor to Aztlan. This saddened Motecuhzoma I, causing him to weep. The myth came true when his heir and namesake Lord Motecuhzoma II lost to the Spanish conquerors.

See also Coatlicue; Huitzilopochtli; Motecuhzoma II, Lord
Suggested reading:

Codex Mendoza. 1997. As reproduced in *The Essential Codex Mendoza.* Commentary by Frances Berdan and Patricia Rieff Anawalt. Berkeley: University of California Press.

Durán, Fray Diego. 1994. *The History of the Indies of New Spain.* Trans. Doris Heyden. Norman: University of Oklahoma Press.

Townsend, Richard F. 1992. *The Aztecs.* London: Thames and Hudson.

MOTECUHZOMA II (XOCOYOTZIN), LORD

Time period: Postclassic

Cultural group: Nahua-Mexica

Motecuhzoma Xocoyotzin (Mo-te-koo-zo´-ma Sho-ko-yot´-zin), the ninth Chief Speaker of the Mexica or Aztecs (Nahua, ruled ca. 1502–1520), symbolizes the potential greatness of the Mexica, their demise, and the possible return of indigenous control. On the one hand, he's depicted as a powerful, skillful, and learned ruler who consolidated Mexica power. On the other hand, he lost to the Spanish; so he also appears as a fearful man, who vacillated at inopportune moments. But in the end, his rule and power has not been completely lost; and according to some myths, Motecuhzoma II may even return some day.

Following on the heels of his uncle the great Chief Speaker Ahuitzotl, Motecuhzoma II was the first to rise to power through his military achievements. He conquered some forty-two towns, which served to consolidate Mexica power by quelling rebellions and filling in gaps. Even Tlaxcala, the Mexica's great enemy just to the east, found itself slowly being hedged in by Motecuhzoma II and his allies; if the Spanish had not interrupted these maneuvers, the province might very well have been brought under Mexica control during Motecuhzoma's rule. He was said to be refined and discreet, to carry out his offices with great seriousness, and to be a skilled astrologer and philosopher, a firm judge, and capable in all arts, both civil and military. Moreover, he appears to have imposed a new order on the Mexica, one in which he himself was held with tremendous esteem and fear; an order that apparently was more dictatorial and less consensual than previous forms of governance.

But he also is said to have caved into the Spanish, thereby seriously debilitating the Mexica's chances at victory. At least some of these less flattering stories were probably told after-the-fact of Conquest, mythologically explaining how the Mexica had their world turned upside down. Storytellers relate how many omens predicted Motecuhzoma's downfall. A drought preceded the Conquest; a comet appeared, moving from where the sun set to where it rose; old women dreamed that a great river smashed his palace to smithereens, and old men dreamed that the Huitzilopochtli temple burned to the ground—not a good sign for the only leader able to talk directly with that fierce patron deity. Some say fire really did burn Huitzilopochtli's temple to the ground, and water only made the flames grow higher. Others say the goddess Cihuacoatl wept at night, crying, "My beloved sons, now I am about to leave you!"; and that the support beam of the House of Song, the place where warriors ritually sang and danced, sang out "Woe my evil rump! Dance well, for you will be cast into the water!" Fishermen caught a grey, crane-like bird with a mirror in its head. In the mirror, Motecuhzoma saw a number of men approaching, mounted on deer; but before his astrologers could explain this image, it disappeared. The Chief Speaker became so frightened that he tried to escape to Chapultepec where a cavernous opening led into the Underworld; but he failed at this when a vision of what he was doing warned his ritualist, who then came and talked him out of it.

At several points, Motecuhzoma II even tested Cortés, trying to figure out who he was. Was he really the returning Quetzalcoatl ready to take back his rule from the Mexica, for example? Early on at least, Cortés never comprehended enough about Mexica worldviews to make this claim, which resulted in an encounter of mutual misunderstanding. He accepted Motecuhzoma's gift of the garb of four deities (including Quetzalcoatl's) who empowered rulers; but he refused to eat the gift of food spattered with human sacrificial blood, and the magicians trying to feed him this found they could not magically control him. Finally, as Cortés approached the city, Motecuhzoma's magicians met not him on the road, but the Mexica deity Tezcatlipoca tied in ropes; the god told the Mexica they were already defeated, and he presented them with a vision of Tenochtitlan's neighborhood civic buildings in flames.

Perhaps out of fear, perhaps out of not knowing what to expect, Motecuhzoma welcomed Cortés and his army into Tenochtitlan. The Spanish quickly took him prisoner. Eventually, he died either at the hands of his own people, who had become fed up with his ineffectual rule, or at the hands of the Spanish, who in the last desperate moments of their occupation of Tenochtitlan, killed him along with several Nahua leaders they had imprisoned. The rebellious Mexica already had elected a new ruler and declared war against the conquistadors; sustaining enormous losses, the Spanish narrowly escaped the city. These stories often suggest that Motecuhzoma II failed because he had become overly proud and greedy. Had not the goddess Coatlicue already told his predecessor and namesake Motecuhzoma I that the Mexica would fail for just those reasons? Or, perhaps his new, but rather self-centered dictatorial order could not meet the extraordinary demands placed upon him by the Spanish.

Motecuhzoma II continued to live through the centuries after the Conquest, periodically resurrected in the form of rebellious indigenous leaders such as Can Ek, who claimed to be his spirit. And today he lives on in dances about the Conquest, where his role can be seen in two completely opposite ways. Their official tale is that Cortés battles Motecuhzoma II, wins, and converts the pagans to Christianity. The opposite, unofficial tale is that Motecuhzoma triumphs over Cortés, wins back his rule, all the while poking fun at the Spanish, Euro-Americans, and the Church. The first tale publicly presents the approved story, the second quietly brings to light private indigenous thoughts criticizing Euro-American rule and religion; the first maintains the status quo, the second resists and challenges it. In La Danza de los Matachines performed in New Mexico Indian towns, the public message says the dance is about the conversion of the Indians to Christianity, but the dancers enact a private, more critical message as well. A young girl wearing native dress plays the part of Motecuhzoma's mythical daughter Malinche. She goes to the spirit realm and brings the vanquished Motecuhzoma back to life. In one year that this dance was performed, Motecuhzoma called on his spirit warriors to help fight a great bull. This bull wore a T-shirt emblazoned with the words "The Saints," making an obvious symbolic link between the bull and Euro-American saints. Two native grandfathers then chased the saintly bull down, captured him, and castrated him with a toy laser gun. A sign was even hung on the bull's neck saying "Bull for Sale." The next day, an ancient traditional dance called the "Turtle Dance" was performed. And so the so-called "Conquest" was conquered, and the dance floor cleansed for a far more important event.

See also Acamapichtli, Lord; Ahuitzotl, Lord; Canek; Cihuacoatl; Coatlicue; Cortés, Fernando; Cuauhtemoc, Lord; Huitzilopochtli; Malinche; Motecuhzoma I, Lord; Nahual; Quetzalcoatl; Tezcatlipoca

Suggested reading:

Durán, Fray Diego. 1994. *The History of the Indies of New Spain.* Trans. Doris Heyden. Norman: University of Oklahoma Press.

Harris, Max. 1997. "The Return of Moctezuma: Oaxaca's *Danza de la Pluma* and New Mexico's *Danza de los Matachines.*" *Drama Review* 41, 1 (T153): 106–134.

Sahagún, Fray Bernardino de. 1953–1982. *The Florentine Codex: A General History of the Things of New Spain.* Trans. Arthur J. O. Anderson, and Charles E. Dibble. Monographs of the School of American Research no. 14. Santa Fe: School of American Research; Salt Lake City: University of Utah Press.

Townsend, Richard F. 1992. *The Aztecs.* London: Thames and Hudson.

NAHUAL (NAGUAL)

Time period: Postclassic–Contemporary

Cultural group: Mesoamerica

A nahual (Naʹ-wal) or nagual, is a spirit being or animistic entity closely associated with a human being. Exactly how, however, varies with time and place.

Among some groups, each person has his/her own nahual acting as a double, a shadow, or protective spirit. Nahuals often are animals such as dogs, horses, opossums, or jaguars, or natural forces such as lightning or meteors. Should one harm another person's nahual, one may harm the person who belongs to that nahual, or at minimum, make him/her very angry. When one is asleep one's nahual can go wandering, something one will see in one's dreams. One can send one's nahual out to perform a task, use it as an advisor, or even turn into it by shifting one's shape from a human to that of the nahual. The pre-Hispanic god Quetzalcoatl's nahual told him how to trick the Lords of the Dead so that he could steal the bones from which people were to be made. And a contemporary Salvadoran story tells about a woman who, on the night of a full moon, would get down on all fours on a particular rock. Turning first three times in one direction, and then three times in another, she turned into a huge pig. She then frightened people bringing their packages home from market because she wanted to steal them. But one night, a neighbor saw her do this, so he hid the rock upon which she had performed her shape shifting turns. When she returned to the spot, finding the rock gone, she turned three times in one direction, and three times in the other anyway, but nothing happened. Unable to turn back into a person, she remained a pig for the rest of her life.

The tradition of nahuals bears great antiquity, reaching from the present far back into pre-Hispanic times. Present day patron saints of towns or "hearts of the people," like their pre-Hispanic forebears, have their own nahuals to help them guard their towns. These nahuallies make nocturnal patrols, giving off evil airs to ward off rival nahuallies. Many today say that each sign of the zodiac has its own nahual; a belief, which is surely related to the ancient idea that each day sign of the divinatory calendar had its personal deity or nahual. Among the K'iche' Maya, the day a child is born determines its nahual. But, one does not tell the child what its nahual is until s/he is old enough to use the knowledge responsibly, otherwise the child might blame the nahual for her/his own bad deeds. Nor do children learn the nahuals of their siblings until they are old enough to act wisely.

In some places, professionals called nahuallies are people adept at prophesy, naming children, and treating illnesses; they sometimes also harm people. Great beings of pre-Hispanic times, such as the Mexica Chief Speaker Motecuhzoma II or the god Tezcatlipoca, often were reputed to be effective nahuallies. Now local curanderos or healers may hold similar reputations. Such individuals are often considered very powerful, even a bit frightening, however helpful or necessary they may be to the community. The linguistic root of the word nahual means to make something clear or audible. In other words, a nahualli's main task is to make things clear to others, and one of his/her main tools for doing so will be speech. Indeed, chants, songs, and poems play a central role in Mesoamerican rituals. It is no accident that a Nahua ruler like Motecuhzoma II was called "Chief Speaker;" like present-day healers, these high-placed governors often controlled events through their words. And it is said that a tiny figure of the Mexica war patron and sorcerer Huitzilopochtli danced in the hand of another sorcerer as a portent of the great ruler Quetzalcoatl's downfall. Like present-day healers, ancient magicians and soothsayers could send their nahuallies out on errands or could shift their shapes into distinctly out-of-the-ordinary forms.

See also Ajitz C'oxol; Calendar Deities; Devil; Dogs; Feathered Serpents; Huitzilopochtli; Motecuhzoma II, Lord; Quetzalcoatl; Saints; Sun; Tezcatlipoca
Suggested reading:

López Austin, Alfredo. 1988. *The Human Body: Concepts of the Ancient Nahuas.* Trans. Thelma Ortiz de Montellano and Bernardo Ortiz de. Montellano, Vol. 2. Salt Lake City: University of Utah Press.

Vogt, Evon Z. 1969. *Zinacantan: A Maya Community in the Highlands of Chiapas.* Cambridge, MA: Belknap Press.

1-DEATH (HUN CAME) AND 7-DEATH (VUCUB CAME)

Time period: Classic–Contemporary

Cultural group: K'iche' Maya

1-Death and 7-Death are the principal lords of Xibalba, the K'iche' Maya underworld. They rule and assign tasks to each of the lords of the underworld, thereby controlling events within their sphere.

In the Popol Vuh story of the Hero Twins Hunahpu and Xbalanque, the twins' uncle Hun Hunahpu and father Vucub Hunahpu anger the Xibalba lords by making thunderous noises over the lords' heads while playing ball. (In K'iche' mythology, the ball court is the earthly

Figure 63. 1-Death, Hun Came (Justin Kerr Archives, file no. 7795)

entrance to the underworld.) In retaliation, 1-Death and 7-Death invite these uncle-father twins to play a ballgame so that they might defeat and kill them;

through trickery, the lords of the underworld do indeed defeat and sacrifice the uncle-father twins. Nevertheless, the next generation, the Hero Twins, trick, defeat, and sacrifice 1-Death and 7-Death just as the death lords had done to the twins' uncle and father. They thereby avenge their uncle's and father's deaths.

1-Death is a common figure throughout Mesoamerica as a deity of the Underworld. The Yucatec Maya called him Cizin; the Mexica called him Mictlanteuctli. For the K'iche', 1-Death shared his exploits with 7-Death, his twin counterpart; 1-Death, however, was the dominant one of the pair. Historically, 1-Death has origins early in Maya prehistory, appearing on Maya sculpture and pottery as far back as the Classic period.

See also Cizin; Devil; Hero Twins; Underworld and Caves, Deities of the
Suggested reading:
Taube, Karl. 1993. *Aztec and Maya Myths.* Austin: University of Texas Press.
Tedlock, Dennis, trans. 1985. *Popol Vuh: The Definitive Edition of the Mayan Book of the Dawn of Life and the Glories of Gods and Kings.* New York: Simon and Schuster.
Thompson, John Eric Sydney. 1970. *Maya History and Religion.* Norman: University of Oklahoma Press.

OPOSSUMS

Time period: Preclassic–Contemporary

Cultural group: Mesoamerica

Opossums are archetypal thieves, tricksters, mythic openers of obstructed passages, and mediators between light and night. Their strange physical traits lend themselves to themes of regeneration as well. Odd little holdovers from the Cenozoic era, these nocturnal marsupials appear everywhere in Latin America. Opossums scavenge for a variety of grains, fruit, insects, and carrion. Females have two uteri and two vaginas; their babies are born prematurely and complete their natal growth in their mother's pouch. Males have a bifurcated penis and oddly placed testicles. A Trique myth says this happened when Opossum inappropriately climbed on the back of his daughter-in-law at her wedding to dance; his members have been stuck in that position ever since. Both males and females are endowed with opposable toes, a hairless prehensile tail, and a body so strong that it can withstand many hard blows. They are known to be fierce fighters, defending themselves against enemies like jaguars or rattlesnakes, which may explain why the Chilam Balam of Chumayel says that the years associated with opossums were also associated with abusive rulers. Of course, when feigning death seems the better part of valor, opossums also "play possum." The Maya Dresden Codex linked Grandfather Opossum with the end of a dying year, and the new year with an opossum "coming back to life."

At Tlapacoya, in the Preclassic era (around 1000 B.C.), someone buried a figurine of an opossum in a building dedicated to Quetzalcoatl as Ehecatl (that is, in his wind aspect). Buried with it were twenty female figurines with children in their arms, a bride's trousseau, a wooden cradle, and human bodies curled into the fetal position. Such maternal imagery perhaps prefigures later myths joining opossums with childbirth and nursing. Moreover, throughout time, opossums have shared a great deal with Quetzalcoatl although not always as Ehecatl. Alfredo López Austin points out

Figure 64. Old fire god. Opossum stole fire from a similar deity. (Museo del Templo Mayor, Mexico City)

that both are said to steal fire; discover corn; initiate the dawn, the rain, and open the pathway of the sun; they are associated with the four quarters, the moon, maguey, and dismemberment; enjoy Coyote as a rival; and appear as an old man.

Opossum images were so common in the Zapotec region during the Classic period, that some feel the animal must have been a god, although we do not know for sure if he was like Quetzalcoatl. One ceramic figure shows a richly robed opossum; another, a man dressed as the beast. Ears of corn hang around the neck of one, perhaps recalling myths linking Opossum with corn's discovery. Also during the Classic period, a workshop at Teotihuacan produced molds for making small clay opossums. In Postclassic Mixtec codices, opossums were linked with New Year celebrations, the ball game, crossroads, decapitation, the moon, and pulque. This strange creature fascinated King Ferdinand and Queen Isabella of Spain, who had never seen marsupials before. Today, some of these ancient mythological themes survive alongside a number of new ones.

Actual opossums are thieves of the first order, often snitching corn and other goodies from granaries and storerooms. Mythologically, one of the most important things they steal is fire, without which people's lives would be much poorer. A contemporary Huichol myth tells how some people discovered fire; then, because they didn't want others to get it, they guarded it closely. One night Opossum came by and asked to stay a while. They didn't trust her, but she assured them she only wanted to warm herself. Next day she thanked them very much and said she was warm enough to leave. They searched her all over but didn't find the little coal hidden in her pouch. Next night they saw a fire lit on another mesa top, and the night after, several more on other mesas; then they knew it was useless to try to recover it, since now fire was all over the world. In a Cora myth, the sky-dwelling Old One fell asleep by his fire. Opossum took some with his tail, withdrawing it little by little. Old One awoke and accused him of stealing his fire. Opossum replied: "No, No! I'm only blowing on it." Old One fell back to sleep. While he was snoring, Opossum slowly got up, sliding the fire to the cornice of the house. Just then, Old One woke up and saw what he was doing. Leaping, he caught Opossum at the edge, but the fire slid off to earth below. This made Old One so mad that he beat Opossum into little pieces with his cane; the pieces caught on fire and fell over the edge too. When this happened, Old One quit, yelling: "You're not going to steal fire from me, Opossum!" This is how fire fell to earth.

But just as actual opossums can take a great deal of beating without dying, and can come back to life after playing possum, so too can the mythic Opossum regenerate. The Huichol also say that after Opossum stole fire, people pursued her, caught her up, and beat her into many little pieces. They left her for dead. After a bit, she regained consciousness and began thinking about this problem. Beginning to get up, she put all her pieces—skin, hair, sandals, hands, top of her head, brains, everything—back in place. She was all right again and very happy. Then she thought: "Oh dear! Maybe they took that little piece I hid in my pouch." But she looked, and there it was. Taking it, she began to blow it gently into life—*wiwiwiwiwiwi*. Because Opossum brought them fire, the Huichol never eat the animals. The Cora also say that Opossum reconstituted himself after falling to earth.

Other contemporary Mesoamerican tales say Opossum was rewarded with her pouch because she brought fire to warm Mother Mary and the Christ Child. In a less salutary version of this story, the Nahua tell how Opossum wrapped his tail around a burning piece of wood to take it to the shivering Christ Child; but when he noticed that the embers had singed off all the hair on his tail, he cried: "Ah, Jesus! Ah, Jesus!" That is why he has no hair on his tail, and apparently why people invoke Jesus's name when they do something dumb.

As a thief extracts things from difficult places, so Opossum removes the obstacles from blocked passages, opening them up. The ancient Nahua believed an opossum tail made one of the best medicines for extracting splinters or foreign objects from the flesh and even bone, successfully and quickly completing a difficult childbirth, loosening the bowels, and clearing phlegm from the throat. Like all medicines, if misused, it could also produce disastrous results. They said that a dog who one night ate an opossum's tail was found at dawn dragging its intestines behind it.

Perhaps because s/he is such a good extractor, Opossum can bring the dawn, extracting it from the underworld. In the Popol Vuh, Opossum held back the dawn so that Xbalanque had time to carve a new head for his decapitated twin, Hunahpu; and only those who can help the dawn emerge could hold it back. López Austin argues that both Opossum and his frequent mythic challenger Coyote act as intermediaries between light and night. Coyote comes from the day and announces the coming of the night; Opossum comes from the night, announcing the day's coming. He also argues that Opossum travels the underworld's watery pathways, sometimes even standing in for the rain gods, the Bacabs.

Sometimes Opossum's watery pathways are on Earth's Surface. According to a Mazatec myth, at the beginning of time, the animals argued over whether rivers should be straight or curvy. To resolve the conflict, they sought out Opossum, looking in one tavern after another. Finally they found him happily getting drunk, singing, and playing his guitar. "Oh, Grandfather Opossum, should rivers be straight or crooked?" Opossum replied: "You've lost your heads! How can a river be straight? Its current will be too strong. You must make the river curvy with small whirlpools, where one can peacefully fall asleep in one's boat while fishing!" The animals applauded him for his wisdom. Indeed, Opossum is as wise as he is foolish. He brings us fire, only to burn his tail; or as a woman, she hides it in her pouch only to be beaten to pieces. Of course, s/he can put her/himself back together again—and in the end, get warm by the fire, enjoy a good drink, or snooze while fishing.

> ***See also*** Earth, Agricultural, and Hunting Deities; Hero Twins; Moon;
> Quetzalcoatl; Sky Deities and Beings; Sun; Underworld and Caves, Deities of the
> ***Suggested reading:***
> López Austin, Alfredo. 1993. *The Myths of the Opossum: Pathways of*
> *Mesoamerican Mythology.* Trans. Bernard Ortiz de Montellano and Thelma
> Ortiz de Montellano. Albuquerque: University of New Mexico Press.
> Sahagún, Fray Bernardino de. 1953–1982. *The Florentine Codex: A General*
> *History of the Things of New Spain.* Trans. Arthur J. O. Anderson and
> Charles E. Dibble. Monographs of the School of American Research no. 14.
> Santa Fe: School of American Research; Salt Lake City: University of Utah
> Press.

PACAL

Time period: Classic

Cultural group: Maya

Reputedly the greatest lord to rule the city of Palenque (Chiapas, Mexico), Pacal (Pa-kal´) lived from A.D. 603 to A.D. 683. He was both a historical and a mythic

Figure 65. Pacal's sarcophagus lid, showing him descending into the underworld (drawing by Kay A. Read)

figure, as we know from extensive hieroglyphic writings and images in Palenque sculpture and architecture. His long reign and extensive building program gave him the aura of a great ruler. However, it is how his descendants remembered him after his death that makes him an important mythic figure. In fact, for centuries after Pacal's death, the Palenque rulers and his descendants revered him as an important ancestor with close connections to the cosmos. Lord Pacal's sarcophagus lid portrays him beginning his journey through the afterlife, entering the underworld Xibalba like a setting sun. Some have interpreted this image as symbolic of Pacal's transition from the earthly role of ruler to that of powerful ancestor. Other sculptures and building facades also are dedicated to Pacal and celebrate his divinity and affinity with the cosmos, providing some indication of his close association with a sun deity similar to Kinich Ahau.

See also Hero Twins; Kinich Ahau; Quetzalcoatl; Sky Deities and Beings; Sun; Underworld and Caves, Deities of the

Suggested reading:

Schele, Linda, and David Freidel. 1990. *A Forest of Kings: The Untold Story of the Ancient Maya.* New York: William Morrow.

Sharer, Robert. 1994. *The Ancient Maya.* 5th ed. Stanford, CA: Stanford University Press.

QUETZALCOATL

Time period: Postclassic–Contemporary

Cultural group: Mesoamerica

One of a number of Mesoamerican feathered serpents, Quetzalcoatl (Ket-zal-ko´-wat) was an important—albeit not the most important—deity among the Postclassic Nahua. With the Conquest, he rose to ascendancy, and today he occupies a major spot in Mesoamerica's mythology. Because of his ancient heritage and his many post-Conquest transformations, he has become extraordinarily complex. Quetzalcoatl's personality displays two distinctive, occasionally intertwined sides, each of which has many permutations. The first—his creator side, in which he participated in the creation and destruction of the cosmos and moved the wind—appeared largely in ancient oral traditions. The second—his culture hero side, in which he legitimated emerging states and provided a morally upright governance model—appeared first in oral tradition, but literary traditions quickly picked up these themes and expanded tremendously upon them. Today, Quetzalcoatl's creative side survives only loosely among the many wind deities in folk traditions, whereas his culture hero side deeply permeates literary mythology presenting nationalist symbols and social criticism.

Various Postclassic Nahua stories describe how Quetzalcoatl created the cosmos along with his sometime competitor Tezcatlipoca, or with Tezcatlipoca's counterpart Huitzilopochtli. Quetzalcoatl and Tezcatlipoca are two of four sons born to the creator couple Tonacateuctli and Tonacacihuatl. After waiting 600 years, this old couple tells them to create the world. In one version, Quetzalcoatl and Tezcatlipoca fight violently with each other; first one vanquishes the other, then the other vanquishes the first. With each battle, one of the four ages is destroyed and replaced by another. The fifth and final age is governed by Tezcatlipoca, leaving the door open for Quetzalcoatl's triumphant return; this possibility becomes mythically important sometime around the Conquest, and now underlies much of the literary mythology. In another version, Quetzalcoatl and Tezcatlipoca cooperate, first creating fire, and later, a rather half-baked sun followed by the first man and woman, Oxomoco and Cipactonal, whom they tell to work the earth and weave. They also place the Lord and Lady of Death, Mictlanteuctli and Mictlancihuatl, in the underworld; make the thirteen skies; form the earth from the fish-lizard Cipactli, whom they twist in half; and produce all the rain gods from Tlalteuctli and Chalchiuhtlicue.

But Quetzalcoatl's role was not restricted to the cosmos's creation; many stories describe how he helped create much of the world's basic stuff. He participates in the Fifth Age's formation: first, by sacrificing all the gods; then, by gently blowing on the stalled sun to set it in motion. After the Fifth Age is created, the time comes to create people who will live in that age; so the gods tell Quet-

Figure 66. Quetzalcoatl (right) and Tezcatlipoca (left) (Codex Borbonicus, Museo de América/Art Resource)

zalcoatl to go to the underworld and retrieve some bones from Mictlanteuctli and Mictlancihuatl. Mictlanteuctli tells Quetzalcoatl he can have the bones only after he blows a conch-shell horn with no holes. Quetzalcoatl tricks the lord by calling some worms to drill holes in the horn, and bees to make it buzz. He tricks the lord a second time with the help of his nahual, who tells him to yell out that he's leaving the bones behind, while actually sneaking off with them. When Mictlanteuctli finds out, he sends his minions to dig a pit in which to catch Quetzalcoatl. Being a trickster, Quetzalcoatl occasionally messes up. He falls into the pit, scatters the two bundles of bones (male and female), thereby mixing them up, and lies there unconscious. When he comes to, his nahual tells him he's ruined them; but oh well, that's the way it goes. So Quetzalcoatl gathers them up and takes them to Cihuacoatl, who grinds the bones like corn, and using some of Quetzalcoatl's blood, fashions the first people.

People have to eat, and Quetzalcoatl helps with that too. He meets a red ant carrying a corn kernel. "Where did you get that?" Quetzalcoatl asks. "Over there!" the ant replies. Quetzalcoatl changes himself into a little black ant and follows him to a great mountain filled with good things. But then Quetzalcoatl doesn't know what to do; the mountain is too big to carry, although he tries. So Oxomoco and Cipactonal cast lots and discover that the god Nanahuatzin should open the mountain. Nanahuatzin (probably lightning) strikes a great blow, and out fly all kinds of corn and seed. But the rain gods instantly snatch it all away. Quetzalcoatl, in fact, is often associated with the rain gods, as the god of wind. He puffed the sun into motion, swept the roads, moved storm clouds, and destroyed the second of the five ages by blowing everything away. Rain ceremonies often celebrated Quetzalcoatl-Ehecatl because this windy god kept the world moving.

Quetzalcoatl's importance as a culture hero appears less clear than his cosmic role, for his many stories present quite a diverse record. As 1-Reed (Ce-Acatl), or Topiltzin-Quetzalcoatl, he probably once was a real ruler who in bearing Quetzalcoatl's name also bore some of the god's powers. Some mythological histories say 1-Reed was conceived when the warrior-god Mixcoatl forcibly lay with Quetzalcoatl's warrior-woman mother; Mixcoatl had been unable to defeat her in battle, so he defeated her this way. Another tale says his mother swallowed a bit of jade, causing his conception. Family rivals killed his father; so when 1-Reed grew up, he sought them out and avenged that death. In so doing, he took control of Tula and the Toltecs. One might understand these myths as tales of internecine warfare and internal political conflict. 1-Reed–Quetzalcoatl wins in the end; for he founds a line of rulers who took his title until the fall of Tula in A.D. 1070 under the reign of Huemac-Quetzalcoatl. They say that Huemac-Quetzalcoatl inaugurated the first human sacrifice; however, archaeological evidence suggests that the practice dates back to the Preclassic Maya.

Other stories say that under Topiltzin-Quetzalcoatl's wise rule, Tula became a center of prosperity, artisanship, and good order. The ears of corn grew as large as a person's arm, the amaranth as tall as a palm tree, and cotton came in many colors; and because all was so plentiful, produce sold at low prices and no one lacked for anything. Moreover, the gold, jade, and feather work were of the highest quality. Tula's chaste Topiltzin-Quetzalcoatl practiced great austerities, did not practice human sacrifice (according to some stories), and maintained good order over a vast area. In these tales, the Toltec heritage models good society, and Topiltzin, good governance. If an upstart group like the Mexica wanted legitimacy, they needed to marry into this line, which they did. Western historians believe that the cult of the feathered serpent emerged around A.D. 900 at Xochicalco in the Mexican highlands and spread from there throughout Mesoamerica, as far south as Guatemala and Chichén Itzá in the Yucatán, where he appeared as Kukulcan. Some scholars think that Topiltzin-Quetzalcoatl traveled to Chichén after he left Tula, but recent archaeological evidence causes others to contest this.

Mythologically, Topiltzin-Quetzalcoatl's rule collapsed because of sorcery and immorality. Tezcatlipoca's magic worked against the Toltecs because Quetzalcoatl had become neglectful of his duties. Many portents led up to their fall; the Toltecs danced and drank too much, they lost in battle, and a local mountain burned. Tezcatlipoca even appeared in the marketplace with a tiny Huitzilopochtli dancing in his hand. The onlookers stoned him to death, but the stench from his body killed many of them, and disposing of the corpse killed many more. In the end, the "dead" Tezcatlipoca made the survivors drunk. In other stories, Tezcatlipoca led Quetzalcoatl astray with pulque and women; ashamed, Quetzalcoatl left Tula and traveled eastward, marking the landscape as he journeyed toward the sea. The Mexica spoke of large rocks as landmarks left by Quetzalcoatl, believing that he sat and rested on them.

Sixteenth-century stories describe him disappearing in many different ways. In one, Quetzalcoatl went eastward and burned himself up. He became the Hero Twins' uncle and father, and his heart rose as the morning star; he vanished into the underworld, and after eight days, reappeared as Venus. In another, he left Cholula for Tlilapan, where he died, his body was cremated, and he became either a star or a comet; and in still another, when he reached the sea, he climbed aboard a raft of serpents and sailed away. Yet another claims that after a series of conquests, Quetzalcoatl simply sickened and died, and his body was burned. Fray Diego Durán (1971) offers at least three more stories, some echoing common folk tales and others the Bible. In the first, as had Nanahuatzin, Quetzalcoatl cracked open a mountain and disappeared into it. In the second, he cast his cape upon the sea, made a sign with his hand, and sailed off. And in the third, just as God parted the waters for Moses, Quetzalcoatl parted the sea with his staff; he and his followers marched through safely but the water engulfed their pursuers. Some believe that such obvious Christian elements suggest that unlike the stories about his role in creation, Quetzalcoatl's culture hero stories had not grown old enough by the Conquest to acquire much consensus. Quetzalcoatl's return in the form of Cortés arose not as a prediction of the Conquest but as an after-the-fact, mythic explanation for it.

Some sources do, however, say that Motecuhzoma II believed Cortés might be the returning Quetzalcoatl, ready to overthrow the rule of Tezcatlipoca-Huitzilopochtli. Upon the first sighting of Cortés's ship off the coast of Veracruz, Motecuhzoma sent out messengers with food for the captain. He told them that if Cortés ate it, it would show that he was the returning god; and if that were true, Motecuhzoma wanted first to die, after which Cortés could take possession. Motecuhzoma also sent the strange Spaniard clothing of four gods—special garments that probably gave his own rulership its power—at least one set of which belonged to Quetzalcoatl. But if the nervous Motecuhzoma believed Cortés to be Quetzalcoatl, others probably did not, for the Mexica themselves may have deposed Motecuhzoma when tensions mounted, and they certainly fought back the invaders most ferociously. Moreover, Cortés's own actions discouraged most post-Conquest mythic remainders; it quickly became painfully clear that Cortés was not the morally upright Quetzalcoatl.

New stories developed that led to Quetzalcoatl's ascendancy as an all-important mythic figure in literary traditions. Durán thought he might have been the wandering apostle Saint Thomas. This explained both where Saint Thomas went after Christ died and why it seemed as though native tradition sometimes echoed Christian teachings. The seventeenth-century Creoles picked up this mythic interpretation and expanded it into a full-blown support of nationalism; because Saint Thomas–Quetzalcoatl predated the Spanish, Mexico could claim its own distinctive moral heritage. Quetzalcoatl becomes an evangelizer, and the noble and chaste foe of human sacrifice (which was encouraged by the Devil); he promoted a belief in a creator god, prophesied the Conquest, and promised to return to restore his own righteous rule. By the eighteenth century, Mexico was able to anchor itself in a noble history separate from Spain and without human sacrifice, enabling it to move toward independence.

After Mexico's achievement of independence, Quetzalcoatl momentarily disappears, although Maximilian briefly represented either a true or a false return in some stories. But revolution in the twentieth century really did bring Quetzalcoatl's return. *Indigenismo* triumphed, and Quetzalcoatl with it. Immortalized by Mexico's top muralists, he represented various noble interpretations of indigenous traditions. José Clemente Orozco made him an emblem of the tragic human condition, comparable to Prometheus. Diego Rivera depicted him as the great moral hero, bringer of freedom and learning, and the source of legitimate Mexican society. Rufino Tamayo painted him as the bright-feathered serpent locked in eternal cosmic battle with the dark jaguar Tezcatlipoca. Quetzalcoatl also fascinated writers and scholars. As a dual lord of sky and earth, Quetzalcoatl became, for D. H. Lawrence, the prototype of the perfect Mexican society founded on a natural, indigenous aristocracy. Writing in a manner mythically like the old friars describing Saint Thomas fighting the Devil, scholar Alfonso Caso described Aztec history as a battle between forces of good and evil, with Quetzalcoatl representing the good. Now this great culture hero has reversed what began at the Conquest; his return represents not the Spanish overcoming the Indians, but the Indians overcoming the Spanish. Although Quetzal-coatl has all but vanished from many folk traditions, his actions, if not his name, survive in cosmic tales about the wind, which still moves rain clouds and blows worlds away. In some places, San Sebastian apparently has taken over Quetzal-coatl's role as the road sweeper; a lightning bolt, not Quetzalcoatl, often meets the ant; and an opossum may steal the corn.

> *See also* Chalchiuhtlicue; Cortés, Fernando; Devil; Dogs; Earth, Agricultural, and Hunting Deities; Feathered Serpents; Hero Twins; Huitzilopochtli; Kukulcan; Motecuhzoma II, Lord; Opossums; Pacal; Tezcatlipoca; Underworld and Caves, Deities of the

> *Suggested reading:*

> *Codex Chimalpopoca.* 1992. As reproduced in *History and Mythology of the Aztecs: The Codex Chimalpopoca.* Trans. John Bierhorst. Tucson: University of Arizona Press.
>
> Durán, Fray Diego. 1971. *Book of the Gods and Rites and the Ancient Calendar.* Trans. Doris Heyden and Fernando Horcasitas. Norman: University of Oklahoma Press.
>
> Lafaye, Jacques. 1976. *Quetzalcoatl and Guadalupe: The Formation of Mexican National Consciousness, 1531–1813.* Chicago: University of Chicago Press.
>
> McVicker, Donald. 1997. "Quetzalcoatl." Pp. 1211–1214 in *Encyclopedia of Mexico: History, Society, and Culture,* vol. 2, ed. Michael S. Werner. Chicago: Fitzroy Dearborn.
>
> Sahagún, Fray Bernardino de. 1953–1982. *The Florentine Codex: A General History of the Things of New Spain.* Trans. Arthur J. O. Anderson and Charles E. Dibble. Monographs of the School of American Research no. 14. Santa Fe: School of American Research; Salt Lake City: University of Utah Press.

RAIN AND WATER DEITIES

Time period: Preclassic–Contemporary

Cultural group: Mesoamerica

Rain and water deities constitute perhaps the largest, one of the oldest, most pervasive and complex group of gods and goddesses in Mesoamerica. This should come as no surprise when one considers the often difficult climatic conditions in the region; for much of Mesoamerica, water comes at a premium for only about one half the year, and it may not come in a desirable form. It can both nourish crops and destroy them with frost or floods. Yet life cannot continue without water. Therefore, these most important deities of moisture cover all aspects of water, including the unexpected, such as the fiery rainfalls and rivers of volcanic eruptions, and drought. The deities of water were created at the beginning of the cosmos, and sometimes cause its destruction. Their products seep, flow, pour, cascade and crash throughout the entire sky and earth; and the deities respon-

sible for this are male and
female, young and old, and interact with both plain folk and roy-
alty. Their age is immense,
easily dating back to the Preclassic period, and their variety is
almost mind-boggling. Nevertheless, a surprising continuity
has existed throughout the ages.

Like a giant terrarium, ancient Mesoamerica had water
constantly cycling through its
cosmic topography. The salty sea

Figure 67. A shell artifact (Museo del Templo Mayor, Mexico City)

water became sweet as it passed into the land, through the underworld, and up
inside the mountains where the water deities stored it. The Mexica claimed that
their high mountain basin, Lake Texcoco, actually originated from the sea. They
even performed an experiment to prove this. Some men located a point along the
seacoast where water was sucked in, and cast a sealed gourd into it. Then people posted around Lake Texcoco watched for it; and lo and behold, it appeared
bobbing on the lake's surface a few days later. The Spanish historian Fray Diego
Durán thought it likely true that the gourd indeed had traveled underground all
the way from the sea, for a large portion of the basin was salty. Emerging from
the underworld, water fell back over earth's surface to the sea as rain, hail, frost,
snow, springs, creeks, rivers, and river-like lava flows, for volcanoes were said to
rain fire upon the earth. Moreover, the sky was even said to consist of water.

An ancient Nahua story tells how the rain and water gods Tlaloc and
Chalchiuhtlicue gave birth to all the water deities. They lived in a great lodging
in whose patio stood four huge clay pots, one for each of the four cardinal directions. Each pot contained a different type of water: the first with good gentle
rains for sprouting crops, a second with nothing but spider webs and blight, a
third with frost, and a fourth with drought. The inhabitants on earth's surface
received the contents of whichever pot the gods opened. The Mixtec Codex Borgia shows not four, but five rain gods: one is good and controls flowery jade-rain;
the second, however, controls nasty fiery-rain; the third, fungus-rain; the fourth,
windy-rain; and the fifth, flint blade-rain. It's not clear exactly what each is, but
they're surely similar to the kinds of good and bad rains held in the Nahua pots.
And like those Nahua pots standing at each of the four directions, the Maya rain
gods, the Bacabs, held up the four differently colored corners of the cosmos.

Many say that, when the gods release their waters, they whack the pots with
great lightning sticks, thunderously cracking them open and spilling their contents

onto earth. The contemporary Yaonáhuac say that the gods crack whip-like lightning bolts to tame the storm clouds. In very ancient times, often these lightning sticks or whips looked like snakes similar to the fire-serpent wielded by Huitzilopochtli when he vanquished his sister Coyolxauhqui on the mountaintop. A Classic Maya ruler's heir inherited the symbol of rulership, a lightning stick mannikin scepter; the Maya rain god Chac also wielded this serpentine stick. Today, gods wielding lightning often are brash, young men like Huitzilopochtli, while thunder gods are aged. This probably has historic roots, for the pre-Conquest Huaxtecs depicted an elderly man leaning on a serpent-shaped cane.

In a sixteenth-century Nahua story, the god Quetzalcoatl discovers that corn and many wonderful grains are locked inside a great mountain, but he is unable to get them out. So, the god Nanahuatzin cracks the mountain open; then the blue, white, yellow, and red rain gods snatch all the seeds away. Likewise, the present-day Yaonáhuac say that the young lightning bolts discovered the corn; but no matter how much they crashed and thundered, they could not open the mountainous granary. Finally they called for Old Thunder-Bolt, or Nanahuatzin, who succeeded. This strenuous activity tired him so, that he asked the lightning bolts to wait while he took a brief nap, but they had no patience. They grabbed all the corn leaving poor Old Thunder-Bolt nothing but debris. Similar tales to this one are told all over Mesoamerica today.

Wind works closely with water gods because it moves clouds and stirs up waves. Quetzalcoatl-Ehecatl controlled the wind among the Nahua and Mixtec, so it is not surprising that he was honored in the same ancient sacrificial ceremonies that honored the rain gods. Some contemporary Nahua say that two kinds of wind exist, one moves rain from the sea, the other from the mountains. Once upon a time, a little cloud had to find out where his wind hid before they could be friends and be puffed through the sky. But like water, wind can be dangerous too. Each of the Mexica five ages perished in ways that sound similar to the bad waters held by the rain gods: the first was eaten by jaguars (rain gods usually sport jaguar fangs); the second by wind; the third by a rain of fire; the fourth by a great flood; and the fifth by drought and earthquakes.

Clearly today's watery gods and their ancient ancestors share a long-lived continuity. A preclassic Olmec-style rock carving at Chalcatzingo, Morelos, depicts a cave shaped like an earth monster's mouth; from its great maw emerges misty clouds raining upon corn, and a ruler sits at its entrance. In Mexica times, rulers bore responsibility for assuring a properly moist world; to accomplish this task, they embodied Tlaloc's powers along with those of other deities. Now Nahua still speak of a watery underground dwelling called Talocan, or the place of Tlaloc, which one enters through a great mawlike cave. One goes to this cave to make offerings to its inhabitants; some even travel in their dreams through this world. And silent sheet lightning courses through a Maya day keeper's blood to call attention to something happening in a dream or on a particular day. These diviners use such electrically spasmodic sensations to explain events or predict the future (see Nahual). They, as did the ancient rulers, also hold responsibility for rituals bringing rains.

If Tlaloc still lives, so does Chac. One Yucatec Maya story tells of the time when Chac wanted a servant, so he stole a young boy and took him to his sky home. But the boy proved quite a problem. He could not obey instructions. One time, in spite of being told not to, he looked in the hole left by a yam he had just dug up for Chac. Below he saw his home. So he got a rope and let himself down through the hole. But the rope reached only part way; and since he could not climb back up, he was left dangling in the wind until Chac found him and hauled him back. Another time, he swept all of Chac's party guests out of the house thinking they were nothing but dirty old frogs. Finally, wishing to play at being Chac, the boy borrowed the god's windbag, gourd, ax, and drum. With these he made a terrible rainstorm, which he could not stop, and the storm mashed the boy. Chac borrowed implements from another Chac to stop the disaster, then he revived the boy by making nine passes over his body. Well, Chac had had it with him, so he sent him home. When the boy arrived he asked his mother if the storm had done a lot of damage. When she said that yes it had, he told her he had caused it and what fun it had been!

In some areas, Saint John (see Saints) and angels have taken the place of the rain gods; and sirens or mermaids have replaced Chalchiuhtlicue and other goddesses. In response to offerings of tobacco, coffee, tamales, and bread, San Juan will send rain, or a siren will release her water from the mountains. In some Nahua towns, San Juan makes the clouds emerge from the ocean, and thunder is the sea's great roar. People celebrate his festival just as the summer rains begin, and they try not to distract him lest he forget his duty. But he can get overly rambunctious too. Once he caused so much rain that many people died; chasing him, the angels threw many clouds at him forcing him down. They tied him to the sea's bottom, so that he couldn't cause anymore damage.

Another Nahua story tells how once a woman could produce many big fat fish simply by washing her hair in the water from the local river. But when her husband found out how she produced these fish he grew upset, telling her that she had been feeding him the filth from her hair. He kicked her out. Sadly—for now she would have no children—she went to bathe in the river with other village women. Diving gracefully into the water, she emerged half fish and half woman, to the fearful amazement of all. Climbing to the top of rock, she played a lovely song on her guitar, and all her children, the fishes, gathered around to listen. Stories say that if you do not respect the siren, taking her children needlessly or not compensating her for her losses, she will retaliate. Many a hapless fisherman has found himself caught in her grips because he was not heedful. If this happens, he may have to give her one of his own children as a return payment for having taken so many of hers. Perhaps this is why the ancient Mexica sacrificed children to the rain gods annually; they needed to repay them in kind. Now all that is required is a soda or a bit of chocolate.

See also Bacabs; Chac and the Chacs; Chalchiuhtlicue; Christ; Coyolxauhqui; Devil; Earth, Agriculture, and Hunting Deities; Feathered Serpents; God L; Huitzilopochtli; Ix Chel; Jurakan; Malinche; Moon; Nahual; Quetzalcoatl; Saints; Sky Deities and Beings; Tezcatlipoca; Tlaloc and the Tlaloques; Underworld and Caves, Deities of the

Suggested reading:

Bierhorst, John, ed. 1986. *The Monkey's Haircut and Other Stories Told by the Maya.* Illustrated by Robert Andrew Parker. New York: William Morrow.

Durán, Fray Diego. 1971. *Book of the Gods and Rites and the Ancient Calendar.* Trans. Doris Heyden and Fernando Horcasitas. Norman: University of Oklahoma Press.

Landa, Diego de. 1978. *Yucatan before and after the Conquest.* Trans. William Gates. New York: Dover.

Sahagún, Fray Bernardino de. 1953–1982. *The Florentine Codex: A General History of the Things of New Spain.* Trans. Arthur J. O. Anderson, and Charles E. Dibble. Monographs of the School of American Research no. 14. Santa Fe: School of American Research; Salt Lake City: University of Utah Press.

Taggart, James M. 1983. *Nahuat Myth and Social Structure.* Austin: University of Texas Press.

SAINTS

Time period: Colonial–Contemporary

Cultural group: Mesoamerica

Mesoamerican saints often carry personalities and powers not borne by their more "official" namesakes or counterparts. Officially, saints in the Roman Catholic Church once were living persons who led exemplary lives. Sometime after their deaths, the Church recognized these individuals by canonizing them, making them Church saints. The Church's faithful invoke the names of saints in prayers, honor their memory by dedicating altars or whole churches to them, celebrate masses and special festival days dedicated to them, and sometimes even preserve their relics as precious remains worthy of particular honor. Saints serve as intermediaries between God and people, pleading on behalf of the prayerful for their special needs. Properly speaking, because of his sacred character, only God can be worshiped; saints should be venerated or offered great respect for their human virtues. They themselves do not perform miracles; only God can do that.

Figure 68. Plaques proclaiming miracles attributed to the deceased Salvadoran Archbishop Oscar Romero, Divine Providence Hospital, San Salvador, El Salvador (Kay A. Read)

The twelve apostles who journeyed with Jesus Christ; his mother Mary; various martyrs who died for Christian causes; and others of high character who present fine role models are among the many who have been canonized.

Unlike the official saints of Roman Catholicism, popular saints in Mesoamerica tend to be linked with local histories and to bear personalities and powers suited to their particular locales. Often these mythic folk are well-known Catholic saints, such as John, Thomas, Michael, Lucia, or the Virgin Mary; in Colonial times, Christ and the Cross became saints. Even today, a town or region might claim its own saint, unknown in Rome. These local saints, whether officially recognized or not, may appear to the faithful in the forms of statues or clouds, and may demand their own churches, much as the old gods required houses. As patrons of particular localities, they establish family and communal landholdings and give a community its identity; their special days therefore are celebrated moments in a group's annual ritual calendar.

Some local saints are associated with ancient Mesoamerican religious themes such as *nahualism* (see Nahual), enabling them to use their powers to help individuals, families and lineages, and towns. In many cases, a saint took over the job of a community's patron deity. In one colonial Nahua town, two elders dreamed that Santiago (St. James) was to replace their former patron deity Quail-Serpent. And so it was. Saints may heal the sick, make the poor prosperous, bring rain, support a farmer's or community's crops, or lead peasants seeking retribution and equality into often violent rebellions. Some local saints incorporate into their personalities classic Catholic taboos such as sexual transgressions that may be shared with pre-Conquest mores.

The historical circumstances surrounding the emergence of Mesoamerica's saints contributed to their uniqueness. The pre-Conquest tradition held that many if not all things of the world held a potentiality for embodying a large variety of powers. The Nahua called these powers *teo,* and everything from gods and mountains to bad little boys could embody them. When the Spanish first brought Catholicism to New Spain, indoctrination in the new religion's subtleties often proved minimal; and because conversion was both rapid and superficial, indigenous converts naturally understood this foreign worldview in their own terms. Saints took on powers not always discernible to the priests: It was sometimes difficult to tell the difference between the powers that made amazing things happen in the ancient Mesoamerican world and the miracles that also caused extraordinary occurrences in the medieval Catholic world. So even in urban areas, where Catholic education was generally more thorough, powerful miracles might be assigned ancient interpretations by indigenous Mesoamericans.

This birth of powerful local saints was encouraged through the centuries that followed by the isolation of the Mesoamerican "Popular" or "People's Church," which tended more and more to embrace popular interests and traditions. The official Church lacked sufficient numbers of clerics to meet the needs of the peasants living in the countryside, so it was common for a priest to visit a parish only once in three or more months and to stay no longer than a day or two at a time. The rest of the time, local folk saw to the day-to-day management of the church and conducted lay worship services, although they could not say mass. As a result, local communities had ample opportunity to incorporate a wide variety of folk traditions that were not historically integral to the official church but that the locals often saw as perfectly "Catholic." In this way, Catholic saints came to move the winds, bring rain, and sometimes even commit transgressions never contemplated by their Roman cousins.

In the town of Ocotlan, just outside Tlaxcala in the Mexican highlands, the Virgin Mary appeared to a peasant named Juan Diego, just as her sister Guadalupe had appeared to a different Juan Diego near Mexico City. It was an early spring evening in 1541, at dusk, when she called sweetly to him to come to where a spring sprang from beneath her feet. The holy water healed people of the smallpox that was ravaging the town. Eventually—so the story goes—the town's skeptical friars followed Juan Diego to an unusually fat tree that bore a statue of the Virgin in its middle. They placed the image in a small side alcove of their small church, but every night she bumped San Lorenzo (St. Lawrence) from his place of prominence, until the friars finally gave up and placed her in his stead, giving San Lorenzo the side chapel.

Like many Mesoamerican saints, the Virgin of Ocotlan, while probably a manifestation of the Spanish Virgin of Balbanera, nevertheless appears today in a concrete statue to help peasants in need, and she acts in very human ways. At present-day Zinacantan, San Miguel (St. Michael) similarly communicates with the faithful, diagnosing illnesses and prescribing cures. People also have found talking saints in caves, in the form of small pictures or statuettes, which they carried home and stored in boxes. San Lorenzo once was a talking saint in Zinacantan. People found him in the woods, dressed in tatters and very hungry. They brought him to the center of town, where they built a church over him. But the elders did not like a saint who talked, so they threw hot water over him to silence him. In the same area, much earlier, San Sebastián, with the help of his brother and sister, survived the deadly spears and arrows of Nahua and Spanish soldiers. His heart, which hung like a target outside his body, could not be pierced. Later the saint and his siblings were transformed into statues. Eventually a book told the villagers that San Sebastián wanted to stay where he was, with a drum that had belonged to his brother, and with his heart-target. So they built a church around him, and this is how he appears today. According to the official Church, San Sebastián was killed by arrows and then brought back to life; his form of death compares well with some pre-Conquest sacrifices in which the offering's heart was pierced by arrows.

Saints often led movements of resistance or popular rebellions against Spanish or Ladino authorities. Between 1708 and 1713, in highland Chiapas, four movements occurred, perhaps in reaction to an earlier attempt to stamp out nahualism. In three, the Virgin descended from heaven, promising to help the Indians; in each case, they built her a chapel on the spot and made offerings to her of food and incense. The fourth occurred in Chenalho. The statue of San Sebastián sweated twice, so the peasants built him a chapel. And then, the town's patron San Pedro (St. Peter) began to emit rays of light, thoroughly frightening everyone into thinking the world was coming to an end. The peasants performed many penances in response. The church officials burned the chapel.

In 1867, the Cuscat rebellion rose up in Chamula, against the harsh economic conditions of the Indians. Local saints and the Mother of God led the revolt. It all began when young Augustina Gomes Checheb saw three stones drop from heaven while tending her sheep; these stones passed to the local official Pedro Diaz Cuscat. Through Augustina and Cuscat, the stones talked to people; then, Augustina miraculously gave birth to several clay figurines, thereby becoming the Mother of God. The figures were installed as saints in a chapel, despite of the local priest's disapproval. On Good Friday, worshipers traveled to the entombed Christ in San Cristobal, where they actually sacrificed a boy between 10 and 11 years old. The sacrifice of the boy symbolically replaced the passion of Christ, allowing the Indians to reject all worship of Ladino and White gods; now they worshiped deities of only local origin. Using the cofradía system, the Indians also assigned saints to each ranch, thereby replicating the ancient social system as well. Eventually the authorities imprisoned Cuscat and Augustina; but a Mexican schoolteacher, Ignacio Fernandez Galindo, took their place, declaring that he was St. Matthew, his wife was St. Mary, and his companion was St. Bartholomew. Tensions led to the outbreak of armed conflict, which petered out around 1871.

More recently, Archbishop Oscar Arnulfo Romero was killed because he supported the peasants' cause during a civil war in El Salvador. Peasant goals often crossed with those of El Salvador's official Church, and Archbishop Romero was the Church's primary representative. At first, he had opposed the rebels, but he was converted to their cause after another priest, along with several peasants and children, was gunned down on the road to town. This opened the archbishop's eyes to the plight of the peasants, and he became a staunch critic of the military's brutality, the wealthy's greed, and the official Church's role in both. On 23 March 1980, Romero told Salvadoran soldiers not to obey military orders to kill; the next day, while saying mass, he was shot by highly trained marksmen, who fled in a shiny black car with opaque windows. On the tenth anniversary of his death, the official Church began motions to canonize him, a move considered moot by some within the Popular Church, who already venerated Romero. Although the canonization process is not yet complete as of this writing, the People's Church has assigned Romero the role of martyr and saint by popular consensus; numerous miracles of healing have already been attributed to him, and he has become the patron of more than one local congregation.

Saints can do many things. Among the Tzotzil, San Miguel can protect you from your enemies; in Oxchuk, Santa Lucia can cure a child of sickness of the eyes; and the water of the Virgin of Ocotlan can cure a variety of illnesses. San Simón or Maximón (Grandfather Simon), who also sometimes goes by the name of Judas, is well known for his ability to help the hopeless. He, however, is not an official saint, although he bears some slight resemblance to various biblical Simons. His primary shrine, at San Andres Itzapa, is maintained by a local cofradía, but many others can be found elsewhere, even in people's homes. Surrounded by written testimonials to the aid he has given people, San Simón's carved wooden statue at San Andres sits upright on a blue ceramic dais. He sports a broad-brimmed Stetson, a faded suit that was once either blue or grey, a crimson tie at his neck, and a shawl around his shoulders. A floral towel covers his lap and legs, and he wears rubber boots. The saint's right hand grasps a silver-tipped cane; his left remains empty so that it can receive the banknotes folded in half that people offer him. People also used to burn candles and copal at his feet, before he was accidentally set on fire; since then, people burn their offerings at a slight distance.

A number of saints have taken over the job of the ancient rain and wind gods. According to some contemporary Nahua, the old thunder-and-lightning people found the baby San Juan (St. John) inside a calabash. They offered him tortillas and coffee, but he didn't want either. Instead, he grew up very large and strong eating nothing but the smoke from copal offerings burned in braziers, and could strike down any enemy. When he grew larger, he went screaming through the fields, so they built him a house at the bottom of the sea.

"Do you like this house?" they asked.

"Yes, I like it. Now I won't leave," he said.

So they told him, "If you don't go, it's all yours, all the water. When God's children make you an offering, throw the clouds up so it rains on earth." The storyteller then tells us that that is why they play music, so that the clouds, which are alive, will come and rain. They also say that because he was forever looking at the sky, San Juan never sees the people celebrating his festival before the rain comes, and they certainly don't want to distract him lest he forget his duty. St. John's feast day falls on 24 June, just three days past the summer solstice, during the rainy season.

Among the Yucatec Maya, San Miguel receives the most bread at rain ceremonies because he is the chief of the Chacs. The Chortí Maya say San Lorenzo is one of the wind gods who carry the rain that makes the corn grow. He also blows the first breath into newborn children and takes it away at death, and he carries away evil winds that curers extract from sick people to make them well. Many of the shrines of San Sebastián were built over those of Quetzalcoatl in his wind form, and it is said that he "sweeps the road," just as the Feathered Serpent did in olden times. Although Fray Diego Durán compared Santiago with the sun, and Cortés and his soldiers used to yell "Santiago y a ellos!" ("[for] St. James and against them!") when they charged into battle, the Totonacs now say that Santiago is the God of Thunder. This may relate to the official St. James, whom Jesus called one of the "sons of thunder" because of his extreme zeal, but it probably doesn't hurt that Santiago's feast day occurs during the rainy season, on 25 July.

But saints' activities are not always completely noble, serious, or even particularly helpful. In the town of Santa Lucia, the story goes that Santa Lucia used to "talk with" San Tomás (St. Thomas) of Oxchuk; in other words, they were having an affair. She loved him so much that she gave him her eyes. This frightened San Tomás a great deal, so he gave them back to her. She never spoke to him again. They say Santa Lucia caused lightning to strike Oxchuk's church because she was so angry. But lightning also struck the church of Santa Lucia so strongly that it had to be rebuilt; that was the fault of San Tomás. They also say that the coupling of the two saintly lovers produced corn, beans, and wheat. Durán thought that Quetzalcoatl was the noble San Tomás; if that is so, then San Tomás apparently had lost his nobility and taken over the philandering side of Quetzalcoatl.

And nor is San Pedro always completely serious. The Nahua tell trickster tales in which San Pedro or his human namesake do some pretty silly things. In one, San Pedro helps a bored shepherd raise the dead, after which the two of them share a chicken for dinner. The shepherd, however, secretly eats the liver himself. Then San Pedro splits the money they received from their amazing feat into three piles.

"Why did you divide it into three when there are just two of us?" asked the shepherd.

"Because the third pile is for the person who would have eaten the liver, but strangely enough, we enjoyed a liverless chicken," the saint replied.

"Oh, well, I ate the liver," said the shepherd, picking up the money. San Pedro then warned him not to try raising any more dead people, and retired to heaven. Of course the foolish shepherd did, and of course he got into trouble with the Devil for trying. In another tale, San Pedro's human namesake fooled a priest by stealing his horse and then selling it back to him after he had whitewashed it to disguise it. Unfortunately, he also stupidly told the priest to wash the horse, thereby revealing his lie.

> *See also* Chac and the Chacs; Christ; Cortés, Fernando; Devil; Feathered Serpents; Nahual; Quetzalcoatl; Sun; Underworld and Caves, Deities of the
> *Suggested reading:*
> Bricker, Victoria Reifler. 1981. *The Indian Christ, the Indian King.* Austin: University of Texas Press.
> Lockhart, James. 1992. *The Nahuas after the Conquest: A Social and Cultural History of the Indians of Central Mexico, Sixteenth through Eighteenth Centuries.* Stanford, CA: Stanford University Press.
> Nash, June. 1985. *In the Eyes of the Ancestors: Belief and Behavior in a Mayan Community.* 2d ed. Prospect Heights, IL: Waveland Press.
> Tedlock, Dennis. 1993. *Breath on the Mirror: Mythic Voices and Visions of the Living Maya.* San Francisco: HarperCollins.

SKY DEITIES AND BEINGS

Time period: Preclassic–Contemporary

Cultural group: Mesoamerica

The Sky is the opposite of the Underworld, and soars far above earth's surface, which lies sandwiched between the two. In many, many Mesoamerican cosmologies, when day rules the Sky, night governs the Underworld; and when night governs above, day rules below. Both the Sky and the Underworld are watery realms, but the upper forms the liquid walls of a great house, whereas the lower is the damp inside of a great beast; dividing the two, earth's surface serves as both a floor to the first and a roof to the second. Sky and Underworld together encase a dry, airy, inner home in which reside humans and other beings. But unlike the Underworld, the Sky cannot be entered by a living person. Perhaps this is so because humans cannot penetrate the walls of the cosmic house within which they reside; they can only pass through doorways or openings into the world below. Various nonhuman beings can and do pass along pathways coursing through the Sky's watery walls, like swimmers flowing with a river's currents. Depending on the mythic source, deities, saints, and ancestors dwell in the Sky; celestial objects such as the sun, moon, planets, and stars move through its many channels; serpents form Sky's riverways, passing into the Underworld; and birds fly through the warm air-bubble caught inside the celestial walls and earthly floor, occasionally traveling (as do most sky-beings) into the Underworld and out again. In spite of historical and geographical diversity, five related themes appear frequently in numerous

Figure 69. The sun and moon from the Primero Memoriales, *fol. 282r (courtesy of Ferdinand Anders)*

celestial myths: (a) the motions of celestial objects; (b) the Sky's role in creation; (c) the cosmic space Sky helps form, and its inhabitants; (d) the role of water and clouds; and (e) the activities of ancestors and the dead, and their relationships to those still living on earth's surface.

The Sky had claimed its important mythical place in cosmic dramas by the Preclassic era. (Significantly, the earliest recorded dates also originated in this era.) Among the Olmec, a celestial plane rose above an earth-dragon floating on the ocean's surface; a fish governed the sea below. The Sky was ruled by a great solar bird-monster who helped grow the plants sprouting from the earth-dragon's back and who created the patterns of time with his motions. The Olmec carved designs commonly called skybands, of alternating suns, moons, stars, and darkness. Atlantean figures held up the sky, one at each of the four corners of the cosmos: The Olmec oriented their buildings and urban plans to celestial motions and the universe's four quarters and cosmic center. In the late Preclassic era, the people of Izapa carved depictions of a long-lipped god, part fish and part human—a probable precursor to the rain god who sent clouds and lightning into the sky's realm. Reminiscent of Olmec carvings, these Izapa artifacts also depict a solar bird-deity, a vulture-precursor to the Postclassic Popol Vuh's 7-Macaw, the false sun whom the Hero Twins defeated before they themselves claimed the celestial realm. Like the twin heroes in that later story, two figures etched on Izapan stones shoot and kill the great solar bird, and one loses his arm in the fight.

By the Classic period, the Sky had become a complex topography through which celestial beings traced their paths. The ancient Mayans likely saw the Popol Vuh's creative events unfold in the Sky's motions; and as did the Olmec, they oriented their urban centers to align with these movements. Likewise, in Oaxaca at Monte Albán and in the Valley of Mexico at Teotihuacan, Mesoamericans coordinated their buildings with the local terrestrial landscape and celestial events. Like many, many others, the Teotihuacanese followed the motions of the Pleiades, noting that it underwent a heliacal rising the same day the sun passed across its zenith. Every fifty-two years, the Pleiades' constant appearance in the night sky prepared the Postclassic Mexica for the sun's nadir, which occurred on a particular autumnal day when the rainy agricultural season was giving way to the dry season of war. At midnight on that date in the year 2-Reed, the Mexica doused all their fires and set a new one in the chest cavity of a human sacrificial offering, feeding the offering's heart to the fire. Every temple and hearth fire in the entire domain was started anew from that one conflagration. It was believed that if this meal was not accomplished, a new sun could not be born because it lacked sufficient nourishment; instead, nocturnal forces would devour all, and the Fifth Sun or Age would end.

With Christianity's introduction in the Colonial period, the cosmos's inhabitants shifted around a bit to accommodate the new deities. Some of the newcomers took over the jobs of some (though certainly not all) of the old patron, wind, or rain gods, and accordingly located themselves on Earth's Surface, in the sea, or in caves. But the celestial nature of Christianity made the sky a favored location. God, Christ, or both at once usually became the Sun, and Saint James or Santiago sometimes took over Venus's job as the Sun's partner and his path the Milky Way. Guadalupe claimed the old pre-Conquest Sun's rays, and the Moon. Of course, the Moon, Venus, and the Milky Way—like many other indigenous beings—continued in clearly pre-Conquest forms right up to the present, in spite of the changes the Conquest brought. And for many today, the inhabitants of both upper and lower realms continue to interact—sometimes pacifically, sometimes not—as they go their often diverse and complicated ways through this cosmic apartment building.

The sky can seem a remote place, beyond the reach of mere humans. As if responding to this sense of distance, the Mesoamerican dead often depart for the Sky's waterways (usually after visiting the Underworld first), and for some, babies come from that faraway place. However, while the Sky and its inhabitants may seem distant (after all, what human can fly or swim there?), its rules are not. Celestial objects move according to highly regularized astronomical laws; their motions structure all existence, and govern all life by diurnal and yearly patterns. The Sun and its companions determine when people will rise from bed, eat, and return again to their nightly slumbers; celestial motions dictate the wet and dry seasons, when people will plant, harvest, hunt, and wage war. Remote though it be, the Sky therefore is not a mysterious place; its rules are clear and theoretically discernable, actually powerful on a daily basis, and even sometimes humanly controllable.

Such powerful, theoretical clarity may help explain the nature of sky mythologies, especially those involving the motions of celestial objects. Astronomical stories generally take one of two forms. The first stresses a strong narrative, telling an often exciting story. But when one looks closer, astronomical information lies embedded in the narration, for the tale's characters act on several levels, at least one of which describes celestial motions, coordinating them with the story's mythic actions. The Hero Twins of the Popol Vuh are not just stupendous siblings who create the cosmos; they also play the roles of actual celestial objects—Venus, the Sun, and the Moon—whose motions really do appear in the sky. Such information may remain hidden to the audience, however, if they are not trained in the complex astronomical system of divinatory knowledge.

The second, more obvious form stresses astronomical knowledge over mythical narrative. The story line may be weak but the tale's structure both strong and theoretically clear. The Mexica myth of the 4-Suns follows a deceptively simple narrative pattern. Each sun or age contains some sort of inhabitants, who live in a particular kind of dwelling and eat a particular food, and each is laid out and then destroyed. The important element throughout is that each age lives for an exact period of mathematically calculable time, whose years coordinate exactly with the solar calendar. This quasi-story is more about astronomical calculation than heroic deeds or events; nevertheless, it was extremely important, for the Mexica Fifth Sun also would live according to that same calendrical pattern. Each previous age had lasted 676 years, or 13 x 52 years; so too would the Mexica Fifth Sun. Such precise knowledge gave people hope that they could control the Sky's effect on terrestrial life through sacrificial rituals; for this reason, every 52 years, the Mexica gave birth to a new sun.

The mathematical dimensions of celestial myths reflect complex astronomical patterns. For example, the Mexica associated the Milky Way with no less than three deities, Citlalicue and Ilamatecuhtli (both goddesses who wore starry skirts), and the god Mixcoatl, whose name meant "Cloud Serpent," and whose black face bore white stars. For many, the Milky Way was a celestial path made either of clouds lit by the night sky, or water flowing like a great celestial river. In one Classic Maya myth carved on bone, the Milky Way in its east-west position became a canoe carrying the Maize God into the Underworld. There he would set up three hearthstones, which would rest at the Place of Creation; these stones were three stars in and near Orion (Alnitak, Saiph, and Rigel). It was here that the first fire would be drilled; the nebula (M42) at the constellation's center was said to be the fire's smoke.

The Classic Maya Lord Pacal (A.D. 615–683) is shown on his sarcophagus lid sliding down the Milky Way (depicted as a great tree) into the earth monster's skeletal mouth. Today's K'iche' say that the black, starless cleft in the Milky Way is the road to Xibalba, the Land of the Dead, and that the Hero Twins' twin fathers were Venus at the end of its morning cycle. At this time, the planet rests near the Milky Way's black cleft, as though ready to descend into the Underworld, where it will disappear before rising as the Evening Star. The twins' twin half brothers, 1-Monkey and 7-Monkey, move through the night sky as Mars in its retrograde motion. And whereas Lord Pacal became a new sun upon death, just as did the Hero Twins, his heir Lord Chan Bahlum lived by the motions of Jupiter, coordinating all his life's major events with that planet's movements. In the 1930s, the Milky Way was Santiago's or Venus's Way, to the Cakchiquel Maya of Panajachel. When Venus appeared in the morning, it was time to grind corn for tortillas; and if the Milky Way appeared very clear at night, the new day surely would dawn cold. They also said that horses must lie down at 3:00 in the morning when Jupiter appeared, otherwise they would be injured; horses already knew this, and this was why they stumbled at that hour if out traveling.

Creation often involves the restructuring of space and its inhabitants after their sacrificial destruction. A great flood collapsed the walls and roof of the Postclassic Mexica Fourth Age. In the "Historia de los Mexicanos por sus pinturas," Tezcatlipoca and Quetzalcoatl traveled to the center of the earth, where the four crossroads met. With the help of four others, they hoisted the celestial roof with all its stars back into place; then the two gods made two great trees to hold it up. Afterward, Quetzalcoatl and Tezcatlipoca created the Milky Way, and Tezcatlipoca turned it into the god Mixcoatl (Garibay, K. 1985, 32–35). Later, the sun and moon were created out of the sacrifices of two gods, Nanahuatzin and Tecuiçiztecatl, who leaped into a fire, as did the Maya Hero Twins in the Popol

Vuh. Today, in a recreation of the cosmos's creation, Chortí diviners ritually hoist the four quarters of the sky into place beginning each 25 April. They do this every night until the rains return. In Panajachel, they said that the Sun or God the Father created everything on earth. But for the Tzeltal, the sun is the youngest of three brothers—God the Father, Jesus his Son, and the Holy Ghost or K'osh—whose mother is Grandmother Moon. K'osh, the brightest in more than one way, eventually tricked his elder siblings, turning them into wild and domestic pigs. After burning the forest to create a cornfield—against the wishes of a great bird who guarded it—he took his brightness into the sky. That is why, every day, darkness follows light.

Maintaining this cosmic space also may require sacrificial destruction either to sustain the living cosmic beings or to create what is necessary for their sustenance. The Mexica said that male warriors who had died in sacrificial rituals captured the sun each day from the Land of the Dead's inhabitants and carried it to its zenith at noon, whereupon dead women warriors captured the sun from the men and carried it down to feed the western-facing earth monster. In Panajachel, they said that the sky met the earth at the horizon, far across the sea. This is where the Lacantunes lived; unfortunately for them, the Sun ate one of them each day as it rose in the east, and another when it set in the west. According to the Cora, Opossum used to live in Old One's house, way up in the sky. Old One was so annoyed at Opossum for trying to steal his fire that he beat him into little pieces, which ignited and fell over the edge onto earth's surface. After landing, however, true to the sacrificial-transformative formula, Opossum pulled himself back together, and now people have fire with which to warm themselves and cook their food.

The Sky's space, like Earth's Surface and the Underworld, is divided into four quarters. Four roads radiate from the center, creating the crossroads at which Quetzalcoatl and Tezcatlipoca met to create the Mexica cosmos. The K'iche' say that the red road moves east; the black, north; the white, west; and the yellow, south. The black road is the cleft in the Milky Way, which leads to the underworld of Xibalba. The ancient Maya said that the roots of the great Milky Way tree lay in the south and its tip arched to the still dark spot near the North Star around which all stars rotated. At creation, the Maya gods made a house divided into eight: four corners, and four sectors. In early Colonial times, the Yucatec Maya said that four trees planted by four skybearers, the Bacabs, held up the sky; in later myths, these four leafy skybearers joined with the four Chacs, or rain gods, to do double duty.

Sometimes the sky is said to contain thirteen levels. The sixteenth-century Mexican *Codex Vaticano Latino* depicts these as vertically arranged, rising to the highest one, in which sits the creator couple. In seventeenth-century Oaxaca, the thirteenth god was called the "God of the Church's Light," and intervened in all aspects of life; the twelfth was a solar god of the hunt. It's unclear, though, whether these two deities sat on celestial levels above all the others in some hierarchy such as that in the *Vaticano Latino*, because the other eleven gods seem associated largely with earthly locations and follow no obvious order, much less a hierarchical one. Moreover, some contemporary myths say that these thirteen celestial layers form the sides of a pyramid with seven steps leading up and six leading down; and in examples of both contemporary and ancient Maya mythic systems, clouds also create thirteen layers with seven rising up and six leading down. The strict vertical depiction in the *Vaticano Latino* may indicate a Colonial re-mythologization of the Mexican myths. The document's annotator draws a clear parallel between this cosmos and a medieval European scheme when he claims that the thirteenth level contained God, or the "first cause" of all. This Spanish scribe probably was attempting to make sense of the strange Mesoamerican cosmos in his own hierarchical terms, just as the Mesoamericans were making sense of his equally strange Spanish cosmos in their own way.

At the first dawn of Mexica time, the sun's rosy rays spread through the half-lit celestial walls like dye spreading in a pool of water. Pools of water also spread in the Panajachel sky. When God made gentle movements, rain fell bit by bit; but when he moved forcefully or suddenly, then it came down in a torrent. Twelve angels did the work of God's rainmaking; each had a gourd that was uncorked during the rainy season, and filled during the dry. If too much fell, they had made a mistake. Clouds heralded rain but also hid the holes in the Panajachel sky through which it fell. Among the Chortí, celestial beings beat the clouds to encourage rain to fall. The rainmakers among the Yucatec Maya are four giants in the sky, and go by the names "Working Angels" or "Owners of the Jar Men." Like the Chacs, their ancient precursors, they stand with the four sky-bearers at each corner of the universe. These skybearers are subservient to the rainmakers; if lightning strikes the earth, it is because a rainmaker became angry with a skybearer and threw his stone axe at him but missed. Lightning often has been imaged as either a stone axe or a snake. The manikin scepter held by Classic Maya kings was a deified axe with a serpent foot; frequently Chac wielded this weapon as well. The Mexican Postclassic Tlaloc also often wielded lightning imaged as a serpent, and thunder cracked when the Tlalocs broke their water jars.

Others besides rain gods inhabited the ancient, watery skies. Like a rain god wielding lightning, Huitzilopochtli attacked his sister Coyolxauhqui with a fire serpent. Two of these hot celestial serpents bear the sun on their backs, arching along the famous Sun Stone's surface. Some modern-day writers have asserted that Huitzilopochtli is the Sun attacking his sister the Moon, but there is little evidence for this claim, which may be based on nothing more than a contemporary academic myth that assumed the sun must always be male and the moon female. However, feathered serpents do often appear decorated with sky symbols to show the demarcation between sky and that which lies below; their gaping mouths are passages into the Underworld. The words for snake and sky are homophonous in Maya, a linguistic suggestion of this serpentine image.

In addition to the great vulture-macaw false sun, who sat in Preclassic skies and whom the Hero Twins defeated, other birds traveled the Mesoamerican skies. Four birds sat atop the four great trees that held up the pre-Conquest sky, a different one for each tree; and each of the thirteen days of a Mesoamerican "week" claimed its own bird, representing a basic count of the Sun's diurnal travels. During the day, owls hid away in forest and caves; when the night skies rose over earth's surface, they flew out into the air above. The screech owl, or Muan Owl, sometimes is identified with the thirteenth celestial level, clouds, rain, and maize, which makes sense if one accepts the graduated pyramid rather than the hierarchical layers as the pattern of the celestial levels. In the pyramidal model, the Owl would sit on the final and lowest (not the highest) step, at the Underworld's western door. This would link him appropriately, like the maize god, both with the rain gods residing inside mountains and caves and with water's nocturnal fertility. New growth could occur only in close conjunction with the Underworld's watery death.

Yet the underworld Land of the Dead was not the only destination of ancestors and the deceased, who also traveled to the sky to become stars, clouds, birds, and butterflies, all of which could help those living on earth's surface. The Classic Zapotec in Oaxaca depicted the ancestors along with various deities in the upper portions of stone carvings, which corresponded to the sky. Ancient and contemporary Maya have said that rain and celestial clouds, as well as the smoke of incense, contain the stuff of souls—the powerful matter that keeps the universe's beings alive and moving. In Yucatec Maya, *tzak* means to conjure both spirits and clouds. The ancient Maya conjured up their cloud-sitting ancestors by ritually spilling sacrificial blood and burning incense. Today, the Maya of Yalcoba say that the pink clouds of dawn and dusk are the deserving, deceased relatives. And the Totonac dead, after wandering for four years, turn into birds, butterflies, clouds, stars, and planets who help the Sun to rise and move along its westerly path.

Stars were people who had died in Panajachel, and babies came from the skies, where they had been stars, following the sun. People continued on this solar path to the west and death, where they met the sky once again. It was said that the soul stayed on Earth's Surface for three days, visiting all of the places it wished to visit and saying goodbye to everyone. Then it started on its way to Heaven, which was a beautiful path filled with both obstacles and dangers. If one committed some wrongdoings during life, one had to stay awhile in the Underworld to pay off one's debt before rising into the sky. Just about everyone did this; for after all, who is perfect? Heaven was a great city with the best of everything. God the Sun, and all of the apostles, saints, and dead people who had paid for their sins could be found in its center. Saint Peter would let you in if you were worthy; otherwise you might sit outside the great city for years and years until God finally let you in to be judged. Thus, the Mesoamerican Sky is sometimes a living being in its own right and other times a place, a kind of upper story, in which particular beings reside and move around, and from which they influence the quality of life on Earth's surface. In either form, it is always distant, complex, intricate, and absolutely central to both life and death.

See also Bacabs; Calendar Deities; Chac and the Chacs; Earth, Agricultural, and Hunting Deities; Feathered Serpents; Fifth Sun; Guadalupe, Virgin of; Hero Twins; Moon; Opossums; Pacal; Quetzalcoatl; Rain and Water Deities; Saints; Sun; Tezcatlipoca; Underworld and Caves, Deities of the

Suggested reading:

Freidel, David, Linda Schele, and Joy Parker. 1993. *Maya Cosmos: Three Thousand Years on the Shaman's Path.* New York: William Morrow.

Joralemon, Peter David. 1996. "In Search of the Olmec Cosmos: Reconstructing the World View of Mexico's First Civilization." Pp. 51–59 in Elizabeth P. Benson and Beatriz de la Fuente, eds., *Olmec Art of Ancient Mexico.* Washington, DC: National Gallery of Art.

Garibay, K., Angel María, ed. and trans. 1985. *Teogonía e historia de los Mexicanos: Tres opúsculos del siglo XVI.* Mexico City: Editorial Porrúa.

Knab, Timothy J. 1995. *A War of Witches: A Journey in the Underworld of the Contemporary Aztecs.* New York: HarperCollins.

Read, Kay A. 1998. *Time and Sacrifice in the Aztec Cosmos.* Bloomington: Indiana University Press.

Tedlock, Dennis, trans. 1985. *Popol Vuh: The Definitive Edition of the Mayan Book of the Dawn of Life and the Glories of Gods and Kings.* New York: Simon and Schuster.

SUN

Time period: Preclassic–Contemporary

Cultural group: Mesoamerica

The sun god claims a long and complex history. He defines the cosmos and time itself; he often endures a split personality, sometimes even becoming two different beings, and shares his powers with rulers, gods, and saints. Following a westerly path through the sky during the day and an easterly path through the underworld by night (always keeping the north to his right and the south to his left), this powerful being continues to circumscribe the boundaries of Mesoamerican cosmoses in much the same manner as he has for centuries. Time itself springs from his movements; and corn, good health, and drought spring from his heat. It is therefore not surprising that many stories have been and continue to be told about this mythological being, without whom the cosmos could not function.

A celestial bird-monster probably ruled the Preclassic Olmec sky; his solar warmth and energy made things grow, and his path measured time. As early as the Preclassic, the Maya employed a four-petaled glyph called *kin,* which signified at once "sun" and "day." After all, it is the sun's motion that creates both space and time. For many Classic and Postclassic Maya, Kinich Ahau, the sun-faced lord, probably represented the Sun or Itzamna as he moved through the sky during the day. But as he moved into the underworld in the evening, the sun became a jaguar. The pre-Conquest Nahua sun had a similarly split personality. Called *Tonatiuh* (the word also means "age"), he rose like an eagle in the morning sky and descended like a jaguar at night. Central Mexicans created many solar disc images, with the sun's rays emanating outward at the cardinal and intercardinal points, as on the Sun Stone. Such discs often appeared in conjunction with particular Central Mexican rulers, as did the *kin* sign with Maya rulers. Mesoamerican rulers shared the sun's powers, and when they died, they too traveled to the underworld. The same trajectory was followed by the Hero Twins in the Popol Vuh, and by the Classic Maya Lord Pacal of Palenque. Once the Hero Twins had vanquished the Lords of Death, one rose as the heir, and the other, as the moon; when Pacal died, he passed on his power to his son, and rose as the sun. The cycle of death and life reflected in the sun's movements is traced in the architectural structure and the wall friezes in buildings at Palenque and throughout Mesoamerica, and appears also in objects connected with rulership. Given that rulers bore the sun's powers and marked time with their rule, it makes sense that Motecuhzoma II sent Cortés a cape with solar symbols decorating its surface when he first landed on the coast of Veracruz; was the stranger a ruler, perhaps even the new one to come? Fray Diego Durán noted that for the Spanish, Saint James, or Santiago, shone like the sun. After the Conquest, the sun in native mythology became Christ, or God. For some, it was both at once; for others, the solar god had nothing to do with Christ. Today, many mythological beliefs about the sun persist: Every year at the Equinox, thousands gather at the great pyramids in Teotihuacan. In 1999, as the new millennium approached, many of those worshiping at the pyramids voiced their hope that the sun would bring peace, physical fortification, and spiritual energy to earth.

Many peoples tell and have told stories of three or four previous ages or "suns" that preceded the present ones. The Postclassic Nahua said that their age, the Fifth Sun, was born of a great fire from which both an eagle and a jaguar escaped. This

Figure 70. A sun deity on an incense burner from Palenque, Chiapas, Mexico (Kay A. Read)

sun resulted from the gods' sacrifice and it could be kept alive only by similarly divine, sacrificial nourishment: Fray Bernardino de Sahagún reported rituals in which the heart was cut from a live warrior's body and offered to the sun. Just as the gods had sacrificed themselves to make the sun, people too must sacrifice their lives to keep it alive; for if the sun were to die, all would perish.

Both the ancient Nahua gods Huitzilopochtli and Tezcatlipoca also seem to bear some of the sun's powers. The K'iché' say that after they left a mythical place called Tollan to seek their home, the sun rose for the first time at Patohil, Pauilix, and Hacauitz. There the Sun showed himself for the first and last time to be the person he was. His hot, shining countenance dried up the soggy, muddy earth; and then all at once, the gods and the first animals suddenly turned to stone, which is how they remain today. If they had not, all those original voracious beasts—the puma, jaguar, rattlesnake, and yellowbite—might have given nothing but grief to humans, perhaps even preventing them from having their "day" or time. The Zapotec, however, say that the sun was created by a great lightning god named Cocijo, as were the moon, stars, earth, the seasons, days and nights, plants and animals, and rivers and mountains. Cocijo exhaled across the unformed, and everything emerged from his breath.

The Sun brings warmth and prosperity to the earth's surface. He nourishes the good health of both corn and people. When a Postclassic Nahua child was born, the midwife turned its small head toward the hearth fire to capture the sun's heat stored there. She then invoked the names of various deities including Tonatiuh and Tlalteuctli (Sun and Lord of Earth), also called "Our Mother, Our Father the Sun." Since a newborn rapidly loses body heat when first born, this was both a symbolic gesture and a physical necessity. As was true in Colonial times, today Christ often appears in local mythology as the sun. At Easter, the Sun-Christ struggles against the forces of darkness. The Kanhobal Maya say that when Christ died, he ascended a golden ladder, from which he shines down on the earth. The Tzeltal Maya relate that during the third creation or age, Jesus offered to be the sun because Lucibel or Lucifer was not giving enough light. Jesus ascended as the sun, and his mother Mary became the moon.

Other stories describe the sun in less glowing terms. The Chantino of Oaxaca say that the sun and moon were very bad little children who killed their adoptive parents. The Kekchi tell a story of a young hero who courts a beautiful woman. This Sun Lord first tries to fool her with a fake deer, and when this fails, he turns himself into a hummingbird. Entranced, she captures him and makes him her pet; but that night, she wakes to find him lying beside her in bed. She's worried because her magician father will be very angry if he finds out. So after darkening her girl's father's magical vision-giving stone with soot and filling his magic blowgun with chilies, the two escape. When her father discovers them gone, he manages to see where they went by peering through a little spot that Sun Lord unfortunately had left unbesmirched. After choking on the chilies in his blowgun, he loses his temper completely and seeks their death. He demands that a reluctant lightning god Chac create a great storm. But through shape-shifting and other magical acts, the young couple survive. Sun Lord places his beloved on a deer and sends her into the sky as our heavenly mother, the moon. Other stories tell how a young Sun tricks a brother into climbing a tree. There he either turns his sibling into a monkey or a pig. And so this long-lived and powerful being shapes the world both ancient and present, in ways both noble and violent; the Sun's character may be creative, supportive, heroic, hungry, nasty, silly, or gentle. But without him, the world would not exist.

See also Chac and the Chacs; Deer; Hero Twins; Itzamna; Kinich Ahau; Moon; Nahual; Sky Deities and Beings; Underworld and Caves, Deities of the

Suggested reading:

Bierhorst, John, ed. 1986. *The Monkey's Haircut and Other Stories Told by the Maya.* Illustrated by Robert Andrew Parker. New York: William Morrow.

Preston, Julia. 1999. "An Ancient Sun Melts Mexico's Modern Stresses." *New York Times,* 23 March, International section, p. A.4.

Sahagún, Fray Bernardino de. 1953–1982. *The Florentine Codex: A General History of the Things of New Spain.* Trans. Arthur J. O. Anderson and

Charles E. Dibble. Monographs of the School of American Research no. 14. Santa Fe: School of American Research; Salt Lake City: University of Utah Press.

Tedlock, Dennis, trans. 1985. *Popol Vuh: The Definitive Edition of the Mayan Book of the Dawn of Life and the Glories of Gods and Kings.* New York: Simon and Schuster.

TEZCATLIPOCA

Time period: Postclassic–Colonial

Cultural group: Nahua

A Nahua deity of some antiquity, Tezcatlipoca (Tez-kat-lee-po'-ka), or Smoking Mirror, played an extraordinarily important role in Postclassic Mexica life. Fray Bernardino de Sahagún called him a "true god" whose abode was "everywhere—in the land of the dead, on earth, [and] in heaven" (1953–1982, Bk 1:5). As god of the night sun, the night wind, and the cosmos's four quarters (each of which was controlled by one of his four aspects), he played a key role in cosmic creation; oversaw life events both good and bad; educated people and passed judgment on their actions; controlled success in war; legitimated and delegitimated Mexica rulership; and by the end of the Conquest, to some he had become the Devil himself. Tezcatlipoca seemingly has more names than any other Mexica deity, a fact that testifies to the age and depth of his cult. Fray Diego Durán reports that Tezcatlipoca's main festival "excelled even that of Huitzilopochtli", the Mexica patron god who shared some of Tezcatlipoca's powers (1971, 426). With the exception of the rain deities, on whom all life depended, no god was more central to Mexica mythology.

Historically, Tezcatlipoca appears to share a number of traits with God K and the other two gods of the Classic Maya Palenque Triad that legitimated rulership (Schele and Miller 1986, 48–51). Although not exactly alike, Tezcatlipoca shows the clearest affinity with God II (also called "K," or the Manikin Scepter): Both claim a serpent-shaped foot, smoke, and an obsidian mirror as major insignia; both also lay some claim to bloodletting. But Tezcatlipoca shares a few traits with the Triad's other two figures as well. As did God I, Tezcatlipoca wears a shell pendant and earrings; and like God I's namesake of the Popol Vuh, Hunahpu, Tezcatlipoca helped create the cosmos. And like God III in his underworld, jaguar form, Tezcatlipoca claims a close relationship with those felines of the night; in addition, he is the sun as it passes through the underworld, and the patron of war. Although one cannot show direct ancestry between Tezcatlipoca and the Palenque Triad, the links are suggestive.

Of course, Smoking Mirror's insignia also differ from those worn by his possible ancestors. Among the Mexica, he was usually painted black from head to toe, and depending on the circumstances, his attire could include flowery decorations made from popcorn (representing the dry, warring season); a net cape sometimes decorated with skulls and crossbones (for death and the underworld); four arrows in his right hand (used to punish wrongdoers); a deer hoof on his right ankle (for swiftness, agility, and might); a gold headband adorned with an ear and speech glyphs (because he was a good listener); bells on his ankles (he brought music to earth); and other items too numerous to list. Various stories and calendrical or ritual associations also tie him to monkeys, owls, and quail; the first perhaps represent music, and the second and third, the underworld. Indeed, Tezcatlipoca represented a large portion of life's pleasure and pain.

He and Quetzalcoatl created the cosmos together—sometimes in competition, sometimes in cooperation. Like the Palenque Triad gods, both were sons of parents who predated the present era. Those born to Tonacateuctli and Tonacacihuatl included two Tezcatlipocas, the red (called Camaxtli in Tlaxcala) and the black (the eldest and worst); Quetzalcoatl (god of wind); and the Mexica war god Huitzilopochtli (the smallest of all). This same story describes the powerful Tezcatlipoca as knowing all thoughts and hearts, and existing in all places. Another story tells how Tezcatlipoca became upset with Tata and Nene, an old couple who survived the flood that had destroyed the Fourth Age. When the pair came ashore in their cypress log boat, they lit a fire by rapidly twirling a stick in some dry tinder, and cooked some fish. But the fire smoked the skies, which annoyed the star gods so much that Tezcatlipoca cut off the couple's heads and attached them to their rears, thereby creating the first dogs. Tezcatlipoca also was one of several gods who sent Quetzalcoatl to the underworld to retrieve the bones with which people would be made, and he was among the gods who sacrificed themselves to create the Fifth Age.

But not all creation is serious. One storyteller describes how Tezcatlipoca, who sometimes appears as a monkey with a mirror on his back, gave rise to sacred music. One day, Tezcatlipoca created a black god of wind and told him to go get music from the sun. First, the wind went to the sea, where he called Tezcatlipoca's helpers: a turtle, a mermaid, and a whale. These three formed a bridge upon which the wind god crossed the ocean. When the sun saw him coming, he warned his musicians not to answer him, or else they would have to follow the wind back to where he came from. But when the wind arrived, he didn't speak to the musicians; instead, he sang to them. One of them, unable to resist the call, answered. Of course, he had to follow the wind back to earth, and that is how people got music for praying and dancing. The Colonial-era teller of this story adds that this music includes the organ one hears in Christian churches.

In pre-Hispanic times, Tezcatlipoca served as a potent deity leading both the Mexica and their enemies into war. Smoking Mirror also controlled many of life's good and bad things. All Mexica had shrines to him in their houses, and he could bring people whatever they needed. Folks who properly cared for him and behaved in an honorable fashion could receive a successful and prosperous life as their reward. Those who did not or who broke their promises and otherwise behaved dishonorably might be punished with leprosy, pustules, swelling of the knees, cancers, itches, and hemorrhoids. In that case, only praying to Tezcatlipoca and owning up to one's misdeeds helped.

One had to watch out for Smoking Mirror (so named because one could not easily see him), for this skilled *nahualli* or magician (see Nahual) appeared in many places at many times, shape-shifting into many things. Sometimes this was helpful; if a coyote suddenly sprang out at you, Tezcatlipoca was warning you that robbers were nearby and you ought to go home. At other times, it was an ill omen; if a passing skunk left its smell in your house, Tezcatlipoca was saying that the householder would soon die. Or sometimes how one acted affected the outcome. If you heard the sound of an ax splitting wood at night, Tezcatlipoca was lurking nearby and would appear as a headless creature whose split chest made a sucking noise with every breath. Then you should grab him and hang tight until he promised to give you three or four bloodletting thorns before you let him go. If you did, he would reward you with riches and success in war. But if you ran away, then you would suffer disease, slavery, or even death. A child named on Tezcatlipoca's day called 1-Death would be protected, rich, and honored, but only if he or she performed rituals properly and behaved well. A school called the Telpochcalli was housed at Tezcatlipoca's temple in Tenochtitlan; parents, both rich and poor, sent their young boys and girls to serve Tezcatlipoca and receive a good training. It makes sense that a god who judged the worth of people's actions also might bless the children and their education.

Tezcatlipoca's major feast occurred during the fifth month of the Mexica calendar, Toxcatl (3 May–22 May), at the end of the dry, warring season, just before the spring rains fell. They honored him on the first day of this month. A young man, perfect in his physical beauty, played Tezcatlipoca's role for a year before the festival. He was trained to play the flute, to sing, and to speak, joyfully entertaining everyone. This youth lived in luxury for the entire year, and enjoyed the pleasures of four women for twenty days before the festival. Tezcatlipoca's temple, courtyard, and participants were then decorated with many beautiful strands of popcorn strung on strings and dried flowers, symbolizing the fruition of the dry season. On the festival day, the beautiful young Tezcatlipoca willingly mounted the temple's eighty steps, breaking a flute on each. At the top, the priests took out his heart, decapitated him, and rolled his body down the steps; his head was strung on the skull rack to dry; and a new youth was chosen for the next year's ceremony. The Mexica also honored Huitzilopochtli during Toxcatl. Both he and Tezcatlipoca served as patrons of war; shared the same odd foot, ending in a snake or mirror; and wore a netted cape. At this time, Huitzilopochtli's image was taken to the temple and placed upon a serpent bench.

Like Huitzilopochtli, Tezcatlipoca could either lead the Mexica to victory or leave them to their own demise. When Cortés neared Tenochtitlan, Motecuhzoma II sent some nahuallis to cast spells on Cortés before he could do them harm. On the way, the nahuallis met a drunken man bound around the chest with eight ropes; he came from one of Cortés's allied Indian groups, the people of Chalco. The strange gentleman wanted to know why the Mexican nahuallis had bothered to come. Motecuhzoma might be overcome by fear, but there was no help for it, for he had already committed great wrongs and had abandoned his people. The Chalcan told the nahuallis to turn back, and magically showed them a vision of Tenochtitlan's neighborhoods on fire. Thereupon the man simply vanished; that's when they realized they had been speaking to Tezcatlipoca.

After the Colonial period, Smoking Mirror disappears from the scene, perhaps because the Spanish saw him as a great devil and worked hard to eliminate him; Sahagún called Tezcatlipoca Lucifer himself. As the underworld vanquisher of Quetzalcoatl and the Toltecs, Tezcatlipoca played that sinister role well. In one tale, he stole Quetzalcoatl's magical rain mirror, thereby causing drought; in other stories, he led Topiltzin astray. Today, Tezcatlipoca is primarily found in literary mythology, where he appears as a dark figure, recalling his mythic past as the feathered serpent's foe. Some of his magical abilities live on in contemporary folk tales about lightning and the underworld, although these abilities no longer are connected with his name. Little else of this complicated and multifaceted Nahua deity survived the violent watershed of Conquest.

See also Cortés, Fernando; Devil; Earth, Agricultural, and Hunting Deities; Fifth Age; Huitzilopochtli; Motecuhzoma II, Lord; Nahual; Quetzalcoatl; Rain Deities; Sky Deities and Beings; Underworld and Caves, Deities of the

Suggested reading:

Codex Chimalpopoca. 1992. As reproduced in *History and Mythology of the Aztecs: The Codex Chimalpopoca.* Trans. John Bierhorst. Tucson: University of Arizona Press.

Durán, Fray Diego. 1971. *Book of the Gods and Rites and the Ancient Calendar.* Trans. Doris Heyden and Fernando Horcasitas. Norman: University of Oklahoma Press.

Sahagún, Fray Bernardino de. 1953–1982. *The Florentine Codex: A General History of the Things of New Spain.* Trans. Arthur J. O. Anderson and Charles E. Dibble. Monographs of the School of American Research no. 14. Santa Fe: School of American Research; Salt Lake City: University of Utah Press.

Schele, Linda, and Mary Ellen Miller. 1986. *Blood of Kings.* New York: George Braziller; Fort Worth: Kimbell Art Museum.

TIZOC, LORD

Time period: Postclassic

Cultural period: Nahua-Mexica

Lord Tizoc (Tee´-zok), the seventh Chief Speaker of the Mexica or Aztecs (ca. 1481–1486), is more known for what he did not do than what he did. Most histories see him as a weak and ineffectual ruler. Symbolically he is the counterpoint of success, for he failed at his job and reaped the results of that failure—an early death.

Lord Tizoc was the second son of Lord Motecuhzoma I (Ilhuicamina) (ruled ca. 1440–1469) and preceded the great ruler Lord Ahuitzotl (ruled ca. 1486–1502). If Ahuitzotl is the symbol of arrogant success, Tizoc represents insipid failure. It is said that in his first war, he lost 300 warriors. As a last ditch effort, he sent in a troop of young inexperienced boys. Normally such boys would not fight, but simply observe. This time, however, they saved the day by routing the enemy and capturing forty enemy warriors to sacrifice at Tizoc's upcoming coronation ceremony. Since a ruler's first war was a demonstration of his powers, this proved a very inauspicious beginning.

His coronation foretold the nature of his reign. Amidst much gift giving and dancing, Lord Tizoc told the throng that they should enjoy life now, for one's days are numbered and one cannot dance after death. Indeed, he died early. Tizoc ruled for only five years, during which he spent much time in seclusion, failing even to complete the main temple's rebuilding, and his conquests apparently numbered very few. This seems to have frustrated his people so much that someone in his own court used sorcery to poison him. After his death, the Mexica found themselves in such a weakened position that potentially unsympathetic cities could afford to decline invitations to Lord Ahuitzotl's coronation. Some evidence, however, does suggest that he may have accomplished more than most histories let on. Thus for some at least, Tizoc mythically (if not tangibly) represents the depths of poor rulership and the deadly rewards of failure.

See also Ahuitzotl, Lord; Motecuhzoma I, Lord

Suggested reading:

Codex Mendoza. 1997. As reproduced in *The Essential Codex Mendoza.* Commentary and edited by Frances F. Berdan and Patricia Rieff Anawalt. Berkeley: University of California Press.

Durán, Fray Diego. 1994. *The History of the Indies of New Spain.* Trans. Doris Heyden. Norman: University of Oklahoma Press.

Townsend, Richard F. 1992. *The Aztecs.* London: Thames and Hudson.

TLACAELLEL

Time period: Postclassic

Cultural group: Nahua-Mexica

The Tlacaellel (Tla-ka-eh´-lel) was a high ranking official in the Mexica or Aztec government. At times the Tlacaellel seems to have held as much power as the Chief Speaker or ruler, governing alongside him in a dual rulership. This office was also called the Cihuacoatl or Snakewoman, for it took its powers from an extremely effective goddess and woman warrior of the same name. The Tlacaellel largely took care of internal affairs within Tenochtitlan, while the Chief Speaker handled mostly external affairs having to do with lands beyond Tenochtitlan's door. Symbolically the Tlacaellel was the matron or lady of the Mexica house, while the Chief Speaker was its lord.

During Lord Acamapichtli's reign (ca 1369–1403), the Tlacaellel appears to have played a secondary role to the Chief Speaker, but shortly before the reign of Lord Motecuhzoma I (Ilhuicamina) (ca. 1440–1469), the rulership of the Mexica had become a partnership. The Tlacaellel's primary duty was domestic and military counseling par excellence. Other duties included governing the city when the Chief Speaker was at war, receiving prisoners of war and visiting dignitaries in the ruler's absence, grandly welcoming the ruler home from battle, governing the city neighborhood that included the temple of the goddess Cihuacoatl, and judging elite crimes. The Chief Speaker, on the other hand, controlled their farmlands and its work force, expanded the Mexica territory through war and negotiation, harvested sacrificial offerings through war, and safeguarded the royal ancestry and its political ties through shrewdly arranged marriage alliances. Like the lady and lord of a very large household, the Tlacaellel's duties kept him largely at home watching over the house, while the Chief Speaker's duties frequently took him out to the countryside and into foreign lands.

It is said that Motecuhzoma I was born on the same day as his Tlacaellel, the latter having auspiciously arrived just before dawn. Another story relates how once the office of the Chief Speaker was offered to the Tlacaellel, but he declined it declaring that he already had the powers of a king and needed no more. Instead he suggested that the young Ahuitzotl (ruled ca. 1486–1502) become king, and he would personally train him. Ahuitzotl's arrogance did not get the better of him until after his valued counselor died. At times the Tlacaellel was given the same burial rites reserved for rulers, but on one occasion his embalmed body was carried into battle to posthumously apply his superior military powers against their enemies. It worked—they won.

However, by the time of Lord Motecuhzoma II (Xocoyotzin) (ruled ca. 1502–1520), the Tlacaellel's influence had begun to wane; maybe because of a short succession of men holding the office, none staying long enough to consolidate its power. Bit by bit, Motecuhzoma II reduced the Tlacaellel's duties to merely acting as a glorified gofer for the ruler, even executing his sometimes distasteful demands. In the end, the Mexica may have paid dearly for this change in governance, for the lack of a skilled advisor may have hurt their chances of victory over the Spanish. One of the omens prophesying the Mexica's downfall was the Tlacaellel's goddess Cihuacoatl crying in the night: "My dear children, now I am about to leave you." Perhaps she did.

> **See also** Acamapichtli, Lord; Ahuitzotl, Lord; Cihuacoatl; Motecuhzoma I, Lord; Motecuhzoma II, Lord
>
> **Suggested reading:**
>
> Durán, Fray Diego. 1994. *The History of the Indies of New Spain*. Trans. Doris Heyden. Norman: University of Oklahoma Press.
>
> Read, Kay A. 2000. "More Than Earth: Cihuacoatl as Female Warrior, Male Matron, and Inside Ruler." Pp. 51–67 in *Goddesses and Sovereignty*. Ed. Elisabeth Benard and Beverly Moon. New York: Oxford University Press.
>
> Sahagún, Fray Bernardino de. 1953–1982. *The Florentine Codex: A General History of the Things of New Spain*. Trans. Arthur J. O. Anderson and Charles E. Dibble. 12 books, 13 parts. Monographs of the School of American Research no. 14. Santa Fe: School of American Research; Salt Lake City: University of Utah Press.

TLALOC AND THE TLALOQUES

Time period: Preclassic–Postclassic

Cultural group: Central Mexico

Tlaloc (Tla´-lok) was an ancient Central Mexican god of storms who, along with the goddess Chalchiuhtlicue, controlled all forms of water or lack thereof. Tlaloc, Chalchiuhtlicue, and the Tlaloques (Tla-lo´-kays) lived in Tlalocan. There the Tlaloques guarded the waters of the universe's four quarters. These waters were kept in mountains like great pots; and when it was time to release the water, the Tlaloques broke their pots with sticks, letting the water spill out. Tlaloc's great age and pervasive nature mark him as one of the most important Nahua deities, something understandable in Central Mexico's semiarid environment.

Tlaloc's image appears with lightning bolts on vases as early as 100 B.C. at Tlapacoya in the Valley of Mexico. Of course we do not know if the town's residents called him "Tlaloc," for that is his Nahuatl name and we do not know what language they spoke at Tlapacoya; nor do we know if that Preclassic god served his people in exactly the same way as Tlaloc in the Postclassic period. Nevertheless, Tlaloc's imagery remained remarkably consistent for many centuries, which indicates (if nothing else) his centrality to Central Mexican worldviews. A storm god bearing Tlaloc's goggled eyes and fang-filled mouth appears as one of the most important deities at the great urban center Teotihuacan (ca. 200 B.C.–A.D. 650/750).

According to Esther Pasztory, he even may have served as the city's patron god, sharing his power with a goddess who perhaps was older than he.

At the Nahua Mexica city Tenochtitlan, however, Tlaloc was older than their patron god Huitzilopochtli. Both these deities shared the Templo Mayor, which stood at the ritual center of the huge city. Tlaloc's small house rested atop the northern side of the pyramid, while Huitzilopochtli's rested atop the southern. Their houses marked the sun's travels along the eastern horizon: Tlaloc's marked the summer solstice and wet agricultural season; the gap between their houses marked the fall and spring equinoxes; and Huitzilopochtli's marked the winter solstice and the dry warring season. Symbolically, agriculture and war combine in the caches hidden within the pyramid's bowels. These clearly show the importance of water and nature's fertility over war's activity. Therein one finds buried many of Tlaloc's pots; numerous shells, coral, and other treasures from the sea; and a multitude of water fowl, fish, and other aquatic animals. These are often associated with sacrificial offerings, indicating that war and hunting helped feed this fertile abundance. In fact, in front of Tlaloc's house stood a chacmool, a sculptured man sitting on the ground, his open mouth exposing his teeth, and he is holding an empty bowl probably intended for sacrificial offerings of heart and blood.

The Nahua tell a story of how Tlaloc came to be. The world was created by Huitzilopochtli and Quetzalcoatl. As part of that task, the two gods created Tlaltecuhtli and his wife Chalchiuhtlicue. Tlaltecuhtli was a great toadlike earth monster wearing Tlaloc's face. In fact, Tlaloc's name means something like "inside the earth," a wonderful metaphor for the moist underworld. This story goes on to explain that all the deities of water were born from Chalchiuhtlicue, and that the water gods lived in a great lodging, in whose patio stood four huge clay pots of water. One pot contained very good water, fine gentle rains for sprouting crops. But, the other three were very bad: one contained blight and spider webs; another contained frost; and the last contained drought. The rain gods stood in the four quarters of this house and, depending on which pots they chose to break with their sticks, sent their contents flying to Earth's Surface.

To honor Tlaloc and the Tlaloques, the Mexica celebrated a number of rituals during the driest season until the spring rains good for sprouting were falling. They also celebrated a ritual at the very end of the rainy season, when a thunderstorm or two could still crash through the skies. During the dry season, children were sacrificed on Mount Tlaloc and at the mountain abodes of other rain deities to give them nourishment and strength, for the Tlaloques would need that to break the appropriate pots. Once the rains had started, people sacrificed amaranth cakes and ate a stew made of the flesh of sacrificed slaves, thus sharing their meal with the deities who made all food possible, but who also could send blight, killing frosts, and drought. Tlaloc displayed his dangerous powers by consuming one of the four ages preceding the Mexica Fifth Sun. Volcanic action demolished the Third Sun or Age 4-Rainstorm by raining fire down upon earth's surface from a mountain; Tlaloc's face signifies this age. If the Fifth Age was to continue, people needed to keep these gods well nourished.

If people attended to Tlaloc properly, he could help in wonderful ways. The Mexica defeated the Toltecs, the previous people in power, with Tlaloc's help; the storm god sent drought upon them, while bringing fresh rains to the Mexica. It's not surprising then that one of the four deities from whom Mexica rulers gained their power was Tlaloc, or that Motecuhzoma II made a gift of Tlaloc's garb to Cortés when he first appeared on the coast of Veracruz. After all, life itself depended on this deity. Needless to say, Cortés did not appreciate the significance of this gift.

> **See also** Bacabs; Chac and the Chacs; Chalchiuhtlicue; Christ; Cortés, Fernando; Earth, Agricultural, and Hunting Deities; Feathered Spirits; Fifth Sun; Huitzilopochtli; Jurakan; Motecuhzoma II, Lord; Rain and Water Deities; Sky Deities and Beings; Underworld and Caves, Deities of the
>
> **Suggested reading:**
>
> *Codex Chimalpopoca.* 1992b. As reproduced in *History and Mythology of the Aztecs: The Codex Chimalpopoca.* Trans. John Bierhorst. Tucson: University of Arizona Press.
>
> Durán, Fray Diego. 1994. *The History of the Indies of New Spain.* Trans. Doris Heyden. Norman: University of Oklahoma Press.
>
> Pasztory, Esther. 1997. *Teotihuacan: An Experiment in Living.* Norman: University of Oklahoma Press.
>
> Sahagún, Fray Bernardino de. 1953–1982. *The Florentine Codex: A General History of the Things of New Spain.* Trans. Arthur J. O. Anderson and Charles E. Dibble. 12 books, 13 parts. Monographs of the School of American Research no. 14. Santa Fe: School of American Research; Salt Lake City: University of Utah Press.

UNDERWORLD AND CAVES, DEITIES OF THE

Time period: Archaic–Contemporary

Cultural group: Mesoamerica

When one enters the Underworld through one of its cave openings, one passes into a world that is the reverse of the one above. As the bright air rises far above dry Earth's Surface, the dark, wet, subterranean Underworld extends deep below. One world depends on the other; for without both sides of this cosmic coin, the universe would fall out of balance, bringing such disasters as extreme drought or flood. When the two are in balance, the upper world provides the warmth and light of the sun, and the Underworld provides the moisture and nourishment of water, sometimes provided by beings who live in the Underworld or beyond the

Figure 71. The mouth of Loltún Cave, Yucatán, Mexico (Kay A. Read)

bubble covering Earth's Surface. Both the dry air above and the wet realm below are absolutely necessary to the growth and health of those living sandwiched between, on Earth's Surface. But at times the underworld almost seems to take precedence over the upper; for without destruction, creation could not happen, motion would stop, and things would stagnate. The Underworld provides the cosmos with the damaging forces that people may not particularly like but nevertheless know are both necessary and inescapable. Life cannot exist without death, for life rises from the disintegrating, nourishing corruption of the Underworld, like plants springing from dark, rotting loam. The complex, interior realm of Earth houses the forces of night, spawns disease, encases death, and consumes food that is absolutely the opposite of the Upper World's nourishment. At times, Mesoamericans conceive of the Earth as female and the Sky as male; occasionally, the terrestrial realm is viewed as male. More commonly, both the upper and the lower worlds are ungendered, although each harbors its own distinctive male and female beings.

The Underworld is one of the earliest mythic themes in recorded Mesoamerican history. The ritual use of the Loltún Caves in Yucatán suggests the importance of the Underworld even in the Archaic period; the burial of early Preclassic era family members beneath the floors of their houses suggests later cosmologies in which the Underworld houses the dead and the Upper World takes the shape of a human abode. By the time of the Preclassic Olmec, the Underworld begins to appear as a significant part of mythology. A great dragon was said to float on the sea's surface; from this beast's body sprouted all manner of plants. Mountains along its back housed storm clouds, lightning, thunder, and rain; and its mouth formed a cave-like portal to the Underworld. Thus the dragon's back served as the Earth's Surface, on which humans and other beings lived, while the dead dwelt in its guts, and ancestors emerged from its mouth onto its earthy spine. Olmec rulers often appear in the Earth Monster's mouth. In one depiction at Chalcatzingo, the ruler sits on a throne in the terrestrial mouth, from which mist and clouds issue; outside, falling rain produces crops. Then, as today, certain springs and caves served as points of connection between Earth's Surface and the Underworld. In fact, the core of this early Underworld imagery remains remarkably stable throughout centuries of mythic development, although its details vary.

The Classic Maya often depicted the Underworld's entrance as the great mouth of a feathered serpent; like the Olmec dragon, this beast separated the Sky from the Underworld. The K'iche' Popol Vuh offers one of the most comprehensive depictions of the ancient Maya Underworld. Honeycombed and river-laced like Loltún caves, the Hero Twins traveled down into this dangerous subterranean world in order to eventually defeat and control the gods of death, such as the delightful 1-Death and 7-Death, Pus and Jaundice Masters, Bone and Skull Scepters, and Bloody Teeth and Bloody Claws. In order to defeat them, the Twins sacrificed themselves and returned disguised as fishermen, then musicians; after their final victory, they reemerged into the Upper World as the Sun and the Moon. The Sun traveled the sky above during the day and the Underworld by night, while the Moon traveled above by night and below by day. From this point forward, the Upper World was opposed to the Underworld, yet joined with it by the motions of the Sun and Moon; life now balanced death. The Classic Maya Lord Pacal of seventh-century Palenque also traveled into the underworld to reemerge as the Sun, while his heir stood on the head and strength of the water-lily god, perhaps a Classic throwback to the Preclassic Olmec earth-dragon. These Maya rulers, like their Olmec mythological ancestors, claimed a heritage from the Underworld, and like the Hero Twins, they journeyed through it in order to achieve control of its moist forces for the benefit of the living.

Pre-Conquest Nahua sources likewise tell of the great female, aquatic, reptilian monster Cipactli, whom Tezcatlipoca and Quetzalcoatl (after turning into huge snakes) twisted into two parts. One half produced the sky, and the other, the earth. From her hair and hide came trees, flowers, and plants; from her eyes and nostrils came springs and caves, and from her mouth, the valleys and mountains. But this sacrifice now demanded a sacrifice in kind, for she cried for human hearts and could not produce fruits without human blood. The Mexica depicted the Earth Monster as a great toad or crocodile-like being. From its open, toothy mouth hung sacrificial blades; its matted hair sometimes sported insects; snakes often belted its waist, wrists, and ankles; and claw-mouth signs of death and the Underworld adorned its clawed hands and feet. The sun was swallowed each evening into its dark insides, only to be captured each morning by the souls of sacrificed warriors who fought the agents of death. But at noon, the souls of dead women warriors fought the men to recapture the Sun, and then carried him back to the Earth Monster's mouth at dusk. Quetzalcoatl also traveled to the underworld to retrieve the bones of the dead, which Cihuacoatl ground in her metate and used to mold people

Figure 72. Mictlantecuhtli, Lord of the Dead, Codex Magliabechiano, fol. 79r, (Art Resource)

as though she were patting out tortillas from corn meal. Having been born of the Underworld, the Mexica also said that their dead traveled back to the Underworld and the Land of Death. There they reached a great river, where little yellow dogs carried them across to the other side and they simply disappeared.

When the Spanish arrived, the dark Underworld became the land of the Devil, and the Sky, the land of the new Father God and his solar-inspired son Christ. An imported Spanish depiction of Hell as a monster with a great mouth from which Christ rescued Adam and Eve and other Holy Fathers from the Devil, happened to fit very nicely with the ancient Mesoamerican Earth Monster, although the newly converted understood redemption in their own particular ways. For them, the Christian devils took on many roles of the old gods of death, water, and the Underworld, quickly moving from the European fiery Hell into the dark, dank, and river-laced passages that lay under Mesoamerica's earthly surface. For some at least, the underworld contained four parts: a hell of the damned, a place for unbaptized children, purgatory, and the limbo of the Holy Fathers whom Christ would come and release. These dead fathers became ancestors of the living, whom Christ brought to life according to foreordained, ancient prophecies (Burkhart, 1996, 124, 244). And in seventeenth-century Oaxaca, the several deities governing the underworld, death, and disease all came to be called "gods of hell," "demons," or "Lucifer," whereas their more celestial counterparts remained simply "gods"; nevertheless these terrestrial deities continued to perform their ancient functions of curing disease and caring for the dead (Berlin 1988, 18–24).

In contemporary times, the underworld differs from place to place. Caves serve as openings into its subterranean depths, as may rocks and trees; but those depths are described in varying terms. Most still consider life down below to be in some way the reverse of life above. And, although those reversals can be described in various ways, the Underworld is still wet and houses the dead and ancestors; it still serves as the source of disease and various potent deities, and the place where the Sun goes at night while the Moon travels above. Moreover, as before, its gender sometimes is clearly female, and at other times male; not particularly clear; or clearly unimportant.

Some Nahua of highland Mexico still describe the Underworld as partitioned into four cardinal lands, although these lands are very different from their Colonial-Christian predecessors. The dream traveler enters each through actual caves, streams, sinkholes, pools, or wells. Death and wind govern the northern land; women, the western; heat, the southern; and the ocean, the eastern land. Modern Nahua depict the Underworld as the exact same four-petaled flower that inhabitants of the ancient Classic highland site of Teotihuacan drew, suggesting that these modern mythic landscapes may be ancient indeed. The lords and ladies governing the contemporary Nahua Underworlds can help or hurt people who travel through their depths. They can also send to those living on Earth's Surface rewards or retribution for their past deeds. But only they can choose to do this; the most that humans can do is present these subterranean governors with respectable requests.

The contemporary Totonac also echo an ancient mythology of fate when they say that gods guide souls to a Land of the Dead governed by Linin. If one dies tragically, perhaps by drowning or murder, the god Aksini metes out punishment, making the deceased wander for four years. During this time, they call to unsuspecting people traveling near streams, and try to trap them. When their four years are up, the dead go to help the Sun rise each day, thereby making sure that Linin doesn't get him. Finally, like their Maya counterparts, they turn into stars and planets; or like their ancient Nahua warrior counterparts, into birds and butterflies; or like some southwestern Pueblo peoples, into clouds.

Some modern deities of the Underworld control one's destiny less by ancient standards that recognize fate's importance than by Christian standards based on retribution and redemption. For the Cakchiquel Maya of Panajachel in the 1930s, the Devil became the dark master, the paradigmatic cruel landowner, extracting harsh labor for people's sins. But his interior land, called the Hill, was not always dark and forbidding. People often described the Hill as a lush interior land with a topography like that of earth's surface; it even contained villages, roads, churches, and farms. One entered it through caves, or from behind big rocks and great trees. If one were out in the woods on Earth's Surface and mysteriously heard dogs barking or church bells ringing, it meant that one of these passages had opened. Then one had better leave immediately, or one might soon meet up with the Devil. After all, God best protects people when they are gathered together in their towns, not when they are alone in the forest. Nevertheless, it was in this lush Underworld land that one served time after death, doing harsh labor to pay for one's misdeeds; so even if one avoided the Underworld in life, one probably would not avoid it in death.

If the Panajachel world could be a beautiful land in which the dead did hard labor, it also could be a dark and forbidding place from which the living might nevertheless profit. A story is told of a poor man caught by robbers one day. He had nothing for them to steal, so they made him do some errands for them in a distant town. They told him to take a short-cut through a dark, nasty passage penetrating the innards of a local mountain. On the path, the poor man met a Christ-like figure who stepped down from his cross and told him he could go no further. But he simply knocked the pseudo-Christ to the ground, as the robbers had told him to do, and continued on his way. When he had successfully completed his errands, the thieves released him; and he now had a darn good story to tell his neighbors.

This counter-Christ reminds us that the Underworld is always the opposite of the upper. Some Panajachel said that if a town existed on Earth's surface, its counterpart existed below, only upside-down. So if buildings rose forty stories high in Mexico City, companion buildings extended forty stories below into the Underworld. After working off their debts for the Devil in the Hill, the dead rose to the sky to be with God as stars or planets.

Both the Cakchiquel of Panajachel and the K'iché say that Earth is their mother and sky is their father. Nevertheless, in stories about the Hill, the Panajachel interior landscape's gender is never mentioned; and it is clear that both male and female ancestors and saints live with God the Father in the sky. Among the ancient Nahua, a male and female couple governed the Land of Death, and another couple governed the thirteenth sky; the Devil in his underworld abode was clearly male and shared his home with a number of female inhabitants; and for the contemporary Nahua of the highlands, both helpful and harmful male and female beings of ancient origin inhabit the Underworld, while male and female Christian saints inhabit the upper world. For the Kekchi, however, the Earth is a lord, not a lady, and he bears the most vital importance of all their deities, being sharply separated from the weaker celestial gods Our Lord Sun, Our Mother Moon, and Red Star (Venus). In a somewhat different vein, Hispanic feminist poet Gloria Anzaldúa (1987, 46–51) reinterprets ancient tradition to equate the Mesoamerican Underworld with the Nahua goddess Coatlicue and with Anzaldúa's own idea of a dark earth mother who devours Anzaldúa, thereby dissolving painful oppositions arising from her sexuality and cultural heritage. This dissolution enables her to be reborn.

Cooking fires, food, and comestible sacrifices also reflect oppositions between the lower and upper worlds. In the Underworld they burn bones in their cooking fires, not sticks. Moreover, they don't eat the same things there. The ancient Mexica said that the Lord and Lady of Death ate human hands and feet, stew made of beetles that lived in damp places, tamales smelling of beetle gas, and atole made of pus that they drank from a skull. The K'iche' say in the Popol Vuh, however, that proper sacrifices to the Gods of Death are not to be blood sacrifices, like the hands, feet, and blood that fed the Nahua Earth Monster and her Underworld inhabitants, but only creatures of the night, clotted sap, and the mean and the nasty. Owls and quail (both nocturnal birds) also were common sacrificial meals offered to the Underworld beings by the pre-Conquest Mexica.

A widespread myth says that one must not eat the things of the Underworld, lest one be doomed to stay there forever. The Panajachel constantly reminded hapless Underworld travelers to avoid the food if they wished to escape. And a Lacandon myth tells of a man who, having been drawn into the Underworld by Death Maker's daughter, was hidden by the god's wife under a blanket of chilies grown on Earth's Surface. When Death Maker appeared with the Sun on his shoulder (for he was carrying him through the Underworld), he smelled the chilies and was absolutely revolted; normally he only ate tortillas of bracket fungi, beans of the larvae of green flies, and corn paste made from the decayed flesh of dead human beings. Death Maker's wife warned the man not to eat the food, even if it looked like that on Earth's Surface. Following her advice, he eventually won the upper hand by forcing Death Maker's daughter to eat a tortilla made of real corn, thereby making her his true wife.

The Underworld is also home to the rain gods, and thus not only provides the rotting nourishment required by chilies and corn grown above but also the rain that sustains them. Throughout present-day Mesoamerica, caves are the homes of a variety of dwarves who guard game, crops, and wealth. These dwarves are most likely the relatives of ancient dwarf-like rain gods who lived in caves and mountains and decided what kind of moisture to send: gentle rain, harsh thunderstorms and lightning, damaging frosts and hail, or funguses and rot; or they might decide to simply withhold all moisture, thereby causing drought. Likewise, among the contemporary Kekchi, the earth lord Tzultacaj is the master of the forest and its animals, and controls all rain, and the Lacandon's cave-dwelling rain god Metzabok burns copal to cause rain to fall. In sum, without the creatures of the underworld and its caves, those living on Earth's Surface could not survive. Heaven may be nice for some after death, but the living rely on what goes on beneath them, and it is there that they pay their debts.

See also: Chalchiuhtlicue; Christ; Coatlicue; Devil; Earth, Agricultural, and Hunting Deities; Feathered Serpents; Hero Twins; La Llorona; Moon; Quetzalcoatl; Rain and Water Deities; Sky Deities and Beings; Sun; Tezcatlipoca; Tlaloc and the Tlaloques; Yum Kaax

Suggested reading:

Brady, James E. 1989. "An Investigation of Maya Ritual Cave Use with Special Reference to Naj Tunich, Peten, Guatemala." Ph.D. dissertation, University of California at Los Angeles, Department of Anthropology.

Burkhart, Louise M. 1996. *Holy Wednesday: A Nahua Drama from Early Colonial Mexico.* Philadelphia: University of Pennsylvania Press.

Joralemon, Peter David. 1996. "In Search of the Olmec Cosmos: Reconstructing the World View of Mexico's First Civilization." Pp. 51–59 in Elizabeth P. Benson and Beatriz de la Fuente, eds., *Olmec Art of Ancient Mexico.* Washington, DC: National Gallery of Art.

Knab, Timothy. 1995. *A War of Witches: A Journey in the Underworld of the Contemporary Aztecs.* New York: HarperCollins.

Tedlock, Dennis, trans. 1985. *Popol Vuh: The Definitive Edition of the Mayan Book of the Dawn of Life and the Glories of Gods and Kings.* New York: Simon and Schuster.

YUM KAAX (DIVING GOD)

Time period: Classic–Contemporary

Cultural group: Yucatec Maya

The Diving God, or the pre-Conquest Yucatec Maya god of maize known as Yum Kaax (Yoom Kash´), seems to be closely associated with agriculture and fertility. However, like many Maya deities with multiple sides to their personalities, this god has other associations as well—with death and sacrifice. The Maya codices portray him with maize imagery, but he also appears as a sacrificial offering, eyes closed in death and entrails falling out of his midriff. The association of agriculture and fertility with death makes sense from the standpoint of Maya natural and cosmological orders. Agriculture, and more specifically the growth of maize, takes place through a cycle of life and death. To create a maize plant, one must destroy the life of the land; that is, one must burn the vegetation to clear a new

Figure 73. Yum Kaax, the Diving God, Codex Tro-Cortesianus, *pl. 35a (Museo de América/Art Resource)*

field and must bury the maize seed in the earth. Maize is also the epitome of new life, being both the material of human creation and the basic unit of the Maya diet. Today we can only surmise the gist of the myths behind the pictures of the diving figure on temple ruins, the codical figures with their maize offerings, and the sacrificial figures; no one knows for sure what those myths entailed.

See also Earth, Agricultural, and Hunting Deities; Underworld and Caves, Deities of the

Suggested reading:

Landa, Diego de. 1978. *Yucatan before and after the Conquest.* Trans. William Gates. New York: Dover.

Taube, Karl. 1992. *The Major Gods of Ancient Yucatan.* Washington, DC: Dumbarton Oaks Research Library.

$$4$$

ANNOTATED PRINT AND NONPRINT RESOURCES

BOOKS AND ARTICLES

Adams, Richard E. W. *Prehistoric Mesoamerica.* Norman: University of Oklahoma Press, 1991.

An introductory textbook to the archaeology and history of ancient Mesoamerica. This book explores the prehistoric cultural and historical development of Mesoamerica before Spanish contact.

Abreu Gomez, Ermilio. *Canek: History and Legend of a Maya Hero.* Berkeley: University of California Press, 1979.

A fictional reconstruction of the Yucatec Maya during colonial times and the early days of independence. This short, accessible collection of stories is about a young creole man who is part of an old aristocratic family, and a young Maya boy (Jacinto Canek) who works on the estate (translated from Spanish).

Anaya, Rudolfo A. *The Legend of La Llorona.* Berkeley, CA: Tonatiuh–Quinto Sol International, Inc., 1984.

This short, easy to read novel combines one of the many myths about Malinche with the basic myth of La Llorona, thereby creating a new tale. An excellent example of contemporary mythology.

Anzaldúa, Gloria. *Borderlands/La Frontera: The New Mestiza.* San Francisco: Aunt Lute Books, 1987.

An intense, beautifully poetic book describing the author's experiences as a Hispanic woman. Offers the reader a skillful re-creation of themes drawn from primarily academically based mythology about women and pre-Conquest deities.

Aveni, Anthony. *Skywatchers of Ancient Mexico.* Austin: University of Texas Press, 1980.

Explores the interesting and often complex relationships among worldviews, architectural structures, topography, and celestial motions.

Benson, Elizabeth P., and Beatriz de la Fuente, eds. *Olmec Art of Ancient Mexico.* Washington, DC: National Gallery of Art, 1996.

This catalogue for a major exhibition offers a number of excellent short articles exploring various facets of Olmec history, society, and culture, all of which are written by specialists.

Bierhorst, John, ed. *The Monkey's Haircut and Other Stories Told by the Maya.* New York: William Morrow, 1986.

An excellent collection of Maya folktales and myths from highland Guatemala.

Boone, Elizabeth H. *Incarnations of the Aztec Supernatural: The Image of Huitzilopochtli in Mexico and Europe.* Philadelphia: American Philosophical Society, 1989.

A thorough historical examination of the imagery that depicts the Mexica patron deity Huitzilopochtli from pre-Conquest times to the Colonial period.

Bricker, Victoria Reifler. *The Indian Christ, the Indian King.* Austin: University of Texas Press, 1981.

A descriptive study of myths, rituals, and beliefs among some of the Maya people from Chiapas Mexico. This text is best suited for the advanced layperson.

Burkhart, Louise M. *Holy Wednesday: A Nahua Drama from Early Colonial Mexico.* Philadelphia: University of Pennsylvania Press, 1996.

A careful, thorough translation and study of a sixteenth-century Christian play written and produced in Nahuatl for indigenous audiences celebrating Holy Week. Includes not only the play, but also good discussions of the historical context in which it was produced, some of its key religious themes, and its blending of indigenous and Christian worldviews.

Carmack, Robert M., Janine Gasco, and Gary H. Gossen. *The Legacy of Mesoamerica: History and Culture of a Native American Civilization.* Upper Saddle River, NJ: Prentice Hall, 1996.

An introductory textbook on the modern history and culture of Mesoamerica. This book covers the changes and growth of Mesoamerican indigenous cultures from the time of Spanish contact to the modern day.

Carmichael, Elizabeth, and Cloë Sayers. *The Skeleton at the Feast: The Day of the Dead in Mexico.* London: British Museum Press, 1991.

A delightful, solid study of the history of the Day of the Dead and its contemporary practice. Includes many fine pictures.

Codex Chimalpopoca. As reproduced in *History and Mythology of the Aztecs: The Codex Chimalpopoca.* Translated by John Bierhorst. Tucson: University of Arizona Press, 1992.

A sixteenth-century Nahuatl codex containing both the "Annals of Cuauhtitlan (1570), a history of a Mexican Highlands urban center; and a lengthy, at least partly Mexica creation story called "The Legend of the Suns" (1558) (translated from Nahuatl).

Codex Mendoza. As reproduced in *The Essential Codex Mendoza.* Commentary by Frances F. Berdan and Patricia Rieff Anawalt. Berkeley: University of California Press, 1997.

A shortened version of an earlier in-depth, multi-volume study, which includes a reproduction of this important sixteenth-century Central Mexican pictorial document, and a discussion of the codex's history and meaning. The book offers a good introduction to Mexica royal history.

Cortés, Hernán. *Letters from Mexico.* Translated and edited by A. R. Pagden. New Haven, CT: Yale University Press, 1986.

The letters of Hernán Cortés, which were sent back to the ruler of Spain Charles V. These report on the conquest of New Spain in fair detail (translated from Spanish).

Cosío Villegas, Daniel; Ignacio Bernal, and Alejandro Moreno Toscano. *A Compact History of Mexico.* Translated by Marjory Mattingly Urquidi. Mexico City: El Colegio de México, 1974.

A very short, concise history of Mexico beginning with the Paleo-Indian and ending with Mexico in the 1970s; each chapter is written by an outstanding Mexican scholar. It was originally intended as an introductory textbook for the Colegio's students (translated from Spanish).

Díaz del Castillo, Bernal. *The Discovery and Conquest of Mexico: 1517–1521.* Translated by A. P. Maudslay. New York: Farrar, Straus and Giroux, 1956.

A highly readable first-hand account written by one of Hernán Cortés's captains detailing the Conquest of Mexico (translated from Spanish).

Durán, Fray Diego. *Book of the Gods and Rites and the Ancient Calendar.* Translated by Doris Heyden and Fernando Horcasitas. Norman: University of Oklahoma Press, 1971.

A rich account describing numerous ritual and calendrical aspects of ancient Mexica religion written by a sixteenth-century friar (translated from Spanish).

———. *The History of the Indies of New Spain.* Translated by Doris Heyden. Norman: University of Oklahoma Press, 1994.

The very readable and lengthy retelling of Mexica ancient history, which was produced by a sixteenth-century Dominican cleric (translated from Spanish).

Edmonson, Munro S., Translator. *Heaven Born Mérida and Its Destiny: The Book of Chilam Balam of Chumayel.* Austin: University of Texas Press, 1986.

A seventh- through nineteenth-century Maya text containing the history of Yucatán from the perspective of the Maya town Chumayel. It also includes less historical information such as medical, exegetical, astronomical, liturgical, and literary materials (translated from Yucatec Maya).

———. *The Book of the Year: Middle American Calendrical Systems.* Salt Lake City: University of Utah Press, 1988.

A somewhat technical, but extremely thorough treatment of just about all of the ancient Mesoamerican calendrical systems. The author takes the position that all are based on a basic count of the days, making it possible to calibrate and coordinate the many, diverse calendars.

Freidel, David, Linda Schele, and Joy Parker. *Maya Cosmos: Three Thousand Years on the Shaman's Path.* New York: William Morrow, 1993.

A review and interpretation of Classic Period Maya religion, which uses modern examples to trace Maya religion from early creation myths and the earliest sculptural portrayals of myth to the modern rituals and stories of today's Yucatec Maya.

Furst, Jill Leslie McKeever. *The Natural History of the Soul in Ancient Mexico.* New Haven, CT: Yale University Press, 1995.

A delightful book that explores pre-Conquest soul concepts, especially among the Nahua. It does so by drawing comparisons among ancient and current ideas and their relationships to how human bodies function and other physical evidence.

Knab, Timothy J. *A War of Witches: A Journey in the Underworld of the Contemporary Aztecs.* New York: HarperCollins, 1995.

A fictionalized novel about a contemporary Nahua community that includes references to mythology about the underworld, ritual practices, and witchcraft. It has been based on actual ethnographic research. Good in the classroom for exploring Mesoamerican cosmology and raising ethical issues.

Lafaye, Jacques. *Quetzalcoatl and Guadalupe: The Formation of National Consciousness, 1531–1813.* Chicago: University of Chicago Press, 1976.

One of the classic scholarly historical books on Guadalupe and Mexican history. It explores the formation of national consciousness through the imagery of Guadalupe and Quetzalcoatl.

Landa, Diego de. *Relación de las cosas de Yucatán.* Edited and translated by Alfred M. Tozzer. Papers of the Peabody Museum no 18. Cambridge, MA: Harvard University Press, 1941.

A superb source for ancient customs, stories, and descriptions of the Yucatec Maya life during the early years of Spanish Colonialism. Written in 1566, this book describes the Maya culture in extreme detail, both in the text and in the 1941 footnotes.

Lockhart, James. *The Nahuas after the Conquest: A Social and Cultural History of the Indians of Central Mexico, Sixteenth through Eighteenth Centuries.* CA: Stanford University Press, 1992.

An extraordinarily well-researched, detailed study of indigenous history in Central Mexico from the Conquest through the 1700s.

López Austin, Alfredo. *The Human Body: Concepts of the Ancient Nahuas.* Translated by Thelma Ortiz de Montellano and Bernardo Ortiz de Montellano. Salt Lake City: University of Utah Press, 1988.

An excellent source for the worldview of the ancient Mexica, and how attitudes on the human body interplayed with the cosmos and its other beings (translated from Spanish).

———. *The Myths of the Opossum: Pathways of Mesoamerican Mythology.* Albuquerque: University of New Mexico Press, 1993.

Ancient and contemporary mythology surrounding the opossum becomes the device for exploring basic indigenous religious and cosmological concepts. A fine resource for learning about Mesoamerican worldviews (translated from Spanish).

Menchu, Rigoberta. *I, Rigoberta Menchu: An Indian Woman in Guatemala.* Edited by Elisabeth Burgos-Debray. New York: Verso, 1984.

The moving biographical account of a living K'iche' woman about her life, worldview, and her trials in the Guatemalan civil war (translated from Spanish).

Milbrath, Susan. *Star Gods of the Maya: Astronomy in Art, Folklore, and Calendars.* Austin: University of Texas Press, 1999.

An extremely detailed study of Maya deities and their relationships to the sky, which both builds on and alters the classic work of Eric Thompson and others. While it focuses on a study of ancient star gods, the work contains much about contemporary celestial mythology, often drawing parallels between that and the ancient.

Nash, June. *In the Eyes of the Ancestors: Belief and Behavior in a Mayan Community.* Prospect Heights, IL: Waveland Press, 1985.

A highly detailed, thick ethnography of a Maya group in Chiapas, Mexico, which includes a variety of different myths and stories.

Pasztory, Esther. *Aztec Art.* New York: Harry N. Abrams, 1983.

A now classic work discussing the art of the Mexica, which also includes a great deal of introductory material, and many fine photos.

Popol Vuh: The Definitive Edition of the Mayan Book of the Dawn of Life and the Glories of Gods and Kings. Translated by Dennis Tedlock. New York: Simon and Schuster, 1985.

An early colonial K'iche' Maya collection of five creation myths of the K'iche' Maya world, starting from the creation of the world to the establishment of the highland Maya tribes and the primacy of the K'iche' (translated from K'iche' Maya).

Read, Kay A. *Time and Sacrifice in the Aztec Cosmos.* Bloomington: Indiana University Press, 1998.

An introduction to the pre-Conquest Mexica worldview and its attitudes on time and sacrifice.

Redfield, Robert and Alfonso Villa Rojas. *Chan Kom: A Maya Village.* Washington, DC: Carnegie Institution of Washington, 1934.

A classic ethnography of a Yucatec Maya village in the early 1930s containing excellent descriptions of their rituals, stories, and beliefs. This work is accessible to nonprofessionals and professionals alike.

Sahagún, Fray Bernardino de. *The Florentine Codex: A General History of the Things of New Spain.* Translated by Arthur J. O. Anderson, and Charles E. Dibble. Monographs of the School of American Research no 14. Santa Fe: School of American Research; Salt Lake City: University of Utah Press, 1953; 12 books, 13 parts.

A vast and important source on religious, social, and environmental aspects of the ancient Mexica. A sixteenth-century Franciscan friar collected and produced this magnificent set (translated from Nahuatl).

Sandstrom, Alan. *Corn Is Our Blood: Culture and Ethnicity in a Contemporary Aztec Indian Village.* Norman: University of Oklahoma Press, 1991.

An ethnographic account of a modern town of Nahuatl speakers; it documents, among other things, a number of healing rituals and discusses diverse facets of their religious life.

Sexton, James D. *Mayan Folktales: Folklore from Lake Atitlán, Guatemala.* New York: Doubleday, 1992.

An excellent collection of Maya folktales, myths, and stories from highland Guatemala (translated from Tzutuhil Maya).

Sharer, Robert J. *The Ancient Maya.* 5th ed. Stanford, CA: Stanford University Press, 1994.

A superb source for the archaeology and history of the Maya world. This book describes the prehistoric cultural and historical development of the Maya before Spanish contact. One of the best introductions available.

Stephens, John Lloyd. *Incidents of Travel in Central America, Chiapas, and Yucatan.* Illustrated by Frederick Catherwood. New York: Dover, 1969.

A nineteenth-century traveler's and explorer's guide to archaeological ruins throughout Maya world. This book is an excellent source for beautiful drawings of Maya ruins as they were seen in the 1800s.

Taggart, James M. *Nahuat Myth and Social Structure.* Austin: University of Texas Press, 1983.

A scholarly discussion of the relationship between myths and social structure among particular living Nahuatl speakers, includes many translations of myths from their original language.

Tedlock, Barbara. *Time and the Highland Maya.* Albuquerque: University of New Mexico Press, 1982.

A revised ethnography of the K'iche' Maya intended for the lay reader, with rich descriptions of K'iche' rituals and cosmology.

VIDEOS

Pre-Conquest Mexican and Mayan

The Fall of the Maya
Films for the Humanities & Sciences, Inc.
Box 2053
Princeton, NJ 08543–2053
1–800–257–5126

When archaeologists first looked at the ruins of the Mayan urban center of Copan, they concluded that the Mayans were a peaceful people devoted to astrology and the arts whose civilization mysteriously disappeared. But as the remaining structures were examined more closely through a complex system of tunnels, and as the codes of the hieroglyphics were finally cracked, scholars began to understand a quite different reality: This often war-like Mayan center revolved around blood sacrifice. Copan eventually was abandoned because of overpopulation and the resultant destruction of its natural resources.

The Five Suns
Patricia Amlin
University of California Extension Center for Media and Independent Learning
2000 Center St.
Berkeley, CA 94704
1–510–642–0460

This animated video, drawn by hand in the style of the sixteenth-century Nahua, traces an origin myth of ancient Mexican peoples of the central highlands. The video begins by describing how the strong sacred forces battled to create the first four, unsuccessful ages, and then how the deities worked together to create the fifth and final age. In addition, *The Five Suns* looks at the position and responsibilities of human beings in the ancient world, and the necessity of sacrifice to keep the natural forces working and maintain life.

Indians of North America: Aztec
Schlessinger Video Productions
P.O. Box 1110
Bala Cynwyd, PA 19004
1–800–843–3620

The Aztecs, who began as wandering hunters and gatherers, eventually settled on an island in the middle of a lake and became one of the largest, most socially complex, and most advanced civilizations of all time. Skilled builders and masons, farmers, engineers, and artists, the Aztecs practiced a religious tradition that revolved around sacrifice to and respect for cosmic forces. Although they were great warriors, they could withstand neither the Spanish conquistadors nor the diseases the Spanish carried; however, traces of this great civilization still exist in Mexico today.

Lost Kingdoms of the Maya
Columbia Tristar Home Video
10202 W. Washington Blvd.
Culver City, CA 90232

This National Geographic video traces the development of Maya civilization from its ancient origins to its eventual downfall, recreating key historical events for the viewer. Archaeologists have found clues in the hieroglyphics and artifacts of Tikal, Copan, and Dos Pilas, which hint at who the Mayans were, how they lived, and how their society was structured. The video also points out that although the great cities of the Maya civilization were abandoned by the end of the Middle Ages in Europe, many Mayans today continue to practice the ancient traditions.

The Popol Vuh
Patricia Amlin
University of California Extension Center for Media and Independent Learning
2000 Center St.
Berkeley, CA 94704
1–510–642–0460

This truly excellent animated video, drawn in the style of pre-Conquest manuscripts, sculptures, and pottery ornamentation, accurately retells a significant portion of a lengthy Maya creation story, parts of which are traceable to the Pre-classic era. K'iche' daykeepers still recount the same legend today. The video begins with the creations of the three previous ages and then focuses on the exploits of the Hero Twins as they put the universe in order for the fourth and present age. At once mysterious, exciting, and action-packed, the video will introduce viewers to an important myth of the ancient and modern Maya world.

Teotihuacan: City of the Gods
EVN, Educational Video Network, Inc.
1401 19th Street
Huntsville, TX 77340
1–409–295–5767

Dubbed the "city of gods" by Aztecs who lived almost a thousand years later, Teotihuacan at its height (ca. A.D. 500–600) housed between 150,000 and 200,000 people. The huge Pyramids of the Sun and Moon dominated the city; an Aztec legend said that the gods created these huge structures by sacrificing themselves in order to give birth to the sun. Although much of the city has decayed, many larger structures remain, as does an extensive collection of artifacts including masks, sculptures, pottery, and wall murals and drawings. The remains found here and at other, similar sites in the region give archaeologists clues as to the type of people the Teotihuacanese were and the kind of warfare they waged. In fact, the city was burned in the mid- to late seventh century, perhaps by a rival center that competed with Teotihuacan in sacred warfare focused on the planet Venus

Post-Conquest–Contemporary Mexico

Art and Revolution in Mexico
Films for the Humanities & Sciences, Inc.
Box 2053
Princeton, NJ 08543–2053
1–800–257–5126

Narrated by Octavio Paz, this video explores the major role played by art during the Mexican Revolution of 1910, showing how it propelled the confrontation by educating, inspiring, and motivating people to act. Many types of art from this period, including murals, satirical cartoons, and political posters by artists such as Rivera, Orozco, and Siquieros, are discussed. The viewer will not only become familiar with these artists' creations but will also learn about the effects they had on the people and the revolution.

Celebrating the Day of the Dead
EVN, Educational Video Network, Inc.
1401 19th St.

Huntsville, TX 77340

1–409–295–5767

This video explores the Mexican ritual of the Day of the Dead from the viewpoint of the dead themselves. It also looks at the effect the festival has on the living celebrants—in particular, how it shapes their view of the dead. Lastly, it touches on the mythical origins of the festival, the influence of the Conquest and introduction of Christianity on indigenous ideas about the dead, and the economic and social standing of the festival's participants.

Great Cities of the World: Mexico City

Films for the Humanities & Sciences, Inc.

Box 2053

Princeton, NJ 08543–2053

1–800–257–5126

From the ancient past of Toltec peoples to the Aztecs' erection of the great city of Tenochtitlán; the Spanish conquistadores to the last monarchies; the Revolution of 1910 to the modern day, this video explores the history of one of the largest cities in the world: Mexico City. All aspects of the city's identity are explored, including the environment, people, politics, religions, and cultures. The video explores these facets through each of the city's major historical periods, painting a complete and many-sided picture of this great metropolis.

Contemporary Central America

Romero

Vidmark Entertainment

2901 Ocean Park Blvd., Suite 123

Santa Monica, CA 90405–2906

213–399–8877

Oscar Romero began his career as a quiet, bookish priest, but gradually was transformed into an outspoken activist and champion of the repressed peasants in his native El Salvador. When faced with the brutal deaths and "disappearances" of his friends, parishioners, and people, Archbishop Romero found he could no longer remain apolitical, and he became instead a powerful supporter of popular resistance in this country's twelve-year civil war (1980–1992). This film traces his life from the moment of his transformation to his assassination by government-sponsored extremists, and brings home the fact that even after his death Romero continued to live in the hearts of the people for whom he fought.

Tierra Madre, Terra Sacre
Cinema Guild
1697 Broadway Suite 506
New York, NY 10019
212–246–5522

Although *Tierra Madre, Terra Sacre* (Mother Earth, Sacred Earth) was made before the 1996 signing of a peace agreement that ended a thirty-year civil war in Guatemala, it still captures the plight of today's peasant farmers in that country. The Kekchi Indians, members of the Catholic Popular Church, still recognize the earth as their mother and desperately seek to preserve their ancient heritage and culture, which the government and rich plantation owners have been slowly stripping away. Traditional communal values are extremely important to these farmers, yet the landowners deprive them of their social autonomy and sometimes even of the church that supports and empowers them. The video is in English, Spanish, and Kekchi, and includes English subtitles.

WEB SITES

General Mesoamerica

Ancient Mesoamerican Civilizations: Maya, Mixtec, Zapotec, and Aztec
http://www.angelfire.com/ca/humanorigins/index.html

The brainchild of Kevin L. Callahan (University of Minnesota, Department of Anthropology), this site provides a truly fine introduction to the culture and history of pre-Columbian Mesoamerica, offering an overview and description of Mesoamerican writing systems, government structures, the Maya calendar, and Mesoamerican religious beliefs. It also offers links to related web sites.

Arizona State University Archaeological Research Institute
http://archaeology.la.asu.edu

A virtual museum on ancient cultures links the viewer to the Teotihuacan home page, an exhibit on the Templo Mayor of Tenochtitlán, and a guide to the decorated ceramics of Zacatecas, Mexico. The site offers the general public and experts around the world information about Teotihuacan and the Feathered Serpent Pyramid, the Templo Mayor Project, and Zacatecas ceramic types. Documents available for viewing at the site are suited to a variety of readerships and levels of interest and include basic introductory pages, recent excavation reports, and academic journal articles.

Culture and Society of México
http://www.public.iastate.edu/~rjsalvad/scmfaq/scmfaq.html

Offers information on a range of topics relating to current Mexican society and culture. Also serves as the home page for the Internet discussion group "soc.culture.mexican."

Foundation for the Advancement of Mesoamerican Studies, Inc.
http://www.famsi.org/

This site is the home page for FAMSI, a private research granting institution that provides research grant opportunities and posts the resulting research reports. The site also includes pages for the Schele, Kerr, and the Montgomery archives. The Schele Archive is a database where people can search through 1,000 drawings by Linda Schele, organized by culture, site, time period, architectural feature, artifact, and iconography. The Kerr Archive contains several thousand rollout photographs of Maya vases by Justin Kerr, which are organized by vase type and iconographic content. The Montgomery Archive offers drawings by John Montgomery, indexed by culture, site, time period, and iconography. This site is extremely useful to Mesoamerican scholars and very informative for the enthusiast and layperson.

GB Online's Mesoamerica
http://pages.prodigy.com/GBonline/mesowelc.html

An interested and motivated amateur designed and created this excellent web site. His purpose is to share information with fellow enthusiasts in his quest to learn more by focusing on various aspects of Mesoamerican cultural studies. This site contains a variety of information and links about Mesoamerican writing systems, archaeological sites, contemporary native Mesoamerican issues, pre-Columbian art, and the calendrical system.

Mesoweb
http://www.mesoweb.com/

Mesoweb is an excellent web site devoted to the exploration of Mesoamerican cultures: the Olmecs, Maya, Aztecs, Toltecs, Mixtecs, Zapotecs, and others. Run by three scholars—Merle Greene Robertson, Jorge Pérez de Lara, and Joel Skidmore on behalf of PARI (Pre-Columbian Art Research Institute)—the site focuses on a variety of subjects including renewal ceremonies of the contemporary Tz'utujil; recent discoveries at the site of Palenque in Chiapas, Mexico; a report on the adventures of Teobert Maler, an early-twentieth-century, Austrian-born photographer and explorer; and rubbings of Maya sculptures by Merle Greene Robertson. The site also offers an illustrated encyclopedia of Mesoamerican cultures and a collection of short animations referring to each section of the web site. It also includes links to related sites. Although this particular site is in English, some of the links it provides are in Spanish.

Pre-Columbian Archaeology and Related Links
http://copan.bioz.unibas.ch/mesolinks.html

This site does not contain any information itself but does have an extensive list of other web sites covering all types of resources on Mesoamerican cultures, myth, and history. This includes web sites focusing on regions and archaeological sites; museums, universities, and societies; publishers and bookstores; tourism and field study programs; universities with pre-Columbian programs; language and astronomy; and geography, flora, and fauna.

The Pre-Columbian Graphic Arts Web Site
http://members.aol.com/hasawchan/precolart.html

A great site for schoolchildren and laypersons, this highly interactive web site concentrates on the Maya area but includes information on other topics as well. It uses impressive imagery, animation, and sound effects to provide a brief synopsis of ancient Mesoamerican history and a description of the Maya world. The author has posted a variety of different photographs from around Mesoamerica and many museums and archaeological sites.

Maya

The Hudson Museum, University of Maine
www.umaine.edu/hudsonmuseum/worldvie.htm

This virtual exhibit explains and describes the ancient Maya worldview using pieces from the Palmer Collection of Maya. The site does a very good job of describing and explaining very briefly the pre-Columbian Maya worldview and discussing how the artifact images relate to Mayan stories and myths.

Maya Adventure
http://www.smm.org/sln/ma/index.html

Useful to teachers and students, this site features a variety of online educational activities and an ample collection of images from the anthropological collections at the Science Museum of Minnesota. The site also provides information on the Museum's related programs and exhibits, among them "Cenote of Sacrifice" and "Flowers, Saints, and Toads."

Maya Art and Books: The Foundation for Latin American Anthropological Research
http://www.maya-art-books.org

This site was founded with the goal of facilitating academic access to scholarly information about Mayan daily life 1,000 years ago in Guatemala, Belize, Mexico, and Honduras. It offers extensive photographic records of facts about and artifacts of ancient civilizations of pre-Columbian Mesoamerica.

The Maya Astronomy Page
http://www.astro.uva.nl/michielb/maya/astro.html

This page was designed and created by an astronomy graduate student from the Netherlands. It contains information about Maya astronomical knowledge, as well as the relationships of astronomy with Maya mathematics and calendrical systems. Very useful site for the beginner trying to understand Maya astronomy.

Maya Civilization—Past and Present
http://indy4.fdl.cc.mn.us/~isk/maya/mayastor.html

The focus here is on Maya science and art. The web site offers various teaching materials, including maps, and discussions of numbers and vocabulary, as well as a collection of Maya folktales and art objects. It also includes information about K'iche' Maya Nobel laureate Rigoberta Menchu and the modern Mayan peoples of Mexico and Central America.

Maya Multimedia Project: Interactive Popol Vuh
http://www.stanford.edu/class/anthro98a /Browser/home.html

This interactive web site arose out of an anthropology class taught at Stanford University by James A. Fox. The user can tab through a translation of the Maya Popul Vuh creation myths, and while reading the myth, view various images of Maya art depicting scenes from these myths.

Mayan Folktales
http://www.folkart.com/~latitude/folktale/folktale.htm

This web site is a collection of myths and stories from a Q'anjob'al Maya storyteller from San Miguel Acátan, Huehuetenango, Guatemala. Each month additional folktales are added to the web site, making it a great source for individuals looking for Maya stories.

MayaQuest 98
http://quest.classroom.com/archive/mayaquest1998/default.htm

This phenomenal web site follows an organized team of explorers traveling throughout the Maya area in 1998, visiting modern Maya communities and archaeological sites. Every day during MayaQuest 98, the team of adventurers and experts communicated exciting news, interesting information, and difficult dilemmas from their remote camps in the rain forest to interested viewers in school classrooms and elsewhere. Well worth the visit, especially if you are a kid, a teacher of kids, or simply interested in the topics.

Mundo Maya
http://www.mayadiscovery.com

Provides a brief introduction to the Maya world, describing some of the archaeology of the region, the natural environment, the daily life of the Maya, history, handicrafts, a short collection of Maya legends and stories, and other information. One can view this in either English or Spanish.

La Nave Va: Zapatistas, EXLN, Subcomandante Marcos, Chiapas, and Global Struggles
http://www.utexas.edu/students/nave

The center for information on the Zapatistas, this site gives a description of their movement with news and information, as well as archives of past events. It is a good location for learning more about the Zapatistas from their own point of view, offering an insight into one contemporary movement of resistance.

Rabbit in the Moon: Maya Glyphs and Architecture
http://www.halfmoon.org

A great web site, useful to both amateurs and experts. Learn about ancient Maya hieroglyphic writing, or how to write your own name in Maya glyphs; play Bul, a Maya game of chance; or walk up a Maya pyramid. This interactive site includes tons of information on Maya writing, calendar systems, and culture, as well as useful links to other sites.

Ancient and Contemporary Mexico

Aztec Folktales—Teacher Guide
http://www.sdcoe.k12.ca.us/score/aztec/aztectg.html

Produced by the San Diego County Office of Education, this web site is a great resource for teachers and students. It contains a set of interactive activities for students, involving the reading, analysis, and illustration of Aztec folktales. Students may choose to create Venn diagrams comparing various tales; create a poster using folktales and imagery from the web site; or write poems or a letter from the perspective of an Aztec lord.

Fiestas Mexicanas
http://www.mexicodesconocido.com.mx/fiestas/fiestas.htm

Created by the Mexican Secretary of Tourism, this site describes various contemporary indigenous fiestas found throughout México. It lists the fiestas that take place each month, and the towns and regions where they are celebrated, and provides a description and interpretation of each event. The site is entirely in Spanish.

La Llorona—Teacher Guide
http://www.sdcoe.k12.ca.us/score/rona/ronatg.html

This site, created by the San Diego County Office of Education, is another good teaching resource. It offers a number of interactive activities allowing students to explore a retelling of a popular present-day legend using modern trial proceedings, research techniques, and poetry. This is a great web site for teaching students about contemporary Aztec legends and about modern Mexican cultures north and south of the U.S. border.

Mexico Student Teacher Resource Center
http://northcoast.com/~spdtom/index.html

This somewhat idiosyncratic but interesting and useful site provides introductory background on the history of Mexico. It offers limited information on the Aztecs, the history of Cortés, the French intervention of 1861, the dictatorship of Porfirio Díaz, and the Mexican Revolution from 1910 to 1940. In addition, it offers a collection of graphics with detailed captions, and a guide for research.

Nahuatl Home Page
http://www.umt.edu/history/NAHUATL

Nahuatl, the native language of the ancient Aztecs and of many Mexican highlanders today, is the focus of this web site. Serving as the home page for the

NAHUAT-L discussion list, the site lists many Nahuatl resources and links to related sites. Among the resources available are books on Nahuatl; the table of contents of *Estudios de Cultura Nahuatl* vols. 1–26 (a Mexican professional journal); Aztec calendar programs; an image of the Aztec Sunstone; the Templo Mayor Museum (includes numerous objects in their collection and information on them and related topics on Mexica); pre-Columbian calendars; the *Codex Mendoza*; and other Nahua manuscripts.

Our Lady of Guadalupe Web Site
http://ng.netgate.net/~norberto/materdei.html

This is an excellent and interesting web site for understanding a worshiper's veneration of Guadalupe as well as her iconography. Not a scholarly or research-oriented site, it offers a believer's view of the chronology of Guadalupe's appearances; stories and myths about her; and prayers and consecrations for her. The site can be accessed in English, Spanish, French, and Portuguese.

REFERENCE LIST

Abreu Gomez, Ermilo. 1979. *Canek: History and Legend of a Maya Hero.* Translated by Mario L. Davila and Carter Wilson. Berkeley: University of California Press.

Adams, Richard E. W. 1991. *Prehistoric Mesoamerica.* Norman: University of Oklahoma Press.

Alarcón, Hernando Ruiz de. 1984. *Treatise on the Heathen Superstitions That Today Live among the Indians Natives to This New Spain, 1629.* Translated by J. Richard Andrews and Ross Hassig. Norman: University of Oklahoma Press.

Anaya, Rudolfo A. 1984. *The Legend of La Llorona.* Berkeley, CA: Tonatiuh-Quinto Sol International.

Anzaldúa, Gloria. 1987. *Borderlands/La Frontera: The New Mestiza.* San Francisco: Aunt Lute Books.

Arora, Shirley L. 1997. "La Llorona." In *Encyclopedia of Mexico.* Edited by Michael S. Werner, 1: 753–754. Chicago: Fitzroy Dearborn.

Aveni, Anthony. 1980. *Skywatchers of Ancient Mexico.* Austin: University of Texas Press.

Baldwin, Neil. 1998. *Legends of the Plumed Serpent: Biography of a Mexican God.* New York: Public Affairs.

Bassie-Sweet, Karen. 1991. *From the Mouth of the Dark Cave: Commemorative Sculpture of the Late Classic Maya.* Norman: University of Oklahoma Press.

Benson, Elizabeth P., and Beatriz de la Fuente, editors. 1996. *Olmec Art of Ancient Mexico.* Washington, DC: National Gallery of Art.

Berlin, Heinrich. 1988. *Idolatría y superstición entre los indios de Oaxaca.* Mexico City: Ediciones Toledo.

Berlo, Janet. 1992. *Art, Ideology, and the City of Teotihuacan.* Washington, DC: Dumbarton Oaks Research Library and Collection.

Berrin, Kathleen. 1984. *The Hungry Woman: Myths and Legends of the Aztec.* New York: William Morrow.

———. 1988. *Feathered Serpents and Flowering Trees.* San Francisco: Fine Arts Museum of San Francisco.

Bierhorst, John, editor. 1986. *The Monkey's Haircut and Other Stories Told by the Maya.* Illustrated by Robert Andrew Parker. New York: William Morrow.

Boone, Elizabeth H. 1989. *Incarnations of the Aztec Supernatural: The Image of Huitzilopochtli in Mexico and Europe.* Transactions of the American Philosophical Society. Philadelphia: American Philosophical Society.

Bradomin, Jose Maria. 1994. "The Sacrifice of Cocijo." In *Myth and Magic: Oaxaca Past and Present,* 44–47. Palo Alto: Palo Alto Cultural Center.

Brady, James E. 1989. "An Investigation of Maya Ritual Cave Use with Special Reference to Naj Tunich, Peten, Guatemala." Ph.D. dissertation, Department of Anthropology, University of California at Los Angeles.

Bricker, Victoria Reifler. 1973. *Ritual Humor in Highland Chiapas.* Austin: University of Texas Press.

———. 1981. *The Indian Christ, the Indian King.* Austin: University of Texas Press.

Broda, Johanna. 1969. *The Mexican Calendar as Compared to Other Mesoamerican Systems.* Edited by Josef Haekel and Engelbert Stiglmayr. Series Americana 4, Acta Ethnologica et Linguistica, No. 15, Institut für Völkerkunde der Universitäte Wien. Vienna: Herbert Merta.

———. 1983. "Ciclos agrícolas en el culto: Un problema de la corelación del calendario Mexica." In *Calendars in Mesoamerica: Native Computations of Time.* Edited by Anthony Aven, and Gordon Brotherston, 145–164. Oxford: BAR International Series 174.

Brundage, Burr Cartwright. 1979. *The Fifth Sun: Aztec Gods, Aztec World.* Austin: University of Texas Press.

Burkhart, Louise. 1989. *The Slippery Earth: Nahua Christian Moral Dialogue in Sixteenth Century Mexico.* Tucson: University of Arizona Press.

———. 1996. *Holy Wednesday: A Nahua Drama from Early Colonial Mexico.* Philadelphia: University of Pennsylvania Press.

Burns, Allan F., translator. 1983. *An Epoch of Miracles: Oral Literature of the Yucatec Maya.* Austin: University of Texas Press.

Cantares Mexicanos. 1985. As reproduced in *Cantares Mexicanos: Songs of the Aztecs.* Translated by John Bierhorst. Stanford, CA: Stanford University Press.

———. 1993. As reproduced in *Poesía Náhuatl: Cantares Mexicanos, Manuscrito de la Biblioteca Nacional de México,* 2d ed. Translated by Ángel Ma. Garibay K. Mexico City: Universidad Nacional Autónoma de México.

Carlson, John B. 1976. "Astronomical Investigations and Site Orientation Influences at Palenque." In *The Art, Iconography and Dynastic History of Palenque, Part III.* Edited by Merle Greene Robertson, 107–117. Pebble Beach, CA: Pre-Columbian Art Research, Robert Louis Stevenson School.

Carmack, Robert M., Janine Gasco, and Gary H. Gossen. 1996. *The Legacy of Mesoamerica: History and Culture of a Native American Civilization.* Upper Saddle River, NJ: Prentice Hall.

Carmichael, Elizabeth, and Cloë Sayers. 1991. *The Skeleton at the Feast: The Day of the Dead in Mexico.* London: British Museum Press.

Carrasco, David. 1982. *Quetzalcoatl and the Irony of Empire.* Chicago: University of Chicago Press.

Carrasco, David, Johanna Broda, and Eduardo Matos Moctezuma. 1987. *The Great Temple of Tenochtitlan: Center and Periphery in the Aztec World.* Berkeley: University of California Press.

Carrasco, Pedro. 1971. "Social Organization of Ancient Mexico." In *Handbook of Middle American Indians.* Edited by Robert Wauchope, 10: 349–375. Austin: University of Texas Press.

Caso, Alfonso. 1958. *The Aztecs: The People of the Sun.* Translated by Lowell Dunham. Norman: University of Oklahoma Press.

———. 1971. "Calendrical Systems of Central Mexico." In *Handbook of Middle American Indians,* vol. 10. Edited by Robert Wauchope. Austin: University of Texas Press.

Cervantes, Fernando. 1994. *The Devil in the New World: The Impact of Diabolism in New Spain.* New Haven, CT: Yale University Press.

Chamberlain, Robert S. 1948. *The Conquest and Colonization of Yucatan, 1517–1550.* Washington, DC: Carnegie Institute of Washington Publication 582.

Chase, Diane Z., and Arlen F. Chase, editors. 1992. *Mesoamerican Elite: An Archaeological Assessment.* Norman: University of Oklahoma Press.

Chilam Balam of Chumayel. 1933. Translated by Ralph Loveland Roys. Washington, DC: Carnegie Institution of Washington.

———. 1967. As reproduced in *The Book of Chilam Balam of Chumayel.* Translated by Ralph L. Roys. Original manuscript 1782. Norman: University of Oklahoma Press.

———. 1986. In *Heaven Born Mérida and Its Destiny: The Book of Chilam Balam of Chumayel.* Translator Munro S. Edmonson. Austin: University of Texas Press.

Chilam Balam of Tizimin. 1982. In *The Ancient Future of the Itza: The Book of Chilam Balam of Tizimin.* Editor and translator Munro Edmonson. Austin: University of Texas Press.

———. 1951. In *The Book of the Jaguar Priest: A Translation of the Book of*

Chilam Balam of Tizimin. Translated by Maud Worcester Makemson. New York: Henry Schuman.

Clendinnen, Inga. 1991. *Aztecs: An Interpretation.* Cambridge: Cambridge University Press.

Codex Aubin. 1893. As reproduced in *Histoire de la nation mexicaine.* Paris: Ernest Leroux.

Codex Borbonicus. 1974. Facsimile ed. Commentary by K. A. Nowotny. Graz, Austria: Akademische Druck u. Verlagsanstalt.

Codex Borgia. 1963. Commentary by Eduard Seler. Mexico City: Fondo de Cultura Económica.

Codex Boturini. 1831. As reproduced in *Antiquities of Mexico.* Edited by Edward King, Viscount Kingsborough. 9 vols. London: Robert Havell.

Codex Chimalpahin. 1982. As reproduced in *Relaciones originales de Chalco Amaquemecan: Escritas por Don Francisco de San Antón Muñón Chimalpahin Cuauhtlehuanitzin.* Translated by S. Réndon. Mexico: Fondo de Cultura Económica.

———. 1997. As reproduced in *Codex Chimalpahin: Society and Politics in Mexico Tenochtitlan, Tlatelolco, Texcoco, Culhuacan, and Other Nahua Altepetl in Central Mexico: The Nahuatl and Spanish Annals and Accounts Collected and Recorded by Don Domingo de San Antón Muñón Chimalpahin Quauhtlehuanitzin.* Edited and translated by Arthur J. O. Anderson and Susan Schroeder. Norman: University of Oklahoma Press.

Codex Chimalpopoca. 1992a. As reproduced in *Codex Chimalpopoca: The Text in Nahuatl with a Glossary and Grammatical Notes.* Translated by John Bierhorst. Tucson: University of Arizona Press.

———. 1992b. As reproduced in *History and Mythology of the Aztecs: The Codex Chimalpopoca.* Translated by John Bierhorst. Tucson: University of Arizona Press.

Codex Cospi. 1968. Facsimile ed. Commentary by K. A. Nowotny. Graz, Austria: Akademische Druck u. Verlagsanstalt.

Codex Dresden [*Codex Dresdensis: Die Maya-Handschrift in der Sächsischen Landesbibliothek Dresden*]. 1962 Edited by E. Förstemann. (Reprint of *Die Maya-Handschrift De Königlichen Bibliothek Zu Dresden.* Foreword by E. Lips. Leipzig: Röder, 1880). Berlin: Adademie-Verlag.

Codex Fejérváry-Mayer. 1901. Facsimile ed. Paris: Duc de Loubat.

Codex Magliabechiano. 1983. Facsimile ed. Zelia Nuttal. Berkeley: University of California Press.

Codex Mendoza. 1938. Facsimile ed. Edited by James Cooper Clark. London: Waterlow and Sons.

———. 1992. Commentary and edited by Frances F. Berdan and Patricia Anawalt. 2 vols. Berkeley: University of California Press.

———. 1997. As reproduced in *The Essential Codex Mendoza*. Commentary by Frances F. Berdan and Patricia Rieff Anawalt. Berkeley: University of California Press.

Codex Perez and the Book of Chilam Balam of Mani. 1979. Edited by Eugene R. Craine, and Reginald C. Reindorp. Norman: University of Oklahoma Press.

Codex Telleriano Remensis. As reproduced in *Codex Telleriano Remensis: Ritual, Divination, and History in a Pictorial Aztec Manuscript*. Commentary by Eloise Quiñones Keber. Austin: University of Texas Press.

Codex Tro-Cortesianus. 1967. Facsimile ed. Commentary by Ferdinand Anders. Graz, Austria: Akademische Druck u. Verlagsanstalt.

Códice Tudela. 1980. Facsimile ed. Commentary by José Tudela de la Orden. Madrid: Ediciones Cultura Hispanica.

Códice Vaticano Latino 3738. 1964. In *Antiqüedades de México*. With a prologue by Agustín Yánez. 4 vols. (Reprint of Vol. 2 of *Antiquities of Mexico*, Edited by Edward King, Viscount Kingsborough. 9 vols. London: Robert Havell, 1831–1848). Mexico City: Secretaría de Hacienda y Crédito Público.

Códice Xolotl. 1980. Facsimile ed. Edited by Charles E. Dibble. Mexico City: Universidad Nacional Autónoma de México.

Coe, Michael. 1973. *The Maya Scribe and His World*. New York: Grolier Club.

———. 1977. "Supernatural Patrons of Maya Scribes and Artists." In *Social Process in Maya Prehistory: Studies in Honour of Sir Eric Thompson*. Editor Norman D. C. Hammond, 327–347. New York: Academic Press.

———. 1984. *The Maya*. 3d ed. London: Thames and Hudson.

———. 1987. *The Maya*. 4th ed. New York: Thames and Hudson.

Colombres, Adolfo. 1982. *Relatos del mundo indígena*. Mexico: SEP.

Cortés, Hernan. 1986. *Letters from Mexico*. Translated and edited by A. R. Pagden. New Haven, CT: Yale University Press.

Cosío Villegas, Daniel, Ignacio Bernal, and Alejandro Moreno Toscano. 1974. *A Compact History of Mexico*. Translated by Marjory Mattingly Urquidi. Mexico: El Colegio de México.

Cross, F. L., and E. A. Livingstone, editors. 1990. *The Oxford Dictionary of the Christian Church*. New York: Oxford University Press.

Cyphers, Ann. 1996. "Reconstructing Olmec Life at San Lorenzo." In *Olmec Art of Ancient Mexica*. Edited by Elizabeth P. Benson and Beatriz de la Fuente, 61–73. Washington, DC: National Gallery of Art.

Davies, Nigel. 1973. *The Aztecs: A History*. Norman: University of Oklahoma Press.

Díaz del Castillo, Bernal. 1956. *The Discovery and Conquest of Mexico: 1517–1521.* New York: Farrar, Straus, and Giroux.

Diehl, Richard. 1996. "The Olmec World." In *Olmec Art of Ancient Mexico.* Edited by Elizabeth P. Benson and Beatriz de la Fuente, 29–33. Washington, DC: National Gallery of Art.

Durán, Fray Diego. 1971. *Book of the Gods and Rites and the Ancient Calendar.* Translated by Doris Heyden and Fernando Horcasitas. Norman: University of Oklahoma Press.

———. 1994. *The History of the Indies of New Spain.* Translated by Doris Heyden. Norman: University of Oklahoma Press.

Edmonson, Munro S. 1988. *The Book of the Year: Middle American Calendrical Systems.* Salt Lake City: University of Utah Press.

———. 1993. "The Mayan Faith." *South and Meso-American Native Spirituality.* Edited by Gary H. Gossen, 65–85. New York: Crossroads.

Edmonson, Munro S., editor and translator. 1982. *The Ancient Future of the Itza: The Book of Chilam Balam of Tizimin.* Austin: University of Texas Press.

Faust, Betty Bernice. 1998. *Mexican Rural Development and the Plumed Serpent: Technology and Maya Cosmology in the Tropical Forest of Campeche, Mexico.* Westport, CT: Bergin and Garvey.

Florescano, Enrique. 1994. *Memory, Myth, and Time in Mexico: From the Aztecs to Independence.* Austin: University of Texas Press.

Fowler, William J. 1989. *The Cultural Evolution of Ancient Nahua Civilizations: The Pipil-Nicarao of Central America.* Norman: University of Oklahoma Press.

Franch, José Alcina. 1993. *Calendario y religiòn entre los Zapotecos.* Mexico City: Universidad Nacional Autonoma de México.

Freidel, David, and Linda Schele. 1988. "Symbol and Power: A History of the Lowland Maya Cosmogram." In *Maya Iconography.* Edited by Elizabeth P. Benson and Gillett Good Griffin, 44–93. Princeton, NJ: Princeton University Press.

Friedel, David, Linda Schele, and Joy Parker. 1993. *Maya Cosmos: Three Thousand Years on the Shaman's Path.* New York: William Morrow.

Furst, Jill Leslie McKeever. 1995. *The Natural History of the Soul in Ancient Mexico.* New Haven, CT: Yale University Press.

Gann, Thomas. 1900. *Mounds in Northern Honduras.* Nineteenth Annual Report of the Bureau of American Ethnology. Washington, DC: Bureau of American Ethnology.

Garibay K., Angel María, editor and translator. 1978. *Llave de Nahuatl.* 4th ed. Mexico City: Editorial Porrúa.

———. 1985. *Teogonía e historia de los Mexicanos: Tres opusculos del siglo XVI.* 4th ed. Mexico City: Editorial Porrúa.

Gibson, Charles. 1964. *The Aztecs under Spanish Rule: A History of the Indians of the Valley of Mexico, 1519–1810.* Stanford, CA: Stanford University Press.

Gillespie, Susan. 1989. *The Aztec Kings: The Construction of Rulership in Mexica History.* Tucson: University of Arizona Press.

Goldin, Liliana R., and Brenda Rosenbaum. 1993. "Culture and History: Subregional Variation among the Maya." *Comparative Studies in Society and History* 35: 110–132.

Gómara, Francisco López de. 1964. *Cortés: The Life of the Conqueror by his Secretary.* Translated by Leslie Byrd Simpson. Berkeley: University of California Press.

Gonzales Torres, Yolotl. 1991. *Diccionario de mitología y religión de Mesoamerica.* Mexico City: Ediciones Larousse.

Gonzalez-Lauck, Rebecca. 1996. "La Venta: an Olmec Capital." In *Olmec Art of Ancient Mexica.* Edited by Elizabeth P. Benson and Beatriz de la Fuente, 73–81. Washington, DC: National Gallery of Art.

Gossen, Gary. 1986. *Chamulas in the World of the Sun: Time and Space in a Maya Oral Tradition.* 2d ed. Prospect Heights, IL: Waveland Press.

Gossen, Gary, editor. 1986. *Symbol and Meaning beyond the Closed Community: Essays in Mesoamerican Ideas.* Albany: State University of New York Press.

Graulich, Michel. 1997. *Myths of Ancient Mexico.* Norman: University of Oklahoma Press.

Haley, H. B., and F. X. Grollig. 1989. "Death in the Maya Cosmos." In *Perspectives on Death and Dying: Cross-cultural and Multi-disciplinary Views.* Edited by A. Berger, 131–145. Philadelphia: Charles Press.

Hancock, Graham, and Santha Faiia. 1998. *Heaven's Mirror: Quest for the Lost Civilization.* New York: Three Rivers Press.

Harner, Michael. 1977. "The Ecological Basis for Aztec Sacrifice." *American Ethnologist* 4, 1: 117–35.

Harris, Max. 1990. "Indigenismo and Catolicidad: Folk Dramatizations of Evangelism and Conquest in Central Mexico." *Journal of the American Academy of Religion* 58, 1: 55–68.

———. 1992. "Disguised Reconciliations: Indigenous Voices in Early Franciscan Missionary Drama in Mexico." *Radical History Review* 53: 13–25.

———. 1993. *Dialogical Theater: Dramatization of the Conquest of Mexico and the Question of the Other.* New York: St. Martin's Press.

———. 1994. "Reading the Mask: Hidden Transcripts and Human Interaction." *Mind and Human Interaction* 5, 4: 155–164.

———. 1996. "Moctezuma's Daughter: The Role of La Malinche in Mesoamerican Dance." *Journal of American Folklore* 109, 432: 149–177.

———. 1997. "The Return of Moctezuma: Oaxaca's *Danza de la Pluma* and New Mexico's *Danza de los Matachines.*" *Drama Review* 41, 1 (T153): 106–134.

———. 1998. "Sweet Moll and Malinche: Maid Marian Goes to Mexico." In *Playing Robin Hood: The Legend as Performance in Five Centuries.* Edited by Lois Potter, 101–110. Newark: University of Delaware Press.

Henderson, John S. 1997. *The World of the Ancient Maya.* 2d. ed. Ithaca, NY: Cornell University Press.

Henestrosa, Andres. 1994. "The Bat." In *Myth and Magic: Oaxaca Past and Present,* 33–37. Palo Alto, CA: Palo Alto Cultural Center.

Heyden, Doris. 1975. "An Interpretation of the Cave underneath the Pyramid of the Sun at Teotihuacan, Mexico." *American Antiquity* 40, 2: 131–147.

———. 1979. "The Many Faces of the Mother Goddess: Deities of Water and Sustenance." Paper presented at the International Congress of Americanists, Vancouver.

———. 1983. *Mitología y simbolismo de la flora en el México prehispánico.* Mexico City: Universidad Nacional Autónoma de México.

Historia de los Mexicanos por sus pinturas. 1985. In *Teogonía e historia de los Mexicanos: Tres opusculos del siglo XVI.* 4th ed. Edited by Angel María Garibay K., 23–90. Mexico City: Editorial Porrúa.

Histoyre du Mechique. 1905. In *Journal de la Société des Américanistes de Paris.* Edited by Edourd de Jonghe, 1–41.

Hofling, Charles Andrew. 1991. *Itzá Maya Myths: With a Grammatical Overview.* Salt Lake City: University of Utah Press.

Ixtlilxochitl, Don Fernando de Alva. 1985. *Obras históricas.* 4th ed. Edited by Edmundo O'Gorman. Mexico City: Universidad Nacional Autónoma de México.

Jones, Grant Drummond. 1989. *Maya Resistance to Spanish Rule: Time and History on a Colonial Frontier.* Albuquerque: University of New Mexico Press.

Joralemon, Peter David. 1996. "In Search of the Olmec Cosmos: Reconstructing the World View of Mexico's First Civilization." In *Olmec Art of Ancient Mexico.* Edited by Elizabeth P. Benson and Beatriz de la Fuente, 51–59. Washington, DC: National Gallery of Art.

Josserand, J. Kathryn, and Nicholas A. Hopkins. 1997. "Tila, Chiapas: A Modern Maya Pilgrimage Center." In *15th Annual Maya Weekend.*

Karttunen, Frances. 1983. *An Analytical Dictionary of Nahuatl.* Austin: University of Texas Press.

———. 1997a. "La Malinche and *Malinchismo.*" In *Encyclopedia of Mexico.* Edited by Michael S. Werner, 2: 775–778. Chicago: Fitzroy Dearborn.

———. 1997b. "Rethinking Malinche." In *Indian Women in Early Mexico.* Edited by Susan Schroeder, Stephanie Wood, and Robert Haskett, 291–312. Norman: University of Oklahoma Press.

Keen, Benjamin. 1971. *The Aztec Image in Western Thought.* New Brunswick, NJ: Rutgers University Press.

Kelley, David Humiston. 1976. *Deciphering the Maya Script.* Austin: University of Texas Press.

Kidwell, Clara Sue. 1992. "Systems of Knowledge." In *America in 1492: The World of the Indian Peoples before the Arrival of Columbus.* Edited by Alvin M. Josephy, Jr., 369–403. New York: Alfred A. Knopf.

Kircher, John. 1997. *A Neotropical Companion.* Princeton, NJ: Princeton University Press.

Klein, Cecelia. 1988. "Rethinking Cihuacoatl: Aztec Political Imagery of the Conquered Woman." In *Smoke and Mist: Mesoamerican Studies in Memory of Thelma D. Sullivan.* Edited by J. Kathryn Josserand and Karen Dakin, 237–277. London: B.A.R.

Knab, Timothy J. 1995. *A War of Witches: A Journey in the Underworld of the Contemporary Aztecs.* New York: HarperCollins.

Krickeberg, Walter. 1966. *Altmexickanische Kulturen.* Berlin: Safari-Verlag.

Lafaye, Jacques. 1976. *Quetzalcoatl and Guadalupe: The Formation of Mexican National Consciousness, 1531–1813.* Chicago: University of Chicago Press.

Landa, Diego de. 1941. *Relación de las cosas de Yucatán.* Edited and translated by Alfred M. Tozzer. Papers of the Peabody Museum. Cambridge, MA: Harvard University Press.

———. 1975. *The Maya: Diego de Landa's Account of the Affairs of Yucatan.* Translated by Anthony R. Padgen. Chicago: O'Hara.

———. 1978. *Yucatan before and after the Conquest.* Translated by William Gates. New York: Dover.

Laughlin, Robert M., and Carol Karasik. 1988. *The People of the Bat: Mayan Tales and Dreams from Zinacantan.* Washington, DC: Smithsonian Institution Press.

León, Nicolás. 1979. *Los Tarascos: Notas históricas étnicas y antropológicas, colegidas de escritores antiguos y modernos, documentos inéditos y observaciones personales.* Mexico City: Editorial Innovación.

León-Portilla, Miguel. 1992. *Fifteen Poets of the Aztec World.* Norman: University of Oklahoma Press.

Liss, Peggy K. 1975. *Mexico under Spain, 1521–1556: Society and the Origins of Nationality.* Chicago: University of Chicago Press.

Lockhart, James. 1992. *The Nahuas after the Conquest: A Social and Cultural History of the Indians of Central Mexico, Sixteenth through Eighteenth Centuries.* Stanford, CA: Stanford University Press.

Lok, Rosanna. 1987. "The House as a Microcosm." In *The Leiden Tradition in Structural Anthropology*. Edited by R. D. Ridder and J. A. J. Karremans, 211–223. Leiden: E. J. Brill.

López Austin, Alfredo. 1988a. *The Human Body: Concepts of the Ancient Nahuas*. Translated by Thelma Ortiz de Montellano and Bernardo Ortiz de. Montellano, vol. 2. Salt Lake City: University of Utah Press.

———. 1988b. *Una vieja historia de la mierda*. Mexico City: Edicíones Toledo.

———. 1993. *The Myths of the Opossum: Pathways of Mesoamerican Mythology*. Translated by Bernard Ortiz de Montellano and Thelma Ortiz de Montellano. Albuquerque: University of New Mexico Press.

———. 1994. *Tamoanchan y Tlalocan*. Mexico City: Fondo de Cultura Económica.

———. 1996. *The Rabbit on the Face of the Moon*. Salt Lake City: University of Utah Press.

López Austin, Alfredo, Leonardo López Luján, and Saburo Sugiyama. 1991. "The Temple Quetzalcoatl at Teotihuacan: Its Possible Ideological Significance." *Ancient Mesoamerica* 2, 1: 93–105.

López Luján, Leonardo. 1994. *The Offerings of the Templo Mayor of Tenochtitlan*. Translated by Thelma Ortiz de Montellano and Benard Ortiz de Montellano. Niwot: University Press of Colorado.

Love, Bruce. 1994. *The Paris Codex: Handbook for a Maya Priest*. Austin: University of Texas Press.

Markman, Roberta, and Peter Markman. 1992. *The Flayed God: The Mesoamerican Mythological Tradition*. New York: HarperCollins.

Matos Moctezuma, Eduardo. 1990. *Teotihuacan: La metrópoli de los dioses*. Mexico City: Instituto Nacional de Antropología e Historia.

Maxwell, Judith M, and Craig A. Hanson. 1992. *Of the Manner of Speaking That Old Ones Had: The Metaphors of Andrés de Olmos in the Tulul Manuscript: Arte para aprender la lenqua mexicana, 1547*. Salt Lake City: University of Utah Press.

McGee, R. Jon. 1990. *Life, Ritual, and Religion among the Lacandon Maya*. Belmont, CA: Wadsworth.

McVicker, Donald. 1997. "Quetzalcoatl." In *Encyclopedia of Mexico: History, Society, and Culture*. Edited by Michael S. Werner, 2: 1211–1214. Chicago: Fitzroy Dearborn.

Menchu, Rigoberta. 1984. *I, Rigoberta Menchu: An Indian Woman in Guatemala*. Edited by Elisabeth Burgos-Debray. New York: Verso.

Mendelson, Michael E. 1965. *Los Escandolos de Maximón: Un estudio sobre la religión y la visión del mundo en Santiago Atitlan*. Guatemala: Tipografía Nacional.

Mendoza, Arnulfo, and Victor De La Cruz. 1994. "Lorenzo (the Coyote) and Evaristo (the Deer)." In *Myth and Magic: Oaxaca Past and Present*, 71–74. Palo Alto: Palo Alto Cultural Center.

Milbrath, Susan. 1989. "A Seasonal Calendar with Venus Periods in Codex Borgia 29–46." In *The Imagination of Matter: Religion and Ecology in Mesoamerican Traditions*. Edited by David Carrasco, 103–127. Oxford: BAR International Series 515.

———. 1999. *Star Gods of the Maya: Astronomy in Art, Folklore, and Calendars*. Austin: University of Texas Press.

Miller, Mary, and Karl Taube. 1993. *The Gods and Symbols of Ancient Mexico and the Maya: An Illustrated Dictionary of Mesoamerican Religion*. London: Thames and Hudson.

Molina, Fray Alonso de. 1970. *Vocabulario en lengua castellana y mexicana*. Preliminary study by Miguel Leon Portilla. Mexico City: Editorial Porrúa.

Monjarás-Ruiz, Jesús. 1987. *Mitos cosmogónicos de México indígena*. Mexico City Instituto Nacional de Antropología e Historia.

Montolíu Villar, María. 1989. *Cuando los dioses depertaron: Conceptos cosmológicos de los antiquos mayas de Yucatán estudiados en el Chilam Balam de Chumayel*. Mexico City: Universidad Nacional Autónoma de México.

Moreno de los Arcos, Roberto. 1967. "Los cinco soles cosmogónicos." In *Estudios de cultura Nahuatl.*, 7: 183–210. Mexico City: Universidad Nacional Autónoma de México.

Morley, Sylvanus G., George W. Brainerd, and Robert J. Sharer. 1983. *The Ancient Maya*. 4th ed. Stanford, CA: Stanford University Press.

Morris, Earl Halstead, Jean Charlot, and Ann Axtell Morris. 1931. *The Temple of the Warriors at Chichén Itzá, Yucatán*. Publication 406. Washington, DC: Carnegie Institution of Washington.

Motolinía, Fray Toribio de Benevente o. 1971. *Memoriales o libro de las cosas de la Neuva España y de los naturales de ella*. 2d ed. Edited by Edmundo O'Gorman. Mexico City: Universidad Nacional Autónoma de México.

———. 1984. *Historia de los Indios de la Neuva España*. 4th ed. Edited by Edmundo O'Gorman. Mexico City: Editorial Porrúa.

Muñoz Camargo, Diego. 1984. "Descripción de la ciudad y provincia de Tlaxcala: De la Nueva España e Indias del mar océano para el buen gobierno e ennoblecemiento dellas, mandada hacer por la S.C.R.M. del Rey Don Felipe, nuestro Señor." In *Relaciones geográficas del siglo XVI: Tlaxcala*. Edited by René Acuña, 4: 23–285. Mexico City: Universidad Nacional Autónoma de México.

Nash, June. 1985. *In the Eyes of the Ancestors: Belief and Behavior in a Mayan Community.* 2d ed. Prospect Heights, IL: Waveland Press.

Neiderberger, Christine. 1996. "The Basin of Mexico: A Multimillenial Development toward Cultural Complexity." In *Olmec Art of Ancient Mexico.* Edited by Elizabeth P. Benson and Beatriz de la Fuente, 83–93. Washington, DC: National Gallery of Art.

Nelson, Ben A., Andrew Darling, and David A. Kice. 1992. "Mortuary Practices and the Social Order at La Quemada, Zacatecas, Mexico." *Latin American Antiquity* 3, 4: 298–315.

Nicholson, H. B. 1957. "Topiltzin Quetzalcoatl of Tollan: A Problem for Mesoamerican Ethnohistory." Ph.D. dissertation, Harvard University.

———. 1971. "Religion in Pre-Hispanic Central Mexico." In *Handbook of Middle American Indians.* Edited by Gordon F. Ekholm and Ignacio Bernal, 10: 395–446. Austin: University of Texas.

Noguez, Xavier. 1993. *Documentos guadalupanos.* Toluca: El Colegio Mexiquense; Mexico City: Fondo de Cultura Económica.

Orozco, Gilbert. 1946. *Tradiciones y leyendas del Istmo de Tehuantepe.* Mexico: Revista Mucical Mexicana.

Ortiz de Montellano, Bernard R. 1978. "Aztec Cannibalism: An Ecological Necessity?" *Science* 200, 4342: 611–617.

———. 1989. "Mesoamerican Religious Tradition and Medicine." In *Healing and Restoring.* Edited by Lawrence Sullivan, 359–394. New York: Macmillan.

———. 1990. *Aztec Medicine, Health, and Nutrition.* New Brunswick, NJ: Rutgers University Press.

Palomo, Benjamín. 1997. *Hablan los Nahuales.* San Salvador, El Salvador: Talleres Gráficos.

Parson, Elsie Clews. 1936. *Mitla, Town of the Souls: and Other Zapteco-Speaking Pueblos of Oaxaca, Mexico.* Chicago: University of Chicago Press.

Pasztory, Esther. 1983. *Aztec Art.* New York: Harry N. Abrams.

———. 1992. "The Natural World as Civic Metaphor at Teotihuacan." In *Ancient Americas: Art from Sacred Spaces.* Edited by Richard F. Townsend, 135–145, 210. Chicago: Art Institute of Chicago.

———. 1997. *Teotihuacan: An Experiment in Living.* Norman: University of Oklahoma Press.

Paz, Octavio. 1961. *The Labyrinth of Solitude: Life and Solitude in Mexico.* New York: Grove Press.

Peterson, Anna L. 1997. *Martyrdom and the Politics of Religion: Progressive Catholicism in El Salvador's Civil War.* Albany: State University of New York Press.

Peterson, Anna, and Philip Williams. 1996. "Evangelicals and Catholics in El Salvador: Evolving Religious Responses to Social Change." *Journal of Church and State* 38, 4: 873–897.

Phelan, John. 1970. *The Millennial Kingdom of the Franciscans in the New World.* Berkeley: University of California Press.

Pohl, Mary DeLand. 1981. "Ritual Continuity and Transformation in Mesoamerica: Reconstructing the Ancient Maya Cuch Ritual." *American Antiquity* 46: 513–529.

Pomar, Juan Bautista. 1964. "Manuscrito de Jaun Bautista de Pomar, Tezcoco, 1582." In *Poesía Náhuatl.* Edited by Angel María Garibay K. Mexico City: Universidad Nacional Autónoma de México.

Poole, Stafford. 1995. *Our Lady of Guadalupe: The Origins and Sources of a Mexican National Symbol, 1531–1797.* Tucson: University of Arizona Press.

———. 1997. "Virgin of Guadalupe and Guadalupanismo." In *Encyclopedia of Mexico: History, Society, and Culture.* Edited by Michael S. Werner, 2: 1535–1537. Chicago: Fitzroy Dearborn.

Popol Vuh. 1950. In *Popol Vuh, the Sacred Book of the Ancient Quiche Maya.* Translated by Adrián Recinos. Norman: University of Oklahoma Press.

———. 1971. In *The Book of Counsel: The Popol Vuh of the Quiche Maya of Guatemala.* Edited and translated by Munro S. Edmonson. New Orleans: Middle American Research Institute, Tulane University.

———. 1985. In *Popol Vuh: The Definitive Edition of the Mayan Book of the Dawn of Life and the Glories of Gods and Kings.* Translated by Dennis Tedlock. New York: Simon and Schuster.

Preston, Julia. 23 March 1999. "An Ancient Sun Melts Mexico's Modern Stresses." *New York Times,* International section, p. A4.

Preuss, Mary H. 1988. *Gods of the Popol Vuh: Xmucane, Kucumatz, Tojil, and Jurakan.* Culver City, CA: Labyrinthos.

Quiñones Keber, Eloise. 1995. *Codex Telleriano Remensis: Ritual, Divination, and History in a Pictorial Aztec Manuscript.* Austin: University of Texas Press.

———. 1997. "Nahua Rulers, Pre-Hispanic." In *Encyclopedia of Mexico: History, Society, and Culture.* Edited by Michael S. Werner, 2: 999–1003. Chicago: Fitzroy Dearborn.

Read, Kay A. 1987. "Negotiating the Familiar and the Strange in Aztec Ethics." *Journal of Religious Ethics* 15, 1: 2–13.

———. 1994. "Sacred Commoners: The Motion of Cosmic Powers in Mexica Rulership." *History of Religions Journal* 34, 1: 39–69.

———. 1995. "Sun and Earth Rulers: What the Eyes Cannot See in Mesoamerica." *History of Religions Journal* 34, 4: 351–384.

———. 1996. "Sacrifice, Mesoamerica." In *Harper's Dictionary of Religion.* General Editor Jonathan Z. Smith. New York: Harper and Row.

———. 1997a. "Mesoamerica: Calendrics." In *Encyclopedia of Mexico: History, Society, and Culture.* Edited by Michael S. Werner, 2: 821–24. Chicago: Fitzroy Dearborn.

———. 1997b. "Mesoamerican: Religion." In *Encyclopedia of Mexico: History, Society, and Culture.* Edited by Michael S. Werner, 2: 824–829. Chicago: Fitzroy Dearborn.

———. 1998. *Time and Sacrifice in the Aztec Cosmos.* Bloomington: Indiana University Press.

———. 2000. "More than Earth: Cihuacoatl as Female Warrior, Male Matron, and Inside Ruler." Pp. 51–67 in *Goddesses and Sovereignty.* Edited by Elisabeth Benard, and Beverly Moon. New York: Oxford University Press.

Read, Kay A., and Jane Rosenthal. 1988. "Xochiquetzal and the Virgin of Ocotlan." *American Anthropology Association,* photocopied.

Redfield, Robert, and Alfonso Villa Rojas. 1934. *Chan Kom: A Maya Village.* Publication 448. Washington, DC: Carnegie Institution of Washington.

Reents-Budet, Dorie J. 1994. *Painting the Maya Universe: Royal Ceramics of the Classic Period.* Durham and London: Duke University Press.

Rengers, Christopher. 1989. *Mary of Americas: Our Lady of Guadalupe.* New York: Alba House.

Ricard, Robert. 1966. *The Spiritual Conquest of Mexico.* Berkeley: University of California Press.

Riley, G. Michael. 1997. "Cortés, Fernando (Hernán)." In *Encyclopedia of Mexico: History, Society, and Culture.* Edited by Michael S. Werner, 1: 352–55. Chicago: Fitzroy Dearborn.

Robertson, Donald. 1959. *Mexican Manuscript Painting of the Early Colonial Period: The Metropolitan Schools.* New Haven, CT: Yale University Press.

Rodriguez, Jeanette. 1994. *Our Lady of Guadalupe: Faith and Empowerment among Mexican-American Women.* Austin: University of Texas Press.

Roys, Ralph Loveland, translator. 1965. *Ritual of the Bacabs: A Book of Maya Encantations.* Norman: University of Oklahoma Press.

Sáenz, César A. 1976. *El Fuego Nuevo.* Seria Historia 18. Mexico City: Instituto Nacional de Antropología e Historia.

Sahagún, Fray Bernardino de. 1953–1982. *The Florentine Codex: A General History of the Things of New Spain.* Translated by Arthur J. O. Anderson, and Charles E. Dibble. Monographs of the School of American Research no. 14. Santa Fe: School of American Research; Salt Lake City: University of Utah Press.

———. 1979. *Códice Florentino.* Facsimile ed. Manuscrito 218–220 de la Colección Palatina de la Biblioteca Medicea Laurenziana. Mexico City: Archivo General de la Nación.

———. 1982. *Historia general de las coses de Nueva España.* 5th ed. Mexico City: Editorial Porrúa.

———. 1993. *Primero memoriales.* Photos by Ferdinand Anders. Oklahoma: University of Oklahoma Press.

Sandstrom, Alan. 1990. "Nahua Myths: Puyecaco, Ixhuatlan de Madero, Veracruz, Mexico."

———. 1991. *Corn Is Our Blood: Culture and Ethnicity in a Contemporary Aztec Indian Village.* Norman: University of Oklahoma Press.

Sarukhán Kermez, José, et al. 1995. *Dioses de México antiguo.* Mexico City: Antiguo Colegio de San Ildefonso.

Schele, Linda, and David Friedel. 1990. *A Forest of Kings: The Untold Story of the Ancient Maya.* New York: William Morrow.

Schele, Linda, and Mary Ellen Miller. 1986. *Blood of Kings.* New York: George Braziller; Fort Worth: Kimbell Art Museum.

Schellhas, Paul. 1904. *Representations of Deities of the Maya Manuscripts.* Papers of the Peabody Museum 4, 1: 1–47. Cambridge, MA: Peabody Museum of Archaeology and Ethnology, Harvard University.

Séjourné, Laurette. 1989. *El Pensamiento náhuatl cifrado por los calendarios.* Mexico City: Siglo XXI Editores.

Serna, Jacinto de la. 1953. "Manual de ministros de indios para el conocimiento de sus idolatrías y extirpación de ellas." In *Tratado de las idolatrías, supersticiones, dioses, ritos, hechicerías y otras costumbres gentílicas de las razas aborígenes de México.* Commentary by Francisco del Paso y Troncoso, 1: 47–368. Mexico City: Ediciones Fuente Cultural.

Sexton, James D. 1992. *Mayan Folktales: Folklore from Lake Atitlán, Guatemala.* New York: Doubleday.

Sharer, Robert J. 1994. *The Ancient Maya.* 5th ed. Stanford, CA: Stanford University Press.

Siméon, Rémi. 1981. *Diccionario de la lengua Náhuatl o Mexicana.* 2d ed. Mexico City: Siglo Veintiuno Editores.

Starr, Frederick. 1896. "Popular Celebrations in Mexico." *Journal of American Folk-Lore* 9: 161–169.

———. 1908. *In Indian Mexico.* Chicago: Forbes.

Stephens, John Lloyd. 1841. *Incidents of Travel in Central America, Chiapas, and Yucatan.* Illustrated by Frederick Catherwood. New Brunswick, NJ: Rutgers University Press.

———. 1969. *Incidents of Travel in Central America, Chiapas, and Yucatan.* Illustrated by Frederick Catherwood. New York: Dover.

Stracke, Claire T., and Richard J. Stracke. 1997. "Popular Catholicism." In *Encyclopedia of Mexico: History, Society, and Culture.* Edited by Michael S. Werner, 2: 1130–1131. Chicago: Fitzroy Dearborn.

Stuart, L. C. 1964. "Fauna of Middle America." In *Handbook of Middle American Indians: Natural Environment and Early Cultures.* Edited by Robert C. West, 1: 316–383. Austin: University of Texas Press.

Sugiyama, Saburo. 1989. "Burials Dedicated to the Old Temple of Quetzalcoatl at Teotihuacan." *American Antiquity* 54, 1: 85–106.

———. 1993. "Worldview Materialized in Teotihuacan, Mexico." *Latin American Antiquity* 4, 2: 103–129.

Sullivan, Thelma D. 1983. *Compendio de la gramática Náhuatl.* Mexico City: Universidad Nacional Autónoma de México.

———. 1988. *Compendium of Nahuatl Grammar.* Edited by Wick Miller and Karen Dakin. Salt Lake City: University of Utah Press.

Taggart, James M. 1983. *Nahuat Myth and Social Structure.* Austin: University of Texas Press.

Taube, Karl. 1992. *The Major Gods of Ancient Yucatan.* Washington, DC: Dumbarton Oaks Research Library and Collection.

———. 1993. *Aztec and Maya Myths.* Austin: University of Texas Press.

Tax, Sol. n.d. "The World of the Panajachel: As Told by Its Maya People in 1936 and 1937." Unpublished manuscript, Native American Educational Services (Chicago).

Tedlock, Barbara. 1982. *Time and the Highland Maya.* Albuquerque: University of New Mexico Press.

Tedlock, Dennis. 1990. *Days from a Dream Almanac.* Urbana: University of Illinois Press.

———. 1993. *Breath on the Mirror: Mythic Voices and Visions of the Living Maya.* San Francisco: HarperCollins.

Tedlock, Dennis, trans. 1985. *Popol Vuh: The Definitive Edition of the Mayan Book of the Dawn of Life and the Glories of Gods and Kings.* New York: Simon and Schuster.

Tezozomoc, Don Hernando Alvarado. 1980. *Cronica Mexicana.* 3d ed. Mexico City: Editorial Porrúa.

———. 1992. *Crónica Mexicáyotl.* Translated by Adrián León. Mexico City: Universidad Nacional Autónoma de México.

Thompson, John Eric Sydney. 1930. *Ethnology of the Mayas of Southern and Central British Honduras.* Anthropological Series 17 (2). Chicago: Field Museum of Natural History.

———. 1939. *The Moon Goddess in Middle America.* Carnegie Institution of

Washington Publication 509, Contributions to American Anthropology and History no. 29. Washington, DC: Carnegie Institution.

———. 1970a. "The Bacabs: Their Portraits and Glyph." In *Monographs and Papers in Maya Archaeology*. Edited by William Rotch Bullard, Jr., 471–485. Papers of the Peabody Museum 61. Cambridge, MA: Peabody Museum of American Archaeology and Ethnology, Harvard University.

———. 1970b. *Maya History and Religion*. Norman: University of Oklahoma Press.

Torquemada, Fray Juan de. 1969. *Monarquía indiana: De los veinte y un libros rituales y monarquía indian, con el origen y querras de los indios occidentales, de sus poblazones, descrubrimiento, conquista, conversión y otras cosas maravillosas de la mesma tierra*. Introduction by Miguel León Portilla. Mexico City: Editorial Porrúa.

———. 1975–1983. *Monarquía indiana: De los veinte y un libros rituales y monarquía indian, con el origen y querras de los indios occidentales, de sus poblazones, descrubrimiento, conquista, conversión y otras cosas maravillosas de la mesma tierra*. Mexico City: Universidad Nacional Autónoma de México.

Townsend, Richard F. 1979. *State and Cosmos in the Art of Tenochtitlan*. Washington, DC: Dumbarton Oaks Research Library and Collection.

———. 1992. *The Aztecs*. London: Thames and Hudson.

Treviño, Adrian, and Barbara Gilles. 1994. "A History of the Matachines Dance." *New Mexico Historical Review* April: 105–125.

Turner, Victor. 1974. *Dramas, Fields, and Metaphors: Symbolic Action in Human Society*. Ithaca, NY: Cornell University Press.

Umberger, Emily. 1987. "Antiques, Revivals, and References to the Past in Aztec Art." *RES*. 13: 63–105.

Vail, Gabrielle. 1996. "The Gods in the Madrid Codex: An Iconographic and Glyphic Analysis." Ph.D. dissertation, Tulane University, New Orleans; University Microfilms, Ann Arbor.

Vaillant, George C. 1944. *Aztecs of Mexico: Origin, Rise, and Fall of the Aztec Nation*. New York: Doubleday.

van der Loo, Peter. 1987. *Códices, costumbres, continuidad: Un estudio de la religión Mesoamerica*. Indiaanse Studies 2. Leiden: Archaeologisch Centrum R.U.

van Zantwijk, Rudolf. 1985. *The Aztec Arrangement: The Social History of Pre-Spanish Mexico*. Norman: University of Oklahoma Press.

Villagutierre Soto-Mayer, Don Juan de. 1983. *History of the Conquest of the Province of the Itza: Subjugation and Events of the Lacandon and Other Nations of Uncivilized Indians in the Land from the Kingdom of*

Guatemala to the Provinces of Yucatán in North America. Translated by Brother Robert D. Wood, S.M. Culver City, CA: Labyrinthos.

Vivó Escoto, Jorge A. 1964. "Weather and Climate of Mexico and Central America." In *Handbook of Middle America Indians.* Edited by Robert Wauchope, 1: 187–215. Austin: University of Texas Press.

Vogt, Evon Z. 1969. *Zinacantan: A Maya Community in the Highlands of Chiapas.* Cambridge, MA: Belknap Press.

Wauchope, Robert, editor. 1964–1976. *Handbook of Middle American Indians.* 15 vols. Austin: University of Texas Press.

Weaver, Muriel Porter. 1993. *The Aztecs, Maya, and Their Predecessors.* 3d ed. New York: Academic Press.

Wisdom, Charles. 1940. *The Chorti Indians of Guatemala.* Chicago: University of Chicago Press.

Zantwijk, Rudolf van. 1966. "Los seis barrios sirvientes de Huitzilopochtli." In *Estudios de cultura Nahuatl.,* 6: 177–185. Mexico City: Universidad Nacional Autónoma de México.

———. 1985. *The Aztec Arrangement.* Norman: University of Oklahoma Press.

GLOSSARY

Aztecs   *See* **Mexica**.

Aztlan   The Mexica's mythical place of origin; home to Huitzilopochtli and his mother Coatlicue. It is told how the Mexica used to live on this lush island surrounded by marshes and lagoons. Because they ate humble foods such as corn, illness was unknown among them and people never died; they could even move from youth to age and back again whenever they wanted. But when their patron deity Huitzilopochtli led the Mexica ancestors from Aztlan, everything turned against them. Thick brambles closed over Aztlan, hiding it; stones wounded them; and prickly trees and bushes stung them. They could never return.

During his reign, however, the Mexica ruler Motecuhzoma II sent magicians on a dangerous magical flight to visit Coatlicue in Aztlan. One-third of them perished on the way. Coatlicue told the survivors that soon Huitzilopochtli would return to her, abandoning the Mexica; he would lose all the towns over which he held power, in the order in which he had conquered them. Moreover, the Mexica were doomed because they had grown heavy with their fancy foods and riches.

Ballgame   An indigenous Mesoamerican game in which two teams attempted to strike a solid rubber ball through a stone ring or against markers to gain points. Mesoamericans often played this game in an I-shaped ball court made of two long structures—essentially, an alley with two end zones. The scoring rings were set vertically, high up, in the center of each side of the alley. Sometimes decorated markers were placed in the end zones. Points were calculated when a player from either team hit the rubber ball through the rings or onto the markers. The players could not touch the ball with their hands or feet but could only strike it with their wrists, elbows, or hips. Outcomes varied greatly. Sometimes the audience was involved, losing items of wealth to the winning player every time the opposing team scored. Occasionally the winning team sacrificed the losing players, decapitating them or throwing them down temple stairs, trussed up like human balls.

Mythic stories of the ballgame abound throughout Mesoamerica, showing that it was and remains intimately involved in mythology and ritual.

Binding-of-the-Years, New Fire Ceremony   A pre-Conquest Nahua ceremony performed every fifty-two years, believed to give birth to a new sun that would travel its celestial and underground path for another fifty-two years. This ceremony occurred when the solar and divinatory calendars both ended on the same day, an event coinciding with the rising of the Pleiades and the beginning of the dry season. Among the Mexica, the ritual took place on top of a small mountain just outside of Tenochtitlán. All of the fires in the entire domain were extinguished, and a new fire was sparked in the chest cavity of a sacrificial offering whose heart had been removed. If the fire priest could not spark the fire, it was feared that the new sun would not be born and all would be eaten by the forces of night. After the new fire was lit, a runner carried the flame to the main temple in the center of Tenochtitlán, to light a new fire there. From there, runners carried fire to all other temples throughout the domain; and from these fires, people sparked their household hearths.

Bloodletting   The ritual drawing of blood from the human body to nourish and sustain various beings or to repay a debt incurred by having been nourished and sustained by other beings. Endemic in pre-Conquest traditions, bloodletting continued to play a role in post-Conquest traditions as well: The offering of blood was an integral part of continuing ancient religious patterns, and fit well with Christian notions of sacrifice and communion. In ancient times, bloodletting ranged from sacrificial slaughter of birds and animals, or human sacrifices, to the more common practice of autosacrifice, or the piercing of one's tongue, earlobe, or thigh in order to spatter blood in the direction of the recipient. The recipients of these comestible offerings included celestial and earthly deities as well as patrons of kinship lines. According to mythological tradition, the deities themselves had offered their blood to create humans, and continued to offer their resources, if not their blood, to create food and housing for humans. Hence, humans were in their debt, and had to work to sustain the living forces of the cosmos, if those forces were to continue sustaining them.

Catholicism   In Mesoamerica, the faith, worldview, and practices of the Roman Catholic Church introduced by the Spanish conquerors in the early sixteenth century. Officially, the Church is the visible society of baptized Christians professing the same faith under the invisible head of Christ and the visible head of the Pope and Bishops in communion with Christ. Unofficially, the "Popular" or "People's Church" professes a wide range of faith positions and admits to many folk practices not necessarily accepted by the official church. Many of these may have more affinity with widespread ancient worldviews and practices, and at times may even run counter to official Catholic doctrine. Nevertheless, the diverse members of the Popular Church usually consider themselves fully Christian and Catholic, even if they do not always agree with the official Church.

Central Mexicans   The peoples of the Mexican highlands, whose main cultural centers are the ancient cities of Teotihuacan and Tenochtitlán (today, the modern city of Mexico City), situated in the Basin of Mexico. This area coincides roughly with the modern Mexican states of the Federal District, Mexico, Morelos, Tlaxcala, and adjacent portions of Pueblo, Hidalgo, Queretaro, Michoacán, and Guerrero.

Cerros   An early Preclassic Maya city located in eastern Yucatán, Mexico, and the northern end of the modern country of Belize. Cerros is a comparatively small Maya site, notable because of its beautiful, elaborately decorated, terraced temples. One of these temples has a series of painted stucco-model masks that symbolize a model of the cosmos and represent the ritual and mythic path of the sun and the center's kings.

Chichén Itzá   The Postclassic-era Yucatec Maya capital city, located in north-central Yucatán, near the modern Mexican city of Mérida. This urban center, one of the largest in the Maya area, covers an area of at least five square kilometers, and its landscape is relatively densely crowded with buildings and other architectural structures. Today, Chichén Itzá is a protected archaeological site and a favorite destination of tourists from around the world. This city plays an important role in the mythic history and stories of the Yucatec Maya.

Chilam Balams   Pre-Conquest and Colonial-era Maya manuscripts that present mythic histories of particular towns and their royal lineages. These manuscripts originated in northern Yucatán and have survived to the modern day. They generally record continuous native histories starting from the tenth century and continuing through the end of the nineteenth. Each draws its name from its town of origin. In Colonial times, the Chilam Balams were translated into phonetic Yucatec Maya and Spanish. The earlier manuscripts or codices, written in hieroglyphs on paper or deer hides, no longer exist.

Codex   A pre-Conquest or Colonial-era manuscript that usually contains pictorial elements and that was produced by indigenous artists. Codices vary in subject matter, ranging from local town histories to ritual and calendrical texts. They are most often named after their location, the person who discovered them, former owners, or their places of origin. Pre-Conquest and very early Colonial manuscripts were painted on deer hide or paper made of a particular tree bark, which was coated with a thin layer of plaster. Traditionally, the early codices were rolled or folded accordion- or screen-style. Colonial-era codices usually were painted on European paper and bound in book form.

Cofradías   Socioreligious fraternities dating to early Colonial times. Originally, they formed because towns and villages held property communally and performed work cooperatively. After the Conquest, governing groups formed to organize community land use and labor, including duties in the local church. The records of who owned what and did what work were held in a box, or *cofra*—hence the name. At that time, both the land and church often were governed by a particular saint, in much the same way as a patron deity had governed temples and land in ancient times. In the eighteenth century, state governmental and political forces began to usurp much of the cofradías' economic power; therefore, cofradías today are limited primarily to ritual church activities, often centering their worship around the local saint, although these ritual activities still contain a significant social component.

Conquistadors   The Spanish warriors and military personnel who traveled in the early sixteenth century with Hernán Cortés and others to conquer the lands and people of New Spain, or Mesoamerica.

Creoles   Children of Spanish ethnicity, born in Mesoamerica, often to poor immigrants. Creoles slowly developed into a small middle class. By the nineteenth century, they had become a highly educated group, most of them having been trained by Jesuit priests in humanist philosophy, and generally advocated independence from Spain.

Díaz del Castillo, Bernal   A captain in Hernán Cortés's army who witnessed and wrote an invaluable account of the conquest of Mesoamerica, called *The Discovery and Conquest of Mexico: 1517–1521* (see the Annotated Bibliography).

Divination, Divinatory Calendar   A cycle of 260 days in the indigenous calendrical system, consisting of 20 thirteen-day "weeks" called *trecenas* in Spanish (20 x 13 = 260 days). Called the *Tonalpohualli* in Nahuatl and the *Tzolkin* in Yucatec Maya, this calendar was and still is often used for divination. The most propitious times for naming a newborn, marrying, taking a trip, closing a business deal, or waging war were identified by reading this calendar. Probably the oldest calendar in Mesoamerica, its origin is unknown; nor are we certain which celestial cycle, if any, it marked. In ancient times among Central Mexicans, the seventy-three divinatory rounds ended on the same day as the fifty-two solar rounds, at which time the Binding-of-the-Years ceremony occurred.

Durán, Fray Diego   A sixteenth-century Dominican friar born in Spain and raised in Mexico. Fluent in Nahuatl, he collected stories and information on the Nahua, recording them in two important volumes: *The Gods and Rites of the Ancient Calendar,* and *The History of the Indies in New Spain* (see the Annotated Bibliography). He intended these works to be used for the training of priests unfamiliar with indigenous Mesoamericans.

Encomienda A Colonial system that awarded *encomenderos*—for the most part, Spanish conquerors—rights to the goods and labor of specified groups of indigenous people in return for educating them in Christianity. Unfortunately, the system was much abused, and the Spanish government in the mid-sixteenth century was forced to take steps to alleviate the extremely harsh treatment many of the Indians were receiving.

Epidemics In Colonial Mesoamerica, waves of European diseases, especially smallpox, that decimated the indigenous population. The effect was extraordinarily disastrous because native populations had no natural resistance to these diseases, never having been exposed to them before the arrival of the Spanish. Smallpox contributed significantly to Hernán Cortés's success; in combination with other factors, it reduced the Indian population by 90 percent by the end of the sixteenth century.

Farabundo Martí National Liberation Front (FMLN) The revolutionary army of guerrillas who waged civil war in El Salvador (ca. 1980–1992). Named for the esteemed revolutionary Farabundo Martí, who was executed in a rebellion in the 1930s, the FMLN consisted of five separate but allied organizations with somewhat differing political ideologies, all of which sought to change the political and economic situation responsible for the extreme hardship suffered by peasant populations. Today the FMLN is a political party in the new, democratic system.

Four or Five Ages A widespread and very ancient genre of creation myth that conceives of the present world as the fourth or fifth created in a series. The previous worlds or ages all failed or were destroyed, each in its turn. In some versions of this story, especially very early ones, the present age is also foredoomed. In contemporary versions of this myth, often God, Christ, Joseph, or the Devil participate in the creation and destruction of the ages.

Hidalgo y Costillo, Father Miguel A Jesuit priest from Dolores, Mexico, who on 16 September 1810 freed the prisoners in his village and locked up the Spanish authorities in their stead. Calling to parishioners from the doorway of his church, he summoned them to join him in overthrowing the oppressive Spanish government, and garnered tremendous support. This cry, or *grito de Hidalgo,* began the Mexican war of independence from Spain, which was won on 27 September 1821.

Kaminaljuyu A late Preclassic-era Maya city located in the southern Guatemalan highlands, in the Valley of Guatemala. Having both a dense population and extensive cultural offerings, this large and powerful city also supported long-distance trade links with other areas of Mesoamerica, especially Teotihuacan and Central Mexico. The site of Kaminaljuyu lies under today's Guatemala City, and most of the ancient city's remains have been destroyed by urban expansion and modern settlement.

K'iche' Maya   A large and historically important Maya group that live today in the Guatemala highlands. The K'iche' were the largest group of Maya that the Spanish encountered during their conquest of Guatemala, and they controlled a huge portion of the highlands. Through myth and history, they trace their origins to the legendary Toltecs. They continue to maintain a rich tradition of native myth and storytelling.

La Venta   An early Preclassic Olmec city, inhabited from 1400 to 600 B.C. Located in the Gulf coast Mexican state of Veracruz, on an island in a large wetland area, La Venta is famous for its pyramid shaped like a volcano and its large stone representations of the heads of Olmec kings. The site is and was considered a cultural center early in Mesoamerican history and myth.

Ladino   A Spanish-speaking Indian who adapted to the new culture during Colonial times. Today, however, this term usually means someone who is either a mestizo—a person of mixed European and Indian heritage—or a non-Indian.

Landa, Fray Diego de   The first Catholic bishop of Yucatán, appointed in the sixteenth century. He collected stories and information on the early Colonial Yucatec Maya, recording them in the important book *Relación de las cosas de Yucatán*. He wrote the book in response to charges concerning his strict methods of governance, which included burning both thousands of native texts, and Maya natives at the stake (see the Annotated Bibliography).

Loltún Cave   A cave located in northern Yucatán that has had historical and mythic importance throughout Mesoamerican history. This cave contains sculptures and representations of people probably dating back to archaic times and up to the modern day, suggesting that it has been a center of ritual and mythic importance for millennia.

Maize, Corn   The staple food of Mesoamerica. Cosmologically and mythologically it plays an enormous role. Maize is the paradigmatic food, symbolic of all food crops, and often is equated with various deities, the sun, rulers, people, and a healthy cosmos. As corn lives, so too does the cosmos and its beings.

Maya   People living largely in the Yucatán peninsula, from the semiarid northern end down to southern tropical rainforests, along the Pacific coast, and across the forested mountains of Guatemala. All Maya people speak a Mayan language, of which there are approximately thirty, not all of which are mutually intelligible. Thus, among the Maya, many different groups exist, including the Yucatec, the K'iche', the Kekchi, the Lacandon, the Cakchiquel, the Tzotzil, the Tzetzal, the Tzutuhil, the Mam, the Mopan, and others. Throughout the Postclassic and Colonial periods and up to the present day, Maya groups have migrated around the Maya region. Nevertheless, in general, today's groups live in the same areas where they lived in pre-Conquest times.

Mexica, Aztecs   The Nahuatl-speaking group based in Central Mexico that dominated a significant portion of Mesoamerica from about 1350 until 1521, when the Spaniards defeated them. Their urban center Tenochtitlán now lies under Mexico City. The name *Aztecs* is a somewhat imprecise label popularized by nineteenth-century scholars, and *Mexica* is probably closer to what they called themselves.

Mexico, Basin or Valley of   In pre-Conquest times, the large, extraordinarily rich wetland area lying at ca. 8,000 feet in the middle of the central Mexican highlands. Bounded by mountain ranges on all sides, the ancient city of Teotihuacan rose along its eastern side, and Tenochtitlán rose on an island toward its western side. In the centuries following the Conquest, the basin has gradually been drained and mostly filled in. Today, Mexico City sprawls at its center.

Mestizo   Today, a person of mixed white, Indian, and in many cases, African descent; although, in the Colonial-era *casta* or caste system, mestizos would not have included persons of African descent. *Mestizaje* is a process whereby cultural and biological blending create a mestizo population—a process that has been endowed with mythological overtones of strength and creativity by some modern Mesoamericans.

Mictlan   The pre-Conquest Nahuatl name for the Land of the Dead, located in the underworld. A damp place of rotting, corruption, and illness, it was populated by numerous deities, animals and birds of the night, and the dead. The sun traveled through Mictlan when it was night above Earth's surface. Today, Mictlan still exists in similar forms among the Nahua.

Mixtec   People living in what is now the Mexican states of Oaxaca, Guerrero, and Puebla, beginning ca. 1300 B.C. They overlapped with the Zapotec in the area, and they are most known for their codices, eight of which offer genealogical histories of the royal families. the Mixteca style of painting influenced some Mexica styles.

Monte Albán   The largest and most prominent ancient city in the Valley of Oaxaca, Mexico. Monte Albán is located atop a large, central ridge that overlooks the three major arms of the valley. There formal public architecture was arranged around several central courtyards, and the dwellings spilled down the terraced hillsides. This densely populated city, home to approximately 5,000 Zapotec, was founded early in the Preclassic period and occupied almost until the Spanish Conquest.

Nahua   People living largely in central Mexico, whose language is Nahuatl. In pre-Conquest times, the Mexica of Tenochtitlán and the inhabitants of many neighboring urban centers were Nahua. Because of Nahua migrations in the late Classic and early post-Classic periods and the prevalent influence of the Mexica, Nahuatl loanwords are common in other Mesoamerican languages, and towns called by Nahuatl names can be found as far away as El Salvador. Today, Nahuatl speakers live throughout central Mexico; and there are even a few who still speak Pipil (a Nahua dialect) living in El Salvador.

Oaxaca   A cultural region that coincides approximately with the modern state of Oaxaca, located in southwestern Mexico along the Pacific coast. The Oaxaca culture area is largely defined by and dominated by the Valley of Oaxaca, where most of the population lives. The population is ethnically mixed and includes Mixtecs and Zapotecs.

Olmec   A group of people and an ancient culture that existed in southern Mexico on the Gulf coast from 2,250 to 300 B.C. The so-called Olmec heartland was situated along the Gulf of Mexico in the modern Mexican states of Veracruz and Tabasco. In the past, scholars saw the Olmec as a "mother-culture," because it was one of the earliest expressions of Mesoamerican civilization. The Olmec built several large cities with temples, sculptures, and art, but are best known for their sculptures of large stone heads weighing between two and three tons each, representing Olmec kings or mythical ancestors. Today the native people of this region speak Olmec languages but are no longer identified as Olmec.

Palenque   A late Classic Maya city located at the foot of the mountains overlooking the Gulf coastal plains in the Mexican state of Chiapas. This site is famous for its beautiful architecture and sculpture with buildings distributed across the landscape. It is best known for the hieroglyphic texts on the buildings and sculpture telling about its royal and mythic history. Even today, this city is an important part of the mythic history and stories of many modern Lacandon Maya people. Today, ancient Palenque is a protected archaeological site near the modern town of Palenque, Chiapas, and a favorite tourist attraction.

Popol Vuh   An important ancient text of the K'iche' people of highland Guatemala. The Popol Vuh is a collection of five connected myths that describe the creation of humans, the exploits of the Hero Twins, and the forming of the various Maya tribes of the Guatemala highlands.

Popular or People's Church (Iglesia Popular)   See Catholicism

Protestantism   Christian groups that separated from the Roman Catholic Church during the Reformation (in the sixteenth century). In Mesoamerica, mainline and evangelical Protestants began missionary efforts in the late nineteenth century. Evangelical Protestant groups underwent particularly rapid growth in the 1960s and 1970s, mostly in the Central America. Hence, today, Protestantism in Mesoamerica often is identified with evangelical Protestantism. Evangelical Protestantism stresses Biblical scripture over the authority of the institutional church, and personal experience over theological doctrine, and teaches that salvation in the afterlife depends on individual conversion to and continued practice of the faith.

Rebellions   Native revolts against harsh Spanish or governmental rule and social and economic abuses began in the sixteenth century and continue at present. Between 1531 and 1801, rebellions against Spanish rule were particularly frequent. After independence, they continued primarily in the areas of ancient Maya settlement, which correspond roughly to today's southern Mexico and Central America. One could argue that the Central American civil wars of the twentieth century were continuations of peasant rebellions that began almost 500 years before, and that the most recent Zapatista rebellion in Chiapas, Mexico, is a modern form of these revolts.

Sahagún, Fray Bernardino de   A sixteenth-century Franciscan friar who produced a twelve-volume, medieval-style encyclopedia on the Nahua called *The Florentine Codex: A General History of the Things of New Spain*. One of the more sympathetic and intelligent collectors of data on the Mexica, Sahagún employed indigenous students in administering a questionnaire to town elders as part of his strategy. This incredibly vast, absolutely invaluable collection was reproduced in three languages: Nahuatl, Spanish, and Latin (see the Annotated Bibliography).

San Lorenzo   An early Preclassic Olmec city located near the Gulf coast of Mexico. San Lorenzo is the earliest known Olmec center, inhabited from 1700 to 900 B.C. The site is located on the edge of a river, atop a large ridge that overlooks open country, with mountains in view to the west. It is particularly famous for its great number of stone sculptures.

Sandinistas   Rebel guerrillas who won the Nicaraguan civil war in the late 1970s and ran the government until the early 1980s. They had named themselves for the assassinated Augusto César Sandino, who led rebel troops in the late 1920s and early 1930s. In the 1980s, social tensions led to renewed conflict, which continued until 1990, when an anti-Sandinista president was elected. The Sandinistas continued to influence politics into the late 1990s.

Solar Calendar   A cycle of 365 days in the indigenous calendrical system consisting of 18 twenty-day "months," called *metztin* in Nahuatl, plus five extra days, called *nemontemi* (18 x 20 = 360 + 5 =365). Called the *Xiuhmolpilli* in Nahuatl and *Haab* in Yucatec Maya, and governed by the sun's motions, this calendar structured the yearly agricultural and seasonal ceremonies. Because these rituals often were celebrated and controlled by the state, the calendrical round all but disappeared after the Conquest. Prior to Spanish rule in central Mexico, a Binding-of-the-Years ceremony was held when 52 solar years ended at the same time as 73 rounds of the divinatory calendar.

Tenochtitlán   The late highland Mexican, Postclassic capital city of the Mexica, located on an island in the Basin of Mexico. This city of 150,000–200,000 served as the nexus of a vast domain. It had four administrative sectors, and the great Templo Mayor arose from its center. Highly efficient, raised-mound agricultural fields called *chinampas* ringed the island. Hernán Cortés and his army, amazed at the city's vastness and splendor, centered their conquest efforts on Tenochtitlán. Mexico City now stands atop its remains.

Teotihuacan   The highland Mexican, early Classic capital city of the greatest domain ever in Mesoamerica. This city of 150,000–200,000 probably set the patterns for urban structures and relations all over Mesoamerica, trading with people as far away as modern Honduras. Its original name is unknown, for the Mexica gave the city its present name, Teotihuacan, which means "The Place Where the Gods Were Created." Mythologically, the Mexica Fifth Sun was born in this city, as were the age's people, and Mexica ancestors traveled there before coming to Tenochtitlán.

Toltecs, Tula   *Tollan* or *Toltecs* can refer to one of two things: either the residents of the highland Mexican, Postclassic city of Tula and Tollan the home of Topiltzin Quetzalcoatl; or the residents of any number of urban centers that lived and died before the Conquest. Residents of Teotihuacan, for example, were sometimes considered Toltecs. In this sense, *Toltecs* carries the nuance of "revered ancestors," and Tula (or Teotihuacan), of the venerated ancestral home.

Venus   The deified planet who closely follows the sun as both the morning and evening stars. Venus is one of the most significant celestial objects in Mesoamerica. In ancient Nahua mythology, Quetzalcoatl was the morning star and the dog-like Xolotl the evening star; but Venus has an extraordinarily long history in Mesoamerica, and its glyph appears everywhere.

Xibalba   The K'iche' Maya underworld and land of the dead. Xibalba was a dreadful, frightening place where those who did not die a violent death went. It is not the same as the Christian hell, for it did not matter whether one had sinned or not; this was where all the souls of the dead went. Xibalba was a location of supernatural geography, where the dead may have to go through trials of fortitude. It was also where the deities of the Underworld and caves lived. The Hero Twins of the Popol Vuh traveled through this land on their quest to conquer the Lords of Death. Having accomplished their goal, they arose as the Sun and the Moon, which then made their daily travels through both Xibalba and the celestial world.

Zapatistas   A rebel group in Chiapas, Mexico, that protests against unfair economic and social conditions. Named for the famed Mexican revolutionary leader Emiliano Zapata. The Zapatistas revolted on 1 January 1994. The revolt, far less violent and shorter than previous rebellions, has used computer technologies to its advantage, and continues to negotiate with the Mexican government for improved conditions. Its mysterious poet-leader Subcommander Marcos and his partner Ramona have become folk heroes in Mexico.

Zapotec   People living in the Valley of Oaxaca, whose language is Zapotec. The Zapotecs established and lived in the great city of Monte Albán. By the end of the Postclassic period the Zapotecs had abandoned Monte Albán and were living in separate communities throughout the Valley of Oaxaca, just as the Mixtec started to migrate into the Valley of Oaxaca. Today, Zapotec speakers still live in the Valley of Oaxaca, continuing their long, rich tradition of myth and folklore.

INDEX

About the Authors

Kay Almere Read is an associate professor of comparative religion at DePaul University in Chicago. She is the author of *Time and Sacrifice in the Aztec Cosmos* (Indiana University Press, 1998) and numerous articles.

Jason J. González is a graduate student in anthropology, specializing in Maya archaeology, at Southern Illinois University at Carbondale. He has extensive fieldwork experience and is the author of several articles and conference papers.

Mosquitoes,
Malaria
and Man

of the genus *Anopheles,* is one small chapter in the mostly unwritten history of man's relationships with the rest of nature. It is a history of ecological entanglements, mostly unrecognized at the time, many of which by revealing the attitudes brought to the war on mosquitoes throw unexpected light on some of the more usual concerns of history.

The war on mosquitoes began in the high noon of the White man's empire, at the end of the nineteenth century. At the time when Ronald Ross in colonial India discovered that mosquitoes transmit malaria, only one important nation remained independent in that part of the world— Siam, which buffered British Burma and British India from French Indochina. The British were in Singapore and the Federated Malay States; the Dutch, in Java and Sumatra; the Germans, in New Guinea. The Pacific was dotted with outposts of empire mostly French and British. So was the Caribbean. The scramble for Africa[3] in the last three decades of the century resulted in the partition of almost the whole continent among the British, French, Germans, Portuguese and Belgians. Even the Italians, entering the competition late with—as Bismarck put it—"such a large appetite and such poor teeth," had taken a small bite out of East Africa. The United States, having at last filled in its continental slice between Canada and Mexico, fought a little war with Spain in 1898 to acquire Cuba and the Philippines and began actively to hanker after Panama. Between 1870 and 1900 Britain, France, Russia, Germany, Italy and Belgium added more than 10 million square miles and 120 million people to their dominions. The only lands thereafter left that had never been under European domination were Turkey, Arabia, Mongolia, Siam, Japan, a scattering of small islands and Antarctica.[4]

Success produced an ecstasy of self-congratulation. Few doubted that, as the European way was clearly the predestined one, White industrial man could take over the world and make it bloom as never before. Some minds popped with greed and jingoism and imagined their own countries growing ever bigger and richer. Others held to the earlier idealism, so fortunately coincident with self-interest, of empire as the beneficent spread of civilization to barbarians, and dreamed of the near approach of a world in which science, business and Victorian virtue would triumph. The historian Carlton Hayes, who had gone through high school before the end of the century, recalled during the agony of World War II the special excitement of those years of success. "I saw those last decades of the nineteenth century then—and for almost thirty years afterwards," he wrote, "as a stage, indeed a glorious stage, in the progress of Europe and our Western civilization toward ever greater liberty, democracy, social betterment, and scientific control of nature."[5]

The ultimate spread of Western civilization was seen at the turn of the century to hinge in large part on the "scientific control of nature." Equatorial Africa, the principal arena of nineteenth-century empire, had notoriously resisted White settlement. The West coast in particular was so disease-ridden that a military posting to such colonies as Sierra Leone, Lagos or the Gambia throughout the eighteenth and nineteenth centuries was considered tantamount to a sentence of death. Except for the highlands of East and Southern Africa no part of the continent was healthy. Tropical Asia and tropical Latin America were hardly more hospitable. Everywhere in the tropics the White man languished and died, wasted by the heat and ravaged by disease, above all by malaria.[6]

When Caliban in *The Tempest* thought to wound the foreign master who had enslaved him in his own land he called to his aid his native fevers. "All the infections that the sun sucks up / From bogs, fens, flats on Prosper fall and make him / By inch-meal a disease."[7] Seventeenth-century English audiences could be expected to recognize the fitness of that curse. Englishmen already familiar with the deadly fevers of tropical lands could easily believe them to be a spell laid by their hostile and savage possessors. By the end of the nineteenth century the new scientific understanding of disease seemed only to confirm its association with savagery.

In the brilliant light of the research of Pasteur and Koch and their successors, it began to appear in the last decades of the century that most, perhaps all, disease was caused by microscopic forms of life which invaded and parasitized the body. As doctors simultaneously found ways to resist some of these invasions, the conquest of disease seemed a near and even, to some, an inevitable prospect. With weapons in hand to destroy the lower forms of life that made men ill, Europeans could move into the tropical lands and supplant the lower forms of human life who were then in possession. The battle against disease and the battle for civilization were demonstrably one.

Europeans early observed that tropical diseases—malaria above all—so often deadly to White men seemed scarcely to affect Blacks. They took that fact as further evidence of the hierarchy of species and races in which they were first and would be master. An Italian doctor in 1870 speculated that the inferior races shared the immunity to malaria of the lower animals to whom they were more nearly kin. After mosquitoes were identified as carriers of the fever it seemed possible to some that Blacks were spared because of the "offensive odour from their persons" or because of their thick skins.[8]

The supposed racial difference in susceptibility to disease helped to define the mission of empire and the role of the doctor in it.* Disease was seen as the ally of barbarism. Only disease permitted backward, slothful races of man to ride best what were obviously the richest lands on earth, so letting their riches go to waste. With the conquest of disease, General Gorgas, cleanser of Panama, wrote, the White man "most eager in his pursuit of wealth" could take over and "produce many times the amount of food now produced in the temperate regions."[9]

So the war against malaria was launched not primarily as a humanitarian crusade to save lives but as a campaign to wrest resources from the grasp of Caliban and exorcise his curse. In seventy-five years both the tactics and purposes have undergone many changes which it is the business of this history to detail. But much of the early militancy persisted throughout.

The dominant view of malaria and mosquitoes has been that they are unqualified and unnecessary evils; the dominant aim has been simply to get rid of them. Each time a new offensive weapon offered new hope, enthusiasts imagined that malaria would soon be wiped out. Only when the latest hope lay dashed did any considerable number of malariologists shift their thinking from an adversary to be conquered to an adversity to be tamed, mitigated and lived with.

Those who hold with the militant view will see this history as a record of a war lost despite important victories on some battlefields. Many of those who took part in the most recent battles do in fact now suffer a sense of defeat. In extenuation some of them point out that their failure is not unique, that in fact one can find very few grand victories in such grand undertakings. (The conquest of small pox may be one, but the final word on that is not in.) That is true. It may also be instructive. Failure so universal, so apparently ineluctable, must be trying to tell us something. The lesson could be of course that we have proved incompetent warriors. It could also be that we have misconstrued the problem.

---

* Actually there is a racial difference. The Negro genetically is relatively resistant (compared to Whites) to one form of malaria. This has been strikingly demonstrated among Negro Americans. Besides that true racial immunity (or tolerance) there is an inherited immunity to another (the malignant) form of malaria that is indigenous to sub-Saharan Africa. This is produced by the sickling trait, an inherited abnormality of haemoglobin. Children with sickling genes from both parents (homozygotes) are likely to develop severe and often fatal anaemia. But those with genes from only one parent have a mixture of normal and abnormal haemoglobin that usually does not bother them and does give them resistance to the malignant malaria parasite. Geneticists have used sickling as a classic example of the survival of normally disadvantageous genes in an environment where they confer a special advantage.

The attempt to exterminate forms of life which compete too successfully with us may be as mistaken in principle as it has generally proved in practice. In the fight against malaria the most enduring gains have been made by gradual, complex social and economic as well as physical and medical changes that have together altered the terms of competition between man and disease organisms in man's favor. Those changes too are part of this history—the hopeful part. Dramatic failures in battle not only shed light on undramatic evolutionary progress but have often prepared and promoted it.

So the story may be read many ways—as probing relations between man and nature, as illuminating the motivation and consequences of colonialism, as documenting the problems of public health administration, as reaffirming the interrelations between disease and social and economic conditions, as well as recounting the struggles of some unusual and a few heroic people against what they rightly or wrongly identified as the enemy. In sum it offers, I think, no simple meanings. And that may be the most important point of all.

2 / Laveran's Germ

It was not inevitable but it was fitting that the two men who made the basic discoveries that unlocked the secrets of malaria were both military men, both sons of military men. Doctors Alphonse Laveran and Ronald Ross served their respective countries' armies in posts of empire—Ross in India, Laveran in Algeria. Ross's father fought in the great Indian Mutiny of 1857 and became eventually a general in the British Army. Laveran's was a doctor who also served in Algeria. Ross, a complicated and chronically maladjusted man, was nevertheless the true son of his father and of his time and circumstance, one who viewed life as a struggle and himself as a soldier perpetually in battle with people and forces that sought, from stupidity or maliciousness, to frustrate him and hold back the course of human progress. Laveran appears to have been a gentler man, more purely a scientist by temperament, taste and long profession. Yet the devotees of science were not indifferent to the struggle for progress. On the contrary, they were among its generals. Laveran like Ross was egotistical, ambitious and endowed with the seemingly limitless energy, patience and optimism that are indispensable traits of discoverers.

Charles Louis Alphonse Laveran was pitched into the study of malaria when he was sent to Algeria in 1878.[1] He was then thirty-three. Besides his medical preparation, he had a degree in public health (from L'École du Service de Santé of Strasbourg) and had spent four years as aggrégé professor of epidemic medicine at the Army's medical school in Paris, Val de Grâce, occupying the chair that had been established for his father. He

7

does not appear to have had special interest in malaria himself or clinical experience with it. But there were at Val de Grâce four doctors who had worked extensively on the disease: F. C. Maillot who in years of practice in North Africa had developed successful quinine therapy, Léon Colin who made careful studies of the epidemiology, and Achille Kelsch and P. J. Keiner, who investigated the pathology. Laveran of course knew them and their work and had in fact carefully studied Colin's principal text in preparation for his examinations for the aggrégé degree.[2]

The work of Kelsch was a direct forerunner of Laveran's, even though Laveran never mentions it in any of his books or papers. Kelsch's attention as a pathologist had been drawn to one of the remarkable peculiarities of malaria: In the blood vessels of people who died of the disease were innumerable tiny black particles, often so numerous in certain organs (especially the spleen and liver, sometimes the brain) as to color the whole organ an abnormal slate grey.

By the 1870s when Kelsch began work the phenomenon of the malarial black pigment was well known though not at all understood.[3] Heinrich Meckel, a German pathologist, is generally credited with having been, in 1847, the first to describe the pigment. Another German pathologist, T. Frerichs, in 1858 demonstrated that the black particles consisted of degraded haemoglobin from the red blood cells. He thought the degradation might occur through a slowing or stoppage of circulation in the capillaries. It would thus be a product of pathological changes brought about by the disease. One doctor theorized that malaria fever destroyed the haemoglobin, another believed circulation of the degraded haemoglobin caused the fever. The critical mystery was why whatever happened happened only in malaria.

At least three doctors probably had the mystery under their microscopes but did not realize what they were looking at. Meckel himself described the pigment as sometimes contained in round, ovoid or spindle-shaped bodies. Rudolf Virchow, one of the great German pioneers in pathology, saw much the same thing a year later. So did Professor Kelsch, who was working in Algeria at the time Laveran was teaching in Paris, and seems to have just missed anticipating Laveran's discovery by some six years.

Kelsch, like Meckel and Frerichs, observed the black pigment almost always contained in white blood cells, or, as he put it, "in cellular elements that more or less conform to the white corpuscles of the blood." But occasionally he found it free and occasionally "enclosed in a hyaline body [clear protoplasm]" which he differentiated from leucocytes but did not otherwise describe.[4] Without much doubt these were the parasites that cause the disease *and* the black pigment.

From *Chanteclair*, 1909

The Wellcome Institute for the History of Medicine

Charles Louis Alphonse Laveran

As a pathologist Kelsch pursued his research chiefly in autopsies. But he had occasion in Algerian hospitals to take blood from a thousand living malaria patients. He found the pigment in the blood of almost all of them and recognized that its presence was a "precious" diagnostic tool. He also discovered that the pigment appeared to come into being at the moment of the access of fever.

These findings in retrospect put Kelsch on the threshold of an open door. Why did he not go on through? Perhaps because the key question—what happens uniquely in malaria?—was not his kind of question. As a pathologist he was concerned with the physiological changes brought about by disease and not with the processes of disease itself.[5] Like all pathologists he examined dead material. Even when drawing fresh blood from malaria patients he would routinely have killed it before examination.

The usual process is to prepare a thin smear of blood on a glass slide, dry it, fix it chemically and then stain it.* Various elements in the blood react differently to the dye, taking on contrasting colors that reveal their forms and often their internal structures under the microscope. But they are also, alas, fixed in the attitudes of death. In stained blood where nothing moved, it was not then possible to be sure that the hyaline bodies were anything but normal cells of some sort. So Kelsch passed by the brink of discovery, abandoned the mystery of the black pigment and went on to study another pathological problem that interested him more: the havoc that malaria wreaks among the red and white blood cells.[6] That destruction was indeed dramatic and significant but it was only a by-product of the main event that Laveran by contrast kept steadily in view. From the beginning the central challenge for him was the uniqueness of black pigment in cases of malaria.

For two years after his arrival in Algeria in 1878, Laveran went over old ground familiarizing himself with the pigment phenomenon (melanism) and confirming for himself that it characterized malaria and only malaria. What happened in malaria and in no other disease?

Kelsch had ascertained that the pigment was formed at the time the fever came on. That observation, whose implication Kelsch ignored, must have been useful to Laveran who, unlike Kelsch, wished to understand a living

---

* Marchiafava and Celli (1883) described their method, adapted from that devised by Koch and Paul Ehrlich, as follows: Having cleansed and pricked the skin, they spread a drop of blood thinly on the glass microscope slide and dried it by passing the slide two or three times over the flame of a spirit lamp. The dried blood was then stained by adding a drop of methylene blue dissolved in water or in alcohol. They then washed the slide in distilled water, gently of course so as not to wash away the specimen that was now slightly stuck to the glass. After drying in air the specimen was preserved in oil, cedar, balsam or garofano.

process. Laveran began to examine fresh blood, liquid and unstained. Though his microscope had only about half the power thereafter considered necessary to properly see what he was looking for, he found it quickly.

It has been said he was lucky. But he was following a series of clues and asking the right questions. When in his autopsies he found pigment contained in transparent cellular bodies, he assumed that these were leucocytes, or white corpuscles: that was plausible, since a function of some leucocytes is to destroy or scavenge alien elements in the blood. When he turned to fresh blood he again saw leucocytes containing black pigment, but alongside them were other clear bodies that also contained black fragments but did not at all resemble the white blood cells. They appeared in two basic shapes, crescents and spheres. Laveran called the first the No. 1 body, the second No. 2. *He suspected they were parasites.* How to prove it?[7]

That was where he got lucky. On 5 November 1880, he took a blood sample from a twenty-four-year-old soldier who was suffering relapse from a fever picked up a year earlier. Dr. Laveran had already found large quantities of crescents in the soldier's blood. Now he was looking at a sphere, a No. 2 body, through his microscope. "I was astonished to observe," he wrote, "that at the periphery of this body was a series of fine, transparent filaments that moved very actively and beyond question were alive." Two days later he found more of these filamented bodies. He was, he says, filled with joy. All doubt vanished. He wrote at once to the Academy of Medicine in Paris to report his astonishing find and stake out his claim to have been the first to make it. Then he went back to his work. Having met the parasite, he now had to get to know it through repeated observations. These in fact were to extend over four years. But before the end of one he knew enough to write a book, *La Nature parasitaire des accidents de l'impaludisme*, in which he described and pictured the new parasite with a wealth of detail.[8]

He wrote, for instance, that the filaments, which he now called flagella,* were slightly swollen at their free ends and that now and then they detached themselves from the spheres out of which they had come and swam off, stirring up the red corpuscles in a highly visible turmoil. He had also concluded that his several bodies were in fact all forms of the same creature: He had seen the crescents gradually fill out and become spheres, just as he had seen the spheres subsequently become flagellated and dispatch their flagella into the unknown. There was no resemblance whatever be-

---

* Because in form and liveliness they resembled the hairlike appendages of certain microscopic organisms whose "beating" (flagellating) movements enable the organism to "swim."

tween his parasite and any other normal or abnormal element of the blood: Whoever sees the flagellate bodies in violent motion, he wrote, could have no doubt that he is looking at a living parasite. "This curious spectacle converts the most incredulous."[9]

A curious spectacle indeed. It was the first glimpse of one form of one species of a genus of protozoans now known as *Plasmodium*. They are one-celled animals that live a part of their complicated life inside red blood cells. There they literally eat their host out of house and home, growing on the digested contents of the cell, and multiplying asexually to feed and grow some more. The black pigment is the residue of their metabolism, which fitly, like droppings along the trail, led to their discovery. Kelsch's finding that malarial patients had greatly reduced numbers of red cells along with an abundance of black pigment, is thus neatly explained.

Yet for about four years, Laveran's discovery was either ignored, explained away, or rejected as simply beyond belief. It could be easily ignored since few medical journals appear to have reported it, and none with any enthusiasm. Though the reports of Laveran himself were harder to explain away, several experimenters thought he might have been deluded by special deformations of the red or the white blood cells. The fact that these deformations could not possibly behave in the lively way he had described was passed over in silence, perhaps in order not to impute hallucinations to a fellow scientist. Then there were those who read Laveran, who had no plausible hypotheses of their own to account for the phenomena he described, but who nevertheless simply refused belief. "Nothing," wrote the great Dr. William Osler of Baltimore, perhaps the premier blood specialist of his day, "excited my incredulity more than [Laveran's] description of the ciliated [flagellated] bodies. It seemed too improbable, and so contrary to all past experience that flagellate organisms should occur in the blood."[10]

Past experience at that time not only excluded flagellate organisms in the blood; it also strongly suggested that the cause of the disease ought to be a bacterium of some sort. Several bacteria had in fact already been identified as cause of intermittent fevers. The most recent, announced in 1879, only a year before Laveran's, by two investigators in Italy, Edwin Klebs and Corrado Tommasi-Crudeli, had been backed by the most impressive scientific "proofs" of any so far. Klebs and Tommasi-Crudeli found in the swamp mud and waters of a highly malarious region of Italy a bacillus which on being injected into rabbits produced a variable fever that they thought resembled malaria. The rabbits moreover developed black pigment in the blood, as well as enlarged spleens, another well-known sign of malarial infection in humans.

Although the Italian bacillus did not reign any longer than it took other scientists to repeat the experiments and fail to confirm the conclusions, dethronement of the malarial bacillus did not open minds to Laveran's claims. There remained a strong presumption in favor of another bacterium likely to be resident, as was the *Bacillus malariae,* in the swamps that were notoriously the breeding places of malaria. That presumption took a strongly prejudicial flavor from the successes of the new science of bacteriology which was just then building on the work of Louis Pasteur and Robert Koch. Koch in the late 1870s was just emerging from the obscurity of a country physician in Posen to the role he achieved by century's end of something like the greatest man in the world. His prestige and Pasteur's, as well as bacteriological fashion, almost certainly delayed serious efforts to test Laveran's work, though Koch himself made a special point in 1880 of warning that there might be other agents of disease beside bacteria. As usual, orthodoxy infected disciples and schools, more virulently than it did their founders.[11]

Laveran's germ besides seeming improbable at the time was also extraordinarily difficult to catch in the act of wriggling on a microscope slide. In the first decade only one observer is on record as certainly having come upon the parasite in human blood by himself, with the aid only of descriptions and drawings. All others who eventually confirmed Laveran's findings had to have the animal personally pointed out to them by someone who had already recognized it.

The process of passing revelation along by hand had begun when Laveran showed the germ to his colleague, Dr. Richard, in Algeria. It continued in 1882 when Laveran went to Rome. His purpose was to find out whether there was a parasite in Roman malarial blood like that in Algerian blood. There was. He found it and showed it to two Roman doctors who were well on their way to becoming the world's first malariologists. They were Ettore Marchiafava* (a favorite and notably loyal student of Tommasi-Crudeli) and his long-time collaborator, Angelo Celli, who after years of distinguished research would become one of the first historians of malaria.

Marchiafava and Celli, who still considered that the *Bacillus malariae* was the most likely agent of malaria, were not impressed by Laveran's demonstration. They said later that he had shown them only dead parasites, which they had seen before. If so, that is surprising. Laveran of all

---

* Marchiafava, a brilliant and attractive man, served as the personal physician to three Popes as well as to the royal house of Savoy. He was made professor at the University of Rome at the age of thirty-six.

people was aware of the ambiguity of the parasite dead. He realized that the Italians were not getting anywhere because they insisted on staining their blood samples. Surely he must have pointed that out; the spectacle that he said would convert the incredulous was to be seen only in fresh blood. At any rate, the Italians persisted in their ways for another year or two. Then they too switched to fresh unstained specimens, detected the parasite, and reported it without a word about Laveran's visit of two years before. Laveran was annoyed. This first coolness between competing scientists of different nations was precursor to bitter me-first battles ahead.[12]

It was some time in 1884 that the Italians first spotted in fresh blood a colorless, very active little animal which they were delighted to believe had not been seen by Laveran. It appeared sometimes in the shape of a ring, did not contain black pigment, was small and forever in motion, contorting its peripheries like a feeding amoeba. It was, indeed, feeding. For this was the young form of Laveran's parasite that having just entered the red corpuscle had begun to surround and ingest haemoglobin. Marchiafava and Celli thought it looked rather like the large masses of protoplasm with several nuclei that zoologists called plasmodia. Eager to have a name that would distinguish *their* form from Laveran's flagellated body, they suggested calling it *Plasmodium malariae*.[13]

In the autumn of 1884 and throughout 1885 Marchiafava and Celli patiently examined hundreds of blood slides, fresh and stained, to assemble in effect a series of motion picture frames which portrayed the parasite's feeding, accumulation of black pigment, and gradual enlargement almost to fill the host cell, by that time emptied of itself. The next step seemed to be division. This they did not observe, but they did find in the blood tiny bodies which did not move in the characteristically lively, amoeboid way. The investigators assumed that these little ones represented a new generation destined to reinvade red cells, feed again, grow again, divide again endlessly.

At the same time Camillo Golgi was making similar observations. A brilliant researcher whose primary interest was the nervous system, Golgi had closely followed the work of Marchiafava and Celli in Rome and then in Pavia carried on by himself. He confirmed the Roman doctors' findings and made one more, the most remarkable since Laveran's: All the parasites present in the blood, he observed, divided almost simultaneously *and at regular intervals*. The moment of division, moreover, coincided with the onset of fever.[14]

Golgi worked first with quartan fever, so called because the victim's temperature peaks every fourth day, counting (Roman style) the first attack as the first day. (The interval between attacks, in other words, is seventy-two hours.) Golgi showed with a series of blood slides that a new generation of quartan parasites (now called *Plasmodium malariae*) appeared every seventy-two hours. But he, too, failed to observe the actual process of division, though he speculated that the parasites described by Laveran in the form of rosettes (*corps rosaces*) were in fact about to segment.

That was correct. The parasite at that point has in fact reached its maximum growth and its nucleus is undergoing mitosis, to produce several daughter nuclei of varying numbers up to thirty-six. At the moment of segmentation each daughter nucleus, having gathered protoplasm around itself, must break out of the containing parental membrane as well as the membrane of the host cell. As millions of parasites thus burst free in a matter of an hour or so, the effect is not surprisingly explosive for the host, though the precise mechanism by which fever is thereby induced remains unclear even now.

Finding that division coincided with attacks of fever, Golgi predicted and later proved that what was known as tertian fever was caused by a different species of parasite (now called *Plasmodium vivax*), which went through *its* life cycle in only forty-eight hours. Irregular fevers whose ups and downs followed neither a three- nor a four-day cycle, Golgi showed, were double or triple infections by either quartan or tertian parasites, several broods of the plasmodium being simultaneously present in the blood stream. Tentatively Golgi identified the parasite which caused malignant malaria (usually known in Italy as estivo-autumnal fever) as a third species characterized by the crescent sexual forms first observed by Laveran. In the most common form of malignant malaria, fever rose every forty-eight hours, and it consequently went by the common name of malignant tertian. But there was also a well-known form in which attacks of high fever came daily. Marchiafava believed the tertian and quotidian diseases were caused by different parasites which he proposed to distinguish. Golgi thought correctly that there was only one, since named *Plasmodium falciparum*. But it was then hard to be sure because *P. falciparum,* as it was later shown, in its youth leaves the peripheral blood to grow and divide in internal organs; only its sexual forms can ordinarily be discovered in blood pricked from the finger. Golgi did not solve the riddle. About 1893 he ended his brilliant detour into malaria research and returned to the neurophysiological work that in 1906 would win him a Nobel prize.

Italian research confirming and extending Laveran's discovery quickly toppled the skepticism that doctors had remarkably held to all but unanimously for five years. Beginning in 1885 acceptance spread throughout the world largely through personal contacts. Early that year Major George

Sternberg of the U.S. Army was in Rome as American delegate to the International Sanitary Conference. Already a well-known worker on malaria and yellow fever, Sternberg during his stay in Rome was made an honorary member of the Italian Royal Academy of Medicine and was welcomed to Marchiafava's laboratory where Marchiafava showed him Laveran's germ. Sternberg, who had been looking for it off and on ever since 1880, was an instant convert. He in turn demonstrated the parasite to Americans, particularly to the doctors of the Johns Hopkins Medical School, recently founded but already outstanding in America. Among them after a year of hesitation was Dr. Osler, who reported his conversion in the *British Medical Journal* in 1887.

Osler's paper was read by a doctor in India, Van Dyke Carter, who had tried before and failed to find the parasite. With Osler as guide Carter succeeded at last and published his findings, though, curiously, the candle he lit in India cast such a feeble light among his brethren in the Indian Medical Service that for nearly another decade the know-nothings could go on commanding space in the local medical journals. Laveran meanwhile had had a chance to show the parasite to Louis Pasteur, who, he says, was much impressed. Perhaps along about this time an English doctor* also visited Marchiafava and brought the truth and the technique back to Dr. Patrick Manson, who would in time pass them along to Ronald Ross. Finally a Russian scientist, V. J. Danilevskii, working independently in Kharkov, had found parasites in the blood of frogs and birds and observed their similarity to Laveran's. Before the end of the decade Osler could write that he knew of no qualified pathologist working in a region where malaria was prevalent who still doubted Laveran's findings.[15]

Yet there were laggards. Among them were both of the men who would finish first in the final race to pin the transmission of malaria on the mosquito. In Italy, Professor Giovanni Battista Grassi, perhaps the most eminent living zoologist, reserved judgment: The parasite, if it was a parasite, he argued, had to have a nucleus and none had yet been found; it also had to eat and no one had definitely shown that it did.[16] So Grassi waited for the last tittle of evidence. That came only in 1889 with the researches of Celli and another colleague, Guarnieri, followed in the next three years by his own investigations in collaboration with a doctor in Catania. Ross faced just the opposite difficulty, almost total ignorance of the literature and even of the techniques of microscopy. It would take him many more years to catch up with the men who had laid the ground for his own lifework, years even to find out what that work was.

---

* See page 33.

3 / Ronald Ross, the Unlikely Hero

Ronald Ross wanted by turns to be a painter, a composer, a mathematician, a poet and novelist. The one thing he clearly did not want to be was a doctor. That was his father's idea. General Sir Campbell Ross, his son was to write admiringly, "was a typical soldier, straight, stern, downright, and greatly experienced in the fierce campaigns against the warlike hill-tribes of India . . . Of rights, grievances, and politics he was oblivious; he had no delusions about the equality and liberty of men; and his own watchword was Service—a far nobler thing."[1] General Ross, with no delusions about the equality of the young, decided his eldest son would join the Indian Medical Service. Despite having "no predilection at all for medicine," the boy at seventeen nevertheless acquiesced cheerfully enough, reflecting that the life would be easy and allow him leisure for shooting and riding and such other hobbies as he "might have a mind for." So it was arranged entirely by the General, who during his last home leave in 1874 physically delivered his son to the appropriate hospital in London (St. Bartholomew's) for the appropriate training. Then Sir Campbell went back for his final tour of duty in India, leaving his wife and family in England. In 1880 he would retire and during the twelve years following, until his death in 1892, would be promoted to full general and receive his knighthood. Not so much a typical soldier as a highly successful one.

But if he expected his son similarly to succeed he must have died disappointed. Even in 1894, twenty years after being deposited at the starting gate at St. Bartholomew's, Ronald Ross was still looking for something

17

interesting and important to do. He had been quite right about his disinclination for medicine. He did not like it at St. Bartholomew's, where he spent five years treating his studies as impertinent digressions from playing the piano and the flute and composing "fragments."

During a holiday in 1875 he had met a poet and begun to think seriously of becoming a poet himself. He had written some verse, trying his hand at it as he had at painting—his father was a devoted Sunday watercolorist—and at music. Only the poetry took; it would increasingly absorb him. He would become serious, indeed, about it and throughout all his other careers—army dilettante, amateur mathematician, medical researcher, novelist, sanitarian—he wrote verse. John Masefield, his friend in later years, professed to admire it but most of what appeared in print was published at the author's expense, and that judgment now seems nearer right. Ross's vision was generally conventional; his imagery was stiff with classical allusion, his language was elevated and awkward. As in everything else he aspired in his poetry to greatness, to great thoughts, transcendent visions and a poet's fame. Even when he wrote most evidently in the grip of strong personal feelings as in his long poem "In Exile," on which he worked for some years in India, the off-stage crackle of Olympian thunderbolts all but blotted out his own voice. Yet he would retain all his life his poet's enthusiasm and energy for writing. One would have to say that he succeeded in becoming a poet even if he did not succeed as a poet.*

In the meantime, though he was not thinking seriously about it at all, he was becoming a doctor. He squeaked through examinations in 1881 for the easiest medical license he could get—membership in the Society of Apothecaries in London. He did scarcely better in his examination for the Indian Medical Service. By dallying in his studies he qualified two years later than he might have, and arrived in India only after his father's retirement and departure. With no claim to preferment he found the ranks of junior medical officers in India overfilled and promotion a long way off. There was not even a proper job at the start. Assigned to a British station hospital in Madras, where his official duties hardly took two hours of the day, he had leisure in abundance. One would not have said that he had prospects.

The service he had joined (the IMS) offered more obvious opportunities for a pleasant life than for professional attainment. After Queen Victoria took over the governance of India from the East India Company in 1858, the IMS which had been in existence since 1764 became the purveyor of

---

* According to Ross, John Masefield was extravagant in his admiration of "In Exile," calling it "a wonderful work" that kept him awake half the night.[2]

medical services to both the civil and military branches of the Government of India. It was accordingly itself divided into a civil and military branch. The latter supplied medical officers to the native regiments under British command (a separate Army Medical Branch functioned with White units). The civil branch comprised doctors who treated and advised British officialdom, ran the base hospitals and dispensaries and ministered to the British-run prisons. Officers of both branches had the right to take private patients for fees, but the opportunities for a significantly lucrative practice were greater by far in the Civil Branch whose officers were normally stationed for relatively long periods in the principal cities.

All those recruited as surgeon lieutenants had to spend the first two years in military service, but most applied thereafter for transfer. The historian of the IMS confesses that the chance of a well-paid practice in the so-called Presidency towns, Madras, Calcutta and Bombay, was "always one of the chief attractions of the Service."[3] The Presidency towns and a few others also had medical colleges, appealing to the very few who were mainly interested in research and professional development.

None of this was for Lieutenant Ross. There is no evidence that he even thought of transfer to the Civil Branch until after he had begun working on malaria and begun also as a family man to feel most sharply the pinch of low pay. He started out as one of the minority who according to an ambitious brother officer "found the light work and greater opportunities for sport and social amenities in military stations so congenial that they remained in the military side throughout their service."[4] But if the work was light it was also dull: little surgery, repetitive cases of fever, dysentery and blistered feet. It suited a man without professional ambition, or one who thought he wanted to be almost anything other than a doctor.

For some years the qualities most essential to Ross's eventual triumph—his great energy and extraordinary resilience—seemed to conspire to prevent him from gathering his forces to do a job he could handle. Like a man trying to solve a maze by running through it as fast as possible, Ross first plunged into the reading and writing of romantic poetry, and then into teaching himself mathematics and attempting to solve grand mathematical problems. It does not seem to have occurred to him for the first six or seven years that he might achieve in medical science the eminence he so evidently craved.

By the time it did, he was getting married to a girl at home, of whom history and her apparently always devoted husband have preserved hardly more than her name—Rosa Bessie Bloxam. That was in 1889. Ross later saw the year as a turning point. But, romantic though he was, he attributed the turning not at all to his marriage. On the contrary, the marriage appears almost as consequence of the profound discouragements he had suffered up to them. He wrote in his memoirs:

> For six years, I had toiled outrageously at almost everything, sparing neither body nor mind; solitary toil which I never mentioned to my friends. [This is reference chiefly to his heroic struggles with mathematics and particularly his determination, typical in all his undertakings, to do something creative and original.] Now [in 1888 when he applied for a furlough home] had come the reaction . . . I could work no more—nor even play; my ponies browsed unsaddled, my books rested unread. Then, moreover, my faith died—the greatest of all faiths, the faith in labour; and I was overcome with the horror of the *cui bono*. What was the use of anything?

He felt he was living in a cemetery.

Presumably Rosa Bloxam had something to do with his recovery of faith, which was typically rapid. There are hints that she exerted strong influence on him throughout his life but no more than hints. Ross has hidden his wife and family almost completely from history with a reticence unusual even in a Victorian officer of the British Army. One does not know even how he met her or what sort of person she was. Although in their rather frequent separations they corresponded, often daily, the letters have apparently been destroyed. In his published memoirs and in his surviving papers Rosa Bloxam is utterly silent and undefined.

If his decision to return to medicine had been made before he left India, surely it would have been reinforced by his marriage. To succeed in his career was an obviously more promising approach to supporting a family than dabbling in mathematics or storming the literary world with gothic romances. At any rate, while he was in England he got at last some relevant medical training: He took a diploma in public health, a certificate newly offered jointly by the Royal College of Surgeons and The Royal College of Physicians. He also arranged a two months' extension of his leave in order to go back to St. Bartholomew's for a course in bacteriology with one of its most distinguished British practitioners, Dr. Edward E. Klein, who had just identified the microbe of scarlatina and would later add substantially to the knowledge of the organisms causing hoof and mouth disease and typhoid fever.[5]

Ross returned to India with a little knowledge of microscopy, superb confidence in that small knowledge, and fresh determination to make his name. Perhaps he is right in his speculation that he was the only doctor in the Indian Medical Service of the day to have had even that much training in bacteriology. (Though certainly there were others, such as Van Dyke Carter, who were far more expert and experienced.)[6] Without question he felt himself to be a lone missionary among the heathen, and he began soon to preach on two themes: that the vast majority of supposed malarial fevers were really intestinal in origin and that Laveran's so-called parasites were probably nothing more than blood cells misshapen by faulty techniques used to examine them.[7] The self-confidence with which he drew that conclusion is as remarkable as his apparent ignorance of the ten years of observation that had not merely established the reality of the parasite but also detailed a good part of its life history in the circulating blood.*

Yet these early papers were impressive—impressive for the enthusiasm with which young Ross wielded the microscope whose new-found powers entranced him, impressive for the ingenuity with which he set up and tested hypotheses, impressive for the logical rigor with which he took off from false premises to arrive at impeccable conclusions. In particular they impressed one very important person in London, Dr. Patrick Manson.

Due for another home leave in 1894, Ross was advised to call on Dr. Manson when he got to London. Manson, he was told, could show him Laveran's parasite. Ross in fact on his arrival in London in March 1894 called first at St. Bartholomew's; but there the chief pathologist also told him, "Go and see Manson."

Several others in London could have shown Ross the parasite—if they had had one to show. But malaria, once prevalent in the United Kingdom, was by then virtually unknown. Dr. Manson, as chief surgeon of the Seamans' Hospital, was one of few who routinely had access to cases of malaria contracted by sailors and others in the tropics. Already without question the outstanding expert in tropical diseases in England, Manson was a warm, patient, avuncular doctor of fifty to whom it must have seemed natural to refer inquiring young men. Finally, it was well known in London medical circles that Manson had a special interest in malaria; he was working at that moment on a theory that malaria might be transmitted by mosquitoes.

On the afternoon of 9 April 1894, Ross called on Manson at 21 Queen Anne Street, just off Harley Street, where then as now the medical elite of London put out their discreet brass nameplates. The doctor was out but that evening Ross received a note of apology and an invitation to come around the next morning if possible. Manson wrote that he thought Ross

---

* Later in life Ross returned to his mathematical studies and worked out a "new" algebra only to discover that his new principles had all been described long before in the literature which he had not bothered to consult.

had missed seeing the plasmodium because of "the technique you employ." It would give Dr. Manson great pleasure to be of service "for I am quite sure you can do good work and have the patience to do it."[9] This was extraordinarily perceptive, both to recognize the quality of patience in Ross, whose more obvious traits at this time were naive enthusiasm and arrogance, and to see that patience above all was what would be needed for the work he had in mind: proof that mosquitoes could infect people with malaria.

Ross appeared, saw the parasite, and was immediately converted.[10] Still more important he was charmed, as were so many others, by Manson, a tall, handsome man with a gentle manner and playful sense of humor. Without that attraction, which seemed from the beginning to have a strong filial flavor, Ross might still have escaped his destiny. He was already being diverted again. Home leave was precious. He was enjoying himself with family and friends. The Rosses decided to spend the summer with another couple in Switzerland. When they left the young doctor's head was full of two new romances, one to be called *The Spirit in the Storm* and published in 1896. Afoot in the awesome Alps he became obsessed with visions of tenderness and passion and dreams of literary fame. What compared to this was a microscopic parasite?

Home in England in the autumn, he settled down to writing. Within a few months he finished both *The Spirit in the Storm* and a verse drama that would not be published until twenty years later. He was also drawn back to Manson. From the latter part of 1894 through the early months of 1895 the two men spent many hours of many days together. Manson had already adopted Ross as a disciple; Ross had slipped, gladly for the moment, into the role. In the time remaining before Ross returned to India, Manson tried to fill him with the lore and learning of his own long years of work with tropical diseases especially in China. He passed on above all his own fervent belief in the mosquito theory of malaria.

4 / The Mosquito Theory

From the time of classical Greece to the mid-nineteenth century, diseases for most doctors in the Western tradition were outward manifestations of internal disharmonies of the four humors of the blood. What caused the upsets were subjects for philosophical speculation rather than for scientific investigation. Causes in any event hardly mattered, since the treatment— bleeding and purgation—would be the same. Agues and intermittent fevers during most of the Christian era were lumped with other maladies for therapy and were not in any other essential way distinguished from the rest.

Malaria nevertheless always asserted some claim to be special. It had, as it were, a personality that set it a little apart, at least for those disposed to wonder at all. The characteristic rise and fall of intermittent fever, though mimicked in some other diseases, was generally seen to be distinctive.* A decimator of populations as serious, if not as dramatic as the plague, malaria, unlike the plague, stayed on year after year. Sometimes subsiding almost below notice, and sometimes surging abruptly to carry off thousands, it was always there, a part of the environment. Indeed, more than any other disease it appeared to *be* a special malignity of the environment.

---

* From about the middle of the seventeenth century Europeans knew of a specific remedy for intermittent fever in the bark of the cinchona tree, but the fact that the bark (or specifically the quinine it contains) affected only malaria was obscured because most doctors thought fever to be a single phenomenon. Its therapeutic record accordingly was spotty and its diagnostic value was lost.

Most commonly in the experience of Europeans, malaria was a sickness of wetlands. Hence the French name, "paludisme" (or less often "impaludisme") from *palus,* Latin for "swamp." Varro and Vetruvius in the first century before Christ warned of the diseases bred in swamps. Columella in A.D. 100 urged farmers not to build near a marsh "which breeds insects armed with annoying stings . . . and crawling things deprived of their winter moisture and infected with poison by the mud and decaying filth, from which are often contracted mysterious diseases."[1] The Pontine marshes near Rome were notorious fever breeders for centuries, and malaria was often called by the English "Roman fever." But in England, too, the fens were unhealthy. When Pip in *Great Expectations* meets Magwitch in the marshes he worries lest his new friend catch the ague. For Shakespeare the "infections the sun sucks up" came from bogs, fens and flats.

Yet obvious as it was that swamps were unhealthy it was almost as obvious that people could sicken elsewhere. As the amateur epidemiologists looked more closely they perceived a special malignancy in disturbed land, woodlands newly cut, soil newly plowed. Its most numerous victims, moreover, were those who did the cutting and plowing.

Marshes and newly plowed land had in common an unusual quantity of decaying organic matter exposed to the air. It was reasonable to suspect that decay was physically unhealthy. The suspicion seemed confirmed by the fact that malaria flourished particularly in spring and late summer and autumn, seasons of the plow and the harvest—before plants blanketed the soil and after they had died. Healthy places seemed to be those where there was little or no organic decay or where wind dispersed its vapors; high mountains, breezy hillsides; bedrooms above the ground floor; deserts; the sea. That malaria seldom if ever struck at sea was one of the most remarkable of its peculiarities, especially considering the very high incidence among sailors who came ashore. Where could one get further away from vegetative decay than in mid-ocean, and where be in closer contact with it than in the low-lying lands beside the sea? "The influence of the soil in the production of malarial fevers," wrote one doctor in 1878, "scarcely needs comment."[2]

But how that influence was exerted was the subject of much comment and disagreement. Some thought the poison was chemical, though none of the attempts to find a specific gas, beginning with Lancisi in 1695, turned up anything even remotely likely to produce the symptoms of intermittent fever. Some thought it immaterial, a special maleficent force whose nature could not be precisely defined. A few thought it might be alive. "Minute animals," declared the Roman writer, Varro, "invisible to the eye, breed there [in swamps] and, borne by the air, reach the inside of the body by way of the mouth and nose, and cause diseases."[3] Lancisi, the noted eighteenth century Italian physician, speculated about a living contagium and wrote so vividly about animalcules which could be inhaled and would then multiply in the blood that the supposed creatures became widely known in Italy as the "serafici."[4] At the end of the century, Giovanni Rasori developed a remarkably consistent theory about disease organisms. He taught his medical students at the University of Pavia that contagious diseases were propagated indefinitely as "organized beings develop and multiply in certain circumstances." Though invisible, the contagia, he thought, were distinct species that always bred true; a particular disease therefore could propagate only itself and no other. Malarial miasmas contained contagia that had lived and reproduced in a swamp before entering people as parasites. In the body they caused fevers "more or less quickly according to their species." This extraordinary guess, so close to the true explanation of malaria, had to remain a guess until suitable microscopes made it possible to look for the serafici.[5]

Whatever the toxin, it was most often thought to exude from mud and stagnant water and infect the ambient air. To the lay mind in particular the menace of miasmas drifting whitely over bogs and fens seemed obvious. That a man inhaling foul, dank air would become sick needed no proof. So it seemed to Italians who began, perhaps in the eighteenth century, to refer to the cause of fever as *mal' aria,* bad air. Horace Walpole apparently first brought the word back to England in 1740. With, and later without, the apostrophe it became in English also the common term for the agent of ague even among those who thought that bad water or bad germs were really responsible. When the true pathogen was found the "malaria" label shifted readily to the disease itself.[6]

Air could be poisoned equally by blowing over the decayed and decaying vegetable matter exposed when woodlands were cut or furrows turned. Just as the poetic consonance between miasmas and ague was for many as satisfying as the common-sense relation between wet feet and head colds, so the notion that uncovering decay could release agents of sickness and death commended itself as just what one would expect. Perhaps the subconscious summoned up such metaphors as the violation of graves, the opening of Pandora's box. More rationally it could be argued that if the poison was formed in the soil—and this was the all but unanimous belief— then it must escape more abundantly when the soil was cleared and cut open.

To get around the objection that all fertile soil contained decaying matter, whereas not all places were malarious, an ingenious explanation was offered: The cause of disease might be not a specific organic poison but a kind of energy normally harmless to people because growing plants absorbed most of it, converting it to live and therefore healthy tissue. In this view the malarial contagium was not really a pathogen at all but an excess of idle power for which the devil found work. A "vegetative force," as Dr. Léon Colin called it in 1870, emerged from the soil to strike at man unless it were "used up by a sufficient quantity of plants." The concept verged unfortunately on the mystical, as Dr. Colin was embarrassed to note. Observing that other diseases were beginning to be attributed to the very specific physical inroads of bacteria, he apologized for the vagueness of his explanation. Yet it did seem to "explain" better than any other hypothesis such peculiarities of malaria as its prevalence in autumn when vegetative growth slows and gradually ceases, as well as the special and well-known dangers of night air when the suspension of photosynthesis prevents plants from exploiting and depleting the force.[7]

A myth current at the time tended to support Colin's hypothesis: Monks of a Trappist monastery located in the highly malarious Roman Campagna, were believed to have escaped malaria by planting eucalyptus trees on the monastery grounds. The trees were supposed to act both as a shield against "telluric" poisons and as an aromatic antidote. But, alas, they did neither. *The Lancet,* reporting the success so far of the experiment in 1876, also noted that "at the beginning of March a strong wind setting in from the Pomptine [sic] marshes laid up a few of the brotherhood with malarious fever."[8] In fact the brotherhood would soon be decimated and the monastery abandoned.[9]

Miasmas, thick and thin, were for most people the most likely agents of fever. But others held that the poison seeped from the soil into water and made people sick when they drank it. The hypothesis by comparison with the miasma theory had for many an appealing directness. It brought malaria into the family of gut diseases along with cholera and typhoid. It could account for the fact that only some people in malarious places got sick, and not all, as one would expect if the poison were absorbed by breathing. It was strongly supported moreover by a dramatic incident often recalled. In July 1834 eight hundred French soldiers embarked at Bône, Algeria, in three vessels bound for Marseilles. Two of the ships made an uneventful trip. But the 120 men who sailed in the third, the *Argo,* came down with malaria almost to a man. Thirteen died; ninety-four who were treated in Marseilles with quinine were cured. On investigation it was found that the *Argo* alone had taken on drinking water drawn from a swamp. It seemed a powerful coincidence.[10]

Some were convinced; some were not. "That *drinking water* is the most frequent means by which malaria is introduced into the system is a firmly established truth," wrote one doctor in 1891.[11] "The evidence . . . is conclusive," wrote the great Dr. William Welch of Johns Hopkins in 1889, "that many infectious agents—and here the malarial germ should prominently be mentioned—can be and often are conveyed by air."[12] And so it went. As Marchiafava wrote later, most early observers held to "a prudent eclecticism" admitting the possibility of many different pathways by which germs might enter the body.[13]

For most laymen it made no difference. The important fact was that the germ lurked in foul water, unkempt land, vegetative decay. In a word, like so many other diseases, it was spawned by filth. That was an old and seminal idea in human history.

The book of Leviticus not only commanded the leper to cry "Unclean! unclean!" but minutely prescribed how he must cleanse himself and his dwelling. Classical Greece by turning the physician's attention inward to the harmonies of the body discouraged speculation about contagion. But in time speculation revived under the terrible instruction of plague. Next to quarantine and flight, the chief measures against plague were the cleansing of houses, persons and effects. An English treatise in 1720 further recommended demolition of the buildings that housed the victims and prevention in the future by reducing crowding and clearing the slums. Some English cities in the eighteenth century took tentative steps in that direction with the Improvement Acts.[14]

The progress of the ensuing public health movement is not our business. What is important here is to observe that publicly organized defenses against disease were mostly shaped before the causes of disease were known and that they were organized, notably in England, by laymen on the lay assumption that filth equals disease. Emphasis on environmental improvement instead of on treatment of the sick tended to discourage attention to the causes and cures of specific diseases. If cholera, plague, typhoid and the rest arose from filth it was better to clean house than to waste time studying the dirt. Emphasis on cleaning up the slums attached sanitarians to other liberal movements and gave their work a strong reformist flavor. Attack on disease became in some sense an instrument of social engineering. Malaria considered as a disease of rural decay, spawn of an ill-kempt, savage and uncultivated land, yielding to good husbandry and civilization, fit the pattern and invited similar countermeasures.[15]

The geography of malaria as mapped by early observations is in fact the habitat of anopheline mosquitoes.* And water, as everyone saw, is indeed the key. All mosquitoes spend their youth in water. Although the eggs of some can survive in soil or on plants for many months none will hatch until wetted; the larval stage emerging from the egg is an aquatic animal. Though air-breathing it cannot live dry-shod. Larvae feed on minute particles of organic matter. Swamps excel in the production of such food. Puddles in a cow's footprint will provide quite enough for some species.

Like the caterpillars that metamorphose into butterflies, mosquito larvae feed, grow and molt until they are ready to become adult. They then develop pupae with relatively hard shells and cease to feed. In due course the adult mosquito steps out of the pupal shell, rests a little on the surface of its birthplace, then flies off to its brief but enthusiastic career of producing more eggs and more larvae. Normally the adult does not fly far, which accounts for the usual concentration of malaria in the immediate vicinity of breeding places. It normally does not fly high, which is why people sleeping above the ground may escape being bitten. It is a weak flier and cannot forage in windy places. A few species can go to sea by breeding in water containers on shipboard, but it is rare for an adult mosquito to fly out even a few hundred yards from shore except when carried by the wind. Many species can survive winters in a temperate climate but only in hibernation. The female will not bite or lay eggs in temperatures lower than 16° C. Most of the malaria-carrying species bite after sundown, which is why the miasmas of night were—and still are—particularly dangerous. Adult mosquitoes are so thin that they are unusually susceptible to being dried out; accordingly they venture out and about more often when the air is damp than when it is dry.

Now and then from classical times onward observers remarked on the remarkable coincidence between the prevalence of mosquitoes and intermittent fevers.[16] But so strong was the common-sense opinion that the germ must dwell in the muck, that those who suspected mosquitoes whispered against the wind. It is true that the suspicion of mosquitoes was ancient and fairly common among the folk, well established according to the explorer Humboldt among the tribes of the Orinoco and, according to Robert Koch, also among tribes of East Africa.[17] If only great scientific minds had listened to the wisdom of the people, a distinguished parasitologist wrote in 1949, the secrets of malaria might have been exposed much sooner.[18] Perhaps so, but an intellectual chasm yawns between an old wives' tale that happens to be true and a scientific hypothesis that can be

---

* For details on the life history of mosquitoes, see Chapter 17.

shown to be so. The few doctors who tried to put together testable hypotheses from observed associations between mosquitoes and fever had few facts to go on; they had to invent cause-and-effect linkages out of whole cloth.

One of the more imaginative of these was the work of an American physician, John Crawford. Crawford worried chiefly about yellow fever, a terrible periodic scourge of Baltimore where he practiced in the early 1800s, and thought mosquitoes might be responsible. He imagined that yellow fever and "every other fever" was produced by eggs "insinuated . . . into our bodies," just as diseases in caterpillars were caused by injection into *their* bodies of eggs of the parasitic flies. Published in 1807 in *The Observer and Repertory of Original and Selected Essays in Verse and Prose, on Topics of Polite Literature*, the theory won instant ridicule for its author. Crawford refused to admit error, was ostracized by his peers, and eventually lost his practice. In the current state of science he was helpless to prove his point even though he was more nearly right than anyone else would be for ninety years.[19]

On the etiology of the disease he was for instance closer to the mark than another doctor who holds a more honored position in medical history as a prototypical author of the mosquito theory. Louis Beauperthy, a French doctor practicing in Caracas, wrote forthrightly in 1854 that "intermittent fever is a serious disease spread by and due to the prevalence of mosquitoes." But he based that assertion essentially on the coincidence of mosquitoes and fever in warm weather and virtually simultaneous disappearance of both when it got cold. As to the pathogenic mechanism he speculated that the mosquitoes sucked up poisons from the decomposing vegetable matter in swamps and along the seashore, which they then injected into people as a snake injects venom.[20]

Rasori, whose comprehensive theory of contagion has been noted, had at least a passing thought that mosquitoes might carry the contagium when he himself came down with fever in Mantua after being tormented there by mosquitoes.[21] But even he could hardly pursue the idea. Like Crawford, Beauperthy and a few other good guessers he had neither precedent nor chart by which to navigate. To believe that invisible animals which might travel by way of insects into human bodies was to embrace all at once a very complex process for which there was not a scrap of evidence. The basic notion that parasites might shuttle between different species of animal (metaxenie) was conceived in Rasori's day (in 1790 by Peter Christian Abilgaard).[22] But it would be another half century before parasitic organisms began experimentally to be associated with disease and before a persuasive body of evidence for metaxenie began to emerge.

Early and recurrent theories of insect transmission of malaria may have been useful, as the medical historian Harrison Shryock believes, in keeping mosquitoes under suspicion and periodic scrutiny.[23] But, as they were intrinsically less plausible than the theories of filth, foul drinking water and insidious miasmas, they could not hope to prevail until underpinned by a lot more facts about disease and about insects.

The first important work on the role of insects in transmitting disease was done by Dr. Patrick Manson in China during the 1870s, when he showed that mosquitoes might be vectors of the disease colloquially known as elephantiasis from the gross swellings, particularly of the legs and scrotum, that it often produces. Two other doctors, Timothy Lewis in Calcutta and Joseph Bancroft in Brisbane, had found the parasite responsible, a filarial worm.* The adult female filaria lodges in a lymph node where she causes the obstruction that leads to the elephantine deformities, and devotes her relatively long life to procreation. Her young are born alive, and unlike their mother, move freely in the blood stream, tiny living threads so slender that they pass through the smallest lymphatics. Filarial embryos found in the blood are always enclosed in a delicate membrane; they can neither feed nor move of their own volition. Therefore, Manson reasoned they must complete their life cycles somewhere else.

In a parallel with Ross's own story, Manson had found out about filariae when he was on home leave from China in 1875 and on his return embarked on long years of research in comparative intellectual isolation. He was at it for seven years, as he combined research with a full and lucrative medical practice.

Reasoning that the worm embryos in their envelopes could never fend for themselves but must drift endlessly and aimlessly with the blood currents unless rescued by an outside agent, Manson decided to see whether the bloodsucking mosquito might not be such an agent. He began in the classic way, feeding his insects on patients known to have filariae in their blood, and then looking to see what happened inside the mosquito.

"I shall not easily forget the first mosquito I dissected," he wrote:

> I tore off its abdomen and succeeded in expressing the blood the stomach contained. Placing this under the microscope, I was gratified to find that, so far from killing the filaria, the digestive juices of the mosquito seemed to have stimulated it to fresh activity. And now I saw a curious thing. The little sac or bag enclosing the filaria, which hitherto had muzzled it and prevented it from penetrating the wall of

---

* Now classified in two genera, *Wuchereria* and *Brugia*.

the blood-vessels in the human body, was broken through and discarded.[24]

Over a period of many months, in many more dissections he followed the development of the liberated filariae, which bored through the stomach walls of the mosquito into the thoracic muscles. There they underwent metamorphosis, increasing in size and developing a mouth and alimentary canal, manifestly preparing to enter a new human host.

Manson, whose delight in the ingenious ways of nature was ebullient and often poetic, speculated that the embryos were born in sacs to prevent their burrowing prematurely into human tissue, and thereby missing their rendezvous with a mosquito in the blood stream. In his later researches he discovered another beautiful adaptation for filarial survival: the embryos appeared abundantly in the blood at night but were difficult to find in the morning. He believed (wrongly, as it turned out) that the comings and goings were not a response to the activity of the human host; it was, he thought, the onset of night, not of sleep, that brought the embryos out into the peripheral blood. Could it not be that the filariae had evolved to appear in numbers at just the time of day when their prospective mosquito hosts normally fed?

Manson did not complete his proof. He did not follow the development of the filariae to full maturity and discover that they proceed into the mosquito's head, enter the sheath of her proboscis and at the moment of biting slide down through the puncture wound into a new human host. He missed that largely because he knew nothing about mosquitoes and had read somewhere that they fed only once in a lifetime of a very few days. That misinformation, apparently never questioned and never checked, cost him dear. It made his own research difficult, even as far as it went, since without food his mosquitoes did in fact die in a few days. Invariably they died before the matured filariae set out on their final journey through the mosquito to the point of exit. Also he had to close by speculation the unobserved portion of the cycle of transmission: from mosquito back to man. Plausibly he elected to believe that the mosquito after laying its eggs died in the water. People drinking that water would then imbibe the filarial worms.

Possessed of a truly creative mind that was always perceiving connections and resemblances between disparate phenomena, Manson was sometimes beguiled by the harmonies of imagination. So in time he became as assured in asserting the reality of his invented chapter in the life of the mosquito as he was in describing facts of observation. Perhaps that was in part due to his power to command the belief of others through the force

Sir Patrick Manson

and charm of his personality, and so in turn to convince himself. He was, Ronald Ross has reported, forever followed by a covey of adoring young doctors who hung on his words and encouraged him to sound assured even when he was not. In his writing is the same engaging mixture of whimsical charm and authority. Though many doctors at the time severely criticized Manson's habit of indulging unsupported speculations, he had always a forum and remained a voice to be listened to. Perhaps, too, as Ross had also asserted, Manson was dilatory in checking his own hypotheses because he found research physically difficult. He was struck by gout in China at the age of twenty-six and suffered from it throughout his life—often totally crippled for days or weeks. Ross says his hands were so unsteady that it was not easy for him to use a microscope.

In any event, the drama of the filariae became for Manson the model for his speculations on malaria, supplemented and slightly modified by the published results of the research of others. It was not until a year after his return to England from China in 1889 that he first read Laveran's reports. His reaction is not on record. It may be that like most others he was skeptical and that his skepticism was overcome by personal demonstration, possibly by a Dr. Plimmer, who reportedly was himself shown the parasite by Marchiafava in Rome.[25] When convinced, he was most struck, as

Laveran himself had been, by the phenomenon of exflagellation, the release from the parasite of hairlike appendages and their final detachment from the parent body apparently headed for an independent existence. What struck him of course was their resemblance to filariae. Laveran, it will be recalled, had asserted that these flagella were the "true" parasite, that is to say its mature stage, and had even speculated that they might be picked up in this form by mosquitoes for transfer to a new host. Just like filariae, Manson thought, and proceeded to explore some seminal analogies.

This was in 1894. He published his speculations in the *British Medical Journal.*[26] Plasmodia, he observed, like filariae, had no means of their own to escape from the human blood stream; to continue their career they had to have outside help. What more likely than a bloodsucking insect? He was impressed with the fact that the flagella were never found in the blood when drawn, but appeared only a half minute or more later (a fact noted in 1889 by Sakharov and confirmed in 1892 by Grassi). That would be just what one would expect if the flagella represented a metamorphosis preparing the parasite for life outside man. What triggered the change? He had experimented with filariae and found that if the blood slide holding them was chilled and then warmed slightly the embryo worms could be seen to withdraw to one end of their enclosing sheaths, thence to rush forward with great force as though trying to break out. He thought the chilling which thickened the blood either provoked the worm to these efforts at escape or at least favored their attempt. The thicker blood, he thought, would tend to hold the sheaths and so permit the worm inside to apply greater force to rupturing them. Just such a chilling and thickening took place when human blood was sucked into the mosquito's stomach.

The red blood cells that enclosed the malaria parasite seemed to him analogous to the filarial sheaths. In the blood stream the sheaths had prevented the filariae from boring holes in the wrong host; the enveloping red cells protected the young parasites from being devoured by phagocytes (white blood cells that function as scavengers and predators to rid the blood of alien elements). "The filaria is sheathed to prevent its committing suicide; the plasmodium is sheathed to protect it from being murdered." Like the filariae, plasmodia, he thought, escaped only after the blood was drawn out by the mosquito. In both cases the triggering mechanism seemed to be the slight drop in temperature. Flagella and filariae arriving in the mosquito gut then begin their metamorphosis. Manson confessed he knew nothing about the transformations of the flagella; that is what he wished some doctor, in India perhaps, would study. (He did not announce that he already had Dr. Ross in mind.)

By contrast he felt moved to describe in picturesque detail the final link in the cycle as though he had actually observed it: The female mosquito, he wrote, having fed "seeks out some dark and sheltered spot near stagnant water. At the end of about six days she quits her shelter, and, alighting on the surface of the water, deposits her eggs thereon. She then dies, and, as a rule, falls into the water alongside her eggs." Man might then become infected by drinking the water. Alternatively the plasmodium might pass directly to a new generation of mosquitoes, skipping man as follows: The larvae, emerging in due course from the eggs, eat everything in reach "and one of the first things they eat, if they get the chance, is the dead body of their parent, now soft and sodden from decomposition and long immersion." That incestuous cannibalism would pass the plasmodia to the larvae and thence to the adult insect.

Nearly every part of the analysis, as it turned out, was wrong. The attempt at detailed analogy between filariae and plasmodia went badly awry. The drama of death and filial ingratitude in the swamp was a highly ingenious and quite misleading amalgam of the facts and fictions of the day. Yet taken as a whole Manson's "mosquito theory" was a brilliant imaginative construction that not only pointed in the right direction for research but provided a logically consistent scheme that could be tested, proved, modified or discarded, step by step. Perhaps not least important, it was presented, both in the first sketch of 1894 and in the fully developed form in lectures of 1896, with a verve that was itself a challenge particularly calculated to excite a man like Ronald Ross, who was both scientist and poet.

5 / Follow the Flagellum

Ronald Ross, newly accepted into the very small company of malariologists, lost no time in announcing his accession. Before leaving England, while finishing his romance and his play in verse, he wrote an essay on malaria and submitted it for the Parkes Memorial Prize offered every three years by the Netley Hospital for the best paper on the subject by a medical man. He won. About the same time he wrote and sent to the *Indian Medical Gazette* a paper mildly titled: "A List of Natural Appearances in the Blood Which Have Been Mistaken for Forms of the Malaria Parasite." The title recalled, as surely it was meant to, Ross's contributions to the same journal a year earlier in which he scoffed at Laveran's so-called parasite and at those inexperienced users of microscopes who were misled by mangled red corpuscles. Now his point was to distinguish carefully those same counterfeit forms from the *real* parasite. The paper was a neat bridge from error to enlightenment; he was off in a wholly new direction without seeming to have shifted his ground. It thus served his intellectual needs. But the tone was unnecessarily offensive. "While the identification of the malaria parasite," he began, "presents little difficulty to anyone who has seen it under the microscope . . ." From one who had so recently seen it for the first time himself that was too grand. Without warrant he patronized his brother medical officers in India, including the handful who not only had had longer experience with the microscope than he but had also found the malaria parasite before him. Sadly it presaged the troubles ahead for this proud and prickly man, who could never pass an empty

35

Ronald Ross and his portable microscope, Darjeeling, May, 1898

pulpit without getting up to preach or pick a quarrel with the congregation.[1]

However, just as characteristically and more endearingly, he was once more engrossed and almost literally wild with enthusiasm in his new quest. He could not wait. During his spare time in England he had invented a portable microscope, and he had one of them with him on the ship to India. He began dissecting cockroaches on shipboard because they had parasites that he thought were much like plasmodia. Having left behind his wife and children, who were to join him later, he was full of the happy thought that he would come back to get them himself in eight or nine months after he had completed his proof of Manson's theory. Then he could land in England to lay his specimens and his victory before Dr. Manson and the world of science.

Finding on his arrival in Bombay that he had to wait over a couple of days before joining his regiment in Secunderabad, he went straight to the hospital where he examined cases of tertian fever. His observations on these cases were the first entries in notebooks that over the next four years were to record almost daily the progress of his research. The doctor was at last enthusiastic about being a doctor, at least one of his own kind. He would need to be.[2]

His task is simply stated: To study *Plasmodium,* not in man, but in the mosquito, "a thing which had never been yet attempted."[3] He had to demonstrate first that plasmodia could and did live in the mosquito, and then find out what happened to them inside the insect. In that quest he was to encounter almost every imaginable obstacle.[4]

He began with a handicap that would have been insuperable for a lesser man: ignorance of almost everything he needed to know. Of bacteriology he knew what he had picked up in the short course he took in London during his holiday; of microscopy, what he had taught himself in the previous three or four years puzzling out the appearances of normal blood, besides what he had been able to learn from Manson. He had read at least one of Laveran's treatises, but none of the Italian papers that for ten years had been describing ever more refined and sophisticated observations of the blood cycle of the parasite. Most of these would have been inaccessible to him anyway, since the only foreign language he had was a little school French. He seems to have taken back to India only one malaria text, a book that had just been published in England containing translations of an Austrian text (Julius Mannaberg, *On malarial parasites*) and the Marchiafava–Bignami paper of 1892 (*On aestivo-autumnal fevers*) reporting the uniqueness of the parasite with crescent forms that caused malignant malaria.[5]

Cut off from the literature, he remained ignorant of a new method of staining blood slides, invented in 1890 by the Russian bacteriologist Romanovskii. By 1895 when Ross began work, the Romanovskii stain was already opening up for Italian, German and American workers brilliant new insights into microbial structure. Ross, who by contrast scarcely knew the pre-Romanovskii methods, spent hours and months experimenting with fixing, staining and preserving specimens almost as if he were the first in the world to face the problem. He subscribed to the *British Medical Journal*; that and his correspondence with Manson would provide his only contact with scientific work outside India during the long lonely stint.

Serious as were these multiple deficiencies in Ross's training and experience, they were trivial compared to his total ignorance of the speciation, physiology and behavior of mosquitoes. As already noted, little enough was known to anyone at that time. Nevertheless, had Ross called at the British Museum before leaving England, as Manson recommended, he would at least have learned to recognize different species of mosquitoes and so to have been on guard against assuming that as an experimental animal one mosquito was like another. It happened ironically that, through no fault of his own, he just missed a still greater helping hand: During his year in England an Italian zoologist, Ficalbi, published the first taxonomy of the mosquitoes of Europe.[6] This could have spared Ross literally years of work. But Ficalbi does not appear to have been known for some years afterward even in England, much less in India.

On arrival at his regimental headquarters in Secunderabad Ross was greeted by an "awful" heat and dry wind "like the blast of an engine furnace." In hindsight he might have likened it rather to a prophetic blast from hell; it was the first of so much to go wrong. The heat was too much for the mosquitoes; they would not bite. It was too much for the parasites; the phagocytes were so stimulated that they "gobbled up" all free forms of plasmodia in twenty minutes.[7]

The heat was not, for the moment, too much for Ross, fresh on the job and armored against it with enthusiasm. But he minded it and would mind it increasingly. The difficulty of working in the relentless heat of India was among the constant refrains in his letters of the next four years. He railed against the heat as if it were in the end a personal enemy, one of many that maliciously or mindlessly made things as hard as possible for him.

Yet even while recounting frustrations he plotted new assaults on the problem that now obsessed him. He poured out his frustrations, his findings, his plans in his first letter home to Dr. Manson with an exuberance that catches one up even now:

Up to date I have failed to get a single mosquito to lay hold, which I think is because I have had to catch them. I am now breeding numbers and have a net ready for use . . . Four cases in my hospital have hitherto given negative results; but I am at present engaged in looking at the parasite rather than for it. I am delighted and surprised at numbers of cases and ease with which they can be found. My microscope is invaluable . . . When present, the parasites generally swarm—1 or 2 in three fields about [fields of the microscope, i.e., that portion of the specimen to be seen through the eyepiece at any one given setting of the instrument]. Today however the two cases in my hospital show not a trace of any, but I am off to them again after sundown . . . Evidently the laws of these sudden appearances and disappearances must be made out if possible. All the cases are beautiful! and I am wild with excitement; but these mosquitoes! They *will not* bite. I tried them on myself for experiment, but having been caught they are frightened I suppose. I expect a crop of new ones in one of my bottles this evening and hope a fever case will show itself to suit . . . I am touting round the country for cases . . .

2ᵈ May. All my mosquito grubs [larvae] have been killed owing to my foolishly putting the bottles in the sun. I have consequently started a new lot . . . I have had two more negative cases. Unfortunately the principal medical officer here seems to be putting me on every duty conceivable; but I shall go and look for cases at the civil hospital again tomorrow . . .

Please excuse the scrawl; and give my kind regards to Mrs. Manson and your son . . . Don't trouble about reply to my verbosity.

Manson of course replied. And so began a remarkable correspondence.[8] For four years Ross reported to Manson on average once a fortnight, more frequently when he was working mostly on malaria, less when he was stuck on other duty. He told Manson in meticulous detail everything he found and all the vicissitudes of his troubles with the Army. Manson offered advice, hypotheses, encouragement, reported on new scientific discoveries he had read about, described the various ways in which he tried constantly to push aside stones and open doors for Ross. It was an unusual relationship that took unusually constructive advantage of the special gifts of both men: Ross's wide-ranging curiosity coupled with indefatigable industry constantly led him into byways; Manson's flair for integrative theory, coupled with his remoteness from Ross's work bench, enabled him constantly to steer the investigation back to the main line. Hew to the main proof, he would say over and over, and leave the details to lesser men. In the end it was at least as much Ross's unflagging interest in masses of detail as Manson's grasp of the larger relevances that led to success. Both talents, and both men, were essential to the work.

Ross, as noted, began his research in the most direct way possible: He caught (and later raised) mosquitoes, fed them on patients whose blood was known to contain parasites, dissected the mosquitoes and looked for parasites in their stomachs. The first point to be settled was whether the mosquito stomach was fit habitat for plasmodia. Apparently straightforward, that question proved not easy to resolve with scientific precision.

Laveran had been able to identify the malarial germ as a living parasite because it continued not only to live in blood drawn from the body and smeared on a microscope slide but underwent development there, the crescents swelling into spheres and the spheres occasionally sprouting flagella. Ross discovered that blood taken from the mosquito's gut immediately after it had fed on a malarial patient displayed the same forms, which underwent the same evolution. But the processes were similarly short-lived. If the flagella emerged and broke loose, the sphere that gave them birth would shrivel and die. If the flagella failed to emerge, the sphere died anyway. As for the flagella, they swam off and disappeared. Essentially the same phenomena were seen in finger blood as in blood ingested by a mosquito. All one could certainly deduce was that nothing in the mosquito immediately damaged the parasites. But why should it? Before the digestive process began, the mosquito's stomach was little more than a container, no more to be expected actively to affect the blood than the specimen slide itself. The negative finding was not enough.

Ross began to look for signs that the parasite fared better inside the mosquito than on glass. He set up controls—a blood smear from a patient's finger, another from a mosquito's stomach—watched, timed and recorded the changes of the parasite in each. He did it again and again, worried lest he might prejudice the results by failing to prepare each specimen in an identical way.

He wrote Dr. Manson on 12 May 1895:

> Today, I have been at work on three mosquitoes. One had no parasites, by which I could see that he* had got into the net [sheltering the patient] after biting someone else outside (the moisture of the

---

* Ross knew that it was the female that sucked blood, but military man that he was he persisted in calling her "he."

net [which he had wet to encourage the mosquitoes' appetite in the hot dry weather] is attracting outside gentry). The other gave no more certain results, though I got him twenty minutes after biting and examined the blood pure. I have been trying control specimens on ice, too . . . I find both spherules and spent-crescents [crescents that had shriveled and died without turning into spheres] in different conditions of the same control specimen; which is irritating because I cannot satisfy myself as to cause. At last, this evening, however, my dull brain suggested the proper course—to try dry *smears*. I got a half-hour mosquito [half an hour after feeding] and smeared his blood with the needle on cover glass, inverted the same after drying in air and simply laid on slide . . . *Nothing but spherules.* A control finger blood made in same way, gave, of course, *all* crescents and no spherules; while a finger blood, which had been kept for two hours and was then opened and dried, gave *mostly crescents and a few spherules.*

This last experiment then seems to me to *prove* that the crescents undergo change into spherules in the stomach of the mosquito as outside; and to *suggest* that they do so faster than in control specimens . . .

The point of the experiment of course was to show that finger blood immediately dried to prevent development of the parasites outside the body would show—as it did—no spheres; whereas in blood that remained fluid a half hour outside the human body, but inside the mosquito's, the spheres *would* grow. As there were more of them after half an hour in the mosquito than after two hours in fluid state on a glass slide, it appeared the mosquito environment did not merely permit but actually encouraged their development.

After six months' more work, and examining more than a hundred mosquitoes in this way, he had to be content with that very tentative conclusion: In the first minutes of liberation from the human body the parasites appeared to feel so much more at home in the mosquito that nearly all of them rounded out to prepare themselves for the next stage, as compared to only about half on the laboratory slide.[9]

The next and, according to Laveran, ultimate stage was emergence of the flagellum. This is, microscopically speaking, a highly dramatic event not wholly understood to this day. The transformation begins with a mysterious agitation of the particles of black pigment within the spherical parasite. Here is how Ross observed the event in his "first perfect specimen" of mosquito blood:

About twenty minutes had elapsed since the mosquito had begun sucking; and the haemoglobin was of course much diffused. The blood swarmed with perfect spherules, not very large . . . but showing an almost eruptive movement of the pigment as if flagella were about to burst forth in a moment. [But] I looked in vain for flagellated organisms; not one was to be seen to my surprise. In a very few minutes the pigment-oscillation (the intensity of which was much greater than in the control specimens) began to quiet down. Many of the spheres were *shaking,* but, as I have said, not one was flagellate . . .

Next day [18 May 1895] I began with a finger-blood specimen . . . Then I made two more liquid mosquito specimens at about ½ an hour, my 18th and 19th mosquitoes [of a batch raised from larvae].

Up to date I had observed only two flagellate bodies, both in finger blood. I was astonished I did not meet more. Always the spheres seemed ripe for flagella, but they did not come (temperature of air 95° F.). Now, directly I looked at mosquito 18 I saw flagellate organisms in every field [of the microscope]. I saw nine altogether in a few minutes, but instead of counting them I wasted my time looking at them. Two fields held two each and I could have found numbers, I do not doubt, if I had looked at once over the specimen. As it was the spectacle afforded by mosquito 18 was amazing. All the spherules seemed bursting with excitement and exceedingly numerous. In contiguous fields I noted [an average of 10 to a field] . . . But when I came to examine special fields I found,

Sixty parasites in one field.

Seventy-two in the next! all swarming and ready to burst. I think you will confess that no one has had such an experience as this in finger-blood. On looking through mosquito 19 I found the same swarms of spheres, but no flagellate organisms. I lit a cheroot, went home (though it was only 12 noon) and slept for three hours; the spectacle of flagella had ceased after about 10 minutes.

Next day [at] 11.50 I made specimen of a fresh mosquito (21) at ½ an hour, with a presentiment of what I was going to see . . .

Flagellate organisms everywhere; one or two in every field. I must have seen 30 or 40 though I examined only a few fields, being hardly able to tear myself away from individual organisms. The flagella were excessively fine, quite invisible in open spaces and seen in haemoglobinous serum and clot; but the flagellate organisms were unmistakable because they were being dragged about all over the field generally, or were quivering and being shaken as a dog shakes a rat. The manifestation nearly ceased in a few minutes . . .[10]

After that excitement, as moving to the poet as to the scientist, he became all scientist and following a day's rest put to himself some hard questions:

1. Are all the masses of pigment met with *spent* spherules or merely broken ones? [Not, as it developed, an important question.] 2. Why do spherules often seem to become spent after a little, *without* the escape of flagella? [Very important because it was a clue to what the flagella really were.] 3. How is it that I have never been able to observe a swarming spherule become flagellate, all flagellate organisms seen by me having been so when I came upon them? [Merely the luck of the draw apparently.] 4. Is the greater number of parasites in mosquito only apparent? [Yes and no; there *are* likely to be greater numbers by volume in the mosquito but only because she concentrates the blood by extracting serum in the process both of sucking and digestion.]

The fact that only some spheres put forth flagella continued to worry him. If Manson and Laveran were right and the flagella represented the mature form of the parasite, why did such a large proportion fail to mature? As there seemed no way at the moment to put that question to experimental test, Ross returned to the main trail. "Tomorrow [30 May]," he wrote Manson, "I begin the second step—watching the flagella. Please send me advice."

Manson had two kinds of advice: one political, the other scientific. He was caught up in Ross's quest almost as if it were going on in his own laboratory. When in June the mail boat from India brought no letter from Ross:

I was terribly disappointed for I thought you had fallen sick, or that you had got a check, or that you had given up the quest. Above everything don't give it up. Look on it as a Holy Grail and yourself as Sir Galahad, for be assured you are on the right track. The malaria germ does not go into the mosquito for nothing, for fun or for the confusion of the pathologist. It has no notion of a practical joke. It is there for a purpose and that purpose depend upon it is its own interests—germs are selfish brutes.

But before pushing on, Ross should systematize his findings so far and publish to establish his position as a serious researcher. Manson suggested therefore the preparation of a series of slides to show the development of the parasite in mosquito blood. If Ross would send a set to London, then at the July meeting of the British Medical Association, "armed with a series of such preparations I could speak with an authority of your work which could not be controverted and you may be sure I will give you a good shove and help you so far as I can to get the ear of the authorities in India who may be in a position to forward your investigations."*

For his scientific counsel Manson drew chiefly on his experience with filariae, into which the myth of the short abstemious life of the mother mosquito seemed now inextricably woven. Though in sum he merely advised Ross to look for the mature parasite wherever it might be, he tended to draw Ross's attention most urgently to those exit points by which the parasite might escape from the mosquito into water. Examine the dung, and the eggs before and after they are deposited, "for I have an idea that the beast gets into them and so into the larva and becomes more or less a permanent parasite not only in the individual mosquito that sucked him in but in the progeny of this mosquito." Make an artificial marsh in which mosquitoes may breed and die, let it dry up, pulverize it, then have someone breathe the dust or drink it in water solution. "Dulce et decorum est pro patria mori," he added. "But don't do it yourself."

But since the plasmodia, of course like the filariae, spent time inside the mosquito, "I should keep mosquitoes to maturity," he wrote, "and tease them up in salt solution and examine their tissues one by one searching inside all cells for something like the plasmodium. I question if he will be pigmented but I am fairly sure that he is intercellular. This too will be a long and difficult task. But it is not without hope."

Ross said he would do it but didn't Manson "think that the flagella ought first to be found free in the stomach? Staining etc. must be tried. As soon as this is done I shall go on to follow your advice exactly about the tissues." That was quite reasonable on the assumption both Ross and Manson made, following Laveran, that the crescent and spherical forms were in fact cysts, rather like seed coverings into which the parasite gathered its protoplasm preparatory for its journey from the human body to the outside.[11] Exflagellation then became explicable as the process by which

---

* Ross omits these passages from his quotation of Manson's letter in the *Memoirs* (p. 154), leaving the clear implication that Manson wanted the specimen slides for his own purposes. It is a sad reminder that Ross wrote the *Memoirs* long after he had broken completely with Manson because he believed his old friend and mentor had robbed him of due credit for his work.

the parasite in a sense was born again out of that cyst or seed capsule, taking shape, in Manson's terms, as a flagellated spore. One difficulty in either proving or disproving that notion was that the tiny, almost transparent flagellum was clearly visible only when in violent motion, and by the methods Ross was using it was unstainable: [12]

I said I was going to watch free flagella [he wrote a week after getting Manson's advice]. With my usual luck I found a beauty in my very first specimen and watched it for three solid hours exactly, without taking my eye off him . . . What he did you will think interesting.

He riggled [sic] around for 20 minutes like a trypanosoma, so that I could hardly follow him. Then he brought up against a phagocyte and remained so long that I thought the phagocyte had got hold of him. Not a bit; he was not killed or sucked in; but kept poking him in the ribs in different parts of the body. I was astonished; and so, apparently, was the phagocyte. He kept at this for about ¼ of an hour, and then went away across two fields and went straight at another phagocyte! He pushed into this in several places with one end for a long time; and the phagocyte seemed to rear up and try to get round him, but could not. At last the phagocyte seemed to give up and flattened itself against an air-bubble, the flagellum still poking away at him. After 50 minutes . . . movement became much slower and I thought the animal was dying[13]—when a very curious thing happened; a third phagocyte came at him with mouth open right and straight across the field, but had no sooner got near him when the flagellum left his fallen foe and attacked the new one, holding on and shaking like a snake on a dog. In one minute the third phagocyte turned sharp round and ran off howling!!!—I assure you. I won't swear I heard him howling, but I *saw* him howling. He went right across a whole field, the flagellum holding on to his tail . . . This continued for five minutes, the poor phagocyte literally *legging it,* after which the flagellum left him and went away. By this time the beast had become more visible and had a large swelling in the middle. I watched him steadily, and his movements gradually became slower . . . At last this swelling moved to one end nearly of the beast and became very large and distinct, until after three hours the creature evidently died—at any rate, curled up and ceased to move. Isn't this interesting? I think it shows, first that the phagocytes have no more power over free flagella than over trypanosomes; secondly the beast was evidently attacking the phagocytes, probably mistaking them for some other kind of cell—so I judge by its leaving the phagocytes after a time.

He did not know what it all meant but it had been a great show. "The spectacle of the first mosquito, [in which he had found an unusual abundance of free flagella] was really wonderful," he wrote. "I shall dream of it. Good night. So was the fight between the flagellum and the three phagocytes. I shall write a novel on it in the style of 'The Three Musketeers.' "[14]

Splendid material for romance, but what was he to make of it for science?* The vision of the Three Musketeers was followed by "5 days of severe work up against a brick wall"—the brick wall being the inexplicable behavior of the flagella which so rapidly disappeared. What to do? Grasping at straws, he tried a flea on one accommodating patient, quite without results—no flagella at all—and a bug (bedbug?) that refused to bite. Then he changed tack.

Manson had suggested exhaustively searching the tissues of adult mosquitoes for something that looked like a plasmodium. Ross decided he would do that but he was not sure the animal he sought would in fact look like a plasmodium. After metamorphosis, he thought, it might take unexpected forms. So he determined to seek out all the parasites in the mosquito's body and by various tests see if they might be one stage in the development of flagella.

It was a singularly courageous step into the dark, taken because there seemed no other way to go. As he later remarked, he cast aside all guidance. Instead of working from the known to the unknown, he went off in search of anything he could find anywhere he could find it.

---

* Manson's Goulstonian Lectures (Manson 1896a) before the Royal College of Physicians in London, in which he developed his mosquito theory at full length, cited Ross's observations as further evidence that the flagellum was the mature form of the parasite seeking to enter a cell.

6 / Diversions

From March when he arrived in Secunderabad through the summer and autumn of 1895, Ross had good if not ideal working conditions considering the isolation and backwardness of medicine in India and the almost total lack of research facilities. At least he had leisure and malarial patients, which is to say he had just about all that the Indian Medical Service could give him. He lived as a bachelor with two fellow officers, both of whom he thought "first-rate fellows," in a bungalow near the regimental grounds, and not far from the Secunderabad Club. Without family responsibilities, he had time enough, despite his research, to play golf and tennis. He says he would have kept ponies as well except that he expected from one week to the next to be transferred and put on a special research assignment.[1] The routine medical duties of his post probably demanded scarcely an hour a day.

He not only expected transfer; he began three weeks after his arrival in Secunderabad to stump for it with his usual directness and energy. He wrote to General Sibthorpe, surgeon general of the Madras command (one of three, it will be recalled, into which the British Army in India and the Indian Medical Services were then split) to ask the general "if you see the opportunity" to "make use of my services" in a special investigation of malaria "from the microscopical point of view." He tried a little pressure: "I have been studying the subject for years and have lately, during furlough, sat at the feet of Patrick Manson, who is very keen on such official investigations being made."

If General Sibthorpe received the letter* he could not have been pleased at being so importuned by a major he did not know. He was certainly much displeased a month or so later to learn that Ross had written to his secretary requesting transfer to the Civil Department and wondering if the general would be "willing to apply for my services." The general would not. He sent the letter to the principal medical officer of the Madras command with endorsement: "Ross does not appear to be aware of the regulations governing such applications." The PMO Madras forwarded it to the PMO of the S&B District "for favour in calling upon Surg. Major Ross to explain why he failed to adopt the procedures laid down in para. 28 AR I Vol V." All of which was officialese for hot water into which Ross had foolishly fallen. "A very nasty letter," Ross commented, "which knocked me over."

Ross had shown himself a channels-jumper, special anathema to the military mind which sees clearly that hierarchy is the essence of the system and that whoever does not respect it is both dangerous and unworthy. The incident was not mentioned again but Ross's subsequent difficulties suggest that it was not forgotten.

Ross's work at this time did not suffer. It is in fact not easy to see what line of research he would have taken had he been put on special assignment. Having deduced all he could from comparing finger-blood and mosquito-blood samples, totally frustrated in his efforts to "follow the flagella," he was now floundering, as he all but admitted to Manson. Worse—he had picked up a false scent. Obedient to Manson's thesis of water transmission, Ross found some native volunteers and began dosing them with "mosquito water," a brew whose recipe he provided in his letter. "Dear Dr. Manson," he wrote on 5 June:

> I am in a state of great excitement and have no time to write you a full letter this week as the post goes out today. One of my "certain experiments" which I mentioned has come off.
>
> On 17 May I took four full mosquitoes from the crescent case, Abdul Kadir, and put two in one bottle and two in another with a little water. They were kept in a cool place until 25th when they were found dead on the surface of the water. In one of the bottles very small mosquito grubs were found, showing that the mosquitoes' eggs had been hatched. The contents of this bottle, minus the dead bodies of the mosquitoes, was given to a native, Lutchman, on 25th at 8.0

---

* The copy in the Ross Archives is undated and lacks a salutation; it is identified in Ross's handwriting as written to Sibthorpe but with no indication whether it is a draft or copy of an original actually dispatched.

a.m. on payment, after full explanation of the nature of the experiment. The contents of the other bottle was given to another native in a similar way. I think myself justified in making this experiment because of the vast importance a positive result would have and because I have a specific in quinine always at hand.

Lutchman is 20 years old, a healthy looking young fellow who *says* that he has never had fever. Yesterday [June 4] he was all right. This morning at 8 a.m. (exactly 11 days from drinking the water) he came to the hospital-assistant complaining of head-ache. Tem. 99.8. Looking ill. Temperature has been taken every half hour and rose to 101.4 at noon, since when (1.30) it has been declining. This looks very promising. Incubation [period] agreed closely with former experiments. The type ought to be either quotidian or summer tertian according to Marchiafava . . . Three [blood] specimens carefully examined give no results; but such are not yet to be expected . . . Chances are greatly against accidental fever, because out of the whole regiment I am getting only 3 or 4 cases weekly . . . A third man drank mosquito water on 31 May . . .

Lutchman's fever lasted three days. Ross could find no parasites in his blood, or none that he could be sure of. There were some ambiguous ring forms. But he kept hoping for crescents.* Meanwhile, so eager was he to believe, that after reporting all his reservations he concluded nevertheless: "On the whole I think that this result [the three-day fever at just the proper interval from the presumed infection] occurring in my first case, is very encouraging." The other two men who had drunk the water remained obstinately healthy.

Manson was enthusiastic. He found Ross's letter written in the high excitement of the first day that Lutchman came down with fever "supremely interesting and, if the experiment you describe turns out to be something more than a mere coincidence, you may be congratulated on having clenched [sic] the whole matter of the role of mosquito as alternative host of the malaria parasite." The finding of crescent evolution in the mosquito had been interesting, but it did not prove the mosquito theory. "Your experiment on malariating a man with mosquito water does prove it if repeated experiment gives similar results."

Although repeated experiments never again did give similar results, the Lutchman case long lingered in the minds of both Ross and Manson. It

---

* Manson persuaded him that the ring forms were in fact parasites.

seemed to them, if not evidence, at least a sign; it was hard to believe that the man's fever had been mere coincidence after his drinking what had so long been thought such a dangerous brew. Neither Ross nor Manson retreated from the conviction that such waters could convey the disease.

In fact Ross was embarking on a new series of "malariating" experiments, using this time as the infective agent not dead mosquitoes but parasites he found in them that were then called psorosperms. They were cysts like tiny barleycorns that contained the spores of one-celled parasites of mosquitoes. In mosquito pupae he found long, sluglike gregarine parasites which he ascertained were the parents of the psorosperms, since he actually found psorosperms inside them. "So far as I have gone," he wrote Manson in a letter in which he appeared eager to convince himself that he was on the right track, "the gregarines live in the pupae, the psorosperms in the mosquitoes. They seem to be hard encysted little bodies capable of enduring much rough usage, and may be discharged either in the faeces or when the insect dies and breaks up."*

He went on to argue that if the mosquito was an alternative host for the malaria parasite, then it must be capable of living in the insect without recourse to man. Malaria, in short, must be a disease of mosquitoes; "the germ must take only an excursion into men for change of scene and refreshment, so to speak." Possibly it got into man almost by accident as when he drank from *"isolated pots of drinking water"* in which the psorosperms lurked. That would account for the spotty distribution of the disease which unlike plague struck only a few individuals at a time even in malarious regions. He continued plying volunteers with psorosperm water. In one trial two of three developed slight fevers in four to six days. Even though he found no parasites in the men's blood he concluded, "I think that the psorosperms bring on some reaction, *probably malarial*. The cases strike me as malarial, [the absence of parasites being] due to *insufficient doses*."

Manson felt it necessary at last to write somewhat more sharply that the psorosperms were interesting but "don't quit the thread. Follow up the flagellum." After seeing Ross's stained preparations of the gregarines, he was more than ever sure they had nothing to do with malaria. They were too big and they spent too much of their time in a free state.[2] Ross never debated the point. Nor did he abandon psorosperms though he did devote

---

* Ross's gregarines belong to a protozoan order that is parasitic in the digestive tract or body cavity of insects and other arthropods. It is never found in vertebrates.

less attention to them and reported even his more hopeful experiments in low key.

On 8 September 1895 Ross was suddenly ordered to Bangalore, a British enclave within the independent state of Mysore in South India. Bangalore, periodically swept by cholera, was experiencing a fresh outbreak. The British residency surgeon, Lieutenant Colonel A. F. Dobson, an old friend of Ross's, had persuaded the Resident (the chief British civil service administrative officer) to bring in Ross to help clean up the native quarters which had repeatedly been seed ground for epidemics. Ross thought he had been chosen because of his almost unique possession of a diploma in public health. It seems more likely that Dobson saw the need for an autocrat and a Hercules and reached for the man he knew who most nearly fitted that role, above all in taste and talent for command, and a capacity for hard work.

Without question Dobson got the right man. As if he had been sent to the front, Ross established headquarters in a tent that he had pitched in the grounds of the posh West End Hotel. There he proceeded to organize his army: consisting of one clerk, several sanitary inspectors, and lots of "peons" for the cleanup squads. A carriage was at his disposal night and day and he appears to have used it night and day. Inside of forty-eight hours he had drawn up, in his own words, "an ultimatum" to the Bangalore municipality, listing sanitary deficiencies they had to repair at once. He followed with many more manifestoes "while every hour I rushed off to see the cases of cholera scattered over the station. Within five weeks I sent the Resident six emergency reports and extracted 5,000 rupees from the Municipality for the necessary work!"

Ross as sanitary czar of Bangalore was so clearly in his element, it seems surprising that he and everyone else had so long neglected the talent for command that underlay his success. Now, at least, both he and his friend Dobson recognized the happy fit between man and job. Dobson, due for home leave, recommended that Ross take over his post as acting residency surgeon, and the recommendation was accepted. Ross was delighted even though it meant a serious setback for his malarial work.

Bangalore, where he had been posted for a time just before his marriage, was one of the pleasantest cities in India for a British expatriate. It had a large British colony, military and civilian, and a lively social life. There were hills nearby where one could escape the worst of the heat. Not least attractive for IMS officers, it was a civil post that carried extra pay and an opportunity for private practice. Ross sent for his wife and three children to come out from England. They arrived with the children's nurse in No-

The London School of Hygiene and Tropical Medicine
Major and Mrs. Ross (center) at the Banjalore Bicycle Club, 1896

vember. Ross settled in for an assured stay of something over a year at least. He hoped it would last much longer.

As acting residency surgeon he undertook to carry out his own sanitary recommendations. The task was Augean. Houses in the native quarters lacked even primitive toilets. The streets were open sewers. Ross worked out a pattern of drains to mitigate the nuisance. He ordered the daily collection of excrement for which he imposed a small tax on the householders. That caused great resentment; not only had they never paid before but they were accustomed to making a little money by accumulating their wastes for a week or more and then selling them to contractors who peddled them as fertilizer. Ross persisted. Almost daily he made rounds of the slums like a doctor perambulating the wards. Determined to master the situation by knowing every detail himself, he even accompanied the scavengers on their dawn collections. He was ingenious and tireless in devising remedies. The grumbling of his patients did not bother him. He enjoyed a good fight. In the midst of the ruckus over his scavenging tax, he broke off a letter to Manson to work on his *"speech* for tomorrow. I have imposed a scavenging tax," he told Manson, "on the public here, who are howling in the press, we expect a row at the municipal meeting tomorrow. I'm going to give it them." He kept the letter open and next day added: "Gave it them with great success. Tax passed [;] my services applied for six months from date."

But his best efforts could not cleanse Bangalore in a year nor banish the cholera. A new epidemic struck the city in the summer of 1896. Twice checked by the closing of certain public wells, it took hold again in August, as he recalled in his *Memoirs,*

> in the worst parts of the town called North Blackpully and the East General Bazaar—areas swarming with slums and containing about 20,000 of the poorest people. There were 582 wells here within a space of about one-quarter of a mile square, most of them within private tenements where we could not easily touch them owing to "caste prejudices"—that is gross superstitions.
>
> We did what we could. We closed the wells in batches; we disinfected them over and over again; we told the people to boil their drinking water and provided it ourselves; we gave them hot coffee and medicine early in the morning; we disinfected backyards, drains, and rooms occupied by the dying. All in vain. The Angel of Death had descended amongst them and smote the poor wretches right and left. They died within twelve hours. Secondary cases [directly infected by the ill] were numerous; where a child died today, the mother or father would be dead to-morrow. The people, usually so patient and good, were stricken with terror, cried to their gods, formed processions, and glared at those who tried to help them; and the heavy rain washed the reeking filth of the streets and latrines into the shallow poison-pools they called wells.
>
> It was a dreadful time . . . Then suddenly, as usual after about a month, the pestilence cleared and vanished like an evil thunder-storm. But 219 cases were reported during that time, of which about 150 died; and probably very many of the cases and deaths were not reported at all in the final rush and terror.

It does not seem a heavy death toll. But as usual in pestilence, terror outran death; British doctors in India, like sanitarians in England, were particularly impressed with cholera because it was so clearly the viper that nested in filth, so horrible in its own manifestations, so easy in theory, so difficult in practice to wipe clean from the earth:

> Great is Sanitation [Ross wrote in 1923 with the splendid Victorian vision still bright in his mind], the greatest work, except discovery, I think, that a man can do . . . What is the use of preaching

high moralities, philosophies, policies, and arts to people who dwell in . . . appalling slums . . . ? Your job, Sanitarian, is plain! You must wipe away those slums, that filth, these diseases . . . We shall reach the higher civilization, not by any of the politicians' shibboleths, methods of government, manners of voting, liberty, self-determination, and the rest, all of which have failed—but first by the scientific ordering of cities until they are fit for men of the higher civilization to dwell in. We must begin by being Cleansers.[3]

In 1896 there was some danger that Ross might be putting sanitation even ahead of discovery as his own greatest work. At least Manson feared so. When Ross wrote that he was working from 6.30 in the morning until midnight, and had practically no time for parasites, Manson merely commented shortly that he was sorry Ross was off malaria and on cholera. He worried lest someone else, particularly some foreigner, beat Ross to the tape. Now that his protégé, like the proverbial hare, had turned aside to clean sewers in Bangalore he saw the tortoises coming on. "Laveran," he wrote just after the bad news from Ross in September, "is inclined to take up the mosquito hypothesis and I have no doubt that by next summer the French and Italians will be working at it. So for goodness sake hurry up and save the laurels for old England."

It was about this time that Ross opened a correspondence with Laveran, enclosing a paper on the crescent–sphere–flagella transformation, which he had read to the South Indian Branch of the British Medical Association a week before Christmas. Aware that Laveran "long ago had conjectured" that mosquitoes might transmit malaria, Ross was "happy to believe that the discoverer of the parasite was also the first to guess the mode of infection." But he was careful to note that his own work had been stimulated by Manson, who had arrived "at the same theory." Laveran was gracious and encouraging—the first professional besides Manson to appreciate his work. The rapid transformation of the crescent had not before been described, Laveran wrote. "I urge you strongly to continue these researches, to examine with care a large number of mosquitoes collected in malarious places . . ." Then he might try giving malaria to man by the bite of the mosquito.

That the mosquito might transmit the parasite while biting seems, curiously, to have occurred to Ross as a serious possibility only a few weeks before he got Laveran's letter. He published the conjecture in February 1896, citing it as an alternative mode of transmission to deposit the parasite in water or on the skin. Perhaps that last possibility conceived during his flirtation with psorosperms helped turn his attention to the mosquito's bite. For it was in the act of biting that he believed the psorosperms were released. In May 1896 he noted that mosquitoes, in feeding, injected saliva into the wound—clearly a possible route of entry for the parasite. "I shall experiment in this direction," he told Manson, "and shall also dissect the head." The historian is moved to shout across the years: "That's right; right on!" Yet Ross was still two years from his landfall in the new world.

7 / The Bite

Ross had gone on studying malaria in Bangalore as he found time and patients. But the old sense of urgency was missing. Effectively the work on malaria had such low priority that during the whole of 1896 Ross accomplished little more than to refine previous observations and confirm previous deductions. He did carry through some pretty experiments bearing on a tangential but nevertheless important question: as the crescent–sphere–flagella transformation never occurred until the parasite was outside the human body, it must somehow know when it is outside. How? Manson and others thought the clue was temperature.

Ross showed that temperature did not matter. The key stimulus he believed was the increased density of the blood as it lost moisture after being drawn out of the body. By keeping finger-blood samples away from the air with a vaseline seal he could prevent the evolution of spheres altogether and start it up as he wished simply by removing the seal. "The vaseline experiment," he told Manson, "is *immense.*" Delighted as much, it seems, by the elegance of the experiments as by the significance of the results,* he wrote a paper which he sent to Manson for submission to the *British Medical Journal.* In high spirits he saw himself on the verge of uncovering still more secrets.

---

* For the mosquito theory it did not really matter whether temperature or density was the trigger, since either could point to the mosquito as the predestined environment.

This time Manson was not impressed. He had just read a note in *The Lancet* reporting that exflagellation could be induced by *adding* water to the blood sample. He had tried it himself—once. It worked. Setting his single experiment against dozens that Ross had made under careful controls, Manson concluded Ross was grasping at another will-o'-the-wisp. He took it upon himself to hold up Ross's article.

Ross was not annoyed but grateful, and went back to his microscope. He had not seen the paper that Manson had read, partly because he did not take *The Lancet,* partly because Manson told him the author's name was "Walker" whereas in fact it was "Marshall."[1] But he could repeat the experiments. For good measure he got three other doctors to work with him. They found that a trace of water added to the blood sample permitted the familiar transformation, but did not speed up exflagellation. He tried it over and over, along with his vaseline experiments. "No," he concluded firmly at last, "I have not been mistaken . . . Exposure to air (abstraction of water) is *necessary* to transformation. This is a law." What Marshall and Manson had witnessed was a mechanical effect: The extra water caused the crescents to swell and burst their sheaths, but this apparent mechanical facilitation worked only *after* some exposure to air had increased the density of the blood. He would add a note to his journal article and then it should be published. That was done.[2]

It was a small step but a satisfying one—the sort of finding that carried esthetic appeal as well as intellectual conviction. Ross, as he announced, had discovered a law, a necessary condition governing observed phenomena, that could be neatly demonstrated and that fitted the known facts to that point. He was less happy in his efforts to test a much more critical hypothesis: that mosquitoes might transmit malaria by their bite.

All during the summer of 1896 he worked at it. In the Bangalore hospital he had a rare case of triple malaria, a patient whose blood contained the parasites of tertian, quartan and malignant fever, all three together. He had also a subject, Mr. Appia, the assistant surgeon, who was willing, eager, to be bitten in the cause. "I let loose on him," Ross wrote, "18 mosquitoes fed 3 days previously and 6 mosquitoes fed the previous day." Four days later Mr. Appia lay in a net with fifteen of the mosquitoes that had bitten him before, along with five others that had been fed two days previously. The assistant surgeon was loyally determined to get the fever, if he could. But for all his patience and courage, he could not. Two other volunteers similarly failed.

The failure was not of course conclusive—an old scientific adage says you cannot prove a negative—and it was less discouraging than it might have been, for it gave Ross a chance to join a controversy, a chance he always relished.

The controversy he joined was in progress that summer between Dr. Manson and the Italian, Amico Bignami. Manson in March had worked out his mosquito theory in a series of lectures (the Goulstonian) that were published in the *British Medical Journal*. Bignami read these and immediately sprang to the attack with a mosquito theory of his own, which appeared in July.*

Bignami's central contention was that the mosquito passed on the parasite in its feeding, not in its dying. As evidence he put special store by the old inoculation experiments, mostly done by Italians, which since 1886 had shown that transfusions of infected blood reproduced the disease in healthy persons. Of course they should. A creature residing in the blood ought to pass with that blood into a fresh victim. And what more simple and direct way could be imagined for the parasite to get into the blood than by a needle penetrating blood vessels? Bignami reasoned that the mosquito's proboscis could also function as such a needle, giving the parasite a much more direct means of entry than by detour, as Manson would have it, via lung or gut. The supposition was plausible and was made more so by recent discoveries in America that a cattle parasite, similar to plasmodia and cause of a fever similar to malaria, traveled from beast to beast by the bite of the tick.[4]

The classic work of Theobald Smith and F. L. Kilbourne on Texas or Southern fever, published in 1893, was indeed impressive, as much for the ingenious experimental design by which the authors reached their conclusions as for their revelation of one of nature's more ingenious patterns of survival. In 1889 Smith and Kilbourne found the cause of Texas fever— a protozoan parasite that like *Plasmodium* lives inside the red corpuscles, consumes the haemoglobin, divides and bursts out, to renew its cycle in fresh corpuscles.† As in malaria the outstanding symptoms that occur as the red cells are progressively destroyed are periodic high fevers and gross anaemia. Smith and Kilbourne suspected that the parasite was carried by ticks, which had long been believed by ranchers to cause the disease. In the next three years they set up experiments to test every permutation of

---

* It was promptly translated and printed in *The Lancet* for November.[3]

† They discovered the parasite in 1889 and named it *Pyrosoma bigeminum* ("pyrosoma" because it was pyriform or club-shaped, and "bigeminum" because it normally was found two to a cell). Actually a Romanian scientist, V. Babeš, a little earlier (1888) working on a fever of oxen had discovered the same organism.[5] Smith and Kilbourne studying Babeš' reports concluded that the diseases were the same and the parasite probably very similar if not identical. The organism has since been assigned to the genus *Babesia*.

possible contagious conditions: infected cattle with ticks and without ticks, ticks alone, fields with ticks but without cattle, fields without ticks. What they found was both astonishing and unarguable.

Since ticks normally spend their lives on a single animal, the Texas fever parasite could not be carried directly to a fresh host; it has had to develop a remarkable technique of passage through the eggs of the female into the next generation. The engorged female drops from an infected beast and lays infected eggs on the ground, where they then develop into infected young ticks. These climb aboard grazing animals—at once if they can, three or four months later if necessary—and, when they bite, pass on their inherited protozoa.

The fact that ticks are not at all like mosquitoes—they are not even insects, but eight-legged arachnids—except in the single respect that both suck blood seemed to zero in on the bite as the avenue of contagion. Thinking along these lines Bignami was one of the first scientists to note and take seriously an anecdote long current, that General Gordon had avoided malaria in the Sudan by conscientiously sleeping under mosquito netting.[6] On the other hand he thought the weight of the evidence was against Manson's notion that the parasite in encysted form passed ultimately through air or water into man. If that happened one would expect malaria to behave like other epidemic diseases, sweeping up its victims wholesale wherever people breathed a common malarial air or drank a common malarial water. In fact the fever was notably selective.

With one final argument against the Manson theory, Bignami strikingly revealed the direction of his thought. If Manson were right, he reasoned, a person suffering from malaria would be able to introduce the disease into any previously healthy place in which there were mosquitoes. We know now that they can, but Bignami could find no record of any such introduction. Therefore, he concluded, man did not pass the parasite to mosquitoes. What is most interesting in this analysis is that in criticizing Manson for a hypothesis that made man a carrier he set up in opposition a hypothesis that made the mosquito the carrier. The adversaries thus divided a circle in half and debated which half more nearly resembled the whole. They did so because both accepted the traditional view that the malarial germ belonged by nature in the environment. Bignami was chiefly interested in how it got from the environment into the human blood. Manson was chiefly interested in how it got out and back where it belonged. For Bignami the mosquito was an inoculating syringe; for Manson she was a pipette and transport system. Neither perceived that her proboscis might be, as in fact it is, a two-way passage, both entrance and exit.

Laveran, it will be recalled, had first become convinced that the pigmented forms peculiar to malarial blood were living organisms when under his microscope he saw one of them put out flagella. For him exflagellation thereafter remained the primary revelation and he came to explain it as the emergence of the true parasite from the cyst in which it had endured inside the human blood stream. Manson, as we have seen, readily accepted that interpretation in the main because it seemed to fit the model he had already worked out of the life cycle of the filaria.

But the Italians were conditioned from the beginning to look for other models. Ever since Marchiafava and Celli had seen the amoeboid form in whose peripheral writhings they found *their* revelation, Italian research gave primary emphasis to those. Italian observers rarely witnessed exflagellation and therefore considered it exceptional. Once they had ascertained that it only occurred some minutes after the blood had been drawn, some (most notably Bignami himself and Professor Grassi) concluded that this must be one way the parasite died. The lashing about, the detachment of threads of protoplasm and the consequent collapse of the sphere they explained as agonistic forms.

It was a scarcely tenable theory. Since countless parasites visibly died without any such contortions and since the phenomenon of exflagellation was most impressive just for its extraordinary liveliness, the agonistic view never fitted even the observed facts. Would it then have been maintained with such tenacity had it not seemed the most plausible alternative to the opinion of Laveran? In any event, their views of flagella reinforced the Italians in their emphasis on the life of the parasite in the blood, making them naturally more curious about how it entered the red corpuscle to live its most vital days than how it got out.

Some time in the late autumn of 1896 Ross heard about the Bignami article, presumably from a scientific news item. He was angry. He knew that Bignami was attacking Manson; he suspected that the Italian was trying to appropriate the mosquito theory, spreading "his six legs over your nest and calling it all his own." Ross decided to make use of the otherwise sad obligation to report failure in his biting experiments to cut down Bignami's pretensions. And he did so in a paper delivered at the end of October.* It would have been like Ross to try utterly to demolish his Italian rival and the bite hypothesis. But he had by now become too imbued with the real complexities of what he was investigating to lay about

---

* He hadn't then read Bignami. Manson enclosed a translation with his letter of 12 October, which must have reached Ross only a few days later. Ross's remark in his *Memoirs* that the Bignami article came from Manson as a bombshell seems exaggerated.

him in the old confident way. He ended his paper with the admission that his experiments might not mean much because the mosquito he used, a large brindled one, "may not be the one in which the malaria parasite is capable of thriving."[7]

So the theory of transmission by bite did not go out the window with Bignami, and Ross's saving speculation had once more brought him to the inner door to the treasure. Actually he had been there at Manson's suggestion—but without the key. Little as Manson knew about mosquitoes, it had occurred to him almost a year and a half earlier that the parasite might not develop in just any old mosquito. He wrote to Ross: "Another hint I would give you. Send specimens of the mosquito for identification of species. Possibly different species of mosquito modify the malaria germ; that the differing degrees of virulence depend on the difference of species of mosquito that has served as alternative host to the parasite."

Ross did all his early experiments with mosquitoes of two genera, *Aedes* and *Culex*. He referred to the former as "brindled"; it appears to have included two species, one of which was *Aedes aegypti*. The Culex mosquitoes were mostly *Culex fatigans* which he called "grey" or "bar-backed." Both mosquitoes are in fact a menace to man: *Aedes aegypti* is the chief vector in Africa and the Americas of yellow fever; *Culex fatigans* transmits the filarial worm as well as viruses of encephalitis. But neither can host the parasite of human malaria.*

Ross had begun strongly to suspect as much toward the end of his duty in Bangalore. In February 1897 he was making plans to seek out new varieties to experiment with. This he thought he might do on a brief leave which he would spend in "the most malarious spot known" in India. He was expecting Dr. Dobson's return from England at the end of the month. Ross's appointment as acting resident surgeon would then end. Ross still hoped, however, that it would be made permanent.

It was not. Dobson reclaimed his job and Ross was out of work. For the first time in his long campaign to get himself assigned to special research duty, he had a chance to put in his bid at official request: The Government of India wired asking what they could do for him. Ross of course replied, "Put me on malarial investigation." He might have left it at that or sent

---

* *Aedes aegypti* has had several names, most common of which were *Stegomyia fasciata* or *calopus*. (*Stegomyia* is now considered a subgenus of *Aedes* but is sometimes retained in the name as *Aedes* [*Stegomyia*] *aegypti*.) *Culex fatigans* is now generally called *Culex pipiens fatigans* and considered a subspecies of the mosquito whose type subspecies, *Culex pipiens pipiens*, is perhaps the commonest of the twilight and night buzzers and biters all too familiar to inhabitants of temperate Europe and North America.

along some of his scientific papers to support his qualifications. But he could not resist a touch of belligerence. He enclosed with his letter a copy of an editorial Manson had written for the *British Medical Journal,* entitled "A Neglected Responsibility of Empire."[8] In it Manson scolded British authorities in India for not pushing the study of malaria and not making suitable use of the talents of Ronald Ross. "So they have it plump," Ross wrote to Manson, "and if they refuse I shall be so disgusted that I shall not care to serve much longer." He would have his assignment by right and not by favor, or he would not have it at all.

Whatever the government might decide—and they would take their time about it—he had to leave Bangalore. He did not complain but was wistful at the end of an especially happy time, happy despite—or perhaps in part because of—the strain of his duties as he had defined them unsparingly for himself. At one point, he had been driven literally to exhaustion and forced to seek a five-day respite in the hills. But now on the eve of departure he took the greatest satisfaction in reviewing his year and a half in battle against the guardians of filth and the apostles of sloth. "It has been a regular campaign for me. I have defeated them in a score of pitched battles!"

That was the best part. But life in Bangalore in other ways had charms when there was time to enjoy them. Notwithstanding all his furious campaigning he had some time—for the club and an occasional game of golf, for friends and home life with his wife and children. At first the Ross family lived at the West End Hotel, but after Dobson left for England they moved with Nanny into his house.

Ross enjoyed having the children with him. Had he stayed he might have kept them. "One can help ones children here," he wrote, "almost as well as in England." All in all he thought he had one of the best appointments open to a medical officer in India, in "perhaps the best station in the country" and "the best climate." These were all "serious matters to a man with a family."

Probably they were at least as serious for his wife, who Ross suggested was not strong and dreaded separations. They had been separated a lot, often because Ross insisted on her going to the hills in the worst of the hot weather. Even when together, they had led an unsettled life; Ross had changed station every two or three years since he joined the service. As often as not they had lived in hotels or briefly in borrowed houses. She would have liked to settle in Bangalore. Ross, had he been able to stay on planned to hire some assistants and set up a laboratory to continue his malaria research. He dreamed of arranging with the authorities so that half his time might be devoted to such research. It would have been a more gentlemanly life; it might have been a productive one. Yet it might also have appeased Ross's demons making the great malaria investigation no longer seem to him his one big chance, desperately to be pursued and snatched from an otherwise hostile world. What is certain is that in leaving Bangalore on 27 March 1897 he resumed his quest in earnest; and soon his demons were starved and howling.

8 / Dapple-wing

Sigur Ghat, a valley of coffee plantations, may not have been the most malarious spot in India, but it would do. Besides a notorious incidence of fever, it offered other advantages for research. British planters had a material business interest in Ross's work. Since tea and coffee grew for the most part in well-watered, fertile areas that were also prime mosquito habitat, malaria continually raided their work force. Ross would be welcome at Sigur Ghat. The place, moreover, was only a half hour's bicycle ride from Ootacamund, to which Ross sent his wife and children even before he himself left Bangalore. "Ooty" was "a bit of England" in the round Nilghiri Hills—a landscape of downs and eucalyptus trees, 8,000 feet above sea level and quite free of malaria. They rented a cottage. There Ross could first take a three-week holiday and then use it as a base for his work.

While momentarily expecting assignment to a special malaria investigation, Ross applied for and was granted two months' privilege leave. He got his equipment together, picked two servants (one of whom was the Lutchman who had been made sick by mosquito water), climbed on his bicycle and set out to find the mosquito that carries malaria. He actually left Ooty at 4 p.m. by bicycle on Thursday, 22 April 1897, headed for Kalhutti which was a three-mile pony ride from the top of the Sigur Ghat canyon and about halfway down. At Kalhutti he dined with two planters, Nash and Kindersley, and spent the night in the guest bungalow. He was encouraged to note that the butler attending that bungalow had the fever.[1]

The next morning he rode with Kindersley to the bottom of the canyon and thence four miles across a spur into another valley where Kindersley had his estate, "Westbury." The ground there was under irrigation, the coffee plants just beginning to flower. The air was "teeming with heat and moisture." Ross walked around for an hour and a half looking for grubs. He found none, yet the place was certainly feverish. In the blood of the young son of a servant he found many parasites of the malignant variety. Another had an enlarged spleen. After lunch he found parasites in the blood of another servant, one of four more he examined.

On Saturday he took samples of water from the pool from which the workers at Westbury drank. He found the water full of green "flagellulae," "just the size and shape of mosquito gregarines." No mosquito larvae. All Sunday morning he searched for "grubs" without luck. In the evening he went to spend the night at Nash's plantation.

At eight that evening he felt pains in his liver. At eight-thirty he was seized with chills. By twelve he was delirious with high fever. The fever lasted two hours then broke and allowed him to sleep. The next morning he felt well, but on examining his own blood he found the telltale "amoebulae" of *Plasmodium.*

How baffling malaria can be, Dr. Ross was now to rediscover from his own case. The most obvious fact was that he had come within the last four days from Ootacamund, where malaria was unknown, to a highly malarious valley and suddenly contracted the fever. Dr. Ross dosed himself heavily with quinine, and brought his fever under control. Ross the investigator made some trial assumptions and Ross the mathematician some calculations.

"Now I slept every night at Kalhutti inside a mosquito net and with closed windows and doors . . . ," he wrote Manson. "Neither of my two servants who also slept at Kalhutti has had fever yet. We all drank boiled water and milk religiously. I must watch developments before judging where I got the fever but think I got it at Westbury . . . on Friday the 23d. This gives about 60 hours incubation." In fact the minimum elapsed time between inoculation of the parasites and their appearance in the peripheral blood with the first onset of fever is five and a half days. Ross did not know that. Supposing instead an incubation period of forty-eight hours, he calculated that he must have admitted twenty-five million parasites into his body on the day of infection. If he had breathed these, the contaminated air must have held sixty-two sporozoa to the cubic inch. That, he thought, was a transparent absurdity. It was only a little easier to believe he might have swallowed that number in the cool tea he had drunk with watered milk. The true explanation, as Ross long afterward bethought, was that he had visited the ghat briefly some two weeks previously and had been stung by a mosquito. But he had no reason to recall that at the time.

In fact what perplexed him most was that he had found so few insects and no breeding places. He went home to his cottage in the hills, rested a couple of days and then returned to the search. On his second visit to the ghat he seemed in luck. He wrote Dr. Manson:

> Another five days in the jungle have reversed the position of affairs in favour of the mosquito theory, but only just as I was beginning to give it up. I started to Kalhutti again on the 5th. On the 6th I went to Sigur, the bottom of the Ghat, and spent the whole day there hunting for mosquito pools and examining dew, puddles, etc. Not a mosquito grub to be found. There is a resthouse there and in it I found a native with fever. He said he had arrived on 17 April and had been attacked with fever four days afterwards (he may have contracted it on the way). On my intimating that I wanted to examine his blood after breakfast he disappeared. I found however a family of nine Kusbahs living all their lives at Sigur in a spot supposed to be absolutely deadly: not one of them had ever had fever, they said, and certainly none of the seven men and children had spleen. They drank river water. I encamped at this spot during the day on the 6th and 7th inst. returning four miles up the ghat to Kalhutti in the evening. I found not a single mosquito grub anywhere but caught a mosquito full of blood in the resthouse. This mosquito was small with wings striped *brown* and white. The Kusbahs (aborigines) informed me that sometimes mosquitoes are so numerous at night that fires are required to keep them off . . .
>
> On Sunday 9th I examined water of puddles, mud, everything—not a sign of a mosquito. There was not a mosquito in this bungalow either. I then offered a reward for every mosquito alive or dead, brought to me and went to bed feeling that mosquitoes could play no essential part in the propagation of malaria . . .

Monday he went back to Nash's plantation:

> After breakfast on the 10th an intelligent native brought me five very small mosquitoes. I jumped with astonishment at the sight of them and told him to take me where he had found them. Instead of taking me to the servants' huts he led me into the neighbouring jungle. It was then midday. He sat down; in one minute four or five mosquitoes had fastened on his black legs and arms, one was on my hand

and several were prospecting my trowsers [sic]. I let the one on my hand bite me, which it did in a few seconds, giving a sharp pain like a bee sting. One on the native's legs filled itself in about a minute. These insects abounded in the darkest parts of the jungle, which however was not a large jungle but rather thin scrub and thorn.* I searched everywhere for the grubs but could not find a pool of water anywhere, though it had been raining over night. Anyway the adult insects swarmed everywhere in the wood. In the evening we looked again for grubs, and at last discovered some in a small pool in a rocky ravine almost entirely sheltered from the sun by thick overhead vegetation and fully half a mile from where we had first found the mosquitoes . . .

The discovery impressed him both because the mosquitoes were so numerous and hungry and because on Nash's plantation it was the men and children who chiefly succumbed to the fever, seldom the women. The men and children worked and played in the scrub woods while the women did their housework and tended the gardens unbitten. He had grubs of the forest mosquito collected, intent on using it in new experiments. For the moment he almost overlooked the single brown mosquito with striped (actually spotted) wings, the mosquito he was later to name, in his strictly Anglo-Saxon taxonomy, the "dapple-wing." (It was in fact an anopheline, belonging to the one genus of mosquito capable of nurturing plasmodia and passing them to people.) He *almost* overlooked it, but he did not: He observed the dapple-wing and recorded it because it was different, even though its uniqueness at that moment seemed only to assure that it had no relevance to his problem. That may have been his finest moment; at least it helps explain why Ross eventually achieved his success and deserved it: He had, like all first-rate scientists, a deep unreasoned respect for facts that no preconception or bias or will to believe could thrust aside. As easily misled as other men by appearances and plausibilities, he nevertheless took pains while following wrong trails to record a tiny fact that was not on his way and did not accord with the currently plausible. And he would remember it.

Mosquitoes of the genus *Anopheles* are particularly easy to distinguish from those belonging to other, non-malaria-carrying genera. They are flagged by two characteristics they share with no others. Virtually all the common dangerous ones, when they rest, tilt their bodies head down, tail up

---

* They were probably a sylvatic species of *Aedes* that breed in water-filled holes in trees.

at about a forty-five-degree angle to the surface; other mosquitoes hold themselves more or less parallel. The second difference is in the appearance of the proboscis. In culicine mosquitoes, which include the ordinary annoying varieties, the mouth parts appear to be three, because the feelers, the palpi, on either side of the central bundle of mouth parts* being much shorter can be distinctly seen. Anopheline palpi are the same length as the proboscis which thus appears to be single and somewhat thicker.

There are other distinguishing characters which though found occasionally in other genera nevertheless are typically anopheline. Anopheline females lay eggs singly (by contrast to the *Culex,* which produces scores of them, glued together in rafts) in the shape of elaborately sculptured boats, often attached at their ends in open geometric patterns. The larvae on emergence lie just beneath the surface of the water, parallel to it, and feed on surface minutiae. Culicine larvae attach themselves to the surface by an anterior breathing apparatus and hang head down, feeding on suspended matter in the water. Finally, most of the common vectors of malaria have, as Ross noted, spotted wings, a pattern actually produced by alternating light and dark segments of the wing veins.

So distinctive are the anophelines, it is remarkable that Ross missed seeing one during two years of intensive collecting, studying, experimenting with many hundreds of insects. It is always easy of course to overlook what one is not looking for.† Ross apparently did little of his own collecting; the "grubs" from which he raised his experimental insects were gathered by his native servants. Where he worked the common anopheline species bred by preference in small, often ephemeral collections of water. Ross's collectors would reasonably have visited larger and more dependable pools where they could net the most grubs with the least effort. Ross himself did not know at first that he ought to be seeking out different kinds of egg and larvae. Surgeon and medical doctor in the narrowest sense of one trained to doctor people, without even the most rudimentary training in entomology, or in any branch of zoology for that matter, Ross had first to discover painfully the questions to be asked before he could begin to think about where to look for answers.

He spent all the rest of his time in Sigur Ghat and the last days of his two months' leave with the forest mosquito and its parasites, of which he had soon described nine varieties. He was particularly excited about the

---

* Seven in all though they appear to the naked eye as a single lancet. See Chapter 17.

† Christophers (1904) noted that *Anopheles culicifacies,* probably the commonest anopheline where Ross worked, is secretive in its habits and easy to overlook even where abundant.

"green flagellulae" he had seen in the drinking water at Westbury on his first visit; a similar organism turned up in the stomach of a Sigur Ghat mosquito. Under the microscope he watched it burst out of hard little spores or cysts, elongate and put forth a single flagellum with which to swim—a "wonderful" spectacle. He was happy also to calculate that the little green animals were abundant enough in Westbury waters, and common enough in their host mosquito, to meet the requirements of the mathematics he had worked out for his own infection. To be sure, his flagellulae bore no resemblance to plasmodia in any of their known guises, but he was willing to make allowances. So much was still hidden. If after he had worked out the flagellulae cycle in the mosquito and found no form recognizably plasmodial, he was prepared to conclude "that the alternative form (in the mosquito) differs morphologically from the human form and that the changes between the hosts are of a complete nature. . . ." Didn't Dr. Manson think so?

Manson did not. Again he was worried that Ross was away off the track. He confessed that Ross's investigations showed "the problem is much more complicated than at first sight one would think." But, he added, "you won't get forrader [forwarder] unless you hang on to the flagellum. Stick to it and try by all sorts of microscopical device to hang on to its tail and get, so to speak, dragged with it to its destiny. Working with these other forms is more or less blind groping; sticking to the flagellum is following the leader."

But how could you follow a leader that wriggled under your microscope lens normally for only a few minutes and then disappeared as completely as a drop of water in the sea? Ross had an idea: The flagellum was so delicate he doubted he could ever hang on to its tail all the way into mosquito tissue, but once there and matured into "firm spores," it might be entrapped. For such spores, he might have to dissect thousands of mosquitoes and each examination at that time was taking him two hours. He was not dismayed. The flagellum "must either develope [sic] in the mosquito or be evacuated by it . . . [T]he things are there and *must* be found! It is simply a matter of hard work."

That he wrote so cheerfully of such a daunting prospect is the more remarkable in that a month earlier he had been at the edge of despair. All during his two months' leave he had been trying to line up a job, anything better than reversion to his old post with the native regiment in Secunderabad. To go back meant taking half the pay he got in Bangalore. It meant another separation from his family for whom Secunderabad offered no decent accommodation. It meant probable transfer in a year's time with the regiment to Burma, again without his family. Perhaps worst of all it meant accepting continued official indifference to his merits and accomplishments.

Ross poured out his gloom and grievances to Dr. Manson. His leave was almost over. "Here then my work must end for the present as I have only a week's more leave and must get some walking and cycling for my health. I fear however that you will be much disappointed to hear that the present is likely to finish my microscope work for ever and a day, though I certainly hope it will not be so . . . I return to Secunderabad on the 16th" he concluded. "It is raining heavily here. No more malaria work possible."

Angry and frustrated, he was also unwell. The weakness following his short sharp attack of malaria lingered; perhaps, too, he suffered reactions to the massive doses of quinine that he had taken daily ever since. He was alone. His wife remained in Ootacamund for a time after he returned to Secunderabad, and then moved to Bangalore. Ross was a bachelor again. "I felt my first violent reaction against the microscope, and could scarcely bring myself to look through mine for a month." It was hot, and suffocatingly still. The Great Monsoon that brings the rains to India each June was late.* In dust and heat and dryness he came as close as he ever would allow to a human cry of despair:

> What ails the solitude?
>   Is this the Judgement Day?
> The sky is red as blood;
>   The very rocks decay . . .
>
> The world is white with heat;
>   The world is rent and riven;
> The world and heavens meet;
>   The lost stars cry in heav'n.

But he was soon recovering. "I have been doing a little work here," he wrote not a month later but less than a fortnight after his arrival in Secunderabad, "(can't resist it)." He was also feeling better. His writing probably helped. The verses just quoted are from his long poem "In Exile," on which Ross worked during most of his stay in India and into which, as the title indicates, he sloughed off for sublimation his periodic discontents. But

---

* The monsoon had failed also in 1896, reducing the yield from non-irrigated crops to less than half of normal, and in some places to zero. The widespread famine continuing into 1897 increasingly absorbed the attention of government and incidentally provided an excuse for avoiding such other avoidable expenses as special malaria investigations.[2]

also he had a telegram from Leslie to say Ross would be appointed "soon" to the Foreign Office as requested, although Leslie could not say when. "So," Ross wrote with a palpable blotting of tears, "that puts the matter all right and removes my *grievances.*" In fact Leslie's "soon" proved infinitely elastic; the appointment never did come through. But the expectation gave Ross the necessary respite. He could go back to the mosquito hunt in earnest.

9 / Mosquito Day

With his research at last riveted to two guide rails—the fate of the flagellum and the appropriate species of mosquito—Ross could now settle into the hard, patient, systematic work at which he excelled. He began with three varieties of the brindled (*Aedes*) mosquito; for ten days he did nothing but dissect these, after feeding them on malarial blood, and painstakingly search their tissues. No results. "Well, I must double or treble this work . . . I see my course clearly now—it is to make an exhaustive search on these lines—I shall not miss a cytozoan, a spore, an amoeba, or a flagellum, believe me." After another week, still without results, he thought he was on the point of declaring that either the brindled mosquito was the wrong species or the flagella develop in forms so delicate or so rare that they are indistinguishable from cells. In either event he would push on and must eventually succeed. "I must discover America if I continue to sail along this parallel westward far enough." But he was not hardened to the trials of the voyage:

> [T]he weather became very hot again in August [he recalled in his *Memoirs*]. At first I toiled comfortably, but as failure followed failure, I became exasperated and worked till I could hardly see my way home late in the afternoons . . . [I worked in a] dark hot little office in the hospital at Begumpett [hard by Secunderabad], with the necessary gleam of light coming in from under the eaves of the ver-

anda. I did not allow the punka [ceiling fan] to be used because it blew about my dissected mosquitoes, which were partly examined without a cover glass and the result was that swarms of flies and of "eye-flies"—minute little insects which try to get into one's ears and eyelids—tormented me at their pleasure, while an occasional *Stegomyia* revenged herself on me for the death of her friends. The screws of my microscope were rusted with sweat from my forehead and hands, and its last remaining eyepiece was cracked!

But he was about to be lucky. He had three natives collecting mosquito larvae for him. A few days before the middle of August one of his men brought him a bottle containing larvae that were strikingly different from those that metamorphosed into the familiar grey and brindled species. By coincidence, on the morning that these hatched, an assistant in the hospital called Ross's attention to a small brown mosquito with speckled wings that sat on the wall with her tail sticking up. It was another anopheline, like the single one he had noted in Sigur Ghat.* He trapped it, killed it with tobacco smoke and dissected it on the spot. "While I was doing so . . . the worthy Hospital Assistant (who had pointed out the anopheline) ran in to say that there were a number of mosquitoes of the same class which had hatched out in the bottle that my men had brought me yesterday." They were big browns with dapple-wings. Ross lost no time. He had a patient, Husein Khan, in whose blood swarmed numerous crescent forms of *Plasmodium*. At 12.25 p.m. Husein stripped and lay under a mosquito net into which Ross introduced ten of the big browns. New and hungry, they gorged themselves within five minutes.

He killed two twenty-five minutes later, hoping to catch the process of exflagellation. He found nothing. On the 17th he discovered that two mosquitoes had died in the night. Dissecting two more in haste and excitement he spoiled the specimens. Of the original ten he had now just four left. He killed one, found nothing.† Despite these failures, tiresomely familiar from the past two years, his special excitement continued. It survived the discovery on the 20th that another of the insects had died. "After a hurried breakfast at the Mess, I returned to dissect the cadaver . . . but found

---

* Though not necessarily of the same species. Experts are reluctant to try to guess what species Ross actually dealt with. The mosquito on the wall might have been *Anopheles culicifacies,* a common and important vector in India and Ceylon, and the larger ones possibly *A. stephensi,* found mainly in cities in India.

† The *Memoirs* say he found "vacuolated cells" but did not pay attention to them. These are not recorded in the notebook.

nothing new in it." Now he had only two mosquitoes left. Just after noon he decided to sacrifice one of these "although my eyesight was already fatigued," and he had only one more chance.

The dissection was good. "I noted at once some cells in the stomach rather more distinct than the usual very delicate stomach cells.* Altogether there were a dozen of these lying mainly towards the upper end of the organ." Aware of the importance of what he saw, he described them meticulously. "They varied from 12 to 16 μ† in diameter [about twice the size of the asexual form of the parasite in the human red blood cell] and were full of stationary vacuoles. The outline was sharp but fine and not at all amoeboid, the shape spherical or ovoid, the substance rather more solid than that of the neighboring cells." But in fact they would not have been distinguishable from the stomach cells except to one who had examined as many as Ross had in his long and seemingly futile search. "Now I am so familiar with the mosquito's stomach that these bodies struck me at once; and you may imagine how much more struck I was when on focusing carefully I found they contained *pigment indistinguishable in colour, shape, etc. from that of the haemamoeba* [Plasmodium] in finger blood! It was black or dark brown (not blue, or yellowish or greenish like the cell granules, debris etc.), not refractive on up focusing, consisting of little balls or rods, sometimes oscillating rapidly within a small range in parts of the cells . . ." There were further technical details. Good scientist that he was, he recognized that any report of something new would meet with searching skepticism. However convinced the original observer might be in the presence of the revelation vouchsafed to him alone, he must prepare to answer the objections of those still in the darkness, and somehow make them see too. That could be done, if it could be done at all, only by the facts so precisely delineated that they could not possibly be taken for other facts configuring a mirage.

He fixed and sealed the peculiar cells to send to Dr. Manson.

"On the 21st I killed my last brown mosquito 5 days after being malariated [fed on malarial blood] and rushed at the stomach. The very same bodies (!) only larger, more distinct, and with a thicker, perhaps double, outline (sometimes). There were 21 of them . . ." The exciting implication was that they had grown! If only he had had another mosquito to

---

* In the *Memoirs* Ross overdramatizes this, implying that he left the examination of the stomach tissues of the mosquito to the end (which would not make sense) and almost neglected it entirely in his fatigue (which would have been wholly unlike him). In fact these implications are contradicted in his letter to Manson, quoted here and in the *Memoirs*, page 228.

† μ = micron = 1/1000 mm.

examine on the sixth day. But not only did he have no more fed; he had no more browns at all. So he went back to the brindled and tried them again on his malaria case. He wanted to be sure that he had not overlooked those peculiar cells before. In eight examined he found not a single pigmented cell. Suppressing his excitement, he methodically set down his conclusions "(provisionally) 1. The pigmented cells appear to exist in malariated brown mosquitoes but not in brindled ones. 2. They are larger on the fifth than on the fourth day. 3. They occupy only one part of the stomach [the esophageal end]. 4 They become more distinct under formaline [the chemical he used to fix his preparations]. 5. They are sometimes intracellular (?). 6. They have pigment exactly like that of the malaria parasite."

Then he allowed his excitement rein:

> The remarkable thing about them is undoubtedly the pigment. I have never seen this before in any mosquito (I have now examined hundreds—or a thousand). It always lies in the cells and is not scattered outside them or in any other cells. In short it is as distinctive a feature of them as it is of the *haemamoeba. No other bodies but these two that I have ever seen contain such pigment; and it is the same exactly in both* . . . Wait now. You will say at once (as I used to think) that the parasite in the mosquito cannot have pigment, because this is known to be derived from haemoglobin and the mosquito has no haemoglobin. Has it not though? Why its stomach is full of it, and these cells which lie in the wall of the stomach, perhaps almost touching its contents, could easily absorb unlimited haemoglobin. Anyway there's the pigment, just like what we see in our old friend.

He itched to get on with more experiments. But "one difficulty remains—to get more brown mosquitoes. I may add that it is a filaria bearing species. One of my old patients has a very rare filaria and I found one kicking in the *tissues* of a 24-hour mosquito."

> I must first keep my mosquitoes alive for more than 5 days by giving them a second feed [the secret that eluded Manson and that Ross picked up, apparently by observation, though he does not say so], in order to see whether the pigmented cells develop spores. By their appearance on the 5th day, I imagine sporulation will begin at about the 7th day [a shrewd guess, exactly right]. If spores form, the parasitic nature of the cells is established taken together with the pigment, leads to an obvious inference.
>
> Next I have to see whether unfed brown mosquitoes or the same

fed on healthy blood do or do not possess these cells, and whether malariated ones always possess them.

All this is only a matter of a little work. Unfortunately I can't get any more of these brown devils . . .

So he indulged reflection and the pure joy of discovery:

It is of course unlikely that these cells are mere ordinary cells which have absorbed pigment granules from the stomach contents by amoeboid action. The cells are too few and the pigment too scattered and scarce—not like that of a pigmented spleen cell for instance. Besides, why should they not exist in the brindled insects?

That was his directional clue: to prove that the cells with pigment were unique to the new variety of mosquito and only to those fed on malarial blood. If they were, then his two years of failure with the greys and the brindled were satisfactorily explained without impugning the mosquito transmission theory, and the connection between the cells and malaria was established. That should be simple enough once he got some more mosquitoes. So long as he had none, like an artist he could take pleasure in his handiwork:

Can do nothing else but look at my pigmented cells. They keep beautifully in formaline. The pigment, though much more scanty in comparison to the size of the cell, is absolutely identical in character with that of the haemamoeba. I have never seen anything like it before except in the haemamoeba. Wonder if I am really on it at last! If not, what can these cells be? Something very unusual.

In the next couple of days, though he could find no more larvae of the brown mosquito, he did catch several adults in the ward. These were the smaller browns. As they presumably had had no chance at malarial patients and contained no pigmented cells, they helped to show that the cells were probably "peculiar to malariated brown mosquitoes."

During the next week he had half a dozen men prowling the environs for grubs, but all they could find were the larvae of *Culex* and *Aedes*. At the end of the week he had to go to Bangalore to see his wife, who had just moved down from Ootacamund. He took with him mounted specimens showing his "wonderful pigmented cells" in the fourth- and fifth-day mosquitoes, because "John Smyth [whom he had earlier instructed in Laveran's parasite] is there I think and some other men who have got a little knowledge of the malaria bug. I'll make them write descriptions," he told Manson, "which I will send with a short note of my own to the B. M. J.

[*British Medical Journal*]." He was anxious to put the discovery on record, with testimonials, right away, since he anticipated that it might be some time before he could find the cells again," and in the mean time some lucky Italian or American who has happened to hit off the right species of insect, may polish off the whole business."

He sent his historic paper to the "B. M. J." early in September under the title, "On Some Peculiar Pigmented Cells Found in Two Mosquitoes Fed on Malarial Blood." It appeared in the issue of 18 December. The slides had gone to Manson, and after examining them Manson appended this note of cautious endorsement to Ross's paper: "I am inclined to think that Ross may have found the extracorporeal phase of malaria." The force of that puff, such as it was, was somewhat deflated by another appended note from a Dr. Thin, a prominent conservative member of the British medical profession. Dr. Thin thought Ross's alleged parasites were in fact nothing but the ordinary epithelial cells of the stomach that had undergone some unspecified change. In fact he had no doubt about it. The *hrrmph* of Dr. Thin's expert pronouncement is all but audible even now.

In fact considerable caution seemed called for. Ross was admirably discreet in his published paper. But in private he was inclined even then to inflate his discovery. He wrote Manson, "I really believe the problem is solved, though I don't like to say so . . . I have hardly restrained myself from wiring 'pigment' to you [in accord with their previous agreement that he would cable proof when he got it—Manson had a special registered cable address, 'Finically,' ready to receive the word] but fear you would think I had gone mad. Well I know pigment by this time. *I am on it.*"

Since pigment had been uniquely associated with malaria for twenty or thirty years, and from the time of Laveran had been the nameplate of the parasite in nearly all its forms, Ross had reason enough to think he was "on it," that the pigmented cells were in fact an incarnation of *Plasmodium* in the mosquito. Yet strictly speaking there was no proof. He had followed the flagellum only to its disappearance a few hours after entering the mosquito's stomach. Then he had discovered the development of the cells some four days later. What happened in the days between? He could only deduce ("guess," an unfriendly critic might say) that the flagellum was father to the pigmented cell. The unobserved process of transition from flagellum to encysted cell on the stomach wall of the mosquito was to remain notably a gap in Ross's research which some of his detractors would argue later impugned his proof. At this time without question it was an open invitation to skepticism.

He did not know what became of the cells either. He thought they were headed for sporulation but he had not seen that. He thought the emerging "spores" would represent parasite forms destined for an independent existence outside the mosquito, and that they would turn out to be the final extracorporeal form which would re-enter the bodies of men by water, excreta on the skin or possibly inoculation. But almost all of this was still speculation. Considering the remaining unknowns, Ross's great discovery was a long way from proof of the theory of mosquito transmission; yet it was the first radically new fact in the natural history of the parasite since Golgi's discovery of the reproductive cycles in human blood. As such it justified Ross's excitement, and even his decision to mark the 20th of August 1897 as "Mosquito Day."

Ironically his next discovery muddied the waters. On 18 September, shortly after his return from visiting his wife in Bangalore, he happened in the hospital ward to catch one of his familiar grey mosquitoes (probably *Culex fatigans*) feeding on a patient who had tertian fever. He caught it, dissected it and was delighted to find its stomach full of pigmented cells, quite a bit larger than those he had found before. Now, all his previous experiments had been carried out with mosquitoes raised from larvae. He thus knew not only what they were but where they had been; he knew that they had fed only at his own invitation. The *Culex* was a stray. Because he had caught her in the act of sucking malarial blood he assumed that was where she had picked up her infection. It seemed to strengthen his case and he wrote a supplementary note for the *British Medical Journal* to report incautiously that he had four cases of pigmented cells—the two original, the small anopheline bred from the larvae he had personally discovered, and now the grey.* By claiming the grey at this time he confused the very important fact he was on the point of demonstrating—that anophelines and only anophelines can be vectors of the fever in man. He also opened himself to the charge, later lodged by Professor Grassi, that in all his experiments he had used wild-caught mosquitoes with an unknown and probably promiscuous history.

The mistake, perfectly understandable in the euphoria of the moment,†

---

* In fact since *Culex* cannot carry human malaria, the grey must have fed before on a bird whose parasites, similar to man's, the similar cells derived.

† He was encouraged in error by the fact that hitherto he had experimented exclusively with cases of malignant fever, the kind caused by the species of *Plasmodium falciparum* that has crescent forms. He had so limited himself because according to Manson the flagellum was the key and it was easiest to detect exflagellation in *P. falciparum*. Now he reasoned that although only the browns would transmit *falciparum* it remained possible that the parasites of tertian might be adapted to the greys. This is an interesting instance of a correct intuition pushed to misleading extremes. Following Manson, Ross tended to believe not only that the parasite was selective as to its mosquito host but that each species of *Plasmodium* might have a preferred mosquito.

might have been immaterial had Ross had a few more months to nail down his proof. He had begun working with the small anophelines (probably *A. culicifacies*), one of which he had already successfully infected. They were inconvenient animals to work with. They will not breed in captivity. It was hard to get them to bite; they did not easily pick up the parasite; and they were fragile and died young with discouraging regularity. Nevertheless there seems no reason why he could not have handled them in time. But there was no time.

The end came suddenly. On 23 September he fed four of the little white-winged browns. They were his last. The next day he had orders to proceed to Bombay at once. He understood that he was to be sent to the front on active service. He left Secunderabad on the 26th.

A long-threatened war had at last broken out. Though it was a minor fracas with a border tribe, the army took no disturbances lightly in a land that the British Raj then saw as both vulnerable and precious. Ross was a military doctor; he accepted that. He went toward the front, if not cheerfully, at least without recrimination. A taste of action even might have pleased him despite the frustration of putting off his investigations for several months, just at the point where he thought he could see victory.

But he never got to the front. His orders posted him to Meiwar Bhil Corps, in Kherwara, Rajputana. The name of Rajputana Ross thought had a pleasant ring, since that state boasted one of the best medical services in India. If he was not to go to war, perhaps at last he would get his Resident Surgeoncy.

A look at the map would have disabused him. In a land crisscrossed by railroads, no tracks passed through Kherwara. None came closer than fifty miles. When Ross set out with his servant, Lutchman, no one could tell him how to go. For three days he circled Kherwara by rail, at last alighting fifty-six miles away; then he had a wait of six days before hiring a two-wheeled horse carriage, a *tonga,* to complete the journey into exile.*

There were only two other Englishmen at the post, the commandant and his adjutant. Ross's job was to replace a junior medical officer on sick leave. His duties were routine regimental doctoring. There was no malaria. Professionally the situation could not have been worse. It was so bad that Ross was sure someone had deliberately done him in, as punishment perhaps for having talent and making the brass hats and dawdlers uncomfortable.

---

* For his initiative the Army made him pay a fine: It was thought he should have waited and gone by *dawk,* a relay service using horses or a sedan chair, which was the only available public transport.[1]

At once he began typically energetic struggles to escape—anywhere. Authority riposted with ice or fire: "Your application will remain on record," said one. "I don't understand what this officer mean[s]," said another— "He was sent to this command by H. E. [His Excellency] the commander in chief & here he will remain until H. E. orders him away."

Manson meanwhile was pulling all possible strings in London. With anxious eye cocked at the competitive laboratories in Italy, France, America and Germany, he was if anything even more upset than Ross at the interruption in the malaria investigation. Manson's reports that he had the ear of the Secretary of State for India and saw good jobs in prospect for Ross must have been heartening. At the same time the letters from London full of Manson's lively life, his recent appointment as adviser to the Colonial Office, his work on his great text, *Tropical Diseases*, which was just about to be published, his shooting holidays in Scotland, his hobnobbing with the medical and political great of the English capital—all this must have made difficult reading for the exile in Kherwara who was inclined at best to feel put upon by life. For four months Ross languished in that wilderness.

10 / The Flagellum Caught

If Ross were to be kept long from his work, it was the Italians who on past showing seemed most likely to solve the riddle. Yet Italian work in fact was in the doldrums. By 1894 Golgi in Pavia, and Marchiafava and Celli in Rome, had completed their differentiation of the species of parasite with descriptions of the blood cycle of *Plasmodium falciparum*. Thereafter, silence. Except for Bignami's single, and highly important, paper in 1896, the Italians published nothing between 1894 and 1898.

They had come to an apparent end of the particular line of research they had followed from the start. Following the initial discoveries of Marchiafava and Celli and the brilliant intuitions of Golgi, they had worked systematically to develop the blood cycle of all the known species of malaria parasites. This work elucidated the nature of the disease, the various forms of fever, and the action of quinine as a therapeutic in suppressing the multiplication of the asexual forms. The alternative cycle of the parasite outside the human body presented a different kind of research problem. Having rejected the Laveran–Manson thesis that the flagellum was the parasite in traveling gear on its way to a new life, they did not expect to find anything in the blood sucked into the mosquito's stomach. Most of them believed with the Russians, Mechnikov and Danilevskii, that the alternative, extracorporeal forms were spores that passively survived in the environment waiting to be picked up and reintroduced into man's blood. Professor Grassi, exceptionally, thought they would be found to be amoebae capable of reproducing themselves by division in their free state.

In either event the parasite outside the body was unlikely to look like or act like the parasite inside. How then might it be recognized? The reasonable answer seemed to be that the alternative forms must also occur in such close association with malaria as to be indictable on their own. Hence the continued emphasis in Italian research on collecting materials, including finally mosquitoes, from "malarious" localities.

On the whole the Italians showed only spasmodic interest in the problem of transmission. What work they did was mostly in testing whether the bite of "malarious" mosquitoes could cause the disease. The earliest of these experiments were done with birds.

Ever since Danilevskii in 1890* had described haematozoa in birds so similar to plasmodia in people in appearance and behavior that he and some others thought they were identical animals, there had been available to malariologists a convenient experimental animal. The doctors were remarkably slow in exploiting it—possibly because they were doctors, not zoologists. At least, interestingly, it was Grassi, trained in both medicine and zoology, who initiated systematic experiments with birds. That had been in 1890, directly after Danilevskii's publication. Most of the laboratory work appears to have been carried out by Grassi's colleague, Dr. Feletti, and the work continued only so long as Grassi remained in Catania where Feletti lived. The Grassi–Feletti research usefully distinguished species of bird parasites and perhaps most importantly showed that one could work effectively with birds.[1]

Grassi turned again to birds (mainly pigeons) in 1896–97 when after four years' absence from the malaria field he was tempted back by the theories of Manson and Bignami. Now ensconced (since 1895) in a professorship in Rome, he discussed the mosquito hypothesis with Bignami. He also found a new colleague, Antonio Dionisi, whom he persuaded to work with pigeons in his laboratory while he, in poor health, left the capital.

Faithful to the Italian school's emphasis on how the parasite got *into* the blood, Dionisi began by trying to infect healthy young birds with mosquitoes collected in malarious places. Not surprisingly he failed. Then he set out to discover whether adult birds could be bitten. His was the first incontrovertible evidence that they could be—an important result.† He looked next for infected birds on which to feed his mosquitoes and exam-

---

* He discovered the bird parasites in 1885–86.

† He had at first used unfledged nestlings, for it was generally thought that adult birds were armored against the bite by feathers. They are. But as Dionisi found, there are enough uncovered parts of the bird's body (around the eyes for instance) to make them vulnerable.[2]

ined the fed insects, as Ross had been doing for two years. Again the odds were hopelessly stacked against him and he found nothing.*

In notable contrast to Ross, Dionisi abandoned his search at that point and reverted to his original shotgun approach, of trying to malariate the birds by means of adult mosquitoes collected where malaria was prevalent.[3] Thus thrown back on a method that in view of the multiple complexities of mosquito transmission was statistically doomed, Dionisi and Grassi for the moment were out of contention. And since Grassi appears to have taken on himself the role of directing at least Roman research (which included most of the top investigators), the men of Italy, ambitious though they undoubtedly were, were less to be feared in the malaria sweepstakes in 1897 than their form indicated.

On the other hand, a remarkable discovery was made this year in North America. For fifteen years or so, the most divergent views had been held as to what the crescent and flagellate forms of the parasite really were. Crescents were thought (by Laveran) to be encysted forms from which the flagella develop, or (by Golgi) stages in an unspecified long-term cycle connected with the well-known phenomenon of relapses in malarial fever, or (by Grassi and Feletti) separate species, or (by Councilman of Johns Hopkins) a spore form, or (by Bignami and his colleague Bastianelli, and Manson) sterile forms since they were not known ever to divide, rudimentary forms of a second cycle that could not be completed in the human body.[4] Flagella had been variously interpreted as degenerative (Grassi and others), as resting states (an American, Dr. Dock) or as extracorporeal forms destined for the mosquito or, as Mannaberg believed, for a saprophytic existence nourished by decomposing organic matter. The crescents are indeed rudimentary forms of a second cycle, but all speculations about the flagella were very wide of the mark.

In 1897 a French parasitologist, P. L. Simond, following up work done in Germany by three researchers including the great Schaudinn, was tracing out the developmental stages of one genus of coccidium (*Eimeria*) similar to *Plasmodium* and found in the blood of rabbits and salamanders.[5] Mechnikov in 1890 had remarked how closely the flagellate form in salamanders resembled Laveran's. All this Simond confirmed. He further noted that each of the flagella consisted of a thread of chromatin (the complex substance that contains the genes) enclosed in a thin layer of protoplasm.

---

* Grassi (1899a) says Dionisi failed only because he had the bad luck to pick the parasite of pigeons then called *Halteridium* (now *Haemoproteus columbae*) whose reproductive cycle had not been demonstrated at the time Grassi wrote. *H. columbae* is transmitted not by mosquitoes but by ectoparasitic flies (Garnham, 1966).

More remarkably, the flagella on emergence seemed to take *all* the chromatin the parasite had. Once the little whips were formed Simond could detect neither chromatin nor nucleus in the transparent sphere now exflagellate. Considering this fact—that all the genetic material seemed to have been extruded—along with the extreme agility and activity of the extruded threads before and after they detached themselves from the sphere, Simond concluded that in a general way the combination "is characteristic of the male sexual element in living things." The flagella, he thought, behaved remarkably like spermatozoa.*

But of course! Why had the resemblance been so long overlooked? Not only had observers watched the excited wriggling of the sperms (microgametes is now their technical name) and noted the slightly bulbous heads, but many had also noted the flagellum's literally headstrong predilection for bumping into things. Ross's report on the flagellum that "attacked" three phagocytes was the most dramatic, but there had been other similar observations. Ross witnessed another, similar "attack" himself later and so did Manson. Since they both expected the flagellum to penetrate a gastric cell of the mosquito these attacks seemed to them but ill-judged efforts by the creature to play its proper role. Much earlier the American investigator, Councilman, reported watching flagella which after becoming detached "swim rapidly through the blood, and whenever they come in contact with an obstacle, as for example, with a blood corpuscle, they do not attempt to pass around it, but continue to push against it . . . [Sometimes having succeeded in making a dent] the filament remains actively in motion, pushing against the corpuscle."[7]

It remained for two American medical interns, students of Dr. W. S. Thayer at Johns Hopkins, to demonstrate that Simond's intuition was correct. Thayer, a Boston doctor, who was a member of that first remarkable faculty gathered by the Johns Hopkins Medical School, had not only done clinical work himself on malaria, which was prevalent in Baltimore, but made himself master of the literature. He was interested in the possibilities which he says Laveran first suggested to him for experimentation with birds, and persuaded two of his students, Eugene L. Opie and W. G. MacCallum, to follow up that research in the summer of 1896.[8] Opie and MacCallum found large numbers of parasites† in English and swamp spar-

---

* Also in 1897 Schaudinn and Siedlecki had announced that the threadlike extrusions of parasites of the genus *Eimeria* were gametes; but it does not appear that Simond was aware of their paper.[6]

† These were *Halteridia* (*Haemoproteus columbae*). Though in behavior much like *Plasmodium*, they are assigned to a different genus chiefly because of two important differences: Only gametocytes are present in blood and their insect hosts, as already noted, are flies, not mosquitoes.

rows, blackbirds, crows and one great horned owl. The parasites were so numerous and so relatively large that they permitted the study of exflagellation "with the greatest facility." But it was only the following summer (1897) that the great discovery was made, by MacCallum alone working at his home near Toronto.

In Dunnsville, Ontario, there were lots of sick crows about, recognizable to him by their ruffled plumage, a queer croak and an unnatural quietness. They appeared to be watched over by other crows on high. But though quiet they were not easily caught. MacCallum tried in vain to shoot one without killing it. Then he heard of a boy who had two crows as pets, and he cycled over to take a drop of blood from each. When he got home he saw in the blood a parasitic form he had never observed before. Reasoning that the form must have developed during his rather slow ride home, the next morning he fetched the crows to his laboratory. Their fresh blood samples displayed the shapes familiar to him from his work with Opie in Baltimore. He and Opie had actually distinguished two forms, one with granular and opaque protoplasm, the other clear. It was the clear (hyaline) form invariably that put out flagella. MacCallum decided that he must get both forms together in one field of his microscope and settle down to watch.[9]

"The granular forms (having escaped from the red cells after the blood was drawn) lie quiet beside the nuclei and shadows of the red corpuscles which lately contained them," he reported later,[10] "but are soon seen to be approached by the flagella which, having torn themselves away from the hyaline organism from whose protoplasm they were formed, struggle among the corpuscles. These flagella . . . swarm about the granular spheres, and one of them plunges its head into the sphere and finally wriggles its whole body into that organism." The entry of one locks out the others and "they may be watched circling about, vainly beating their heads against the organism. The flagellum which has entered continues its activity for a few minutes and the pigment of the organism is violently churned up." Then it becomes quiet until in about fifteen minutes a "conical process" appears. Soon the whole cell has become fusiform. "This spindle-shaped organism moves forward with a gliding motion . . . Red corpuscles lying in its path are either punctured . . . or passed over and dragged along by the adhering posterior extremity." In an intense infection the corpuscles are destroyed in great numbers. Even leucocytes "fall victims to the destructive force of these organisms which have been seen to dash through them, scattering the granules into the plasma . . ."

He could observe no more. On the glass slide the spindle organism which he called a "vermicule" and which is now known as the oökinete (or mobile egg) had no place to go. In fact it was headed for the stomach wall of its insect host where it would lodge to continue its development. On the slide it gradually lost its energy and disintegrated. MacCallum concluded "from their great powers of penetration that [the vermicules] may be the resistant forms that escape the body during life into the external world." Though that was wrong, his conclusion that he had witnessed fertilization, not battle as Ross imagined, was just right and just as Simond had predicted.

It happened that the zoological section of the British Association for the Advancement of Science was holding its annual meeting in Toronto that summer. Young Dr. MacCallum had a chance to read his dramatic paper to a distinguished audience that included Lord Lister. The frock-coated English doctors, though sweltering in record heat, listened with lively interest and Lord Lister himself got up to move a vote of thanks.[11]

Ross received a copy of the Simond paper typed for him by Mrs. Manson; he heard eventually about MacCallum's discovery. But he evinced only mild interest. (His principal comment on getting the Simond piece was that he must get Mrs. Ross a typewriter.) As for MacCallum he wrote later that it seemed to him immaterial whether the flagella were, as MacCallum probably correctly supposed, sexual or whether, as Laveran supposed, they entered directly into the mosquito's stomach walls. Though he thought it an interesting problem, he himself would make no effort to repeat MacCallum's experiment. That was odd. While one could, in a crude way, view the oökinete as merely carrying the flagellum into its predestined nest in a gastric cell, Ross's failure to include the fertilization process in his own analysis left, as already noted, a large hole in his own eventual proof.

11 / Pigeons and Sparrows

In his exile at Kherwara, Ross had once more come close to despair. He was lonely. He missed his wife and children. He chafed at the thought of the military dunderheads who out of jealousy, retribution or mere ineptitude had inflicted this "punishment" on him. Worst of all he was idle. Kherwara, never a particularly malarious spot, was enjoying its healthiest season in ten years.

On the first of February Ross had a telegram from Surgeon General Cleghorn: "Government India sanctions your appointment on special duty under Director General [IMS, Civil Branch] for six months. Rupees one thousand per mensem.* Your transfer may be delayed."[1] Delay or no, it was most welcome news that "relieves me of all anxiety." He was finally to have his special malaria duty and while waiting he spent idle hours looking for mosquitoes, trapping an occasional dapple-wing in his warm bathroom, and discovering that the brindled species (*Aedes aegypti*) seemed to breed exclusively in pots around houses—an observation that would take on significance later when the brindled mosquito in the Americas was indicted as the prime vector of yellow fever. Ross was interested now only in nailing down proof that they were not hosts of *Plasmodium*.

He expected a delay of two months; in fact his orders arrived in less than two weeks. He was to proceed at once to Calcutta. He had six months assured him for the work, and another six months if he needed them, with

---

* His normal regimental pay was R/800 a month.

no responsibilities but to his research. Yet ironically the assignment put on him new and very heavy pressures. At various times past, when Ross had demanded official notice of his interest in malaria research, he had expressed interest also in kala-azar, a serious disease especially prevalent in Assam, which he and others believed was a form of malaria. Now the army had obliged. Knowing nothing of the demands of research, the bureaucrats thought to get both jobs wrapped up in two official reports delivered on schedule. Six otherwise idle months should be ample, with six more in reserve. One of the first questions General Cleghorn put to Ross on his arrival in Calcutta was when he planned to go to Assam. With the monsoon, Ross said, and that was accepted. Thus he was on sufferance in Calcutta until the rains came, perhaps in four months; before then he felt he must have his *proof*.

In Calcutta he had the use of the laboratory—it was the only one maintained by the Government in India—in which Lieutenant Colonel D. D. Cunningham for many years had investigated various diseases. Cunningham was on home leave and soon to retire. His laboratory in a separate porticoed brick building, near a large European hospital, a native hospital and two jails, was well suited to Ross's needs. Equipment was adequate; there were two Indian assistants (though he was to replace both) and appropriately swarms of both grey and dapple-winged mosquitoes in the dusty corners.

All he needed besides were cases of malaria. He found it inconvenient, as he said, to use patients at the European hospital because there they expected treatment, not experimentation, "and the papers might talk." At the native hospital where patients were naturally less important to the papers, he found few cases. So he began a "touting system with a constant flow of backsheesh" to bring in walking reservoirs of parasites from the city. Enough came so that he could continue work. In addition he sent "boys out to get me grubs from distant parts and [I] poke about myself after them. Am flooding some ground at the laboratory to imitate a rain-puddle." But that still did not keep him busy. "I have also bought some sparrows and will examine their blood tomorrow."

This was the first step on the road to success, seemingly taken only as a last recourse under pressure of his deadline and the lack of human subjects.[2] Why had he so long avoided procedures that had been used successfully by the Italians and that today seem so obviously attractive? In October 1896, Manson had written: "Were I in a hot place I would try to work this point out [the fate of the flagellum in the mosquito] in birds rather than in man." Manson noted the abundance of material and the ease of working with it, a constant and reliable source of blood parasites and no worry about finding willing patients "squaring the man, accusations of homicide and so forth." Ross, then in Bangalore, merely replied that he had already tried some "pigeons, doves and parroquets" without results. But such perfunctory effort was not like him.

That he was so long in trying again suggests that, being intent on solving the *human* problem, he regarded experimentation with birds as a detour to be accepted only if the main road were hopelessly blocked. After his frustrations at Sigur Ghat he wrote that he might have to come to working with "frogs, lizards and birds." He came to it out of his almost total frustration in Kherwara, deciding, "I will try my best with the blue-rock pigeons." He had some success. He wrote Manson later:

> I told you that I had found Halteridium in a wild pigeon. Well I shot several more of these birds, together with doves, finches, etc., and found Halteridium in some of the first only. But none of the birds had any kind of ectoparasites—ticks, fleas, etc., though I searched them very carefully with a lens. Then I bethought me of Major Cole's [the commandant's] tame pigeons. These are persecuted by a horrible kind of black horseflies which live among their feathers . . . They suck large quantities of blood from the poor birds . . . I set to work and examined 30 of the flies. The blood in the stomach when fresh contained numbers of Halteridium, showing that the tame pigeons are also infected; but there were no pigmented cells in the stomach or other tissue of the flies.

Manson wrote to encourage this line of research. He had just read and been much impressed with MacCallum's paper reporting sexual conjugation of *Halteridium* in crows. Again he commended the paper to Ross, and Ross for the first time was able to find a copy in Calcutta soon after his arrival. Perhaps that was decisive.

The plasmodia of birds, that is to say the species of parasites then known as *Proteosoma* (now *Plasmodium relictum*),* could be transmitted by mosquitoes. But *Halteridium,* as already noted, could not. Ross had to discover that trap himself and avoid it. As his difficulties in finding good human malaria cases and infecting dapple-wings continued, he "set hard to work on birds." The zoological garden agreed to have their keepers catch crows, larks, sparrows and pigeons and "send them over," though Ross would have to pay for the pigeons.[3] Out of the first batches he found

---

* See Chapter 14.

mostly *Halteridium* in the pigeons, nothing in the sparrows and larks. He fed his grey mosquitoes indiscriminately on the cageful of mixed birds. In fresh blood from one mosquito he rediscovered MacCallum's "vermicule," looking and behaving just the way MacCallum described it. Had all the infections been invasions of *Halteridium* as he thought, he would have found no pigmented cells at all in the stomachs of his mosquitoes. In fact he did find them in one insect only. That was luck, but he had managed it carefully:

> You remember that on the 12th [of March 1898] I obtained a number of greys fed on a crow, two pigeons, and several larks and sparrows. Out of nine of these I found pigmented cells in one only. Then I fed mosquitoes on the crow and pigeons and lastly on the crow alone and a few on the pigeons alone. Of these[,] 35 in all were carefully examined—no pigmented cells. Where then did the pigmented cell fellow come from in the first series? Probably from the larks and sparrows. Hitherto I had time only to examine a few of these, in which I found nothing; but now, on the 17th, I went through them more carefully, and found *proteosoma*, Labbé,* in three larks and one sparrow. What if the pigmented cell [in the] mosquito had come from one of these? It was easy to find out. On the night of the 17th to 18th March, 10 grey or barred-back mosquitoes were fed on the three larks . . . On the morning of the 20th I judged these mosquitoes to be ready. All except one were alive. I was so excited that at 8 a.m. I could hardly dissect the first one.
>
> It contained pigmented cells. I now had to come home for breakfast and could scarcely sit it through. When I returned at 10 a.m. I set to work on the rest of the mosquitoes. The second and third of them contained no pigmented cells, but certain peculiar *clumps*. Of the remaining six, four contained more or less numerous pigmented cells [the other two exhibited more *clumps*] . . . This, compared with the past negative results could be interpreted in only one way. I felt that the theory was proved.†

---

* Labbé is the name of the biologist who first described and named *Proteosoma*. It is usual in technical literature thus to add the discoverer's name to that of the species he first described to make identification doubly secure.

† He tried repeated experiments in feeding *Culex* mosquitoes on crows whose blood he ascertained to contain only *Halteridia*. He never found the pigmented cells (coccidia) and therefore concluded in his notebook: "This suggests that the coccidia are derived only from proteosoma."

Well, not quite. When the excitement subsided, he set out systematically to find out what happened to the pigmented cells. He guessed that they would sporulate, that is burst and release spores, probably in a relatively hard resistant form suitable for an independent life outside the mosquito. He had already estimated that that might happen on the seventh day after feeding. From now on his attention was fixed on that critical sabbath: "I think something funny happens on the seventh day."

He had traced the development of the pigmented cells meticulously to that point:

> The cells begin to be noted certainly after one day (sometime between 24 and 48 hours after feeding)* as small bodies from 4 to 10 μ [microns] or so, profusely pigmented, lying in the stomach wall, sometimes in the external muscular coat, and apparently not intracellular. They increase steadily in size. On about the fourth day they generally lose all traces of pigment, reaching at that time a size of about 30 to 40 μ. They then begin to protrude from the external wall of the stomach into the body cavity. On the sixth day this protrusion is generally complete. . . .
>
> At this stage the bodies may reach nearly 60 μ . . . they are full of clear fluid containing a few large vacuoles and numerous bright refractive granules, or rather globules . . . At this stage I thought sporulation would commence; on the contrary it seems to me that the cells burst or disappear; because in mosquitoes kept after 6 or 7 days . . . the largest sized cells are rarely to be found, while a few wrinkled empty capsules may often be seen still attached to the stomach wall . . . It seems likely then that some trick of nature takes place at this point . . .

But what? His competitive spirit was roused. "There is a hand to hand fight with nature; she always has some nasty trick to evade me just as I am getting hold of her. But we will have it all out in a short time."

He had scarcely written that when he discovered that the trick, the nasty evasion, was not nature's but his own clumsiness. "I have been bursting the coccidia in making the specimen." The answer to that he soon found, following a tip from Manson, was to add a slightly stronger salt solution to slides on which he did his dissections. But that had to wait. His stock of fed

---

* Note here the one- to two-day gap that he never filled. He explained that he was afraid of spoiling averages by earlier dissection.

mosquitoes temporarily exhausted, he set two hundred more to feed. How convenient to have the birds at hand! "What an ass I have been not to follow your advice before," he wrote Manson, "and work with birds. Technique *much* easier."

Again he was on the verge of discovery and halted. This time he interrupted himself for reasons showing the multiple strains he was under. It had become terribly hot in Calcutta. As usual he felt the heat keenly. He was also worried: He had to produce an interim report after three months for the Surgeon General which he felt might decide whether he would be allowed to finish or not; he was fretting about the investigation he still had to make of kala-azar; and he was "burning to work with the human *Plasmodia.*"[4] So he decided to leave Calcutta to go off into the foothills of the Himalaya, the Terai country, where he knew there was a lot of human malaria and had heard there were also diseases similar to kala-azar.

Adding surely to his restlessness was the fact that his wife and children, after joining him briefly—they lived together six weeks in a boarding house—had just been driven out of the city by the heat. When they went to stay in the mountains at Darjeeling he moved into bachelor quarters near the laboratory with an old acquaintance, Dr. F. P. Maynard, now editor of the *Indian Medical Gazette.* Maynard's company was pleasant but the bachelor life offered a temptation which Ross could seldom resist to prolong his hours of work.

As soon as he got permission he took ten days' leave to visit his family and then went to stay at Kurseong on the mountain railway between Darjeeling (8,000 feet elevation) and the Terai plains. He took with him two servants, Lutchman and his laboratory assistant, Mahomed Bux, whose salary he had just raised to 16 rupees a month; they carried onto the train cages full of sparrows, pigeons and larks. As he remarked, it was to all appearances a lunatic departure.[5]

Out of the break in Kurseong came his official report, "Report on the Cultivation of Proteosoma, Labbé, in Grey Mosquitoes," finished and submitted on 21 May 1898. But otherwise his work did not progress. So far as birds were concerned, he discovered that it was *Halteridium* not *Proteosoma* country, and for more than a month he found not one infected mosquito. As for human malaria, there was not much of it and what there was he could not touch. The natives, especially those who worked on the local tea plantations, had become suddenly terrified of doctors.

The terror harks back to 1896 when bubonic plague broke out in Bombay—imported, it was believed, from Hong Kong. It was the first visitation at Bombay in 184 years. That is perhaps why the first mild cases early in the year went unreported.[6] In the autumn the disease raged out of control.

Some 20,000 deaths were reported in the first six months; 200,000 people left the city. The disease spread, though greatly lessening in severity, through 1897 and 1898. (Altogether it is estimated 300,000 died.)[7] Although no other parts of India suffered as did Bombay, the fear of plague reached all.

Fear not only of the plague but of its alleged cure. In 1897 a French doctor, Haffkine, got permission of the Indian government to try out a plague vaccine that he had developed.* Since out of the first 3,000 inoculated only one contracted the disease, the inoculations were judged a success and were continued. The serum contained killed bacilli. There was a risk that some bacilli might remain alive to spread the disease instead of immunity to it: so thought one prominent Bengali doctor, who expressed his fears in the *Calcutta Journal of Medicine*.[8] It seemed obvious to the people that if you stuck a man with a needle you put him in jeopardy, and if afterward he fell sick it was because of poison injected by the needle. In early 1898 the word was out in Bengal to beware the white man with his needle of germs.

Perhaps Ross's frustration at not getting the right birds or the right mosquitoes for his experiments was conveyed to his man Mohamed Bux, whose job it was to collect both. In any event Mohamed got notably reckless. One day, spotting a sparrow in a bazaar where plantation workers lived, he took a pot shot at it. It is not recorded whether he hit or missed but he scared two counties—or at least two tea plantations. The tea workers heard that the servant of a white man was shooting coolies to have them inoculated with the plague. Hundreds dropped everything and fled the area.

The manager of one estate was apoplectic. He had Mohamed Bux arrested and when Ross appealed for his release, flatly refused. It was not, he said, a simple case of shooting a bird but of "firing off a Gun in the middle of the Bazaar. The consequence is the Company has lost thousands of Rupees, by tea spoilt in the factory & coolies bolted & mounds of leaf spoilt on the Garden & on top of this your servant had the cheek to tell me behind my back what did he care for me." Far from letting him go, the angry manager was resolved to "get him as much as I possibly can . . . [because he had lost a number of coolies] & possibly at the end of this season might lose my billet over it."[9]

Mohamed was eventually released but a deputation of the planters, who were generally friendly, called on Ross with the local magistrate to ask him please to desist from further experiments. With an imperious snort for

---

* The plague bacillus was identified by Yersin in 1894.

Manson's benefit at the "native" who "is really nearer a monkey than a man" Ross gave up and asked permission to return to Calcutta.[10]

He had little of substance to show for his six weeks away from the laboratory (except of course the report, on which he had spent ten days). But he had succeeded in rededicating himself to his task. As he in his *Memoirs* recalled his experience, romantic vision, self and the memory of his father curiously entwined.[11]

> My pleasure at returning to those great mountains, which I now saw again for the first time after years of my early childhood, may be imagined. My work lay mostly in the gigantic trench, somewhat like the Sigur Ghat, which leads up northward from the plains to Darjeeling, richly wooded, with a torrent at the bottom of it, and broken foothills on either side . . . The railway ran up the east side of the trench, and Kurseong was perched near the top of the steep declivity looking out at the plains to the south and, from a point on the road, to the eternal snows of Kinchinjunga to the north. But at that season the heights were haunted by immense clouds; and even during the ten days I spent at Darjeeling I saw the mighty mountain but once—suddenly, after a day's rain, breaking out, like the phantom of another world lit by the setting sun, above the rolling and grumbling legions of mist— just as my father before me painted it.
>
> Those days were for me days of victory—spent among the magnificent mountains which are themselves symbols of victory. They stand gazing down for ever upon the plains of common earth . . . victors over Time and Fate. So, I thought, we poor creatures who must toil below may sometimes by our own efforts haply reach some higher summit . . .

For Ross communion with the mountains of his childhood seems to have brought not so much refreshment of spirit as a tune-up of his adrenalin pump. He did not return to work free from the pressures and worries that made him leave Calcutta; he returned in fact temporarily ill, but hardened (or numbed?) to mounting tensions by the brief ecstasy of ego as his special duty crossed the halfway mark.

He had failed in his petition to be relieved of responsibility for the kala-azar project. He had only two months to go on his assured term of special duty. It was clearly not enough even to finish the work on bird malaria, much less work out the cognate problems of human malaria, and still less to combine these with what promised to be an exceedingly difficult investigation of the frequently described ambiguities of kala-azar.

12 / Ross's Cycle

In Calcutta the heat was "awful." If only he hadn't spent all that time in the Terai he might have finished working out the *Proteosoma* cycle and then might have gone home to England. Ross was now eligible for a pension (after seventeen years' service) and though he had decided nothing, his thoughts turned more and more to getting out, to leaving India and its insupportable heat. A meeting of the British Medical Association was to be held at Edinburgh in July; it would have been nice if he could have attended himself to deliver to all the doctors at home his own account of lonely victory hardly won in India.

But the reality was that there was everything to do at once and no time to do any of it. Thus confronting the impossible Ross found, as usual, only one course: As it was unthinkable to give up, he could only drive himself to work all the harder. Back then to the mystery of the Sabbath when the fully grown pigmented cells, the coccidia, burst and disappeared.

Toward the end of June, he wrote Manson: "I think I am on the verge of another great advance." Using a strong salt solution for his dissections, he discovered that the mature coccidia were striated in such a way as to make them "look sometimes like caterpillars contained in an egg." He wondered if sexual division might be in progress:

> No, I think it likely that the striations are due to the coccidia, or some of them, being packed full of *germinal threads* 10 μ in length which are *scattered into the living insects coelom* [abdominal cavity]. I say this

95

on the experience of one insect only of 8th day examined this morning. It contained many mature proteosoma coccidia deeply striated; and also swarms of small bodies *feebly moving* in the salt solution and evidently escaped from the body cavity of the insect. I thought that by pressure I could force similar bodies out of the coccidia. The bodies are not bacteria; they taper at both ends and are broader in the centre, which appears capable of some change of shape.

Later he succeeded in bursting one of the coccidia with a needle and saw a multitude of rods pour out.[1]

He observed the "rods" repeatedly and described them minutely. Though he was inclined at first to think they were spermatozoa or possibly "naked spores," the rods did not fit into any of the scenarios he had imagined for the life of the parasite. "Nature probably makes some extraordinary effort here in order to complete the life cycle. What the dickens she is going to do next I cannot imagine at all. Great difficulties may however be feared owing to the absence of hard spores. But I am trying to turn the position by blind attempts to infect healthy sparrows." After further observations he found the rods too numerous to be spermatozoa and too oddly behaved. They sometimes issued from *all* the coccidia and "[t]hey evidently get into the insect's circulating fluid for some reason."

He pushed on hoping for results that Manson could announce at the Edinburgh meeting, even though the continued heat and hard work were making him "thoroughly ill." Now he pursued the "germinal rods" as once he had tried to follow the flagellum. On 29 June he found them in the stomach scales and in the thorax [the midsection of the tripartite insect body]. "Very numerous in the thorax," he noted, "but I can't locate them anywhere there." He seems to have been expecting them to lodge in tissue to continue development like the filariae. On 2 July he found some in the head, and the next day, Sunday, noted "extremely numerous rods attached to head . . ."

But let him tell the story in his letter to Manson of 6 July:[2]

> I hope this letter will reach you at Edinburgh. [It did.] If so, it will be opportune; because I feel *almost* justified in saying that I have completed the life cycle, or rather perhaps one life cycle, of proteosoma, therefore in all probability of the malaria parasite. I say almost, because though I think I have siezed [sic] the final position, I have not yet occupied it with my full force.
>
> My last letter left me face to face with the astonishing fact that the

germinal rods were to be found in the thorax as well as in the abdo-men. Instead of the hard resisting spores we expected to arrive at— spores easily seen and followed—here were a multitude of delicate little threads, scarcely more visible than dead flagella and poured out amongst the million objects which, under an oil-immersion lens, go to make up a mosquito. I dare say you imagined my consternation. I could not conceive what was to happen to the rods.

Well, I was in for a battle. It was, I think, the last stand—on the very breathless heights of science. I am nearly blind and dead with ex-haustion!!—but triumphant. Expect one of the most wonderful things.

The rods were evidently in the insect's *blood*. By merely pricking the back of the thorax and letting its milky juice flow into a minute drop of salt solution thousands of proteosoma—coccidium—rods could be easily obtained. The question was what next?

I now divided my insects before dissection between the thorax and abdomen and examined each part separately. It was found that the rods were often *more numerous in the thorax than in the abdomen;* there were even cases where scarcely one could be found in the ab-domen (the coccidia having evidently burst some days previously as shown by their empty capsules), while numbers (4 or 5 in a field) could be detected on teazing [sic] up the thorax and head.

Here however I was brought up standing. Sometimes the rods were more common in the head, sometimes in the thorax. I went at mos-quito after mosquito spending hours over each, until I was blind and half silly with fatigue. The object was to find if possible a place or structure where the rods accumulate; or to discover some further de-velopment in them. Nothing.

On the 4th however, after pulling out the head by its roots (oeso-phagus etc) from the thorax, some delicate structure dropped out of the cervical aperture of the latter. This proved to be a long branching gland of some sort, looking like a coil of large intestine, and consist-ing of a long duct with closely packed refractive cells attached to it. I noticed at once that the rods were swarming here and were even *pouring out* from somewhere in streams. Suddenly to my amazement it was seen that many of the cells of this gland *contained* the germinal rods of *proteosoma–coccidia within them.* Looking further, the cells of one whole lobe of the gland were simply packed with them, and on bursting the cells the rods poured out of them just as they pour out of the original coccidia.

The rods were quite unmistakable, having the tapering, flattened and vacuolated structure peculiar to them. They are identified at once and no structures like them exist in the normal mosquito. Here they were in the cells of the gland. The cells were not *coccidia*. They are only 25 μ in diameter, have a very thin outline and contain a perfectly clear fluid, without granulations or oil-drops such as the coccidia possess. The rods lay within them quite irregularly and motionless except for brownian movement [like the dancing of particles in gas caused by the collision of molecules]. In one lobe almost every cell contained numbers of rods; in other lobes only one or two cells contained them. By the attachment of the cells to the central duct, it seemed quite easy for the rods to pass on occasion from the former into the latter.

Now what was this gland? Will you believe it, I examined two whole mosquitoes without finding it again? What with the scales, the debris of muscles etc, I could not come upon it. A third mosquito gave the same result, until I opened up the *head* itself. There was the gland *attached by its duct which led straight into the structures somewhere between the eyes.* The cells were again packed with germinal rods.

I have found the gland now altogether in seven mosquitoes. In six of them the cells were packed (especially in some lobes) more or less with germinal rods. In the seventh I could find only a small piece of gland, which was free from rods.

I still experience, however, the greatest difficulty in dissecting out the gland itself. It appears to lie in front of the thorax close to the head, but breaks so easily in the dissection that I cannot locate it properly. In the second mosquito however there was no doubt, as shown by evident attachment, that the duct led straight into the head-piece, probably in to the mouth.

In other words it is a thousand to one, it is a *salivary gland*.

I think that this, after further elaboration, will close at least one cycle of proteosoma, and I feel that I am *almost* entitled to lay down the law by direct observation and tracking the parasite step by step—

Malaria is conveyed from a diseased person or bird to a healthy one by the proper species of mosquito and is inoculated by its bite.

Remember however that there is virtue in the "almost." I don't announce the law yet. Even when the microscope has done its utmost, healthy birds must be infected with all due precautions.

I say *one* cycle. I think it likely there is another. I continually observe that only a portion of the coccidia contain germinal rods. The rest, I now think, give rise to the black sausage-shaped bodies shown in Plate I, fig. 20 of my report, which I believe may be the true spores of the parasite, meant either for free life or to infect grubs.* Oddly enough, in old mosquitoes these bodies get carried away into the tissues—unless they are some disease of the insect. I will attack this next.

7th . . . I dissected two healthy mosquitoes this morning and began by dividing the head and anterior third of the thorax from its middle third by means of a razor, and then carefully breaking up the anterior third. In both cases the glands were found and their ducts were traced straight into the head.

In all probability it is these glands which secrete the stinging fluid which the mosquito injects into the bite. The germinal rods, lying, as they do, in the secreting cells of the gland, pass into the duct when those cells begin to perform their function, and are thus poured out in vast numbers under the skin of the man or bird. Arrived there, numbers of them are probably instantly swept away by the circulation of the blood, in which they immediately begin to develop into malaria parasites, thus completing the cycle. No time to write more.

The experiments in infecting healthy birds began by accident. To keep his infected mosquitoes alive long enough for the full development of the parasite to take place he had been refeeding them on healthy sparrows. Just after he wrote Manson of his triumphant finding of the salivary gland, he examined three of these birds. On 20 June their blood had been perfectly clean; now three weeks later it was swarming with parasites "more proteosoma than I have *ever seen before.*" Over the next weeks he carried out controlled experiments and reiterated them until he was entirely satisfied that proteosoma inoculated by the bite of the grey mosquito into a healthy bird invariably caused parasitaemia.

The first of these experiments he was able to communicate to Manson in time for the British Medical Association meeting. So the proof exposed to the scientific world in July 1898 was complete, if not airtight. Considering how difficult it remains to grasp the remarkable life cycle of plasmodia that Ross discovered—its sexual complexities, the microscopic fecundity of the hundreds of cells implanted on the walls of one mosquito's stomach each capable of bearing thousands of protoplasmic threads (now called sporozoites), each a complete individual, the migration of the sporozoites, so nearly unerring, through the tissues of their host to its head and salivary

---

* In fact these are degenerative products of a failure in the reproductive process (see below, Chapter 14), but in mimicking spores they gave Ross a long, hard run.

gland, ready there to drop down the mosquito's tubular mouth as soon as she lowers it into their next animal home—considering that despite the comparative sophistication of our science and the understanding of biochemical process, the insect cycle of the parasite remains for us a miracle of adaptation—one can believe that the report at Edinburgh in July 1898 caused, as it is said to have done, "quite a furore."*[3]

Dr. Patrick Manson was such a well-known and attractive speaker that any lecture of his drew a good audience. Asked to make a presentation to all sections of the meeting in joint session, he packed the benches of the pathological theater of the University of Edinburgh.[4] Yet he almost didn't make it at all. In June he had suffered a severe attack of "general gout." He was laid up for "three weeks of solid misery and pain," enjoyed a few days remission and then was hit again in the middle of July. Only his determination to present the proof of his mosquito theory got him to Edinburgh two weeks later, still ill and "hardly able to hobble about." When, after beginning his lecture, he had to stand to demonstrate points by diagram, he did not dare sit down again, and as he could not see his prepared manuscript lying on the table, he had to proceed extempore.[5] His presentation was simple, lucid, and glowing with the warmth both of the speaker's personality and of the pleasure in discovery. Manson himself appears to have been impressed with the reaction of his audience, for he wrote to Ross: "The fat is thoroughly in the fire now & you may expect now to hear more of yourself than your modesty may care for." He noted that Lord Lister was "taking a very great interest." William Osler was there from Baltimore, "very much interested," and Manson gave him one of Ross's papers.[6] The meeting offered a unanimous resolution of congratulation to Ross and Manson.[7]

Sweet victory for both! Yet the savor was less for Ross. This was *his* moment, or at least *their* moment, yet only Manson had been present for it. He had been scrupulous in giving Ross the credit; but still it had been Manson's announcement, in Manson's voice; and Manson received the applause. Years later Ross went out of his way to collect memories of those who had been in Edinburgh that July, as though straining still to hear the clapping of hands and, perhaps still sweeter, the exclamations of amazement that in 1898 he was left only to imagine 6,000 miles away.

Moreover, though Manson might be painfully prostrated with the gout—he went right to bed on his return from Edinburgh "frightfully weak & unable to tackle anything but necessary work"—Ross was not only in

---

* For detailed recapitulation of the life cycle of *Plasmodium* see below, Chapter 14.

miserable health himself but also under the inhuman, unremitting pressures of his assignment to finish with malaria and then get on with kala-azar already weighing on him "like a nightmare." He had already applied for a six months' extension of his special duty. That meant that he could not come home as he had thought he might in September. He was longing for a sniff of the cold of England. He was also, he said, financially "nearly ruined from having to live in hotels everywhere—the family in one place, myself in another."

The syndrome of lamentations was as usual—bad weather, poverty, hard work and ill health. Accepted at face value these reiterated as a kind of chorus in his letters portray a man sunk in all the minor miseries of an unappreciated life. The portrait is false. Even at his most complaining Ross almost always was at the same time working, thinking, even playing at high speed expending energy prodigally and joyfully. This time his complaints were prelude to a hope that Manson might get him ordered home right away to take charge of a commission on malaria that was about to be set up by the Royal Society. To go home under orders rather than on furlough prior to retirement would save him money; it would also produce the necessary urgency in the interests of the service to force cancellation of his kala-azar duty. But like so many of Ross's schemes to circumvent bureaucracy this came to nothing. The commission was formed without him, and he had to go to Assam and study kala-azar. It was one of the most frustrating and depressing times in his life, and perhaps the only time he did a bad job. Believing when he went to Assam that kala-azar was a particularly pernicious kind of malaria—as the last student of the disease had affirmed—Ross duly proved to his own satisfaction that malaria it was. Yet the symptoms of kala-azar and the course it takes are so different from those of malaria that Ross had to develop hypotheses unsupported by observation in order to make the two distinct etiologies even seem compatible.*[8]

But that in the end was not important. The worst of his kala-azar work, which occupied him into February 1899, was that it kept him from completing his investigation of malaria. He had no chance to show that the life cycle of the parasite causing human malaria was identical with that which he had demonstrated in birds, and to follow the lead of the dapple-wing to the incrimination of *Anopheles* as the sole vector.

---

* Kala-azar in fact is caused by a different parasite, identified in 1902 by Leishman and independently by Donovan; the disease is now called Leishmaniasis. It was Ross who generously proposed that the kala-azar parasite which he had missed be called *Leishmania donovani.*

13 / The Roman Quarrel

The last lap went to the Italians. They would complete, round out and refine Ross's discoveries as earlier they had Laveran's. Ross was later to declare that they did nothing he could not have done as well and would have done in a matter of weeks had he only been allowed to by the British Army. Well, maybe. Yet it does appear that in this last stage the superior techniques, facilities and even reputation of the Italians were all but essential to the job.

In fact Ross himself at that time welcomed them to it. In November 1898, bogged down in the kala-azar study and literally sick of it, he wrote to a former IMS officer then resident in Rome asking him to convey felicitations to Bignami and Grassi for their success to date in identifying the vector and confirming the mosquito cycle of the plasmodium. "I will do everything in my power," he wrote, "to help the Italian savants whose splendid work on malaria is so well known." Grassi from his side was reported to be cordially disposed, familiar with all that Ross had done and to have spoken of it "in the highest terms."[1]*

Yet in a matter of weeks these polite exchanges were swept away by a furious quarrel that was to embitter Ross for the rest of his life and impugn Grassi's scientific integrity.[2] Ironically the rivalry that touched it off seems

---

* The notes to this chapter provide further discussion of the controversy as well as documentation for anyone particularly interested in trying to apportion blame.

Giovanni Battista Grassi

not to have been between Grassi and Ross at all but between Grassi and Robert Koch.

The Italians began work in the middle of July 1898. By that time Ross's proof was complete and partly published. Before the end of the summer the results were all public both in his official report circulated to the Italians, among others, and in Manson's Edinburgh lecture printed in two British journals.[3] Grassi's colleagues were familiar with all of this. They knew that the two main tasks left were to demonstrate that the parasite of human malaria went through a cycle in the mosquito similar to that of Ross's *Proteosoma,* and to identify the mosquito that transmitted human malaria.

Grassi organized and divided up the work. Antonio Dionisi, who had worked with birds in 1897, was to test Ross's findings by repeating his experiments. Bignami, despite his earlier failures, proposed once more to prove his own mosquito theory by infecting volunteers by mosquito bite. Grassi himself would survey certain well-known feverish and healthy places in Italy and by comparing their mosquito populations try to deduce which were the dangerous species. Once he had found them, the final work could proceed, following Ross's trail through the mosquito to ascertain the cycle of the human malaria parasite. This job would be done by Bignami and a colleague, Giovanni Bastianelli.

The research strategy was sound enough but it had to be carried through in a most unscientific rush. Bignami had scarcely lined up his volunteers and collected his mosquitoes, Grassi had hardly departed Rome, when with much fanfare Koch arrived in Italy. From the Italians' point of view Koch was as much an interloper in their field as Ross and his immense reputation made him much harder to swallow.

Koch in fact had never shown a great deal of interest in malaria, though he claimed to have developed a mosquito theory of his own as early as 1883.[4] Lately, however, he had been recruited for the last stages of the investigation by the German government which sent him on official mission to German East Africa to solve the malaria problem. He was just back from Africa now and came to Italy avowedly to finish the job. Sponsored by the German government, and at the invitation of the Italian, he had given himself a couple of months to wrap things up. Genius that he was, it seemed that he might just do that. And if he did he was sure, on the record, to take full credit. His report from East Africa mentioned neither Ross nor the Italians; it read indeed as though Koch had been the first ever to consider the problems.[5]

For Grassi, premier zoologist of Italy and perhaps the world, Koch's mission was an insult to him and to Italian science. Not only had his government extended every official courtesy but it also put at Koch's disposal free facilities and assistants for research such as no native researcher had ever enjoyed. Worst of all, some of the politicians and newspapers talked as though Koch were bringing scientific enlightenment to a dark continent.

Grassi left Rome about the middle of July. Koch arrived triumphantly in Milan on 14 August. "In Milan for several days is the illustrious bacteriologist, Professor Koch, who in these last years has set the whole world talking." Other newspapers announced more matter-of-factly that Koch had come to complete malarial studies he had begun in Africa. Thereafter reporters followed his travels, reporting minutiae like crumbs from the prophet's table: He visited Maggiore Hospital yesterday; he would go to Pavia today; at Pavia he extracted some blood from a patient and went to make some observations in the laboratory of Dr. Mariottini; then he returned to Milan.[6]

So it went until Koch's departure at last from Rome on 2 October. No wonder Grassi, whose sense of his own importance quite equaled Koch's, was miffed on his re-entry into Rome in late September after what he called "most fatiguing experiments."[7] It seemed to Grassi that he and his colleagues were being ignominiously shunted aside. While in India the amateur Ross who did not know one mosquito from another was claiming that he had done it all, Koch had invaded Italy itself to make off with whatever bits of laurel might remain. Grassi said he felt as though he were back in the epoch of Austrian dominion over Italy, or, to mix epochs, as though Koch were a new Caesar repeating from day to day, "Veni; vidi; vici"; or—any allusion could serve his bitterness—as though Koch meant to show once more that "only in the cloudy north was it possible for the star of science to shine for the illumination of the sleepy brains of the degenerate Italian race."[8]

Grassi in September had some interesting but necessarily spotty data from his survey. In places he had looked there were notably different mixes of mosquito populations that could be correlated with the presence and absence of malaria. For instance, he thought he had found an "intimate relationship" between the virulence of disease in the Roman Campagna, certain areas of Lombardy, Venetia and Tuscany, and the abundance in all of them of *Anopheles claviger*. In the woods of Rovellasca, on the other hand, and in the zoological gardens at Naples where *Culex elegans* predominated, there was no fever. In a doctor's house in Tuscany where he stayed—culex mosquitoes, no fever; at a nearby foundry—lots of fever among the workers and lots of anophelines (called "zanzaroni" locally, instead of standard Italian for mosquitoes, "zanzare").[9] All this was interesting but decidedly anecdotal evidence. It was not the stuff from which a careful scientist would wish to draw conclusions at all.

Probably Grassi ordinarily would have been reluctant too. But now he felt driven to publish at once to put in his claim lest Koch should meanwhile have solved the riddle himself.[10] With such caution as was possible in those circumstances he named three species as "enormously suspect": *Anopheles claviger, Culex penicillaris* and *Culex malariae*. As a deduction from statistical evidence which made not the slightest claim to being statistically reliable, such a finding could at most be a starting point for further research. And in fact it was. But another year would pass before Grassi could get around to the necessary rigorous experiments which finally eliminated *Culex* while incriminating most anophelines. At the moment, as he later revealed, he had no suspicion himself that *Anopheles* was the real and sole culprit, even though Ross's 1897 experiments had pointed the finger at spotted wings, a characteristic unique to the genus.[11]

Even more notably rushed was Bignami's publication. During the summer he had been able to do only two experiments, seemingly because he could get only two volunteers. Both were patients in a hospital for nervous diseases. Both were bitten repeatedly by wild mosquitoes caught near Porto, a notoriously malarious place, and by mosquitoes reared in the laboratory from larvae collected in the Roman Campagna. Bignami did not identify any of the insects, and both trials failed.

In October he tried again using the three species that had been found enormously suspect by Grassi, along with the volunteer who had been bitten in his first experiment. In November this man obligingly developed a fever and parasites appeared in his blood. Grassi was called in to look at the mosquitoes. He verified all three of his suspects but thought that since so few of the anophelines had been used they could be exonerated.

With only one success out of three tries, in experiments using mosquitoes which, unlike Ross's, had not been experimentally fed on known infected blood, Bignami nevertheless claimed complete proof of transmission by bite. So patently circumstantial was the link between bite and fever that Bignami himself had to rest his case on his inability to think of any other source of his man's illness. Yet like Grassi he published at once and scarcely hedged his conclusions.[12]

Both men were too experienced in the ways of science to have crawled so far out on a limb but for two circumstances: One was the urgency of beating Koch into print—they could, if necessary, edit or even retract later—and the other was Ross's work establishing a high probability that human malaria was conveyed by the bite of particular species of mosquito with speckled wings. The fact, in other words, that their work confirmed deductions made probable by Ross's enabled them to draw conclusions with a confidence that their own evidence did not warrant.

Grassi's first publication of his summer's work appeared in two journals in early October.[13] There he announced that his colleagues, Angelo Celli, Amico Bignami, Antonio Dionisi and Giovanni Bastianelli, were even then experimenting with the mosquitoes—"le zanzare e i zanzaroni" (*Culex* and *Anopheles*)—selected by him as probable vectors. "We hope therefore to arrive at a definitive solution to the question."[14]

In fact only the joint research that Grassi had allotted to Bignami and Bastianelli, beginning about that time, entered directly into competition with Koch.* "Working rapidly" they observed and described the evolution of the parasite of human malaria in an anopheline mosquito. It exactly duplicated the process that Ross had observed in *Proteosoma;* they could not have been surprised, since they had before them while they worked a copy of Ross's own official report. The first paper on this research was

---

* Dionisi decided to work on parasites in bats. Celli was working independently on the problem of immunity.

finished on 28 November, the second on 22 December 1898. Grassi sent copies of one or both to Koch "as a Christmas present." Recalling that moment later, he wrote: "Since Koch had not yet published anything, we could declare that the victory was completely ours!"[15]

So intent had they been on the race with Koch that they almost overlooked Ross. Their December paper described the cycle of *Plasmodium* in the mosquito as if it were all a fresh revelation. Only at the end did they refer to Ross's discoveries, in these words: "It [the life cycle of *Plasmodium*] finds in large part confirmation in that observed by Ross for proteosoma of birds in the *grey mosquito*."[16]

When he read that, Ross was stung to instant anger. Today the most elementary dictate of scientific good manners is to acknowledge first and precisely any earlier research on which one's own is based. That code was not so well established then. Yet even in the most charitable reading, the Italians' brief, ambiguous and belated mention of their immense intellectual debt to Ross's pioneering work was so perfunctory as to be seriously misleading. It seemed to set their work on a footing equal and parallel with Ross's. In fact they had followed Ross's published procedures step by step to demonstrate (importantly but not originally) that the plasmodium of human malaria behaved in the mosquito exactly as Ross said *Proteosoma* behaved. If their paper was not quite piracy, as Ross alleged, neither was it fair play, and Bignami and Bastianelli in effect apologized later by dissociating themselves from Grassi's increasingly arrogant contentions.[17]

Ross, once launched in anger, was never to pull back. He engaged in a lifelong polemic to quash all Italian pretensions and reassert with everdiminishing qualifications that he and he alone had demonstrated the transmission of malaria by mosquitoes. Grassi, no less egotistical and stubborn, fought him all the way.[18]

Once the quarrel swung uncompromisingly into all-out attacks and counterattacks, the simpler truths were so twisted by passion that it is difficult to recognize them even today. They remain, nevertheless, quite simple. Ross might have completed his proof with human malaria, but he did not; Grassi with Bignami and Bastianelli did. Ross flagged the dapplewing mosquito as a probable vector; Grassi showed that it was *Anopheles* and that all its generic sisters were also guilty. Ross clearly is not entitled to the whole credit for the whole proof, simply because he did not finish it. On the other hand it makes no sense or justice to couple the names of Ross and Grassi together as co-discoverers—as is often done—without noting the very large difference between the explorer at the helm and those who rode his decks and helped make a landing.

Ross was vindicated in the end with a knighthood and the Nobel prize in medicine, then only the second ever awarded. But his terrible obsession with righting the record cost him many friends and much good will that might have eased his second career as a battler in the field against malaria. As for Grassi, he made such an implacable enemy of Koch that Koch spoke of him as a charlatan without either ethics or brains. In 1902 when Ross was recommended for the Nobel prize, the committee considered splitting it with Grassi. Koch's violent opposition was probably decisive in preventing that.

The ragged ends of the many divergent hypotheses about the life of the malarial parasite that had grown over the years, were in 1898 and 1899 trimmed to the consensus that now gathered around Ross's discovery. Koch while working in Rome had succeeded in demonstrating the genetic material, chromatin, in the flagella and showed his preparation to Doctors Bastianelli and Bignami.[19] They accepted this as final disproof of the notion that flagella were agonistic forms, to which the Italians had clung so long. MacCallum's discovery of fertilization, so far as I can tell, was never overtly challenged or publicly confirmed but lay around in the scientific consciousness until it became commonplace. The first hours of the parasite in the mosquito, including fertilization and the lodging of the oökinete in the stomach wall, which both Ross and the Italians omitted from their descriptions of the life cycle, were eventually filled in.

A relict of the past more difficult to tidy up was the notion that the malarial germ lurked in malarious places quite independently of either man or mosquito. Almost everyone believed—though there was and obviously could be no evidence—that malaria existed where man did not. Since transmission of the disease from man to man by the bite of the mosquito could not account for that, it seemed there must be another pathway to infection. Thus Dionisi defended his apparent diversion in 1898 to the study of parasites in bats on grounds that animal malaria might explain that supposed phenomenon.[20] Koch, on the analogy of the parasitic cycle in Texas fever, in 1899 still expected to find that mosquitoes could in some way bequeath their parasites to their offspring. Ross, as noted, was beguiled with the "black spores" that he thought might be stages in an alternative life cycle that would bypass man.

These ideas lingered but lost their force as no evidence appeared to support them. Moreover, it had always been hard to imagine that a parasite adapted to life in two hosts could in addition have a third existence contending with the quite different rigors of living free. It does not. The extraordinarily complicated life of the parasite as Laveran, Ross and the Italian savants exposed it has been found since to be even more complicated, but it lives in only two homes: the vertebrate host and the mosquito.

14 / The Three Lives of *Plasmodium*

After four years of research Ross had described in part the development of one species of *Plasmodium* in one species of mosquito. He thus made landfall on a vast continent of knowledge that is still being explored. The parasite with which Ross worked, *Plasmodium relictum,* is now reckoned as just one of twenty-five species that infect only birds. Others have evolved to parasitize the blood of mice and rats, flying squirrels, porcupines, bats, lizards, snakes and other reptiles, ungulates and primates. Eighteen species have been identified in lemurs, monkeys and higher apes.*

Man is normally host to just four†: *Plasmodium vivax,* cause of the seldom fatal and commonest form of malaria (formerly known as tertian or benign tertian, now most often simply as vivax malaria); *Plasmodium ovale,* the rarest of the four species, native to the West coast of Africa and so like *vivax* in appearance and effect that it was not differentiated until 1922; *Plasmodium malariae,* distributed in inexplicably spotty fashion throughout the world and cause of the generally mild but often extraordinarily tenacious quartan fever; and *Plasmodium falciparum,* named for the unique crescent shape of its gametocytes and most lethal of the four, a

---

* Some of these animals and others are also host to other genera of protozoa closely related to *Plasmodium* and sometimes causing similar disorders. See Garnham (1966).

† Human beings have occasionally been infected by species normally parasitic on monkeys.

parasite needing long warm seasons to flourish, now most common in Africa but a threat everywhere in the tropics.

Ross actually observed only a portion of the life cycle of *Plasmodium relictum* in the grey mosquito—from fertilized eggs on the mosquito's stomach walls (oöcysts) to the threadlike sporozoites that lodged in her salivary glands. He then proved that healthy birds were almost invariably infected by the bite of mosquitoes previously fed on parasitized birds, providing that sufficient time had elapsed to let the plasmodia complete the cycle he had witnessed. Finally he noted that mosquitoes discharge saliva in the course of feeding. From these facts by reasonable deduction he closed the loop of the parasite's extraordinary career through man and mosquito. He deduced that the oöcysts had derived from the crescents and spheres ingested by the mosquito with her blood meal, though he had not in fact seen these pass into the mosquito nor even watched the process of fertilization. At the other end of the transmission chain, he supposed that sporozoites were injected with saliva into the new host to enter the blood and resume the familiar asexual cycle of eating, growing and dividing. But neither he nor anyone else had found sporozoites in the puncture wound of birds or man. No one indeed had found the sporozoite naturally occurring anywhere outside a mosquito. Nor would anyone for many years.

There remained great white places on Ross's map. He presumed, for instance, that sporozoites entering a man's blood burrowed straightaway into red cells, and once inside transformed themselves into the pale little amoebae that Celli and Marchiafava had called "plasmodi." That seemed direct and plausible. But Professor Grassi for one doubted it. The nucleus of the sporozoite and the nucleus of the youngest "amoeba" or schizont in a red corpuscle were so different, he thought, that a considerable process of development would be required to convert one into the other. In his summing up in 1901 of the research to date on malaria, Grassi suggested that there ought therefore to be a third parasite cycle somewhere in the body to carry out the necessary transformations.[1] He was exactly right. But no one paid much attention.

Even Grassi himself did not pursue the matter because in 1903 the eminent German parasitologist, Fritz Schaudinn, claimed to have settled it. The sporozoite, said Schaudinn, goes directly into the red cell; he had seen it happen. In a warmed, dilute drop of his own blood drawn from a blood blister he got from rowing, Professor Schaudinn placed ripe and ruptured oöcysts from an infected mosquito and watched through his microscope for six hours without let. He described how during the first hour two sporozoites pushed into red corpuscles, first making a dent, then striking through the cell membrane with their fine pointed tails and at last pulling their bodies inside by peristaltic jerks.[2]

Parasitologists are certain now that nothing of the sort happened, that it could not have happened. Whatever Schaudinn saw, it was not a sporozoite entering a red cell. Yet so great was his reputation and so persuasive the circumstantial detail with which he described his observations that for a generation they carried the weight of revealed truth, proof against the repeated failures of everyone else who tried it to reopen the window he supposedly looked through.

Schaudinn's curious delusion lay like a spell over subsequent investigators. Compounded of plausibility and authority (the vestments of truth), it was difficult to shake off. Yet many wished to do so: Schaudinn's picture of the parasite emerging from the mosquito and resettling at once into its old warm blood habitat did not jibe with certain other facts. Some of these—the curious phenomenon of long-term relapses for instance—were known at that time; others emerged during the following three decades. Many began appearing in the 1920s out of new laboratories that enjoyed a boon unusual in medical research, an abundance of human guinea pigs.

It was known for years, perhaps even in ancient Greece, that the insane, or some of them, might recover their sanity after an attack of malaria. But only after World War I was this still not wholly explained reaction turned systematically to the treatment of mental illness. It began with a Viennese psychiatrist, Wagner-Jauregg, whose successes after 1922 prompted Britain, the United States and Rumania to set up special treatment units to use malaria as therapy, especially for syphilitics suffering general paresis. These people had heretofore been considered hopelessly insane. But in Britain during the first five years of the special unit, a fifth of the nearly 3,000 treated with malaria walked out of the hospital to function as human beings again. Many more were substantially helped.[3]

Two ways deliberately to give a person malaria are to have him bitten by a mosquito previously fed on malarial blood or to inject that infected blood into his veins directly. Both methods were used in the special hospitals. Both produced satisfactory fevers. In other respects, however, the transfused and the bitten patients had strikingly different experiences. The transfused came down with fever almost immediately; the bitten not for a week or more. If given appropriate doses of quinine the transfused showed no signs of illness at all; the bitten became feverish about on schedule as though they had not been treated. Once cured, those receiving blood injections stayed cured, those bitten relapsed weeks or months later. How did the two groups differ? Only in this: Whereas one had taken in sporozoites from the mosquito's salivary glands, the other received the blood forms of the parasite as these had developed in another human body. If Schaudinn had been right and the difference between a sporozoite and a blood schizont is only the few seconds or minutes it takes the former to find and get inside a red blood cell, then drastic differences in the behavior of the blood-induced and the mosquito-induced diseases simply could not be explained.

Suppose instead that the sporozoite, unaffected by quinine, takes a considerable time to metamorphose into the vulnerable blood forms; suppose that it makes this change somewhere outside the blood stream where quinine cannot reach; suppose that not all the sporozoites mature at once or that, maturing, they elect for some reason to remain hidden long after some of their fellows have moved out into the blood, so that for weeks or months they may continue to be sheltered against antimalarial drugs and other hazards in the open blood. Such a sequence of events would fit the facts and explain them admirably. This turned out to be more or less the truth, though difficult to prove.

Hypotheses, evidence and scientific interest built slowly until the middle 1930s, when amidst shades of the great international competition of some fifty years earlier, British, Italian, American and German investigators converged on the problem and in about a dozen years solved it. In Italy Giulio Raffaele working with birds—another echo of the past—in 1934 found and described avian parasites developing in the internal organs of infected canaries inside a special kind of cell that lines many internal organs, and manufactures blood elements. The parasite contained none of the typical malarial black pigment because, not being in a red cell, it was not feeding on haemoglobin. Yet there was no doubt of its identity.[4]

Others—Italians, British, Germans and Americans—confirmed and extended Raffaele's findings.[5] By 1937 most experts had no longer the slightest doubt that plasmodia in birds went through a third life cycle inside the vertebrate host but outside the blood. And so, nearly everyone believed, must it do in man. Grassi and his colleagues had taken only a few months to retrace Ross's steps and show that the human species of the parasite developed in mosquitoes just as the bird species did. Now it took ten years to demonstrate that the bird–man analogy also held in part for the third cycle. The trouble of course was that people as experimental subjects, no matter how cooperative, have special disadvantages. They cannot be taken apart like mosquitoes and birds to look for sporozoites, and they are very large: immense haystacks in which to look for a handful of sporozoite needles that might hole up literally in any one of billions of body cells.

The first important step narrowing the search was taken by N. Hamilton

Fairley during World War II. With the help of army volunteers Fairley measured the duration of the third cycle by establishing that from the moment of infection *Plasmodium vivax* took precisely eight days to appear in the blood stream; *P. falciparum* took just five. So doctors now knew when to look, but still not where.[6]

In 1947 P. C. C. Garnham, working in Kenya, found a monkey malaria parasite developing in the liver cells.[7] That was a clue but unfortunately the particular parasite (*P. kochi*) is not an especially close relative of human parasites. Garnham soon thereafter came back to London where he joined Colonel H. E. Shortt in research begun before the war at the London School of Hygiene and Tropical Medicine, home of the Ronald Ross Institute. Shortt was working with rhesus monkeys that host a parasite (*P. cynomolgi*) so like *P. vivax* that it can give people malaria. Where *cynomolgi* lodged it seemed altogether likely that *vivax* would also be found.[8]

After many failures Shortt, now with Garnham's help, decided to better the odds of the haystack by vastly multiplying the number of needles. The two of them set 500 infected mosquitoes to feed on a single rhesus and then for good measure injected the animal with the insects themselves ground up in monkey serum. Seven days later the monkey was sacrificed and specimens of all his organs taken for microscopic examination. Despite the clue unearthed by Garnham, Shortt—as he later admitted—was "obsessed" with the bird work and expected the parasites to lodge in the special cells of the reticulo-endothelial system as they do in birds.

It was twenty-one days before Shortt got around to examining sections of the monkey's liver, where almost at once he found what he described as an ovoid body with vacuole and nuclei-like granules. This, he thought, was "IT!" But having suffered many disappointments, he schooled himself to patience. It was a Friday afternoon. He put the slide away, deciding "to let the excitement simmer over the week-end and to re-examine it on Monday." When he came back to it neither he nor Garnham had any doubt. They called in the great protozoologist C. M. Wenyon "as the supreme authority." After examining the preparation, Wenyon, in the authentic tones of historic utterance, said, "Well, that seems to be all right."*[9] Shortt and Garnham promptly sent off a brief note to *Nature,* just to stake their claim to primacy in the discovery. "These results," they wrote in conclusion, "appear to confirm the almost universal belief in the existence of a

---

* It is interesting that more than ten years earlier Wenyon had also been called in to certify the tissue phases of a bird parasite, whose discovery by Colonel S. P. James in 1937 had first triggered Shortt's own quest.

pre-erythrocytic* stage in the mammalian malaria parasite."[10] Suitably sober words which nevertheless did not muffle the ring of triumph.

Now they knew where to look for *Plasmodium vivax* in people. They found a subject, a mental patient needing malaria therapy and willing to undergo the special added discomfort of an operation to remove a small slice of his liver. The experiment began with the feeding of 3,600 mosquitoes on patients whose blood contained *vivax* gametocytes. These insects were kept in cages for fourteen days with sustaining meals of rabbit blood while the parasites developed. At the end of that time the 2,010 insects that were still alive were put to feed on the volunteer on two successive days. Next, doctors dissected out the mosquitoes' salivary glands, mixed the remaining sporozoites in a plasma and saline solution and injected them into the patient. It is unlikely that any human being ever before had been so massively invaded by the parasites of malaria.[11]

Again the doctors let just one week pass, to catch the parasite on the last day of its third cycle when presumably it would be most easily visible. A surgeon then cut out a small section of the patient's liver—a minor operation—and technicians began preparing it for examination. But Shortt could not wait; the normal processing would take several days. He put a bit of the tissue in a bottle with a very strong fixative, one in which the specimen would spoil if left too long, and took a train for London. There he delivered the main specimen to his lab for processing. His own bit, after a surreptitious washing in a station lavatory, he took with him to a field station near his home in Hertfordshire. There he worked through the night—shades of Ross on the final scent—and found, though not until the exhausted hours of the early morning, what he was looking for.[12]

The work of confirming, refining and extending these observations for each of the four species continued for several years.† Although some obscurities persist, the main events in the three lives of *Plasmodium* are now well attested. It is time to review them.

A thoroughly infected anopheline mosquito ready to pass on malaria may have 5,000 to (exceptionally) 100,000 or more sporozoites in her salivary glands. As constrictions of the proboscis force the sporozoites to

---

* "Before the blood forms." Later usage has tended to drop the term in favor of the more general "exo-erythrocytic" for all stages of development outside the red corpuscles, whether occurring directly after the inoculation of sporozoites or later in the course of the infection and leading, for instance, to relapses. Both are scientifically useful but clumsy terms for which the simpler "tissue cycle" will do well enough here.

† Because of the difficulty of finding carriers with sufficient numbers of gametocytes to infect large numbers of mosquitoes the tissue cycle in *P. ovale* was not observed until 1954, and in *P. malariae* it has been described only from a chimpanzee (Garnham, 1966).

pass through single file it seems unlikely that more than 1,000 ever leave in a single feeding, and the numbers are usually much smaller.*[13] In the blood the sporozoites appear to be carried directly to the liver and apparently most of them get there, although how and why is not clear.

By painstaking work over a period of four years two German investigators managed to backtrack on the trail of the sporozoite in birds to find it in tissue cells five hours after inoculation.[14] The youngest form seen in primates has been two days old. It is then minute—about two thousandths of a millimeter (2 μ) in diameter—but already well established. Indeed the next day it begins the process of splitting its nucleus preparatory to reproduction. Over the next several days (from five to fifteen altogether, depending on the species) it rapidly grows to fifty times the diameter, more than 100,000 times the volume, of its second-day size.

The nuclei go on dividing until at ripeness the creature, still inside the liver cell, is in effect a package of thousands of incipient individuals. When its time comes, it ruptures; each nucleus picks up a tiny bit of cytoplasm from the mother store and emerges as a new individual. Now called a merozoite, it heads for the next habitat, a red blood cell. A single schizont derived from a single sporozoite of *Plasmodium falciparum* has been estimated to contain 40,000 merozoites at maturity.

So long as the parasite remains in the liver cells neither we nor apparently any of its other mammalian hosts suffer. The sojourn in the liver is a period of latency—of symptomless infection—which continues even after the emergence of the merozoites until these have become numerous enough by division to cause the first onset of fever. Ordinarily one can expect this state of latency to last a week or two, the time required for the parasite to complete its tissue cycle and take over in force in the blood. But sometimes it lasts much longer.

In Holland until about forty years ago there used to be well-defined, though small, outbreaks of malaria in the early spring before the warming weather could have permitted mosquitoes to transmit it. These attacks were found to be due to parasites which had been injected by mosquitoes the previous autumn and during the winter had lain dormant in the bodies of their human hosts. In Russia, scientists identified a distinct hibernating strain of the *vivax* parasite consistent in its behavior and clearly evolved to cope with northern European winters. We now know that hibernation takes place in the liver, but not how the creature times its sleep and its awakening.

---

* Some minimum is needed to produce malaria and experiments now under way are trying to find out what that is.

No less mysterious are the probably similar mechanisms underlying the phenomenon of malarial relapse, which occurs only in *vivax* and *ovale* malaria. The best guess at the moment is that the relapses are caused by late-developing sporozoites that are under genetic control.

When the mature liver schizont bursts to scatter its offspring, certain kinds of white blood cells, known as phagocytes, swarm into the neighborhood as to a feast. And that is just what they are there for. As their name indicates they are cells that eat and what they eat is any small matter in the blood that is chemically tagged as alien. We are pleased sometimes to regard these hungry cells as soldiers of the blood ready to defend us against invasions of microbes. But it is doubtful that there is a militant streak on either side. Parasite and phagocyte are equally sensibly concerned with turning into food whatever edible comes their way.[15]

Phagocytes in the liver do actually devour a good many of the young merozoites, but not all. Those that escape proceed to *their* feed. It is of the essence of successful parasitism that neither side should ever take the last swallow. A host must exact such toll of the parasites as will check their voracity well short of fatal damage. The parasite must, as it were, be willing to suffer those losses in order to keep its own literally lethal vitality from destroying the host and consequently itself. This system of mutual frustration producing an effect of mutual forbearance generally works well in malaria. Ecologically the man–mosquito–parasite relationship is a highly stable system, a "balance of nature" we would like very much to upset. And can't.

Merozoites that are not eaten enter red blood cells at once. Or, reversing the proposition, merozoites able at once to enter red cells escape being eaten. Although occasionally the parasites—particularly those of the species *falciparum*—may cling for a time to the outside of the blood cell, most, and probably all, penetrate it within minutes and develop inside it. The fact is that merozoites are almost never found free-swimming in blood plasma, suggesting that the open plasma full of phagocytes is indeed a sea of sharks.

How the parasites enter a blood cell is still unknown. But electron microscopes and sophisticated biochemical techniques have begun to throw some light on the process. It is thought that the merozoite finds the cell by means of special minute organelles which make first contact with the cell membrane and after penetration disappear. That a chemical attraction is set up between the cell and the parasite has been made clear by experiments that have "washed" the cell membrane with enzymes and thereby prevented penetration.[16] Clearly this whole subject is of immense theoretical interest to immunologists and of practical interest to malariologists. If the red corpuscle could be assisted chemically to repel invaders one might have at last an inoculation for malaria that could conquer the disease.

The young merozoite is again very small. (It is remarkable how many times during its life this one-celled parasite scales down to another infinitesimal youth as if testing the lower limits of viability.) Most commonly, it looks at first in the cell like a tiny ring as it surrounds a bit of haemoglobin and begins to feed. After a while the central feeding vacuole that suggests a ring disappears and the nucleus begins to divide. Basically it begins to repeat in blood the asexual growth and multiplication process it has just gone through in liver cells. Now the process, however, is much quicker and less ambitious: Depending on the species, growth and division in human blood takes from 48 to 72 hours, producing not more than thirty-six young and usually fewer. The splitting of the nucleus takes place entirely before there is any division of the cell protoplasm, as it did in the liver cells. At the climactic moment the parasite, again a schizont, bursts all at once, shattering its own membrane and that of the host cell, and spilling its progeny into the blood plasma. And once more—tireless cycle!—the new brood, who resume the title of merozoites, seek out *their* own red cells and all is to do over again.

After two or three of these blood cycles the density of parasites in the blood is such that their precipitous release periodically causes paroxysms of fever. Characteristically beginning with sensations of shivering cold or rigor, the fever may reach 105 degrees Fahrenheit or even higher. Seldom, if ever, fatal in itself, it lasts typically three or four hours, terminated by profuse sweating and then relief accompanied by a sense of weakness. Thereafter the fever may resurge every day, every other day or every third day for one or two weeks, depending on the species of parasite and the number of broods present concurrently in the blood.

If no drugs are taken, all forms of malaria hang on for at least six months, sometimes for years, and bouts of fever periodically recur. The early reappearances are generally recrudescences and not relapses. Parasites remain in the blood after the initial attack, but, tamed by the body's immunity, they multiply so slowly as to cause no fever. Then weeks later, presumably through a relaxation of the immune defense, they suddenly resume an explosive reproduction and the fever returns. (As noted, true relapses, which do not occur in malignant or quartan fevers, are presumed to be the product of fresh blood cycles initiated by delayed release of merozoites from the liver cells.)

Destruction of the red blood cells of course causes anaemia. After multiple and untreated infections, the anaemia may become severe and debilitating. Ordinarily the body cell factories can make good the losses as soon as the infection ends.

Far more serious is the special effect that the *falciparum* parasite of malignant malaria has on the blood cells. It makes them sticky. Two days or so after the young ring form has gotten established and begun to grow, the red cells which it infects disappear from the circulation. The reason is that they have been trapped in sinuses and vessels deep in the body. There the infected cells clump together, stick to white cells and cling to the walls of the blood vessels. So they block and slow the movement of the blood, while inside them the parasites enlarge and divide. Repeated division and reinvasion of fresh cells may so clog the capillaries as to deprive that part of the body of oxygen. If this happens in the brain, as it frequently does, the victim goes into a coma and usually dies. A massive enough congestion in any vital organ may result in death. Indeed it is chiefly this special propensity for development in the inner organs of the body that makes *falciparum* alone of the human forms of malaria a killer. Recent experiments have shown knoblike protrusions on blood cells infected with *falciparum* parasites and it is possible that these knobs brush so close to cells lining the capillaries as to permit the formation of chemical bonds between the lining and the blood.[17]

It is not entirely fanciful to regard these knobs in the evolutionary sense, as youthful rough edges that unnecessarily make life hazardous for both parasite and host and which would probably in time be lost. *Plasmodium falciparum* shows other signs of being less well adapted to life in us than its sister species. It has the shortest cycle of development in the liver and is the most prolific. Whereas *Plasmodium vivax* prefers young blood cells and *Plasmodium malariae* has nearly as strong a preference for old ones, *falciparum* invades them all indiscriminately. The result is that whereas *malariae* choosing senescent cells rarely survives in more than about 5,000 of those cells per cubic millimeter, and *vivax* with its prejudice for the young may infect 50,000, in fatal cases of *falciparum* more than one million cells have been found parasitized in each cubic millimeter of blood. Indeed, there is one record of more than double that density.[18]

Since successful parasitism evolves toward accommodation, perhaps ideally toward a fully cooperative commensalism in which the interests of both animals are served, the reckless behavior of *P. falciparum* suggests that it is new to its host. Perhaps we have not had evolutionary time to develop effective controls over its fecundity, and it has not had time to oust the killers from its genetic main line.

After several rounds of multiplication in the red cells, *Plasmodium* begins producing male and female gametocytes, usually in suitable proportions. Different in structure and behavior, the gametocytes nevertheless appear to arise spontaneously from asexual division.[19] They take longer to mature than the asexual forms (four days instead of two in *vivax*; ten days in *falciparum*). When mature they fill their home cells and become dormant, causing their host no further trouble. Total numbers are bafflingly variable. Though in a general way related to the severity of the infection, identical experimental infections have sometimes produced masses of gametocytes in one patient and none at all in another.[20]

This variability lengthens the odds against the parasite's finding a mosquito host even where malaria is common.[21] When a mosquito does happen to bite someone with a suitable concentration of gametocytes, there then takes place inside her stomach another lottery at unfavorable odds for *Plasmodium*. First, the mosquito must of course happen to be of the right kind. Although many species of *Anopheles* will experimentally host the parasite, only a few are regular vectors; most of the others are relatively inhospitable. Then the temperature must be right. If it is, the males after violent trembling will put forth sperm. Up to eight apiece are possible but sometimes fewer actually emerge. Now the mosquito's stomach we would say is a very small place. But for the flagellum which has to find one of possibly a few score or at most several hundred female parasites among perhaps 30 or 40 million globules of blood, it is a trackless sea in which it can swim only a little way during the few minutes it lives.

S. T. Darling, one of the brilliant early students of malaria, in the 1920s measured the meals consumed by mosquitoes of the species *Anopheles albimanus* (which are small eaters), and the number of gametocytes in each cubic millimeter of the blood on which he fed them. Thrice-fed insects, he calculated, should host 1,632 fertilized parasite eggs. On average they in fact contained only 50. In short, 97 percent of the female parasites that reached the mosquito's stomach died there virgin.[22]

One cannot assume of course that comparable mortality holds in all insects. Certainly the number of parasites that succeed in establishing themselves varies widely, from a few to many hundred. What happens in successful fertilization, it will be recalled, is that a fertilized female becomes herself the offspring (zygote) as her own nucleus merges with that contributed by the flagellum. The new creature stretches out and heads for the mosquito's stomach wall. Though microscopic it has a complicated structure that includes a tapered forward end armed at the tip with a relatively rigid collar. This, as two recent investigators put it, "presents a spearhead for thrusting through the epithelial layer" of cells lining the mosquito's gut.[23] Once through, it rounds out and settles down. Now called an oöcyst, it grows over a period of about nine to ten days, although the actual time required for development is dependent on temperature.*

The oöcysts in growing emerge normally on the outside of the stomach walls as nearly perfect spheres, looking remarkably smooth even at the highest magnification and reflecting light so that they glisten like tiny glass beads. Inside, the parasite's nucleus is dividing rapidly. Toward maturity the nuclei, of which there may be ten thousand, have gathered wisps of cytoplasm around them in the long, thin, curved needles that will become sporozoites.[24]

Released into the insect's body cavity, the sporozoites swarm with the circulating fluids throughout her organs. When they reach the salivary glands they bore through the cell lining and come to rest. They may survive there as long as the mosquito lives. But if she happens to have a longer than average life (if, for instance, she goes into hibernation) the sporozoites gradually lose their vitality.[25]

At every stage of *Plasmodium*'s remarkable travels the odds against its continuance are overwhelming. If a mosquito manages to pick up the parasite from an infected person—not, as we have seen, a likely event to begin with—she must then stay alive for the ten to twelve days that the sporozoites need to develop and lodge in her head. In many species the odds are much against that. One notorious vector, *Anopheles culicifacies,* responsible for much of the malaria of India and virtually all of that of Ceylon (Sri Lanka) has, it has been calculated, only one chance in two hundred of passing the parasite along. In some species the odds resulting from high mortality are worsened still further by the mosquito's comparative indifference to whether she bites people or beasts. The parasite's chances of closing its circuit become four times less likely if the mosquito chooses a human being only every other time it goes in search of a meal.

Malaria, in short, is a most improbable disease. Yet it has demonstrated a durability and a resistance to attack second to none. The ramifications of that paradox are the matter of the rest of this book.

---

* Temperatures higher than the optimum may shorten the cycle; lower temperatures may prolong it up to a month or prevent it altogether. Both deviations cause some mortality. Hence Ross's "black spores."

15 / "A War of Extermination..."[1]

When Ronald Ross first came upon the oöcysts, his wonderful "pigmented cells," protruding from the stomach walls of a dapple-wing mosquito, he exulted in a typically stiff, self-conscious poem:[2]

> This day relenting God
>   Hath placed within my hand
> A wondrous thing; and God
>   Be praised. At His command,
>
> Seeking His secret deeds
>   With tears and toiling breath,
> I find thy cunning seeds,
>   O million-murdering Death.

In truth he did not much exaggerate the importance of what he had done. He had uncovered quite remarkable facts about a quite remarkable form of life, extending a long string of microscopic observations that for a generation had been literally exploring new worlds. Like the earlier discoverers, he opened up brilliant new prospects for conquering disease. Each new discovery coming hard on another had already suggested to some that the road to immortality was open. A quarter of a century earlier, another Englishman, dazzled by the new science, had written: "Disease will be extirpated; the cause of decay will be removed; immortality will be invented. . . . Finally, men will master the forces of Nature; they will become themselves architects of systems, manufacturers of worlds."[3] Ross was perhaps less sanguine—or naive—yet essentially he shared the vision and welcomed his own discovery as inevitably a step toward a millennium being prepared for the world by industrial civilization.

The nineteenth century was pre-eminently a time when science and technology not only were making Western man immensely powerful but were doing so more rapidly than he could explore the problems to whose solution the new powers might be applied. Instead of struggling in the traditional way to use limited knowledge and often makeshift tools in meeting unexpected crises or in incrementally bettering his lot, he found himself with an "excess" capacity so impressive that it seemed possible to issue a general challenge to nature, forestall its hostile initiatives and in effect solve problems in advance. The mood was rather like that of a man of modest means who, having suddenly doubled his income, feels immensely rich because he has not yet discovered how expensive the life of a rich man is.

Ross was challenged and moved by the excitement of scientific discovery but, as he often said himself, it was the "practical" implications of his malaria work that he most valued and that he himself yearned to realize. He had felt most happy and fulfilled as sanitary czar of Bangalore, never as scholar with a microscope. He left India early in 1899 disgruntled that he had not had the chance to complete his research on the transmission of human malaria. He had even a passing thought that he ought to stay on and not leave all those beautiful still-to-be-done experiments to the Italians. But no sooner had he stepped aboard ship than he was swept with relief to be going home, and freshly exhilarated by the prospect of a crusade against malaria.[4]

Yet he had no personal plans. Once again a place was found for him. Once again Patrick Manson played a leading role. Manson had founded a School of Tropical Medicine in London, and when the University of Liverpool showed interest in a similar school, as medical adviser to the Colonial Office he gave it active encouragement. He thought moreover that Ronald Ross might be just the man to start it off as the first lecturer. Ross, after delivering to Manson his final report from India in a meeting of which, interestingly, he could afterward recall not a single detail, went up to talk to the new school's sponsors.[5]

He found that the job would pay him only £250 a year and even that in the long run would be contingent on success in raising an endowment by public subscription. For the nonce the pay would be guaranteed by annual contributions of Alfred Lewis Jones, a wealthy trader and directing partner of a Liverpool shipping firm. It was not much and miserably insecure. But with his Indian Medical Service pension of £292 a year he thought that he would get along, even somewhat better than he had in India. The teaching, he supposed, would be minimal (it was—three students the first year) and the opportunities would probably be generous for frequent travel to the tropics. If he did not have an understanding on that score before he took the job, he got one soon after. He settled in Liverpool in April 1899, fired off his inaugural lecture as a challenge to the world to extirpate malaria at once, and by July was on board ship for Sierra Leone to see what he could do himself.[6]

Sierra Leone was the first of Britain's West African colonies (established in 1787 and made a colony in 1807). Until near the end of the century it was British West African headquarters for trading stations and settlements on the Gold Coast and at Lagos. Sierra Leone itself in its founding and history mixed idealism, racism and business with that air of doing what comes naturally—a kind of sociological primitivism—characteristic of, if not unique to, the nineteenth century. It began as a place to dump London's Black poor, largely ex-slaves from North America and the West Indies. The largest contingent of early settlers was a group of Loyalist slaves who after the American Revolution had escaped to Nova Scotia and who were removed out of the cold, at their own urgent request, to constitute what were afterward known as the Settlers of Freetown, capital of Sierra Leone. After 1807, when the British Parliament outlawed slave-trading (in which British merchants were heavily engaged), Sierra Leone became again the dumping ground for the liberated, known in the local social hierarchy as the Recaptives.[7]

Sierra Leone was a Black settlement but firmly governed by Whites. It prospered by trade with the interior sufficiently to survive and always enjoyed in the councils of Westminster a privileged position because of its political usefulness in the antislavery cause. By the end of the century, when the scramble for Africa had partitioned virtually the whole continent among European powers, Sierra Leone, originally a small mountainous peninsula consisting of Freetown and some satellite villages, extended a "protectorate" deep into the hinterland. A railroad was pushed inland. Alfred Lewis Jones, who owned the Sierra Leone Coaling Company, established the colony's first bank. But the disease-ridden coast was still the White man's grave. A project to make it safe for Europeans took on new urgency.

Ross was never sure whether Alfred Jones understood or believed the mosquito theory of malaria or indeed the possibility of making the tropics healthier by sanitation. Whether from skepticism or penury, Jones refused to screen his own ships. But he did provide free passage on one of them for

Ross, Ross's assistant, Dr. H. E. Annett and Dr. Ernest E. Austen, entomologist of the British Museum of Natural History, for their expedition in the summer of 1899.

Otherwise they could not have gone. The Colonial Office from which Joseph Chamberlain steered the course of Empire contributed £20, matching another £20 offered by the India Office. Manson wangled a grant of £100 from the British Medical Association.[8] That was all they had. Dr. Austen spent part of the BMA money on his personal kit, which cost him altogether £ 12–15, and included collecting bottles, mosquito veils and thin leather gloves to protect him at his work. He also took a gun and may have taken his bicycle, though he worried up to the last minute whether he should. "[I]t has pneumatic tyres," he wrote to Ross, "& I fear it is only too probable that they would speedily get punctured by thorns."[9] Other supplies they got as gifts from well-wishers and merchants, an aluminum medicine chest for instance, from Burroughs, Wellcome. They had letters of introduction to the acting governor of Sierra Leone.*

Such was the advance guard of the armies of extermination that landed in Freetown on 10 August 1899. It had two tasks: to complete the great malaria investigation by proving that mosquitoes transmitted the parasite to man (confirming, in other words—though not in words that Ross ever used—the work of Grassi and his colleagues), and to reconnoiter the habitat of incriminated mosquitoes and plan their destruction.[10]

They were lucky. Austen almost at once picked up and identified the two species that were and still are the main vectors of malaria throughout sub-Saharan Africa: *Anopheles gambiae* (then called *costalis*) and *Anopheles funestus,* small, dark and appropriately named. Both were found where malaria was prevalent and both, on dissection, proved to be loaded with pigmented cells. Ross succeeded in cultivating some of these cells by feeding the little black *funestus* on a soldier with malaria. But the Army wouldn't let him close the cycle and test whether the insect would pass on the disease to another. He had to be content with the fact that since there were no other mosquitoes around, these had to be the ones that did the transmitting. The "proof" was acceptable enough because Ross in his turn could now rest easy in the knowledge that Grassi had already been over the ground. Indeed, he had had word just before leaving England of the results of Grassi's spring and summer experiments of 1899, which incriminated all anophelines while exonerating *Culex*.[11]

---

* Sir Frederick Cardew, the governor, was in London defending himself on charges of having precipitated a war by unwise taxation.

As for the anopheline breeding places, Ross found just what he expected: that the eggs were chiefly laid in middle-sized puddles, big enough not to dry up too fast and small enough not to shelter fish. Freetown had lots of puddles. Though Ross found it a charming town—charming in its setting on and between hills that peaked at just under two thousand feet—its charms lessened on closer acquaintance. The typical two-story frame houses were small and overcrowded; many were dilapidated; the unpaved streets were reasonably well drained in the center of town where most of the Europeans lived, but elsewhere the heavy seasonal rains scoured out deep pits and puddles. There was no town sewerage. Each householder dug his own cesspit, sometimes under the house, sometimes in the yard, and cleaned it only as often as suited him. The British health officer angrily characterized the whole town as one gigantic cesspit.

But either Ross did not stay long enough to see the herculean problems presented by Freetown or else his optimism simply would not let him see them. He thought mosquito breeding could easily be controlled. He wrote to Lord Lister: "We all agree if the local authorities will set themselves heartily to the task, Freetown can be freed of the insects at a trifling cost. We carefully made a map of the whole town, locating all the *Anopheles* puddles. There are only about 100 of these altogether, lying mostly in clusters. All could be drained at little cost and most could be swept out with a broom."[12] To the acting governor he reported still more optimistically that "if all or most of the Anopheles pools in a locality be systematically treated with oil twice a week for a month or two such a blow will be struck at the prevalence of the insects there that they will not be able to recover their ascendancy for a long time."[13]

The governor's health officer, Dr. William Prout, was by no means convinced that Ross had the right idea about how malaria was spread. He was ready to admit that mosquitoes carried the germ but thought the anopheline larvae might pick it up out of the puddles where they fed. In any case he agreed that the puddles ought to go, as he had himself repeatedly urged, "though it was not based on the mosquito theory."[14] He obediently engaged one man to oil the puddles shown on Ross's map.

Ross left in September pleased with his results, though "we cannot answer for the carrying out of" the recommended anti-mosquito measures. His reports appeared in the *British Medical Journal*. Manson sent congratulations: "You have held up the torch once more . . ." Alfred Jones gave the returning crusaders a homecoming banquet. Ross treated the Liverpool Chamber of Commerce and its wealthy merchant members to a "rather fiery" denunciation of the public indifference that permitted malaria to continue its evil work. Then he waited for the logical sequel: "Weary though I was of the tropics, I expected to be called to the front again at any moment—this time in charge of a worthy army."[15]

In fact Ross's reports were shelved ("put by") at the Colonial Office—which, as always, feared recommendations that threatened new expenses.[16] In Freetown the war delivered into the care of one man with an oilcan was not surprisingly making no headway at all. Two members of the Royal Society's Malaria Commission (J. W. W. Stephens and S. R. Christophers), which it will be recalled had been appointed in 1899 at the instigation of Dr. Manson, dropped in to check up. Stephens and Christophers had the time and the appropriate skepticism to re-examine the bases of Ross's optimism. They noted that his mapped puddles appeared to have been treated faithfully with petroleum for several months but that whenever the treatment stopped, larvae reappeared in all of them. (That was just what one would expect though Ross had clearly claimed more lasting benefits.) Ross had seriously understated the number of breeding pools. He had drawn his conclusions from the observations of a single rainy season; other seasons' puddles followed a different set of configurations. And during the rest of the year—as Ross could not have seen—a large breeding population of mosquitoes survived the dry season by using relict pools in the beds of two streams that ran through town. Finally, Ross had overlooked the runoff of springs and various collections of waste water in which Stephens and Christophers found larvae. The two men in short so altered the appreciation of the enemy's force in Freetown that for them the victory that had seemed to Ross so simple and cheap receded out of practical reckoning altogether.*

The Royal Society promptly published these reports and Ross read them.[17] He read too of a scattering of efforts elsewhere: in Hong Kong, where Dr. J. C. Thomson was reported to have had some success in reducing the breeding of mosquitoes; in Lagos, where Governor William MacGregor, himself a doctor, was waging a small but many-pronged campaign of public education, quinine for school children, and drainage; in America, where Dr. Alvah Doty was clearing Staten Island, New York, of malaria mosquitoes; in Havana, where the campaign against yellow fever mosquitoes had begun.[18]

Ross grew restless. He threatened to raise money by public subscription, levy his own troops and storm the enemy under the noses of the do-nothing colonial officials and their unbelieving medical advisers. A wealthy Scot

---

* Ross in his *Memoirs* disparages all these "corrections" of his findings as signifying no more than a self-serving pessimism.

heard the threats, wrote for details, liked what Ross told him and sent £1,000 without strings. Gratefully Ross took the money, with half of it signed up an assistant for a year, and in 1901 went back to Freetown to raise an army.[19]

Sierra Leone had a new governor, Sir Charles King-Harman, though the skeptical Dr. Prout was still on the job. They tolerated the new expedition, indeed gave it cooperation though they were evidently somewhat bemused. Ross, who had based his advocacy of an attack on *Anopheles* on grounds that it could be highly selective and therefore economical in men and money, now decided to eliminate all mosquitoes of all species from Freetown. The breeders in domestic water containers, which he had ignored before, had just been proved to include *Aedes aegypti,* vector of yellow fever.* Other culicines spread filariasis and perhaps other diseases. All mosquitoes notoriously were a nuisance.

Perhaps with the thought that a clean sweep would be likely to produce an improvement sufficiently impressive that people would then be willing to keep it up, Ross organized two battalions of mosquito fighters, an anopheline gang and a culicine gang. The former were to sweep, fill, channel, drain and oil the puddled streets and yards. The latter were to remove the accumulated domestic rubbish from the yards of Freetown, which had never in its history had a garbage collection so far as anyone could recall. Twin tasks for seven maids and Sisyphus. Ross's assistant, Dr. Logan Taylor, who stayed on in Freetown for eighteen months, was afterward to be remembered there chiefly as the man who carted away the rubbish.[20] He and Ross had from thirty to forty men at work, mostly hired by them, some contributed by the government. Ross calculates that the six in the culicine gang in eight months got rid of 2,257 cartloads of trash—broken bottles, calabashes, buckets, empty tins, all the domestic throwaways capable of holding rainwater and hence of sheltering mosquito larvae. All apparently were hauled away by the one bullock cart recorded in town.

It was a memorable cleanup. Half the town was cleaned before Ross left and Dr. Logan kept heroically at it thereafter. But somehow the job never got finished. When C. W. Daniel, the third member of the Royal Society Malaria Committee, came down in the autumn of 1901 to check up, he thought that something like twice the effort would be required: another European supervisor to assist Dr. Logan—only a European, he thought, would be capable—and about 100 workers.[21]

One trouble, as Ross observed on his return the following year, was that

---

* There had been an epidemic of yellow fever in Freetown in 1884; twenty people had died. Fyfe (1962), 445.

the government moved so slowly in grading the streets it was necessary to divert a labor force to oil the persisting puddles so as to keep mosquito breeding in check: too few men then remained to keep up with the draining and filling. As for the householders, they were apparently grateful enough for their cleaner yards but not in the least disposed to keep them that way.

Whether a larger, more extensive effort might have got results was not to be tested. The government had decided on a different "solution": removal of the two hundred or so Europeans in Freetown to the hills, where they would be protected by isolation from the reservoir of parasites in Black blood.*

Segregation had been earnestly recommended by Stephens and Christophers. Along with their observation of many more mosquito breeding places than Ross had allowed, they had noted the affinity of adult insects for the natives. During the day resting mosquitoes were rarely to be found in European houses, but clung in great numbers to the dingy walls and thatched ceilings of one-room native huts in which sometimes twenty people slept on a dirt floor. They believed that native houses—and Black bodies—acted as magnets in a community, drawing in and concentrating even very small populations of mosquitoes. They did an experiment indicating that a native sleeping in a tent would attract vastly more mosquitoes than a White man. The popular notion that Blacks were less often bitten than Whites they showed to be false; Blacks were bitten more but felt it less. Dissection of the insects collected in native houses revealed a high percentage with infected glands. The Stephens–Christophers conclusion: The greatest danger to the health of Europeans lay in their spending the nights near native huts.[22]

For authority this was a singularly appealing conclusion. The governor, Sir Charles, was already much tempted by the prospect of a White settlement in the hills.[23] Even at 700 feet it was notably cooler, "fresh and even exhilarating," Stephens and Christophers wrote, "and one experiences the greatest relief after residence in Freetown with its most enervating, foul atmosphere."[24] The exurbanites moreover would be able to tap mountain streams and springs for a water supply that would be far healthier than the contaminated shallow wells of Freetown. Now solidly backed by scientific opinion, Sir Charles found the coincidence of convenience and good reasons irresistible: He sent off an urgent request to the Colonial Office for permission to build a railway and survey for the new town. "No reasonable

---

* Then and afterward Ross railed against native sloth and official incompetence. He never mentioned the government's decision.

outlay should be objected to."[25] Chamberlain, who had strongly favored the railroad into the interior, to which this would be an administrative add-on if not precisely a spur on the ground, also found the idea appealing despite its expense.

Construction of the railway began at the end of 1902. The two-and-three-quarter-mile line ascending to 1,100 feet above Freetown was completed by January 1904 at a cost of £35,000. Meanwhile, 250 acres were cleared for the hill station on which the government would build twenty-four bungalows at an additional cost of £25,000. To speed construction timber was imported from England.

In building the town, authorities had to extinguish a number of shadowy land titles deriving from earlier grants to ex-slaves. They also decreed that no native buildings were to be permitted within a mile. The Whites were not of course expected to do without their Black house servants, but these were a minor danger; Stephens and Christophers had shown it was native children, not the semi-immune adults, who provided the principal reservoir of malarial infection.

Presumably the hill station worked as malarial prophylaxis for Europeans. At least there were no further complaints. Social segregation hardened in the colony. Sir Charles hoped that business would follow the refugee householders up the hill but in fact there were almost no White entrepreneurs in Sierra Leone any more; everybody was an employee of absent firms or government.[26] They remained so few, moreover, that the railroad was never able to pay its way. After World War I automobiles began carrying commuters up and down the hill; the last passenger train ran in 1929, and the tracks were pulled in 1931.

In the town below everything returned to normal—the filth, the mosquitoes and the parasites. Freetown, for all its continuing importance to the British Empire through two world wars, remained for another fifty years a notorious center of hyperendemic malaria.[27] ·

16 / "...Wherever Economically Possible"[1]

The failure of attacks on mosquitoes to reduce malaria in Freetown could perhaps be fairly discounted—as Ross discounted it—on grounds that the attacks were never more than half-hearted and were too soon abandoned. But there were other failures in the making that called more seriously into question the practicality of a war on anophelines.

At Lagos, Sir William MacGregor, governor and medical man, in 1900 launched a full-scale public health campaign. It was badly needed. In a population of about 33,000 Blacks and Whites, more than 2,200 died each year. Illness among Europeans was all but universal and chronic. It included the governor. Seven months after his arrival he wrote a friend: "I could not affirm that I had ever been quite well a day and a night in West Africa . . . [F]or weeks at a time my head is so light that I dare not try to turn around quickly." And later he wrote: "I have an invincible, selfish, irrational objection to being buried in these swamps."[2]

The swamps were those in the midst of which Lagos was built. Determined to drain and fill them, Sir William set convict labor to work on the task. At the same time he campaigned to arouse the people to the realities of malaria. He had pamphlets published and distributed describing what malaria was and how to protect oneself against it—by screening, using mosquito nets at night and taking quinine. He arranged public lectures and organized a society of the native ladies of Lagos—many of whom, he noted, had been educated in England—to administer quinine to school children. He made the drug widely available and free.[3]

130

Setting his face against the segregation of Europeans, Dr. McGregor resolved to make Lagos healthy for the natives, on whom, he observed, the ultimate prosperity of the colony must depend. Dangerous sentimentality, said Dr. Stephens, at least until the native could be properly educated and trained to decent standards of sanitation.[4] It was an idealism certainly that reached too high for that day. Although Sir William spent as much as ten thousand pounds a year—Ross at Freetown, it will be recalled, had barely five hundred at his disposal—it was "painfully apparent that what is being done at Lagos against malaria is far short of what is required."[5] He only hoped that it was a good beginning and if continued for two or three years would demonstrate enough success so that the people and government of Lagos would be moved to carry on.

But it was not continued. Sir William almost died of a severe attack of malaria in the autumn of 1903. Even before hearing of his illness, the Colonial Office had decided to terminate his appointment. ("He has not been altogether a success at Lagos.")[6] His successors, perhaps forewarned by his example, lacked his enthusiasm for public health and possibly, too, for benevolent societies of Black ladies. In the end, all that the governor proved was that one could expend a great deal of money and labor on public works, doing all the right things, without in the least affecting the health of the community. Because it was one of the very few places where an effort was made on behalf of the native residents, defeat at Lagos cast a particularly long and depressing shadow. It was soon reinforced by another highly publicized failure.

Drs. Stephens and Christophers, having observed and recorded the inadequacy of the work at Freetown, in 1901 went on to India to advise the government on an experiment there in mosquito control. Neither man was then familiar with India, yet the two of them had to choose and design the experiment quickly. They feared their commission could expire at any moment and they would have to go home. So without reconnaissance they decided on a large British troop cantonment at Lahore, in the Punjab, known as Mian Mir. From a distance Mian Mir looked like a fair testing ground: Outstandingly malarious (for years the incidence of malaria averaged only a little less than 100 percent and in epidemic years might rise to over 300 percent), and appealingly dry (rainfall amounted to only about twenty inches a year). With so little rain they reckoned it would be comparatively easy to eliminate the casual water in which it was then supposed that anophelines chiefly bred, and with so much malaria, any improvement ought to be dramatically obvious.

"It was only on arrival at Mian Mir," they reported to the British Medical Association, "that we found the whole place to be a network of irrigation canals."[7] This was an extraordinary admission. Records of Mian Mir clearly showed that although the Army had suffered fever there from the time of its construction in 1851, the incidence had more than doubled in 1867 immediately after a spur from the main irrigation channel in the area was brought into the cantonment. It was thereafter that the place acquired its evil reputation.

Mian Mir was built on a plateau some 700 feet above sea level, almost perfectly flat and underlain at a depth of four feet by an impervious subsoil known locally as khunkur. After the canals were dug, the water scarcely moved in them and the weeds and algae flourished. So did the mosquitoes. It was ideal breeding water, close to unlimited sustenance in the barracks and native bazaars. The khunkur moreover assured that in the autumn rainy season every small depression in the flat tableland would make a fresh nest for more mosquito eggs, with water that would neither spill out nor seep underground.

From the mosquito's point of view—and the sanitarian's—the place was immense. Twelve square miles were dotted with officers' quarters, gardens, maneuver and parade grounds, troop barracks and the bazaars or villages that housed native servants, families and hangers-on. On average there were 3,900 army officers and men in occupation, along with 8,800 natives.

Yet the prospect was not at first daunting for Dr. Christophers,* who with Captain S. P. James of the Indian Medical Service took on the Mian Mir project in September 1901. If topography favored the mosquito, people had some offsetting advantages. The barracks were well built with good sanitary arrangements. Though large in itself the post was isolated from other large settlements. As a community under discipline it had manpower that could presumably be commandeered for whatever task needed to be done.

The plan was simple: Depress the mosquito population by clearing and oiling the irrigation ditches, remove infected persons from the immediate vicinity of mosquito breeding places, administer quinine in both preventive and curative doses. Work began in the spring of 1902 and continued through the following year, at the end of which James and Christophers took stock. The results were profoundly discouraging. Though millions of larvae surely had been slaughtered, adult mosquitoes were as numerous as ever in the barracks. Ross thought that broods were hatching in the canals

---

* Stephens left India at the end of 1901. Christophers returned to England in 1902, joined the Indian Medical Service and the next year came back to Mian Mir. James was on the job steadily and full time.

between applications of oil.[8] But the main trouble seems to have been constant immigration from outside the attack area, both of larvae by water and adults by air. The attack had been planned on the assumption that mosquitoes could not fly more than half a mile. But one species almost certainly flew in from a village two and a half miles away. Operations took in not more than a quarter of the whole cantonment area. Clearly it was not enough. "It must be admitted," James wrote, "that although we have been given, practically speaking, a free hand in matters of expenditure and in the amount of labour employed, and although my own services and those of a hospital assistant have been confined exclusively to this work, we have, up to the present [end of 1903] made but little impression on the number of *Anopheles* mosquitoes."[9]

Nor was there any demonstrable reduction in malaria. It was hard to extract the possible effects of the control measures from data that so much more strongly reflected annual fluctuations in mosquito breeding due to weather. But at least the achievement, if any, was not obvious. As for prophylaxis by quinine, it was the old and ever-repeated story: Few men took their pills as directed, and when mustered for administration by command and under the general's eye, so many were unavoidably absent on special duties that a sizable reservoir of parasites could always escape.

The almost total failure of the first two years was not the end at Mian Mir. The Army got its back up. If canals were the trouble, why not get rid of them? One observer had earlier predicted that removal would be bitterly fought by those who valued the revenues accruing from rental of the cantonment grasslands, and by the ladies in love with their rose gardens and the padre devoted to his church groves, and indeed by the whole company of Englishmen who would "miss the pleasant greenery that relieves the natural hideousness of a singularly ugly place."[10] But sentimentality was not to prevail.

The year 1903 was a bad one. The hospitals at Lahore were full of fever cases "of the worst type," wrote Surgeon General Hamilton, the principal medical officer, "and it required no trained eye to see that four fifths of the men that one met in the roads should have been in the hospital."[11] Mian Mir at this time was under command of Major General F. W. Kitchener, younger brother of Lord Kitchener of Khartoum recently installed as commander in chief in India. Well connected, General Kitchener was also open-minded and vigorous. At the end of the year Dr. Hamilton advised him that if malaria was to be checked irrigation must be stopped. Kitchener promptly issued the order.

In the summer of 1904 some four or five hundred British and Indian soldiers were put to work full time filling all the canals and cuts within 800 yards of quarters. General Kitchener himself supervised the project. "At certain periods General Kitchener suspended all military work, except station duties and musketry, and every available man was put on fatigue duty."[12] In addition he organized twelve-man squads during the rainy season to sweep, fill and oil puddles. He enlisted the cooperation of householders to clear up domestic water. One engineer regiment spent a large part of its time for two years trying unsuccessfully to fill a great pit, in which puddles formed and mosquitoes bred. All this work went on until 1909. "It would not be easy," one observer commented, "to find an example of equally thorough and painstaking operations."[13]

Then once again in 1909 the Army took stock. Incredibly, nothing had changed. The abundance of adult mosquitoes was undiminished. The rate of enlarged spleens among native children was 66 percent, which is to say that two-thirds were still being infected. They were being infected mostly by insects flying in from beyond the range of operations. In military terms, the enemy had abandoned only her forward outposts; the main positions to the rear were intact. Even with an army to command, Kitchener could not undertake to drain and fill the whole twelve square miles, especially since much of the work would have to continue indefinitely through the procession of rainy seasons. There seemed nothing to do but call off the attack.

Failure at Mian Mir was particularly impressive because it was so expensive. Indeed, it was so exceptionally expensive not just in money but in the use of involuntary labor that even had it succeeded, it could rarely, if ever, have been emulated. That was the lesson that the Government of India took to heart. There had never been any thought of trying to protect the native populations of the subcontinent. Now Mian Mir seemed to show that even cantonments of the British Army could not be defended against mosquitoes en masse.

The end of the Mian Mir experiment in 1909 coincided with a serious epidemic. As a result of it the government called a conference out of which emerged the Malaria Survey of India, the first malaria research institute in the world and destined to become one of the most distinguished. That much more research was needed, especially research into the dynamics of the mosquito, was a fair conclusion to draw from Mian Mir, but there was a sense too in which the establishment of the institute represented a withdrawal from action.

Ross was especially bitter. "It proved nothing at all," he wrote of Mian Mir in 1910, "and its only effect was to retard antimalaria work in that and other countries for years."[14] Some historians have echoed that view.[15] Mian Mir was unquestionably discouraging and served for many years as a convenient exhibit for malariologists who for various reasons were luke-warm, or even hostile, to the strategy of larviciding.* But Ross was ba-sically wrong: Mian Mir proved a great deal. It proved that attacks on anopheline breeding were not necessarily cheap and easy. It proved that the mosquito was a much more formidable enemy than had previously been admitted, especially in its adaptability to attack, its capacity to cover con-siderable distances and make use of, as it were, secondary breeding places, when those of first choice were closed. It proved above all that in malaria control every local situation needed to be reconnoitered and a tactic tailored to it.

A strange irony of the battle of Mian Mir was that Army authorities were so obsessed with cleaning out mosquito breeding places that they over-looked the simplest and most effective control available to them—screen-ing the barracks. This was not done until 1926, "in despair" as one officer wryly put it. In the first year thereafter malaria cases dropped to one fifth.[16]

If the principal lesson of Mian Mir was that mosquitoes, well en-trenched, tenacious, adaptable, are difficult and may be impossible to defeat, that lesson was both confirmed and enriched by the work at the same time of Dr. Malcolm Watson in Malaya, even though in history (as in the eyes of Ross) Malaya was as brilliant a success as Mian Mir was a failure.

Dr. Watson, fresh from medical school, went out to the Federated Malay States in January 1901 to take the post of district surgeon in the district of Klang south of Kuala Lumpur. Most of the district was a rich coastal plateau rapidly being covered with rubber plantations. The town of Klang, its administrative and trading center, in 1901 had 3,500 people, a large proportion of whom were more or less chronically ill with malaria. Dr. Watson, of course, had no training in tropical diseases—no one at the time had—but he had read Ross's papers and when, on arrival, he found the Klang hospital packed with fever cases he decided perforce that malaria was to be his principal business.[17]

There was always plenty of malaria in Klang as throughout Malaya, but 1901 happened to be a particularly bad year. It got so bad by autumn that Dr. Watson found only three houses in the European section of town free of it, and none at all in the native town. In November the Chinese mer-chants of Klang closed their shops for three days, when processions and

---

* As for instance the League of Nations Malaria Commission. See Chapter 19.

religious rites were staged in an effort to lift the curse. By the end of December almost 600 deaths had been recorded, most of them directly or indirectly attributable to malaria.

In the light of Ross's discoveries, Klang's affliction seemed easy enough to explain. It and its newly opened satellite town, Port Swettenham, five miles down the River Klang, were sited and constructed as though the purpose had been to make life as convenient and abundant as possible for mosquitoes and plasmodia. Twenty-two acres in the middle of Klang town were marsh; Port Swettenham arose literally from a mangrove swamp that was flooded every spring by the seasonal high tides. The rain was abundant all year round, collecting everywhere in low-lying ground, in small depressions and shallow wells—all of which bred mosquitoes in profusion. Dr. Watson found them also swarming in the jungle and secondary forest which together comprised almost half the acreage of the town.

Opportunities for the parasite were hardly less rich. Temperatures, ideally warm, varied little from month to month or from day to night. Endemically established in the native population, the parasites had continually new supplies of non-immune blood to invade, as the planters brought in fresh supplies of labor. There was an irony in this, too, and a curious appearance of man conspiring to serve the interests of his enemies.

Most of the planters in the Klang district came from Ceylon, where they had grown coffee until they were wiped out by the depredations of malaria among their workers. These workers, mostly Tamils imported from South India, suffered as Whites did because they had no native immunity. When the planters moved to Malaya it was to plant coffee again and import more Tamils to work it. Again they failed, this time because the Malayan coffee could not compete in the world market with Brazilian. Hoping not to have to move again, the coffee men began interplanting rubber trees. By 1904 these began to replace coffee in large areas and a new and long prosperous industry was born in Malaya. But the unfortunate Tamils, still without immunity from malaria, had only found a new place to sicken and die by thousands. Some estates were such notorious killers that British law enforceable in India and Malaya forbade the importation of Tamils to work them.

Planters thus disadvantaged often recruited Chinese, who had no greater immunity but proved hardier because they ate better, used mosquito netting and generally took better care of themselves. But the Chinese, organized in strong guilds, exacted double wages to compensate their risk.

From a quick review of the scene—the crisis of 1901 allowed no time for detailed study—young Dr. Watson drew the obvious conclusion that the watery breeding places of Klang and Port Swettenham had to be dried up. He proposed in Klang to cut back the bordering jungles and drain the central marsh, and in Port Swettenham, besides draining and filling the wetlands, to build dikes to keep out the high tides. His tactic was quite simply to reduce the number of mosquitoes in the immediate vicinity of houses. At the time he did not know what kind of mosquitoes they were or whether they carried malaria. The tactic and the assumption underlying it were in short identical to those applied in Mian Mir.

Neither his medical superior, the state surgeon, nor the colonial administrators asked for further evidence. The colony's labor force—its very capacity to function—was at risk. If as Watson suggests, there was thought of abandoning the site altogether, it was evidently worth a lot more in Klang than in Freetown to try first to move the mosquitoes. Young Dr. Watson found the government almost embarrassingly cooperative and generous: They not only promptly accepted and set aside money for his plan but in the end spent twice as much on it as he recommended.

The causes of their generosity were two: Dr. Watson's control measures worked, and the resulting reduction in malaria directly profited the planters for whom the government had a special care. Hospital admissions for fever dropped in the first year (1902) to a third, and in 1903 to a tenth, of the 1901 figure. Deaths from all causes in Klang and Port Swettenham fell from 582 in 1901 to 144 in 1902. That meant a lot more working hours in the plantations.

Watson was not cleverer than Ross, just luckier. He, like Ross, had been trying simply to get rid of mosquitoes in town by clearing out the breeding places. In fact he succeeded not in reducing the number of mosquitoes but in changing the species. When he had the jungle cut from around the town of Klang, the pools and puddles were exposed to the sun. It happened that the chief local vector, *Anophels umbrosus,* will not lay eggs in full sunlight and so withdrew as the trees were cut. Her place in the sun was taken over by another species that happened not to carry malaria. Mosquitoes continued to thrive in Klang but the sickness fell away. Dr. Watson had similar luck at Port Swettenham. The vector there was *Anopheles sundaicus,* a species that lays its eggs by preference in brackish water. When, preparatory to drainage, the Port Swettenham marshes were diked to keep out annual encroachments by the sea, the water freshened and *sundaicus* was driven out.

Dr. Watson was lucky but he did not rest on his luck. In time—and he was to spend twenty-eight years in Malaya—he discovered these facts and others along the same lines that for a while suggested a bright new hope for malaria control. When, after 1907, as an employee of rubber planters he began working to reduce malaria in the hills back of the coastal strip, he found another species acting as the main vector—*A. maculatus.* Since it liked sunny waters, clearing the jungle to plant rubber enlarged its habitat and spread malaria. Furthermore the hill species bred in clear streams, which unlike pools and swamps could not simply be eliminated. Watson's solution, one adopted by many planters, was to install tile and concrete drain pipes underground on those portions of the estates where workers were housed.

Fascinated by the fine tuning of the environment through which it seemed possible to be rid of just those species of mosquito that one wished to destroy, Watson generalized his experience as a tactic that another malariologist would call "species sanitation." Like so many others who first climb small peaks Watson thought he could see forever. He spoke of a time to come when by precisely manipulating the physical and chemical nature of breeding waters one would "be able to play with species of *Anopheles,* say to some 'Go' and to others 'Come,' and to abolish malaria with great ease, perhaps at hardly any expense."[18]

The notion of species sanitation proved a great boon to science, as it made eminently practical the detailed study of mosquito behavior and genetics. As a tactic, however, it had serious limitations. Watson had happened upon three vector species with idiosyncratic life styles in a setting where it was just possible to use controls that discriminated against them. Such species and such settings turn out to be exceptional. Even in Malaya, Watson greatly exaggerated both the success and the general applicability of his techniques.

In 1911 malaria raged throughout the country with a severity comparable to that of ten years earlier.[19] This appears not to have been a true epidemic but rather a climactic coincidence of local outbreaks that had different local causes. Collectively, however, these spoke eloquently of the real difficulties of winning a war against the mosquito, not just cheaply but at any cost. One difficulty was that even the most carefully and solidly constructed system of land drainage, normally installed at considerable expense as a permanent solution, was not permanent: It had to be not only maintained but constantly extended and adjusted as people built, farmed, cleared forests, did all the environment-changing things that people inevitably do to make a living. New houses and railways in Port Swettenham, for instance, soon blocked the old drainage patterns; malaria returned. The authorities had to spend substantial sums to banish it a second time. Klang suffered a return as well. As prospering rubber planters extended their estates from the hills to the outskirts of town, they extended also the habitat of *A. maculatus,* the hill species of malaria mosquito. The countermeasure was to extend also the subsoil drainage systems that had "solved" the problem on the estates. And that cost still more money. Some plantations started up new mini-epidemics by building new workers' dormitories close to the edge of the jungle, where the *A. umbrosus* mosquitoes still held undisputed possession. Ineffective drainage in the federal capital, Kuala Lumpur, brought the disease to nearly epidemic levels there in 1911 as well. A serious outbreak occurred in Singapore, where little control had thus far been attempted.

The special Malaria Advisory Board appointed in 1911 in response to the emergency found little to cheer about. Despite some local successes in reducing malaria, improvements, the board reported, had not been maintained. There was no machinery to ensure that "continuity of policy and extreme thoroughness" which were essential to the war against malaria. It proposed itself as the required machinery and set its aim as "the extermination of anopheline mosquitoes in all thickly populated centres and, wherever economically possible, in rural areas."[20]

But there in a casual modifying clause, "wherever economically possible," was the catch—an admission of practical helplessness in the midst of a declaration of war. Singapore, Kuala Lumpur, Klang, Port Swettenham—even Freetown, for that matter—given the proper sense of urgency and the proper technical advice could control (not exterminate) mosquitoes and so reduce (not eliminate) malaria. So could rubber estates and White settlers going it on their own. But to do so was expensive. The expense if defrayed from a public treasury could only be justified when the costs divided by the number of people protected (or by their political or economic importance), gave a ratio that seemed reasonable to those who controlled the purse.*

Unfortunately malaria is essentially a rural disease, a disease that flourishes where mosquitoes can find unlimited breeding places, where enough children are born each year to provide fresh blood habitat for parasites, and where adults are so few and so poor that a collective effort of defense is unmanageable or seems prohibitively costly in relation to the lives saved. The disease flourishes where settlement is scattered; defenses are practicable only where it is compact.

Kings, lords and burghers once walled citadels, and towns, against marauders, but the peasantry whose labor supported them had to work exposed outside. It would be hard to fault the lord for failing to palisade a countryside, or equally the early battlers against malaria for putting to one side the major problem in order to define a smaller one they could hope to

---

* See Chapter 27.

deal with. A crusade for human life, organized selectively, could easily become a defense of the privileged. And sometimes did. The technical difficulties of helping the Black masses could easily serve to excuse complacent neglect. And sometimes did. Yet it is hard to see how the first fighters could otherwise have retained the optimism to act at all and so to keep alive the possibility of extending the fight later on.

17 / Appreciation of the Enemy

In military terms the first attacks on mosquitoes were useful chiefly in developing the enemy position, revealing strengths, dispositions, complexities of behavior, and reserves of resourcefulness, unsuspected at the outset. In success as in failure they taught the need for more knowledge. For the first time mosquitoes became the subject of widespread and serious scientific inquiry. It is scarcely an exaggeration to say that all we now know about mosquitoes has been learned in the past seventy-five years.[1]

"In these minute nothings," wrote Pliny the naturalist, musing on insects, "what method, what power, what labyrinthine perfection is displayed! Where did Nature find a place in *culex* for all the senses?"[2] Today optical and electron microscopes, biochemical techniques, and old-fashioned methods of patient observation applied with increasing sophistication have lighted some of the mysteries—and, as always, deepened others. In sum, new knowledge, while leaving much unexplained, has given people the power to deal more intelligently and so, potentially at least, more effectively with the enemy. Pliny's sense of wonder remains.

Minute nothings in contest with large animals have one striking military advantage: They can mobilize vast numbers in small space and little time. One female mosquito, depending on her species and environment may lay from a little less than 50 to about 500 eggs in her first brood, slightly fewer in each subsequent delivery, of which there may be eight or ten before she dies. Taking 200 eggs as an average clutch and assuming half of these will hatch out females, then the theoretical progeny from a single insect in five generations would be twenty million. As each life cycle from egg to egg takes under good conditions something like two weeks, those twenty million could be the produce of one favorable North American summer. In some tropical localities where reproduction goes on all year round, one female could theoretically be ancestor to mosquitoes numbering twice ten to the twenty-sixth power—a quite unimaginable quantity. In practical terms the calculus means simply that were one to wipe out 99 percent of a given mosquito population the survivors could quickly make good the losses.[3]

Small size, a short life and enormous fecundity give the mosquito another advantage that in an enemy is even more daunting than mere numbers: adaptability. In going through a large number of generations in a short time, the mosquito achieves a genetic fine tuning to its environment, able to change as the environment changes. In each population of a single species individuals differ more or less significantly from each other in their inheritance. They not only have variant combinations of similar genes but may now and then produce a mutant gene governing a new trait. Mutation is rare and only a minute proportion of mutants can live at all, much less profit from their difference. But with the multiplying factor large enough these long shots often come home.

A species, for instance, that has always hatched in fresh water may by mutation produce larvae capable of surviving higher concentrations of salt. The new talent, being genetically determined, will be inherited and through opening up vast new habitat it may profit its possessors and make them abundant. Or consider resistance to pesticides, regrettably familiar in our time. Within certain populations of insects individuals appear with genes enabling them to metabolize into harmless substances poisons that kill their cousins.* With saturation poisoning of the environment the susceptibles are cleared from the mosquito niche and resistant mutants fill in. These are dramatic examples. The bread-and-butter value of genetic plasticity is that it enables an animal to penetrate into and exploit a subtle variety of small environments and so collectively to survive the destruction of any one.

So long as one regards the individual as the essential expression of life, viability and most of the traits conducing to it appear as properties of the person. The death of the individual is the symbol, and the personal reality, of extinction, and for all its inevitability tends to be seen as a defeat. Conversely vitality is discovered in personal vigor. The weak are those easily carried off by disease or by their enemies. The strong are those who stand longest against adversity.

* See note, page 232.

Another quite different perspective derives from seeing persons as ephemeral vessels, rather like cells of the body, in ever-shifting aggregations sharing the larger life of the species. In that perspective there is a sense in which the vulnerability of the individual can become a source of strength because in dying easily he readily makes room for the more fit. Species death is held at bay by the ease with which individuals allow themselves to be replaced by fresh vessels of the common heritage. Mosquitoes in hundreds of millions of years on earth have become so marvelously plastic, shaped to fit such a variety of environments, that one must believe they will survive as long as the earth they have so totally occupied.

A female mosquito's reproductive exuberance demands quantities of protein to build and nourish her young. Hence her voracious appetite for blood. Her gorged gut may contain from one to more than four cubic millimeters of blood, and she may suck twice that much in order to concentrate the haemoglobin solids from which she takes nourishment for herself and her eggs.[4] From our blood store of some five million cubic millimeters, the loss is minute. For the mosquito the gain is immense. An average meal comes to two and a half times her unfed weight. That in human terms translates as four hundred pounds of beefsteak for a light eater. There are records of even more prodigious capacities, of virgin females taking in fifteen times their own weight in blood. One glutton mosquito from Sumatra has been said to go on sucking long after her stomach is full, excreting not just plasma but whole blood while she eats.[5] As each cubic millimeter of normal human blood contains from five to six million red cells, a normal mosquito meal would consist of from forty to fifty million cells, any one of which, it will be recalled, might contain another whole animal, *Plasmodium*. Such is the vast cosmology of the small!

Blood is not essential to the welfare of individual mosquitoes. Males of all species subsist entirely on juices of plants, fruits and flowers. Females in nature may now and then also suck up juice, particularly for the sugar to fuel a long flight. In the absence of hosts they, too, may survive exclusively on a vegetable diet. In a few species neither sex bites. Oddly, the commonest of these vegetarians, belonging to the genus *Toxorhynchites,* are carnivorous in their youth: Their larvae prey voraciously on the larvae of other mosquitoes. One remarkable mosquito of the genus *Malaya* neither bites nor sucks plant juices. It dines in forests of bamboo by waylaying a bamboo-feeding ant, inserting its proboscis down the ant's throat and stealing the ant's meal. For reasons no one understands, the victim peaceably submits and when released continues quietly on its way.[6]

All the mosquitoes that concern us are blood-feeders belonging to the genus *Anopheles,* of which there are about 200 recorded species. With some exceptions—most notably among the islands of the Pacific (including New Zealand)—anophelines flourish wherever man does. Yet they are not dependent on man except for passage now and then to new worlds. They have evolved of course on animal blood long before there were people. Many anophelines still will not bite man at all. Few are so domestic as to dine on us exclusively. Even among the notorious vectors of malaria, by definition man-biters, some evidently regard us as second choice and bite only when they cannot find a pig or a cow.[7]

A female mosquito normally will bite only when roused by biochemical messengers that periodically make their rounds. One call comes at intervals of between twenty-three and twenty-five hours, the circadian rhythm familiar to all who live in mosquito country. *Culex pipiens pipiens,* the nuisance of temperate-zone summers but so far certified harmless, emerges every evening about dusk and stays to browse the bedrooms at night. Night-biting is extremely common, especially among malaria vectors, but it is not universal. *Aedes aegypti,* the vector of yellow fever, for instance, bites most often in mid-morning. All mosquitoes tested have firm preferences and keep quite regular hours.[8]

The mechanism controlling ciracadian rhythms is unknown: It is not a direct response to daylight and darkness. Night-biting insects kept entirely in the dark continue the twenty-four-hour cycle, resting in the hours they had known as day and getting up to hunt in their erstwhile evenings. They observe this schedule, however, only if they have had one experience of change from light to dark. Ingenious experiments have shown that the biological clocks are set by darkness following an instant of light no matter how brief. From the first dusk the mosquito thereafter reckons her days and nights.

As the purpose of blood is to feed and mature the eggs, the mosquito needs to bite and ordinarily will bite only often enough to keep eggs coming. Blood stimulates the eggs to rapid growth, maturing them in from two to five days. While they mature the mother seems inhibited from taking blood meals, though occasionally she will have a little something if tempted.

When the time is right and there are eggs to ripen, the mosquito goes in search of food. Even then she does not appear aware of external realities, the presence or absence of hosts in her vicinity, or of atmospheric indicators that might assist her to locate a meal.[9] In quiet air she takes off in any old direction and continues to fly at random. Only if there is a mild breeze will she strike and keep a heading into the wind. The British entomologist, J. S. Kennedy, in classically elegant experiments showed that she does not "feel" the wind, much less scent it. She sees it. Discovering that in total darkness mosquitoes in a breeze continued to fly in all directions, Kennedy built a cage with a striped moving belt on the floor. As the stripes moved simulating a passing landscape, four-fifths of his experimental insects flew to overtake them. At six inches above the floor their flight speed exceeded the speed of the moving stripes by almost precisely the average rate of mosquito flight in still air. Kennedy reasoned that like passengers in a stationary train watching the train on the next track pull out, his insects thought they were moving backward and flew strongly enough to reverse that illusion. When the stripes were speeded up, the mosquitoes flew faster, achieving ten times their normal speed of about three-tenths of a mile an hour. When they could no longer fly fast enough to hold their own, they alighted.[10]

Perhaps this visual reaction to wind has evolved because of the potential advantage of coming on hosts upwind the more easily to pick up other sensory signals. But it does not appear in any direct way to be a tracking tactic. Only when the mosquito has come within attack range (to be measured in yards at most) are her senses clearly alerted to the presence of a host.

Seventy-five years ago Professor Grassi noted that people who talked a lot seemed to be bitten more often than those who kept their mouths shut.[11] If that was indeed a fact, the special attraction of the garrulous could have been the extra breath they exhaled—hot air, in short. Many experimenters since have observed that mosquitoes respond to an increase in ambient carbon dioxide. The gas appears to make them more active and possibly alerts other probing senses.[12]

Among these is a "nose"—chemical receptors located on the insect's antenna that experimentally have been shown capable of detecting and tracking odors over distances of several hundred yards. There is no evidence, however, that in nature mosquitoes depend on that sense. Indeed, experiments designed to find out what a mosquito smells and what difference it makes to her have yielded the sort of equivocal results that fill quantities of scientific papers all coming in the end to a confession of essential ignorance. Mosquitoes can discriminate odors—that much is clear—and sometimes seem to do so, but with an inconstancy that suggests they are obedient for the most part to other stimuli.[13]

Some observers think the hunt for food remains largely random until the insect is close enough to feel the warmth of her prospective victim. "There can be no doubt," wrote Sir Rickard Christophers in his monumental study of *Aedes aegypti,* "that the effective factor . . . causing *A. aegypti* to attack to feed are warm convection currents set up by the host."[14] These of course strike her only when she is overhead on the final approach. So positioned she has been shown to land more often on skin at normal blood temperature than on skin that has been cooled several degrees. The attraction moreover is greater when the ascending warm currents of air are also appropriately moist as they would be from a mildly perspiring host. (Excessive moisture appears to be a repellent.) In all this there is nothing astounding: The mosquito seems sensibly conditioned to home on those beams of warmth, moisture and odor most likely to come from its host.

Nor can it be surprising to learn that mosquitoes also use their eyes. They may even be like us in this respect, acting as if the obvious way to find something were to look for it. We have seen that they navigate visually. The compound eyes that they share with other insects are relatively crude instruments compared to the mammalian eye, but for the huntress's purposes effective. Each composed of between 350 and 500 separate fixed lenses (ommatidia) that project separate images on the retinal cells, the two eyes cover most of the head surface and almost meet in front and below. Together they give the insect a horizontal plane of vision of nearly 225°. The eyes perceive light and dark, as well as form (at least in gross outline); they discriminate size, possibly color within limited range, and motion to which the mosquito is highly responsive.

Mosquitoes (chiefly species of *Aedes*) that haunt in vast multitudes the brief summers of the northern prairies and tundra will attack any prominent object presumably seen by them as silhouetted against the sky when they hunt at about two feet above the ground.[15] A mosquito in Africa that cruises at about the same height will fly over and ignore people who are lying down but will instantly launch a ferocious attack on an uplifted head or hand.

Some years ago Dr. A. W. A. Brown and colleagues in Canada set up dummies to test the perceptions of *Aedes* mosquitoes.[16] They made the bodies of heated water tanks and the heads of toilet bowl floats with mouth holes through which carbon dioxide could be released. They dressed the manikins in various kinds and colors of cloth. Their mosquitoes, showing no obvious ability to distinguish the dummies from human hosts, did show a fairly consistent preference for the dark and rough materials: dark red flannel, navy serge, black drill and the olive drab of soldier suits. They preferred the materials of whatever color that reflected the least light. That confirmed the striking preference shown in other experiments for dark skins. Perhaps it is an evolutionary hangover from the mosquito's much longer familiarity with dark, furred and feathered animals than with naked man who has been bleached to boot. Or there may be comparative safety in the camouflage of dark surfaces to favor the survival of insects attracted to them.

To recapitulate, a female mosquito ready to bite—one may in shorthand call her "hungry," though hunger in the sense of craving for nourishment has apparently nothing to do with it—is roused at her usual hour of day or night, flies upwind, sees something that looks like a host, flies on into a rising column of warm, moist air slightly richer in carbon dioxide than the air elsewhere, picks up odors of hospitality on the sensilla of her antennae, spots if possible a darkish landing area and comes in to bite. That seems to be the standing operating procedure, and all quite sensible as tactics even if we don't know how the insect works them out.

But there are also quirks of taste that seem oddly idiosyncratic in a creature presumably programmed to practicalities by her inheritance. For instance, the popular notion that some persons are tastier than others for mosquitoes seems to be a fact. In one old experiment four Africans switched huts nightly and before morning killed and counted the mosquitoes inside.[17] One man attracted more mosquitoes than the others for nine nights running, another for six. On the thirty-fourth day of the experiment a new man replaced one of the original four and took the lead at once, holding it for ten nights. Possibly individual differences in body odor, perhaps due to different populations of skin bacteria, may account for such preferences.

More baffling are the results of another experiment that set out to compare the individual attractiveness of four men and three women. As in a chess tournament they were matched against each other in every possible combination of pairs. No one came in a clear favorite, but the men as a group collected decisively more bites than the women.[18]

Within seconds of landing, the mosquito will have thrust her stiletto mouth parts through the skin to begin her probe for blood. The bite is quick and looks effortless, but mechanically it is a most elaborate process.

Collectively a mosquito's mouth parts are called the proboscis—an awkward word that misleadingly calls to mind the elephant's trunk, but there seems to be no other. To the naked eye the proboscis looks like a single fine hair; in fact it is made up of seven parts. An outer sheath, called the *labium,* encloses six stylets. The labium does not penetrate the skin but bends against the surface when the bundle of stylets is inserted. This inner bundle is in turn partly enclosed by a deeply grooved beak, confusingly called the *labrum* (with an "r"). The sides of the labrum curl downward to touch each other along most of its length, thus forming a nearly closed tube through which the insect sucks blood. The tip of the labrum is trimmed to a point like a quill pen. At the other end where it enters the mosquito's head, it is underlain by a slender stylet, the *hypopharynx,* that makes it airtight.

The hypopharynx also contains the salivary duct through which saliva is pumped into the puncture wound. Inside the labrum are a pair of *maxillae* and a pair of *mandibles*. The maxillae are important cutting tools, finely serrated at their business ends. The mandibles, extremely delicate even by mosquito standards, are flattened at the apical ends and in some species are also finely toothed. Though they thus look like weapons, they are so extremely fine and so adherent to the labrum within which they lie that they probably do not contribute materially to the biting process. More likely they serve simply as covers to close the end of the labrum when it is not in use. The six stylets are compacted and stiffened by a viscous fluid.[19]

Much of the biting process can be deduced from the structures but not until 1939 was it actually observed. In that year two experimenters, R. M. Gordon and W. H. R. Lumsden, built a window for the purpose. They had noted that in the nearly transparent webbing between the toes of a frog's hind foot one could, in a good light, see the blood capillaries clearly and in detail. So they made a piece of apparatus in which the foot of an anesthetized frog could be held under a microscope and transluminated from below. A glass tube with a gauze-covered window in one end held a mosquito (*Aedes aegypti*) upside down under the frog skin, close enough to bite through the gauze. Being upside down bothered the mosquito not at all and the experimenters looking through the microscope were able to watch the whole process of probing, penetration and sucking.

First a circular shadow appeared on the frog skin as the insect's labium approached and touched it in several places apparently seeking the right spot to enter.* The watchers could not see just how the first prick was made but it appears to be a straightforward push in by the mosquito with legs braced and thrusting with her neck muscles.[20] Once inside, the teeth of the maxillae catch in the flesh, and while they hold, the tip of the labrum drives down; the two maxillae then alternately take a deeper hold, acting rather like ratchets as the point continues to penetrate by minute forward thrusts and withdrawals "after the manner of a pneumatic drill."[21] Possibly the mandibles assist in the cutting but Gordon and Lumsden were never able to see them in action at all.

Thus far the process was about as the anatomists had deduced. The big surprise was that, when part of the way in, the labrum bent sharply at right angles and began probing parallel to the skin. So effortless was this maneuver that the proboscis appeared to swim like an eel in water. How the

---

* Or perhaps merely to confirm the fact that she is touching skin. The tip of the labium is equipped with sensory organs that have been shown to be sensitive to sugar and apparently alert the insect to feed on nectar.

mosquito manages that has never been explained; it is hard to reconcile with the stiffness that the bundle of stylets must have to thrust through the skin and which is presumably achieved by the tubular structure and the viscosity that enable the slender instruments to reinforce each other. A fluent needle remains a paradox for us but for the mosquito it is a great convenience. With it she can enter and probe in all directions for food to the limit of her reach and if she finds a capillary can point her open mouth directly into the flow of blood.

Surprisingly she makes only haphazard use of her power, apparently because the labrum does not have any sense organs to inform the mosquito of where it is. Gordon and Lumsden often watched the stylets come so close to a capillary as almost to touch it and then move away. Sometimes the mosquito drove through a capillary without stopping to feed. Only if the tip of her mouth happened to enter a pool of blood spilled by the ruptured vessel would she recognize her luck. Then her powerful twin pumps came at once into action to suck up the extravasated blood. For the mosquito this "pool-feeding," which is the technique used exclusively by some bloodsucking insects such as horseflies, is a dangerously slow process. Because the pools are generally too small to satisfy her hunger she has to move on looking for others. She may be ten minutes in feeding thus, by contrast to about three when she strikes directly into a capillary.

That a mosquito will remain motionless so long, at such risk to herself, is striking evidence of the evolved priorities of the species. As blood is essential to reproduction, the female is conditioned to get it at any cost. Skittish and evasive at other times, she is fearless in the nourishment of her eggs. Christophers noted that *Aedes aegypti* could be removed from the skin during feeding only by force and that when removed she would try to go back, if she could, to finish her meal.[22] Those of us whose chief business with mosquitoes is trying to swat them know how comparatively easy they are to crush on the skin. No doubt such dedication to the reproductive meal takes a high toll. But the species can afford it. Odds of even 100 to 1 against the individual are favorable for the species: It needs only one to finish and get away to make good the loss of the hundred.

Before she sucks blood and often at intervals thereafter, the mosquito releases saliva in little bursts. Why is not altogether clear. As the saliva appears to be secreted into tissues rather than into the blood, it may serve to stimulate the flow of blood in the area of penetration. In some species but not all it acts as an anticoagulant.[23]

What mosquito saliva does to people is all too clear. Besides being the medium in which the sporozoites of *Plasmodium*, and the viruses of yellow fever, encephalitis and the rest transfer to us, it is the cause of the charac-

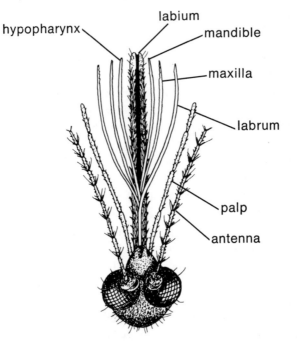

Dorsal view of mouthparts
of female mosquito (after Boyd 1946)

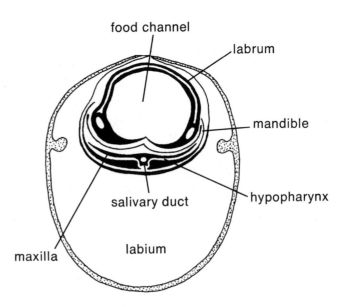

Cross-section at middle of proboscis (from Boyd after
Robinson after Vogel 1920)

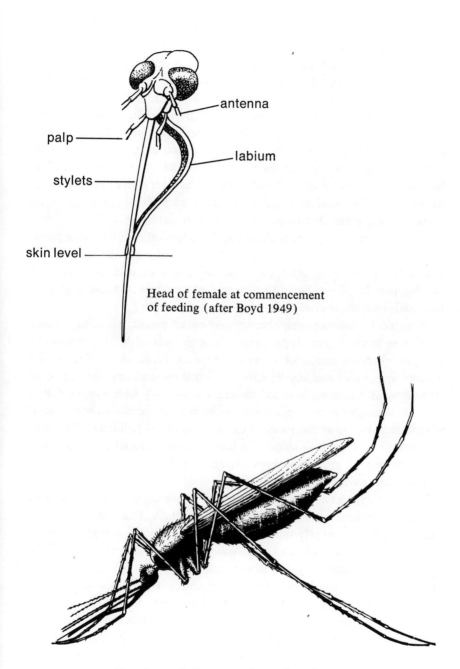

palp

antenna

labium

stylets

skin level

Head of female at commencement
of feeding (after Boyd 1949)

Female anopheline mosquito resting after meal

teristic itch. Or rather it is the provocation, for itching is actually produced by the body's immune reactions to the saliva. It is something we learn through bitten experience. Although individuals differ, most can take the first few bites of their lives without any reaction. They progress then, as Kenneth Mellanby showed, through three stages of suffering back to indifference.[24] Stage one: itching wheals only twenty-four hours or so after the bite; stage two: immediate wheals fading after ten or fifteen minutes and then recurring periodically for perhaps several days; stage three: a few minutes' itch at once, nothing thereafter; stage four: no reaction at all. This final achievement of immunity unfortunately is a very small boon to be so hardly won: The sensitizing substance in the mosquito's saliva is peculiar to the species; immunity to one is no use against another.[25]

Having completed her meal the mosquito relaxes the muscles that power her maxillae, allowing their teeth to drift inward from the edge of the wound. She pulls the stylets out by small successive wrenchings of her neck and leg muscles. Then away to a resting place where she can digest her meal and ripen her ovaries for egg-laying.

Most fed mosquitoes seek obscure and covert places: surfaces, corners of a room farthest from light, caves, the underside of leaves, crevices in bark, overhanging banks of a stream, pigsties, cattle sheds. The choice depends on species and opportunity. All agree on shunning the light after feeding which for many was an attractant when they were hungry.[26] Presumably through the millennia there has been an especially strong survival advantage in hiding at this moment close to biological fulfillment. The dark cool places also tend to shield the insect against excessive evaporation, always among the gravest of threats to an animal with such relatively huge ratios of body surface to volume.

When the eggs have ripened in from one to five days, the female goes in search of suitable water in which to deposit them. Only three kinds of natural water are entirely unsuitable and never contain mosquito larvae: the open sea, large lakes and swift-flowing rivers. Some species find the particular conditions they like in foul, stagnant pools or even in sewage; some choose the quiet banks of clean streams; some lay eggs in irrigation ditches, rain barrels, cemetery urns, pineapple plants, tree holes, rain-filled footprints, salt marshes, fresh marshes, roof gutters, beached fishing boats, discarded rubber tires, coconut shells, beetle borings in bamboo cane. To track down mosquito breeding places is to be reminded what a well-watered world this is.

Although mosquitoes share among them such a variety of breeding places that only total desiccation of the globe could close them all out, most species have a firm and narrow preference—for shade or sunlight, for water that is fresh or brackish, clean or stagnant, in pool or puddle or old tin can. Gravid females of some species seem to look for water, which they apparently see as a dark patch on the ground. Some appear to feel for it, flying an inch or two above the ground and constantly dipping to touch.[27]

When she finds a patch that is indeed water the mosquito hovers bobbing up and down before alighting. Apparently by touch she can discriminate temperature, relative salinity, and degree of pollution. If these are not to her liking she flies on. Anophelines, if satisfied, either alight on the surface and extrude their eggs one at a time or scatter them in flight over the water. One mosquito belonging to the colorful tropical genus *Sabethes,* which breeds in bamboo, hovers two or three inches away from a suitably large hole in a water-filled cane and by a spasm of her abdomen flicks the eggs inside, one at a time, like someone pitching a quarter into a toll box.

Many species of *Aedes* put their eggs in water-to-come, laying them dry at the edges of a pool or on the sides of a container or in moist depressions in the ground. The larvae develop but stay inside the shells until rain or high water submerges them, days or perhaps months later. An ingenious adaptation to the vagaries of climate, this patience in the egg permits *Aedes* to colonize small and ephemeral collections of water that other species cannot use.[28]

Mosquito eggs are heavier than water and need special flotation structures to ride the surface. In anophelines these are twin air-filled floats bulging amidships like pontoons. The egg itself is boat-shaped with upturned ends to ride the ripples of its normally quiet waters. Laid singly, the eggs often join up end to end, one adhering to the next in sometimes intricate geometric patterns that further enhance their seaworthiness. *Culex* species normally lay eggs in parallel rows that stick together. Each culex egg is so shaped that when joined side by side they form a slightly concave raft that floats nicely like a curled leaf.

Under favorable conditions a mosquito embryo completes its development in about two days. Then by means of a spine on its head it apparently cracks the egg and by swallowing fluid swells enough to break off the cap of the shell. Through this hole the embryo wriggles out, seeks the surface and expels the fluid from its tracheal system, replacing it with air.

The emergent creature bears little resemblance to an adult mosquito except that its body has the characteristic three-part insect form, segmented into head, thorax and abdomen. Anopheline larvae uniquely lie just beneath the surface and parallel to it, breathing through one end, feeding through the other. By means of constantly waving mouth brushes they set up tiny vortices on the water surface that carry into their gut whatever is floating in the neighborhood. They swallow everything that is small enough to pass inside, digest what is digestible, excrete what is not.

Larvae live only to eat and grow. They are literally free-living embryos whose development into adult form has been temporarily delayed by special juvenile hormones. This hormonal inhibition lasts while the larvae grow through four moults (or instars), enlarging and shedding their outer cuticle four times. After the fourth moult they enter the pupal stage. All during this time—about ten days on average—the adult mosquito has actually been developing within the larva but without affecting its outer form. Adult tissue has differentiated gradually and grown in so-called imaginal buds on the larval surface. Metamorphosis is thus already well along by the time the pupa is formed. Nevertheless the final transformation into adult, in as little as a day and a half during warm weather, remains (like the more celebrated transformation of caterpillars into butterflies) the kind of marvel that familiarity cannot diminish.

What is believed to happen is that the juvenile hormones at last turn off in the pupal stage, releasing the brake on maturing processes and letting them proceed along genetically predetermined lines. In simplest terms, the adult structures speed up their delayed growth while the embryonic ones wither and are reabsorbed. The great insect physiologist V. B. Wigglesworth regards insects which like mosquitoes go through complete metamorphosis as being two organisms existent in a single individual, and metamorphosis as the resumption of an interrupted embryonic development.[29]

Of the final act A. N. Clements has written:

> The first sign of emergence is the appearance of a small amount of air beneath the pupal cuticle, at the bases of the respiratory siphons and elsewhere. The abdomen is slowly raised to a horizontal position and shortly after this the pupal cuticle splits . . . A minute later the thorax of the adult, which is quite dry, rises into view . . . . [The insect] can be seen swallowing air by regular contractions of the pharyngeal pumps [one of the two that will later pump blood] and this air slowly distends the stomach, forcing the adult up and out of the pupal skin. The longitudinal split extends further back and transverse slits appear while alternate movements of the abdomen and legs disengage the body from the surrounding cuticle . . . The various appendages are freed from their sheaths, in the case of the mouth parts and legs partly by muscular action, and the insect steps on to the water.[30]

All this takes about fifteen minutes. For about another fifteen the newborn mosquito rests from its exertions on the surface of the water. Then it tries its wings in short flights. After about an hour it leaves its birthplace.

In the short life of the mosquito everything happens quickly. Not least sex. Males of most species cannot copulate until a day or two after emergence. They are born with the sexual organs at the end of their abdomens pointing the wrong way (downward), perhaps to enforce infant celibacy. These take a couple of days to twist around and point up. Most females are ready at once, or after an hour or so. In one species (*Opifex fuscus*) the male scurries over the surface of breeding waters to seize pupae and copulate with females before, in a manner of speaking, they are born. Males embracing a pupal case have no way of telling the sex of its occupant until they try to mate. But if mistaken they simply try again and no harm appears to be done.

Most mosquitoes are only a little less precocious. Mating in fact commonly takes place at the larval nursery within a day or two of emergence. Short-lived animals obviously cannot afford to waste time in the virgin state and the place where they are born is certainly the most convenient and the surest rendezvous.

Many species, however, have found in male swarming another way to get together, although the reproductive importance of this behavior is not clear. Males at half light may go into a dance about some rare and prominent landscape feature—a bush, a tall tree, a light or dark patch of ground, even a single leaf if it stands out alone. One dance pattern in a breeze has been shown to consist of a short rush upwind toward the marker until it is just about to be lost to peripheral vision, and then a drift back. In still air the insects fly in all directions but maintain a tight formation as though held magnetically to the marker. At dusk in the tropics huge swarms have been seen over the treetops looking like plumes of smoke. A swarm may contain thousands of individuals or only one; what defines it is the flight pattern of the male and his orientation to a landmark.

A female, perhaps attracted also by the landmark, now and then joins in. When she does she is immediately recognized by the lower hum of her wing beat.* A male promptly seizes her with his legs—there is no courtship—and copulates at once. The act, lasting only a few seconds, may be completed on the wing or the pair may drop to the ground and finish there.[31]

In some species mating within the swarm is common; in others it is rare.

---

* The vibrations are normally slower by 100 to 200 cycles per second than those of the male's wings.

Some experts therefore think that swarming behavior must have arisen in response to other, unknown needs, and that sex may be incidental, like bumping into a girl at the opera. It is, to be sure, tempting to see the swarm as reproductive insurance, offering unmated females a second chance. If so, even when takers are few, the species could significantly gain by the increased fecundity—and the males, after all, have nothing else to do. In the face of slight and ambiguous evidence, however, it is more prudent to conclude that one does not really know.[32]

Within fifteen minutes of copulation sperms have passed, probably by swimming, into a special storage vessel in the female called the spermotheca. There they will remain normally for the lifetime of the female, who need never mate again, though by chance she may do so. At each ovulation sperm is released from the spermotheca to fertilize the eggs as they pass by on their way out through the oviduct.

Since the continuity of the species demands that the eggs be both well-nourished and fertile, the female's body is normally conditioned to require both blood in her gut and seed in her spermotheca before she will lay. But fed and unmated females sometimes lay eggs, which of course do not hatch. In some species females mated but unfed will lay one brood that does hatch. To provide the necessary yolk to nourish the embryos as they develop inside the eggs, the mothers expend their own protein stored in the larval stage. They can do so only once. Autogeny, as the bloodless reproduction is called, though probably useful in keeping families going temporarily when hunting fails, is not an alternative tactic. Blood for the bloodsuckers is an absolute necessity. Without it individuals may appear scarcely affected, but the species will die.

18 / Victory in Panama

Ross was always chagrined that his own country so notably failed to push the campaigns against malaria that he believed his discoveries had made possible. As evidence of the imperial opportunity that Great Britain had missed he would point to Panama, where the United States in behalf of its new and still tiny empire warred on mosquitoes in the decade before 1914 with the drive and concentration of force that Ross urged in vain on his countrymen. Panama, Ross thought, showed what could be done with the will, the cash, and the right man in charge.[1]

The right man happened to be another army major and medical doctor, William Crawford Gorgas, who was about Ross's age and like him endowed with an energy that he could apply singlemindedly in the absolute conviction that he was right. Gorgas cut his battle plans for Panama in Havana where immediately after the American occupation of Cuba he fought and defeated yellow fever and *Aedes aegypti*. That was a fact of critical importance not only for the Panama campaign but for the subsequent war against *Anopheles*. It turned out to be an apprenticeship in tanks for warfare in the jungle.

In the first place the disease was different. Yellow fever, though often mistaken for malaria before the causes of either were known, runs a quite different course both in the body and in the community. It is caused by a virus, submicroscopic, subcellular, a parasite that does not feed on host cells like *Plasmodium* but makes itself a part of them in order to use their substance to its own ends. Probably the virus evolved in the mosquito.

157

"Ronald Ross (right) with William Crawford Gorgas en route to Havana aboard the *SS Advance,* September, 1904

Undoubtedly they have lived together a long time, becoming so well adapted that mosquitoes suffer no harm and the viruses once in occupation remain in the tissues of the insect's body so long as she lives. Man, by contrast, can entertain the virus only for a few days and in a state of violent conflict, which ends either in his death or in the extinction of the invaders and the establishment of a lifetime immunity against them. In that brief, hostile association man acts less as a host than as a point of transit where viruses, if they are lucky, can change mosquitoes.[2]

Yellow fever is a killer. Though probably no more often fatal than *falciparum* malaria, it seems to be. Most infections are so light that they go unrecognized. When the characteristic symptoms do develop, mortality may be as high as 70 percent and is seldom less than 20. Death comes quickly and with terrifying terminal agonies that include extreme delirium and vomiting masses of black blood. Because the virus can establish itself only among people who have never before been infected, yellow fever, unlike malaria, is always epidemic: It strikes without warning when non-immune persons visit places where the mosquitoes are infected, or when, conversely, those mosquitoes (or sometimes human carriers) are transported into the midst of susceptible populations. It has thus characteristically been a scourge of seaports, especially those having regular trade with tropical countries.

In the second place, the mosquito *Aedes aegypti,* long thought to be the sole vector, is different from *Anopheles.* Known historically by many names, *A. aegypti* has familiarly and conveniently been called by her enemies "steg" (after the subgenus *Stegomyia,* to which she belongs). She is so thoroughly domesticated that she bites people almost exclusively, breeds in barrels, gutters, tin cans, any sort of domestic water container, and lives her whole life in and around the house.* With such habits it was natural for her to go to sea; through long voyages she could breed in water tanks and buckets aboard and dine on the crew. If infected she had a good chance of cycling the virus through a sailor to at least one new generation. That must have happened, and probably several times, for yellow fever almost surely evolved in West Africa and traveled to the western hemisphere not earlier than the sixteenth century, presumably on European ships.[3] The virus took hold in a few West Indian and Latin American ports busy enough to constantly renew the stock of susceptibles. Havana was an early fever base in part because of its attraction for buccaneers. Once the sugar trade with North America was flourishing the fever began regular raids from Havana on Boston, Philadelphia, Baltimore, New York, and New Orleans.

So costly were these raids—a New Orleans epidemic of 1878 traced to a single ship from Havana took 6,000 lives[4]—and so certain was it that they all came from Cuba, that an itch to clean up Havana is reckoned by some people to be one of the causes for the war with Spain in 1898.[5] In any event, when American troops did occupy the city in January 1899, sanitation squads under Major Gorgas were ready to go to work at once. Gorgas had the full backing of the new governor, Major General Leonard Wood, himself a medical doctor.[6]

As yellow fever was then believed to breed like so many other diseases in filth, Gorgas went after sewage and garbage and dirt in the streets. With characteristic vigor he had made Havana shine by spring, and seemed to have made it healthy.[7] But that, it turned out, was only because the weather was cool, American troops were confined to barracks and immigration from Spain had stopped. The virus had no one to attack. The

---

* An entomologist in 1931 captured a number of stegs in Brazil and released them in the jungle. They failed to maintain themselves. But in their native West Africa they may breed in tree holes at some distance from human habitation. Strode (1951).

summer changed all that. As things returned to normal, yellow fever came back to Havana: A good-sized epidemic struck in the fall of 1899, and the following summer brought the worst one in twenty years.

That was when Walter Reed (another medical major) and three colleagues arrived to investigate. They were sent by George Sternberg, the man who had brought Laveran's revelation to the United States and who now, still one of the foremost bacteriologists in the country, was also surgeon general of the Army.

Some twenty years earlier a Cuban doctor, Carlos Finlay, had claimed to have proof that yellow fever was transmitted by mosquitoes—"stegs" to be precise, and Dr. Finlay was precise on this point.[8] Unfortunately his experiments were not. So although he has fair claim to priority for the hypothesis, it was left to Dr. Reed, assisted by Dr. James Carroll, Dr. Jesse Lazear and Dr. Louis Agramonte to prove it. They did so in one of the best known and most dramatic investigations in medical history.[9]

With the help of heroic soldier volunteers, Reed showed that yellow fever was picked up by mosquitoes from the blood of victims during the first three days of their infection, and only then. The microbe, whatever it was (and it would not be found for another generation), took twelve days to mature inside the mosquito. Thereafter the infected mosquito's bite invariably gave yellow fever to anyone who was not immune. In separate experiments Reed showed that filth, even the foulest leavings of fever victims, had nothing to do with the infection.

Reed and Gorgas discussed the next step.[10] Both men were impressed by the fact that all the fevers experimentally induced had been light. Might that not be because the mosquitoes under the controlled conditions of the laboratory transmitted relatively few germs? If so, populations might be immunized by such bites against more serious infections. The inference seemed reasonable, but when the two men tried it in the summer, three of seven volunteers in the experiment died. Gorgas was "very much disappointed." Reed thought that at least the tragic results were "very strong confirmatory evidence of our observations of last fall and winter."[11]

If people could not be immunized,* perhaps the victims could be isolated during the first three days when they were infective. That worked well in hospitals but by the time the sick came there they might have been harboring the virus for a couple of days and have been bitten many times. It occurred to Gorgas that nevertheless one might effectively quarantine any house where fever struck and kill all the possibly infected mosquitoes in and near it.

---

* Today, of course, immunization by a vaccine is the main defense.

This he set out to do. Following each report of a fever case, fumigation squads went in, sealed up the house along with its immediate neighbors and burned pyrethrum (a natural insecticide derived from a species of chrysanthemum) at the rate of one pound to an average-sized room (1,000 cubic feet). That was typical Gorgas overkill.[12] Yet it failed. The trouble was that mosquitoes could pick up the virus from people who showed no signs of the disease and never reported themselves ill.

Having thus run through the more attractive apparent options, Gorgas came at last to the simple, hard one: Destroy the mosquitoes. That, in a city which got its drinking water from rain cisterns, was a daunting prospect. Inspectors in the spring of 1901 found 26,000 collections of domestic water that held mosquito larvae.

Gorgas issued an order. Every householder was to dump, oil or screen every container of water on his property on penalty of a $10 fine. To enforce the order, Gorgas divided the city into twenty districts, each in charge of an inspector who would check every house in it once a month. The army worked smoothly; the people in general cooperated; fines rarely had to be imposed. Gorgas' own cleanup squads at the same time were out draining ditches and oiling them. Mosquito larvae by the millions, it is said, poured from Havana's sewers. And by the summer of 1902 yellow fever had been driven out.

The western hemisphere was not made wholly safe thereby, but it was now much safer than it had been since the seventeenth century. An epidemic in New Orleans in 1905 was the last to strike any North American city. War on the disease worldwide was of course only just started but thanks to Reed and Gorgas the world now knew how to wage it.

Dr. Gorgas in Havana was a man in his element. He had found not only the job that exactly suited his taste and temperament but also a cause that gave a driving purpose to the rest of his life.

A gregarious Southerner, soft-spoken and gentle in manner, he was also a military man to the core with a love of battle and an enthusiasm for command. His father, Josiah, had been a professional soldier and had married the daughter of a former governor of Alabama. When the Civil War came, Josiah Gorgas, though from Pennsylvania himself, chose the Confederacy and became General Lee's chief of ordinance.[13]

Josiah admired Southern institutions and the Southern way of life, including slavery. Long before the war he remarked that his wife Amelia "could be quite happy if she could see herself twelve or fifteen years hence the mistress of a hundred bales of cotton and forty or fifty ebony faces."[14] William grew up with a small slave of his own, who in the ironic euphemism of the day was an "inseparable companion."

The Gorgas family spent most of the war in Richmond, capital of the Confederacy. Friends of President Jefferson Davis, they were warmed by the purest fires of patriotism and lost causes. It is reported that William, just eleven when the war ended, came to a stiff salute as the train carrying him and his mother from Richmond passed the prison where Jefferson Davis was alleged to be held.

William Gorgas always wanted to be a soldier. Denied an appointment to West Point, chiefly because his grades were not good enough, he decided at the age of twenty-two to study medicine in order to join the medical corps. This roundabout way into uniform, he followed to the letter: He did well enough in medical school and was commissioned in 1880.

For twenty years thereafter nothing marked him out from all other reasonably competent Army surgeons who were carrying out the generally routine assignments of their postings. Perhaps the most important happening of the two decades was that in 1884 he caught and almost died from yellow fever. On recovery he attended the sister of his commanding officer's wife, who had also fallen desperately ill with the fever. Gorgas in fact was preparing to speak the few words necessary over her grave. Instead she too recovered and not long afterward married him. When the Spanish-American War came along he applied to go to Havana because he was immune to the fever. He was accepted for perhaps no better reason.

Gorgas never had any doubt that it was the systematic destruction of mosquito larvae that wiped out yellow fever in Havana.[15] The lesson was deeply impressed on him because he had been himself so deeply involved in the work. A front-line commander, he had prowled Havana streets, peered into rain barrels, rung doorbells, checked the work and the inspectors, until his white hair and strikingly handsome face were known throughout the town. When success came, Gorgas must have felt it to be personally his as indeed it was.

From the heart of Havana the sanitation squads had gradually pushed out into the suburbs. There more and more they were dealing with the breeding places of *Anopheles,* and more and more Gorgas deliberately aimed the campaign at the elimination of malaria as well. He believed by 1902 when he left that this too had been a success. *Anopheles* he thought had been thereby proved a no more formidable enemy than *Aedes aegypti,* one that could be defeated by the same means.

In the autumn of 1902 Gorgas wrote personally to Surgeon General Sternberg to report the success of antimosquito work in Havana and to suggest that similar measures could be equally effective in Panama, where the United States was about to take over the construction of an Isthmian canal from the French. Sternberg agreed. He would recommend further-more that Gorgas be put in charge.*

Panama was one of the unhealthiest places on earth—at least for the non-immune immigrants, Black as well as White, imported by the French to work on the canal. In the first eight years, from 1881 to 1888, the hospitals built by the French at Ancon and Colon recorded deaths from disease of more than 5,500 (a death rate among employees of 63.1 per thousand). The actual toll was undoubtedly much higher. The canal company headed by Ferdinand de Lesseps ran the hospitals but let out the digging work to private contractors. For each worker hospitalized the company charged the contractors a dollar a day, a strong incentive to let them sicken and die elsewhere. Bunau-Varilla, the great engineer-promoter of the canal, wrote in 1892 that only one out of five workers arriving in Panama could stay more than a few months on the job, and many of those who did stick it out were so weakened by illness as to be almost useless.[16]

Working before the etiology of either malaria or yellow fever was known, the French could do little to make Panama healthier. Instead they tried to give it a healthier reputation. Company propaganda continually scoffed at reports of disease. "Panama is an exceedingly healthy country," de Lesseps told a large Paris audience in 1880 after a few days' visit to the Isthmus during its short dry season.†[17] In 1883 a new director general of works, determined to prove the diggings safe, moved his family out. Within three months of their arrival, a son, a daughter and her fiancé were dead; the poor man's wife died about a year later. All were victims of yellow fever.

De Lesseps' canal company failed in 1889. Another company was formed to carry on the work but never commanded the resources needed. Both companies were victimized by financial manipulators as voracious as

---

* To prepare the way, Gorgas was ordered to New York to take part in planning for the canal and presumably to be on hand when the key appointments were made to the Panama Canal Commission authorized by Congress to direct the work. In fact Gorgas had almost a year to wait. During that time he went on orders to Egypt to have a look at Suez, and then a few months later to Paris to study the records of the French experience. In Egypt he visited Ismailia, where Ross had worked, but concluded that the conditions were so different that the lessons of Suez could have little relevance for Panama.

† Among those tempted by company propaganda was Paul Gauguin, who went out in 1887, thinking to settle and eventually paint in a tropical paradise. He took a job digging on the canal and shortly wrote home of his miserable existence swinging a pickaxe "from five thirty in the morning to six in the evening, under tropical sun and rain. At night I am devoured by mosquitoes." Mercifully he was fired after less than two months and went to Martinique; Tahiti and paradise enow were just over the horizon.

the mosquitoes of the Isthmus. Gersten Mack, who has done the most thorough study of building the canal, believes, however, that neither peculation nor disease caused the failure. The critical fault, he thinks, was de Lesseps' resolve, unsoundly based and stubbornly held, to build the canal at sea level. With existing techniques and within the resources and the time available, that could not be done. Correspondingly when the Americans had bought out the French company and concluded the appropriate treaties with the New Republic of Panama, it was the decision to use locks that presented them with an entirely new opportunity of success.

America's other opportunity, to greatly reduce the cost of the canal in lives, might have been overlooked entirely but for Gorgas.[18] Few laymen, including President Roosevelt, were convinced by the experience in Havana of the dangers of mosquitoes. It still seemed more reasonable to attribute disease to filth, and more natural to regard it as one of those things people had always endured and always would. The first chairman of the Isthmian Canal Commission, Rear Admiral John G. Walker, is said to have read Reed's reports with total disbelief: The idea that mosquitoes might be dangerous made him laugh.

Gorgas, ordered to Panama at last in June 1904 as sanitary adviser to the commission, had still to prove himself and his methods. He brought with him $50,000 worth of supplies and a first-rate staff.* With these he went to work with characteristic energy and directness, first to rid Panama City of yellow fever. Since the city was less than a tenth the size of Havana he reckoned that he might as well fumigate all the houses right away. The fumigators started at one edge of the city and worked their way systematically through to the other. Promptly fever broke out behind them. They went back and made another sweep, and then a third. They extended the fumigation to Colon. Altogether Gorgas' men burned 300 pounds of sulphur and 120 pounds of pyrethrum, the entire year's supply for the whole of the United States and all that could be found on the market. At the same time other squads were emptying, covering, oiling water receptacles.

Panama citizens bore it all patiently enough, if perhaps skeptically. The governor of the Zone and his chief engineer looked askance. They deplored the expense and doubted the value. Their doubts appeared justified: in April 1905 the fever recurred, and within a month had sparked what looked like a full-scale epidemic among newly immigrant canal employees.

---

* It included J. L. LePrince, who with A. J. Orenstein organized sanitary engineering works throughout the Isthmus, and that careful and expert scientist, Henry Rose Carter, who had worked closely with Gorgas in Havana and who in Panama served as his director of hospitals. Dr. S. T. Darling, later to be a Rockefeller Foundation staff member, was in charge of the laboratory.

The Governor demanded that Washington relieve Gorgas, Carter and all the others who persisted in the mosquito delusion and replace them with men of practical views.[19]

Out of the whole American community in the Isthmus 187 came down with fever and 57 died. Although this was mild compared to past epidemics, that was no comfort, for the toll was also undiscriminating: Some of the dead were high officials. The only advantage for the privileged was that they could get out. And many Americans did, among them the chief engineer. That was useful as the new chief engineer, John F. Stevens, supported Gorgas. Washington stood firm.

The sanitation work went on just as though it were succeeding, and in fact it was. Amid appearances of defeat the battle against yellow fever had actually been won. The epidemic of 1905 was to be the last. One more doubtful case was diagnosed in May 1906; since then there have been none.

Malaria, however, was not to give up so easily. Gorgas mounted his attack on *Anopheles* all along the 47-mile railroad from Panama to Colon that would be substantially the line of the canal. Although the work was at first limited to a few hundred yards from where canal workers slept, and never extended more than a mile or so on either side of the canal, there remained even so about 100 square miles (one-fifth of the total area of the Zone) to be cleared of waters that could breed mosquitoes. As no one then knew which species were dangerous and which were harmless, the war in fact took on all of them indiscriminately. In tropical jungle country with high annual rainfall, that was an immense undertaking. So long as the construction went on it was as frustrating as cutting off the Hydra's heads. The excavation and the continual shifting of heavy equipment meant thousands of new depressions that filled with rain and harbored larvae. Workers housed in tents and temporary barracks were helplessly exposed to bites.

Gorgas saw to it that he had the forces to cope. To protect 80,000 people (including natives) in thirty villages and camps he commanded between 1,200 and 1,300 laborers in twenty-five sanitary districts, each with its inspector, and disposed an annual budget of between $300,000 and $350,000. For himself he maneuvered skillfully to get the autonomy he was sure the job demanded. By 1907 his department was reporting directly to the chairman of the commission; he was at last a member of that commission himself. Perhaps most important of all, his successes in Havana and in eliminating yellow fever from Panama had given him prestige far more valuable than the organizational charts that safeguarded his independence.

When President Roosevelt made a three-day visit to the Zone in November 1906 he was notably and ostentatiously cordial and on departure insisted on waiting at the dock until Gorgas could be found to say goodbye. It was soon after his return to Washington that Roosevelt nominated Gorgas to be a member of the commission in a message on the canal that Gorgas thought was "a corker." That moment, Gorgas wrote, "probably marks the acme of my career."[20]

Presidential favor was especially helpful at that juncture. By the spring of 1907 the entire canal commission had retired, drifted away, or resigned, including Chief Engineer Stevens. Roosevelt, who had detested the idea of a commission from the beginning, now decided to put the military in command. His new commission, appointed in April, respected the forms decreed by Congress and included two civilians; but its chairman, Colonel George W. Goethals, with assignments also as chief engineer and president of the Panama Railroad, was designed to become, and almost immediately did become, commander of the Zone and all its works. Colonel Goethals enjoyed the exercise of power and was soon directing the construction work and governing his people like a patriarchal despot. Gorgas was already established as a despot in his own realm. Conflict between the two was inevitable. For the next seven years, until the canal was completed, Army society seldom lacked a fresh anecdote about a run-in between the two. Goethals was openly contemptuous of Gorgas' sanitation department; Gorgas regarded his chief as merely an impediment to good work.[21] But both men were politically untouchable; both were in jobs they loved. They had to get along.

Gorgas attacked the mosquitoes of Panama by all available means. His men drained swamps and other breeding places if they could; if they could not, they cleared out weeds and spread a concoction of carbolic acid, resin and caustic soda, invented and manufactured in the Zone. If there were windows for screening they were screened or bed nets were supplied. When there was no way to keep the mosquitoes out they were killed by hand.

That technologically primitive tactic was first tried in 1908 in a temporary tent camp where it seemed not worthwhile to go to the trouble and expense of treating breeding places. The next year 1,200 workers who were rebuilding a section of the railroad had to live in box cars. Gorgas had these screened. Besides screening the cars, the sanitation department hired "unlettered West India negro laborers at a compensation of ten cents an hour" to swat mosquitoes inside, or to trap them in glass tubes containing chopped rubber bands soaked with chloroform, an ingenious invention of Gorgas' engineer, Joseph LePrince. It was surprisingly effective.[22]

In his first three years' work, Gorgas cut the incidence of malaria in the Zone by more than half and kicked off a steady decline that carried the rate of sickness from a high in 1906 of more than 800 out of every thousand canal workers to only 16 in a thousand in 1916. Deaths from disease among employes dropped from almost 40 per thousand in 1906 to 8.68 per thousand in 1908 and stayed below that figure for many years thereafter.[23] Gorgas talked of victory and predicted the total elimination of both yellow fever and malaria within a few years. It would not be long, he told the class of 1907 at Cornell, before "life in the tropics for the Anglo-Saxon will be more healthful than in the temperate zone."[24]

Victory it was, even when qualified by the fact that at the end the enemy remained in the field with undiminished powers of recuperation. But how many such victories could the world realistically expect—or afford? Gorgas had reduced malaria to the status of a minor public health problem in Panama at a cost of about $350,000 per year, about $3.50 per person protected. At a time when laborers could be hired for a dollar a day or less that was not a trivial amount. The United States paid the bill without serious cavil because the canal was thought to be essential to American security. Panama was difficult terrain but it was also tiny. Where else was it likely to be thought worth $3 million and ten years of sustained effort to suppress mosquitoes in a hundred square miles? And how often would the troops be available under tight military command such as Gorgas exercised? In Panama if standing water needed treatment it was treated, whether it was on private property or public, politically inside Gorgas' jurisdiction or outside. If Gorgas thought houses should be screened, soldiers put up the screens and inspectors checked to see that they remained in good condition. If quinine pills were indicated, the men under military discipline were lined up and made to take them.[25]

Dr. Malcolm Watson, among the many admiring visitors to the Canal Zone, thought that the "real triumph" of the Americans was the "perfection of the whole Canal administration."[26] He doubted that Gorgas' example could be followed, because there were no more Gorgases and no more Roosevelts to back them. Rubber company directors, he thought, would not want to grant their estate medical officers anything like the authority Gorgas enjoyed. Nor, he added, would medical officers be likely to want such authority. If not company directors, how much less politicians!

Whether or not Gorgas was indeed so entirely unique, his example was slow to inspire imitation even in the United States, which had backed him with its riches and acclaimed him as its hero. L. O. Howard, one of the most distinguished entomologists of his day and author of the then authoritative work on mosquitoes, noted sourly in 1912 that "almost nothing had been done" in the United States up to that time.[27] There was, it is true, a war on against mosquitoes in New Jersey brilliantly and at last successfully waged under command of the state entomologist, John B. Smith. The aim of that war was to remove a nuisance and so raise property values along the Jersey shore. It was therefore obviously worth the cost.*

The other early American success was the victory of Dr. Alvah H. Doty over *Anopheles* in Staten Island. In 1901 when Doty began work, one-fifth of the inhabitants of Staten Island suffered from malaria. Doty, the health officer of the Port of New York, launched a systematic campaign to eliminate mosquito breeding on the island, climaxed in 1905 by massive reclamation of a swamp along the coast where during four years of work nearly a thousand miles of drainage canals were dug. In 1909 it was hard to find a mosquito on the island. The cost ($50,000) had been high considering the very few acres protected, cheap considering the value of the island. Dr. Howard wryly noted another contemporaneous campaign in the New York region where a very wealthy man induced authorities to dry up certain marshes near Brooklyn so as to get rid of mosquitoes that annoyed his race horses.[29]

But in the South where malaria was a serious problem, wherewithal for the battle was much harder to find. Health boards were slow to accept the mosquito theory. Town councils were reluctant to vote the money. Washington with millions for Panama offered no support. Only as national associations formed, as propaganda contributed to an increase of knowledge and public pressure, and as, here and there, a local success proved politically and economically attractive—only very slowly by these means did serious antimalaria work come to the South, becoming notable only after World War I. And it was not until after World War II that malaria was at last driven out of the North American continent.

---

* One booster declared that suppressing the salt-marsh mosquito and reclaiming both farm and resort land ought to increase the taxable value of New Jersey by more than half a billion dollars in twenty years.[28]

19 / Italy and Koch's Way

Freetown, Lagos, Mian Mir, Malaya, Panama, Staten Island—these were the most considerable attempts in the first twenty years after Ross's great discovery to reduce malaria by attack on the breeding places of anophelines. There were a few stirrings elsewhere. In Hong Kong, Dr. J. C. Thomson in 1900 and 1901 surveyed breeding places in and around town and eliminated many.[1] In Ismailia, the Suez Canal company town on the shores of one of the bitter lakes, Ronald Ross in 1902 advised on the formation of mosquito brigades to clear standing water and cover or oil cesspits. That work continued for years supplemented later by the conversion of a large swamp into a golf course, and the town was made relatively healthy. Ismailia proved again the power of lots of money, applied by an autocratic government to a very small area.*[2] In Algeria two brothers, Étienne and Edmond Sergent, began in 1902 a lifetime of experimental work on malaria control by every means. Although they did not eliminate malaria from Algeria, the Sergents operated a useful test ground for control methods that were carefully designed and meticulously reported to the rest of the world.[3] Finally, in 1907 the colonial government of Mauritius consulted Ross on how and where to attack malarial mosquitoes and over the next fifteen years more or less followed his advice—but with such delays,

---

* Though twenty-five years later the brigades were still at work and there was still malaria in Ismailia.

169

Angelo Celli

such lack of system and such penny-pinching that the net effects were negligible.*

In Italy a different approach was shaped and directed by Professor Angelo Celli, the doctor who with Ettore Marchiafava was first in Italy to confirm the existence of Laveran's parasite. Whereas Ross and Gorgas thought of malaria control in military terms and sought above all to drive *Anopheles* from the vicinity of human habitations, Celli, an intellectual, historian and passionate social reformer, saw it essentially as a social problem. Fever, he believed, was both cause and result of the miserable, impoverished lives of the majority of Italian peasants especially in the central and southern provinces. A lifelong Roman, Celli was deeply influenced by his observations of the landless agricultural workers, the *braccianti,* in the fever-ridden plains of the Roman Campagna. "Poor leaves detached from the tree, at the mercy of the wind," another Italian called them.[4] More literally in Celli's view, they were at the mercy of absentee landlords and greedy labor contractors (*caporali*).

---

* For the story of how malaria came to Mauritius, see Chapter 21.

In a course of lectures on malaria in 1899 Celli devoted long and elo-
quent passages to describing the plight of the *braccianti*. In a second edition, prepared the following year, he greatly elaborated these as though
especially to underline the point for a larger audience, even though the
book was intended and long used chiefly as a medical text.[5]

The *braccianti* of the Campagna mostly lived in villages in the hills back
of the coast which were comparatively healthy. But they got no advantage
from that. Those days, anywhere from 100 to 200 a year, when they hired
themselves out in order to subsist at all took them into the highly malarious
plains below, and at just those seasons when mosquitoes were most abundant. They worked under the worst possible conditions. Badly paid by the
caporali, who could withhold their wages at will to repay usurious loans,
they had to buy at exorbitant prices from landlords' stores food that was
normally inadequate and often toxic.* Those who had any shelter at all
were crowded into windowless straw and cane huts whose dark and fetid
interiors offered ideal feeding and resting places for mosquitoes. Most lived
entirely in the open, wearing clothes that scarcely protected them against
cold nights, much less against insect bites. Tired, ill-fed and constantly
exposed, they suffered terribly from the so-called Roman estivo-autumnal
fever.

When in 1899, Celli, like others in Italy, cast about for ways effectively
to use the new knowledge of malaria, having the *braccianti* in mind he
thought most readily of defending people rather than of warring on pests.
His first experiments in late 1899 were to protect railway workers by
furnishing them with head nets and gloves, screening and burning chrysanthemum flowers in the stations.[6] Dr. Manson on a visit to Italy was so
impressed with the results that he especially urged the railroad administration to do more. Eventually the technique was widely adopted. Exported to
Algeria, it was put to effective use there by the Sergent brothers.

But it was an answer to no more than one small problem. Screening
could protect only those who lived in houses that would take screens and
who could stay inside when the mosquitoes began to bite—in short, people
whose way of life was as different as could be imagined from that of the
peasants in the Campagna. That perception is what drove Celli to urge
economic reform as the first line of attack on malaria. The peasants had to
prosper to afford decent housing (and screens), eat well and not be forced
to work late or sleep in the fields. So the public health doctor found himself

---

* Pellagra, a disease caused by nutritional deficiency—chiefly found among those
living on a diet of corn—was a common and devastating scourge of the Italian
peasantry.

in a text on malaria urging a law to fix a minimum wage, and other laws to regulate conditions of work. "The first step," he wrote, "should be to abolish the exploitation of workers by the so-called *caporali*. But alas no one thinks of that!"[7] Still less was anyone thinking of changing the feudal patterns of landownership, which in southern Italy had survived unification. Yet that, Celli believed, was what was needed. It was the engrossment of the land by a "small but omnipotent band of proprietors, privileged more than they deserve," and exercising rights to use and abuse without restraint, that kept the peasants impoverished, that frustrated state efforts to reclaim and resettle new lands, and that was finally "the greatest enemy of public health."[8]

He was right. But while working for social change the good doctor had to take care of his patients as well as he could. He considered of course trying to get rid of mosquitoes. The first Italian experiment in mosquito control in 1899 was in fact a success. Claudio Fermi eliminated malaria from the small penal island of Asinara, north of Sardinia, by suffocating mosquito larvae while screening the prisoners and administering quinine. Fermi thought the antilarval measures most important and tried throughout a long career to promote them in Italy.[9] But Celli was discouraged. After one trial of larviciding he and a colleague concluded that it had no general relevance for malaria control in Italy. There were just too many breeding places; they could not all be drained and to keep clearing them of weeds and oiling them was too expensive.

"The problem of the destruction of mosquitoes," Celli wrote, "is soluble experimentally; but practically it will only be so when the economic interest wishes it."[10] Realistically he thought the economic interest would wish it infrequently and that the destruction of mosquitoes therefore would never be possible on a large scale.[11] That left quinine as the most promising antimalarial means at hand. Celli took it up, at first rather tentatively, then with growing partisanship.

When first Laveran, then Celli and many others saw that quinine actually destroyed plasmodia in the blood cells, the ancient therapeutic appeared in a wholly new light. It was not merely a drug to ease fever and assist the recovery of the sick; it was a weapon against the disease itself.

Robert Koch was most impressed. Accustomed to seeking out vaccines with which to counterattack invading bacteria, he found killing plasmodia in the body with a drug a much more congenial notion than eradicating mosquitoes in the environment. It was a straightforward medical approach and he thought it would be simpler in practice. In 1899 he wrote that quinine systematically administered to both new and relapsed cases could wipe out malaria in nine months.[12] That was the earliest and certainly the most extreme claim ever made for quinine treatments as a general prophy-laxis against malaria. It asserted what then appeared theoretically possible under perfect conditions for dosing carriers and preventing reinfection. Reality would require considerable revision.

Koch in 1900 went to New Guinea, then a German colony, to have a look at actual conditions. There he worked out a regimen of quinine treat-ments designed to extinguish all parasites in the blood in two months. It seemed to work and became the basis for the "Koch method" that with modifications was widely adopted particularly in southern Europe (Italy, Greece and Spain). But Koch also discovered an important difficulty: Many persons with parasites in their blood did not feel ill enough to see a doctor. To reach all carriers with quinine therefore it was necessary to screen the blood of all "suspected" persons. Who were the suspected? Koch found them to be chiefly the immigrants and the children.[13]

Koch's finding that the blood of very young children, those under five, constituted the principal reservoir of parasites in areas endemic for ma-laria, was of major importance for malaria control. But it was also dis-couraging, since infants would always be particularly hard to reach and dose effectively. Koch confessed that blood examinations were troublesome and time-consuming, but minimized the difficulty. He returned from his few months abroad highly optimistic. Like almost everyone else he could not resist building global generalizations on a brief and special experi-ence. His method of treatment he thought "could make every malarial place free or almost free of malaria."[14]

Celli was attracted but at first skeptical. He had noted, as had others, that quinine did not kill the sexual forms of *P. falciparum,* the familiar crescents. "Even, when giving quinine every day by subcutaneous injection, and in large doses for a whole month," he wrote, "I have not often suc-ceeded in destroying the crescentic forms."[15] But perhaps quinine would in some way interfere with passage of the gametocytes into the mosquito. In 1900 he did a series of experiments—with discouraging results. *Anophe-les* feeding on patients undergoing quinine treatment did become infected, and Celli found that "the sexual cycle develops in spite of the treatment. Consequently," he concluded, ". . . a complete rational prophylaxis by means of this disinfection, notwithstanding what Koch says about it, is not easy, nor is it always possible." As quinine could not interrupt transmission it could not do much for the peasants of the Campagna who, by remaining in malarious areas, would be constantly reinfected.

Nevertheless one must go ahead. "Without exaggeration, and without excessive optimism," he wrote in 1901, "we must continue to get quinine used as much as possible; we must administer it promptly, assiduously and in greater quantities than Koch prescribed."[16] Having so decided, Celli swallowed his reservations and put all of his considerable prestige and energy behind promoting quinine therapy and prophylaxis.[17] He lobbied successfully for the law of 23 December 1900 that set up a state quinine service (Azienda del Chinino di Stato) to manufacture and sell quinine at reasonable prices. Profits accruing to the service were reserved for quinine subsidies, special investigations and prizes. Another law the following year entitled all workers to get treatment for malaria at the expense of their employers, and required landowners to carry out and pay for controlling surface water on lands. That was not quite the thoroughgoing social reform that Celli wished to see but it did attack a root problem in recognizing malaria as the occupational disease that it was indeed among Italian peasants.

Unfortunately action under the law was much less impressive. The steady stream of legislation that Italian governments for twenty-five years directed against malaria, extending the availability of quinine, tightening the responsibilities of landowners to protect workers and reduce mosquitoes, providing for compulsory reporting of malaria, requiring the screening of all quarters housing state employes, is one significant measure of how little actually got done.

But quinine seemed an almost instant success. The state service sold 2,242 kilograms, chiefly in sugar-coated tablets, in its first year of operations (1902–3). Sales climbed rapidly to exceed 24,000 kilograms five years later. Gratifyingly deaths from malaria fell from a high of over 15,000 in 1900 to a low of just over 2,000 in 1914, on the eve of war which as always would be on the side of the mosquito.

Celli's early doubts were overwhelmed. He considered the case for quinine proved. Some later observers have agreed. Yet on closer examination the case was really not nearly so strong as it looked.[18] Long before anyone knew what malaria was and before any measures had been taken against it, the fevers had begun to withdraw from Europe. Precisely why is still not clear but it certainly had to do with developing intensive agriculture and general economic improvement.* In Italy malaria was probably also retreating steadily out of the north, where temperatures were less favorable for the reproduction and transmission of plasmodia and where economic development was concentrated. Cheap and widely available quinine superimposed on this "spontaneous" trend must certainly have accelerated it. Yet in the absence of any good statistics at all on malaria

---

* See below, Chapter 22.

morbidity, as distinct from mortality, it is not possible to know just what was happening, much less to isolate the possible impact of the drug.

That fewer people died from the fevers can safely be attributed at least in part to wider use of quinine. To that extent the Italians' decision to emphasize drug treatment was amply justified. On the other hand, in almost certainly exaggerating its efficacy, Italy developed over the years an exclusive attachment that tended to discourage alternative strategies that might in some circumstances have been more effective. There was in that attachment a patriotic flavor: Italy in the forefront of malaria research remained in the forefront of the efforts at control. As the Italian way based on quinine prophylaxis spread to other nations, most notably Greece, Spain and Algeria, Celli and others took considerable pride of paternity on behalf of their country.[19]

It seems likely, however, that early success with quinine, and early discouragement with alternative methods, abetted by nationalism and economic interests and by inertia in the end restricted the antimalarial campaign more than Celli ever intended. Despite his enthusiasm for quinine and what amounted almost to a vested interest in it when he himself became president of the state quinine service, he continued to see as the ultimate objective those basic land reforms that would give the peasant a healthier, more prosperous deal. The fight against malaria, he wrote in 1908, should aim to "maintain a man in health first of all . . . and with this healthy man to undertake land and water reclamation and management [*bonifiche idrauliche e agrario*] for the total redemption of the land from malaria."[20]

The reclamation and resettlement of waste and disease-ridden lands, called *bonifica* (bonification) was an ancient Italian dream embodied now and then in official policy and here and there even realized. The ideal included banishing disease, especially as applied to the Campagna—where since the days of ancient Rome malaria had notoriously been the prime cause of the land's desolation, and where the presence of the fever so near the capital was an embarrassment as well as a menace. But more basically *bonifica* meant economic development to take care in an overwhelmingly agricultural country of the rapidly multiplying poor. It could also be a political safety valve for relieving pressure on successive governments to do something about land reform. As few politicians found it attractive to take on the big landowners in an effort to force them to disgorge farms for the peasants, bonification offered a political alternative: new-minted lands to dangle before the land-hungry *braccianti*.[21]

In practice the *braccianti* got little. The major benefits went, as they so often did, to the northern provinces, Italy's healthiest and most prosperous.

Not only was most of the reclamation work done there, but only in the north was malaria closely associated with swampy ground. Elsewhere the malaria vectors bred in rivers, pools and puddles. Drainage schemes scarcely touched them. Moreover, as central and southern Italy were subject to torrential seasonal rains, diked and drained lands were constantly reflooded. A law of 1901 did recognize that general drainage might not meet the requirements of mosquito control and prescribed supplementary care of puddles and canals, *piccola bonifica*. But not until 1923 did the law link bonification with flood control.

Bonifica, ordained and encouraged by a steady stream of legislation, was popular with successive Italian governments. They spent large sums on it. By the mid-1920s nearly four million acres (about one-sixteenth the area of Italy) had been reclaimed, were in the process of reclamation or were scheduled for it.[22]

Yet during the first fifty years the new lands did not materially reduce the number of the landless rural poor, and their impact on malaria, confined to the north, remains ambiguous. In view of a striking coincidence between areas of marshlands and of endemic malaria in the northern provinces it is reasonable to assume that they became healthier in part because they were being dried out. The fact remains however that malaria declined also where no drainage or any other antimalarial measures were taken.

Italians themselves had little faith in either *grande* or *piccola bonifica* as specifics against fever. Dr. Lewis Hackett, who came to Italy in 1924 on behalf of the Rockefeller Foundation, found among them a "note of extreme pessimism" after their twenty-five years' experience. He wrote: "Apart from a few political enthusiasts (*Fascisti*) who cite the favorable results obtained in the North of Italy by the immense expenditures of Government money on large-scale drainage operations, and who hold that control of malaria is now a financial rather than a scientific problem, the majority of scientists feel that very little if any progress has been made of late in rural malaria control on a sound economic basis."[23]

As for the Campagna, it was subject of repeated legislation and nearly continuous experimentation in every conceivable kind of control—all discouraging. When Hackett visited he found things unchanged not just over the past twenty-five years but over the past several thousand. "The mode of life," he wrote of Celli's miserable seasonal workers, "is as primitive as anything I have seen in the tropics . . . one would have to go back to Cro-Magnon days for a parallel."[24] And like Celli here and throughout the malarious regions to the south, Hackett concluded that what was needed was to bring "civilization" to the region and create a vigorous working class.

20 / Rockefeller and the American Way

Two battlers against *Plasmodium* in the island of Corsica wrote in 1913, on the eve of that other war: "The fight against Malaria can only be a long job. All who have fought this tenacious disease are unanimous in recognizing that. Efforts are never immediately crowned by success. Whatever prophylactic measures are used their good effects are only felt after many years and only then if they are applied rigorously and under supervision of vigilant experts."[1] That was a fair summing up of the first dozen years.

Those disposed to be discouraged by the difficulties uncovered found their blackest pessimism justified in World War I. Italy lost most of the ground so painfully won; deaths from malaria soared—in 1918 reaching the numbers (though not quite the rate per million population) of 1898. In Malaya control efforts stopped. Panama, where the canal did not open until August 1914, was again a bright exception—in large part because America was not immediately drawn into war and because the Zone was a military installation. And again the exception proved little of general applicability.

Worst of all the war demonstrated that public authority—military commands above all—had simply not gotten the message. Despite abundant expert warnings of the dangers of malaria—amply authenticated by history, despite expert advice on how to counter those dangers—armies of both the Allied and Central Powers blundered into anopheline territory quite unprepared. In 1915 hundreds of thousands of non-immune Greek refugees reached Macedonia from Asia Minor, Caucasus and Thrace and stoked the malarial fires before the Allied landings at Salonika. The resulting epidemic of 1916–17 prostrated the invading forces as well as the German and Bulgarian defenders. Whether the Allied thrust might otherwise have succeeded was a moot point; it would at least have been less costly. In Palestine 5 percent of the British occupying forces in 1918 were hospitalized with fever; in the highly malarious Jordan valley the figure was 8 percent.[2] In one small sector the army devoted 123,900 man days to clearing and oiling mosquito breeding places—without which, according to their historian, "the force would have completely melted away."[3] Nowhere were troops entering malarious zones properly warned of the dangers, trained to avoid them or issued protective nets or quinine.

The war closed out the first generation of experiments in malaria control on a sour, even a bitter, note. Yet there was a useful lesson: The enemy was tougher than the optimists of the beginning believed and crusades were much more difficult to manage. New beginnings, if there were to be any, demanded reassessments of the problem and fresh deployments of force. For that, a new institution was happily at hand with just the combination of talents, resources and naivety needed for innovation.

When at the end of the robber-baron century, John D. Rockefeller began to divest himself of some of his oil millions, he first set up in 1901 the Rockefeller Institute for Medical Research. That choice reflected the conviction of his closest adviser, Frederick T. Gates, that health and hygiene were the most neglected "elements of civilization."[4] Two years later Rockefeller money launched the General Education Board, whose work was particularly directed toward the Southern states. In a few years the Board had determined that the mental and physical torpor characterizing so many poor Southern children (and adults as well) was neither native stupidity nor laziness but the physiological result of infestations of hookworm. Accordingly Rockefeller in 1909 funded the Rockefeller Sanitary Commission to launch a campaign against the parasite.

Four years later (in May 1913), old John D. Rockefeller set up his crowning philanthropy, the Rockefeller Foundation to promote "the well-being of mankind." Success in the interim against hookworm encouraged the trustees of the new foundation not only to continue and widen that war but also to look for similar opportunities to challenge other diseases. What they wanted, and thought they had found when at last they authorized a war on malaria were openings to apply existing scientific knowledge to public health through relatively cheap and simple techniques.

The man first commissioned to look for such openings was a Southern educator named Wickliffe Rose, who as head of the Rockefeller Sanitary Commission was already running the hookworm war. Rose was not trained in medicine and his selection underlined the Foundation's determination to support social action not medical research. It also meant that Rose would have to find and heavily depend on technical advisers. In fact he made a grand tour in 1914 to look for them. He talked with Malcolm Watson in Malaya and with Ronald Ross among others in London.[5] On his return he found himself sufficiently impressed with the case for taking on malaria to authorize some preliminary trials of tactics.* But he had also found a more urgent task.

In July he went to see Dr. William Gorgas, who was now surgeon general of the United States. It was then just a month before the Panama Canal was to open. Gorgas was worried, as were many others, that yellow fever, still a periodic scourge of Latin American ports, might travel on ships through the canal to Asia where it had never been known. Asia, he thought, had been spared until that moment because *Aedes aegypti* could not live through the long, cold sea passage around the southern tips of Africa or South America. Swift transport through the canal would immensely improve their chances. Dr. Manson had expressed the same fear as early as 1903.[7] Those who went ahead and built the canal anyway had by their own lights been gambling with millions of lives.

Gorgas' idea, put at the eleventh hour to the Rockefeller Foundation, was to end the gamble by eliminating the disease. He thought a successful outcome was not only possible but probably easy. Henry Rose Carter, who took part in these and later talks, guessed it might take a couple of years; at most, he estimated, there remained after Havana only five or six other endemic foci of the disease in the southern hemisphere.

The prospect of a quick, decisive victory over a major disease which, if successful, could save half the world from its visitations was obviously attractive. In May 1915, the Rockefeller Foundation announced that it was "prepared to give aid in the eradication of this disease in those areas where the infection is endemic and where conditions would seem to invite co-operation for its control."[8] Gorgas was to lay on the campaign and later to lead it.

In the summer of 1916, when with Carter and three others he reconnoitered South America, he discovered that for once he had been too pessimistic: There were not five or six endemic centers but only one, at Guayaquil, Ecuador. The four months' trip yielded an even greater bonus for the Foundation as it turned into a triumphal tour that opened all doors. Gorgas, handsome, charming and now a major general, was quite the most

---

* These first took place in the American South in the summer of 1915 and involved two small towns in which mosquito control was compared with quinine treatments as to both cost and effectiveness.[6]

famous doctor in the world.* Political leaders and leading citizens of South America all wanted to pay him homage. Some of his fame and charm brushed off on the Foundation for which he worked and assured a welcome for their men for a generation thereafter, during which time they did vital work in Latin American countries on both yellow fever and malaria.

But the year 1916 turned out not to be auspicious for public health programs. Plans were shelved for two years. Then, three days after the Armistice, General Gorgas retired from the Army, joined the Rockefeller Foundation full time and took command of the interrupted yellow fever campaign. The work of destroying breeding places of *Aedes aegypti* in Guayaquil began at once—in November 1918—and seven months later Dr. W. E. Conners, in charge, could announce complete success. Yellow fever was gone from Guayaquil.[10] It has never returned.

The confidence of Gorgas seemed more than vindicated. Success put the Gorgas stamp indelibly on the Foundation. Scientists and sanitarians employed by it—and during nearly forty years in action against disease it employed a large proportion of the best—were always to show a strong bias for bold and radical solutions. Almost without exception they wanted to extirpate malaria, not merely reduce it. Whatever other reasons there may have been, one surely was that the core staff—Gorgas, Carter and Samuel T. Darling, the former chief of the Panama laboratories—were all Havana and Panama men, conquerors of *Aedes aegypti,* the mosquito that happened to be the most vulnerable of all to direct attack on its breeding places. Their colleagues and successors tended to be those who held similar views.

The public health club at that time was in fact small and close-knit. The successor to Wickliffe Rose as head of the Foundation's health programs was Colonel Frederick F. Russell, another Army doctor, who had worked as a bacteriologist under General Sternberg. He was appointed to the Foundation post in 1923 with the active support of such Rockefeller board members as Dr. William Welch, Sternberg's and Gorgas' teacher, and Dr. Simon Flexner, another of Welch's students and an old friend.†

It was under Russell, a short, stout man who liked to be called "General" once he had made that grade, that the Rockefeller Foundation's work against malaria really got under way.[11] It is worth noting, moreover, that

---

* In 1914 Gorgas, visiting England, had received an honorary D.Sc. degree from Oxford at a special convocation and had been hailed by the *Daily Mail* as a man who held the whole world in his debt.[9]

† A third strong Russell supporter was Dr. Hermann M. Biggs, New York State commissioner of health and a dominant figure in the American public health movement.

Lewis W. Hackett (right) with Miss Lindsay (center) and unidentified companion in a field camp in Albania, 1930

the campaign against yellow fever continued and prospered, for some years inevitably setting standards for what were at first necessarily more tentative forays against malaria.

The attack on malaria developed as an expanding series of experiments, first in the Southern states, then into Latin America, Europe and at last Africa and the Far East. It was a remarkable, unique effort—the first international attack on what had always been seen as an international problem, and the first adequately funded attempt to find out scientifically what worked and what the cost would be. The method was to employ public health doctors, administrators and occasionally engineers and detail them for tours of duty in foreign lands where they worked with local professionals, often in new institutes or services developed jointly with Foundation and national staffing and financing.* Like diplomats the Foundation men were transferred frequently, carrying with them an ever richer mix of experience that exerted increasing influence on tactics worldwide. It happened, largely because of two unusual men, that the Foundation's influence built up chiefly in two centers. The first of these was Italy, where

---

* With Foundation support malaria research institutes were set up by the governments of twenty-six countries.[12]

Dr. Lewis Hackett arrived in January 1924 to investigate with the Italian government the possibilities of cheap and effective control of malaria mosquitoes.*

"I was sent to Italy with only the most fragmentary knowledge of malaria," Dr. Hackett later wrote.[13] Then not quite forty, he had been trained as a doctor and public health administrator, had worked for the Foundation briefly in Panama, on hookworm in Guatemala and then for six years in Brazil where he was concerned mostly with health services. Yet, he observed wryly, by grace of being an American he was expected to teach Grassi, Bastianelli and Marchiafava how to control malaria.

Besides being an American, fortunately, he was modest, diplomatic, bright, energetic and willing to learn. He had also a sense of humor. It amused him for instance that he spent his first nine months in Italy touring the beautiful and romantic countryside peering into drains, dipping for *Anopheles* larvae and counting the "number of spleens of children under 12 reaching to the umbilicus."[14] He was amused later, on a similar tour of Albania, by a small boy who watched him crawling on hands and knees around a house in search of mosquitoes and remarked, "Even if I were a Christian I wouldn't do that."[15]

He found some of the Italians proud and suspicious and his own position as an American missionary difficult. Public health officials were at first touchy about the implication that they, who were first and longest in the field against malaria, had anything to learn or that their government needed charitable assistance. Later, after Hackett had completed his survey and recommended a few modest local experiments in mosquito control, they were dismayed that a great and rich American organization should have set its sights so low.[16] They themselves thought in terms of centralized national efforts—a legacy in part from the state quinine monopoly which in a literal way sought to dose the nation from Rome. They had hoped Dr. Hackett would provide money for more health centers, more ambulances which by saturating the country with quinine would complete the triumph of the Italian way.

The fact is that Hackett found himself in profound disagreement with the Italian way. Not only did he doubt the efficacy of quinine, or rather its adequacy as the sole weapon against malaria, but he was convinced that malaria by its nature was a local phenomenon which could be effectively attacked only through a thorough understanding of the local conditions that allowed it to spread. Above all he thought that the defeat of malaria

---

* The other was Brazil, where Fred L. Soper developed his faith in eradication strategies. See Chapter 23.

demanded defeat of the mosquito. It was this latter conviction that brought him into sharp conflict not merely with the heirs of Celli (including Celli's widow, Anna) but also with dominant international opinion as expressed by the distinguished experts who formed the first Malaria Commission of the League of Nations.

The League Commission, set up in 1924, was important as the first step toward the collective action against malaria that would later be developed so brilliantly under the egis of the World Health Organization. But its mandate was cautiously restricted to stay well clear of any implications of international interference in national affairs: It was to investigate and report on the present status of malaria and malaria control, especially in Europe, and estimate world needs for quinine.* In fact the 1924 commission looked only at Europe, visiting the Kingdom of the Serbs, Croats and Slovenes, Greece, Bulgaria, Romania, Russia and finally Italy in August.†

By the time the commissioners reached Italy they had had four months of travel and were "fed up" with it.[17] The visit was cut short. They collected most of their information from the department of public health. Perhaps they would have done so in any event, since their chairman was Alberto Lutrario who had only just ceased to be head of that department. Still, they were rather rudely in a hurry. Only three men in Italy at that time had been consistently involved in mosquito control work. They were Claudio Fermi, who kept doing experiments and failing to follow them up;[18] Professor Grassi, who had worked long discouraging years in battle against *Anopheles* in Fiumicino; and Alberto Missiroli, a much younger man, who had had a subordinate job at the health department until Hackett picked him up to be director of the new malaria experiment station which the Foundation in cooperation with the Italian government established in Rome in 1924. The commission put two-thirds of their collective nose out of joint. Members spent one hour at Fiumicino, the hour before lunch. Grassi, then seventy years old, not only had a lifetime of work to show them but his mind was teeming with new ideas born of the despairing realization that he still had not solved the problem of malaria.[19] The commissioners were not interested. As for Missiroli, he put on a demonstration in the use of a new larvicide, Paris green, eager to show that there were effective ways to kill mosquitoes. The commission members dutifully watched the spreading of the poison, but they never came back to check the kill.[20]

---

* The terms of reference are an interesting reflection of the already wide acceptance among experts of Koch's way as practiced in Italy.

† A second tour covered the rest of the malarious world in 1927.

Later Hackett had lunch with two of the most influential members, N. H. Swellengrebel, the Dutch professor with whom Hackett would have closer associations in subsequent research, and Colonel S. P. James of the Indian Medical Service—the officer, it will be recalled, who had been in charge of the failed experiment at Mian Mir. Hackett liked them both "immensely"[21] but was appalled at their wholly negative attitude toward mosquito control. Colonel James warned that U. S. methods would not work in Europe, asked Hackett if he had ever been in India and then "announced that no one could know malaria without going to India."[22] Professor Swellengrebel, who was to draft the bulk of the commission report, wholly admired the Italian attack which he conceived to have two main prongs: reduction of mortality and improvement of social and economic conditions. So far as *grande bonifica* made people better off he thought it indirectly prophylactic; but in his view neither it nor *piccola bonifica* had any effect on mosquito numbers and therefore could not be held to be antimalarial measures. This was a conclusion he had already arrived at in studies in his native Holland, where land reclamation could often be shown to have increased malaria, never to have reduced it.[23]

The commission's final report was revisionist in spirit, even as to the utility of Ross's discovery. "As a result of hard-worn experience during the past 25 years," the commissioners wrote, "the belief is gaining ground that the discovery of the mosquito cycle of the disease, of fundamental value though it was, revealed only the most important link in the epidemiological chain and that many auxiliary factors, of which at present we know only a few, play an important part in the epidemiology of the disease." The commission accepted Professor Swellengrebel's view that malaria was a social disease that like tuberculosis responded to "measures of social hygiene" such as good nutrition and housing. These were wise and useful observations but in context appeared defeatist. The commission nominated quinine as the only effective basis for antimalarial campaigns and dismissed "the alternative, the long and costly effort called for to wage a really victorious anti-anopheles war."[24]

Hackett was angry at a conclusion he felt was unjustified and that only made his own work more difficult. There was worse to come. Three years later the second League Commission report, this one drafted largely by Colonel James, reiterated all the negative points in even stronger language. At the time of Ross's discovery, the second League Commission observed, it had been universally believed "that a single simple method" had been found to defeat malaria. "Since then nearly three decades have passed, and such a method is still to seek . . . The history of special antimalarial campaigns is chiefly a record of exaggerated expectations followed sooner or later by disappointment and abandonment of the work."[25]

Colonel James and the commissioners admitted that in the light of this record they never conceived that their job was to see how malarious areas might be made healthy. Few, if any, nations could afford that. Rather, they meant to examine measures that might be "adopted in order that malaria may cease to be an important cause of sickness and death."

Futile campaigns against *Anopheles* might make matters worse. Colonel James, addressing the malariologists of the world assembled in Rome in 1925, reported that in Eastern Europe the commission "saw some sad occurrences where all the doctors in certain localities were out in the fields fishing for *Anopheles* larvae . . ." while people lay sick in bed without medical care.[26] In the official report that extraordinary observation led to an extraordinary generalization: "It is safe to say that in some countries of Eastern Europe with very limited resources hardly anything has retarded the effective control of malaria so much as has the belief that, because mosquitoes carry malaria, their elimination should be the object of chief concern and expenditure."[27]

No wonder the mosquito fighters were furious. After the first report Hackett, fearing that the pessimism of the commission would powerfully confirm the Italians in theirs, protested to a League official. He particularly objected to the closed-mindedness that seemed to settle on a simple formula and rule out experimentation. "Are we approaching the dark ages of malariology?" he asked with an emotionalism he later regretted.[28]

After the second report Hackett's unhappiness found echoes all over the world. In the Far East, Sir Malcolm Watson, near the end of his long battle in Malaya publicly attacked the commission's findings as "damn nonsense."[29] Americans were particularly irritated by a special report which discounted all their efforts at mosquito control and attributed the decline of malaria in the United States entirely to natural causes. The U. S. Surgeon General wrote to Geneva suggesting that the commission would not want to lend its authority to conclusions so hastily drawn from "contradictory and often insufficient premises."* [30]

The League responded by calling a meeting in June 1928. Dr. Hackett went with six other members of the Rockefeller Foundation. Colonel James, who appears to have been largely responsible for the American report, was there to defend himself. But if there were confrontations they were all off stage. The official conclusions muffled the quarrel by giving

---

* In fact the report was never published.

everyone his due. The subcommittee charged with examining the methods of malaria control advocated by the League Commission enunciated nine principles that it said represented the consensus of "malariologists of the old and the new world." The first eight endorsed the flexibility of attack dear to Dr. Hackett's heart, the ninth asserted that the first duty of health authorities was to assure the treatment of the sick.[31]

But there was no real reconciliation of views. The League of Nations officially, and the members of its Malaria Commission individually, continued to regard drugs as the main line of defense against malaria.* The staff of the Rockefeller Foundation who soon came to dominate malaria control work continued tirelessly to promote the war on *Anopheles*.

Just as Ronald Ross had opened the first phase of the universal war with a skirmish in the puddled streets of Freetown, so Dr. Hackett now similarly deployed for small-scale battle in phase two, setting up two field stations, one in the toe of Italy (Calabria) and one in Sardinia, to experiment with larval control. His principal weapon was to be Paris green†—a remarkable new larvicide that would have been worth the League Commission's closer attention.

Traditionally the accepted ways of killing mosquito larvae were either to dry up the pools in which they lived before they could complete metamorphosis into adult form, to suffocate them by laying down a film of oil that clogged their breathing tubes, or to poison the entire body of water in which they grew with chemical compounds such as were used in Panama. In 1920 a French entomologist, Emile Roubaud, remarked what many others knew but had not noticed: the fact that anopheline larvae ingest everything of the right size that drifts into their mouths. Roubaud dusted the water with a lethal chemical, paraformaldehyde, watched the larvae brush it into their mouths and die.[32] Two Americans, Barber and Hayne, after reading Roubaud's report systematically experimented with other substances. The cheapest, most effective and easiest to handle they found was copper aceto-arsenite (Paris green), long in use against pests of food crops, mixed with water or still more effectively with dry fine dust.[33] It was much cheaper than oil. It could not injure the spreaders unless they devoured it in large quantity. It was not toxic or even offensive to cattle and could therefore be used on their watering holes. It did not hurt fish. It could be easily transported in pure form and mixed on the spot, one part to

---

* Over the next decade of its existence the commission promoted various tests of quinine, and synthetics after those began to appear in the 1930s. Its last report, in 1937, noted that the elimination of malaria by drug therapy and prophylaxis "has not hitherto been found possible in practice."

† Called in Paris "Vert de Schweinfurt."

a hundred, with road dust. It could effectively be spread—as would be found a little later—by airplane over large swampy areas inaccessible to any other kind of treatment.[34] It worked in weedy waters where oil did not. There was only one drawback: Unlike oil it did not kill culicine nuisance mosquitoes which fed below the surface. It might therefore meet resistance where people objected as much to being bitten as to getting the fever.* Otherwise it seemed quite to justify Dr. Hackett's enthusiastic assertion that "the discovery of Paris green as a larvicide is the most important addition to our knowledge of malaria control in a decade."[35]

He at any rate was delighted with it. In the first two experiments it cost only a little over nine cents a person to reduce the parasites in the blood of some 18,000 people to "insignificant" levels. That was done in a year. Within three, Hackett could claim to have banished malaria from both experimental towns. Portotorres on the coast of Sardinia, where in 1925 no one not native willingly passed a single night, in 1927 had opened a hotel and was building a bath house. A hundred and fifty school children came from places inland to spend six weeks of the summer in an unscreened school building. Success in Bianconovo in Calabria was comparable.† The experiments moreover were being repeated "in various parts of Italy" with such gratifying and well-publicized results, Hackett told his Foundation, "that several administrative authorities are now greatly interested in antilarval measures, and for this reason our campaign will be extended over a vast zone. . . ."[37]

They were interested because it was reasonably effective and very cheap.‡ Techniques of *piccola bonifica* applied hitherto by Grassi, Fermi, Missiroli and one or two others might work technically but Italy could not afford them on a large scale. Paris green opened new prospects. The Italian government from an initial position of hostility had been so far won over by 1929 that Hackett could write: "It can probably be truly said that no Government in the world is now doing as much anti-larval work in the control of malaria as Italy."[38]

Perhaps that was not saying a great deal, as no one was then doing much. It was significant, however, that Italy from being the most pessimistic about challenging the malaria mosquito had picked up a newly militant spirit. Success with the new larvicide contributed something to that.

---

* This limitation has since been overcome.

† Infant parasite rate at zero for three years. General parasite rate brought from 18 to zero; spleen rate from 56 to 12.[36]

‡ The per capita cost in Portotorres, Sardinia (pop. 6,000) was 12 cents and in Conoro, Calabria (pop. 12,500) it was 8 cents.

Coincidentally there was excitement over a tiny fish, of the genus *Gambusia*, which demonstrated a voracious appetite for mosquito larvae and an extraordinary ability to adapt and thrive far from its native haunts in North America. In 1921 the U. S. Bureau of Fisheries had sent some *Gambusia* to Spain where they were bred up, distributed, flourished on a diet of larvae and multiplied so prolifically that a starter brood of two or three hundred fish could be shipped from there to Italy the next year. Distributed in four lots these also flourished, most notably in Fiumicino where Grassi thought they were responsible for greatly reducing larval populations. Two years later the fish were exported to Corsica where they reputedly had spectacular success; others went experimentally to Russia.[39]

Skeptics observed that predators never extinguish a prey and that nature has a way of establishing a balance among the eaten and the eaters that enables all species, however disagreeable, to survive. But for the moment at least *Gambusia* was an exotic and enjoyed the advantage of a fox first set among the pigeons. *Gambusia,* moreover, by dint of being new, like Paris green could help leaven the pessimism that Hackett noted in Italy in 1924 and that the League of Nations seemed to adopt on behalf of the rest of the world.

Italy, of course, also had Mussolini to inspirit her. Hackett witnessed the Fascists' first more or less legitimate election that in 1924 confirmed Mussolini in power by "a rousing plurality."[40] He also witnessed that same year the murder of the socialist deputy Matteoti at the hands of the Fascisti, which revealed how that power would be exercised. On that he made no comment. Mussolini was to be cooperative with the Rockefeller Foundation, assisting first in the establishment and the funding of the experimental station in Rome, absorbing it later into the department of public health.

Cleaning up malaria may not have been one of the Duce's top priorities but it fitted well enough with his ideas of a bigger, healthier, stronger Italy. He was in particular interested in *grande bonifica*. In his socialist days in 1911 he had spoken of land reclamation along with social reform in the south as steps in "conquering" Italy which he then preferred to foreign and colonial adventures. In power he saw *bonifica* as part of the preparation for greater glories. It could increase production, help anchor peasants to the land, slow immigration, encourage higher birth rates, and build a conservative and relatively docile rural nation. Under him the number of acres reclaimed or scheduled for reclamation greatly increased and control of malaria in the new settlements by screening and larviciding was made mandatory. For the first time in history since *Plasmodium* originally invaded the Pontine marshes, Mussolini made them habitable by combining major drainage with *piccola bonifica* and model farm settlements with screened houses.* It was not of course the first time that dictatorial controls were able to effect gains in public health that eluded individualist societies.[42]

Mussolini, Paris green, *Gambusia,* screens and the fresh determination to fight the causes of malaria all cooperating with a naturally ebbing tide of fever reduced the disease in Italy to an historic low on the eve of World War II. Yet there remained enough carriers in enough endemic areas—the boot, Sicily and Sardinia were the worst—to fuel a terrible resurgence under war conditions. Italy's final deliverance—and Europe's—awaited the coming of DDT.†

---

* The use of screens in Mussolini's Italy appears to have increased rapidly. Hackett wrote: "It is probable that no country in the world except America has adopted screening of houses on such a scale as Italy; yet only five years ago the general application of screening was considered by health officers practically impossible owing to the ignorance and poverty of the rural populations, and the type of construction of the older houses." In the Roman Campagna the year before he had wanted to do an experiment involving mosquito catches in bedrooms, but could find none unscreened.[41]

† UNRRA (1947) reported 55,453 cases in 1939; 441,602 cases in 1945. Presumably these are hospital figures and need to be regarded with considerable skepticism.

21 /A Preference for Pig

When Dr. Hackett arrived in Rome in January 1924, Italy's classic age of malaria research was over, though the aura of past greatness and some of the great themselves lingered. One of the American doctor's first moves was to call on Professor Grassi at the laboratory of comparative anatomy of the University of Rome, where he found "the old man . . . writing, well bundled up in an old cape, with unkempt white hair and short straggling beard, his spectacles resting on his moustache." Grassi, "restless and vehement in manner," was as usual embroiled in and obsessed by quarrels with his colleagues.* A former assistant, he told his visitor, was attacking him. He then spoke with "acerbity" about a former student who had dared question the effectiveness of quinine therapy. But the angriest of his quarrels was the old one with Ronald Ross.[2]

Ross had poked at the embers in his *Memoirs,* published the year before. In a chapter headed "Roman Brigandage" he repeated his charges against Grassi of fraud and plagiarism with all the intemperate exaggerations that years of bitterness had for him hardened into truth. Grassi by now was no less intemperately convinced that Ross was the usurper and that he, Grassi, alone had discovered mosquito transmission of malaria. If only the world could be made to see: Grassi, like Ross, went on rummaging through the

---

* One colleague, Antonio Pais of the Radio-therapeutic laboratory, later told Hackett that Grassi "is impossible to cooperate with, being domineering, grasping and volcanic by nature."[1]

litter of old polemics for the ultimate devastating truth that could be driven through the heart of his rival.

It was too bad—a terrible waste of energy. Yet Grassi seemed to have plenty of that to spare. Over seventy years old, he was teaching comparative anatomy three days a week and getting out at least once a week into the swamps of Fiumicino, where he tirelessly tended experiments in malaria control that had gone on for more than twenty years without success. Now in 1924 he faced one of the worst fever seasons in thirty years, bringing home with more heartbreaking force than ever the consciousness of failure. His experiments, financed by a parsimonious and largely indifferent government at not more than $2,000 a year, never had any chance of making an impact on this ancient and vast region of endemic fever. Meanwhile Grassi's fertile mind reached out for new ideas but none of promise came to him.[3]

The picture of the old man battling on alone in the ancient stronghold of the enemy appropriately symbolizes the end of an era. Of the great malariologists of his own generation, Marchiafava and Bastianelli were still alive but had long been working on other problems. Celli was dead, and at all events his last years had been devoted largely to promoting quinine therapy and social reform. His widow, Anna, continued his work and fiercely guarded his memory against all who might question that his way was the right one.[4]

Missiroli thought Grassi had deliberately driven everyone else out of the field and that malariology in Italy would be resurrected only over the old man's grave. That was harsh. It is true that a resurgence of scientific interest in malaria in Italy did follow closely on Grassi's death in 1925, and that Missiroli himself played a prominent part in that. But more obvious causes than Grassi's departure were the establishment of two malaria institutes, the Rockefeller-supported Experiment Station,* and after 1927 a rival research group, the International Institute of Malaria set up under the Italian foreign office, primarily as a political ploy to attract students from Latin America.[5] These new foci of research moreover coincided with the ripening of a fascinating and extremely important research problem.

This problem began to be defined almost as soon as mosquitoes were incriminated as vectors of malaria. If anophelines transmit malaria one would expect that in suitable climates fever would always be endemic where they flourished, absent where they did not. Indeed, Grassi had asserted the guilt of *Anopheles* on just such observed correlations. But within

---

* Stazione Sperimentale per la Lotta Antimalarica.

a year he had himself found areas where anophelines abounded and no one suffered malaria. G. F. Nuttall, studying the spontaneous disappearance of malaria from the British Isles, could find no relation between areas heavily infested with *Anopheles maculipennis,** the notorious fever vector, and areas where in the past malaria had been endemic. Étienne Sergent in 1902 found more *Anopheles* on the banks of a tributary of the Seine in France, where malaria was extremely rare, than in the most fever-ridden regions of Algeria. Celli with a colleague explored large areas of Tuscany that had once been malarious but that by 1901 were healthy for no obvious reason. The swamps that had bred the anophelines were still there. Ficalbi, the expert taxonomist, declared mosquitoes emerging from them to be indistinguishable from *Anopheles maculipennis,* the species positively incriminated by Grassi and Bignami in their 1898–99 experiments. Tuscan peasants moreover were as constantly exposed to bites as peasants of the Campagna; in fact they lived in identical straw huts (*capanne*) and worked the fields in August, the most feverish month.[6]

Celli confessed bafflement at an "inexplicable exception to the new etiological and epidemiological theory of malaria." He was inclined to think that mosquitoes after a while might become refractory to the parasite and so cease to transmit it. But he never found any explanation that was really satisfactory.[7]

The Sergent brothers continued their observations in France. They noted that the *Anopheles maculipennis* mosquitoes that transmitted malaria in the Vendée, like those in Algeria, were so closely associated with people as to be almost domestic. In the environs of Paris, which were free from malaria, the same insects were much less often found in and around houses.[8] There was the clue: the obvious yet easily overlooked fact that mosquitoes transmit malaria not by their presence but by regularly and frequently biting people.

During a 1901 malaria epidemic in the Italian province of Mantua, inhabitants of Mantua city suffered much more severely than those in the rest of the province. A doctor investigated, found throughout the province enormous numbers of *Anopheles* resting in piggeries and horse and cow barns but very few in peasant homes. City dwellers, he concluded, suffered less because of the presence of mosquitoes than because of the absence of pigs.[9]

Emile Roubaud in 1918 went over the same ground as the Sergents had in 1902, confirmed their conclusion and speculated that the spontaneous

---

* Then known as *Anopheles claviger*.

regression of malaria throughout Europe might be due to an evolving taste of the mosquitoes for animal blood.[10] Why not exploit that taste, he asked, and set up animal barriers to protect people?

But first the fact had to be nailed down. That mosquitoes were found resting in animal shelters did not necessarily mean they had fed on animals. In 1922 two American entomologists studying the behavior of *Anopheles* in Louisiana devised an ingenious procedure that has been used ever since to determine without question the source of a mosquito's meal.[11] In the so-called precipitin test they mixed blood from the insect's stomach with serum drawn from a rabbit that had been injected with, and had developed immunity to, one of eight different kinds of alien blood, from cow, pig, dog, man, etc. If, for instance, a serum was used that contained antibodies from a rabbit injected with a cow's blood, it would "recognize" the cow and the mosquito and signal that recognition by precipitating the mosquito's meal.

With the precipitin test, Hackett and Missiroli surveyed those parts of Italy having lots of anopheline mosquitoes but no malaria. They began in the province of Massa in Tuscany, where Grassi had first brought the phenomenon to the attention of malariologists everywhere. In Viareggio, then as now a popular beach resort, Hackett found a cowshed that housed one cow and at least 4,000 mosquitoes, half of which he identified as *Anopheles maculipennis*, the chief malaria vector of Italy. He collected mosquitoes here and from a livery stable "run by three ladies, who were altogether suspicious of me, and did not quite like me taking their insects." On examination he found the ratio of animal blood to human in the Tuscan mosquitoes to be on the order of 400 to one. That appeared to be about the ratio throughout the non-malarious regions of Italy and was something like fifty times greater than in places where malaria was transmitted.[12]

Hackett and Missiroli made some calculations that strikingly revealed how a taste for animal blood on the part of malaria vectors could eliminate the disease. Suppose every family in a given village had, to start with, one carrier with the infective gametocytes in his blood; the chances of any one mosquito's picking up the parasite they estimated at one in five. The chances of that mosquito's surviving long enough for the parasite to develop and produce infective sporozoites they put also at one in five. Now they knew by observation that only one out of every 400 insects fed on a person, giving odds of 400 squared or one in 160,000 that the same mosquito would bite a second person and so be able to pass on parasites. Now multiply by five (as only one in five will have picked up the parasite) and by five again (as only one in five will survive for a second bite), and the chances of malaria's being transmitted were reduced to one in four million. Black with mosquitoes though the cowshed walls of Tuscany might be, few villages were likely to shelter four million. That was why soldiers could come home bringing with them parasites in their blood, and suffer relapses even in large numbers, without having the fever spread.[13]

For malaria control, diverting a mosquito to an animal was as good as killing it. But could it be deliberately done? What attracted the mosquito to animals? Some thought it might be a simple reversion to tastes developed by *Anopheles* before people existed to be bitten. Others thought the multiplication of domestic animals had opened a new niche that *Anopheles* was evolving to fill. In fact it was hard to demonstrate conclusively any preference at all. In experiments *Anopheles* often appeared an indiscriminate feeder. American observers suggested that mosquitoes might be attracted to the stable, not to the beast.[14] As Europe and North America prospered, more people began living in bigger, brighter houses, with increasingly less appeal to resting anophelines. They would have begun congregating instead in the darker, damper stables and sties, and in time have grown accustomed to feeding on the inhabitants because it was convenient.

Each of these notions was as plausible as it was hard to prove. None fitted all the evidence.[15] All as a practical matter, however, supported the feasibility of deliberate animal screens. And many of these were tried. One experimenter in Italy had a ring of twenty pigsties built around a village and asserted that in a year's time malaria had been so reduced that the government was able to remove the nurse who had been dispensing quinine and thus to recoup the cost of the new pigsties.[16]

Experiments with animal prophylaxis continued but at best it was a clumsy method. Where, moreover, one dealt with a mosquito of more or less indiscriminate biting habits, introduced animals seemed merely to attract more insects to larger banquets that still included people.[17] Through the 1920s and 1930s evidence slowly accumulated that so-called animal deviation was in fact a complicated evolutionary process not easily duplicated by contrivance.

The Sergent brothers in 1903 had noted that *Anopheles maculipennis* mosquitoes in the Vendée were slightly smaller than those around Paris. Emile Roubaud, following up this work in 1920, suggested that the two populations might belong to different races with significantly different genetic makeup. He patiently counted the number of "teeth" on the maxillae (the sawlike mouth parts) of hundreds of mosquitoes from each region, and developed what he called a "maxillary index" that he believed could distinguish animal-biters (zoophilic species) from anthropophilic people-biters. His evidence showed the mosquitoes that were predominantly animal-biters to be larger and to have on average more teeth. That seemed to make sense: Extra teeth would be useful for driving through the thicker hide of cattle.[18]

But, as so often happens, what made sense didn't happen to be true. More malariologists began counting maxillary teeth but no one could confirm a correlation between their number and the mosquito's biting preference.* Nor was there, as a Dutch investigator, P. H. Van Thiel, discovered, any correlation between maxillary teeth and body size.[19]

In Holland at that time an east–west line drawn through Amsterdam divided a malarious northern zone from a southern zone where malaria was rare or absent. Van Thiel, comparing the mosquitoes in each zone, found that those which were most abundant in the north were darker and had shorter wings than the dominant variety in the south. If there was any statistically significant difference at all in the number of teeth, the smaller mosquito was more richly endowed. But the most interesting difference was that the short-wing insects of the north laid their eggs in the brackish water standing in polders reclaimed from the sea. In the south the land was nearly all above sea level and the water nearly all fresh.

Van Thiel at first thought that the short-wings might be handicapped by their early environment, that the salt in the water might stunt their growth and render them more susceptible to infection by the malaria parasite.[20] That was another plausible guess that proved wrong. Professor Swellengrebel and co-workers showed that the two varieties were equally susceptible to infection and that the short-wings were stunted by their genes, not their environment. Short- and long-winged insects bred true in all habitats and when crossed produced larvae that either did not metamorphose at all or else engendered adults that were infertile. In short each variety was a true species belonging to separate breeding populations that were reproductively isolated. Van Thiel came to the same conclusion in further experiments and gave the short-wing the specific name *atroparvus*.[21]

Later experiments showed that *atroparvus,* if given a free choice, actually preferred to lay her eggs in fresh water, but that when long-wings were present, her larvae apparently lost out in competition for food.[22] The use of brackish breeding places thus appeared to be a forced adaptation. It is an interesting case of losers in competition for an ancestral domain display-

---

* The Sergents, for instance, found a very high maxillary index, well above the figure supposed to indicate a zoophilic species, in the most malarious parts of Algeria (Hackett, 1937). Since the maxillae act not as cutting tools themselves but as hooks that hold in the wound and enable the mosquito to thrust in the point of her labrum, a larger number would not necessarily contribute to greater power of penetration. But the biting process was not demonstrated until 1939. See above, Chapter 17.

ing greater adaptability than the winners permitting them to colonize niches closed to the ostensibly more successful species.

The short-wing differed from the long-wing in another way critical for the transmission of malaria. In Holland, long-wings hibernate as adults. In the autumn the female stops producing eggs and develops a fat body on which she subsists through the cold weather without other nourishment. *Atroparvus* also suspends her ovarian activity with the approach of cold weather but then seeks warm places—stables or houses—in which she spends her winter in a sleepy state from which she rouses now and then to take a blood meal.* This periodic feeding through the winter may keep the parasite in circulation within a single family or among a few houses whose inhabitants intimately intermingle—a peculiar feature of Dutch epidemiology that had long baffled the experts.[23]

Identification of *atroparvus* had been difficult because the external, morphological differences separating it from the long-winged species were only statistical. *Atroparvus* tended to be darker on average and its mean wing span was less. But when comparing any two individuals one might not be sure which species they belonged to unless they could be tested by interbreeding.

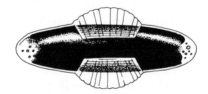

Egg of *A. macalipennis labranchiae*, after Grassi;
identified by him as *A. claviger*

There was another way to be quite sure—a clear and striking difference that had long been overlooked. In the twenty-five years of keen interest in mosquito taxonomy it seems never to have occurred to taxonomists to look at the eggs. Esthetic, not taxonomic interest, first drew Domenico Falleroni to them in 1924.[24] Falleroni, a retired inspector of public health in Italy, was fascinated by the beauty and diversity of anopheline eggs, their surfaces textured in delicate bas-relief and variously patterned in blacks, greys and frosty whites. He began breeding mosquitoes as a hobby and collected them from all over Italy.

Little by little, order appeared in the diversity of egg shapes and patterns. Among the eggs of *Anopheles maculipennis* Falleroni distinguished

---

* Grassi observed the phenomenon in Italy and called it semihibernation.

two main varieties by color: one so dark it was almost black, and the other a light grey. There seemed also to be five typical color patterns. Falleroni, like everyone else until then, thought these latter were mere fancies of nature, but the greys and the blacks he guessed represented different species. He named them after two friends of his, Dr. Messea and Dr. Labranca—director and division chief, respectively, of the public health services—the black for Messea and the grey for Labranca.

It remained for Hackett, Missiroli and a colleague from Germany, E. Martini, to put together the discoveries of Van Thiel and Swellengrebel with those of Falleroni.[25] In time they proved that *Anopheles messeae* with the dark eggs was identical with the Dutch long-wing, predominantly an animal-biter and therefore of slight danger to man. The grey eggs of *A. labranchiae* were laid, like those of *atroparvus*, in brackish water and never turned up in regions where there was no fever. *Labranchiae* was probably a southern representative of *atroparvus*—their ranges did not overlap—but probably also deserved the status of a separate species. In one important respect it differed from *atroparvus;* its taste for man was much more strongly developed and could not be diverted to animals. When all the mosquitoes called *maculipennis* were at last sorted out, five species had been described: the two dangerous ones, *atroparvus* and *labranchiae,* and three generally but not universally harmless, *messeae, typicus* (now called simply *maculipennis*) and *melanoön.*

Hackett believed that out of this work emerged the explanation for the spontaneous recession of malaria from Europe.[26] *Messeae,* in earlier times the principal vector, was more and more diverted by its strong taste for animals as animal husbandry increased and especially as intensive agriculture reduced pasturage and forced the feeding of cattle in stables. Being strongly competitive for fresh water habitat, it tended to drive out the man-biters except along the coasts where man himself by land reclamation often provided alternative breeding places in brackish waters.

The truth of that analysis was confirmed by other observations but its sufficiency was called into question. Emile Brumpt, the French parasitologist, pointed out that malaria receded from certain parts of France where agriculture had not become intensive and where no changes were observable that either reduced the numbers of anophelines, changed the species composition or led to animal deviation. The only constants Dr. Brumpt could find were an increased use of quinine and decreased birth rates that meant fewer infants whose blood offers a major reservoir for *Plasmodium* gametocytes.[27]

In the United States, if animal deviation played a part, so did very extensive land reclamation, notably in the valleys of the Mississippi and its principal tributaries which eliminated vast mosquito habitats. So did the farm mechanization that thinned out rural communities, along with improvement of farm housing and screening, as well as the steadily decreasing price of quinine that made it widely available as a household remedy.

Since a relationship as complex as that between mosquitoes, parasites and man may alter in response to any one or any combination of scores of variables—climatic, economic, biologic—no single explanation of historic change will do. The mechanism of malaria transmission, as has been noted, is extremely sensitive to numbers—numbers of susceptible people; numbers of anophelines and how many of those bite people; the number of gametocytes in the blood of carriers, affecting in turn the number of sporozoites that develop in the mosquito that in turn determine the intensity of infection; and finally the number of days during which the temperature and humidity permit the mosquito to flourish and the parasite to develop at its most favorable rate. Professor George MacDonald after World War II combined the key variables in equations that showed how very slight changes in certain numbers could make the difference between the growth and the disappearance of endemic malaria, and between endemic and epidemic conditions.

Agricultural progress, land reclamation, animal deviation, quinine, screening—these changes have been able in various ways to tip the scales against malaria in temperate climates because they have worked where climatic conditions are relatively marginal for transmission. The same changes have failed in the tropics in large part because *Anopheles* and *Plasmodium,* flourishing through long, wet, warm seasons, can overwhelm with sheer numbers any relatively minor improvements in human defenses.

The brilliant pioneering work on *maculipennis* did not provide a new formula for malaria control. Yet it had practical value hard to overestimate. Besides making possible in some places Malcolm Watson's tactics of species sanitation, concentrating on dangerous species and ignoring others, it forced malariologists everywhere to recognize that detailed knowledge of the biology of the vector mosquito was critical to understanding the epidemiology of the disease and hence to efforts at control. From the 1930s on, species complexes all over the world began to be differentiated* and hitherto inexplicable anomalies in the distribution of malaria were explained. More generally the idea took hold that the better one knew one's enemy the better the chances of fighting her successfully. It was a sound idea—even axiomatic—and ultimately essential for success. In the event it was to prove oddly perishable.

---

* E.g., *umbrosus* in Asia, *gambiae* in Africa, *quadrimaculatus* in North America.

22 / Epidemic

Throughout recorded history malaria has been a resident scourge in most places that have known it at all. But it can of course travel, invade new territories and strike with all the epidemic fury of the classic pestilential diseases such as yellow fever, cholera, influenza, and the plague.

Some early New World settlements were decimated by what almost certainly were malaria epidemics. Probably colonists brought the parasites with them from parts of Europe, including England, where the fever in the seventeenth century was still endemic though generally mild. The New World provided an abundance of anophelines and, in the southern latitudes, long transmission seasons that allowed a relatively few parasites to multiply and spread explosively among people mostly without immunity. Later as Negro slaves arrived in increasing numbers from malarious West Africa the fever became endemic in the Americas wherever the weather suited, and epidemics were thereafter rare.*

The classic case of a malaria invasion of new lands, and the earliest to be reported in detail, is the epidemic that struck the island of Mauritius in 1866.[1] Mauritius, lying in the Indian Ocean a thousand miles from the African mainland, was then a British colony and virtually an economic dependency of British India. Sugar was produced there by indentured labor recruited in India, and most of it was sent back to India in exchange for

---

* For the distinction between "endemic" and "epidemic" see note page 201.

coffee, rice and grain. The Indian laborers of course also brought in malaria parasites as did the British troops who were frequently posted to Mauritius from India and China, and who arrived "saturated with malaria." In Mauritius, however, all recovered. The fever did not spread, clearly because there were no native anophelines to carry it.

The anophelines came at last out of Africa. They were the notorious *Anopheles gambiae* and *Anopheles funestus,** arriving presumably by ships that docked in Port Louis. Perhaps they had actually been arriving there for years but until some time in the early 1860s had been unable to establish themselves. What is clear is that in 1866 they found conditions much to their liking. Throughout the 1860s, as the sugar industry prospered, more of the jungles of Mauritius had been cleared and planted to cane, and more labor was imported to work the plantations. *Gambiae* likes people and sunny breeding places. Mauritius had plenty of both in 1866 after the very heavy rains of the previous December broke a long drought and caused widespread flooding of the newly cleared lands. *Funestus,* a more indiscriminate breeder, found lots of weedy streams and miscellaneous collections of water that *gambiae* passed over.

The first outbreak of malaria was not in Port Louis but at the Albion sugar estate seven miles to the south, where presumably the recently immigrated mosquitoes were able both to breed in large numbers and to find parasite carriers. During 1866 the fever crept southward three miles along the coast, into a marshy area and simultaneously northward to the capital, which it reached in two months. From its starting point at Albion the epidemic covered between forty and fifty square miles during that first year. In two more years, borne on the current of the prevailing winds, it completed the 104-mile circuit of the island and lapped inland except where high ground kept it at bay. Though slow, the spread of the fever among the 300,000 inhabitants, most of whom had never before been exposed, was inexorable and deadly. In Port Louis more than one out of five died.† So many were ill, it was said, that one could hardly find enough strong men to bury the dead. Throughout the colony as a whole 31,920 people died in 1867, the peak epidemic year.

As so often in epidemics death seemed a palpable enemy in constant relentless pursuit of the living. "Certain it is," the historian of these events, Dr. Andrew Davidson, wrote in 1892, "that many persons who started, say on a journey to the country [in flight from Port Louis] were suddenly

---

* *Funestus* was not identified in Mauritius until 1922 but apparently had been present about as long as *gambiae*. Tonking (1947) believed *funestus* to have been the cause of 75 percent of Mauritian malaria.[2]

† The death rate among victims of fever alone was recorded as 211 per 1,000.

overtaken by death on the way, and dead bodies of such unfortunate wayfarers were constantly met with on the roadsides or in the bushes close to the paths."[3]

No one in 1892 knew that mosquitoes were in fact death on the wing. Yet the facts powerfully impressed Dr. Davidson with the sense of a living agent of destruction. No satisfactory explanation was possible, he thought, without supposing a living organism "growing in its season, becoming quiescent in the winter, spreading from the centre steadily in a more or less regular course where conditions favoured its growth . . ." He considered it "at least possible that the germ of malarial fever may have . . . been carried from some malarious country such as India or Madagascar [as the coffee-leaf disease had been imported from Ceylon] . . . and that having been so introduced, it found the conditions in the colony at that moment favourable to its spread."[4]

The great Mauritius epidemic subsided after 1868 when deaths exceeded 10,000. There would be no repetitions. Malaria, once introduced into the island, settled down to become a constant fact of life and death. As an endemic disease it took annual toll (typically of the very young), developed a saving immunity among those who survived, and established another perennial battlefield in the war against mosquitoes.

In epidemiology that pattern of innocence lost but once is so familiar that the terms "endemic" and "epidemic" normally connote distinctive and mutually exclusive modes.* But there are parts of the world where malaria not only is endemic at low levels but also explodes periodically in killing epidemics. One of these is the northwest corner of the Indian subcontinent, now Pakistan, formerly the administrative districts of Sind and Punjab, which suffered ten serious epidemics between 1869 and 1908. In the latter year Rickard Christophers made the first studies of the mechanism of epidemic malarial outbreaks.[5]

The region he studied is a semi-arid plain verging to the east on the great Rajasthan desert. Its inhabitants depend heavily, and always have, on irrigated agriculture, drawing water mainly from a number of large rivers which drain the northern mountains. Throughout history, too, the Punjab's irrigated fields, singularly difficult to drain properly, have been subject to

---

* "*Endemic* means *in* the population; *epidemic, upon* the population. An endemic disease is visibly present, in greater or lesser frequency, all the time. An epidemic disease may, or may not, be also endemic, but is characterized by occasional rapid and great increases in its morbidity and perhaps its mortality" (Pampana, 1969, 72). A disease which, like malaria, engenders immune responses in proportion to the frequency of infection can be epidemic only in populations which experience it only marginally or not at all (*Ibid.,* 92).

disastrous waterlogging. In normal dry years the rivers and the irrigation works provide the main breeding places for anophelines. Rivers form pools along their banks; irrigation storage ponds overgrown with weeds breed mosquitoes themselves and also spill out into swamps and along irrigation canals that breed still more. Around every village, here as in most of the subcontinent, are borrow pits from which the villagers dig clay to make their houses; relatively impervious, these pits fill readily with water from even light rains.

The country as a whole is not particularly hospitable to mosquitoes. In normal years the main malaria vector, *Anopheles culicifacies,* barely maintains itself in sufficient numbers to keep the parasite circulating. But when now and then heavy rains fall it can, from its scattered refuges, rapidly colonize the temporary waters that appear suddenly in oversaturated lands. Christophers noted that not only had all the Punjab epidemics in the past struck in years of heavier than normal rainfall but also they had affected chiefly those areas most subject to flooding. He noted further that rain did not always bring malaria. It had to be rain following on drought. Why? Perhaps, Christophers thought, drought causing crop failure weakened the resistance of people by malnutrition. He tried out a correlation between the price of grain (surrogate for scarcity), rain and fever and found that it could account for four-fifths of the epidemics. Rainfall made the mosquitoes more abundant; famine made the people more susceptible. "There seems little doubt," Christophers concluded, "that the two factors, rainfall and scarcity, are the determining causes of the epidemic malaria seen in the Punjab."[6]

So they seemed to be also in Sind, where an epidemic in 1929 took more than 40,000 lives.[7] After years of drought, very heavy rains in July and August produced widespread flooding. The floods besides multiplying the nurseries for larvae humidified the air, thus protecting adult mosquitoes from dehydration and so prolonging their lives. The flooding also ruined crops, made people homeless, dislocated trade and caused general economic distress. This came moreover on top of a cholera epidemic in the north that took more than 3,000 lives and persumably left survivors weakened. Students of the Sind disaster noted too that in the twelve years since the previous epidemic a generation of children had largely escaped infection; in 1929, lacking immunity, these were the chief victims, just as they had been in the Punjab twenty years before.

The gross epidemic mechanism was clear enough. Where malaria barely maintained itself year by year (that is, in hypoendemic areas), an explosive increase in numbers of vector mosquitoes was clearly the primary cause of epidemics. That was the wind that fanned the blaze. But how important were such other conditions as might either help or hinder its spread: levels of immunity among the people, general physical well-being, atmospheric humidity, and perhaps additional variables still to be discovered?

These were open questions when in 1934–35 the most unexpected and catastrophic malaria epidemic ever recorded hit the island of Ceylon (now the nation of Sri Lanka). Occurring at a high point of scientific interest in malaria, it was meticulously studied and its riddles and some of the resolutions thereof have become classic in malariology.[8]

Ceylon, a 25,000-square-mile island shaped like a teardrop, lies in the Indian Ocean just north of the Equator. Temperatures hover around eighty degrees Fahrenheit day and night all year round, give or take ten degrees or so. The southwest quadrant, where the capital city, Colombo, is found, and where about two-thirds of the people lived in the year of the great epidemic, is very wet; and so are the mountains that rise to an altitude of 8,000 feet in a compact mass in the south-central part of the island. Up to 200 inches of rain falls in these parts each year—chiefly during a summer and a winter monsoon, though every month has normally at least two inches. The rest of the country is very dry. It has only one annual monsoon from October to January, when nearly the whole year's supply of rain (75 inches or less) falls.

Throughout the dry zone, malaria is endemic or hyperendemic.* In the wet zone the constant rains almost literally wash most of it away. Anophelines, as observed, need water in small portions; they like vestigial or back waters, water that has withdrawn from the main and turbulent hydrologic cycle to evaporate quietly in isolation. In the dry zone the sole Ceylonese vector, *Anopheles culicifacies,* breeds the year round, in rock pools in the beds of streams that seldom have much water in them, in irrigation ditches and in pools leaked from reservoirs. In the rainy season the insects may multiply hugely in casual pools, even in water-filled animal footprints. Thus annual surges occur, mimicking in smaller scale the longer-term cycles of fever in the Punjab and Sind. But because the outbreaks are annual, the reservoir of parasites in the population is never emptied; communal immunity remains high; the depredations of fever are not great in any one year but go on continuously pruning out the very young.

In the wet zone during normal years *culicifacies* are hard to find. They do not breed in the rivers, which are too full of fast-flowing water. If pools form now and then and receive larvae, fresh rains soon flush them out.

---

* I.e., half or more of the children are infected.

Abundant marshes and other wet places suitable for mosquito breeding are usually preempted by other species that are not naturally infected by plasmodia.

Briefly, what happened in 1934–35 was that an extraordinary drought produced in the wet zone conditions very like those normal to the north, and the resultant epidemic swept devastatingly through a non-immune population. When both monsoons failed in 1934 the principal rivers of the southern half of the country shrank to a string of pools and these in the spring began to teem with the larvae of *A. culicifacies*. They hatched and bred through the long summer. Heavy rain in October briefly flushed them out but it hardly mattered; the huge adult population already in being resumed its explosive growth in November when the expected rains from the northeast failed to arrive.

Authorities with long experience could see what was coming in the unclouded skies of April and May. At least they predicted an increase in fever and ordered wider distribution of quinine. But there was really no defense. The drought was quite unprecedented, with less than half as much rain as the seventy-five-year annual average. Moreover the people were unusually vulnerable. Following a mild epidemic in 1928–29 weather unfavorable for breeding diminished the mosquitoes and the fever had receded. In the next four relatively healthy years, many adults got rid of the parasites in their systems. More babies were born to healthier mothers and more of these escaped infection after birth. The proportion of children to adults was thus significantly higher than normal, as was the proportion of non-immune children to immune. It was the children under ten years old who as usual were to take the heaviest casualties.

Anopheles culicifacies struck with apparent suddenness in October 1934, when unusually large numbers of people with fever crowded into hospitals in the vicinity of one of the main rivers north of Colombo, strikingly pinpointing the enemy's base of attack. (It was later to be found that the epidemic was largely confined to the catchment basins of the five major river systems of the south.) By mid-November hospitals throughout the wet zone were filling until in some the fever cases reached ten times the normal number. By mid-December half a million people, or about 10 percent of the entire Ceylonese population, were ill.

During 1935 the epidemic not only continued its rapid spread but intensified its fury. The proportion of malignant *P. falciparum* infections reached well over one-third and deaths, which had been relatively few in the early months, now soared. At last in November and December normal widespread rains refilled the rivers and drowned out the epidemic. By then nearly a third of the people had fallen ill; altogether some 80,000 died.[9]

The Ceylon epidemic dramatically proved that alternation of drought and flooding was the trigger for epidemics and it did not matter whether a normally very dry country experienced unusual rains or a normally very wet country experienced unusual drought. At the point of climatic convergence *culicifacies* exploded. If at that point the people had been relatively free of malaria for long enough (three years at least to allow most of the *P. vivax* parasites to die out in the blood stream), then not only would the fever spread rapidly among non-immunes but it would also take a much higher percentage of lives than normal. The coincidence that the people of Ceylon, like those of Sind and Punjab, met their enemy somewhat debilitated by hard times was suggestive if not conclusive that a lowering of general physical resistance played some part.

Other facts about the epidemic were less easy to understand. Before it broke out there was so little fever in the wet zone that one could look at thousands of blood slides without finding a parasite. In particular the telltale crescents of the sexual forms of *Plasmodium falciparum* essential for transmission were rare to the vanishing point. How then could the mosquitoes, no matter how numerous, find parasites with which to begin the epidemic spread? How, starting from so near nothing, was it possible for so many to be infected so fast?

Colonel Clifford A. Gill of the Indian Medical Service was on the spot collecting facts in the midst of the epidemic.[10] The onslaught he found had struck almost literally overnight. He found one hospital where admissions had doubled on a single day in October 1934; in hospitals everywhere there were large increases in the space of a week. Thereafter hospital admissions peaked every four weeks in four distinct waves, coinciding very nicely with the total incubation time for the parasites in man and the mosquito. After those four waves the epidemic subsided, only to flame up again in greater fury in the spring of 1935. Taking careful note of these rhythms Colonel Gill added one more observation that he thought highly significant: In the first wave there were few deaths, and notably few among the children who were to be the chief sufferers later. Death curves began to peak in imitation of the illness curves only at the tenth week, thereafter to echo faithfully the ups and downs of hospital admissions.

A neat hypothesis fitting all these facts—the sudden emergence out of nothing, the primary and secondary waves and the initially low death rate—struck Colonel Gill: Suppose the epidemic had begun with a series of relapses. These would happen primarily to adults, the most likely to have been previously infected, and would be less virulent than primary infections. Hence the few deaths at the beginning. Once the parasite had been put back into circulation in the blood of the relapsed patients it would be spread in ever intensifying four-week cycles, and infect and kill children, just as had in fact occurred. The second wave in 1935 acting like the first and clearly involving relapses appeared to be a confirmation.

But the Gill hypothesis, ingenious though it was, raised fresh difficulties. There had never been evidence of long-term relapses in *falciparum* infections; *vivax* relapses after more than three years—and it had been five since the last epidemic—were historically rare. Moreover it was at least as hard to explain a sudden rash of relapses striking so many people at once, as to account for an eruption of primary infections. Gill remarked the increased atmospheric humidity in Ceylon at the time, paralleling similar increases noted in Sind and Punjab. He suggested that the damper air might somehow affect the parasite–host balance and trigger the multiplication of plasmodia in the blood. But he had to confess that he had not the slightest idea of how that might occur.

For some time the possibility that relapses might underlie epidemic outbursts remained under serious discussion. But eventually it withered and was trimmed away by Occam's razor: Besides the fact that relapses have been shown definitely not to occur in *falciparum* malaria, the hypothesis offered an over-elaborate explanation of phenomena much more simply explained.

It now seems so obvious that the essential mechanisms of the transmission of disease can be expressed and illuminated by mathematics that it is hard to understand why Ronald Ross's pioneering efforts to develop a mathematics of malaria, beginning in 1904, until about this time had been almost wholly ignored. But during the 1930s George MacDonald—who was to join the Ross Institute in Ceylon in 1937—began brilliantly to work out his mathematical models.[11] The Ceylon epidemic gave MacDonald a chance to demonstrate how with a large enough number of man-biting mosquitoes, a mighty epidemic could grow rapidly from so few carriers that they might easily escape detection by ordinary blood surveys. In fact the equations of malaria transmission showed that it did not matter how small the starting point; everything depended on the rate of reproduction which was a function of the number of man-biting mosquitoes and their survival. The events in Ceylon could be precisely accounted for, Mac-Donald calculated, by an increase of 5.3 times in the numbers of *culicifacies* or equally by a slight increase in longevity.* If each starting infection produced ten others in from 20 to 30 days—the rate which MacDonald calculated might have prevailed in Ceylon—there would be 100 secondary

---

* I.e., a probability of 90 percent instead of 80 percent that one female would survive one day.

cases in 50 days, 1,000 in 100 days and so on. Since the number of carriers and the number of infected mosquitoes increase as functions of each other the multiplication of a few all-but-invisible parasites into devastating hordes can—and does—occur with a speed that will always seem miraculous however mathematically routine.[12]

As for Gill's other main difficulty—the low mortality at the start—there are also simpler alternative explanations: Where both *Plasmodium vivax* and *P. falciparum* are present, as they were in Ceylon, *vivax* will spread faster because it has a shorter turnaround time through the man–mosquito cycle.* That *vivax* malaria is less lethal would account for the low death rate in the beginning. Also, as Christophers pointed out, the intensity of infections must increase gradually in the course of an epidemic.[13] Because there are few carriers at the start, mosquitoes on average will pick up fewer gametocytes and therefore will develop fewer sporozoites. A light injection of sporozoites normally means a light infection. As the carriers increase so will the number of sporozoites, and each person bitten will be likely to have a more serious case. In short here is another of those rolling snowballs that once set in motion, by mutually reinforcing processes of increasing size and accelerating growth, gathers in the avalanche. The insidiously slow takeoff of *P. falciparum* is one of the most worrying threats latent in the current resurgence of malaria, which typically appears for the moment to be causing few deaths and so is arousing comparatively little political concern.

Ceylon was hit in 1968 by another great epidemic, which though far less destructive than the first was a shocking warning of the disease potential still to be reckoned with. And other areas are becoming similarly vulnerable.

---

* About 20 days from one victim to another for *vivax* as against about 35 for *falciparum*.

23 / Toward Total War

The Great Ceylon epidemic spread gloom among malaria fighters. It seemed to show the essential helplessness of man that years of hard and often brilliant work had done really nothing to reduce. Colonel Gill concluded that malaria control in the relatively undeveloped and thinly populated areas which were typical of three-quarters of the island of Ceylon was an insuperable problem. "In so far as this and other similar areas in the tropics are concerned," he wrote, "it may be said that, despite the great advance of knowledge during the past 50 years, the control of malaria, as a practical proposition, is almost as far to seek as it was a century ago."[1] It was precisely in those areas among the rural poor that malaria chiefly flourished and took its heaviest toll. It still is. Mark Boyd, malariologist with the Rockefeller Foundation, carried pessimism a step further. On the eve of World War II, surveying the state of malaria control in the world he considered it all "in a well-nigh primitive condition."[2]

Yet there were still optimists in the late 1930s, as fortunately there always have been in the long mosquito war. As usual they were the handful who first discovered something new and in the moment of revelation were permitted to imagine that now at last they had the key to victory. One discovery was technical (insecticide spray); one, strategic (proof that in some battles at least total victory was possible). These two innovations (both in fact but reconstitutions of old experience) together set the stage for the dramatic entrance during World War II of the "ultimate" weapon—DDT.

208

It has often been observed that great discoveries appear altogether obvious as soon as they have been made. The reciprocal phenomenon is that a lot of "purloined letters" lie around in plain sight for years before anyone notices them. It took surprisingly a full generation to put together well-known and well-publicized facts about insecticides and apply them systematically to the control of malaria.

An important tactic in the battle with *Aedes aegypti* in Havana, it will be recalled, was the killing of adult mosquitoes by fumigating houses with the smoke of burning sulphur, pyrethrum or occasionally tobacco.* The insects might be killed outright by the smoke or merely stunned, swept up afterward and burned. Although the tactic was somewhat less successful in Panama, it continued to be used in campaigns against yellow fever. The principle was sound: It attacked the disease at the most precarious point in the transmission cycle, when the parasite was in the care of a comparative handful of highly vulnerable insects. If one could manage to kill infected mosquitoes within ten days of infection then it would not matter how many others survived; even in the presence of large populations transmission must be halted. This vital point was obscured in Havana by the simultaneous and dramatically successful frontal attack on *Aedes* breeding places. It would not be rediscovered for some years.

Fumigation by smoke required that rooms be hermetically sealed for hours. It was unpleasant, inconvenient, expensive, often damaged household effects and could be used only in relatively sophisticated structures that could in fact be made airtight and kept so. Recognizing all these drawbacks, G. Giemsa (famous for the still-used stain he invented for coloring microscopic specimens) began thinking around 1910 of substituting a fine poisonous mist for the fumigating smoke. He proposed to use pyrethrum, one of the substances burned. The formula he arrived at consisted of pyrethrum powder, glycerine, green soap and carbon tetrachloride (later omitted) diluted in water. He devised a suitable pump and spray nozzles and tried out the insecticide on hibernating culicine mosquitoes in the cellars of Hamburg. It worked very well. In the laboratory he found it also killed *Anopheles maculipennis* most satisfactorily. He supposed that since the malaria parasite took about eight days to develop in *Anopheles,* spraying every seven days ought theoretically to halt transmission of malaria, but he did no experiments to test the theory.[3]

Giemsa's great invention, reported in detail in 1913, was neither disparaged nor adopted; it did not seem very important. Within the decade

---

* Used successfully in cigar factories.

household pyrethrum sprays were in use in the United States against nuisance insects. In 1928, the year of a yellow fever epidemic in Rio de Janeiro, a Brazilian doctor first sprayed to kill *Aedes aegypti*. He reinvented Giemsa's pump on the model of paint sprayers then in use.[4] But no one dreamed that he held in hand a major weapon against mosquito vectors until the 1930s, when South African health officials stumbled on the fact in desperation.

Malaria had long been endemic in much of South Africa, particularly in the so-called low veld. It escaped being a major public health problem only because the plains, suitable mainly for grazing, were so thinly populated. In the 1920s a considerable sugar industry developed in Zululand along the east coast (the province of Natal). To work the estates—there were 650 of these by the end of the decade—planters imported labor from India and from Black Africa outside Natal. Most of these newcomers had no immunity. In 1929 an epidemic of startling severity broke out among the million and a half susceptibles who were concentrated in the sugar-growing region. By the end of the season 2,751 deaths were recorded. For the next six years the fever flamed up again every summer, reaching a peak in 1932 when more than 10,000 died.

Dr. G. A. Park Ross, South Africa's senior assistant health officer, had long since decided that the only feasible counter to malaria among the poor Whites and Blacks, living as they did in generally primitive and widely dispersed conditions throughout the country, was quinine.[5] So now he mobilized and trained special quinine teams and set up free quinine dispensaries throughout the affected land. But the teams found that malaria was the least of their enemies. The tribal witch doctors were pushing their own herbalist cures; the sugar estate managers were skeptical and unconcerned. The people generally, though ready to accept the gift of pills out of politeness, had no faith in and indeed no comprehension of their utility.

Even though the fever was a little less severe in the two years following the 1929 onfall, it was clear that quinine did not have it under control. To spread oil over mosquito breeding places in so large a country was impractical even if the herdsmen had allowed it. (Curiously the use of Paris green seems not to have been considered.) As an emergency measure of last resort Dr. Park Ross suggested spraying with pyrethrum. A few estates agreed to try it. The result was spectacular. One of two adjacent estates which sprayed the barracks of its workers during the summer of 1931 decreased its fever cases by 86 percent while on the estate next door they rose by more than 50 percent.

At the end of that season a cheap pyrethrum insecticide was on the market and in the next three years it was generally used on the plantations, first in the barracks sprayed weekly from the time the first mosquitoes were found until the end of the season, then later routinely in native village huts as a community prophylactic. In the last recorded season (1934–35) fever deaths in the whole epidemic area were down to 119.

Even though the campaign had been improvised and empirical and no one was sure just how it had worked or why, the results were so impressive that at last nearly everyone thought spraying was worth a try.[6] The Rockefeller Foundation, which had assisted Professor Swellengrebel in testing pyrethrum sprays in Holland in 1932, mounted larger-scale experiments in India from 1938 on.[7] Success was such that in 1941 Sir Gordon Covell, head of the Malaria Institute of India, wrote: "The spray-killing of adult mosquitoes is now recognized as a major control measure and . . . represents the most important advance which has been made in malaria prevention in recent years."[8]

In one sense Sir Gordon exaggerated: Spray-killing had already had some notable failures.[9] Where malaria was hyperendemic it did not work at all, being overwhelmed by the sheer numbers of carriers and vectors. Where the vector belonged to a species that normally stayed in a house only long enough to bite and take the briefest digestive rest, the spray worked only when it was used daily in large enough amounts to kill off not just infected insects but also breeding females in such numbers that the whole population declined. In another sense he understated the advance, for even as he wrote the new technique was about to be given an undreamed-of efficiency by loading the spray guns with DDT.

As pyrethrum sprays prepared the way technically and tactically for an age of total insect war to come, a remarkable man was dramatically resurrecting the go-for-broke spirit of William Gorgas, appropriately in Latin America. Appropriately too, Dr. Fred L. Soper also worked for the Rockefeller Foundation and was quite conscious of the heritage of Gorgas.[10] He was a strong, blunt, difficult man who though medically trained always thought of himself as an administrator and sanitarian, in the main-line tradition of the men challenged by filth to get to work and scrub up. Like Gorgas and Ross he was an enthusiast for direct action and had formidable talents for organization and command. The job he did in Brazil in the decade of the 1930s reshaped the strategy of the mosquito war to the present day.

His first enemy was *Aedes aegypti,* the "stegs." The Rockefeller Foundation in 1923 had established a yellow fever service in Brazil. By 1930 when Dr. Soper took charge, two unexpected outbreaks of the fever, in the northeast in 1926 and in Rio in 1928, had shocked the Brazilian government into giving the service a virtually free hand. Fred Soper had just the temperament, energy and force of personality to take full advantage.

He reckoned that previous campaigns had failed because they attacked on too narrow a front. It was not enough to clean out the big port cities traditionally regarded as the sole foci of fever. By the time they were freed of the disease, infected stegs had traveled to other seaside or inland towns. They went by coastal vessels, by road, and perhaps most ingeniously in the baggage of religious pilgrims. *Aedes,* Soper discovered, regularly laid her eggs in water jugs carried by such pilgrims in northeast Brazil. To stop that, Soper found an ally in a ninety-year-old unfrocked priest, Padre Cicero, who was a powerful cult leader among the peasants of the northeast. He asked Father Cicero to let the water jugs be oiled. The old man agreed and did more: He connived at a rumor, soon circulated countrywide, that the oil was good for rheumatism.[11]

For Dr. Soper road blocks to keep the stegs from traveling were only an interim measure. He had already decided that the mosquitoes should be exterminated. But when he talked about that his own best men thought he was crazy.[12] So to start off he merely went about the familiar jobs of ridding the country little by little of *Aedes* breeding places, by emptying, covering and oiling domestic water containers. Like Gorgas he developed and directed a highly disciplined organization. He put his mosquito inspectors into uniform, forbade them to take tips on penalty of instant dismissal. He set over them district inspectors who were specially trained and better paid. If one of these overlooked a single breeding place, he lost a day's pay; if two, he was demoted.* The organization functioned under an extraordinary decree, issued in 1932, that gave inspectors the right of entry into all houses, provided penalties for obstructing their work, made it an offense subject to fine to maintain a breeding place on one's property, made mosquito-proofing of houses obligatory and set forth in minute detail the ways in which collections of domestic water were to be reduced.[13]

It worked. By the end of 1934 *Aedes aegypti* had disappeared. The Foundation, impressed by the success, now openly embraced eradication as its objective and extended the campaign to Bolivia, Paraguay, Peru and Colombia.[14] In Brazil Soper was triumphant but not, as he might have expected, out of a job.

---

* The service once dismissed an inspector who failed to inspect an arsenal that was on his itinerary. His dereliction was discovered because on the very hour when according to the charts in Soper's office he was supposed to be there the arsenal blew up and killed everyone in it (Soper, 1965).

He had a new enemy, which seems to have arrived in Brazil at about the same time as he did. That enemy's arrival might have been missed but for the annoying curiosity of R. C. Shannon, the Rockefeller Foundation's chief resident entomologist. Shannon so irritated his medical associates by constantly roaming the countryside in search of mosquitoes which had nothing to do with their mission that Soper at last, according to a colleague, "cancelled requisitions and trips which did not seem to bear exclusively on the yellow fever problem."[15] It happened that Shannon was off duty on a Sunday in March 1930, when in a flooded area near Natal on the northeast coast he collected the larvae of *Anopheles gambiae*. It was a chilling find. *Gambiae,** the most efficient malaria vector in the world, had never before been found outside Africa. Indeed no anopheline had ever been picked up so far from its native range. The closest precedent was *gambiae's* invasion of Mauritius. But the journey by boat to Natal was more than twice as far and to literally another world. Although Brazil, unlike Mauritius, had other anopheline vectors, it had none nearly so dangerous. The chances of serious epidemics were substantial. And if *gambiae* could establish itself it could spread hyperendemic malaria throughout Brazil.

Beginning in April, malaria struck Natal with unprecedented severity.[16] Soper inspected the *gambiae* breeding places. They seemed to be confined to low-lying meadows recently reclaimed from the sea by dikes and now used profitably to grow hay. Soper observed how easily the invader could be wiped out by opening the dikes and salting out the larvae. But letting in the sea would also destroy valuable hay. Its owners balked. Despite repeated requests authorities procrastinated: The local government lacked power to act against vested interests; the national government was in the midst of a presidential election.

The best that could be done was to dust the breeding places with Paris green. *Gambiae* was gradually extinguished in Natal but not in time. Another worse epidemic struck Natal in January 1931. When that was put down, the word came that *gambiae* had escaped; it was breeding far afield. Soper wanted to pursue it. His bosses at the Foundation were cool. The business of the yellow fever service, New York remarked, was yellow fever; *gambiae* should be left to the Brazilians.[17]

While Soper's men turned energetically and successfully to the attack on stegs, *gambiae* quietly deployed on more favorable grounds. The ironic fact is that Natal was in most respects a miserable place for *gambiae* to make

---

* Or, strictly, three of the five species into which the *gambiae* complex has now been divided.

landfall. Virtually the only suitable habitat anywhere around was in the hayfields made by man. Natal moreover is almost surrounded by lands through which no anopheline could travel, a coastal plain of swift-flowing rivers to the south, mountains to the west and a narrow coastal plain northwards in which the mosquito-friendly river valleys are separated by high, dry, sparsely settled, forbidding plateaus. But though nature thus bars migration, man has opened it up. Natal is a center for trade by small ships that ply the coast, calling at many small ports as coastal ships do. *Gambiae* mosquitoes probably came aboard and jumped ship where they could. Or they may have traveled by truck. In either case they had a long and precarious journey, constantly stopping to breed and renew themselves. It was five years before they were ready to attack in mass in good breeding country more than 500 kilometers north and west along the coast from Natal.

The opening assault in 1938 centered in the valley of the Jaguaribe River.[18] Predictably this is a dry area subject to heavy seasonal rains. Between rains the inhabitants cultivate sweet potatoes in the streambeds of dry rivers. They water the potatoes from shallow wells that tap the high water table through the sand. These wells, without plants or algae and lying in the sun, are just what *gambiae* likes best and in them the invader bred prolifically, to emerge by 1938 in devastating hordes. That year a hundred thousand people in the valley fell ill and twenty thousand of them died. As the people put on black to mourn their relatives the country seemed, in the eyes of one native observer, to darken in the wake of mosquitoes advancing "like hordes of bloodthirsty huns." Many of the valley people fled, the well-to-do to the cities, the poor to nearby villages. The parasites, of course, went with them, so the infection spread.[19]

By mid-1938 the Brazilian government with the Rockefeller Foundation was organizing a counterattack. Early in 1939 the jointly funded Malaria Service of the Northeast came into being, absorbing some of the people from the Yellow Fever Service and taking over its priorities. Soper was effectively in charge. The plan of campaign was modeled on the battle against the stegs but Paris green was to be used generally in place of oil and adult mosquitoes were to be attacked by pyrethrum sprays. The same tight system of hunt and destroy was to be repeated in a country now well accustomed to the uniformed mosquito inspectors.

But few at the beginning were sanguine. *Gambiae* took advantage of the wet season at the start of 1939 to push up the river valleys. In June larvae were found 120 kilometers beyond what had been thought to be their outpost lines. The road along the Jaguaribe River was beaded with houses that formed a continuous village, each house within mosquito flight of its neighbor. No one was sure that the mosquito had not jumped normal barriers during the rains to invade still more favorable country to the north. If so it might be out of reach. One observer talked of a fight perhaps limited to preventing further spread or delaying it for many years.[20]

Everyone, including Soper, recognized that the first engagements had to be defensive. Beginning in the rainy season there was no hope of immediately checking reproduction. Soper tried to build up the morale of his men by emphasizing one seeming success: *gambiae* had been cleaned out of one coastal village. But for the rest he had continually to pull his fighters out of the valley where the worst trouble was in order to stamp out *gambiae* at the edges of its occupation zone. As the dry season came on they worried about running out of money and Soper laid off 250 fighters in the inner core, in order to be sure he could pay the men on the frontiers.

So bleak were the prospects that success coming swiftly, as it did before the end of the second year, was almost anticlimactic. In 1939 the Malaria Service recorded 185,572 cases of malaria in the districts within its jurisdiction; in 1940 there were only 6,124. By the mid-1940s *gambiae's* frontier breeding places had been cleared. Thereafter the workers converged toward the center, pocketing the invaders and systematically exterminating them. On the last day of August, *gambiae* that had been maintained for experimental purposes in a laboratory at the mouth of the Jaguaribe River were killed. Though they were not quite the last in Brazil—the last adult and the last larva were put to death on 9 and 14 November respectively—the war was over. It had been quickly and brilliantly won. Soper and his men celebrated their victory on 7 September, Brazil's Independence Day.

It was a splendid victory, but its meaning could be variously read in accord with the reader's taste. Because it was the biggest battle so far in which spray-killing played a major role, some drew the conclusion that spraying had made the critical difference. Soper thought he had ample proof that antilarval measures by themselves would have sufficed whereas attacks on the adults alone "were never shown to be effective."[21]

He himself, of course, considered the case for eradication as an antimalaria tactic to have been made. He tended to be scornful of the opposing view. To settle for a reduction in the number of vectors was, he thought, "good philosophy for the defeated."[22] He thought so despite the survival of the native Brazilian anophelines in the area of the great battle, which though depleted were shortly to recover their forces. They too might have been extinguished, in Soper's view, if only enough "men, money, and necessary materials" had been expended.[23]

This was the radical view of total war to which Soper remained faithful despite many discouragements to come, and it was to have wide following. Yet like so many of the final answers that have regularly supplanted one another in the history of the struggle against malaria, it was grounded on the most obviously local and special situation. *Gambiae* was not only a foreigner in Brazil but one selected as it were to be as vulnerable as possible to attack by man. The fact that it boarded ship in Africa demonstrates that it belonged to a highly domesticated strain, dependent on man for food and to a large extent for habitat. It could therefore be defeated conclusively, like *Aedes aegypti,* in and around human habitation; it had no wild hiding places. But each of the *gambiae* species in Africa includes many strains, with various capacities to adapt to a large number of different habitats and to feed on animals other than man.

The campaign in Brazil did not prove the general practicability of eradication. It did demonstrate the efficacy—indeed the indispensability—of well-trained, well-disciplined organization under decisive leadership, with full government backing. There is incidentally no single lesson that emerges more often and more clearly from the war on mosquitoes than the truism that it takes good armies to fight winning wars. The remarkable fact is how consistently the routine military requirements of leadership and discipline have been overlooked or rationalized away because they could not readily be met. Secondly, Brazil showed strikingly and tragically how terrible can be the cost of ignoring invaders when they first arrive. And that lesson, alas, was also forgotten almost as soon as learned.

A third lesson worth remarking was less readily apparent, yet important. In the invasion area *gambiae* raised the parasite rate to almost 100 percent. That is to say, everybody in the community became a carrier (though not necessarily infective). Yet as soon as *gambiae* had been defeated the parasites died out until by 1941 the rate of infections returned to the pre-epidemic levels. The local anophelines, feeding in this immense reservoir of plasmodia had been expected to keep the epidemic going after the strangers' departure. Why didn't they? The question was noted at the time but not explored.[24]

The reason throws strong light on the epidemiology of malaria. What the facts say is just what they said in Ceylon: that the prevalence of the disease is not so much influenced by the abundance of carriers as it is by the numbers and transmitting efficiency of the vectors. A lot of carriers in Brazil could not keep malaria at a high rate when the vectors transmitted poorly; a few carriers in Ceylon permitted malaria to reach high intensity when the vectors became numerous and efficient. The facts in Brazil confirmed those in Ceylon and coincided with what the mathematical models worked out by Professor MacDonald had predicted. Still it was not enough. History in due course touched and was burned by those facts again.*

By the time *gambiae* had been defeated in Brazil, the United States was within a few months of being drawn into the war that had already engulfed most of Europe and Asia. Fred Soper along with many of his Foundation colleagues and malariologists everywhere entered military service in or out of uniform. Military leaders in World War II were no more sensitive to the dangers of malaria than they had been in World War I and it took a lot of sickness among the ranks of British and American troops in tropical theaters to persuade field commanders that mosquitoes were enemies sometimes more to be feared and respected than the Germans or Japanese. Yet whereas World War I had set back antimalaria work to the starting line, World War II ended by setting up a brand new starting line, one very near, it seemed, to the finish.

---

* See Chapter 27.

24 / "An Almost Perfect Insecticide"[1]

If a malaria fighter in the 1930s had set out to design the ideal weapon, it might well have been a house spray that needed to be applied only once or twice a year instead of once or twice a week, a pyrethrum with staying power—in a word DDT. In retrospect it seems odd that no one then—and no one, so far as the record shows, in all the history of the mosquito war—ever worked out the requirements of battle and specified means to meet them. The four great weapons discoveries—larviciding oil, Paris green, pyrethrum spray and at last DDT—were made in that order by accident, by scientific curiosity, by a desperate reach into the barrel of old tricks, and by serendipity during the search for an answer to another problem.

Chemists of the J. R. Geigy company of Switzerland had been looking for twenty years for an efficient and safe killer of the clothes moth when in 1941 their man, Paul Müller, synthesized dichloro-diphenyl-trichloro-ethane. He mixed it 5 percent in inert powder, and Geigy called the product "Gesarol," leaving to the British Ministry of Supply the distinction a year later of underlining the initials of the active ingredient and giving it for posterity the name of DDT. The first tests were encouraging. Gesarol killed clothes moths. It killed Colorado beetles which then infested Swiss potato fields. It killed flies, mosquitoes and grain weevils. Best of all it did not seem to have any effect at all on warm-blooded animals. In 1942 Geigy put DDT in a powder designed to kill human lice and called it Neocid. "As soon as the lice came in contact with Neocid," a Geigy chemist announced, "they fell to the ground and . . . were dead in 12 to 48 hours."[2] That in wartime was dramatic news. Body lice transmit typhus, the ancient and perennial scourge of unwashed armies in battle and of civilians in war-ravaged cities.

Through the U. S. military attaché in Berne, the British and the Americans both procured small amounts of the powder with which they began experiments in late 1942 at agricultural stations in Rothamsted and Orlando, Florida, respectively. When the news of Neocid passed through military attachés and scientific advisers, both countries stepped up the pace. Within months they had fully confirmed Swiss results as to both DDT's insecticidal effectiveness and its apparent harmlessness to man. Britain gave the manufacture of DDT the highest wartime priority along with radar and penicillin, two other notable life-savers. Production began in England in April 1943; in America in May.

Now when DDT has been indicted as a killer of peregrine falcons, brown pelicans, sea lions, ladybugs, salmon and thousands more wild friends of man, it is painful to read the encomiums that greeted its birth. Yet DDT in the beginning was in fact the boon it was thought to be; indeed the full extent of its power to benefit man had still to be discovered. It was to be the first weapon effective enough and cheap enough to give to people a potentially decisive advantage in the war against insect pests. That there were also risks was clear then and scientists faced them. The Entomological Society of America in December 1944 hailed DDT as promising an end to pest problems but warned that what killed pests would also kill beneficial insects, the "allies of mankind."[3] They observed that DDT was shown to poison fish and that there had not been time enough to find out whether there might be cumulative effects on organisms in the soil. The U. S. Army and Public Health Service in a public statement a few months later recommended that DDT not be used to kill mosquito larvae where there was danger to fish and that broadcasting the poison from airplanes be done only "with due regard to the possible effects of DDT on beneficial insects and all forms of plant and animal life."*[4]

Ought these warnings to have led to withholding or restricting the use of

---

* Latter-day environmentalists often assume that our difficulties with the side effects of such useful substances as pesticides come from the failure in the first place to understand what those effects might be. So they impute a blindness or carelessness or both to the men of the past, along with a new enlightenment to themselves, and deduce that now with our fresh awareness of problems we are likely to do better. The fact that we got into trouble with DDT *despite* early recognition of the dangers suggests that our new awareness (so far as it is new) may not help us much. At least awareness provided no counterforce to the political and economic pressures that led to the immediate use and eventual overuse of DDT.[5]

DDT until more exhaustive tests of its environmental and long-term consequences could be made? No one then suggested such a thing. It would have been unthinkable to let people die of typhus and malaria on grounds that unwise and prolonged misuse of the saving chemical might eventually cost mankind dear. Moreover the abuses that were at last to threaten a "silent spring" and lead to widespread repudiation of DDT were perpetrated mostly in agriculture, not in public health. This is a critical distinction often blurred in public discussion. It was the farmers, especially the very big farmers, and among them especially the cotton growers, who egregiously ignored early warnings against the indiscriminate, wholesale applications of DDT. It was areal (and aerial) spraying, often in hugely redundant quantities, that established concentrations of DDT in the food chains and killed so many birds and fish. By contrast the malaria fighters, though beginning with broadcast applications of DDT, came in time to use it almost exclusively to treat the interior surfaces of houses. Although precisely what general environmental impact these treatments may have had has never been investigated, the damage must have been less significant than that from agricultural use.

It took some time to learn what DDT could and could not do. As almost always in the history of the mosquito war, the learning process was wholly pragmatic through trials reiterated in different times and places. Directing some of the earliest and most impressive of these was Dr. Soper, for whom it seemed DDT might have been specially designed.

Soper had left Brazil in September 1942, his work well done and his reputation as a kind of General Patton of the anopheline war well established. There was talk of sending him into the other war with the rank of lieutenant colonel. But the offer was a staff post advising others how to deal with malaria. Advising, he told the army, was not his strong point and the rank was too low for the job anyway. In the end he joined as a civilian the U. S. Typhus Commission, which late in 1942 set up headquarters in Cairo. That turned out to be just the right place for him to be.

For one thing, quite unexpectedly, he ran into his old enemy *Anopheles gambiae,* which was again striking out into new territory from its homeland in tropical Africa. This time *gambiae* headed out of Sudan and down the Nile into Egypt, where it had never been recorded before. The new invasion from the outset went the way of the first.

When Dr. Soper landed in Cairo, a year and a half had already passed since the government entomologist of the Sudan first collected *gambiae* larvae from pools along the Nile several miles north of the Sudanese border. That official had reported the fact at least in a scientific journal, and had set up what he hoped would be a barrier to further spread by

Fred. L. Soper (dark suit) on yellow fever inspection tour in Matto Grosso, Brazil

dusting potential breeding places along a six-kilometer stretch of the river with Paris green.[6] This might have been effective if the mosquito had been migrating, as he assumed, by a progression of generations. In fact it appears that *gambiae* was once again traveling by ship, taking advantage of greatly increased wartime traffic on the Nile and of human negligence.

Apparently the first word of the invasion to reach Egyptian health authorities was a report in March 1942 of a terrible outbreak of malaria in Abu Simbel, a village of 3,500 people a few miles inside Egypt.[7] Government investigators reached the village at the end of April to find nearly every one of the inhabitants ill. The best they could do at the moment was bring in drugs. Even these were hard to come by when armies had absolute priority. Almost no insecticides were available.

In the course of the year it became clear that Abu Simbel was an old bridgehead for an enemy that had already advanced some 700 kilometers into Egypt. At the end of 1942 *gambiae* was breeding all along the Nile throughout an area of more than 4,000 square kilometers with a total population of three million. Malaria cases climbed to an estimated 63,000 of which probably 10 percent were fatal.

Dr. Soper having inspected the invasion area wanted, of course, to try for immediate eradication. But he had no official position; he could not commandeer the 150 tons of Paris green he estimated were needed. British and Egyptian authorities thought it more prudent to contain the enemy within the territory it already occupied by breeding barriers and quarantine. Soper could not move them. He left an eradication plan with the health ministry, along with a report of the Brazilian campaign, and returned to his job of controlling body lice.

That work was to occupy him through 1943, in Cairo, Algiers, and at last in Naples. Before it was finished malaria suddenly struck down three-quarters of a million people in Egypt. Shocked, the Egyptian government unearthed Soper's old eradication plan and agreed to ask the Rockefeller Foundation for advice on carrying it out. Soper came over for a reconnaissance. Although he himself could not be spared to direct operations, the government—which in any case did not want an American in charge—took over the project itself. Employing 4,600 men under Sir Aly Shousha, under secretary of health, and closely following the Brazilian model, Egypt wiped out the invaders in six months.[8]

So the lessons of Brazil were inked in: That invasions by exotic species had to be taken seriously and dealt with decisively and promptly, and that such species could be eradicated if systematic and simultaneous attacks could be mounted in a relatively compact area against substantially all their breeding places. Egypt was another limited success of exactly the same order as the first; it proved no more and no less. Yet two successive victories seemed to reinforce each other and to suggest a general validity for the means employed. Eradication might indeed be the right tactic. Soper's stock rose and he was soon in a position to try again.

The successful delousing of Naples in the early months of 1944, just after the American occupation, has come to be regarded as a minor landmark in the history of the war against insects in general because it was the first time that DDT (in the form of Neocid) emerged from the laboratory onto the battlefield. The myth is that it promptly worked a miracle, banished typhus quickly and easily and stood forth as a superweapon like the tank at Cambrai or the A-bomb at Hiroshima. The truth is that Neocid played a very small role. The people of Naples were dusted almost wholly with pyrethrum. Neocid arrived only after the louse, and with it typhus, had been defeated.

But if DDT did not triumph in Naples it did show its remarkable potential. Although no more effective than pyrethrum in killing adult lice, it lay in wait for the next generation. So long as Neocid remained on skin or clothing, nits hatching out died on contact. Thus one application of DDT might remain effective for a month whereas pyrethrum had to be applied at least every week. The gain was not only in greatly reduced expense but reduced public resistance to a procedure so much less of a nuisance. Soper, after the Naples campaign, while recognizing that pyrethrum had done the job, hailed DDT as "all that its champions claim it to be, an almost perfect insecticide."[9]

In wartime Italy it had the almost perfect proving ground. As usual war befriended disease, disrupting all the routines by which settled peoples protect their welfare. On top of the disorganization of the health services, the lack of quinine, the absorption of doctors and nurses into the military and the wandering of the sick and homeless, retreating German armies took another turn of the screw. To slow the Allied advance they systematically breached the dikes in southern and central Italy that had been built over the decades to reclaim the land and dry out anophelines. Many of the great bonification projects reverted to marshland and were promptly reoccupied by *Anopheles labranchiae*. Many were also strewn with land mines, which were even more effective in discouraging the mosquito larviciders than in holding up Allied soldiers.

The Allied Control Commission, which governed Italian territory behind the combat zone,* in the spring of 1944 asked Soper and his Rockefeller Foundation team to see what they could do. Two trials, both in bonification lands reflooded by the Germans, showed that a single spraying of DDT (two grams per square meter) to coat the interior surfaces where feeding mosquitoes rested could halt the transmission of malaria for an entire season. It was simple and it was cheap.[10]

In 1945 the Health Division of the United Nations relief organization (UNRRA) which supplied all the DDT used (and which happened to be headed by another former Rockefeller Foundation staff doctor, Wilbur A. Sawyer), decided on a systematic campaign to sweep malaria out of Italy. The plan was to start in Sicily and Calabria and follow the warming weather up the boot, poisoning resting places of *Anopheles labranchiae* just before the season of its emergence. The campaign got well under way in 1945 when half a million pounds of DDT were expended by eight-man spray teams who covered 135,000 square miles.[11]

By 1946 the Italian government was ready to take over. Professor Missiroli designed a five-year campaign. UNRRA, as it peacefully went out of business, handed over the DDT it had on hand, sold other supplies and equipment to the Italians and donated the proceeds to help pay for the

---

* The commission's man in charge of antimalaria work was Paul Russell, a Rockefeller Foundation doctor in uniform for the duration.

campaign. So equipped, Missiroli's fighters took not five years but only three to reduce malaria deaths in Italy (excluding Sardinia) to zero.*[12] Although DDT spraying would continue in some places for more than ten years, this short, sharp postwar attack effectively marked the end of Italy's ancient curse.

Sardinia, excluded from the mainland campaign, was to be made a special case. UNRRA in 1945 still had a lot of surplus lire. Dr. Sawyer wanted to use them for something of permanent value to malaria control everywhere. His former colleague, Dr. Soper, still dreamed of eradication, not as an occasional special tactic but as the centerpiece of global strategy. He wanted to try it in Sardinia. After some negotiation with Missiroli and other representatives of the Italian government, this was agreed upon.[14] Rockefeller put up $400,000 and assumed technical control; UNRRA contributed 15 million lire. The Italian Ministry of Public Health organized a special entity with full legal powers to organize and direct the campaign.

Soper wanted to get right at it. For one thing UNRRA was to disband at the end of 1946, and its contribution could not be renewed. For another he saw no reason to waste time in lengthy preparations. The enemy *Anopheles labranchiae,* as one of the *maculipennis* complex which had been studied for twenty years by a virtual sub-profession of malariologists, was as well known as any vector. Reconnaissance therefore seemed to him unnecessary. Moreover what he envisaged was no fencing match but attacks of massive irresistible weight. He thought that if it was done right it could be done in a year. The resources available should not be attenuated by dragging out operations.[15]

Perhaps Dr. Soper himself could have brought it off. But he had just set up a Middle East regional health office for the Rockefeller Foundation in Cairo and was not available. Command went to a colleague who, though a good scientist, had neither organizational talent nor drive. His selection moreover was delayed for almost a year while administrative and logistic snags were untangled. A second year was largely lost in demonstrating that he was indeed miscast.

The overall strategic idea was straightforward: It was simply to kill mosquitoes in season and out, by DDT house sprays during the winter when adults sheltered indoors but did not breed, and by DDT larvicide the rest of the year. But there were no detailed plans when winter spraying began at last in November 1946. Neither the houses nor the breeding places had been mapped. Not enough men had been trained even to begin the job properly and there were no training facilities to provide more.

---

* Confirmed primary cases in 1949 numbered just eighty-one.[13]

While the properties of the spray were pretty well known by this time, the larvicide had not been thoroughly tested. In fact the decision to use DDT in preference to Paris green, which after all had gained the victory in both Brazil and Egypt, does not seem to have been even debated much less submitted to the arbitration of experiment.

So began in haste and awkwardness and without its conceptual father, what was to be the supreme and perhaps final test of Dr. Soper's idea. It could hardly have had a more difficult one. Sardinia, about the size of the state of New Hampshire (24,086 square kilometers) is a rugged country, mostly hills and mountains, much of it inhospitable and unsettled. More than 90 percent of the million and a quarter inhabitants at the time of the campaign lived in cities and villages. Because throughout history Sardinia's coasts had been repeatedly raided, almost all the villages were tucked back in the hills. Roads were few. The coastal plain "is fringed with swamps and salt or brackish water lagoons. The river systems have shallow tortuous beds, choked with vegetation and upland mountain swamps are common."[16] Malaria had plagued the land through history. From 1861, when the island became part of the new kingdom of Italy, Sardinia had consistently been Italy's most malarious region.

Anopheles labranchiae had been in occupation at long time. Missiroli, who at the time warned of the tenacity of long-established species, thought it might have been on the island since before the Alps and Mediterranean were formed.[17] Even if, as now seems more likely, it had been there only the few thousands of years since the end of the last ice age,[18] it had had time to mold itself to the variety of its environment and exploit many habitable niches. One could expect in Sardinia a population of individuals with many different ways of life and strategies of survival, not the inbred, homogeneous descendants of a handful of stowaways that had proved so easy to find and destroy in Brazil and Egypt.

At the end of 1947, after one year of spraying and larviciding, there were some who thought Missiroli's pessimism already vindicated. But the only certainty was that Soper's optimism had been unfounded. The tactic had not yet been given a fair test. Dr. John A. Logan took charge. He asked for more money, more men, and more supplies. That had to be: The experiment might have succeeded in a year; it could not fail in a year.*

Battlers against *gambiae* had enjoyed one technical advantage of which they were not duly appreciative: Their enemy bred almost exclusively in weed-free pools in the open, relatively easy to find and to treat. *La-*

---

* South Vietnam might have been "saved" in a short war; it took a very long one to "lose" it.

branchiae larvae grew up among weeds that were sometimes so thick that the water could not even be seen. In such habitat larvicide either did not reach the water at all or spread so unevenly on the surface that many insects escaped. Not even repeated spraying from airplanes flying a few yards above the ground and from helicopters that forced the pesticide downward by the draft of their motors, could get through. The weeds had to be cleared. No mechanical dredges could maneuver in that country, even if any had been available. Flame-throwers in wet conditions did not work and in dry ones proved too dangerous. The job at last had to be done by hand, and it took 24,000 more men, a sixfold increase in the original organization. (The men were easy to find: Sardinia was a poor country with lots of unemployed.)

The summer of 1948 brought some good news. Malaria cases, which had been halved the year before, were halved again. It was getting notably difficult to find either adult *labranchiae* in houses or their larvae in water. But there was bad news as well, noted but not then taken quite seriously: Whereas in Brazil and Egypt, when the periodic collections of mosquitoes had been graphed, the numbers found had declined in a straight line toward zero, a comparable graph in Sardinia had begun to level off well above the zero line. That meant that progressively fewer mosquitoes were being killed per unit of effort. One had either to step up the attack or to continue it for a very long time, perhaps forever. Dr. Logan might reasonably have concluded from this telltale curve, familiar in many forms as predicting diminishing returns and escalating costs, that Sardinia had announced its lesson, that even in the best of circumstances the price of total extermination of *labranchiae* would be prohibitive. But it was hard to let go. UNRRA was out of business but the U. S. Economic Cooperation Administration offered comparable support, reasoning that the death of *labranchiae* would contribute as much as anything to the economic development of the island.

In the final stages of a drive toward perfection an agonizing paradox appears: Holdouts grow ever more tantalizingly scarce and ever more exasperatingly elusive. Dr. Logan's men turned to a concentrated assault on *labranchiae*'s wild stronghold in the northeast part of the island. They sprayed shelters and breeding places there once a week for six weeks running. And when they finished larvae reappeared—not many, just an ineluctable few.

All along Dr. Logan and his staff had assumed that where the mosquito survived it was breeding in water that had escaped attention. Only in 1950 did they bring larvae into the laboratory—not *labranchiae,* because they were too hard to find in numbers, but another anopheline—and for the first time systematically tested their larvicide. To their surprise they found that larvae survived concentrations twenty-five times greater than those that had been used in the field. The larvae did not seem to have developed resistance to the poison; they just weren't taking it in, possibly because the medium in which the DDT was dissolved did not spread an even film over the water. Other mixes gave better results but none, significantly, was perfect.

The campaign continued one more year, into 1951—a total of five years instead of the one originally planned. It cost $12 million ($2 per Sardinian per year), four times the cost of the successful antimalaria campaign in the rest of Italy. Malaria was banished from Sardinia but *labranchiae* stayed on, waiting in obscure lairs until Logan's men left and it could reoccupy the ancient homeland.

Missiroli and others had correctly predicted the failure of the Sardinian project and for the right reasons. Yet it was well worth the effort. Had it not been tried then and there, surely it would have had to be tried somewhere else. The notion of getting rid forever of disease-carrying mosquitoes is inherently too attractive to be abandoned on merely theoretical grounds, persuasive as those grounds now seem in retrospect.

What did the failure say about DDT, the only weapon widely used in Sardinia? Nothing, really, except that the people using it still did not fully understand its peculiar powers and limitations. Spraying to kill adult mosquitoes in the winter was useless. These were not infected insects; they were not biting and therefore not transmitting. The object in attacking them was to reduce the number that could lay eggs in the spring. But in view of the mosquito's reproductive powers, nothing much short of total extermination of overwintering adults would have made a difference and that was not even theoretically possible. The fact was recognized in the second year and routine winter spraying was stopped. The practical futility of broadcasting the poison from airplanes was also observed and that, too, was stopped.

The more general lesson was not so clearly drawn, and would take a good deal more learning: DDT's outstanding value was not that it killed more efficiently than pyrethrum and Paris green—it did not—but that used as a house spray it stood guard over people against an enemy that infiltrated back. DDT at its most efficient was a defensive weapon, in action rather like a vaccine applied to the environment to make it unsuitable for the transmission of parasites. It did not make easier the eradication of anophelines; but it might—it just might—eradicate malaria. That was the next and final test.

25 / Eradication

UNRRA's involvement in the Italian and Sardinian campaigns set a pattern for the postwar years of international cooperation in the mosquito war. UNRRA itself, on its decease at the end of 1946, bequeathed its assets to the new United Nations children's organization (UNICEF) which decided malaria was sufficiently notorious as a killer of children to warrant a continuing investment in malaria control. UNICEF would be from that time until 1973 an important supplier of pesticides and other materials to developing nations. When ECA (the Economic Cooperation Administration) took over UNRRA's role in Sardinia, it set another precedent—for American assistance worldwide. ECA and its successor agencies, now absorbed in AID (Administration for International Development), were to spend $375 million through 1971 in supporting Third World antimalaria programs and for many years would give technical aid as well.

But the principal international agency involved—the one that gave and still gives a global character and something like central direction to the mosquito war—is the World Health Organization, conceived at the United Nations' birthplace in San Francisco in 1946 and formally established two years later. WHO absorbed the Health Organization of the League of Nations along with an interim International Public Health Office that had been functioning in Paris. It wanted to take over the Pan American Sanitary Bureau, which since 1901 had been providing certain health information and advisory services for the Americas. Soper, at the head of the Bureau, successfully resisted that bid. The upshot was that the Bureau remained independent but assumed the functions in addition of a regional WHO office, one of five. The others are in Africa, Europe and the Middle East, Southeast Asia, and the Pacific.

WHO, while still functioning as an Interim Commission, had decided that malaria along with tuberculosis and venereal diseases should head the enemies list. Accordingly it named an expert committee on malaria to formulate strategies, review problems and generally function rather like a board of directors though without administrative authority. The committee, meeting for the first time in April 1947[1] and thereafter at two- or three-year intervals, was as independent as most boards: Its members were bound to be pre-selected for their friendliness to the management that appointed them, but since they represented outside constituencies in the scientific community as well, they also spoke for them.

No strategy was made at the first meeting. The committee was content to note what would clearly be the two most crucial conditions of fighting: on the one hand the powers of DDT, from which they had "hopes of the complete eradication of the disease—and even of *Anopheles*—from entire countries," and on the other the general unpreparedness of people to use it effectively. They refrained at this first gathering from recommending an immediate worldwide campaign. To the contrary they cautioned WHO against encouraging nations that lacked the knowledge, the organization and the trained people to get into a fight they probably would not be able to handle. Considering the spirit of the time and the eagerness of old frustrated malaria fighters to exploit the most promising tactic to emerge in fifty years, that caution was remarkable.

A few nations seemed reasonably well prepared to begin at once. Italy, as noted, was one. There DDT speeded the recovery from the relapse of war and delivered the coup de grâce to an enemy long in retreat from both human and natural pressures.

Another was Ceylon, also a very old battleground. Ever since the great epidemic of 1934–35 Ceylon had had a malaria surveillance service which not only kept watch against a resurgence of disease but accumulated detailed information on carriers and vectors. Pyrethrum sprays had been tried out during the war and DDT substituted in 1945, when the British Army turned over a couple of tons to the health authorities.[2]

Ceylon was ready in 1946 to launch a full-scale DDT campaign. It was an instant success. In the first year the island's death rate dropped from 20.3 to 14.3 per thousand—the largest one-year reduction ever and the first time the index had ever been below 20.[3] That was only the beginning. Within ten years DDT cut the incidence of malaria in Ceylon from about three million cases to 7,300 and eliminated malaria deaths altogether.

What made the achievement especially dramatic was that it began in drought conditions in the wet zone reminiscent of those that had produced the 1934–35 epidemic. The drought in 1950 was the worst since 1934. Conditions in the puddled river beds of the wet zone were again ideal for breeding *culicifacies*. Yet malaria did not increase. When the next year the rains returned to normal, inspectors could collect only 81 adult *culicifacies* from 37,000 houses.[4] That stand against the second great Ceylon drought was a heady victory. At last, it seemed, man and not nature had the upper hand.

Venezuela had not been quite so long in the field. But since 1936 there had been a special antimalaria unit within the government's public health department which supervised the free distribution of drugs and organized local drainage projects to protect the "more important centers."[5] These were the only general control measures but there had been considerable experimentation with pyrethrum sprays. Most important, under the vigorous leadership of Dr. Arnoldo Gabaldón, the malaria service had accurate knowledge of the geography and habits of the country's two principal vectors, *Anopheles darlingi* and *A. albimanus*. Gabaldón knew that both were vulnerable to spray attack. The most obvious difficulties were the size of the malarious zone (as large as Texas), its widely scattered population and poor roads and the fact that malaria was transmitted all year long. Nevertheless Gabaldón decided in 1946, as soon as DDT was available, to proceed at once with a full-scale attack. The attack gathered momentum over the next four years, at the end of which Dr. Gabaldón commanded eighty DDT squads, about half of them motorized, the rest moving on horseback, on foot or in one instance by trolley. The most accessible areas (about three-quarters of the whole) had by then been cleared of *darlingi* mosquitoes. *Albimanus* persisted because it was less compulsively addicted to life indoors, but by the same token it did not seem to be transmitting. Dr Gabaldón was encouraged to think that the remoter regions not yet covered could be similarly cleansed, though at greater cost.

Another decade would show that the gains in Ceylon and Venezuela, though great, were less sweeping and less durable than they had at first seemed. In Greece the battle, even while going well, posted warning signs for the future. Greece, possibly the most malarious country in Europe, had early followed Italy's lead in establishing a state quinine monopoly and in rejecting war on the mosquito as generally impracticable. The country was so poor in the early years of the century that such few mosquito fighters as there were sometimes used olive oil to kill larvae as the cheapest oil to be had.[6] Between 1930 and 1936 a Rockefeller Foundation mission to Greece worked out a number of control techniques and assisted the Greek government in setting up a central service.[7] One of the Rockefeller men was Colonel D. E. Wright, an engineer who had begun his career with Gorgas. Colonel Wright left Greece at the beginning of the war but came back with UNRRA at the end. On his return he brought with him almost unlimited resources of DDT, hand and mechanical sprayers, motorcycles, cars and trucks, even a fleet of eighteen aircraft, and the still exuberant spirit of Panama.[8]

Greece in 1945 began at once to try out DDT and simultaneously to train spraymen. So spectacular were the first results that the government budgeted five times as much money as it had originally planned for a 1946 campaign. Spray teams were paid out of this but were fed by the communities where they worked. In Crete where a simultaneous attack got under way the spraymen were paid as well as fed at the expense of the villages through which they fought. With free supplies from UNRRA and with Greek pilots flying the army aircraft, the £300,000 in the special malaria fund was ample for the uninhibited war that in fact now began.

Year by year the house-spraying expanded until by 1949 every shelter in malarious regions was being treated at least once a year. In addition DDT larvicide was spread generously on mosquito breeding waters both by handsprayers and by airplane. Pilots in two-seater biplanes skimmed the ground at heights of from ten to twenty feet, covering 96,000 acres of swamplands with 20 percent DDT solution. In the first year they made an average of more than five sweeps over the target acreage. With DDT and high spirits to spare on one occasion they sprayed 25,000 acres of olive trees and reported afterward that "we wiped out with one air-spraying—a matter of minutes—a plague of caterpillars."[9] Delighted farmers found they had 25 percent more olives that year. Elsewhere, too, people rejoiced in the spray. They did not care so much about what it might do to malarial mosquitoes; the great thing was that suddenly the flies and the lice and the fleas were gone. Some pilots, presumably with friends in Athens, made an unauthorized early morning pass through a suburb of the capital, and the sandflies were gone. "This was something new," the chief of the WHO Greek mission reported, "and the national clamour for more and more DDT has an appeal no Government can resist."[10]

In the first year the only problems were those of success. Keepers of bees and silkworms demanded to be spared the ubiquitous spray. Some doctors who had made a good thing out of giving private treatment for malaria complained of losing business. It appears that in one year transmission of malaria may have stopped. More than 16 percent of Greek children showed parasites in their blood in 1946, only one-tenth of one percent in 1948. From 1947 on no parasites at all appeared in blood slides taken from infants.

In the second year there was another kind of problem, also apparently minor: While the fever continued rapidly to fade, the flies came back. Because for technical and economic reasons the sprayers were now mixing DDT in an odorless water emulsion instead of in kerosene,* people thought an inferior poison was being fobbed off on them, and the first fine edge of cooperative enthusiasm dulled. The same thing happened simultaneously in mainland Italy and soon thereafter in Sardinia, with the same potentially dangerous impact on public opinion. If people lost interest they would close their houses to the spray squads and the campaign would falter or fail. Professor Missiroli was sufficiently alarmed to call a press conference "to tranquillise the people and to stop the criticisms appearing in the press." In Sardinia Dr. Logan's men mixed chlordane, another chlorinated hydrocarbon, with the DDT and the flies again thinned out.

DDT hadn't changed; the population of houseflies had. In later investigations it was shown that individual flies have several different genes that permit them in various physiological ways to absorb the lethal effects of DDT as well as other insecticides.† Possibly, since these genes existed in populations of *Musca domestica* long before there was any occasion to use them in defense against pesticides, they conferred some other marginal advantages. In any event the advantage became decisive when DDT blanketed the habitat. The Greek saturation attack was rather like a flash flood that drowned whoever could not swim. It left a population of swimmers—a very high percentage of individuals with resistant genes. By interbreeding, their progeny came in a few generations to monopolize the housefly niche.

Professor Missiroli remarked that "nature has dealt us a bitter surprise."[12] Yet it should not have been altogether a surprise. Resistance in insects was well known even though previously not common. As early as 1887 a scale insect in California was reported to be surviving formerly lethal doses of lime sulfur and hydrocyanic acid. In 1928 strains of codling

---

* DDT is almost insoluble in water. For spraying it is dissolved in kerosene, made into an emulsion or, as most commonly now, prepared in wettable powders by chemically coating the grains so that they may be held in suspension in water.

† An insect may resist the lethal effects of contact insecticides such as DDT by changes in behavior (e.g., avoiding contact with contaminated surfaces), by changes in the makeup of its cuticle (cutting down absorption of the poison), by mutant enzymes capable of metabolizing the poisons into harmless substances, or by generally superior hardihood. Some kinds of resistance are controlled by single, others by multiple genes.[11]

moth, the apple pest, were found resistant to arsenic compounds.[13] There were other cases. In hindsight it is easy to understand that the phenomenon had been rare only because before DDT man had been merely skirmishing locally with insects and had therefore seldom applied the selective pressure, the wholesale weeding out of susceptible strains, that became possible with the residual insecticides.

WHO at once sounded the alarm: If flies could become resistant, might not anophelines show the same capacity?[14] Actually WHO's chief malariologist, Dr. E. J. Pampana, lunching one summer day in a Greek country inn noted that not only flies but a few *Anopheles* were "calmly resting on the wall of a bedroom which had been sprayed only two months before."[15] That was disturbing but not of course proof, not even solid evidence. No action was yet called for. The DDT campaign was still clearly pushing the anophelines into retreat and malaria continued to subside.

Not until 1951 did the other shoe fall. In a village in the Peloponnese mosquitoes chased by the spraymen came back within weeks, sometimes within days, to alight on the DDT-covered walls and live to bite again. These insects belonged to the chief Greek vector, *Anopheles sacharovi*. It was another two years before laboratory tests confirmed that they were indeed physiologically resistant. By that time there were signs that the other two vectors were also surviving the spray in increasing numbers. Mosquitoes still died in the attack but enough survived to resume transmission. The curve of malaria cases, which had dipped very close to zero in 1951, turned up again. Perhaps even more ominously, in 1956 mosquitoes, both adults and larvae, showed resistance to chlordane and dieldrin—a group of chlorinated hydrocarbons chemically different from DDT, which had been used chiefly on crop pests in the region. It was the first time resistance had appeared in larvae.*[16]

Resistance clearly altered the balance of force between the attack and the defense. The enemy was newly armored and the attack must change to deal with that. But how? That question raised another: How serious and how widespread was the resistance? It might be partial, idiosyncratic to a few species only, local and even temporary, in which case no more than minor tactical shifts might be needed. But suppose these first incidents of resistance augured a hardening of the enemy worldwide. That must demand a profound shift in strategy, even perhaps a major retreat and regrouping. WHO agonized over these questions for several years, as it

---

* In twelve field tests standard doses of chlordane and dieldrin larvicide achieved no measurable kill at all.

became ever more deeply involved in and responsible for directing the fight.

Enthusiasm for DDT and the wish to try it out had quickly developed their own momentum after 1946 and WHO had been caught up. Within a year or so it was itself pushing to widen the war despite continuing reservations about the ability of most nations in the tropics to field armies of even minimal competence. Its official advisers, the expert committee, in 1949 were clearly impatient. In contrast to the dramatic retreat of malaria in some places, so much of the world still lay victim and was doing too little. The developing nations for the most part were no better organized, or trained to act, than two years before. WHO was obliged to lend a hand. The "function of WHO," they advised, "should be to stimulate and to assist governments which have a malaria problem to apply actively those modern methods of control which have now been shown to be so highly effective and economical."[17] Under the placid official prose burned a missionary zeal.

The committee, it is true, wanted aid to go only to governments that already had a suitable antimalaria organization or wished to establish one. But the principal aid offered, the loan of a demonstration spray team, was frankly designed to first sell the method by showing how effective it was, and then train people to use it. That was assistance but it was also promotion. The sudden and often spectacular reduction of malaria after a demonstration spraying, the committee noted, was the very best form of propaganda to gain public and official support. "In many countries it has been observed that such success immediately brings requests to extend the campaign to neighbouring areas."[18] It did not follow that countries making the requests were necessarily well prepared for extended campaigns.

WHO confronted a genuine dilemma: If developing nations were to take advantage of DDT they had to mobilize, but they were not likely to take on that expense unless convinced that the campaign would work. To show them it would work, WHO and its demonstration teams, of which there were seven in the field in 1949, could hardly avoid overselling: The gist of their persuasive power was the near-miraculous blow that DDT dealt malaria when first used. People witnessing the miracle might indeed decide to mobilize but they would also be conditioned to thinking that the key to success was DDT, not organization. Neither they nor WHO itself were fully aware of the dangers of starting this kind of war without adequate preparation.

Against that background the finding of resistance in mosquitoes cast a shadow of more than life size and very frightening. By 1950 nearly every one of the nations that were ever to undertake systematic antimalaria campaigns dependent on DDT had one under way. In only a handful of these was a victory either accomplished or clearly and imminently in the making. The others were only slowly expanding their coverage as resources permitted. All, even the most successful, were committed to routine spray rounds year after year indefinitely. If the spray were now to prove ineffective, the hopes (touted above all by WHO) of eliminating malaria from the world would crash; nations that had been persuaded to put their money into the campaign would lose it; *Anopheles* would emerge victorious and perhaps this time forever invulnerable; on WHO would fall the blame.[19]

But no sooner were the malaria fighters backed into this corner than they seemed providentially to be offered a way out. Mostly to save money,* the Greeks had stopped spraying in Crete and in the Peloponnese before resistance was discovered. To everyone's surprise, malaria showed no signs of coming back. In Crete—though this would take some years to prove—malaria had actually been eradicated. Malaria control officers in the United States and British Guiana were noting the same thing: that they could stop spraying and malaria did not resurge. Contrary to what everyone up to then had believed, it now seemed that it was not necessary to keep up the defense against mosquitoes; the pool of disease could be permanently dried up and the pumps stopped.

Briefly WHO resisted the obvious and most attractive invitation that was implied. In 1953 it advised nations to continue "control on the established principles."[21] The resistance thing had perhaps been exaggerated. So far only Greece and the state of Tennessee had reported it. In both places the pressures on mosquito populations had been unusually intense as farmers, along with public health authorities and individuals with Flit guns and aerosol bombs, had been drenching the environment with insecticides—inside and outside, from the ground and from the air—for years and in all seasons. Even so they had not yet lost control.

But the notion that resistance might be a local and anomalous event which strategy could ignore did not last long. By the end of that year came word from Lebanon that *A. sacharovi* was resistant there just as it was in Greece. Thereafter, as though a dike had been breached, the trickle of reports swelled from all over the world: *sacharovi* resistant also to DDT in Iran; *stephensi* resistant in Saudi Arabia; *sundaicus* resistant in parts of Indonesia. A switch to the other group of chlorinated hydrocarbons that includes dieldrin was successful for a little while. Then, as noted, *sacharovi*

---

* The demand for petroleum to fight the Korean War had raised the price of DDT. Marshall Plan aid was coming to an end.[20]

in Greece began to survive dieldrin, and in 1956 *gambiae* with resistance to dieldrin turned up in northern Nigeria.

By that time WHO had grasped the nettle. It announced a new strategy of malaria eradication. The Pan American Health Organization under Dr. Soper, not surprisingly, embraced the strategy first and endorsed it at the October 1954 meeting. A year later the World Health Assembly proclaimed it and finally in 1956 WHO's expert committee defined the concept and methods for the guidance of governments who were thenceforth to be urged with relentless pressure to go along.

The essential idea was to overwhelm the enemy before she had time to breed out invulnerable generations. It looked from the Greek experience as though one might reasonably expect five or six years' grace, and as though that would be time enough to eradicate the parasite. If transmission could be interrupted and altogether prevented for at least three years, the parasites unable to escape one host and enter another would virtually all die out. Thereafter vector mosquitoes might defend themselves and flourish as they pleased; their survival could no longer be a threat to people, provided only that one kept close watch over the frontiers of the cleansed areas to detect and properly treat infected immigrants. The results in Crete showed that DDT spraying could in fact halt transmission, bring it to zero and keep it there for five years with precisely the result predicted—the eradication of malaria carriers.

Some malariologists hailed eradication as the right strategy fortunately compelled by circumstances. Others accepted it as the only promising response to circumstances. Still others, particularly those who happened to work in such hyperendemic areas as sub-Saharan Africa, had small faith that eradication would work but could see no alternative. For all, WHO's decision gave at least a welcome new energy and mass to the effort.[22]

Eradication was to be achieved in four stages, each a prerequisite for the next—preparation, attack, consolidation and maintenance.[23] Only the first, the preparatory stage, might occasionally be skipped if a nation had already developed sophisticated knowledge and organization through control campaigns under the old rules. The attack phase, beginning as soon as the organization and plan were considered to be in shape, was defined as "time-limited," although the number of years could not be fixed. Mainly on the basis of the Greek experience, the planners hoped that transmission would be interrupted in the first year. If it did not recur for three successive years thereafter, malaria could tentatively be considered to have been eradicated. The battle then was to move into the third phase: consolidation. After an unspecified but convincing number of years under consolidation without new indigenous cases of malaria, the country would be officially certified as clean and the final phase of maintenance would begin. Since maintenance involved no more than continued vigilance against outside attack it was equivalent to what is usually called peace and might safely continue forever.

The crux of the new strategy lay in the attack and consolidation phases and most particularly in the transition between them. In the attack phase all shelters within the malarious zone were to be sprayed regularly from one to four times a year, depending mainly on how many and how long the seasons were in which mosquitoes were active. There was to be no routine interference with mosquito breeding.

At least a year before the end of the attack, the country should have in operation a surveillance system capable of determining when the transmission of malaria had ceased. The main criteria were two: no parasites at all found in blood slides taken from infants and no recent infections in anyone as ascertained by an army of investigators calling regularly among householders in the attack area.

As soon as the surveillance workers reported transmission ended, routine spraying would stop. The surveillance system would then assume command and the consolidation phase begin. As perfection was not to be expected, there would certainly still be carriers, relapsed and imported cases as well as some possibly overlooked before. It was the business of surveillance to find these so as to assure that every individual was cured by drugs—and there were now drugs which killed both the asexual and sexual blood forms of all four species of plasmodia—and if necessary to call for specially targeted spray attacks where carriers seemed numerous and a focus of infection was developing.

Although not remarked at the time, the war between its attack and consolidation phases not only took new form; it changed weapons. From primary dependence on residual insecticides to kill mosquitoes it moved to primary dependence on drugs to kill parasites. In military terms the consolidation phase was the mopping up of a defeated enemy following a decisive outcome in the main battle. Its purpose was to destroy enemy holdouts in pockets of continuing resistance, round up the strays incapable of organized defense but possibly subversive, and make sure that the territory gained could be held. In war, mopping-up operations follow on the momentum of the main attack, employing many of the same troops and most of the same means. Consolidation in the malaria war required new organization, new means, new tactics. Out of that basic discontinuity grew technical as well as psychological difficulties that will be reviewed later. Even had these been foreseen, perhaps WHO would have gone ahead anyway feeling that it had no choice in the matter. To discontinue spraying as soon as possible was in fact the heart of the eradication strategy, reflecting the near panic over insect resistance in which it was forged. The expert committee, meeting at Athens in 1956, noted the warning of insect resistance as constituting "the basis for the new strategy against malaria proposed by WHO," and they added their own view that "the development of such resistance was more dangerous than the premature interruption of spraying operations."[24]

What that meant was that there would be a bias and continuing pressure to break off attacks as quickly as possible. This would reinforce the natural human impatience to graduate from a lower status into a higher one marking progress toward the goal of final liberation from malaria, which itself brewed a powerful impatience especially among politicians. The ground was thus prepared for delusive victories that would warm the seeds of failure.

26 / India–Model for the World

From the caution of 1947 to the aggressiveness of 1956, WHO had come a long way fast. It not only had developed an attack strategy and the techniques to achieve it, but had subtly shifted out of a purely advisory role into a directing one. Formally the staff had no global command. Each nation would devise, run and pay for its own eradication campaign as each had so far carried out independent control operations. The Malaria Eradication Division of WHO (as it now called itself) had very little money and no international authority to shape or manage campaigns, much less carry them out. It merely provided technical aid. Yet because through the expert committee it commanded a virtual monopoly of professional talent, because it had a plan and a rationale for the plan and because by dint of these advantages it had the ear of such international funding agencies as were interested (USAID and UNICEF in particular), its advice became more and more the prescription to be ignored at the patient's peril; its strategy, the norm for nations to follow on pain of losing both technical and material support.

The disease-fighting strength of nations had not matured nearly so fast. Moreover the first ten years of control using DDT underlined profound differences in fighting conditions in various parts of the world. Even when WHO aimed only to reduce malaria it recognized that in some places the job would be exceptionally long-drawn-out and difficult.

Most difficult without question was equatorial Africa. Climatically ideal for mosquito and parasite, it had, in *Anopheles gambiae,* the world's most efficient known vector and, in patterns of dispersed settlement, nomadism, poverty and illiteracy, the smallest capacity to organize antimalarial campaigns. So daunting were the problems of Africa that they became the subject of two special strategy meetings of the WHO experts. At the first, in 1950, the experts were divided: One group—Professor Swellengrebel prominent among them—wanted to use drugs as the principal weapon. They feared that DDT would work only to reduce malaria so far as to weaken adult immunity and so expose the populations to devastating epidemics. The others, who carried the day, insisted that DDT had a good chance of working and that even to have cut down sickness only a little would contribute so materially to the prosperity of African nations that the risk of epidemic ought to be accepted.[1] Five years later at a second conference they stopped just short of admitting they had been wrong. Control by spraying with DDT remained, they said, "technically feasible," but for all sorts of human reasons it was so difficult in practice that it ought to be supplemented by massive drug therapy. The fact is that the only successes up to that time (except in small experimental areas) had been in the islands of Mauritius and Réunion, both obviously atypical examples with little relevance for the continent.[2]

The African straddle was never resolved. When the decision was made to try for eradication worldwide, Africa was explicitly left out; or rather, to be quite fair, it was put aside as one of the places where malaria could be expected to hang on longest, perhaps safe from effective attack until after the easier battles had been won.[3] But eradication strategy never squarely faced the contradiction between a time-limited campaign announced for the world as a whole and the exceptions that clearly would have to be made for some countries where one could not see the end of the war.

WHO accepted the contradiction mostly because it perceived no choice. To make exceptions for Africa or other similarly disadvantaged places was to admit either that eradication was not in fact globally possible or that alternative strategies were. To the latter WHO, gripped by the fear of insect resistance, could not subscribe. Emotionally, if not logically, it followed that eradication must offer all the hope there was.

One could, moreover, make the chances look better by analyzing the obstacles to be overcome. These were of three broad sorts: special strengths or evasive talents in the enemy (WHO called these "technical" problems); peculiar human customs and habits tending to make people unusually defenseless; and finally the human failures that WHO called "administrative" and "operational." In plainer language these last consisted of whatever changes might be rung on error, incompetence, corruption and indifference in organization and performance.

Where mosquito vectors were vulnerable to attack by house sprays, eradication became in the WHO analysis "technically feasible." If then, despite that vulnerability, eradication was not going forward at the proper rate, the causes must be human. For WHO's own "administrative" and "operational" convenience the distinction was useful. But it had also psychological consequence. Since in most of the world eradication was in fact technically feasible, it became easy to reckon that therefore no "real" or insuperable bars to success existed. Administrative and operational weaknesses were not after all inherent, but aberrational and idiosyncratic. By contrast to the hard givens of mosquito biology, they could indeed seem quite soft and tractable.

In 1956 when eradication was offered from Geneva as the last, best and only hope of finally defeating malaria, the United States and Europe were already on the point of achieving it.[4] In Latin America, Chile had eradicated not just malaria but the vector; Guiana (British) and Venezuela had reduced the disease to a minor public health problem. For Africa there was promise only in the southern part of the continent. Israel among the Middle Eastern nations was within sight of victory. In Asia Sri Lanka (Ceylon) had stopped spraying throughout the island and was settling down to keep watch against a resurgence. Elsewhere in the world the battle was evenly joined. WHO was optimistic but enough difficulties had already appeared in the course of control campaigns to suggest that there would be no more easy victories.

India, big enough to comprehend nearly every possible difficulty, sophisticated enough to develop highly skilled leadership and organized armies, having thus both the worst and the best, may fairly represent what was happening in so many places at once during the first decade of the war for eradication.[5]

Under the experienced leadership of the Malaria Institute of India— founded, it will be recalled, in 1911—that country had experimented extensively with pyrethrum sprays before the war, and with DDT as soon as it became available at the end of 1944.[6] In 1946 the largest control project ever attempted in the rural tropics got under way in the country around Bombay primarily to find out how best to organize a DDT campaign.[7] The government of Bombay state supported the project; the central government took notice, in this the last year of the British Raj, and Mahatma Gandhi found it important enough, amid the final struggles for independence and the agonies of Muslim separatism, to send his blessing. That was important. There were then, and still are, religious purists (as in the Jain sect) who take the proscriptions of *ahimsa* against harming their fellow creatures quite literally and will not kill a mosquito. On this occasion of the trial that would launch India's all-out assault on anophelines with DDT, the doctor who was to become the new nation's minister of health asked Gandhi how he could reconcile his blessing of the enterprise with *ahimsa*. Gandhi turned to Dr. D. K. Viswanathan, the malariologist in charge of the trials. Spraying a house with DDT, Dr. Viswanathan replied, was like putting barbed wire around it. He would not be forcing DDT on the mosquito; if she chose to break into his home to drink his blood and died in the course of her trespass, that was her doing, not his. Gandhi laughed.[8]

The experiments that thus began in Bombay state in the national spotlight continued successfully for ten years and thereafter became the basis for the first tests in India of transition from attack to surveillance.

For pyrethrum spray that had to be applied two or three times a week a purely local organization was needed. The spraymen worked part time and seasonally in the villages where they lived. With DDT that was inefficient; it seemed better to organize mobile teams of full-time workers, each of which would deal with a group of villages. The resultant area service, neat, efficient and centrally controlled, pleased Dr. Viswanathan who envisaged that it might become a permanent fixture in rural India, providing continuing freedom from malaria to each householder perhaps eventually at a small fee that could reimburse the state's costs.[9]

The model attack unit devised in the Bombay experiments consisted of several teams of twenty-two workers with nine stirrup pumps, two men to a pump. For every six men (three pumps) there was one supervisor. A fourth supervisor had charge of mixing and dispensing the pesticide. Finally the whole unit was under the command of a malaria inspector.

In practice during the campaign, in India as elsewhere, these numbers varied considerably. A knapsack sprayer for instance could be operated by one man. Unit size had to be adjusted to terrain and available transport. In India where settlement was dense most of the teams walked. Elsewhere the campaigns depended heavily on trucks that were chronically inadequate and unreliable. What was constant and essential to all organization was a military ordering of responsibilities, which aggregated individuals in basic fighting squads and then pyramided groups of squads, groups of groups and so on. On the firing line, the spraymen needed minimal skills and training. At each higher echelon the talents and knowledge required for command and inspection became increasingly demanding and correspondingly difficult to find. In India the top operational commands were the state governments, the head man normally the minister of health. New Delhi provided financial aid and technical supervision. Almost everywhere else the control and eradication campaigns were national.

By the 1951 census India's population just exceeded 360 million. Each year about 75 million were sick with malaria and about 800,000 died. Virtually the entire 360 million were at risk. Among the 44 species of anophelines in the subcontinent, six were (and are) important vectors of malaria and one or more flourished everywhere except in the high mountains.

The spray attack on them with DDT built slowly beginning in 1953 and concentrated at first in the endemic and hyperendemic areas. According to plan one attack unit (numbering from 130 to 275 men, depending on where they worked) was to protect one million people, and in 1953—when the objective was merely control, that is to say reduction, not eradication, of the disease—125 units were projected. In 1958 when India, with UNICEF and U.S. assistance, agreed with WHO to try for eradication, 160 such units were in operation; 230 more were to be added to cover the entire country. The units were subdivided into sub-units, sectors and sections. The section, or basic attack team manning the spray pumps, operated in a group of settlements containing on average 10,000 people. That meant about 2,000 houses to be sprayed once a season where malaria was seasonal, twice a year where transmission occurred the year round.

The campaign thus laid out was immense not only in overall scope but in the size of the smallest bite. Planners pressed their demands for performance at all levels to the very limits of feasibility. And then they set the tightest possible deadline. Assuming immediate success in ending transmission, attack was to continue just three years. By 1960–61, 365 of the 390 units were to be organized for surveillance, prepared to stop spraying and pass into the consolidation phase.[10]

As in any organized effort everything depended on the command structure and its articulation through the hierarchy of supervisors and inspectors. It was just there, in India and most other nations, that reality most seriously cheated expectations. In the first place it was not always technically possible for inspectors to be sure the spray teams had adequately and completely covered the buildings for which they were responsible.* Experimentally one could put up test papers that might be useful for training, to see whether the DDT in fact reached all the surfaces it ought to, and in

---

* The prescribed spray procedure in normal circumstances was as follows: A compression sprayer filled with 5 percent suspension of DDT wettable powder in water is pumped up to a pressure of 40 pounds to a square inch. The sprayman holds the nozzle of his spray about 18 inches from the wall and makes vertical sweeps at a rate of about 20 inches per second to leave the prescribed deposit of 2 grams of pure DDT on each square meter of sprayed surface.[11] Of course there is some margin for inconsequential error in this procedure but it is nevertheless a fairly demanding routine, especially for the half-trained and halfhearted soldiers who are common enough in any war.

quantities sufficient to do the job. In operations such checks were clearly impracticable. One depended necessarily on the conscientiousness of the men themselves maintained by appropriate morale and discipline.

When the game was new and both the spray teams and the householders were witnessing the miraculous disappearance of ancestral vermin, conscientiousness was a relatively common virtue. It became rarer as the job went on and on, as the vermin became resistant, as the workers tired of the routine and as villagers grew impatient with the everlasting inconvenience. At the same time, of course, malaria decreased and so the benefits appeared ever less worth the effort. At that point only the most vigorous kind of leadership could see the battle through. In fact such leadership was seldom to be had.

Making sure the job was properly done was hardly more interesting than doing it. Yet supervision and inspection were most exacting tasks, requiring intelligence, devotion, skill in handling people. From the very beginning it proved impossible to recruit the right kind of people in the right numbers and to hold on to them. The turnover in India was always immense and the shortages were chronic. Far too many of those who could be persuaded to take the jobs were not the kind of people who could accept or use authority. They were more likely to connive at neglect and even to falsify reports. Partly for this reason the state ministries of health retained in their own hands the exclusive right to hire, fire, assign and reassign field staff. But that made matters worse. It ensured that even those field subordinates who might have been able to exercise command were deprived of the power. Inspectors saddled with malingerers could not punish them or even get them transferred. An exceptional appeal to higher authority might go forward, but in the knowledge that the ministry was unlikely to act if the offender or his friends and family had any political influence.[12]

At various times, especially when things were obviously not going well, national leaders or specially invited missions from WHO and USAID made spot checks of efficiency. One of these in 1970 reported that of 96 spray units then operating in an area containing more than 40 million people, only eleven could legitimately claim better than 90 percent coverage of the houses for which they were responsible.[13] The inspectors then submitted one village to detailed scrutiny. It contained 63 houses. Ten of these had been locked at the time of spraying and were passed by. To fifteen the spray teams had been refused admittance. In another twenty the householders would agree only to having the verandahs, cattle sheds and storerooms treated. One house was overlooked. Thus out of the 63, only seventeen had actually received the treatment required by them all.

A fault almost as serious as not spraying at all was to spray at the wrong time. In some areas temperatures, humidity and rainfall permitted mosquitoes to breed, and parasites to complete their cycles of development, only during certain months of the year. Elsewhere malaria was transmitted all year round but nevertheless peaked in certain months when mosquitoes were most abundant. To be effective, spraying throughout the country therefore had to be timed to put fresh DDT on the walls just before the mosquitoes emerged in critical numbers. It often was not.

In the Bombay test spray area a sharp epidemic broke out in 1958, after six years of spraying had reduced all the malaria indices to almost zero. Here malaria is transmitted during the monsoon, roughly June to November, and the plan was to spray twice during that season with an interval of from ten to twelve weeks between rounds. In fact, investigation revealed that the interval had never been less than twelve and in four out of the six years it had been more than twelve. The epidemic, remarkably, struck at the same time in all the affected villages, suggesting that carriers must have been distributed throughout. That could have happened, the investigators believed, if in the few extra weeks between rounds enough mosquitoes had regularly survived contact with the stale DDT to inject a few parasites annually into fresh hosts. The numbers might remain small enough to escape routine detection yet still assure a well-distributed reservoir of infection such as could feed an epidemic when, as in 1958, the *culicifacies* mosquitoes enjoyed a good breeding year and emerged in "enormous numbers."[14]

The 1970 inspection mission found that this sort of failure had become general where spray attacks still went on. Out of fifty-seven units then operating in areas of year-round transmission, thirty-one had not even scheduled enough rounds to cope with the annual surges of mosquito numbers. In four states where malaria was seasonal, delays of one sort or another had made almost all the spraying wholly unrelated to the seasons.

This of course was very late in the campaign when weariness had overtaken almost everyone. It is an indication of how great a discrepancy could exist between plan and performance without necessarily being reported, rather than a fair measure of the deficiencies that affected either the national control program from 1952 to 1958 or the national eradication program that followed. Nor would it be fair to put the whole blame on the sprayers for such perennial shortcomings as there were. They often faced a nearly impossible task. The monsoon period was likely to be the time to spray, yet the rains it brought could make many villages quite inaccessible, sometimes for weeks. Throughout the country peasants might leave their home villages to work on roads or other construction jobs and live in camps that could not be properly protected by DDT. An epidemic among such workers occurred in Gujarat state in 1960.[15] The Gujarat outbreak significantly took fire in a cattle-grazing area where the road laborers encamped. As herdsmen here and throughout India lived seminomadic lives, they spent many months in the open or in temporary shelters that would normally escape the attention of even the most assiduous spray teams. Malaria had remained endemic among them while the workers from settled villages that had been sprayed for eight years lost their immunity. They were the classic epidemic fodder.*

Finally in extenuation it should be noted that many of the teams had been given too big a job. Even before the eradication campaign began some malariologists thought the attack units, except in the most densely populated areas, would be hard put to cover a million people each. An average allotment of 800,000 people per unit might have been more realistic but that would have meant 100 more units than were actually formed. As the campaign stretched out far beyond its original deadline, the population of India continued to grow by something like 2 percent a year. (Ironically the success of the attacks on malaria was helping it to grow faster.) By 1970 India had well over 500 million people; the units then in operation had on average to cover 1.3 million apiece. No one ever supposed that was a reasonable work load.

The difficulties of the war and the mistakes in prosecuting it were so many and so apparently critical that those who reviewed them had in the end to conclude they proved too much. Despite them, the campaign had remarkable—indeed, for a time spectacular—success. In 1960 the senior American officer working with the Indians congratulated them for providing an "example to the world [that] should do much to further eradication of malaria beyond the boundaries of India."[16]

Each of the nations that were to attempt eradication—fifty-two in all—had a campaign completed or under way by 1960. In 1966, when WHO's expert committee at the special request of the World Health Assembly reviewed progress, the total war had thus been waged five to ten years.[17] There were some impressive overall results. Malaria had been eradicated in once endemic areas inhabited by more than 600 million people and re-

---

* Nomadism of one sort or another was to prove a major obstacle to eradication in most parts of the tropical world. Not only among the Bedouins of the Middle East that come so readily to mind, but also among the tribes of Iran (some two million of them) who move annually between summer and winter quarters, among the Amerindians of the Amazon, among the slash-and-burn agriculturists and illegal gem miners of Ceylon, among migrant workers, often crossing international borders (as between India and Nepal, or Bangladesh and Burma), as well as among the millions of so-called "tribals" within India itself. The nomads because of their mobility readily spread infection, and because of their usually primitive way of life can seldom be effectively protected by any currently feasible antimalarial methods.

duced to an occasional and minor disease for another 334 million. Ten of the fifty-two nations had achieved eradication;* eleven others had banished the disease from some part of their territory.

Among the latter, India and Sri Lanka were outstanding. India had brought the number of malaria cases down from the estimated 75 million in 1951 to about 50,000 in 1961. Sri Lanka, which launched its eradication program in 1959 after twelve years of control, reduced malaria from about three million cases after World War II to just 29 in 1964. Sri Lanka, jubilant, proclaimed that "this year (1964) marks the end of an era."[18] WHO, reviewing the world scene, hailed "an international achievement without parallel in the provision of public health service."†[19]

It was that. Yet it was a significantly smaller achievement than had been hoped. The grand statistics suggested a broadly sweeping victory which closer examination showed had not been won. Of the ten countries where eradication had been achieved, four were in Europe, the other six in the Americas—Chile and five Caribbean islands. As the experts noted, 638 million people still lived where malaria was actively transmitted and still constituted a major cause of sickness and death; 360 million were in Africa and half of these lived where no efforts were yet being made to fight the disease.‡ Despite some successes in experimental programs, victories in Mauritius and Réunion and progress in the south, nowhere in equatorial Africa were there indications that transmission might be stopped. In Asia, counterbalancing success in India, Pakistan had yet to launch any campaign at all in half the country.

But more damaging than any of the specific shortcomings was the fact that an all-out war of extermination had been in progress everywhere for at least five years, and in some places for ten, without yielding one sure victory in any major tropical area. The essence of eradication strategy had been speed in execution. Three to four years in attack ought to have been enough, and if resistance in the mosquitoes had developed at the threatened rate that might have been all the time there was. Now after ten years the strategists were talking not about final victory but about progress toward it taking place in some still indefinite future.

The original idea had been by massive and intensive spraying to end

---

* Not including Taiwan, which was also clear. See below, p. 255.

† Statistics of success are especially tricky. In 1969 the experts reckoned that of two billion people then living in areas formerly malarious, about half were in what could be called consolidation or maintenance areas—that is, no longer routinely exposed to infection. But by 1974 that number had slipped to 800,000,000. It is still slipping.

‡ For the 800 million people living in China, North Korea and North Vietnam, there was no information.

transmission simultaneously throughout areas large enough to hold thereafter, without DDT, against both lingering small foci within the region and incursions from outside. But in practice the massive nationwide campaign was but a statistical generality of many small battles, fought with uneven skills in conditions of disparate difficulty. As victory was not to be had all at once, and as everyone was in a hurry to cut off the spray and show results, the battles began to be called off one at a time—often in relatively small districts wholly surrounded by others where the fight went on. Many of these could not be held and the attack had to be resumed. Both India and Sri Lanka, models for the feasibility of eradication, slipped back a little between 1960 and 1965. It was not much. But in the circumstances even the slightest regression was ominous. The goal of eradication had to be postponed and, by definition, time was on the other side.

WHO was of course concerned but, it would appear, not gravely so. As in the 1950s the campaign leaders had been rushed into a program of eradication by fears of insect resistance, now ten years later they were beguiled into accepting more distant goals by seeing that their fears had been somewhat exaggerated.[20] To be sure, resistance had spread rapidly: From the five species of anophelines proved resistant in 1956, the number had risen to thirty-eight in 1968. But in many places the declining vulnerability was not yet sufficient to interfere with control. In India, for instance, *Anopheles culicifacies,* a major vector widespread in the country as a whole, was shown to be resistant but only in a few isolated localities—not enough to make any real difference. From Sri Lanka when spraying stopped in 1964, reports that *culicifacies* there remained wholly susceptible were encouraging. Most of the thirty-eight resistant species tolerated DDT or dieldrin but not both and so could be controlled by switching insecticides. WHO's pesticide experts concluded that around the Persian Gulf and in several countries in Central America "resistance challenges the outcome of the campaign," but that elsewhere it was still more of an inconvenience than a major obstacle.[21] So there was still time—time, the experts thought, "for a more thorough study and analysis" of the program the better to adapt it to the capacities of those countries still struggling.

In India the 50,000 malaria infections proved in 1961 had become 100,000 by 1965. That was not a great increase and might indeed be factitious since in the interim the detection system had become much more thorough. Similarly in Sri Lanka a few more cases turned up in 1965 than in 1964 but the reason was clearly that a few local foci of infection persisted, mostly in highly inaccessible parts of the island. There seemed no reason for alarm. To all intents and purposes, the major gains were being held and other countries were still moving ahead even if not on schedule.

27 / Relapse

In reckoning lives saved and illness remitted, WHO periodically hailed the eradication campaign as a remarkable achievement. At the same time it always insisted that the essential point of eradication was that, unlike control, it did not merely seek current improvements in health; it was to end malaria once and for all. It was an all-or-nothing effort. There could be no such thing as partial success; either malaria went or the campaign failed. In 1960 it was still possible to be optimistic although some close observers were not.[1] In the next few years the signs of failure could hardly be blinked. The edifice continued to rise and statistically approach completion but the ground under it was in fact softening and beginning to sink.

That ground was the surveillance system on which the strategists had counted to consolidate the spray-gun victories and establish a defense against any return of the fever. The system had been prepared in haste and never properly tested. Even its theoretical basis remained for some years unexamined.[2]

The starting point of malaria transmission is of course the reservoir of parasites in infected mosquitoes or—more often in practice—in human carriers. Whether and how far the disease spreads thereafter depends essentially on how many times on average a person is bitten by a potentially infective mosquito, and how long on average the mosquitoes survive. To interrupt transmission it is necessary only to reduce the biting rate or the life expectancy below some critical number which in any given situation can be mathematically calculated. It is not necessary anywhere to prevent all mosquito bites, much less to kill all vectors. It follows that the transmission of malaria can be stopped by an imperfect attack, one that by error or design permits significant numbers of dangerous mosquitoes to continue to feed. The margins for error are large enough, as we have seen, so that where people are reasonably intelligent and determined and the mosquito does not enjoy all the advantages of climate and terrain, man has a fair chance of success.

Quite different requirements are imposed by the system of surveillance devised to wrap up the victory. The transmission of malaria does *not* depend on *how many* parasites exist initially in a particular area. A single carrier may be enough to launch an epidemic, and was proved to have actually done so in 1956 at Palma de Montechiano in Sicily.[3] It can be shown mathematically that one carrier remaining infective to mosquitoes for eighty days could, in extreme but nevertheless realistic conditions, be the primary source of 5,000 new cases providing only that the vectors bit often enough and lived long enough.

It follows that in order to prevent the resumption of transmission after the battle a detection and patrol system must find and properly treat *every* carrier. It must do so within a few seasons of calling off the attack. For once the spraying stops, the mosquitoes begin rebuilding their population and returning to their human blood meals in numbers as before, assuming that no permanent changes in terrain, temperature or human customs have intervened. In short, the conditions that made malaria endemic in the first place are quickly restored. Thereafter slovenliness such as marked the attack but often did not frustrate it must almost necessarily be fatal. Yet there was every reason to expect not fewer but more errors in the consolidation phase than in the attack.

The job of the basic surveillance workers was even more tedious and repetitive than the job of the sprayman, and more exacting. As the system was set up, teams of field men were to patrol areas in which spray attack had been halted and were to call on every householder in the area once every two weeks during transmission seasons. Anyone reported to have had an attack of fever since the last visit was to be given a dose of antimalarial drugs and to have his or her finger pricked so that a sample of blood could be sent to district laboratories for microscopic examination. If parasites showed up the local inspector would be notified; he then had to find the infected person and get him to submit to a five-day, or preferably a fourteen-day, radical drug cure, capable of destroying all forms of the parasite in his body. If positive cases were found to cluster in a given locality, then spray teams might be recalled to put out the fire.

In addition to this so-called "active case detection," district hospitals, local public health dispensaries and private physicians were under instruction to take blood samples from all patients complaining of fever and also to administer the "presumptive" drug treatment. The doctors also were to give radical cures to patients whose blood was subsequently found positive.

When surveillance began in India, workers were paid (with allowances) three rupees a day (about forty cents), a little more than spraymen got but still a wage for unskilled or semiskilled labor.[4] Although it is not difficult to prepare a blood slide, an indifferent worker in the field could spoil many; although it is proverbially trivial to have one's finger pricked, it is yet unpleasant enough to tempt many persons to avoid it by concealing a history of fever. The teams had a large number of houses to cover every two weeks, some perhaps more than they could handle at best. Quotas appear to have been set as a result of experiments in 1956[5] but as population swelled during the twenty years that followed, the workload for some teams may have increased by half.

Randomly to miss a few houses on the fortnightly rounds was not likely to be serious; but there was evidence in India, for instance, that some teams routinely avoided remote villages and concealed their delinquency by taking an excess of blood samples from families more easily reached. "Passive case detection" in the hands of nurses and doctors was not always more reliable. Many doctors considered the whole routine operation rather beneath their notice, and malaria itself a relatively minor and uninteresting affliction.

In the spring of 1976 a state malaria inspector in Andhra Pradesh in India dropped in unannounced at a rural hospital, well equipped and in charge of two well-trained young doctors. The hospital in the previous month had sent in considerably fewer blood slides than expected, and the inspector asked why. The doctors first answered that they must not have had the normal number of fever cases. But in the end they admitted that during this month the hospital had run out of microscope slides because a technician had forgotten to reorder them. What struck the visitor as probably symptomatic of similar failures elsewhere was not so much the technician's forgetfulness as the doctors' unconcern.[6]

Even when field workers collected far fewer blood slides than they ought to have done, the slides nevertheless poured into district and state laboratories often in quite unmanageable profusion. There, semiskilled technicians sat hour after hour, day after day, hunched over microscopes scanning each stained slide for the telltale outlines of parasites. They made one think of Dickensian clerks perched on high stools and bent over their ledgers in unescapable drudgery. Each microscopist was supposed to spend about five minutes on each slide and to get through fifty a day. One out of every ten slides would be randomly selected to be checked at central laboratories.[7]

As usual, the system was designed to press against the limits of human capacity because no one wanted to put more money or manpower into it than was absolutely necessary. Thus when workers were sick or quit and could not be replaced, the work inevitably piled up. It was not unusual for local laboratories in India to have a two or three months' backlog of unexamined slides. That meant that carriers who ought to have been identified at once and given radical drug cures were left at large for weeks, to infect mosquitoes and pass along their parasites. Even at its minimum the delay between the taking of a blood sample and the report back to the field could tear serious holes in the surveillance. By the time a reasonably prompt report came back (say in a couple of weeks) that a certain individual was infected, he might have left his village or because of false or ambiguous identification at the local clinic have become untraceable.

The only hope that a detection service so laxly operated might escape disaster lay in assuring that it was not too severely tested. Ideally attack was to be continued until no malaria parasites could be found among the residents of a large area so bounded by mountains or the sea as to make regular or casual reintroductions from the outside unlikely. Within such malaria-free consolidation zones, a few small foci of persistent transmission might be tolerated—as for instance encampments where workers slept out of doors—provided that they were isolated and small and discrete enough to be quarantined while attack within them continued. In such conditions surveillance would be required only to pick up the occasional relapsed case and the migrant carrier who now and then might slip through the natural mountain or ocean barriers. But these conditions in fact rarely existed. A retreat from the ideal occurred first in translating theoretical requirements into practicable criteria and then once again in applying these.

To justify calling off the attack and depending on surveillance, the first criterion was proof that malaria was no longer being transmitted. The proof consisted in finding, by interview and blood examinations, that no parasites at all had made their way into the blood of infants under one year old and that no adults had been recently infected on their home ground. In addition the total number of carriers, including persistent old infections and immigrants, should not exceed one in 10,000,* as ascertained by examining the blood of from 5 to 10 percent of the whole population

---

* This was the 1963 criterion, tightened from the five in 10,000 minimum set in 1960.[8]

depending on whether malaria transmission was seasonal or perennial.

That is where the whole system began to spring leaks. WHO time and again warned that surveillance, unlike malaria surveys, could not depend on sampling systems. Indeed to be quite certain that no more than one person in every ten thousand carried parasites, one would have had to examine everyone's blood. That being obviously impossible the next best thing was to examine the blood of all who were suspect because of recent fever. Hence the case detection system. A difficulty never overcome was that there was no good way of testing the effectiveness (or honesty) of case detection. Even when there was no intent to deceive, it was all too easy to seem to meet the criteria statistically by a blood sampling system that left at large a dangerous number of carriers.[9]

The ideal of continuing attack until extensive areas enclosed by natural barriers to transmission were cleared was still more difficult to translate into politically practicable criteria. No error was more egregious in practice than the premature establishment of islands of surveillance surrounded by areas under attack, or conversely the tolerance within large consolidation areas of considerable enclaves without natural boundaries where transmission persisted. The error came in part from the genuine difficulty of deciding just how large a defensible consolidation zone had to be, but in greater part from the manifold political and economic pressures to get off the DDT wherever it seemed even marginally possible. The result was a gerrymandered patchwork of defense zones whose frontiers were certain to be regularly and even massively reinvaded.

Endemic malaria returned to India rather like the turnaround of a tide, slowly at first and then with a broad sweep. From 1961 through 1963 there were less than 100,000 cases in the entire country. In the next three years the number moved from 100,000 to 150,000. In 1967 and 1968 it reached 275,000 and in 1969, 350,000. Then the barriers gave way. Cases doubled in 1970 and doubled again in 1971. At that point about a quarter of the units resumed attack and for the next three years the spread was checked but not rolled back. In 1975 the cost of DDT, a petroleum product, soared in response to the steep increase in oil prices. Malathion, which had to be substituted for DDT where *Anopheles culicifacies* had developed resistance, was still more expensive. India ran short. Almost two and a half million cases were recorded in 1974, and the next year that number once more than doubled.* In 1977 according to some estimates the number of

---

* These are figures for the number of positive blood slides found—i.e., of proved cases of malarial infection. The actual number of infections is undoubtedly much higher.

cases reached at least 30 million and perhaps 50 million. The proportion of potentially lethal *falciparum* infections inexorably mounts as *Plasmodium*'s reconquest of India tragically goes on.[10]

Perhaps even more bitterly disappointing was the reverse that took place in Sri Lanka. Statistically at least, Sri Lanka had appeared on the point of abolishing malaria as early as 1954. But instead of continuing the attack past the point of apparent victory to make it sure, the government yielded to the temptation to save money and progressively stopped spraying in district after district as soon as the criteria were minimally met.* When malaria resurged in 1956 following an abnormal drought, Sri Lanka resumed full attack. In 1957 the endemic dry zone was completely resprayed. The surveillance organization, the oldest and probably the best in Asia, was overhauled. A supplementary budget was approved and the United States offered vehicles and sprayers.[11]

In 1959 the new attack was formally reorganized to set eradication as its target. Within three years thereafter, as noted, Sri Lanka stood once more on the brink of total victory. Or so it seemed. The remaining few cases were in remote forest areas, often among people who lived in temporary camps or houses without walls. Intractable as these holdouts were, they did not appear to threaten the country.

Nevertheless on close examination ominous facts turned up. Among the handful of cases an extraordinarily high proportion were infections of *Plasmodium falciparum*. As *falciparum* infections do not relapse, all of these had to be newly contracted. The Sri Lankan malaria service had outdone itself in collecting blood slides annually—from 16 percent of the population instead of the recommended 10 percent. But a disproportionate number came from the least dangerous areas, where malaria had been moderate, as compared to those where it had been hyperendemic.† Moreover WHO consultants found large backlogs of unexamined slides. In one focus of infection to which several *falciparum* cases were traced, no blood slides at all had been taken by the two apothecaries responsible. A small matter perhaps but the man from WHO noted this "with a sense of uneasiness." The slow, steady rise in cases throughout the country by then (1965), he thought, "suggested that the situation had been smouldering for a longer time than originally realized."[12] Perhaps the most worrying fact in Sri Lanka was that it was proving impossible to seal off the remote foci of infection. After a 1966 outbreak of malaria in a village of 258 people,

---

* Ironically vigilance against recurrences actually cost Sri Lanka almost as much as spraying.

† The examination rate in some high-risk areas was as low as 3 percent.

investigators traced the source to a nearby contractor's camp. They then discovered that workers from that camp had dispersed to 58 other villages and among them eight had carried parasites.[13]

Despite these rumblings of trouble the epidemic that hit the island in 1968–69 was shocking, unexpected and deeply discouraging. The few score cases suddenly multiplied into more than half a million. In a single season parasites reestablished themselves almost throughout the areas from which they had been so expensively driven in the course of twenty years. Sri Lanka went back to the spray guns, reducing malaria once more to 150,000 cases in 1972; but there the attack stalled. *Anopheles culicifacies,* completely susceptible to DDT when the spray stopped in 1964, was now found resistant presumably because of the use of DDT for crop protection in the interim. Within a couple of years, so many *culicifacies* survived that despite the spraying malaria spread in 1975 to more than 400,000 people.[14]

India and Sri Lanka were models for the world: India for leadership and organization in huge compass; Sri Lanka for the most sophisticated vigilance system tied in with countrywide health services. It could be no surprise when other countries partly in consolidation began suffering similar relapses.

Throughout Southeast Asia setbacks have been so general and so serious that WHO officially reported in 1976: "The entire population living in the originally malarious areas is now at malaria risk."[15] Not a single region in a single country where the disease ever flourished can today claim that it has been banished.

In other continents some gains are still being held. The ten countries that WHO certified as having achieved eradication since 1956 have all maintained it. So has Taiwan, which won its battle in 1961 (victory certified in 1965) after a campaign notable for the political will and disciplined organization displayed, particularly in rooting out the enemy from its last strongholds.[16] In some places where the campaign continues it is still making progress, but the encouraging word appears now as the exception, not the rule.[17] In Latin America, Cuba achieved eradication in 1973. Most of Venezuela, most of Argentina, large parts of Brazil and Paraguay are malaria-free and so far holding against re-incursions. Brazil continues a campaign aimed at eventual eradication. Elsewhere the remaining centers of infection are yielding only very slowly or not at all, and fresh outbreaks have occurred. Worst is the situation in El Salvador and Guatemala, where cotton farmers have been drenching their fields with every known insecticide twenty or more times a season and have produced a malaria mosquito resistant to them all.

To the 19 million or so people living in the Middle Eastern countries of Iraq, Syria, Jordan and Lebanon, the eradication campaign had brought, in the opinion of WHO advisers, benefits unequaled by any other public health effort, including the opening up of fresh farmlands.[18] Some gains have been held but malaria, abetted by war, is back. About half of Iraq had been cleared by 1964; all has been re-invaded, in part owing to the war with the Kurds. A million people in Syria who had been protected are vulnerable again. Jordan, near victory in 1967 (only twenty-eight cases detected) slipped back in the war with Israel. Lebanon, which conquered malaria in 1969, held its ground until 1975. But now parasites must have come back in, perhaps with the Syrian army, and spread with the political disorganization. Malaria has also re-invested those parts of Turkey, Iran and Tunisia that had been cleared. The Turkish army carried parasites to Cyprus, one of the first countries to achieve eradication. So far they have been contained. Greece has been re-invaded.

Islands in the Pacific that were formerly malarious, such as New Guinea, still are. The Philippines, which had cleared large parts of the country, slipped back a little in 1975. Sub-Saharan Africa has on the whole scarcely been touched by the antimalaria war. No one now expects to uproot the disease in the foreseeable future, or even materially to reduce its incidence. The hope is only to trim deaths by more widely distributed cheap or free drugs and improvement of general health services.

It is not easy to analyze, much less sum up, worldwide the causes of failure. If the malfunctioning of the surveillance system has been the most pervasive and serious immediate weakness, the causes of that weakness have been many and diverse. Sri Lanka put dependence in the system too soon; Nepal to save money cut it down; India allowed it to be corroded by corruption and inefficiency; Tunisia got careless. In many countries—Iran is one—uncontrolled and often uncontrollable migration and nomadism across their borders has put impossible burdens on the watchmen.

Almost everywhere the economic strain has been highly unpopular. Eradication was sold very largely on grounds that it was a once-for-all effort: Spend now and save later. But vigilance in fact proved nearly as costly as war and much harder for its proponents to continue to justify politically. Critics of the Indian failure in 1972 found a key explanation in the dilemma of "near-success in an environment with an excess of problems clamoring for attention. As malaria recedes to a low level other pressing health and social problems exert irresistible demands for available resources."[19]

If there is a lesson in that, it is perhaps that tries for perfection must not go on too long. Is it only that people get bored? They do. But there is wisdom too in the natural impatience with prolonged blitzkrieg—a perception that because of the massive means it employs, the energies and concentration it demands, and the dependence it places on finding the enemy surprised and relatively defenseless, it must, as Hitler's war machine demonstrated, succeed quickly or not at all.

By 1969 governments whose "eradication" campaigns had become desperate attempts to defend against a resurgent enemy and international organizations who saw no end to the demands on their funds and only diminishing returns from them were both vociferously fed up. The World Health Assembly meeting that year in Boston demanded that the malaria eradicators change course. The formula was to ask for "a more flexible approach" to take account of local conditions, and especially the high cost and "laborious nature of operations" that acted as "restricting factors especially in developing countries."[20] In a word, the developing countries—or many of them—were war-weary. Though not ready to surrender, they wanted a slower pace and lower costs. Perhaps more than anything, though it was not then articulated, they wanted a fresh definition of attainable goals that could make whatever programs they adopted productive and defensible.

WHO gave way to the facts on the one hand and the national pressures on the other. But it was not easy either to abandon the old ways or to find new ones. Eradication had been a jealous idol. For fourteen years it had the exclusive devotion of malariologists in battle. To fight malaria meant to cover the walls of the malarious world with two grams of DDT per square meter, thereafter to collect and read blood slides and administer drugs in doses sufficient to wipe out residual parasites. Intelligence of the enemy was pretty much limited to checking on mosquito resistance. For fourteen years no one had seriously considered any other tactics and no one had been trained to consider any. WHO had pushed eradication with such zeal and held out for it such brilliant promise that its amour propre argued desperately against retreat.

So it gave way very slowly, with many a backward glance at what might have been and a particularly painful sense of failure. For four years the Malaria Eradication Division held on to its name* and to as much of the old strategy as it could. Eradication remained the ideal. Where it was judged impractical, countries might put it off indefinitely by reverting to measures of control. To accept control meant to accept malaria as a continuing incubus and aim only at mitigating the burden, reducing the inci-

---

* Changed in 1973 to Division of Malaria and Other Parasitic Diseases.

dence and the severity of the disease. Essentially the controllers would go on doing mostly the same things the eradicators had done, but under less pressure and with no time limit.[21]

Slowly, however, WHO began to resurrect older tactics that had been superseded by the miracle pesticides: drainage, fill and other kinds of environmental manipulation, larviciding, colonizing mosquito breeding places with predatory fish, domestic defense by house screens, personal defense by netting and repellents.[22] The whole rusty arsenal reappeared and some of the old weapons would actually be used, rededicated to fashion under the name of "integrated control." For environmentalists it was the dawn of a new wisdom; for the eradicators it was a humiliating retreat to the comparative helplessness of the past. In fact it was something less and more than either.

None of the tactics now available for malaria control is new nor is there anything new in the thought of combining various means in integrated programs for keeping the mosquitoes and parasites within tolerable bounds. But return to such tactics is not necessarily retreat. Whether eradication was a wrong-headed and disastrous mistake, as some WHO critics think,[23] or whether it was a bold, necessary and on the whole productive effort that might and ought to have succeeded, as most people in WHO still believe, it had one unqualifiedly negative result: It all but destroyed malariology. It turned a subtle and vital science dedicated to understanding and managing a complicated natural system—mosquitoes, malarial parasites and people—into a spraygun war.

With the failure of that war, the scientists and the managers now are free to come back and work out more realistic and promising ways of coping with *Anopheles* and *Plasmodium*. That will take time—the time needed perhaps to reorient and retrain a generation. Meanwhile in transition the malaria fighters face the psychological dilemma of all who would fight limited wars—a dilemma especially difficult for those who have just lost their bid for total victory. What worthwhile goals are possible short of victory? How can one define the limits of appropriate action and justify them by results? What fresh ideal can kindle at least such faith as induces the farmer season after season to renew his struggle with pests and weather?

If there are good answers, they are not yet in. At the moment WHO appears to be pushing primarily for better general health services and selling them as an important contribution to development. In most countries malaria control has already been partly or wholly integrated into the national public-health establishment. The same workers in the field now may take blood slides to be examined for plasmodia and advise mothers on the feeding of their children. The same doctors may direct antimalaria work as treat the sick in district hospitals. In the short run, the organizations to fight malaria, where they were strong, are bound to be weakened by dilution. Where they were weak—as for instance throughout sub-Saharan Africa—the new policy will help but only very slowly. Whatever can be done to reach out to rural populations with clinics and dispensaries will begin to lay down a base that might start a new war against malaria, or against any other disease. Further ahead the hope is that since health is a condition as indivisible in a community as in a person, all efforts to promote it will be mutually reinforcing. What is considerably more problematic is how effectively and how far the providing of health services improves health, especially in countries where bad health is more obviously a result of primitive living conditions than of lack of doctoring. At least it is a lot easier to relate killing mosquitoes to rolling back malaria.

As for tying public health efforts to development, WHO takes its stand on popular but treacherous ground. One reason eradication failed, the argument goes, is that governments were not convinced it was worthwhile and were unwilling to push it or pay for it. Malariologists neglected to bring out cost–benefit models to prove that it may pay more than it costs to keep people healthy.

Now it is notoriously difficult to put a value on human life, though many economists are perennially willing to try. But the exercise becomes superficially plausible if you assume that development is the social objective, axiomatically to be considered good, by which other values are tested. Then the worth of a man may be reckoned as what he contributes during a normal life span to the gross national product. If he dies prematurely the years of useful labor cut off are lost and constitute a social cost. If he is periodically ill or chronically debilitated, his actual productivity falls short by a measurable amount of his assumed potential. And that is economic loss. All these costs may be charged to malaria if malaria is the villain, along with the direct expenses of treatment, and weighed against the cost of eliminating the disease or reducing it by any given amount.[24]

If the model predicts that fighting disease pays, then the exercise can seem as harmless as it ought to seem superfluous. But suppose the fight is found not to pay. As the whole point of running a cost–benefit model is to sway governments presumed to be responsive to that kind of argument, would they not be under as strong pressure to forgo malaria control when the model lights turn red as to proceed when they are green?

Unpleasant as is that proffered choice, in the name of economic reason, to buy or not to buy lives, there is still a more unpleasant middle ground: To buy certain lives and sacrifice others. WHO has come perilously close to recommending that governments do just that. As a limited war against malaria by definition cannot extend to the protection of all people, a suggested strategy is to concentrate on protecting those people in society whose economic contributions are most important—workers in key industries, producers of cash crops, those who labor to build roads, dams and other capital improvements, in short all those who are useful for development.[25]

This implies a curious and dismaying reversal of values. It used to be argued that development was a good thing because it benefited people; now we seem on the point of agreeing that people are a good thing so far as they benefit development. No one appears to have blushed at the implication that human life was to be protected only as it contributed to the gross national product. No politician appears to have protested the cynicism thus imputed to political leadership. Everyone is busy being "realistic." If you want to do good in a world so obsessed with development that it allows only two kinds of nation, the developed and the developing, you have to prove that doing good is one way to develop.

Failure of the idea of mosquito eradication has in truth left a vacuum. Nations such as India, that came such a long way toward abolishing the ancient malarial scourge, do not want it back; their governments in fact have no real political choice but to continue the fight. (India in 1977 doubled its budget for antimalarial operations.) Yet the warriors remain dispirited, badly in need of fresh purpose.

It may be that the most damaging legacy of eradication has been the mental conditioning it fostered. The eradicators developed military minds: The game, they thought, must go to them or to us, win or be defeated. But there were skeptics of the eradication strategy all along who protested that this was not the real choice in the real world where man habitually copes with recurrent and perennial problems that he can never hope to resolve and put away forever. Protecting ourselves against the malarial plasmodium can be accepted as quite probably a task for all time without being daunted by the prospect.

Malaria fighters have been a mercurial lot, subject to intense enthusiasms and deep discouragements. Yet their own history should hearten them. Unless The End is finally here, current doldrums are also part of that history, they are therefore interlude not culmination.

Acknowledgments

For three years the Ford Foundation, for which I worked as Officer in Charge of the Resources and Environment program, gave me leisure to research and write this book. I am grateful to its president, McGeorge Bundy, for this extraordinary favor and only hope that I may have repaid it in small part. During most of those three years I was based in London as an academic visitor at the Imperial College of Science and Technology. For that appointment and the magnificent hospitality that accompanied it I have to thank Professor T. R. E. Southwood, head of Zoology and Biological Sciences. To work at the college, where I could talk to entomologists and parasitologists of the staff as well as to members of the Resources Management group based at Silwood Park under the direction of Dr. Gordon R. Conway, was of inestimable value. I was thus helped through often unfamiliar technical thickets and stimulated and encouraged as well. When research for the first part of the book (the Ronald Ross story) was finished, I was lucky to be offered five weeks at the Rockefeller Foundation's study center in Bellagio. They were extraordinarily productive as well as enjoyable writing days thanks in good part to the skillful management and hospitality of the director and his wife, Dr. and Mrs. William Olson.

The chief sources for this history have been manuscript collections, scientific papers and conversations with a number of doctors and others currently engaged in the fight. Most important among the manuscripts are the Ronald Ross Archives housed at the London School of Hygiene and

Tropical Medicine, the Rockefeller Foundation Archives at Pocantico Hills, New York, and the unpublished documents in the files of the World Health Organization in Geneva. I am particularly grateful to the librarian of the London School, Mr. V. J. Glanville, and his staff who gave me every possible help during the more than two years that I worked there. Miss Mary Gibson, who had just begun cataloging the Ross papers when I arrived, was particularly kind and helpful. Dr. William J. Hess made me welcome at Pocantico Hills and directed me to the very useful papers of Dr. Lewis Hackett, which are included in the Rockefeller Foundation collection. To Dr. Tibor Lepeš, director of the Division of Malaria and Other Parasitic Diseases of WHO, and his staff I owe an especially heavy debt: for opening the WHO and League of Nations document files to me, for discussing problems with me and recalling events and finally for reviewing the manuscript. My visits to WHO were made especially pleasant and productive by Dr. Joseph H. Pull, who introduced me to his colleagues and shepherded me through the collections. As no one at WHO, or anywhere else for that matter, made any attempt to influence my account or my interpretation of the facts they are obviously blameless for them.

The papers of Dr. William Welch at the Institute of the History of Medicine in Baltimore turned out to have only slight relevance for this task. Nevertheless I spent a couple of very profitable weeks rummaging through the stacks of the Welch Memorial Library, where Mrs. Janet Koudelka not only gave me every assistance but made me feel warmly welcome.

Also of minor utility but nevertheless of great interest were the notebooks of Dr. Alphonse Laveran, which le Médecin Général Fabre kindly allowed me to examine at the Musée du Val-de-Grâce in Paris.

Scientific papers are not exactly ephemera; someone somewhere usually manages to hold on to a copy of everything published, but tracking down journal articles on a single subject like malaria over a period of a hundred years can take one to scores of libraries. I had to content myself with only a few; besides the London School and the Welch Library, I used the collections of the British Museum, the Wellcome Institute and, through the courtesy of Professor P. C. C. Garnham, the Royal Society. In Rome Professor Augusto Corradetti made it possible for me to read in the incomparable collection of Italian journals in the library of the Istituto Superiore di Sanità.

Adequately to acknowledge the help from persons I have formally interviewed or informally consulted is more difficult. A list of names seems no warmer than a general expression of appreciation, which I hereby make to all who will know their contributions if they wish to own them. But an exception has to be made to name Professor P. C. C. Garnham and Dr. Paul F. Russell. Professor Garnham, I am happy to believe, became a friend in the course of advising me and disputing vexed points with me (sometimes successfully) during the three years of my study. He also kindly reviewed the manuscript in the end, corrected many of my scientific ineptitudes, straightened out some of my thinking and reaffirmed some of his disagreements. Dr. Russell, a leader in the Rockefeller Foundation's long fight against malaria, reviewed the manuscript, corrected many blunders and gave me new insights. I am very much beholden to them as I am to my friend Dr. Conway, a systems ecologist, who helped shape, though he may wish to disclaim it, much of the point of view expressed here.

Fully to document the narrative in graduate-school fashion and list the thousand or so sources used would set me a chore I'd rather skip, encumber the book with information few readers could possibly want and add dollars to the price that no sensible person would wish to pay. On the other hand there is particular reason, in a book that goes over much new ground and puts before general readers much information hitherto locked up in documents and specialist publications, to leave blazes along the path so that it may be picked up, backtracked or diverged from by others on a different journey. Accordingly I have tried a compromise. The list of references, reduced by more than four-fifths, provides guidance to frequently used and more durable sources (e.g., the classic papers in the field, along with a few obscure sources that deserve to be better known), and the chapter-by-chapter notes refer as seems necessary to the additional papers that have provided important but local clusters of facts or ideas. The notes are largely bibliographic but also contain supplementary technical information. Sidelights on the text of more general interest have been put into footnotes on the pages to which they refer.

Notes

Chapter 1
Caliban's Curse

Pages 1 through 6

1. Hippocrates studied in Egypt and there are papyrus manuscripts of about 1500 B.C. mentioning diseases that quite probably include malaria. Garnham (1966); Russell (1955).
2. Ronald Ross (1910, 314) wrote: "Sanitation is a form of war. It requires not only money and effort, but also thought, organization and discipline." Lewis Hackett, tongue in cheek, wrote to a friend in 1925 of skirmishing with mosquitoes in Italy: "A telegram would come to G.H.Q. 'Seven Anopheles discovered in Bacigalupi's barn' and then the reserves would be rushed to the spot: poisonous gases would be employed ruthlessly; wells would be poisoned, rivers mined, enemy babies slaughtered, whole battalions chloroformed in prison, homes destroyed, and neutral craft spurlos versunkt just like a real war. . . ." Letter to Florence M. Reed, 5 Aug. 1924, Rockefeller Archives.
3. See Chamberlain (1974), the excellent little book by that name.
4. Hayes (1941); Bismarck quotation on page 141.
5. *Ibid.*, preface.
6. Joseph C. Chamberlain, Colonial Secretary, is quoted in *The Times* of 11 May 1899 as hailing the work of doctors in lessening the unhealthiness of Asia and Africa, opening the latter continent to development. The conquest of malaria and other fevers, he said, would "make the tropics livable for white men." Malaria, according to two Italian doctors, Klebs and Crudeli, (1879), was the principal obstacle to the exploration and colonization of Africa. Robert Koch (1912, 327) wrote in 1898: "We will not be happy

in our colonial possession until we succeed in becoming master of this disease [malaria]."

7. Act II, Scene 2.

8. Diomede Pantaleone ("Del miasma vegetale e della malattie miasmatiche," *Sper. Gior. Critico Med. Chir.* 26 [1870]: 454) wrote: "[N]on solo dunque gli animali inferiori ma le razze umane considerate come inferiori non vanno soggette all' infezione miasmatica ed alle febri che ne risultano." Nuttall (1900) blamed "offensive odours." It was Laveran (1898) who remarked on the coincidence of thick skin and immunity. A lecturer at University College in Ibadan, S. D. Onabamiro, is reported by Russell (1955) to have welcomed the Black alliance with the mosquito: "Let us give thanks therefore to that little insect, the mosquito, which has saved the land of our fathers for us . . . The least we can do is engrave its picture on our National Flag."

9. Gorgas (1915), 290.

Chapter 2
Laveran's Germ

Pages 7 through 16

1. The only biography of Laveran is a short, uncritical memorial: Marie Phisalix, *Alphonse Laveran; sa vie, son oeuvre* (Paris, Masson, 1923). Ronald Ross summed up Laveran's career in an obituary notice in *Proc. Roy. Soc.* vol. B94 (1923).

2. His 1873 notebook contains 27 pages of notes on the work of Léon Colin (1870).

3. An early and detailed account of the pioneers in malaria research is found in Thayer and Hewetson (1895). Details are given also in Scott (1939).

4. Kelsch (1875). Kelsch's other writings on malaria are to be found in *Arch. Physiol.* 3 (1876): 490–550; 5 (1878): 571–611; 9 (1882): 278–324, 458–498 (the last three in collaboration with P. L. Keiner) and *Arch. Gen. Med.* VII ser. 5 (1880): 385–413.

5. A medical colleague (le Docteur Simonin) wrote (*La Presse Med.* (15 Feb. 1911, 129–134), "C'est dans la pratique des autopsies qu'il se révéla, dès l'abord, un maître que peu de cliniciens ont pu dépasser; il était littéralement séduit par l'idée d'arriver à l'aide de constatations matérielles à l'enchainement logique des symptômes ou des lésions observés chez la malade."

6. Kelsch's near miss was early recognized. He is credited with having "already seen in part" the flagellate forms of *Plasmodium* by A. Celli and G. Guarnieri, "Sulla etiologia dell' infezione malarica," *Arch. Sci. Med.* 13 (1889): 307–336.

7. In a communication to l'Académie des Sciences, 24 Oct. 1881, Laveran wrote: "Ces éléments [the spheroid bodies] n'ont pas de noyau et se colorent très difficilement par le carmin, ce qui permet de les distinguer des leucocytes mélanifères avec lesquels ils ont été confondus jusqu'ici." Reproduced in Edmond and Etienne Sergent and L. Parrot, *La découverte de Laveran* (Paris, Masson, 1929).

8. Quotes from Laveran (1881). His first communication is the briefest of

notes in Nov. 1880 *Bull. Acad. Med.* 44 (1880): 1268. A second note was reported to the academy the next month by Léon Colin (*Ibid.* 1346). The 1881 book is the first extended report. It was followed by books in 1884 and 1898. Other reports are A. Laveran, "De la nature parasitaire de l'impaludisme," *Bulls. & Mems. Soc. Med. Hopitaux Paris* 19, 2d ser. (1882): 168–176; and "Des hématozoaires du paludisme," *Ann. Inst. Pasteur* (1887), 266–288.

9. Laveran (1881), 83.
10. Osler (1887), 558. *The Lancet,* which with the *British Medical Journal* kept British doctors professionally informed, reported Laveran's discovery just a year late (12 Nov. 1881, 840–841), noting that Laveran himself had in the past year verified his first report by finding the parasite in 180 out of 192 malaria patients whose blood he had examined. *The Lancet* made no comment here or anywhere else.
11. Medical histories referred to and relevant include Bulloch (1938), Foster (1965), Newman (1932), Scott (1939) and Shryock (1936). Koch's unorthodoxy was commented on by two of the foremost American researchers who felt that their colleagues in general were too conservative. W. T. Councilman and A. C. Abbott, "A contribution to the pathology of malarial fever," *Am. J. Med. Sci.* 89 (1885): 416–429.
12. In 1883 (that is, a year after Laveran's visit) the two Italians (Marchiafava and Celli, 1883) wrote about the "corpicciuoli" in the blood and noted that the hypothesis that they were microorganisms that invaded the red corpuscles "could not be more seductive" but that, they concluded, was no reason for considering it true. Even after the publication of Laveran's book in 1884 they continued to resist the hypothesis. Among Laveran's papers at the Musée de Val de Grâce (Correspondances Diverses, C 156/1) are two letters from Marchiafava, one in Italian, undated, the other in French and dated 9 April 1884. Both dispute the parasitic nature of Laveran's bodies. In the historical account of Marchiafava and Bignami (1892) purporting to detail the steps to discovery there is no mention of Laveran's visit. Laveran (1887) had written: "It is notable that M. Marchiafava does not speak anywhere of the observations we made together at the hospital of San Spirito."
13. Marchiafava and Celli (1886). This is projected as the second of four papers. The first (Marchiafava and Celli, 1883) preceded discovery of the parasite; the third is "Studi ulteriori sulla infezione malarica," *Arch. Sci. Med.* 10 (1886): 185–211; and the fourth is "Sulla infezione malarica," *Ibid.* 12 (1888): 153–189.
14. Golgi (1886) is the first of his publications on malaria. Five more papers were published, 1888 through 1893. All are collected in Aldo Perroncito (1934).
15. Vasily Danilevskii (1852–1939) was professor of physiology at the University of Kharkov. He was unaware of Laveran's work when he found the parasites. When he read Laveran's papers he thought the parasites so similar that they must be identical. His first papers were observations of the blood of lizards, tortoises, frogs and birds. "Matériaux pour servir à la parasitologie du sang," *Arch. Slaves Biol.* 1 (1886): 364–96, 715; 3 (1887): 33–49, 157–176. His conviction that all constituted a single species is

stated in "Sur les microbes de l'infection malarique aiguë et chronique chez les oiseaux et chez l'homme," *Ann. Inst. Pasteur* 4 (1890): 753–759. Osler's summing up is in "On the value of Laveran's organisms in the diagnosis of malaria," *Johns Hopkins Hosp. Bull.* 1 (1889): 11.
16. B. Grassi, "Significato patologico dei protozoi parassiti dell' uomo," *Atti Accad. Lincei* 4 (1888): 83–89.

Chapter 3
Ronald Ross, the Unlikely Hero

Pages 17 through 22
1. Ross (1923).
2. *Ibid.*, 506. A friend of Ross published a biography half of whose pages were devoted to Ross's literary work. R. L. Megroz, *Ronald Ross, discoverer and creator* (London, Allen and Unwin, 1931).
3. Crawford (1914).
4. Rogers (1950), 19.
5. Brand (1965), 79.
6. Patrick Hehir, an officer in the Indian Medical Service, had begun examining malarial blood for Laveran's parasite in 1887, found it and reported periodically thereafter in two local journals, the *Indian Med. Gaz.* (e.g., July 1891, 212) and *The Indian Med. Rec.* (e.g., April 1893, 207–213).
7. Ross published four papers to expose the Laveranian delusion: *Indian Med. Rec.* 4 (1893): 213–215, 310–311; *Indian Med. Gaz.* 28 (1893): 329–336; 29 (1894): 441–443.
8. G. M. Giles, "Recent German researches on malaria: its treatment by methylene blue," *Indian Med. Gaz.* (1892), 326–330. Even the more bookish found the intellectual isolation of colonial India hard to escape. Surgeon Major Giles in 1892 wrote that up to that time he supposed that Laveran's parasite had joined all the earlier microbes of malaria in the discard. "I was astonished when, recently, chance brought to my notice what a mass of literature accumulated in favour of this view."
9. Manson to Ross, 9 April 1894. Ross Archives. See Chapter 5, note 8.
10. "Going to England," Ross wrote later, "I submitted my precious articles, together with a number of photomicrographs which had cost me about a year's labour to Dr. Patrick Manson. He said the kindest things possible about my work, but—showed me the malarial crescent . . . I had never seen such a thing before . . . and I recognised that many months of my life had been wasted in a foolish and immature attempt to disprove what better men had proved." "Surgn.–Lieut. Col. Lawrie and the parasite of malaria," *Indian Med. Gaz.* 3 (1896): 353–356.

Chapter 4
The Mosquito Theory

Pages 23 through 34
1. L. J. M. Columella, *On agriculture,* tr. by Harrison Boyd Ash (Cambridge, Harvard Press, 1941), vol. I, ch. 5.
2. John Spear, "A filth-polluted soil," *The Lancet* (1878): 540. "That malaria

resides in the soil may be taken as an axiom," wrote Dr. J. R. Roberts (*Indian Med. Gaz.* [1891]: 38). Sternberg (1884): 37 proclaimed: "The evidence connecting the production of malaria [the poison, not the disease] with the presence of organic matter in the soil is overwhelming and conclusive."

3. Lloyd Storr-Best, tr., *Varro on farming: M. Terenti Varronis, Rerum rusticarum, libri tres* (London, G. Bell, 1912), bk. I, ch. 12.

4. Thayer (1899), 5. Lancisi's principal book is *De noxiis paludum effluviis* (1695).

5. Monti (1928): quotations from pp. 121, 126.

6. Saul Jarcho, "A cartographic and literary study of the word 'malaria,'" *J. Hist. Med.* 25 (1970): 37–39. Sternberg (1884) defined malaria as "an unknown poison of telluric origin," and noted that chemical analysis had been unable to find any constituent gas in marsh air that had toxic properties anything like malaria.

7. Colin (1870), 14–15. On similar grounds T. J. Maclagan ("On the anti-malarial action of the chinchona compounds," *The Lancet* 2 [1880]: 166) found the autumnal development of malaria "associated with the autumnal cessation of vegetable growth."

8. *The Lancet* (15 April 1876), 585.

9. During the next four years 20 in the monastery died. In 1880 it was converted into a prison. But five years later even that had to be abandoned. In 1902 a few people settled in the area and managed to stay well by screening their houses and taking quinine. Hackett diary (4 May 1924).

10. A. Celli, "Acqua potabile e malaria," *Gior. Soc. Ital. Ig. Milano,* 8 (1886): 226–233.

11. Roberts (1891), 380. See note 2 above.

12. Welch (1920), vol. I, 570–571.

13. E. Marchiafava and A. Bignami, *"La infezione malarica: manuale per medici e studenti* (Milano, Francesco Vallardi, 1902), 78.

14. Brockington (1966); Shryock (1936).

15. E.g., Laveran (1884), 8, comments that malaria likes uncultivated fields, scarcely peopled lands and lands devastated by war but "recoils almost always before man and before civilization."

16. Varro recommended screening to keep out maleficent animals. Cited in Edmond Sergent, *La Lutte contre les moustiques* (Paris, J. Rueff, 1903), 9. Ross (1910), 257, wrote: "[W]hen I went to India in 1881, it was a common saying amongst sportsmen, planters and many residents in that country, that the way to keep off malaria was to use the net under all circumstances." General Gordon always slept under a mosquito net in Africa, both to keep out insects and to filter out malarial poisons. "A note on mosquito nets and malaria," *J. Trop. Med.* 2 (1900): 249–250. One observer interpreted the coincidence of mosquitoes and fevers in reverse. "It is my firm conviction," Dr. Samuel W. Francis wrote in 1874, "that the mosquito was created for the purpose of driving man from malarial districts; for I do not believe that in nature any region where a chill and fever prevail can be free from this little animal." Quoted in Howard, Dyar and Knab (1912), 188.

17. Howard, Dyar and Knab (1912). Koch's comments are in *Deutsche*

Kolonialblatt 9 (1898): 234. Koch mistakenly believed that the words for "mosquito" and "illness" were the same in Swahili. See Garnham (1966), 9.

18. Brumpt (1949), 480.
19. Peller (1959).
20. Sanabria (1968); Peller (1959); Russell (1955).
21. Monti (1928), 128.
22. Janssens (1974). Albert Freeman Africanus King, an Englishman resident in Washington, proposed in 1882 that the remarkable links between mosquitoes and malaria, which he systematically listed, warranted experimentation to test a possible causal relationship. No one took him up. King, incidentally, was the physician who attended Abraham Lincoln at Ford's Theater and helped carry the wounded President across the street to the house where he died. Foster (1965); Howard, Dyar and Knab (1912); Russell (1955).
23. Shryock (1936), 265–266.
24. Quoted in Newman (1932), 207.
25. Ross (1930) says he had this story from Dr. H. G. Plimmer himself but that Manson always implied he had found the parasites unaided.
26. Manson (1894).

Chapter 5
Follow the Flagellum

Pages 35 through 46

1. Issue of December 1894, vol. 29, 441–443. Two years later he would more candidly confess error. (See Chapter 3, note 10.) But that was an occasion when he was attacking another who persisted in ignorance; in the context the assumption of modesty became a weapon in the attack.
2. The notebooks are in the Ross Archives.
3. Ross (1923), 135.
4. Manson (1896) said that he and Ross "fixed on a certain line of experiment and observation which my experience in former years in filaria work seemed to indicate as being likely to lead to some definite result one way or another." The first step was to find out whether the crescent forms inside the mosquitoes were (1) destroyed, (2) flagellated in the same proportions as on microscope slides or (3) flagellated in greater numbers.
5. Published by the Sydenham Society in July 1894. Cushing (1926), vol. I, 399.
6. E. Ficalbi, *Revisione systematica d. Fam. delle Culicidae Europea* (Florence, 1896).
7. Ross (1923), 136.
8. In this and all subsequent chapters dealing with Ross's discovery all quotations, unless otherwise attributed, are from the Ross and Manson letters in the Ross Archives. Many of these have been printed in whole or in part in Ross (1923) and in Manson–Bahr (1927). Quotations here are all drawn from the manuscript letters. Ross frequently used ampersands, but so erratically that I have converted them all to "and" to save editorial confusion.
9. His conclusion is from his draft report to the residency surgeon, 1 Nov. 1895. Ross Archives.

10. A similar account, with some minor discrepancies, was published in the *Indian Med. Gaz.* (March 1896), 109–113, and in *The Indian Lancet* (March 1896), 227–230, 259–262.

11. Laveran, 24 Oct. 1881, cited in Sergent, Sergent and Parrot (1929), wrote: "La nature animée des corps sphériques renfermant des grains pigmentées mobiles et munis de filaments periphériques mobiles est indiscutable. Je suppose qu'il s'agit d'un animalcule qui vit d'abord a l'état parfait, devient libre sous forme de filaments mobiles."

12. Ross in the paper cited in note 10 above wrote: "The flagella are, in fact, next door to being invisible; and we are confronted with some such question as this—'Trace the movements and metamorphoses of that which *cannot be seen.*' Unless we call in the assistance of a theosophist or some such 'occult professor,' it is difficult to know how the problem is to be attacked."

13. The words from "movement" through "dying" are interpolated from the Notebook, vol. I, 40.

14. He saw a similar "attack" a few weeks later. Four flagella just escaped from a sphere poked at a "small lymphocyte which had fixed itself on a small air bubble." They kept at it for four minutes and then movement ceased. Ross called it "<u>a most remarkable</u> phenomenon." (Double underlining his; Notebook, vol. I, 103.)

Chapter 6
Diversions

Pages 47 through 55

1. Ross (1923), 134.

2. Manson to Ross, 21 Oct. 1895. Missing from Ross Archives, copy printed in *Indian Med. Gaz.* (March 1896), 113.

3. Ross (1923), 186. For a brilliant discussion of Victorian attitudes and concepts see Houghton (1957); also Young (1953).

Chapter 7
The Bite

Pages 56 through 63

1. The paper referred to is Robert J. Marshall, "The malaria parasite," *The Lancet* (24 Oct. 1896), 1187.

2. Ronald Ross, "Observations on a condition necessary to the transformation of the malaria crescent," *Brit. Med. J.* (30 Jan. 1897): 251–255. Manson in the same issue commended the paper as elegantly demonstrating the evolutionary nature of crescent transformation, though he did not think Ross had proved that increased blood density was the trigger. "A neglected responsibility of empire," *Ibid.,* 289.

3. *The Lancet* (1896), 1363–1366, 1441–1444; translation by G. Sandison Block.

4. Bignami (1896). Bignami said later (1898) that he had attached great importance to the analogy between malaria and Texas fever in proposing his mosquito theory.

5. V. Babeš, "Sur l'hémoglobinurie bactèrienne du boeuf," *Comptes Rendus Acad. Sci.* 107 (1888) : 692–694.

6. See Chapter 4, note 16.

7. "Some experiments in the production of malarial fever by means of the mosquito," *Trans. South Indian Branch Brit. Med. Assoc.* 7 (1896) : 93–106.

8. See note 2 above.

Chapter 8
Dapple-wing

Pages 64 through 71

1. This and following details of the Sigur Ghat expedition are from Ross's notebook and his draft report on the investigation to the Director General, Indian Medical Services, 12 July 1897. Ross Archives.

2. Statement (1896–97).

Chapter 9
Mosquito Day

Pages 72 through 80

1. The saga of his trip into exile is related in his official letter to the adjutant of Meiwar Bhil Corps, 22 Oct. 1897. Ross Archives.

Chapter 10
The Flagellum Caught

Pages 81 through 86

1. The series of Grassi and Feletti papers begins with "Parassiti malarici negli uccelli," *Bull. Mens. Accad. Gioenia Sci. Nat. Catania* (March 1890), 3–6. Others in the same journal are in issues of April 1890, 2–7, 7–8, and Jan. 1891, 16–20. The final paper is "Contribuzione allo studio dei parassiti malarici," *Atti Accad. Gioenia Sci. Nat. Catania*, Memoria V, ser. 4 (1892). The work was taxonomically important. See Hewitt (1940). Several investigators used birds for experiments (all unsuccessful) in transmitting malaria by blood inoculation; e.g., A. Celli and F. Sanfelice, "Sui parassiti del globulo rosso nell' uomo e negli animali," *Ann. Ist. Ig. Sper. Roma* 1 (1891) : 33–63; Bignami and Dionisi as reported in Bignami (1898b) and di Mattei as reported in Thayer and Hewetson (1895).

2. Grassi and Feletti (1892) (see note to p. 83) flatly denied that mosquitoes bite birds, using that "fact" to discount Laveran's [sic] thesis of mosquito transmission.

3. Antonio Dionisi, "Sulla biologia dei parassiti malarici nell' ambiente," *Il Policlinico* 5 (1898) : 419–424.

4. Welch (1920) reviewed these theories (vol. I, 510–511).

5. P. L. Simond, "L'évolution des sporozoaires du genre *Coccidium*," *Ann. Inst. Pasteur* (1897), 545–581.

6. F. Schaudinn and M. Siedlecki, "Beitrage zur Kentnis der Coccidien," *Verhandl. d. Deutsche Zool. Gesellschaft* 1897; 192–204. C. M. Wenyon (1926) says that Schuberg in 1895 (no reference given) had suggested that the threads emerging from gametocytes of *Eimeria muris* were gam-

etes. Koch (1912) writing in 1899 nevertheless gave Simond credit for being the first to recognize flagella as spermatozoa.

7. W. T. Councilman, "Some further investigations on the malarial germ
of Laveran," *Maryland Med. J.* 18 (1887–8): 209–211.

8. Eugene L. Opie, "On the haemocytozoa of birds," *J. Exp. Med.* 3 (1898):
79–101. Thayer said (*Bull. Johns Hopkins Hosp.* VIII, March 1897) that
it was Laveran who "several years ago" had impressed upon him the
possibility of getting important research results from the study of haematozoa of animals, especially birds.

9. Details from MacCallum in a letter to Lewis Hackett, cited in Hackett
(1937), 162–163.

10. MacCallum (1897a).

11. *Address delivered at the anniversary meeting of the Royal Society on
Friday, November 30, 1900* (London, Harrison, 1900). Account of the
Toronto meeting in Cushing (1926), vol. I, 456–457.

Chapter 11
Pigeons and Sparrows

Pages 87 through 94

1. Manson had written Cleghorn on Ross's behalf and stimulated a distinguished IMS veteran to write also. Although Ross (letter to Manson,
1 Feb. 1898) thought Cleghorn acted before receiving those letters, the
general had had time to get them before issuing orders. Cleghorn told
Manson that he had recommended Ross's special assignment some time
earlier but that shortage of money and men had checked him. Manson to
Ross, 7 Feb. 1898. Ross Archives. Relevant passages from these letters are
not printed in Ross (1923).

2. The myth that Ross turned to birds because a plague scare (see page 92)
deprived him of human subjects has no basis in fact but has proved persistent. See, for instance, Janssens (1974).

3. Letter with illegible signature, 10 March 1898. Ross Archives.

4. Ross (1923), 278.

5. Notebook, vol. II, 46.

6. *Brit. Med. J.* (1898), 586.

7. Statement (1898–99), 27.

8. Cited in *Indian Med. Gaz.* 33 (1898): 230.

9. J. D. Curnow, manager, Marionbad Tea Estate, to Ross, 4 June 1898. Ross
Archives.

10. Ross to Manson, 30 May 1898. The sneer at "natives" is dropped without
ellipses from the transcription of the letter in Ross (1923), 284–286.

11. Ross (1923), 289–290.

Chapter 12
Ross's Cycle

Pages 95 through 101

1. Notebook, vol. II, 73.

2. At the time Ross was writing his *Memoirs* the first four pages of the letter

were mislaid. Ross (1923) accordingly reproduces only the last half. The whole letter has been printed in Russell (1955).

3. T. Edmonston Charles to Ross, 19 Nov. 1900, in *Letters from Rome on the new discoveries in malaria with introduction, notes and postscript by Ronald Ross* (Privately Printed, 1900). Copy in Ross Archives. This publication was part of Ross's squabble with Grassi over who did what first. See below, Chapter 13.

4. *J. Trop. Med.* 1 (1898): 20.

5. The oral and written versions are respectively Manson (1898b) and Manson (1898c).

6. Manson to Ross, 28 July 1898.

7. Printed in *Brit. Med. J.* (1898), 369. Also in Ross (1923), 306–307.

8. Ronald Ross, *Report on the nature of kala-azar* (Calcutta, Supt. Govt. Printing, 1899).

Chapter 13
The Roman Quarrel

Pages 102 through 108

1. Quotations from Ross correspondence with T. Edmonston Charles, in Ross Archives. And see Chapter 12, note 3. Ross thought finding the right species of mosquito might be a long job, especially so long as he believed (as he still did in 1898) that each species of parasite might have a different mosquito host. But demonstrating the mosquito cycle in human malaria, he thought, was merely a matter of repeating his procedures. He wrote Charles (29 Nov. 1898): *"The only difficulty is to find the suitable insect for each parasite. The rest is child's play."* Six years later it had, in his mind, all become easy. The door was unlocked with the finding of the pigmented cells in the dapple-wing mosquito, he told the Nobel prize audience (Ross 1904): "The great difficulty was really overcome [in 1897] and all the multitude of important results which have since been obtained [including his own work of 1898?] were obtained solely by the easy task of following this clue—a work for children." He had by then forgotten that in 1899 (Ross 1899a) he had welcomed the follow-up work of Grassi and company saying that any new observation in science has to be confirmed "by men of recognised scientific standing," not by children.

2. In the course of the quarrel both men lost all sense of proportion and much of their finer sensitivity to truth. Ross was particularly angered by what he thought was Grassi's fiddling with the evidence in two discrepant versions of the same paper. The first was published in *Il Policlinico* 5 (1898): 469–476, and dated 29 Sept. 1898; the second, in *Atti Accad. Lincei* 7 (1898): 163–172, was dated 2 Oct. 1898. The latter made two significant alterations in the *Policlinico* version, both of which tended to inflate Grassi's achievements and belittle Ross's. Ross saw that as a deliberate attempt to knock him off the hill and opened fire. Grassi later (Grassi [1898], 236) alleged that despite the dates (which appear on each of the articles) the version of later date was in fact written first. That would of course mean that his second thoughts were more charitable

or modest than his first. It is odd that he did not think it worthwhile to make that clear while the dates implied just the opposite.

3. Manson (1898b), (1898c).

4. Koch says he thought of the possibility of mosquito transmission in 1883 and 1884 when he was in India on a cholera investigation. He wrote nothing but told R. Pfeiffer, who recorded the suggestion in a note in his *Beiträge zur Protozoen Forschung* (Berlin, 1892). See Koch to Ross, 15 May 1901; Ross Archives.

5. Koch's African reports are: "Berichte über die Forschungsreise nach Deutsch-Ostafrika" (1898) and "Aerzliche Beobachtungen in den Tropen," a speech to the Deutsche Kolonial-Gesellschaft, 9 June 1898. Both appear in Koch (1912).

6. The newspapers consulted in regard to the visit of Koch are *Il Messagero, Il Nuovo Secolo, La Capitale Italiana, Il Populo Romano,* and *Don Chiosciotte di Roma.* Quotation is from *Il Nuovo Secolo,* 17–18 Aug. 1898.

7. Grassi (1900). A year later he referred to the same period as "a few months of holiday." *Il Policlinico,* Sez. Prat. 8 (1901–2) : 474.

8. Grassi (1899). Grassi also accused Koch of delivering an insulting farewell speech to reporters in which he made fun of Grassi and the *Anopheles* theory. I can find no trace of such parting words. *Il Messagero* (4 Oct. 1898) in a page-one story reported only factually on the visit, noting that Koch had ascertained that the Roman fever was identical with tropical malaria, and that he would return to Rome in the spring. In *Il Populo Romano* (3 Oct. 1898) a reporter from Berlin noted that the German newspapers had quoted Koch as having found in Italy not only "great courtesy and a true professional brotherhood but also very great, undoubted progress in every branch of science."

9. Grassi (1898a).

10. In *Il Policlinico,* cited in note above, Grassi wrote: "Il prof. Celli e i suoi amici mi assicuravano che Koch a Roma aveva risolto il punto fondamentale del problema, mentre essi no erano arrivati al alcun risultato! Di fronte a questo disastro scientifico, che ricadeva specialmento sulla scuola d'igiene di Roma, io rivelai cio che nessuno a Roma sapeva, che, cioè, in seguito ad estese ricerche ero venuto nella convinzione che l'anopheles claviger dovesse veramente propagare la malaria." Experiments to test the susceptibility of anopheline and culicine mosquitoes began in June 1899 and continued into August. In these, some anophelines proved positive; all culicines, negative. Grassi (1900).

11. T. Edmonston Charles wrote Ross, 25 Nov. 1898 (Ross Archives), to report that when he called on Grassi in his laboratory Grassi had before him a copy of the *British Medical Journal* containing Ross's 18 Dec. 1897 paper on dapple-wings and pigmented cells (Ross 1897), and that Grassi asserted that he had no doubt from Ross's descriptions that the dapple-wings were *Anopheles claviger.* Grassi in a letter to Charles, 13 Nov. 1902, denied he had seen the Ross paper. In "Per la storia delle recenti scoperte sulla malaria," *Policlinico* (1900), 593–600. Grassi says that Ross's identification of the mosquito by its spotted wings and single, black, boat-shaped eggs was insufficient to distinguish *Anopheles* from some other still undescribed species—which of course is true but irrelevant to the argument.

12. Bignami (1898a) concluded as follows: "Il risultato positivo constituisce, secondo me, *il fatto singulare,* che basta per se solo a dare una base secura all *teoria dell' inoculazione.*"
13. Grassi (1898a) and (1898b).
14. Grassi (1898a).
15. Grassi (1899a).
16. Grassi, Bignami and Bastianelli (1899).
17. In October 1899 they read a paper at the 10th Congress of the Società Italiana di Medicina Interna in which they said: "These researches of Ross, it is apparent to everyone, possess an extraordinary importance . . ." as demonstrating the forms of the parasite in the mosquito "for the first time" and in showing that development could take place in only one species. They concluded: "[N]o one can suspect our perception of the truth to have been obscured by certain recent polemics." Translation from *The Lancet* (13 Jan. 1900), 79.
18. The heart of the Ross–Grassi controversy was Grassi's claim to have worked independently of Ross, that is, to have made his own discoveries without prior knowledge of what Ross had done or what methods he had used. The hard historical evidence is all against that claim, including the plain fact that Grassi *began* his investigations only *after* Ross's results had already been published. In support of it there is only Grassi's assertion that inexplicably in the summer of 1898 he was still ignorant of readily available papers that a serious investigator should have read. Historians nevertheless have tended to accept the boast of independence at least in part. For example, the distinguished protozoologist C. M. Wenyon (1926, vol. II., 910) summed up the controversy thus: "Ross opened up an entirely new field . . . Grassi *may have been,* and probably was, *influenced and guided to some extent by what he had heard* of Ross's discoveries, but nevertheless he and his co-workers were the first to obtain the absolutely scientific proof of the specific relation of anopheline mosquitoes to human malaria . . ." The statement of what Grassi did is perfectly accurate but the words I have emphasized understate Grassi's intellectual debt almost as seriously as Grassi did himself.
19. G. Bastianelli and A. Bignami, "Intorno alla struttura delle forme semilunari e dei flagellati nei parassiti malarici," *Ann. Med. Nav.* (1898), 1202.
20. Antonio Dionisi, "I parassiti endoglobulari dei pipistrelli," *Atti Accad. Lincei* 7 (1898): 254–258, and "Un parassita del globulo rosso in una specie di pipistrello," *Ibid.,* 214–215, where he noted the remarkable similarity between the bat parasite and the plasmodium causing quartan fever.

Chapter 14
The Three Lives of Plasmodium

Pages 109 through 120
1. 2d ed. (1901) of Grassi (1900). See Augusto Corradetti, "L'opere protozoologica di Battista Grassi alla luce degli odierni sviluppi degli scienze," *Riv. Parassitol.* 15 (1954): 190–199.
2. See Bray (1953); Garnham (1966). As late as 1926 a malaria text re-

produced Schaudinn's drawings of a sporozoite entering a red cell (E. Marchoux, *Paludisme* [Paris, Baillière, 1926]), though with the notation: "Chose curieuse, pareille observation n'a jamais pu être faite avec des sporozoites extraits des glandes salivaires."

3. James (1931).

4. Raffaele (1934).

5. E. g., Clay G. Huff and William Bloom working in Chicago ("A malarial parasite infecting all blood and blood forming cells in birds," *J. Infect. Dis.* 57 [1935]: 315ff), Raffaele himself (1936), and perhaps most importantly James and Tate (1937) working with a malarial parasite of chickens, *Plasmodium gallinaceum,* only just discovered by Émile Brumpt. Besides Bray (1953) see Hewitt (1940), especially for early observations of tissue forms in birds by MacCallum and Laveran.

6. Bray (1953).

7. Garnham, P. C. C. "Exo-erythrocytic schizogony in *Plasmodium kochi* Laveran: a preliminary note," *Trans. R Soc. Trop. Med. Hyg.* 40 (1947), 719–722.

8. Details of Shortt's experiments are recalled in Shortt (1951), on which the following account is chiefly based.

9. Shortt (1951).

10. H. E. Shortt and P. C. C. Garnham, "Pre-erythrocytic stage in mammalian malaria parasites," *Nature* 161 (1948): 126.

11. Shortt and Garnham (1948).

12. Shortt (1951).

13. The range of these numbers is enormous. The sporozoite load of *Anopheles gambiae* and *A. funestus* in a part of Tanzania has been estimated to be anywhere from a few hundred to 70,000, with a mean of between 4,000 and 5,000 (Clyde, 1967). An observer in 1945 estimated the number of *P. vivax* sporozoites in the gland of *A. atroparvus* to be 135,000 (Brumpt, 1949). Electron microscope studies of sporozoites in a rodent plasmodium showed the process of exit single file. Charles P. Sterling, Masamichi Aikawa and Jerome P. Vanderberg, "The passage of *Plasmodium berghei* sporozoites through the salivary glands of *Anopheles stephensi,*" *J. Parasitol.* 59 (1973): 595–605.

14. W. Kikuth and L. Mudrow working from 1938 through 1942. See Bray (1953).

15. Shortt and Garnham (1948). F. M. Burnett in *The natural history of infectious diseases* (1953) wrote: "Infectious disease is no more and no less than part of that eternal struggle in which every living organism strives to convert all the available foodstuffs in its universe into living organisms of its own species." Quoted in Cameron (1956), 225.

16. Louis H. Miller, George W. Cooper, Shu Chien and Henry N. Freemount, "Surface charge in *Plasmodium knowlesi* and *P. coatneyi*-infected red cells of *Macaca mulatta,*" *Exp. Parasitol.* 32 (1972): 86–95; Louis H. Miller, James A. Dvorak, Tsugiye Shiroishi and John R. Durocher, "Influences of erythrocyte membrane components on malaria merozoite invasion," *J. Exp. Med.* 138 (1973): 1597–1601.

17. Miller, Cooper, Chien and Freemount (1972), cited above.

18. One million *P. falciparum* per cubic millimeter is said (Sandoshan, 1959)

to be "not uncommon" in Malaysia and patients so massively infected may recover. Brumpt (1949) reports one case in which 44.2 percent of the patient's red cells contained at least one parasite.

19. Garnham (1966).

20. P. G. Shute and M. Maryon, "A study of gametocytes in a West African strain of *Plasmodium falciparum,*" *Trans. Roy. Soc. Trop. Med. Hyg.* 44 (1951): 421–438.

21. The proportion of gametocytes decreases with gains in immunity (Clyde, 1967). A scarcity of gametocytes not only cuts down on the number of mosquitoes infected but reduces the intensity of infection in those that do pick up the parasite (MacDonald, 1973). Nevertheless an important fact of malaria epidemiology is that mosquitoes can be infected by game-tocytes occurring in such small numbers as to escape detection easily. Yekutiel (1960) reports mosquitoes infected by blood containing only one gametocyte to a cubic millimeter. But the normal infection threshold, depending on species of parasite and species of vector, appears to range from about ten to several hundred per cubic millimeter. A rundown of various experiments on infection thresholds is M. Ciuca, G. Lupasco, E. Negulici, P. Constantanisce, A. Cristesco and I. Sandesco, "Recherches sur le pouvoir infectant pour *A. atroparvus* des parasitémies asymptoma-tiques à *P. vivax, P. falciparum* et *P. malariae,*" *Bull WHO* 30 (1964): 1–6.

22. Reported in James (1931).

23. Elizabeth U. Canning and R. E. Sinder, "The organization of the oökinete and observations on nuclear division in oöcysts of *Plasmodium berghei,*" *Parasitol.* 67 (1973): 29–40.

24. The sporozoites measure 0.8μ at their widest by 11μ in length and are enclosed in two membranes. J. Vanderberg, J. Rhodain and M. Yoeli, "Electron microscopic and histochemical studies of sporozoite formation in *Plasmodium berghei,*" *J. Protozoology* 14 (1967): 82–103.

25. Longevities actually observed and reported so far range from 50 to 68 days. But the observations have been of a limited number of strains. It is possible that strains may have evolved in hibernating or semihibernating mosquitoes capable of surviving substantially longer. Experiments are currently under way to try to find out. Personal communication from Dr. J. H. Pull, WHO.

Chapter 15
"A War of Extermination . . ."[1]

Pages 121 through 129

1. Commenting on the distinctive horizontal posture of anopheline larvae Ross wrote to George H. F. Nuttall (28 April 1899) that that would be an important practical fact if "as will probably soon take place, a war of extermination against Anopheles be inaugurated." Ross Archives.

2. Ross (1923), 226. In the draft of the poem in Ross Archives, "relenting God" appears as "designing God." Was there a question of whether God meant to tell or was forced to?

3. Winwood Reade, 1872, cited in Houghton (1957), 36.

4. Ross to Manson, 15 and 24 Feb. 1899. Ross Archives.

5. Ross (1923), 366.

6. Ross (1899a); Ross, Annett and Austen (1900). The Lord Mayor of Liverpool, congratulating Ross on his inaugural address, added congratulations to the university for "this determination to utilise its highest culture to advance the commercial interests of the city." *J. Commerce,* 13 June 1899. Ross Archives.

7. Fyfe (1962); Curtin (1965).

8. Ross to Manson, 1 and 23 July 1899. Ross Archives.

9. E. E. Austen to Ross, 20 July 1899. Ross Archives.

10. Ross (1899a).

11. Communicated in a letter from T. Edmonston Charles, 22 July 1899. Ross Archives.

12. Letter, 2 Oct. 1899; quoted in Ross (1923), 386.

13. Ross, report to Major Nathan, 22 Sept. 1899; quoted in Fitch-Jones (1932), 18.

14. W. T. Prout to Hon. Colonial Secretary, commenting on Ross report (cited above), 21 Nov. 1899; quoted in Fitch-Jones (1932), 23–25.

15. All quotations are from Ross (1923), 386, 389, 330, respectively.

16. Fyfe (1962), 610.

17. J. W. W. Stephens and S. R. Christophers, "Distribution of Anopheles in Sierra Leone, "Parts I & II," *Royal Society: Reports to the Malaria Committee* (London, Harrison, 1900).

18. Ross (1923), 433. See below, Chapters 16 and 18.

19. His benefactor was James Coats, Jr., of Paisley who did not wish his name to be "brought prominently into notice" Ross (1923), 438. Ross's reports on this opening battle were published in the series, *Liverpool Sch. Trop. Med. Mem.,* vol. V, nos. 1, 2 (1901, 1902).

20. Fitch-Jones (1932).

21. [C. W. Daniels] "Reports &c. from C. W. Daniels, East Africa," *Roy. Soc.* (1900).

22. J. W. W. Stephens and S. R. Christophers, "Summary of researches on native malaria and malarial prophylaxis," *Thompson Yates Lab. Rep.* 5 (1903): 221–233. See also S. R. Christophers and J. W. W. Stephens, "The native as the prime agent in the malarial infection of Europeans," *Further Reps. to Mal. Com. Roy. Soc.* (London, 1900). Koch (1912) in his 1900 reports in the *Deutsche Med. Wochenschrift* recommended segregation and so did Edmond Sergent (1903), who wrote that the first antimalarial efforts should be to protect Europeans. "The example and the prosperity acquired will thereafter serve the natives as they emerge from the barbaric state."

23. Ross in his report to Major Nathan (22 Sept. 1899, cited in Fitch-Jones, 1932) had pointed out the happy example of segregated housing in India and observed the excellent hill sites available to the White settlers in Sierra Leone.

24. J. W. W. Stephens and S. R. Christophers, "The proposed site for European residences in the Freetown hills," *Roy. Soc.* (1901).

25. Request sent in August 1901. Fitch-Jones (1932).

26. Fyfe (1962), p. 611, writes: "Thus the Indian model of a racially stratified

society was introduced into Sierra Leone, not shamefacedly as required by prejudice, but openly dictated by medical science."

27. See Colony of Sierra Leone, *Report on malaria in Freetown and district* (Freetown, Govt. Printer, 1946). Copy in WHO Docs.

Chapter 16
". . . Wherever Economically Possible"[1]

Pages 130 through 140

1. See note 20 below.
2. William MacGregor to Arthur Gordon, 18 Feb. 1900; quoted in Joyce (1971), 226.
3. William MacGregor, "Notes on anti-malarial measures now being taken in Lagos," *Brit. Med. J.* (1901) vol. II, 680–682.
4. J. W. W. Stephens, "Discussion on the prophylaxis of malaria," *Brit. Med. J.* (1904), 629–631. The assistant under secretary at the Colonial Office, R. L. Antrobus, in 1908 wrote of the "curious streak of sentimentalism" which made Sir William reject segregation in Lagos. Joyce (1971), 233.
5. MacGregor (1901), cited above.
6. Joyce (1971), 238.
7. Stephens (1904), cited above.
8. Ronald Ross, "The anti-malaria experiment at Mian Mir," *Brit. Med. J.* (1904) vol. II, 632, 635.
9. James (1903); see also Christophers (1904).
10. G. M. Giles, "Cold weather mosquito notes from the United Provinces—North-West India," *J. Trop. Med.* (1904), 120.
11. H. D. Rowan, "Mian Mir (Labore Cantonment) a retrospect and prospect," *J. Roy. Army Med. Corps* XI (1908): 237.
12. R. Nathan, H. B. Thornhill and L. Rogers, *Report on the measures taken against malaria in the Lahore (Mian Mir) cantonment* (Calcutta, Govt. Printer, 1910), 15.
13. *Ibid.,* 45.
14. Ross (1910), 571.
15. E.g., Paul F. Russell, "Malaria in India; impressions from a tour," *Am. J. Trop. Med.* 16 (1936): 653–654. Russell wrote (p. 663): "Mian Mir proved nothing, but it weighed heavily with officialdom." Russell, to be sure, at that time was speaking less as an historian than as an embattled mosquito fighter.
16. Hackett diary, 1 March 1928. Hackett after a visit wrote: "It would occur almost immediately to anyone that screening the barracks and hospitals would probably keep down the amount of malaria enormously. In fact, after all methods of anti-malarial work within financial possibilities had failed, over a period of 25 years, this also occurred to the Army. 'In despair,' as Major Munroe said, 'screening was tried in 1926 in the Amritsar and part of the Lahore barracks.' "
17. Watson (1915) and (1921) are the principal sources. In addition, three papers by Watson fill in some details: "The effect of drainage and other measures on the malaria of Klang, Federated Malay States," *J. Trop Med.* (Dec. 1903); "Anti-malarial measures," *Official Rpt. to Chairman San.*

Bd. (Kuala Lumpur, FMS Govt. Press, 1905); "Twenty-five years of malaria control in the Malay peninsula," *Brit. Malaya* Jan. 1927 (Reprint in WHO files).

18. Identical words in Watson (1921), 217, and Watson (1915), 31. It was N. H. Swellengrebel who coined the phrase "species-sanitation"; Swellengrebel (1938), 56.

19. Sandoshan (1959), 22.

20. Federated Malay States, *Report of the Malaria Advisory Board for the year 1913* (Kuala Lumpur, 1914).

Chapter 17
Appreciation of the Enemy

Pages 141 through 156

1. In 1738 R. A. F. Réaumur, *L'Histoire des cousins* was published as the fourth volume of his *L'Histoire des insectes*. It described in great detail the structure and life history of *Culex pipiens pipiens* (so fully in the opinion of Howard, Dyar and Knab [1912] that he discouraged further research). In any event Réaumur's observations were reiterated for the next 150 years and assumed to apply to all mosquitoes. Ficalbi (1896) was the first mosquito taxonomist. He distinguished three genera, *Culex, Anopheles* and *Aedes*. On the base built by Ficalbi and under the stimulus of Ross's discoveries taxonomists by the end of 1899 had described 122 species. Within a couple of years more than 200 others were identified, 136 new species being described by Theobald in the first English taxonomy. See J. Everett Dutton, "Report of the malaria expedition to the Gambia," *Liverpool Sch. Trop. Med. Mem. #10* (1903).

   Among general works my chief dependence has been on Clements (1963), an excellent and encyclopedic work that ought to be put out in a new edition. Other general sources are Russell, West, Manwell and MacDonald (1963); Christophers (1960); Bates (1949); Mattingly (1969); and Gillett (1971).

2. Pliny, *Natural History* (*Naturalis Historia*) 10 vols. (Cambridge, Mass., Loeb Library). *Culex* apparently meant a mosquito-like creature from a people point of view, i.e., a biting nuisance. The Loeb translation gives "flea"—a misreading for *Pulex?*

3. The theoretical calculation of twenty-four generations a year was made by R. Senior-White in "Malaria transmission in the light of modern evolutionary theory applied to malaria-carrying mosquitoes," *Indian J. Malariol.* 2 (1948): 13–33, in the context of estimating the speed with which mutant genes might penetrate a population. There is, so far as I know, no evidence that mosquitoes in fact approach this fecundity. Dissections in Tanzania of *A. gambiae* and *A. funestus* both of which breed year round, showed maximum completed ovipositions for *gambiae* were 6, for *funestus* 9. (Clyde, 1967). This is remarkably similar to estimates for *A. quadrimaculatus* generations in the southern United States, where breeding of course is seasonal (8–10 ovipositions in Georgia, 7–8 in North Carolina). Luis Vargas, "Malaria along the Mexico–United States border," *Bull. WHO* (1950), 611–620.

4. Russell, West, Manwell and MacDonald (1963) estimate for malaria vectors 2.44 to 3.3 cu. mm. per meal, varying from one and a half times the insect's weight to more than double. Clements (1963) reports tests on *Aedes aegypti* showing an average intake of 4.2 cu. mm. Individuals have been shown to vary enormously from the species norm. Records on *A. quadrimaculatus,* the U. S. vector, show individual meals of up to fifteen times the female's body weight (Boyd, 1949).

5. Reported by Howard, Dyar and Knab (1912), p. 208.

6. Formerly assigned to genus *Harpagomyia.* S. P. James, *"Report on a mosquito survey of Colombo and the practicability of reducing stegomyia and some other kinds of mosquitoes in that seaport* (Colombo, Govt. Printer, 1914), describes a mosquito he identifies as *H. generostris* that breeds in bromeliads in Ceylon. Upon emergence the adult rests on a leaf or stem of a plant along which ants travel. When one happens to approach the mosquito, she thrusts out her proboscis, bringing its bulbous tip in contact with the ant's mouth, collects food and then flies up a few inches to allow the ant to proceed on its way.

7. A northern mosquito (*Aedes canadensis*) has an apparent passion for the blood of turtles. W. J. Crans and E. G. Rockel ("The mosquitoes attracted to turtles," *Mosq. News* 28 [1968]: 332–337) describe watching *A. canadensis* hover hungrily over places where turtles have lain and try to insert their stylets between the scutes of the animal's carapace. Ordinarily the insects feed on the turtle's legs or head and neck. They are often crushed when the turtle pulls in its head. There is also a species (*Aedes longiforceps*) that attacks a fish, the mudskipper, which often lies half out of water between high and low tides. Reported by R. Sloof and E. N. Marks, "Mosquitoes (culicidae) biting fish (Periophthalmidae)," *J. Med. Ento.* 2 [1965]: 16.

8. A. J. Haddow carried out extensive experiments to determine the biting rhythms of mosquitoes ("Studies of the biting habits of African mosquitoes; an appraisal of methods employed with special reference to the twenty-four hour catch," *Bull. Ent. Res.* 45 [1954]: 199–242). He found either single or double peaks of activity during the twenty-four hours, although individual variations were very great, and the pattern for the population appeared to shift from night to night.

9. Clements (1963) remarks that the mosquito in nature probably seeks out her host in response sequentially to a number of different signals. Laboratory experiments remain ambiguous because they cannot reproduce the sequence. Mattingly (1969), 114, writes: "Summarizing, it is probably fair to say that there is a great deal of evidence as to how mosquitoes might locate their hosts, almost none as to how they actually do."

10. Kennedy (1939); Clements (1963).

11. Reported by Christophers (1960), 536. Grassi supposed that the attractant was noise. Other experiments have failed to show that mosquitoes react to noise.

12. Most exhaustive experiments were done by Laarman (1955). See also G. Mer, D. Birnbaum and A. Aioub, "The attraction of mosquitoes by human beings," *Parasit.* 38 (1947): 1–9, and A. A. Khan and Howard I. Maibach,

"Effect of human breath on mosquito attraction to man," *Mosq. News* 32 (1972): 11–15.

13. Clements (1963), 67. Experiments on mosquito reaction to smells include Edwin R. Willis, "The olfactory responses of female mosquitoes," *J. Econ. Ent.* 40 (1947): 769–778; Susan B. McIver, "Host preferences and discrimination by the mosquitoes, *Aedes aegypti* and *Culex tarsalis* (Diptera: Culicidae)," *J. Med. Ent.* 5 (1968): 422–428; Brown, Sarkaria and Thompson (1952) as well as Laarman (1955) and Christophers (1960).

14. Christophers (1960), 538.

15. Howard, Dyar and Knab (1912), 107.

16. The experiments are reported in a series of papers with different co-authors appearing in the *Bulletin of Entomological Research* (1952–1957).

17. Ribbands (1949).

18. Clements (1963), 281.

19. Robinson (1939).

20. Christophers (1960), 484–485; Clements (1963), 137.

21. Gordon and Lumsden (1939).

22. Christophers (1960), 486.

23. Gillett (1971), 61.

24. Kenneth Mellanby, "Man's reaction to mosquito bites," *Nature* 158 (1946): 554.

25. Feingold, Benjamin and Michaeli (1968) made a detailed study of the histopathological changes caused by mosquito saliva. See also the earlier study by R. M. Gordon and W. Crewe, "The mechanism by which mosquitoes and tsetse flies obtain their blood meal, the histology of the lesion produced, and the subsequent reactions of the mammalian host; together with some observations on the feeding of *Chrysops* and *Cimex*," *Ann. Trop. Med. Parasit.* 42 (1948): 334–356.

26. Laarman (1955), 9; Christophers (1960), 530.

27. Clements (1963) generalizes that most species appear to search for water visually and are attracted to dark patches which they then probe to discover if they are wet (p. 304). See also J. S. Kennedy, "On water-finding and oviposition by captive mosquitoes," *Bull. Ent. Res.* 32 (1942): 277–301.

28. *Aedes aegypti* eggs have been known to hatch six months after laying. Another aedine species has survived in the egg for four years. Gillett (1971), 22.

29. Wigglesworth (1939), Bates (1949).

30. Clements (1963), 85.

31. *Ibid.,* 297.

32. *Ibid.,* 302. Females also sometimes swarm, often before migration; Hocking (1953). But mosquito swarms are always of one sex, according to J. A Downes "The swarming and mating flight of diptera," *Annual Rev. Ent.* 14 (1969): 271–298. M. S. Qurashi ("Swarming, mating and density in nature of *Anopeheles stephensi mysoriensis*," *J. Econ. Ent.* 58 [1965]: 821–824) estimated frequent mating in swarms he observed in Iran. He counted streaks in the insect cloud that he believed were made by the amatory swoops of the males.

Chapter 18
Victory in Panama

Pages 157 through 168

1. Ross (1923, 493) wrote: "Everyone knows how magnificently Gorgas maintained the health of the Canal Zone . . . If I had had my way the same thing would have happened in every British colony."
2. Strode (1951); Andrewes (1967).
3. Carter (1931).
4. Sternberg (1890).
5. Victor Heiser (*A Doctor's Odyssey: Adventures in Forty-Five Countries* [London, Cape, 1936], 42) says flatly: "To prevent this danger [yellow fever invasions of the United States] was one of the principal reasons for our going to war with Spain." Gorgas in his "Report to B. G. Leonard Wood, 12 July 1902" (See U. S. Congress, 1911, 237) wrote: "The primary object of the war with Spain was the liberation of Cuba from Spanish domination [this, of course, being the official *casus belli*], but at the same time, the United States had hoped to accomplish a good deal in improving the sanitary condition of the island." The American Public Health Association, at its Ottawa meeting in 1897, called President Mc-Kinley's attention to the recent yellow fever epidemics in Louisiana, Mississippi and Alabama that had taken 16,000 lives and cost $100 million (U. S. Congress, 1911, 132).
6. Wood, a protégé of General Sternberg, had been personal physician to President McKinley just before his assignment to Havana.
7. U. S. Congress (1911).
8. On Finlay's work see, besides U. S. Congress (1911), George M. Sternberg, *Sanitary lessons of the war and other papers* (Washington, B. S. Adams, 1912); and Peller (1959).
9. Popularized above all by Sidney Howard's play, *Men in White*. But there is still no thorough, scholarly account or a good biography of Walter Reed. See Albert E. Truby, *Memoir of Walter Reed: The yellow fever episode* (N. Y., Haeber, 1943); also Kelly (1906).
10. Gorgas (1915).
11. *Ibid.*, 91–92, 95.
12. Reed wrote on 5 June 1901 (Gorgas, 1915, 83–84) that the army had fumigated barracks at Mount Vernon with two to three ounces per 3,500 square feet and found the dose enough to kill *Culex* species.
13. The best biography is Gorgas and Hendrick (1924). There is also John M. Gibson, *Physician to the world: the life of General William C. Gorgas* (Durham, N. C., Duke Press, 1950), which despite its issuance from a university press is undocumented and uncritical.
14. From General Gorgas Sr.'s notebook, quoted in Gibson (1950), cited in note above.
15. U. S. Congress (1911), 3.
16. P. Bunau-Varilla, *Panama; le passé, le présent, l'avenir* (Paris, Masson, 1892). For an excellent history of the canal under both the French and Americans see Mack (1944). Details also in Simmons et al (1939).

17. Quoted in Mack (1944).
18. Dr. Welch and probably Dr. Osler, certainly the two most distinguished medical men of their day, called on President Roosevelt in February 1904 to urge that Gorgas be appointed to the Canal Commission. Roosevelt was not convinced. See Cushing (1926), I, 631–632; Gorgas (1915), 142.
19. Simmons et al (1939).
20. Gorgas and Hendrick (1924).
21. A squabble between them over whether the sanitation department or the quartermaster corps should mow grass to deprive mosquitoes of resting places was the subject of an article in *Outlook*. Gibson (1950), 162. See note 13 above.
22. Orenstein (1912).
23. Figures from Simmons et al (1939).
24. H. B. Allen, *Report on health conditions at Panama* (Melbourne, Commonwealth of Australia, 1913).
25. Hackett (1937), for one, found Panama an unconvincing demonstration of what might be done elsewhere, noting that in the relatively massive effort neither the resources of the people nor the economic worth to them of relief from disease was taken into account. Simmons et al (1939) summed up: "By the expenditure of large amounts of money, certain parts of the narrow, mosquito-infested strip of land, which traverses the Isthmus on either side of the Panama Canal, have been rendered comparatively free from malaria and have been converted into fairly safe places in which to live."
26. Watson (1915), 103. Allen (1913), cited above, found that the essence of the administration was "a benevolent despotism, under a military dictator."
27. In Ross (1910).
28. [Thomas J. Headlee and Mitchell Carroll], "The mosquito must go," *New Jersey Exp. Sta. Circ.* III (April 1919). In Ross Collection.
29. Howard, Dyar and Knab (1912), 444.

Chapter 19
Italy and Koch's Way

Pages 169 through 176
1. *Brit. Med. J.* (1901): vol. II, 680ff, reporting a British Medical Association meeting on 30 July.
2. André Pressat went with Ross to Ismailia and reported separately in "Prophylaxie du paludisme dans l'Isthme de Suez," *Presse Méd.* 61 (1904); offprint in Ross Collection. Sir David Bruce had a look in 1911: "Report on the present condition of Ismailia as regards malarial fever," *J. Roy. Army Med. Corps* (April 1911); copy in Ross Collection. Hackett checked up in 1927, noting that Ross's mosquito brigades were still being "employed continuously" and that "there is some malaria in Ismailia still." Diary, 13 Dec. 1927.
3. Sergent and Sergent (1928).
4. Arrigo Serpiero, Mussolini's adviser on *bonifica,* quoted in Lutrario (1928).
5. Celli (1899) and (1901). The *braccianti* at that time made up more than

half the Italian rural population. Christopher Seton-Watson, *Italy from liberalism to fascism, 1870–1925* (London, Methuen, 1967), 23.

6. Celli's report on the experiment was one of the papers that MacGregor had translated for distribution in Lagos as "The new preventive treatment of malaria in Latium," dated Rome, 19 Oct. 1900. Copy in Celli, Collected Papers, bound in London Sch. Trop. Med. Grassi, in charge of some experiments in protecting railroad workers by screening in Salerno, according to Celli was, in familiar style, claiming pioneering results without acknowledging that others had done similar work before him. Angelo Celli, "Sulla nuova profilassi della malaria," *Ann. Ig. Sper.* 11 (1901). In Collected Papers, cited above.

7. Celli (1899), 162.

8. Celli (1901), 254.

9. Fermi (1935).

10. A. Celli and O. Casagrandi, "Per la distruzione delle zanzare," (Roma, Soc. Ann. Ig. Sper. 9 (1899): 317–354.

11. A. Celli, "La malaria in Italia durante il 1907," *Atti Soc. Studi Malariol.* 9 (1908): 675–729.

12. "Erste Bericht über die Tätigkeit der Malariaexpedition," *Deutsche Med. Wochenschift* 37 (1899), in Koch (1912), 389–396.

13. See his second and third reports in the series cited above, Koch (1912), 397–411. The discovery that large numbers of very young children in endemic areas had parasites in their blood without displaying obvious symptoms of fever was made independently by J. W. W. Stephens and S. R. Christophers of the Royal Society Malaria Commission in observations in Africa and confirmed in India. S. P. James, "Malaria in India," *Sci. Mem. Offs. Med. San. Depts. Gov. India,* New Ser. #2 (Calcutta, 1902).

14. Robert Koch, "Vierter Bericht . . . etc." Koch (1912), 414.

15. Celli (1901), 192.

16. "Sulla nuova profilassi della malaria," cited in note 6 above.

17. Celli with Giustino Fortunato and Leopoldo Franchetti founded the Società per gli Studi della Malaria which both promoted research and lobbied for health legislation.

18. For instance, the dramatic drop in deaths from malaria—from 15,805 in 1900 to 9,908 in 1902—occurred before quinine could possibly have come into play.

19. A. Celli, *Malaria in Italy during 1910,* tr. by N. P. Gorman-Lalor (Rangoon, Govt. Print., 1912). Albert Boddaert ("Les travaux de la Societé Italienne pour l'étude de la Malaria," *Bull. Soc. Med. Gaud* [1901]; offprint in Ross Collection) wrote that the society "poursuit un but à la fois scientifique et pratique pour le plus grand honneur *della patria commune* et au plus grand profit encore de l'humanité toute entière."

20. Celli (1908), cited in note 11 above.

21. Seton-Watson (1967), cited in note 5 above.

22. Lutrario (1928).

23. Hackett diary, 22 Feb. 1924.

24. *Ibid.,* 15–17 March 1924.

Chapter 20
Rockefeller and the American Way

Pages 177 through 189
1. Marcel Leger and J. Arlo, "Le paludisme en Corse; deuxième campagne antipaludique (1913)," *Pub. Inst. Pasteur* (1914). In Ross Collection.
2. [League of Nations], "Reports on the tour of investigation in Palestine in 1925," *L. of N. Docs.* (C.H./Mal/52, Sept. 1925).
3. C. E. P. Fowler, "Malaria in Palestine," *J. Roy. Army Med. Corps* (April 1926); offiprint in Ross Collection.
4. This and much of the background information for this and subsequent chapters that concern the Rockefeller Foundation have been drawn from the manuscript history of the Foundation and from voluminous notes for that history prepared by Lewis Hackett after his retirement. The book was never finished and remains in manuscript and note form in the Rockefeller Archives. A selective and popular history of the Foundation's work in public health is Greer Williams, *The Plague Killers* (N. Y., Scribner's, 1969).
5. Hackett MS. Hist., vol. V, 22–24.
6. Wickcliffe Rose, "Field experiments in malaria control," *J. Am. Med. Assn.* 73 (1919): 1414–1420. The fourteen Southern states in which malaria lingered did not make a serious attempt to extinguish it until 1947. In 1934 these states had reported 131,980 cases, suggesting an actual incidence very much higher. By the time the eradication campaign with DDT was begun, reported cases had dropped below 10,000, but this was largely because of climatic and cultural factors that made life for the parasite increasingly difficult, rather than because of specific efforts at control. Simmons and Upholt (1951).
7. Patrick Manson, *Tropical Diseases: a manual of the diseases of warm climates,* third ed. (London, Cassell, 1903).
8. Strode (1951), 14.
9. Gorgas and Hendrick (1924).
10. F. F. Russell, "War on disease; with special reference to malaria and yellow fever," *Sigma Xi Q.* 13 (1925): 11–32.
11. Hackett MS. Hist., vol. VII, 12.
12. P. F. Russell, "The Rockefeller Foundation's role in malaria control and eradication," *Parasitology* 2 (1967): 15–22.
13. Hackett Hist. notes.
14. Hackett to Florence M. Reed, 5 Aug. 1924.
15. Hackett (1937), 22.
16. "It is disappointing to them," Hackett wrote to F. F. Russell on 18 Oct. 1924, "as Missiroli told me yesterday, to have the I.H.B. [International Health Board of the Foundation] interest itself in such 'small town stuff.'"
17. Hackett diary, 27, 28 Aug. 1924. In a letter to S. T. Darling, 18 Aug. 1924, he quoted another doctor who had accompanied the commission members and who observed that they were "not anxious to do much walking in the hot sun."

18. Hackett diary, 13 April 1924 and 15 July 1924. See page 172 and note, below.

19. Hackett wrote to S. T. Darling, 28 March 1924: "I get the impression that he [Grassi] feels that his active life is drawing to a close and that he has not yet solved the malaria problem. His mind feverishly turns from one theory to another, and he hopes to bring off something big yet before he dies."

20. Hackett diary, 27 Aug. 1924.

21. Hackett to S. T. Darling, 29 Aug. 1924.

22. Hackett diary, 28 Aug. 1924.

23. N. H. Swellengrebel, "Some aspects of the problem of malaria in Italy," *L. of N. Docs.* (C.H./Mal/30, 5 Oct. 1924); Swellengrebel (1938), 193–197.

24. League of Nations (1924).

25. League of Nations (1927).

26. *Compte-rendu du premier Congrès International du Paludisme* (Rome, Senate Press, 1926).

27. League of Nations (1927), 13.

28. Hackett to Ludvig Rajchman, 3 Nov. 1924.

29. Reported in Hackett diary, 29 Dec. 1927.

30. League of Nations Docs. C.H./Mal/107, 15 June 1928.

31. Unpublished materials on the conference include following docs: C.H./Mal/102, 119, 121 and C.H. 736.

32. Hackett (1925).

33. Whorton (1971).

34. Insecticidal dusts were first sprayed on crops by airplane in the United States in 1921. Experiments in dusting Paris green from the air were carried out from 1922 to 1924. Covell (1941).

35. Hackett (1925), 12.

36. L. W. Hackett, "Malaria control through anti-mosquito measures in Italy," *Trans. Roy. Soc. Trop. Med. Hyg.* 22 (1929): 477–508.

37. Hackett Annual Rpt., 1927. Rockefeller Archives.

38. Hackett 2d Quarterly Rpt., 1929.

39. Jacques Sautet, *La lutte contre le paludisme en Corse* (Paris, Masson, 1928), 72.

40. Hackett diary, 6 April 1924.

41. Hackett Annual Rpts., 1930, 1931.

42. On *bonifica* under Mussolini, see Cesare Longobardi, *Land-Reclamation in Italy: Rural Revival in the Building of a Nation*, tr. by Olivia R. Agreet (London, P. S. King, 1936); and D. Ottolenghi, "La bonification intégrale italienne dans le cadre de la lutte anti-paludéenne et de l'hygiene générale," *Riv. Malariol. Suppl.* 14 (1935): 109–114. Both are quasi-official and wholly uncritical. Laura Fermi (*Mussolini*, Chicago, Univ. Press, 1961, p. 299) quotes from a speech of Mussolini's in 1932 when he dedicated a new town in the reclaimed Pontine marshes: "It is here that we have conquered a new province. It is here we have waged and shall wage true war operations. This is the war that we prefer."

Chapter 21
A Preference for Pig

Pages 190 through 198

1. Hackett diary, 13 April 1924.
2. *Ibid.*, 30 Jan. 1924.
3. Hackett to S. T. Darling, 28 March 1924. Also to Mark F. Boyd, 22 March 1924 and to Robert Hegner, 5 Aug. 1924.
4. William Welch, visiting Italy in 1927, wrote in his diary: (Welch papers. See Acknowledgments): "Hackett has had to overcome serious obstacles & criticism, due mainly to international jealousies & reactionary opinion. Main reliance of Italians has been curative & prophylactic use of quinine which is distributed free by the State—antilarval work considered impracticable. The widow of Celli has been among those attacking Hackett's methods. The ambassador from Argentina—[Dr. Fernando] Perez—has led in opposing Anglo-Saxon vs. Latin methods!! and largely through him a 'School of Malariology,' not part of university but under Ministry of Public Instruction and supported by Mussolini—President V. Ascoli (prof. Med. Rome) has been established—Perhaps a good thing & not opposed by Hackett, but motives in creating school were antagonistic. . . ."
5. Ambassador Perez, who was a medical doctor, presided over an international meeting of malariologists in Rome in Oct. 1925, the main purpose of which was to endorse and give publicity to the new institute. *Compte-rendu du premier Congrès International du paludisme* (Rome, Senate Press, 1926).
6. Sergent (1902); Lutrario (1924).
7. Celli and Gasperini (1901); Celli, "La malaria in Italia durante il 1907," *Atti Soc. Studi Mal.* 9 (1908): 685.
8. Edmond and Étienne Sergent, "Essai de campagne anti-malarique selon la méthode de Koch," *Atti Soc. Studi Mal.* 5 (1904); offprint in Ross Collection.
9. Falleroni (1927). The investigator was Dr. Bonservizi. See also Hackett (1937), 28.
10. Missiroli and Hackett (1927). Wesenberg-Lund, working in Denmark, made similar observations at about the same time and came independently to the same conclusions.
11. Bull and King (1923).
12. Hackett and Missiroli (1931).
13. Missiroli and Hackett (1927).
14. Carroll G. Bull and Francis M. Root, "Preferential feeding experiments with anopheline mosquitoes," *Am. J. Hyg.* 3 (1923): 514–520.
15. Hackett and Missiroli (1931).
16. G. Escalar, "Applicazione sperimentale della zooprofilasi in Ardea," *Riv. Malariol.* 12 (1933): 373–380.
17. E.g., Paul F. Russell, "Zooprophylaxis failure: an experiment in the Philippines," *Riv. Malariol.* 13 (1934): 610–616.
18. Roubaud (1921).

19. "Maxillenzahnzahl und Flügellänge bei *A. maculipennis,*" *Beih. Arch. Schiffs-u. Trop. Hyg.* 30 (1926): 67–76.
20. De Buck, Schoute and Swellengrebel (1927); Swellengrebel and de Buck (1938). H. J. M. Schoo, "Malaria in Holland," *Atti Soc. Studi Mal.* (1902); offprint in Ross Collection.
21. Swellengrebel and de Buck (1938).
22. Hackett (1937).
23. De Buck, Schoute and Swellengrebel (1927); L. W. Hackett, "The present status of our knowledge of the sub-species of *Anopheles maculipennis,*" *Trans, Roy. Soc. Trop. Med. Hyg.* 22 (1934): 109–140.
24. Falleroni (1926).
25. Hackett (1937); Missiroli, Hackett and Martini (1933).
26. In Boyd (1949), 1416–1431.
27. Brumpt (1944).

Chapter 22
Epidemic

Pages 199 through 207

1. Davidson (1892) is the best account. Dr. Davidson was visiting and super-intending surgeon at the civil hospital in Port Louis, and professor of chemistry at the Royal College of Mauritius. See also M. A. C. Dowling, "An experiment in the eradication of malaria in Mauritius," *Bull. WHO* 4: 443–461; Ronald Ross, *Report on the prevention of malaria in Mauritius* (London, Churchill, 1909); A. Rankine, "Malaria in Mauritius with suggestions for future policy in regard to this disease," *Colony of Mauritius Pub. #63,* 1951; and Tonking and Gibert (1947).
2. Ross overlooked *A. funestus.* First identification was by Malcolm E. Mac-Gregor, *Report on the anophelinae of Mauritius, and on certain aspects of malaria in the colony, with recommendation for a new anti-malaria campaign* (London, Waterlow, 1923).
3. Davidson (1892), 751.
4. *Ibid.,* 755.
5. Christophers (1911).
6. *Ibid.*
7. G. Covell and Sudebar J. D. Baily, "The study of a regional epidemic of malaria in Northern Sind," *Rec. Med. Survey India* 3 (1932): 279–322; and "Further observations . . . ," *Loc. cit.* 6 (1936): 411–437.
8. E.g., Dunn (1936); Gill (1936), (1938); MacDonald (1973); R. Brier-cliffe, "The Ceylon malaria epidemic, 1934–35," *Sessional paper XXII* (Ceylon, Govt. Press, 1935); T. Stanton, "Malaria epidemic, Ceylon, 1934–1935," ms., *WHO Docs.;* V. B. Wigglesworth, "Malaria in Ceylon," *Asiatic Rev.* 3 (1936).
9. Dunn (1936) estimated *P. falciparum* infections as 36.7 percent of the total in mid-1935. He says that the proportion did not change during the epidemic. Stanton (1935) on the other hand estimated the proportion of *falciparum* in the first wave of cases in 1934 as about 10 percent. Since the total cycle of *falciparum* transmission takes about one and a half times as long as the cycle of *vivax,* one would normally expect the ratio of *falciparum* to *vivax* infections to increase with increasing numbers and longevity of

mosquitoes and the duration of transmission. That supposition, moreover, fits better with the fact of higher death rates in the later stages of the epidemic. Figures on deaths attributable to a particular illness are at best an informed estimate. The best measure of the epidemic's impact is the excess of deaths in the epidemic year over those of other years. In Ceylon, 1935 saw an excess over 1934 of 77,754 recorded deaths, and an excess of 82,162 over the 1925–1934 average. Ceylon, *Report of the director of medical and sanitary services* (Annual pub.).

10. Gill (1936).
11. MacDonald (1937), especially the 1953 paper analyzing malaria epidemics (146–160).
12. Covell and Baily (1932; cited in note 7 above) noted the paucity of gametocytes in the Sind region at the beginning of the 1929 epidemic. They calculated that the epidemic could have taken the course it did from a base point of one gametocyte carrier per 200 population; at that density blood sampling could easily overlook them altogether.
13. Cited in Covell and Baily (1932), 425.

Chapter 23
Toward Total War

Pages 208 through 217

1. Gill (1936), 428.
2. Mark F. Boyd, "Malaria: retrospect and prospect," *Am. J. Trop. Med.* 19 (1939): 1–6.
3. Giemsa (1911) and (1913).
4. The Brazilian doctor was Emygdio de Mattos (Soper and Wilson, 1943a). F. W. Edwards ("Mosquitoes and their relation to disease; their life-history, habits and control," *Brit. Mus. (Nat. Hist.) Eco.* Ser. 4, 1916) recommended "Giemsa solution" for an adult spray to control mosquitoes.
5. Park Ross (1936).
6. Botha de Meillon did some controlled experiments after the fact, which he reported in "The control of malaria in South Africa by measures directed against adult mosquitoes in habitations," *Q. Bull. Hlth. Org. L. of N.* 5 (1936): 134–137.
7. N. H. Swellengrebel and J. A. Nykamp, "Expériences de lutte antianophélienne au moyen d'insecticides contenant du pyrèthre," *L. of N. Docs.* (C.H./Mal/220, 9 Aug. 1934). On the Indian experiments see D. K. Viswanathan, "Malaria control by spray-killing adult anophelines, second season's results; with special reference to the effects of this measure on the longevity and infectivity of *Anopheles minimus,*" *J. Mal. Inst. India* 4 (1942): 393–403; also Thomson (1951).
8. Covell (1941).
9. For instance in Northern Rhodesia and West Africa; Thomson (1951).
10. Soper and Wilson (1943b) write: "[The] consolidated [Yellow Fever] Service was able to take advantage of the ideas and methods developed by the Rockefeller Foundation under the influence of Gorgas. . . ."
11. L. W. Hackett interview with Fred L. Soper, 17–18 Feb. 1951. Hackett Hist. notes.
12. *Ibid.*

13. Soper and Wilson (1943b).

14. O. P. Severo, "Eradication of the *Aedes aegypti* mosquito from the Americas," *Mosq. News* 16 (1956): 115–121.

15. L. W. Hackett interview with W. A. Sawyer, 29 Aug. 1950. Hackett Hist. notes.

16. R. C. Shannon, *"Anopheles gambiae* in Brazil," *Am. J. Hyg.* 15 (1932): 634–663.

17. Fred L. Soper, "Paris green in the eradication of *Anopheles gambiae:* Brazil, 1940; Egypt, 1945," *Mosq. News* 26 (1966): 470–476.

18. M. A. Barber, "The present status of *Anopheles gambiae* in Brazil," *Am. J. Trop. Med.* 20 (1940): 249–267.

19. Soper and Wilson (1943a).

20. Barber (1940), cited above.

21. Soper and Wilson (1943a), 162.

22. *Ibid.,* 234.

23. *Ibid.,* 226.

24. *Ibid.,* 173.

Chapter 24
"An Almost Perfect Insecticide"

Pages 218 through 227

1. See note 10 below.

2. Cited in West and Campbell (1946), from which details of the DDT story have been drawn.

3. West and Campbell (1946), 178.

4. *Ibid.,* 134.

5. Dr. E. J. Pampana, director of WHO's antimalaria work, noted in 1947 how in contrast to the careful experimentation that preceded widespread use of larviciding oil and Paris green, governments rushed to spend "enormous sums of money" on DDT "on the basis of experience gained in foreign countries or very brief and restricted local trials . . ." It seemed humane, he added, to use DDT with the utmost energy (WHO, Exp. Com. Mal., 1947).

6. D. J. Lewis, "A northern record of *Anopheles gambiae* Giles," *Proc. Roy. Ent. Soc.* Ser. B vol. 11 (1942): 141–142; D. J. Lewis, "Observations on *Anopheles gambiae* and other mosquitoes at Wadi Halfa," *Trans. Roy. Soc. Trop. Med. Hyg.* 38 (1944): 215–229.

7. Shousha (1947).

8. Account from Shousha (1947) supplemented by Hackett interview with Soper (Rockefeller Archives) and D. J. Lewis, "The extermination of *Anopheles gambiae* in the Wadi Halfa area," *Trans. Roy. Soc. Trop. Med. Hyg.* 42 (1949): 393–402.

9. Fred L. Soper, W. A. Davis, F. S. Markham and L. A. Riehl, "Typhus fever in Italy, 1943–1945, and its control with louse powder," *Am. J. Hyg.* 45 (1947): 305–334.

10. Fred L. Soper, F. W. Knipe, G. Casini, Louis A. Riehl and A. Rubino, "Reduction of *Anopheles* density effected by the preseason spraying of building interiors with DDT in kerosene at Castel Volturno, Italy, in 1944–

1945 and in the Tiber Delta in 1945," *Am. J. Trop. Med.* 27 (1947): 177–200. Thomas H. G. Aitken, "A study of winter DDT house-spraying and its concomitant effect on anophelines and malaria in an endemic area," *J. Nat. Mal. Soc.* 5 (1946): 169–187.

11. UNRRA, Italian Mission, *Historical report of the health division, Part II, A: Malaria Control Programs* (March 1947).
12. P. Moreschini and E. J. Pampana, "Report on the survey of the anti-malaria organization," *WHO Docs.* MH/307/49 (Italy).
13. Brown, Haworth and Zahar (1976).
14. Wilbur Sawyer at this time wrote that "the success beyond all predictions of the major strategy in the extermination of *A. gambiae* in Brazil had fired the imagination of malariologists everywhere" (quoted in Hackett MS. Hist. IX, 18). But Missiroli (1947) for one was skeptical.
15. Logan (1953), which is the main source of the narrative that follows.
16. Logan (1953), 9.
17. Missiroli (1947).
18. Julian de Zulueta, "Malaria and Mediterranean history," *Parassitologia* 15 (1973): 1–15.

Chapter 25
Eradication

Pages 228 through 238

1. WHO. Exp. Com. Mal (1948–1974). Only excerpts of the report of the first meeting were published.
2. A. Rajendram and S. H. Jayewickreme, "Malaria in Ceylon," *Indian J. Mal.* 5 (1951): 1–124; L. F. Gunaratne, "Recent anti-malaria work in Ceylon," *Bull. WHO* 15 (1956): 791–799; [Ceylon], *Malaria control in Ceylon* (*Report by the Departmental Committee on Malaria*, Colombo, Govt. Press, 1945).
3. Pampana (1951).
4. "Report of WHO advisory team on malaria eradication No. 3—Ceylon, February–June 1957," *WHO Docs.* WHO/AS/102.57.
5. Arnoldo Gabaldón, "Progress of the malaria campaign in Venezuela," *J. Nat. Mal. Soc.* 10 (1951): 124–141.
6. Constantine Savas, "Le paludisme en Grèce: L'oeuvre de la ligue anti-malarienne," *Atti Soc. Studi Mal.* 8 (1907): 137–170.
7. Livadas (1951).
8. M. J. Vine, "The anti-malaria campaign in Greece—1946," *Bull. Who* 1 (1947–48): 197–204; Gregory A. Livadas and George D. Belios, "Malaria control activities in Greece during 1946," ms. WHO Docs.
9. Vine (1947–48), cited above.
10. *Ibid.*
11. Georghiu (1969).
12. Missiroli (1947).
13. On early examples of insect resistance see Russell (1955), 188; also J. R. Busvine, "The significance of insecticide-resistant strains," *Bull. WHO* 15 (1956): 389–401.

14. As in the second meeting of the expert committee on malaria *Bull. WHO* 1: 227.
15. WHO Exp. Com. Mal. (1947).
16. George D. Belios and George Fameliaris, "Resistance of anopheline larvae to chlordane and dieldrin," *Bull. WHO* 15 (1956): 415–423; George D. Belios, "Recent course and current pattern of malaria in relation with its control in Greece," *Riv. Malariol.* 34: (1955): 1–24.
17. Third meeting; WHO Tech. Rpt. #8.
18. *Ibid.*
19. This is the recollection of all the veterans of those days with whom I have talked.
20. Gregory A. Livadas, "Malaria eradication in Greece," *Riv. Malariol.* 37 (1958): 173–191.
21. WHO., Exp. Com. Mal. 5th meeting; WHO Tech. Rpt. #80.
22. Assessments based on interviews with WHO staff and advisers.
23. Eradication plan was outlined in the 6th meeting of the expert committee (WHO Tech. Rpt. #123).
24. WHO (1957a).

Chapter 26
India—Model for the World

Pages 239 through 248

1. WHO, *Malaria conference in equatorial Africa* (WHO Tech. Rpt. #38, 1951).
2. L. J. Bruce-Chwatt, rapporteur at the first meeting, wrote of the recommendations of the second: "It would be an exaggeration to say that it [the recommended use of chemotherapy in Africa] constituted a veiled admission of defeat of residual insecticides, so brilliantly successful in other parts of the world." In retrospect it doesn't seem much of an exaggeration, if any. See L. J. Bruce-Chwatt, "Chemotherapy in relation to possibilities of malaria eradication in tropical Africa," *Bull. WHO* 15 (1956): 852–862.
3. The crucial exception was made in a footnote: "In tropical Africa since there have not yet been demonstrations of any wide areas being cleared of malaria by residual spraying, it seems premature to plan in terms of continent-wide eradication." WHO Tech. Rpt. #123, 8.
4. For the final clearing of malaria from continental U.S.A., see Bradley (1966), Simmons and Upholt (1951) and Russell (1968).
5. The India story has been put together chiefly from articles in the *Indian Journal of Malariology* and the *Bulletin of the National Society of India for Malaria and other Mosquito-borne Diseases,* and from unpublished WHO reports.
6. R. Senior-White, "House spraying with D.D.T. and with Pyrethrum extract compared: first results," *J. Mal. Inst. India* 6 (1945): 83–93.
7. D. K. Viswanathan and T. Ramachandra Rao, "Control of rural malaria with D.D.T. indoor residual spraying in Kanara and Dharwar districts, Bombay province: first year's results," *Indian J. Malariol.* 1 (1947): 503–542; *idem* . . . second year's results," *Ibid.* 2 (1948): 157–210.
8. Viswanathan (1958).

9. Viswanathan and Rao (1948), cited above.
10. Ray (1961).
11. Brown, Haworth and Zahar (1976).
12. From personal interviews with members of the Indian National Malaria Eradication Programme, 1976.
13. Two joint reports by USAID and WHO systematically review the shortcomings: USAID/WHO (1970) and the earlier "Report of consultation with malaria eradication officials of the state of Gujarat, Feb. 5–8, 1968." *WHO Docs.*
14. T. B. Patel, T. Ramachandra Rao and G. J. Ambwani, "An outbreak of malaria in parts of Thana District, Bombay State, India, after several years of successful control," *Indian J. Malariol.* 15 (1961): 71–90.
15. T. B. Patel and G. J. Ambwani, "Report on an epidemic occurring during eradication of malaria in Gir Forest, Gujarat State, India," *Indian J. Malariol.* 15 (1961): 129–137.
16. Ray (1961).
17. Thirteenth meeting; WHO Tech. Rpt. #357.
18. *Report of the Director of Medical and Sanitary Services* (Colombo, 1963–64), 218.
19. WHO Tech. Rpt. #357.
20. The expert committee at its ninth meeting in 1962 noted that resistance had been reported in 24 anopheline species, among which were 15 important malaria vectors but that "in no case, so far, has the prospect of eventual malaria eradication been placed in jeopardy." WHO Tech. Rpt. #243. That remained the dominant view through the 1960s.
21. WHO Tech. Rpt. #443.

Chapter 27
Relapse

Pages 249 through 260
1. A meeting of the Royal Society of Tropical Medicine and Hygiene in February 1962, attended by many malariologists in the thick of the fight revealed unexpected numbers of "heretics who believe there is more to malaria eradication than just spraying with DDT." In fact the chairman at the end expressed surprise "to find that no one has come forward to support the WHO case for total eradication." Colbourne (1962).
2. *Ibid.*
3. Julian de Zulueta, "Report on a visit to Italy from 11–22 March 1957," ms. *WHO Docs.*
4. Ray (1961).
5. T. B. Patel, T. Ramachandra Rao, and P. D. Paranjpey, "A pilot study on the suspension of D.D.T. spraying and the setting up of a surveillance organisation in Kanara District covering the work up to October 31, 1956," *Indian J. Malariol.* 11 (1957): 271–292.
6. Personal observation.
7. Information from interviews with personnel of the India National Malaria Eradication Programme, 1976.
8. WHO Tech. Rpts. #205, #272.

9. Yekutiel (1960).

10. Statistics and analyses of the relapse in India are in S. L. Dhir, "National malaria eradication programme: retrospect and prospects," ms. *WHO Docs.;* USAID/WHO (1970); Scholtens, Kaiser and Langmuir (1972); Wickremasinghe (1976).

11. WHO (1957b).

12. F. R. S. Kellett, "Field visit report on malaria eradication programme, Ceylon, WHO Project: Ceylon 58," *WHO Docs.* SEA/Mal/51, 14 May 1965.

13. A. Gabaldón, "Assignment report on malaria eradication, Ceylon, WHO Project: Ceylon 58," *WHO Docs.* SEA/Mal/59, 12 July 1966.

14. [Ceylon] *Report of the Director of Medical and Sanitary Services* (Colombo, 1964–65); Wickremasinghe (1976).

15. Regional reports compiled for submission to the 29th World Health Assembly. *WHO Docs.*

16. C. T. Ch'en and K. C. Liang, "Malaria surveillance programme in Taiwan," *Bull. WHO* 15 (1956): 805–810; Colbourne (1962).

17. Status of the malaria eradication program as of 1975–1976 from Brown, Haworth and Zahar (1976) and from WHO regional reports in WHO Docs.

18. J. de Zulueta and D. A. Muir, "Malaria eradication in the Near East," *Trans. Roy. Soc. Trop. Med. Hyg.* 66 (1972): 679–696.

19. Scholtens, Kaiser and Langmuir (1972).

20. WHO Off. Rec. #176.

21. WHO, Exp. Com. Mal. 15th meeting; WHO Tech. Rpt. #467.

22. *Ibid.,* 16th meeting; WHO Tech. Rpt. #549.

23. Dr. Tibor Lepeš, present director of WHO's Division of Malaria and Other Parasitic Diseases, said at the 9th International Congress on Tropical Medicine and Malaria in 1973 that some health administrators thought eradication was "one of the greatest mistakes ever made in public health" (Suppl., *J. Trop. Med. Hyg.* vol. 77, no. 4, April 1974). He did not name the critics.

24. See, for example, L. A. Mears, *Economic project evaluation with Philippine cases* (Univ. Phil., 1969).

25. In minutes of their 16th meeting, the expert committee on malaria wrote: "The very slow improvement of health conditions in developing countries is due in part to a continuing uncertainty over the priority to be accorded to health measures in these countries owing to doubts about their contribution to economic development. It has been argued that to compete successfully for resources destined for the physical elements of national growth, the advocates of public health will need to establish a stronger case for the economic benefits of expenditures in the field of health." WHO Tech. Rpt. #549.

References*

ANDREWES, C. H. (1967). *The natural history of viruses* (London, Weidenfeld and Nicholson).

BASTIANELLI, G. and A. BIGNAMI (1899). "Sullo sviluppo dei parassiti della terzana nell' *Anopheles claviger*," *Bull. R. Acad. Med. Roma.* Offprint in Ross Collection.

BASTIANELLI, G., A. BIGNAMI and B. GRASSI (1898). "Coltivazione delle semilune malariche dell' uomo nell' *Anopheles claviger* Fabr. (sinonimo: *Anopheles maculipennis*, Meig.)," *Atti R. Accad. Lincei* 7: 313–314.

BATES, MARSTON (1949). *The natural history of mosquitoes* (N. Y., Macmillan).

BIGNAMI, AMICO (1896). "Le ipotesi sulla biologia dei parassiti malarici fuori dell' uomo (a proposito di un recente scritto del dott. P. Manson)," *Policlinico* 3: 320–339.

——— (1898a). "The inoculation theory of malarial infection: account of a successful experiment with mosquitoes," *Lancet*, 1461–1463, 1541–1544.

——— (1898b). "Come si prendono le febbri malariche," *Ann. Med Nav.*, 1177–1200.

BOYD, MARK, ed. (1949). *Malariology: A comprehensive survey of all aspects of this group of diseases from a global standpoint* (Philadelphia and London, Saunders).

BRADLEY, G. H. (1966). "A review of malaria control and eradication in the United States," *Mosq. News* 26: 462–470.

BRAND, JEANNE L. (1965). *Doctors and the state: The British medical profession and government action in public health, 1870–1912* (Baltimore, Johns Hopkins).

---

* See Acknowledgments.

297

BRAY, R. S. (1953). "Studies in the Exo-erythrocytic cycle in the genus *Plasmodium*." Univ. London thesis.

BROCKINGTON, C. FRASER (1966). *A short history of public health*, 2d ed. (London, Churchill).

BROWN, A. W. A., J. HAWORTH and A. R. ZAHAR (1976). "Malaria eradication and control from a global standpoint," *J. Med. Ent.* 13: 1–25.

BROWN, A. W. A., D. S. SARKARIA and R. P. THOMPSON (1952). "Studies on the responses of the female Aedes mosquito; Part I: the search for attractant vapors," *Bull. Ent. Res.* 42: 105–114. (First of a series; see Chapter 17, note 16.)

BRUMPT, EMILE (1944). "Anophelisme sans paludisme et regression spontanée du paludisme," *Ann. Parasit. Hum. Comp.* 20: 67–91.

——— (1949). *Précis de parasitologie,* 6th ed. (Paris, Masson).

BULL, CARROLL G., and W. V. KING (1923). "The identification of the blood meal of mosquitoes by means of the precipitin test," *Am. J. Hyg.* 3: 491–496.

BULLOCH, WILLIAM (1938). *The history of bacteriology* (London, OUP).

CAMERON, THOMAS W. M. (1956). *Parasites and parasitism* (London, Methuen).

CARTER, H. R. (1931). *Yellow fever: An epidemiological and historical study of its place of origin* (Baltimore, Williams & Wilkins).

CELLI, ANGELO (1899). *La malaria secondo le nuove ricerche* (Roma, Soc. Dante Alighieri).

——— (1901). *Malaria according to the new researches,* Tr. from 2d ed. by J. J. Eyre (London, Longmans Green).

——— (1908). "The campaign against malaria in Italy," *J. Trop. Med. Hyg.* 11: 101–108.

——— and G. GASPERINI (1901). "Paludismo senza malaria," *Policlinico, Sez. Prat.* Offprint in Celli, Collected Papers, bound in Lond. Sch. Hyg. Trop. Med.

——— and G. GUARNIERI. "Sulla etiologia dell' infezione malarica," *Arch. Sci. Med.* 13: 307–336.

CHAMBERLAIN, M. E. (1974). *The scramble for Africa* (London, Longmans).

CHRISTOPHERS, S. R. (1904). "Second report of the anti-malarial operations at Mian Mir, 1901–1903," *Sci. Mem. Offs. Med. San. Depts. Govt. India,* New Ser. #9 (Calcutta, Govt. Print.).

——— (1911). "Malaria in the Punjab," *Sci. Mem. Offs. Med. San. Depts. Govt. India* (Calcutta, Govt. Print.).

——— (1960). *Aedes aegypti (L.): the yellow fever mosquito; its life history, bionomics and structure* (Cambridge, Univ. Press).

CLEMENTS, A. N. (1963). *The physiology of mosquitoes* (Oxford, Pergamon).

CLYDE, DAVID F. (1967). *Malaria in Tanzania* (London, OUP).

COLBOURNE, M. J. (1962). "Prospects for malaria eradication with special reference to the Western Pacific," *Trans. Roy. Soc. Trop. Med. Hyg.* 56: 179–201.

COLIN, LÉON (1870). *Traité des fièvres intermittentes* (Paris, Baillière).

COVELL, G. (1941). *Malaria control by anti-mosquito measures,* 2d ed. (London, Thacker).

CRAWFORD, D. G. (1914). *A history of the Indian Medical Service, 1600–1913,* 2 vols. (London, Thacker).

CUSHING, HARVEY (1926). *The life of Sir William Osler*, 2 vols. (Oxford, Clarendon).

DANILEVSKII, V. I. (1886). "Matériaux pour servir à la parasitologie du sang," *Arch. Slaves Biol.* 1: 85–91, 364–396, 715; 3(1887): 33–49, 157–176, 370–417.

DAVIDSON, ANDREW (1892). *Geographical pathology: an inquiry into the geographical distribution of infective and climatic diseases*, 2 vols. (Edinburgh, Pentland).

DAVIDSON, GEORGE (1964). "*Anopheles gambiae*, a complex of species," *Bull. WHO* 31: 625–634.

DE BUCK, A., E. SCHOUTE and N. H. SWELLENGREBEL (1927). "Récherches sur l'anophelisme sans paludisme aux environs d'Amsterdam," *Riv. Malariol.* 6: 8–39.

DUNN, C. L. (1936). *Malaria in Ceylon; an enquiry into its causes* (London, Bailliere, Tindall and Cox).

FALLERONI, DOMENICO (1926). "Fauna anofelica italiana e suo 'habitat' (paludi, risaie, canali), metodo di lotta contro la malaria," *Riv. Malariol.* 5: 553–593.

———— (1927). "Per la soluzione del problema malarico italiano," *Riv. Malariol.* 6: 344–409.

FAUST, ERNEST CARROLL (1945). "Clinical and public health aspects of malaria in the United States from an historical perspective," *Am. J. Trop. Med.* 25: 185–201.

FEINGOLD, BEN F., E. BENJAMIN and DOV MICHAELI (1968). "The allergic responses to insect bites," *Annual Rev. Ent.* 13: 137–153.

FERMI, CLAUDIO (1935). *Lotta antimalarica: manuale teorico-pratica* (Gallizzi–Sassari).

FITCH-JONES, B. W. (1932). "Hill station," in D. B. Drummond, ed., *Sierra Leone Studies*, No. 18.

FOSTER, W. D. (1965). *A history of parasitology* (Edinburgh & London, Livingstone).

FYFE, CHRISTOPHER (1962). *A history of Sierra Leone* (London, OUP).

GABALDÓN, ARNOLDO (1949). "The nation-wide campaign against malaria in Venezuela," *Trans. Roy. Soc. Trop. Med. Hyg.* 43: 113–164.

GARNHAM, P. C. C. (1966). *Malaria parasites and other haemosporidia* (Oxford, Blackwell).

GEORGHIU, G. P. (1969). "Genetics of resistance to insecticides in houseflies and mosquitoes," *Exp. Parasit.* 26: 224–255.

GIEMSA, G. (1911). Beitrag zur Frage der Steckmückenbekämpfung," *Arch. Schiffs-u. Trop. Hyg.* 15: 533–536.

———— (1913). "Das Mückensprayverfahren im dienste der Bekämpfung der Malaria und anderer durch Steckmücken überfragbar Krankheiten," *Arch. Schiffs-u. Trop. Hyg.* 17: 181–190.

GILL, C. A. (1936). "Some points in the epidemiology of malaria arising out of the study of the malaria epidemic in Ceylon in 1934–35," *Trans. Roy. Soc. Trop. Med. Hyg.* 29: 428–480.

———— (1938). *The seasonal periodicity of malaria and the mechanism of the epidemic wave* (London, Churchill).

GILLETT, J. D. (1971). *Mosquitos* (London, Weidenfeld & Nicholson).

GOLGI, CAMILLO (1886). "Sull' infezione malarica," *Arch. Sci. Med.* 10: 109–135. (First of a series. See Chapter 2, note 14.)

GORDON, R. M. & W. H. R. LUMSDEN (1939). "A study of the behaviour of the mouthparts of mosquitoes when taking up blood from living tissue, together with some observations of the ingestion of microfilariae," *Ann. Trop. Med. Parasitol.* 33: 259–278.

GORGAS, W. C. (1915). *Sanitation in Panama* (London, Appleton).

GORGAS, MARIE D. and BURTON J. HENDRICK (1924). *William Crawford Gorgas, his life and work* (London, Heinemann).

GRASSI, B. (1898a). "Rapporti tra la malaria e peculiari insetti," *Policlinico* 5: 469–476, and *Atti R. Accad. Lincei* 7: 163–172.

———— (1898b). "La malaria propagata per mezzo di peculiari insetti," *Atti R. Accad. Lincei* 7: 234–240.

———— (1899). *Le recenti scoperte sulla malaria esposte in forma populare* (Milano).

———— (1900). *Studi di uno zoologo sulla malaria* (Roma, R. Accad. Lincei).

———— (1903). *Documenti reguardanti la storia della scoperta del modo di trasmissione della malaria umana* (Milano, A. Rancati). Copy in Grassi, *Miscellanea I*, ist. Sup. Sanitá.

———— A. BIGNAMI & G. BASTIANELLI (1899a). "Ulteriori ricerche sul ciclo dei parassiti malarici umani nel corpo del zanzarone," *Atti R. Accad. Lincei* 8: 21–28.

———— (1899b). "Resoconto degli studi fatti sulla malaria durante il mese di Gennaio," *Atti R. Accad. Lincei* 8: 100–104.

———— (1899c). "Ulteriori ricerche sulla malaria," *Atti R. Accad. Lincei* 8: 434–438.

———— (1899d). "Ciclo evolutivo delle semilune nell' *Anopheles claviger* ed altri studi sulla malaria dall' Ottobre 1898 al Maggio 1899," *Ann. Ig. Sper.* 9: 258–271.

HACKETT, LEWIS W. Papers. Rockefeller Foundation Archives.

———— (1925). "The importance and uses of Paris green as an Anopheles larvicide," *Trans. 1st Int. Cong. Mal. Rome,* 158–166.

———— (1937). *Malaria in Europe: an ecological study* (Oxford, OUP).

———— & A. MISSIROLI (1931). "The natural disappearance of malaria in certain regions of Europe," *Am. J. Hyg.* 13: 57ff.

———— & A. MISSIROLI (1935). "The varieties of *Anopheles maculipennis* and their relation to the distribution of malaria in Europe," *Riv. Malariol.* 14: 45–109.

HACKETT, L. W.; P. F. RUSSELL; J. W. SCHARFF; & R. SENIOR WHITE (1938). "The present use of naturalistic measures in the control of malaria," *Bull L. of N. Hlth. Org.* 7: 1016–1064.

HOCKING, B. (1953). "The intrinsic range and speed of flight of insects," *Trans. Roy. Ent. Soc. Lond.* 104: 223–345.

HOUGHTON, WALTER E. (1957). *The Victorian frame of mind, 1830–1870.* (New Haven, Yale University Press).

HOWARD, L. O.; H. G. DYAR; and F. KNAB (1912). *The mosquitoes of North and Central America and the West Indies,* vol. I (of four) (Washington, Carnegie Inst.).

JAMES, S. P. (1903). "First report of the anti-malarial operations at Mian Mir, 1901–1903," *Sci. Mem. Offs. Med. San. Depts. Govt. India,* New Ser. #6 (Calcutta).

———— (1931). "Some general results of a study of induced malaria in England," *Trans. Roy. Soc. Trop. Med. Hyg.* 24: 477–538.

———— and P. TATE (1937). "New knowledge of the life cycle of 'malaria' parasites," *Nature* 139:545.

———— and P. TATE (1938). "Exo-erythrocytic schizogony in *P. gallinaceum* Brumpt," *Parasitol.* 30: 128.

JANSSENS, P. G. (1970). "Le procés du paludisme," *J. Trop. Med. Hyg.* 77 (Suppl.) 39–46.

JARCHO, SAUL (1970). "A cartographic and literary study of the word malaria," *J. Hist. Med.* 25: 31–39.

JEFFREY, GEOFFREY M. (1976). "Malaria control in the twentieth century," *Am. J. Trop. Med. Hyg.* 25: 361–371.

JOYCE, R. B. (1971). *Sir William MacGregor* (Melbourne, OUP).

KELLY, HOWARD A. (1906). *Walter Reed and yellow fever* (Baltimore, Medical Standard Books).

KELSCH, A. (1875). "Contribution à l'anatomie pathologique des maladies palustres endémiques: observations sur l'anémie, la mélanémie et la mélanose palustres," *Arch. Physiol. Normale Path.* 7(2d Ser II) 690–734. (First of a series. See note 4, chapter 2.)

KLEBS, EDWIN and CORRADO TOMMASI-CRUDELI (1879). "Produzione della malaria—esposizione delle ricerche istituite in passato per determinare la natura," *Gior. Ital. Sci. Med.* 44: 396–413.

KOCH, ROBERT (1912). *Gesammelte werke,* ed. by J. Schwalbe, vol. II (Leipzig, Thieme).

LAARMAN, J. J. (1955). "The host-seeking behavior of the malaria mosquito *Anopheles maculipennis atroparvus,*" *Acta Leidensia* 25: 1–144.

[LAVERAN, A.] (1880). "Deuxième note relative à un nouveau parasite trouvé dans le sang des malades atteints de la fièvre palustre," *Bull. Acad. Med.* 44 (2d ser., vol IX): 1346–1347.

LAVERAN, A. (1881). *Nature parasitaire des accidents de l'impaludisme: description d'un nouveau parasite trouvé dans le sang des malades atteints de fièvre palustre* (Paris, Baillière).

———— (1884). *Traité des fièvres palustres avec la description des microbes du paludisme* (Paris, Octave Doin).

———— (1898). *Traité du paludisme* (Paris, Masson).

League of Nations, Health Organization, Malaria Commission (1924). "Report on its tour of investigation in certain European countries in 1924," *L. of N. Docs.* (C.H. 273).

———— (1927). "Principles and methods of anti-malarial measures in Europe: Second general report of the malaria commission," *L. of N. Docs.* (C.H./ Mal/73).

LEPEŠ, T. (1974). "Present status of the global eradication programme and prospects for the future," *J. Trop. Med. Hyg.* 77, No. 4 (Suppl.) 47–53.

LIVADAS, GREGORY A. (1951). "Malaria control in Greece during the last fifty-year period," *Riv. Malariol.* 30: 17–27.

LOGAN, JOHN A. (1953). "The Sardinian project; an experiment in the eradication of an indigenous malarious vector," *Am. J. Hyg. Monograph* #20 (Baltimore, Johns Hopkins).

[LUTRARIO, ALBERTO] (1924). *La malaria in Italia ed i risultati della lotta cantimalarica* (Roma, Lib. Stato).

———— (1928). "Renseignements sur les bonifications," *L. of N. Docs.* (C.H./Mal/122).

MACCALLUM, W. G. (1897a). "On the flagellated form of the malarial parasite," *The Lancet* 2: 1240–1241.

———— (1897b). "On the hematozoan infections of birds," *Bull. Johns Hopkins Hosp.* 8: 235–236.

MACDONALD, GEORGE (1973). *Dynamics of tropical disease: A selection of papers with bibliographical introduction and bibliography.* ed. by L. J. Bruce-Chwatt and V. J. Glanville (London, OUP).

MACK, GERSTLE (1944). *The land divided: A history of the Panama Canal and other Isthmian projects* (N. Y., Knopf).

MANNABERG, JULIUS (1894). "The malarial parasites," tr. by R. W. Felkin; in *Two monographs on malaria and the parasites of malarial fevers* (London, Sydenham Soc.).

MANSON, PATRICK (1894). "On the nature and significance of the crescentic and flagellated bodies in malarial blood," *Brit. Med. J.,* vol. II, 1306–1308.

———— (1896). "The Goulstonian lectures on the life-history of the malaria germ outside the human body," *Brit. Med. J.* 641–646, 712–717, 774–779.

———— (1898a). "Surgeon-Major Ronald Ross's recent investigations on the mosquito-malaria theory," *Brit. Med. J.,* 1575–1577.

———— (1898b). "The mosquito and the malaria parasite (being an address delivered by request in the section of Tropical Diseases at the annual meeting of the British Medical Association, held in Edinburgh, July 1898)," *Brit. Med. J.,* 849–853).

———— (1898c). "An exposition of the mosquito-malaria theory and its recent developments," *J. Trop Med.* 1: 4–8.

MANSON-BAHR, P. H., and A. W. ALCOCK (1927). *Life and work of Sir Patrick Manson* (London, Cassell).

MARCHIAFAVA, E., and A. BIGNAMI (1892). "Sulle febbri malariche estivo-autunnali," *Bull. R. Accad. Med. Roma* 18: 297–464.

MARCHIAFAVA, E., and A. CELLI (1883). "Sulle alterazione dei globuli rossi nella infezione della malaria e sulla genese della melanemia," *Mem. R. Accad. Lincei* ser. 3, vol. 18: 381–401. (First in a series. See Chapter 2, note 13.)

———— (1886). "Nuove ricerche sulla infezione malarica," *Arch. Sci. Med.* 9: 311–340.

MATTINGLY, P. F. (1969). *The biology of mosquito-borne disease* (London, Allen & Unwin).

MISSIROLI, A. (1947). "Riduzione o eradicazione degli anofeli?" *Riv. Parassit.* 8: 141–169.

———— and L. W. HACKETT (1927). "La regressione spontanea della malaria in alcune regioni d'Italia," *Riv. Malariol.* 6: 193–243.

———— L. W. HACKETT, and E. MARTINI (1933). "Le razze di *Anopheles maculipennis* e la loro importanza nella distribuzione della malaria in alcune regioni d'Europa," *Riv. Malariol.* 12: 1–56.

MONTI, ACHILLE (1928). *Giovanni Rasori nella storia della scienze dell' idea nazionale* (Pavia, Ist. Pavese di Atti Graf.).

NEWMAN, GEORGE (1932). *The rise of preventive medicine* (London, OUP).

NUTTALL, GEORGE H. F. (1900). "Upon the part played by mosquitoes in the propagation of malaria: a historical and critical study," *J. Trop. Med.* 2: 198–200, 231–233, 245–247, 305–307; 3: 11–13.

ORENSTEIN, A. J. (1912). "Mosquito catching in dwellings in the prophylaxis of malaria," *Am. J. Pub. Hlth.* 3: 106–110.

OSLER, WILLIAM (1887). "An address on the haematozoa of malaria," *Brit. Med. J.,* 556–562.

PAMPANA, E. J. (1951). "Lutte antipaludique par les insecticides à action réma-nents: résultats des grandes campagnes," *Bull. WHO* 3: 557–619.

——— (1969). *A textbook of malaria eradication* (London, OUP).

PARK ROSS, G. A. (1936). "Insecticide as major measure in control of malaria, being account of methods and organization put in force in Natal and Zulu-land during the past six years," *Q. Bull. Hlth. Org. L. of N.* 5: 114–133.

PATEL, T. B., T. RAMACHANDRA RAO, and P. D. PARANJPEY (1957). "A pilot study on the suspension of D.D.T. spraying and the setting up of a surveillance organisation in Kanara District covering the work up to October 31, 1956," *Indian J. Malariol.* 11: 271–292.

PELLER, SIGISMUND (1959). "Walter Reed, C. Finlay and their predecessors around 1800," *Bull. Hist. Med.* 33: 195–211.

PERRONCITO, ALDO, ed. (1939). *Gli studi di Camillo Golgi sulla malaria* (Roma, Luigi Pozzi).

PLETSCH, DONALD J., F. E. GARTRELL, and E. HAROLD HINMAN (1960). "A criti-cal review of the national malaria eradication program of India," ms. *WHO Docs.*

RAFFAELE, GIULIO (1934). "Sul compartamento degli sporozoiti nel sangue dell' ospite," *Riv. Malariol.* 13: 395–403; 705–706.

——— (1936). "Il doppio ciclo schizogenico di *Plasmodium elongatum*," *Riv. Malariol.* 15: 309–317.

RAY, A. P. (1961). "Review of the national malaria eradication programme," *Bull. Nat. Soc. India Mal. Mosq. b. Diseases* 9: 10–19.

RIBBANDS, C. R. (1949). "Studies on the attractiveness of human populations to anophelines," *Bull. Ent. Res.* 40: 227–238.

ROBINSON, C. G. (1939). "The mouth parts and their function in the female mosquito, Anopheles maculipennis," *Parasitol.* 31: 212–242.

ROGERS, LEONARD (1950). *Happy toil* (London, J. Muller).

ROSS, RONALD, Archives. London School of Hygiene and Tropical Medicine.

——— Collection, College of Physicians and Surgeons, Glasgow. (The collec-tion contains literary and mathematical manuscripts as well as pamphlets and off-prints on malaria.)

——— (1897). "On some peculiar pigmented cells found in two mosquitoes fed on malarial blood," *Brit. Med. J.,* 1786–1788.

——— (1898). "Report on the cultivation of Proteosoma, Labbé, in grey mos-quitoes," *Indian Med. Gaz.* 33: 401–408, 448–451 (also separately pub-lished as pamphlet by Govt. Print. Calcutta, 1898).

——— (1899a). "Inaugural lecture on the possibility of extirpating malaria from certain localities by a new method," *Brit. Med. J.,* 1–4.

—— (1899b). "The malaria expedition to Sierra Leone," *Brit. Med. J.*, 675–676, 746, 869–871, 1033–1035.

—— (1901). "First progress report of the campaign against mosquitoes in Sierra Leone," *Liverpool Sch. Trop. Med. Mem.* V (1).

—— (1910). *The prevention of malaria* (N. Y., Dutton).

—— (1923). *Memoirs* (London, John Murray).

—— (1930). *Memories of Sir Patrick Manson* (London, Harrison).

——, H. E. ANNETT, and E. E. AUSTEN (1900). *Report of the malaria expedition of the Liverpool School of Tropical Medicine and Medical Parasitology* (Liverpool, Univ. Press).

ROUBAUD, ÉMILE (1921). "La différenciation des races zoötropiques d'Anopheles, et la régression spontanée du paludisme," *Bull. Soc. Path. Exotique* 14: 577–595.

ROYAL SOCIETY (1900–1903). *Reports to the malaria committee*, ser. 1–8 (London, Harrison).

RUSSELL, PAUL F. (1955). *Man's mastery of malaria* (London, OUP).

—— (1968). "The United States and malaria: debits and credits," *Bull. N. Y. Acad. Med.* 44: 623–653.

—— and F. W. KNIPE (1939). "Malaria control by spray-killing adult mosquitoes," *J. Mal. Inst. India* 2: 229–237. First of series; others in same journal, 3 (1940): 531–541; 4 (1941): 181–197; 5 (1943): 59–76 (with N. R. Sitapathy).

RUSSELL, PAUL F.; LUTHER WEST; REGINALD D. MANWELL; and GEORGE MACDONALD (1963). *Practical malariology* (London, OUP).

SANABRIA, A. (1968). "Luis Daniel Beauperthy y la transmision de las enfermedades por insectos," *Pagine Storia Med.* 12: I, 1–19.

SANDOSHAN, A. A. (1959). *Malariology with special reference to Malaya* (Singapore, Univ. Malaya Press).

SCHOLTENS, ROBERT G.; ROBERT L. KAISER; and ALEXANDER D. LANGMUIR (1972). "An epidemiologic examination of the strategy of malaria eradication," *Intern. J. Epidem.* (1972): 15–24.

SCOTT, H. HAROLD (1939). *A history of tropical medicine* (London, Edward Arnold).

SERGENT, EDMOND (1903). *La lutte contre les moustiques* (Paris, Rueff).

SERGENT, EDMOND and ÉTIENNE (1902). "Sur les Anopheles de la banlieue de Paris," *Ann. Inst. Pasteur* 16. Offprint in Ross Collection.

—— (1928). "Vingt-cinq années d'étude de prophylaxie du paludisme en Algérie," reprint from *Arch. Inst. Pasteur d'Algérie* vol. 6, nos. 2, 3.

—— and L. PARROT (1929). *La découverte de Laveran* (Paris, Masson).

SERGENT, ÉTIENNE (1902). "Existence des Anopheles en grand nombre dans une region d'où la paludisme a disparu," *Ann. Inst. Pasteur* 16: 811–816.

SHANNON, R. C. (1932). "*Anopheles gambiae* in Brazil," *Am. J. Hyg.* 15: 634–663.

SHORTT, H. E. (1951). "History of recent researches in tissue phases of the malaria parasite at the London School of Hygiene and Tropical Medicine," *Trans. Roy. Soc. Trop. Med. Hyg.* 45: 175–188.

—— N. HAMILTON FAIRLEY; G. COVELL; P. G. SHUTE; and P. C. C. GARNHAM (1951). "The pre-erythrocytic stage of *Plasmodium falciparum*," *Trans. Roy. Soc. Trop. Med. Hyg.* 44: 405–419.

SHORTT, H. E., and P. C. C. GARNHAM (1948). "The pre-erythrocytic development of *Plasmodium cynomolgi* and *Plasmodium vivax*," *Trans. Roy. Soc. Trop. Med. Hyg.* 41: 785–795.

SHOUSHA, ALY TEWFIK (1947). "Species eradication: the eradication of *Anopheles gambiae* from Upper Egypt, 1942–1945," *Bull. WHO* 1: 309–348.

SHRYOCK, RICHARD HARRISON (1936). *The development of modern medicine: an interpretation of the social and scientific factors involved* (Philadelphia, Univ. of Pa. Press).

SIMMONS, JAMES STEVENS, with GEORGE H. CALLENDER; DALFERES P. CURRY; SEYMOUR C. SCHWARTZ; and RAYMOND RANDALL (1939). "Malaria in Panama," *Am. J. Hyg. Monograph Ser. 13* (Baltimore, Johns Hopkins).

SIMMONS, SAMUEL W., and WILLIAM M. UPHOLT (1951). "Disease control with insecticides; a review of the literature," *Bull. WHO* 3: 535–556.

SIMOND, P. L. (1897). "L'évolution des sporozoaires du genre *Coccidium*," *Ann. Inst. Pasteur* 21: 545–581.

SMITH, THEOBALD, and F. L. KILBOURNE (1893). "Investigations into the nature, causation and prevention of Texas or Southern cattle fever," *U. S. Dept. Agric., Bur. Animal Husbandry Bull. No. 1* (Washington, GPO).

SOPER, FRED L. (1948). "Species sanitation as applied to the eradication of (A) an invading or (B) an indigenous species," *Proc. 4th Intern. Cong. Trop. Med. Mal.* (Washington, Dept. of State).

———— (1965). "Rehabilitation of the eradication concept in prevention of communicable diseases," *Pub. Hlth. Rep.* 80: 855–869.

———— and D. B. WILSON (1943a). *Anopheles gambiae in Brazil, 1930–1940* (N. Y., Rockefeller Foundation).

————, D. B. WILSON; S. LIMA; and W. S. ANTUNES (1943b). *The organization of permanent nation-wide anti-Aedes aegypti measures in Brazil* (N. Y., Rockefeller Foundation).

[Statement] (1896). *Statement exhibiting the moral and material progress and conditions of India during the year 1896–97:* 33d number (London, HMSO).

STEPHENS, J. W. W. (1904). "Discussion of the prophylaxis of malaria," *Brit. Med. J.,* 629–631.

STERNBERG, GEORGE M. (1883). "Malaria," *Pub. Hlth. Rep.* 9: 31–54.

———— (1884). *Malaria and malarial diseases* (N. Y., Wood).

———— (1890). "Report on the etiology and prevention of yellow fever," *Pub. Hlth. Rep.* No. 2 (Washington, GPO).

STRODE, GEORGE K., ed. (1951). *Yellow fever* (N. Y., McGraw-Hill).

SWELLENGREBEL, N. H., and A. DE BUCK (1938). *Malaria in the Netherlands* (Amsterdam, Scheltema & Holkens).

THAYER, WILLIAM S. (1899). *Lectures on the malarial fevers* (London, Henry Kimpton).

THAYER, W. S., and JOHN HEWETSON (1895). "The malarial fevers of Baltimore," *Johns Hopkins Hosp. Rep.* 5: 5–218.

THOMSON, R. C. MUIRHEAD (1951). *Mosquito behaviour in relation to malaria transmission and control in the tropics* (London, Edward Arnold).

THORNTON, A. P. (1959). *The imperial idea and its enemies: a study in British power* (London, Macmillan).

TONKING, H. D., and S. GIBERT (1947). *The use of D.D.T. residual sprays in the control of malaria over an area of 16 square miles in Mauritius* (Port Louis, Colony of Mauritius Pub. No. 40).

United States Congress (1911). "Yellow fever, a compilation of various publications: results of the work of Maj. Walter Reed, Medical Corps, United States Army, and the Yellow Fever Commission," *Sen. Doc. 822.*

United States AID and World Health Org. (1970). "Report of the evaluation in-depth of the National Malaria Eradication Programme of India," MS. *WHO Docs.*

VISWANATHAN, D. K. (1958). *The conquest of malaria in India: an Indo-American cooperative effort* (Bombay, privately printed).

WATSON, MALCOLM (1915). *Rural sanitation in the tropics: being notes and observations in the Malay Archipelago, Panama, and other lands* (London, John Murray).

——— (1921). *The prevention of malaria in the Federated Malay States,* 2d ed. (London, John Murray).

[WELCH, WILLIAM HENRY] (1926). *Papers and addresses by William Henry Welch,* ed. by Walter C. Burket, 3 vols. (Baltimore, Johns Hopkins).

WENYON, C. M. (1926). *Protozoology: A manual for medical men, veterinarians, and zoologists.* 2 vols. (London, Bailliere, Tindale & Cox).

WEST, T. F., and G. A. CAMPBELL (1946). *DDT: the synthetic insecticide* (London, Chapman & Hall).

WHORTON, JAMES C. (1971). "Insecticide spray residues and public health: 1865–1938," *Bull. Hist. Med.* 45: 219–241.

WICKREMASINGHE, F. A. (1976). "Review of the malaria situation in Southeast Asia region," ms. *WHO Docs.* (SEA/Mal/Meet. 1/6).

WIGGLESWORTH, V. B. (1939). *The principles of insect physiology* (London, Methuen).

WILLIAMS, GREER (1969). *The plague killers* (N. Y., Scribner's).

World Health Organization (1957a). "Malaria conference for the Eastern Mediterranean and European regions," *WHO Tech. Rep.* 132.

——— (1957b). "Report of WHO advisory team on malaria eradication No. 3, Ceylon, February–June 1957," *WHO Docs.* WHO/AS/102.5.

World Health Organization, Expert Committee on Insecticides (1949–1975) WHO Tech. Reps. (esp. 3d, 8th, 13th, 16th, 17th, 20th & 21st: 4, 153, 265, 356, 443, 513, 561).

World Health Organization, Expert Committee on Malaria (1947). "Report on Dr. Pampana's mission to Greece and Italy," *WHO Docs.* IC/Mal/8, 21 Aug 1947.

World Health Organization, Expert Committee on Malaria (1948–1974). (Reports of the first and second meetings in *Bull. WHO* 1: 21–28; 213–252. Third through sixteenth meetings in WHO Tech. Reps. 8, 39, 80, 123, 162, 205, 243, 272, 291, 324, 357, 382, 467, 549).

YEKUTIEL, P. (1960). "Problems of epidemiology in malaria eradication," *Bull. WHO* 22: 669–683.

YOUNG, G. M. (1953). *Victorian England: portrait of an age,* 2d ed. (Oxford, OUP).

Index